A Rose in Winter

Kathleen E. Woodiwiss

A Rose in Winter

AVON BOOKS NEW YORK

This is a work of fiction. Names, characters, places, and incidents either are the product of the author's imagination or are used fictitiously. Any resemblance to actual events, locales, organizations, or persons, living or dead, is entirely coincidental and beyond the intent of either the author or the publisher.

AVON BOOKS
A division of
The Hearst Corporation
1350 Avenue of the Americas
New York, New York 10019

Copyright © 1982 by Kathleen E. Woodiwiss
Interior design by Kellan Peck
Visit our website at http://AvonBooks.com
Library of Congress Catalog Card Number: 82-13932
ISBN: 0-380-97600-5

First Avon Books Hardcover Printing: December 1997
First Avon Books Mass Market Paperback Printing: October 1983
First Avon Books Trade Paperback Printing: December 1982

AVON TRADEMARK REG. U.S. PAT. OFF. AND IN OTHER COUNTRIES, MARCA REGISTRADA, HECHO EN U.S.A.

Printed in the U.S.A.

FIRST EDITION

QPM   10   9   8   7   6   5   4   3   2   1

Dedicated to those readers who have
written letters of encouragement.
Thank you. You're appreciated.
K.E.W.

A Rose in Winter

A crimson bloom in winter's snow,
Born out of time, like a maiden's woe,
Spawned in a season when the chill winds blow.

'Twas found in a sheltered spot,
Bright sterling gules and blemished not,
Red as a drop o'blood from the broken heart,

Of the maid who waits and weeps atop the tor,
Left behind by yon argent knight sworn to war,
'Til ajousting and aquesting he goes no more.

Fear not, Sweet Jo, amoulderin' on the moor.
The winter's rose doth promise in the fading runes of yore,
That true love once found will again be restored.

One

Northern England / October 23, 1792

"Marriage!"

Erienne Fleming drew back from the hearth and slammed the poker into the stand, venting a growing vexation with the still young day. Outside, the cavorting wind gleefully whipped large, splashing raindrops and stinging shards of sleet against the leaded windowpanes to mock with its carefree abandon the bondage she felt in her spirit. The rolling chaos of dark clouds churning close above the tiled roof of the mayor's cottage mirrored the mood of this trim, dark-haired young woman whose eyes flashed with a violet fire of their own as she glared down into the flames.

"Marriage!"

The word flared afresh in her brain. Once the symbol of a girlhood dream, of late it had become more a synonym for foolery. It was not that she opposed the institution. Oh, no! Under the careful guidance of her mother, she had prepared herself to be a fitting spouse for any man. It was only that her father, that self-same mayor of Mawbry, was bent on matching her to any wealthy purse, regardless of what foppish, obese, or bone-thin caricature of a man bore it to her door. All other desirable traits, including manners, seemed unimportant to him. Indeed, not even to be considered. If the man be rich and willing to wed, then he was a likely candidate for her hand. A sorry lot they had proven to be, and yet—Erienne's finely arched brows drew together in sudden doubt—perhaps they were the best her father could do without the enticement of even a reasonable dowry.

"Marriage! Pah!" Erienne spat the words out in renewed disgust. She was quickly losing the blissful fantasies of youth and beginning to look upon the state of wedlock as something less than pleasant. Of course, it was not altogether rare that a young lady should detest an arranged suitor, but after the sampling she had been subjected to, she held little hope that her father's usual dogmatic nature would greatly improve his selections in the future.

Restlessly Erienne strode to the window and stared pensively through a diamond-shaped pane toward the cobbled road that meandered through the village. The trees that bordered the hamlet were little more than dark, skeletal shapes in the slashing rain. Her gaze drifted down the empty lane, and a dull ache, not unlike a mild dyspepsia, was born in her at the thought that barely an hour separated her from a meeting with an unwelcome suitor. She had not the smallest desire to put on a gracious smile for another simpering buffoon, and she dearly hoped, yea, even prayed, that the road would remain devoid of travelers. Indeed, should a rain-weakened bridge collapse beneath the conveyance bearing the man, and the whole lot fall into the foaming water never to be seen again, she would not grieve overmuch. The man was a stranger to her, a faceless entity identifiable only by a name she had very recently been given. Silas Chambers! What kind of man would he prove to be?

Erienne glanced about the modest parlor and wondered how he would view her home and if his disdain would be apparent. Though the cottage was as fine as any in the town, the spartan furnishings readily conveyed a lack of wealth. Had it not been for the fact that the dwelling was offered with the position, her father would have been hard pressed to provide such lodging.

Self-consciously she smoothed the worn velvet of her plum-hued gown, hoping its outdated style would not be noticed. Her pride had been stung too often beneath the haughty arrogance of mincing fops who saw themselves well above her and felt no compulsion to keep the fact a secret. Her lack of dowry weighed poorly against their heavy purses. She longed to demonstrate to those opinionated oafs

2

that she was as well schooled and certainly better mannered than they, but such an attempt would have brought harsh disapproval from her father.

Avery Fleming thought it unnecessary and imprudent for any member of the fairer sex to be tutored beyond the basics of womanly duties and certainly not in ciphering and the written word. If not for her mother's inheritance and stubborn insistence, such a luxury of schooling would not have been bestowed upon the daughter. Angela Fleming had carefully held back a part of her own wealth to see the matter done, and Avery could say naught, considering he had himself, during the course of their marriage, appropriated the major part of it to support his own widely varied indulgences. Although the same opportunity had been lavishly expended upon Farrell, after less than a year at an advanced seminary, the lad had declared an intense dislike for "the pompous preaching and unjust disciplines of a bunch of stodgy old men" and resigned as a man of letters to return home and "learn the trade of his father," whatever that might be.

Erienne's mind prowled like a foraging hind through the long months since her mother's death, recalling the many hours she had spent alone while her father and brother played at cards or drank with some of the local townsmen or, when they traveled to Wirkinton, with the sailors and tars who came to the port. In the absence of Angela's careful rationing, the family's meager wealth dwindled rapidly away, and with its loss came the ever-constant tightening of purse strings, which in turn brought an increasing pressure from her father to wed. The critical juncture in this process came after the wounding of her brother in a viciously one-sided duel that left his right arm hanging at his side with the elbow fused at an odd angle and the hand beneath it weak and nearly useless. From then on Avery appeared beset by a fever to find her a rich husband.

A sudden anger nipped at the heels of Erienne's memory, and her thoughts quickened with its challenge.

"Now, *there* is one I'd like to meet," she hissed hotly to the room at large. "Christopher Seton! Yankee! Blackguard! Gambler! Roué! Liar!" Whatever name she seized upon seemed to fit. Indeed, a few titles that dwelt upon his lineage flitted through her mind, and she savored the taste of them.

"Aye, to meet that one face to face!" She imagined close-set eyes and a thin, crooked nose, stiff, straight hair sticking out from beneath the brim of a tricorn, narrow, pinched lips twisted in a cruel leer that revealed small, yellowed teeth. A wart at the point of a receding chin completed her creation. The vision was sweet as she finished and set it atop a thin and bony frame.

Oh, if she could just meet that one! Though she might not best him in a brawl, she could certainly flay his composure to her satisfaction. He would smart for a fortnight from the tongue-lashing she would lay upon him, then perhaps he would think twice before wreaking his vengeance on a less than wise and unwary lad, or causing havoc to rain upon an elder.

"Were I a man," she struck a fencing pose and swept her hand before her as if it held a razor-sharp rapier, "I'd fix him thus!" She stabbed once, twice, thrice, then whipped the imaginary tip across her victim's throat. Delicately she wiped the phantom blade and restored it to an equally airy scabbard. "Were I a man," she straightened to stare pensively through the window, "I'd assure myself that braggart knew the error of his ways and henceforth would bend to seek his fortune in some other corner of the world."

She caught her reflection in the crystal panes and folding her hands, struck a demure pose. "Alas, a brawling lad I am not, but a mere woman." She turned her head from side to side to inspect the carefully arranged raven tresses, then smiled wisely at her image. "Thus my weapons must be my wit and tongue."

For a moment she cocked a dark, finely arched brow above a baleful glare which, with the chillingly beautiful smile, could have iced the heart of the fiercest opponent. Woe to the one this lass unleashed her ire upon.

A drunken bellow from outside the house broke into her musings. "Eriennie!"

Recognizing her brother's voice, Erienne hastened into the entryhall and, with a heated admonition ready on her lips, threw open the portal to find Farrell Fleming leaning heavily against the doorjamb. His clothes were badly mussed and spotted, his tan hair like so much tangled straw beneath his tricorn. It was obvious from a mere glance that he had been drinking and carousing the whole night long and, since the hour was near the eleventh before noon, most of the morning as well.

"Erienne, me own fair sister!" he loudly greeted. Stumbling back a pace, he managed to reverse direction and lurched into the hall, flinging wide a spray of icy water from his sodden cloak as he passed his sister.

4

Erienne glanced anxiously up and down the road to see who might have witnessed this debacle and was relieved that on this miserable morn no one was about except a lone rider some distance off. By the time he came over the bridge and passed the cottage, he would see nothing out of the ordinary.

Erienne closed the door and leaned against it as she frowned at Farrell. He had caught his good arm about the balustrade and was trying to steady himself while he tugged feebly at the ties of his cloak.

"Eriennie, give yer li'l Farrell a hand with 'is rebesh . . . uh . . . rebelush garment. It willn't leave me as I bid it." He grinned apologetically and lifted his crippled arm in helpless appeal.

"Fine time for you to be coming home," she admonished, helping him out of the recalcitrant cloak. "Have you no shame?"

"None!" he declared, attempting a gallant bow. His efforts caused him to lose his precarious balance, and he began to totter backward.

Erienne quickly caught a handful of coat and wedged a shoulder beneath his arm to steady him, then wrinkled her nose in distaste as the stench of stale whiskey and tobacco smoke filled her nostrils. "The least you could have done was to come home while it was still dark," she sharply suggested. "Out all night drinking and playing your games, then you sleep the day through. Have you no better pastime?"

" 'Tis pure folly that I've been hindered from honest work an' from holdin' me own in this family. You can blame it on that Seton devil, you can. He did this to me."

"I know what he did!" she rejoined crisply. "But that's no excuse for the way you're carrying on."

"Cease yer harpin'," wensh." His words were more than slightly slurred. "Ye're gettin' to sound more like an ol' maid ev'ry day. A good thing Father has it in mind to marry ye off afore too long."

Erienne ground her teeth in mute rage. Catching a firmer grip on his arm, she tried to direct him into the parlor but staggered as he leaned heavily against her. "A pox on the both of you!" she snapped. "One as bad as the other! Marry me off to any rich man who comes along so you can carouse your lives away. A fine pair you are!"

"So!" Farrell jerked his arm free of her and accomplished an adroit quick step for several paces into the parlor. When he regained his footing on the treacherously heaving floor, he faced his sister and timed his sway like any seasoned salt to the slowing motion of the room. "You resent my sacrifice for your honor," he charged, trying to fasten an accusing eye on her. The task proved beyond his present capability, and he yielded to let his unruly gaze roam where it would. "Me and Father only wants to see ye fairly wed and safe from wayward rogues."

"My honor?" Erienne scoffed. Setting arms akimbo, she regarded her brother with something between tolerance and pity. "If you'd care to remember, Farrell Fleming, 'twas Father's honor you were defending, not mine."

"Oh!" he was at once apologetic and humble, like a small boy caught in a prank. "Tha's right. 'Twas Father." He stared down at his lame arm, swinging it forward to draw her attention to it so he might elicit as much sympathy as possible.

"I suppose in a small way it was also for me, because I bear the Fleming name," Erienne mused aloud. "And after Christopher Seton's slander of it, 'tis hard to ignore the gossip."

Thoughtfully she gazed once more at the rainswept landscape beyond the splattered panes, paying little heed to her brother, who was carefully weaving his way toward a whiskey decanter he had spied on a side table. Much to her disappointment, she saw the bridge was still intact, evidenced by the passing of the lone rider over its cobbled surface. The man appeared in no special hurry, but came steadily on, as if undaunted by the drizzle and assured of all the time in the world. Erienne wished it could be so with her. Heaving a sigh, she faced Farrell and immediately stamped a slender foot in vexation. He had set out a glass and was trying to work the stopper from the decanter with his good left hand.

"Farrell! Haven't you had enough?"

"Aye, 'twas Father's good name I was tryin' to defen'," he mumbled, never pausing in his labor. His hand was shaking as he slopped the glass full. Memory of the duel haunted him. Over and over he heard the deafening roar of his own pistol firing and saw the astonishment and horror on the judge's face as the man stood with the kerchief still in his raised hand. The sight was permanently impressed on his mind, yet at the time he had felt a strange mixture of horror and a blossoming glee when his opponent stumbled back clutching his shoulder. The blood had quickly seeped through Seton's fingers, and Farrell had waited in frozen expectancy for him to crumple. Instead, the man steadied himself, and the surge of relief Farrell had briefly known was abruptly washed away in a tide of cold sweat. The full folly of firing before the signal was given struck him when Seton's weapon slowly raised, for the bore of the pistol halted dead center on his chest.

"You challenged a man well beyond your experience, all because of a game of cards," Erienne chided.

The buzzing in Farrell's head forbade the penetration of his sister's words. Paralyzed by the scene that slowly unfolded in his mind, he saw only the gaping bore that had threatened him that early morn, heard only the thunderous beating of his own heart, felt only the gut-wrenching terror that now tormented his waking hours. On that chilly morn the sting of sweat had been in his eyes, but he had been too frightened even to blink, afraid that the slightest movement would bring a deathbound ball to slay him. The splintering panic had saturated him and torn at his nerve ends until with a bellow of helpless rage and frustration, he had raised his arm and hurled the empty weapon at his foe, never realizing that the sights of the other's pistol were already lifting to a point above his head.

Another explosion of sound had shattered the silence of that early dawn and buried it beneath an avalanche of echoes, turning Farrell's bellow of rage into a shriek of agony. The tearing shock that had seared through his arm had left a burst of white-hot pain throbbing in his brain. Before the smoke had cleared, he had fallen to the chilled, dew-laden greensward and there had writhed and moaned in utter torment and defeat. A tall, silhouetted shape had approached to stand just behind the kneeling form of the surgeon attending his arm. Through the haze of pain he had recognized his tormentor framed against the misty light of the rising sun. Christopher Seton's composure had done much to shame him, for the man calmly attempted to stem the flow of his own blood with a cloth tucked inside the shoulder of the coat.

Farrell had realized in the midst of his pain that by taking an unfair shot he had lost far more than the duel. It was a devastating blow to have one's reputation ruined so completely. No one would accept a coward's challenge, and he found no safe haven from the condemnation of his own mind.

" 'Twas the lad's own foolishness that caused the wound." Seton's words came back to plague him, drawing a whimper of despair from his lips. The man had stated it out boldly. "If he hadn't thrown his pistol, mine would not have discharged."

The judge had replied in a similarly distant and hollow tone.

"He fired before I gave the signal. You could have killed him, Mr. Seton, and no one would have questioned it."

Seton had growled his answer. "I'm not a slayer of children, man."

"I assure you, sir, you are blameless in this matter. I can only suggest that you hie yourself from here before the boy's father arrives and causes more trouble."

To Farrell's way of thinking, the judge had been too forgiving. The desire to make it understood that he was not of the same gracious mood had roiled through him, and he had screamed a string of foul curses, venting his helpless rage on the man rather than face the truth of his own cowardice. Much to his chagrin, the insults had produced nothing more than a bland smile of contempt from his opponent, who had strode away without giving him further heed, as if he were a child to be ignored.

The torturous vision retreated, and reality returned with its hard facts. Farrell faced the full glass before him, but his trembling knees could scarcely bear his weight, and he could not afford to give up the support of his good arm long enough to lift the whiskey to his lips.

"You mourn your terrible loss." Erienne's words finally claimed his attention. "And you're ready to count your life done at two years short a score. You'd be far better off had you left the Yankee alone instead of playing the outraged rooster."

"The man's a liar, and I called him out for it, I did." Farrell cast about for a haven and saw a welcome chair nearby. " 'Twas Father's honor and good name I sought to defend."

"Defend, bah! You're crippled for your effort, and Mr. Seton has not retracted one word of his accusation."

"He will!" Farrell blustered. "He will, or I'll . . . I'll . . ."

"You'll what?" Erienne questioned angrily. "Lose the use of your other arm? You'll get yourself killed believing you can go against a man with Christopher Seton's experience." She threw up a hand in disgust. "Why, the man is nearly twice your age and sometimes I think twice your wit. You were foolish to go after him, Farrell."

"The devil take ye, wench! Ye mus' think the sun rises and sets for yer lordly Mr. Seton."

"What do you say?!" Erienne cried, aghast at his accusation. "I've never even met the man! The most I know about him is some gossip I've heard, and I can't very well rely on that for accuracy."

"Oh, I've heard it, too," Farrell sneered. "Every li'l gatherin' o' twitterin' females is abuzz 'bout the Yankee an' his money. You can see the gleam o' it in their eyes, but without it, he's no better'n anybody else. An' experience? Huh! I've probably had as much."

"Don't you dare brag about those two you nicked," she snapped back in irritation. "No doubt they were more scared than hurt and in the long run just as foolish as you are."

"Foolish, am I?" Farrell tried to straighten himself to display his outrage at such an insult, but a loud belch seemed to deflate his purpose, and he slumped toward the table again, mumbling in self-pity. "Leav' me be, wench. Ye've attacked me in an hour o' weakness an' exhaustion."

"Hah! Drunkenness, you mean," she corrected acidly.

Farrell stumbled to the chair and fell into it. He closed his eyes and rolled his head on the padded back. "Ye take 'at rogue's side agin yer own brother," he moaned. "If Father could only hear ye."

Erienne's eyes flared with bright sparks of indignation. In two steps she was before his chair, catching the lapels of his coat. Braving the rank fumes that issued from his sagging mouth, she bent toward him.

"You dare accuse me?" She shook him until his eyes rolled in confusion. "I will tell you simply, Brother!" Her words were spat out in a half-hissed, half-snarled torrent of verbiage. "A stranger sailed into these northern climes, setting everyone's eyes agog with the size of his merchant ship, and the third day after his arrival in port," she jerked the coat and Farrell in it to underscore her facts, "he accused our Father of cheating at cards. Whether true or false, he had no need to bleat it aloud for all to hear, causing such a panic among the merchants of Mawbry and Wirkinton that even now Father fears they'll throw him into debtor's prison for the notes he cannot pay. Aye, and 'tis for the ease of this predicament that he seeks to marry me off. The wealthy Mr. Seton can hardly care about the havoc he has brought upon this family. I will indeed hold the man responsible for all he's done. But you, my dear brother, are an equal fool, for a heated denial and a failure to enforce it only strengthen the other's cause. Such men are better dealt with in calm deliberation, not youthful bravado."

Farrell stared at his sister in stunned amazement for this attack on his person, and Erienne realized he had heard nothing of what she had said.

"Oh, what's the use!" She pushed him back in disgust and turned away. There seemed to be no effective argument that would point out the folly of his ways.

Farrell eyed the brimming glass of whiskey and licked his lips, wishing she would bring him the drink. "You may be a couple years older'n me, Erienne." He was extremely weary. His mouth was cotton thick, and it took an effort to speak. "But tha's no cause to rant at me as if I were a child." Tucking in his chin, he mumbled glumly to himself, "Tha's what he called me . . . a child."

Erienne paced before the fireplace, seeking that elusive rationale with which she could affect her brother's reason, until a soft sound halted her, and she turned to find Farrell's head lolling limply on his chest. The first low snore quickly deepened into a rich, sonorous example of the art, making her crushingly aware of her blunder in not seeing him directly to his room. Silas Chambers could arrive momentarily, and her pride would pay a heavy toll beneath his scornful smirk. Her only hope would be her father's speedy return, but that too might prove to be a double-edged sword.

In the next halting moment, it dawned on Erienne that the leisurely clip-clop of hooves that had sounded outside for the past moment or two had ceased in front of the cottage. Erienne waited tensely for some indication of the rider's whereabouts, and doom descended when a heel grated on the step, closely followed by a loud rap on the door.

"Silas Chambers!" Her mind leaped apace with her nerves. Glancing wildly about, she wrung her hands in distress. How could his arrival be so ill-timed?

In frantic haste she ran to Farrell and tried to rouse him, but her best effort failed even to interrupt his measured snores. She caught him under the arms and attempted to haul him up, but alas, it was like trying to hoist a loose bag of heavy stones. He slumped forward and slid to the floor, sprawling in a limp, disorganized heap as the room echoed again with the caller's insistent knock.

Erienne had no choice but to accept the obvious. Perhaps Silas Chambers was not worth her concern, and she'd even be grateful for the blighting presence of her brother. Still, there was a reluctance to lend herself and her family to the ridicule that would surely follow his visit. Hoping at least to hide her brother from the casual eye, she pulled a chair around in front of him and spread a shawl over his face to soften the snores. Then with calm deliberation she smoothed her hair and gown, trying to squelch the anxieties that remained. Somehow it would all work out for the best. It just had to!

The persistent summons came again as she reached the door. She laid her hand on the latch, a cool vision of poised womanhood, and swung open the portal. For a brief moment the space seemed entirely filled by a tall expanse of darkly wet cloth. Slowly her gaze traveled up from expensive black leather boots, over a long length of redingote, to the face beneath the dripping brim of his beaver hat, and then her breath halted. It was a man's face, and far and away the most handsome she had seen in many a year. When a slight frown marked the brow, as when she first glimpsed it, the features appeared awesomely stern and foreboding. There was a tense, almost angry look to the crisp, chiseled line of his jaw, the taut cheeks, and the slightly aquiline profile that would have been well at home at sea. Yet humor came quickly, flitting about the features and compressing the tiny wrinkles of mirth at the corners of the eyes. The grayish-green eyes were totally alive, as if searching out every last note of joy in life. They openly and unabashedly displayed his approval as his gaze ranged over the full length of her. The slow grin that followed and the sparkle in his translucent eyes combined to a most disarming degree to sap the strength from her knees.

This was no doddering ancient or swaggering fop, Erienne realized, but a man alive and virile in every fiber of his being. That he greatly exceeded her expectations was undeniably an understatement. Indeed, she wondered why such a man had to resort to seeking a bride by way of barter.

The stranger swept off his hat in gallant haste, revealing a short, thick crop of dark, russet-brown hair. His rich, masculine voice was as pleasing as his good looks. "Miss Fleming, I presume?"

"Um, yes. Oh, Erienne. Erienne Fleming." Her tongue seemed unusually clumsy, and she began to fear that it would stumble and betray her. Her mind had begun to race, forming thoughts totally counter to what they had been earlier. The man was nearly perfect! Without visible flaw! Yet the question persisted. If the man was willing to wed, how could he reach a mature age without being entrapped by at least a dozen women?

There must be a flaw! her common sense raged. Knowing Father, there is a flaw!

Race as it might, her mind was fairly outdistanced by her suddenly active tongue. "Do come in, sir. My father said you would be coming."

"Indeed?" He seemed to digest her statement with a certain amount of amazement. The quirk in his lips deepened into an amused, one-sided grin as he peered at her inquiringly. "Do you know who I am?"

"Of course!" She laughed brightly. "We've been expecting you. Please come in."

As he stepped across the threshold, a faint frown of perplexity furrowed his brow, and he seemed almost reluctant to yield her his hat, riding crop, and gloves. Tucking the latter into the crown of the hat, Erienne laid the articles aside.

"You surprise me greatly, Miss Fleming," he commented. "I had expected to be greeted with resentment, not kindness."

Erienne mentally cringed at the implication of his words. She had not considered that her father would be so tactless as to reveal her unwillingness to wed. How could her parent have even thought that she would resent such a handsome suitor when he was so far above the rest who had come seeking her hand?

Responding with a feigned laugh of gaiety, she carefully expressed her concern. "I suppose Father told you of my reluctance to meet you."

The man grinned knowingly. "No doubt you thought me some horrid beast."

"I am much relieved to see that you are not," she replied, then worried that she had spoken with too much enthusiasm. She gritted her teeth, hoping he wouldn't think her a forward filly, but what she had said was almost an understatement.

Hiding her pinkening cheeks, she reached past him to close the door. A gentle cologne mixed with the pleasant smell of horse and man touched her senses with an acute awareness that left her almost giddy. Certainly no imperfection here!

His long fingers were deft and quick as he unfastened the buttons of his redingote. He swept the garment off, and try as she might, Erienne could find no flaw in those wide shoulders, lean waist, and long limbs. The ample swell of manhood beneath the snugly fitting breeches gave bold evidence of his masculinity, and remembering the cause of his visit, she was suddenly aflutter, as if already a bride.

"Let me take your coat," she offered, trying to steady her trembling voice. The impeccably tailored clothes were to be admired nearly as much as the man who wore them. Yet on someone of less impressive stature, they might have lost much of their flair. The waistcoat, worn beneath a dark green coat, was fashionably short and of a light buff hue that matched the breeches. The leather boots were made to mold the lean, muscular shape of his calves and were turned down at the tops to reveal cuffs of tan. Though the garments were stylish and costly, he wore them with a manly ease that held no hint of a foppish demeanor.

Erienne turned aside to hang the redingote on a peg beside the door. Stirred by the contrast of chilly wetness on the outside and the warmth on the inside, she paused to smooth the raindrops from the rich fabric, then faced him with a comment. "It must have been a miserable ride on a day like this."

The green eyes lightly swept her and catching her own, held them with a smiling warmth. "Miserable perhaps, but with such beauty to greet me, easily borne."

Perhaps she should have warned him about standing so close. It was most difficult to subdue the deepening blush of pleasure while appearing nonchalant. She berated her mind for its spring-halt inadequacy, but her thoughts had become mired in the fact that she was actually entertaining a man who, for once, seemed to fulfill every letter of her desire. Surely there was a flaw. There had to be!

"My father should be back any moment now," she informed him demurely. "Would you care to wait in the parlor?"

"If it would not inconvenience you," he replied. "There is a matter of importance I wish to discuss with him."

Erienne swept around to lead the way but almost froze when she entered the adjoining room. Farrell's shoe jutted obtrusively from behind the chair where she had left him. She was appalled at her own foolishness but realized it was too late to redirect their guest. In an attempt to distract the man, she gave him her prettiest smile as she crossed to the settee. "I saw you coming over the river from the north." She sank to the cushion and silently gestured for him to take a chair. "Do you live somewhere nearby?"

"Actually, I have a town house in London," he responded. He swept back the tails of his dark green coat, revealing its buff lining, and took a seat in the very chair that partially hid Farrell.

Erienne's composure faltered slightly when she considered how ridiculous she would feel if he chanced to spy the undignified heap behind him. "I . . . ah . . . was about to brew some tea," she stated in a nervous rush. "Would you care for some?"

"After such a wet and chilly ride, I would enjoy that immensely." His voice was smooth as velvet. "But, please, don't trouble yourself on my account."

"Oh, 'tis no trouble, sir," she hastened to assure him. "We have precious few guests here."

"But what of this one?" To her overwhelming chagrin he swept a hand toward Farrell. "A rejected suitor, perhaps?"

"Oh, no, sir! He's only . . . I mean . . . he's my brother." She shrugged helplessly. Her mind was too numb to allow a quick riposte. Besides, now that her secret was out, it was probably best to be completely honest, since there was no other logical explanation. "He . . . um . . . imbibed a trifle heavily last night, and I was trying to get him up to his room when you knocked."

Subdued amusement played on his face as he rose from his chair. Dropping to a knee beside her brother, he tossed aside the shawl and lifted a limp eyelid. The snores continued undisturbed; and when the man glanced up at her, his humor had grown more obvious. Strong white teeth sparkled behind a broadening grin. "Would you have need of assistance toward that end?"

"Oh, certainly, sir!" Her own smile would have charmed a sprite out of its lair. "I would be most grateful."

He came to his feet with a movement so easy and quick that it almost made her gasp with surprise. He shrugged out of his coat, confirming the fact that those broad shoulders belonged solely to him, and folded the garment neatly over the back of a chair. The vest had been meticulously tailored to fit the tapering chest that rose from a lean, narrow waist. When he lifted Farrell from the floor, the fabric of his shirt stretched taut for a moment, revealing the flowing muscles across his shoulders and arms. The weight that she had scarcely been able to move was casually laid over his shoulder. He turned to eye her quizzically. "If you will lead the way, Miss Fleming."

"Erienne, please," she bade as she brushed close by him to obey. Again the nearness and the fresh, manly scent of him filled her head, and she hurried into the hall, hoping he would not see the blush that infused her cheeks and neck.

Ascending the stairs, Erienne felt almost smothered by a perusal she knew by instinct never left her. Yet she dared not glance around, afraid she might prove her intuition correct. Indeed, if she had been able to note the admiring attention he paid her gently swinging hips and trim waist, she might have had even more reason to blush.

She ran ahead to Farrell's room to throw back the covers on his bed, and the man followed to dump his burden into the downy softness. She bent over her brother to loosen his stock and shirt, and when she straightened, her heart began to race, for the man was standing much too close again.

"I believe your brother would be more comfortable without his shirt and boots." Glancing down at her, he showed strong, white teeth in a sudden grin as he offered, "Shall I remove them for you?"

"Oh, by all means," she responded, warmed by his smile and solicitude. "But he's lame. Be careful of his arms."

The man paused and looked at her in surprise. "I'm sorry. I didn't know."

"No need for you to be concerned, sir. 'Twas much of his own doing, I fear."

His brow raised in wonder. "You're very understanding, Miss Fleming."

Erienne laughed to hide her confusion. "My brother is of a different opinion."

"Brothers generally are." The grin came back as she lifted her gaze, and his eyes moved leisurely over the fragile features, pausing at length on her soft red lips.

Erienne's senses felt dazed, snared on the brink of time. Distantly her mind observed that the irises behind those dark lashes were a clear green, with a hint of light gray around the inner edge. They glowed with a warmth that brought the color rising to her cheeks and made her heart thump unevenly in her chest. Mentally chiding herself for lacking the poise and aplomb of a highborn lady, she stepped away and began to putter about the room, allowing him to attend her brother. Since he appeared to have the matter well in hand, she did not offer any assistance, preferring to keep a secure distance. The silence grew long and stilted, and feeling a need to speak again, she tried a bit of clever repartee.

"The day has been quite miserable so far."

"Aye," he agreed with equal originality. "A most miserable day."

The deep timbre of his voice reverberated in her breast, and Erienne gave up trying to discern what his faults might be. In comparison to the ragtag collection of suitors who had come before him, he was about as close to perfect as she and her senses could bear.

When Farrell had been stripped to his breeches, the man came away from the bed with the shirt and boots in his hands. She reached to take the articles and was almost startled when his fingers deliberately lingered beneath hers. A warm shock went through her, slowly shredding her nerves. The thought formed in her mind that with all the fumbling, fondling caresses of her various suitors, she had never been affected as deeply as by this casual contact.

"I fear the weather will be much the same until spring," she said in a nervous rush. "Here in the north country, one can expect a lot of rain this time of year."

"Spring will be a welcome change," he replied with a slight nod.

The brilliance of their conversation did little to betray the active minds working beneath. The realization that he might soon become her husband dwelt foremost in Erienne's mind, and she grew curious as to what circumstances had brought such a man here in quest of her hand. Considering the choices her father had presented her of late, she would have felt fortunate if Silas Chambers had been only tolerable-looking and something less than ancient, but he was so much more than that. It was hard to believe her fondest hopes could be completely fulfilled in this one man.

In an attempt to calm her emotions and put a safe distance between herself and this man, she crossed the room and spoke over her shoulder as she put away her brother's clothes. "Being from London, you must find these northern climes quite different. We really noticed the change when we moved from there three years ago."

"Did you come for the climate?" he asked with amusement glowing in the clear green orbs.

Erienne laughed. "If you become accustomed to the dampness, 'tis quite pleasant to live here. That is, if you can ignore all the frightening rumors of highwaymen and raiding bands of Scots. You'll learn about them if you stay here for very long. Lord Talbot complained so fiercely about the Scottish bands raiding the hamlets along the border, my father was brought in as mayor and then a sheriff was appointed to keep the outlands safe." She spread her hands in a gesture of doubt. "I hear many rumors of distant skirmishes and of highwaymen murdering and robbing the rich as they pass in their coaches, but the best my father and the sheriff have done has been to catch a poacher on Lord Talbot's lands. Even at that, the man wasn't a Scot."

"I shall resist the urge to boast of my Scottish ancestors lest I be taken for a highwayman or the like."

She gazed at him in sudden worry. "Perhaps you should take special care not to tell my father. He gets highly upset when any discussion about the Scottish and Irish clans arises."

Her companion dipped his head slightly to acknowledge her warning. "I shall try not to anger him unduly with such a revelation."

She led the way from the room, speaking over her shoulder. "I assure you 'tis not a family trait. I have no reason to dislike them."

"That's encouraging."

Erienne was somewhat dazzled by the warmth in his voice and failed to devote due attention to the stairs. Her slippered foot partially missed the first step, causing her to stumble and teeter precariously on the brink of a precipitous descent. Her breath froze in her throat, but before she could react, a long arm encircled her waist and yanked her back to safety. Caught against his broad, hard chest, she gasped in breathless relief. Finally, tremblingly, she raised her gaze to the face above her own. Filled with concern, his eyes searched hers until gradually the worry left them, to be replaced by a deeper, smoldering light.

"Miss Fleming . . ."

"Erienne, please." Her whisper was subdued and distant.

Neither of them heard the front door being opened or the mingled masculine voices drifting up from below. They were caught in their own private universe and might have remained there undisturbed for several more moments had not an enraged bellow roused them to abrupt awareness.

"Here now! What's the meanin' o' this?"

Still much in a daze, Erienne pulled away and glanced down to the hall below, where her father and another man stared back in equal amazement. The rapidly darkening, wide-eyed face of Avery Fleming was enough to unsettle her composure, but the thing that really roused doubt about the rightness of her world was the coarse-featured visage of the thin, bony stranger who stood beside her parent. He matched her vision of Christopher Seton exactly. All he needed was a large wart on his chin to be her foe incarnate.

Avery Fleming's righteous display of anger fairly shook the house. "I asked ye what's the meanin' o' this!" He gave her no moment to answer before he ranted on. "I leave ye for no more 'an a moment or two an' come back to find ye flauntin' a man in me own . . . *You!*"

Avery threw his hat to the floor, and his sparse hair stood on end. *"Be damned! Betrayed in me own house! By me own kin!"*

Red-faced with embarrassment, Erienne quickly descended the stairs as she tried to shush her kin. "Please, Father, let me explain . . ."

"Ahhh, ye needn't!" he snarled in derision. "I can see it all with me own eyes! Betrayed, it is! An' by me own daughter!" He flung up a hand contemptuously toward the man who came down the stairs behind her and sneered, "With this bloody bastard!"

"Father!" Erienne was shocked at his choice of titles. "This . . ." She also indicated the one descending down the steps. "This is the man you sent. Silas Chambers, I believe."

The raw-faced stranger stepped forward, bobbing his head in a confused, birdlike manner. He jabbed his hat out in front of him to gain their notice and began to stutter, "I . . . I a-a-am, I-I m-mean, h-he . . . he's n-not . . . ooof!"

The last was an abrupt exhalation caused by Avery when he stepped forward and flung his arms wide in a gesture of complete disgust. The gaunt man was brushed aside as the father's discomfiture burst in broad display.

"Ye mindless little twit! Have ye lost yer wits? He's not Silas Chambers!" He thrust a thumb over his shoulder at the bony one. "This one's yer man! Right 'ere!" Then he struck a portly, bowlegged pose and stabbed a stubby finger at the man on the stairs. " 'At one! 'At father-less swine . . ."

Erienne leaned against the wall and shut her eyes tightly. She already knew what her father would say.

". . . 'E's the one what blasted poor Farrell's arm! 'E's yer Mr. Seton! Christopher Seton, it is!"

"Christopher Seton?" Erienne's lips formed the words, but no sound issued forth. She opened her eyes and searched her father's face as if fervently seeking a denial of what she had heard. Her gaze went to the gawky stranger, and the truth was only too clear. He was no different from the rest of the suitors her father had brought for her consideration.

"You foolish ninny!" Avery continued to berate her. "*This* is Silas Chambers! *Not* that conceited scoundrel ye was wrapped up with!"

An expression of stunned horror on her face, Erienne stared up into the green eyes.

Christopher smiled sympathetically. "My apologies, Erienne, but I thought you knew. If you'll remember, I questioned you about it."

The dismay on her face yielded beneath the onslaught of pure rage. She had been duped! And her pride ached for revenge. Hauling back a hand, she let fly a stinging slap to his bronze cheek. "'Tis Miss Fleming to you!"

Rubbing the side of his face, Christopher Seton laughed softly, his eyes still warm and sparkling. Erienne could not bear his taunting gaze and presented her back to him. He admired it briefly before he lent his attention to her father. "I came to inquire about a debt you promised to make good, sir. I'm wondering when I might expect such an event to take place."

Avery's head lowered sheepishly between his shoulders while his face glowed a bright red. Avoiding Silas's inquisitive stare, he mumbled something about paying the debt as soon as he could.

Christopher stepped into the parlor to retrieve his coat and came back shrugging it into place. "I was hoping you could be a bit more specific than that, Mayor. I don't like to intrude on your hospitality too often, and you did promise to pay me within a month's time. As you must be aware, the month has come and gone."

Avery clenched his hands into tight fists but dared not bring them up from his sides lest the movement be taken as a challenge. "You'd best keep yer moldy presence away from here, Mr. Seton. I won't have the likes o' ye servicin' me daughter. She'll be gettin' married, and I'll not see ye hinderin' the nuptials."

"Ah, yes, I did hear some rumors about that," Christopher replied with a sarcastic smile. "After meeting her, I'm somewhat amazed that you haven't been more successful, though it seems rather unjust that she must pay the rest of her life for a debt you made."

"Me daughter is none o' yer concern!"

Though Silas Chambers had jumped as each word was being shouted, Christopher had held a bland smile on his face. He appeared undaunted as he replied, "I hate to think that she'll be forced into a marriage because of a debt owed to me."

Avery gaped at him in surprise. "Aye? Ye wouldn't be thinkin' o' forgettin' 'bout the debt, now would ye?"

Christopher's laughter dispelled the notion. "Hardly! But I'm not without eyes in my head, and I realize your daughter would be a most charming companion. I'd be willing to wait a bit longer for what is due me if you would allow me to court her." He shrugged casually. "Who knows what might come of it."

Avery nearly strangled over the suggestion. *"Blackmail and debauchery!* I'd sooner see her dead than taken up with the likes o' ye!"

Christopher considered Silas, who nervously crushed his tricorn against his chest. When he returned his gaze to the mayor, his mockery was subtle yet direct. "Aye, I imagine you would."

Avery blustered under the jibe. He was aware that Silas was not much to look at, but the man had a modest fortune. Besides, his daughter was better off avoiding marriage to a handsome rake who would get her with a brood of brats. Silas would be suitable enough for her needs. But then, after seeing her with this Seton devil, Silas might be hesitant about offering marriage for fear he might be getting tainted goods.

"There be plenty o' suitors willing to pay the bride price," Avery insisted, just in case Silas had any doubts. "Men what are wise enough to see what treasures she'll bring 'em, and not one of 'em abused her kin."

Facing Erienne, Christopher favored her with a lopsided grin. "I suppose this means I won't be welcomed here again?"

"Get out! And don't ever darken this door again!" she cried, fighting tears of anger and humiliation. Her lips curling with contempt, she gave him a scathing perusal. "Were a twisted, scar-faced, hunchbacked cripple the only other man on earth, I would surely choose him over you!"

Christopher let his gaze glide down her. "As for me, Erienne, were you cast down before me, I would not be wont to cross over you to get to some broad bovine." He smiled in wry humor as his eyes met hers again. " 'Twould be pure foolishness to spite myself for the sake of pride."

"Out!" The word was spat from her lips with vengeance as her arm thrust out in the direction of the door.

Christopher gave a curt, mocking bow of compliance and approached the peg which bore his redingote while Avery seized his daughter's arm and jerked her into the parlor.

"What's this now?" The mayor hissed in an angry demand. "Here I goes out and risks me fine health in a high-blowin' nor'easter to bring yer beau to ye an' returns to find ye throwin' yerself at the likes o' him!"

"Silas Chambers is not my beau!" Erienne corrected in an urgent whisper. "He's just another man whom you've brought to look me over as if I were some horse to be traded. And I wasn't throwin' myself at anyone! I just stumbled, and Silas . . . Mr. Seton caught me."

"I saw what the beggar was tryin'! Had his hands all over ye, he did!"

"Please, Father, lower your voice," she begged. " 'Twas not the way you think!"

As the argument continued and Avery's voice grew louder, Silas Chambers twisted his tricorn in painful indecision. On the verge of panic, the lank, pale-haired, coarse-faced man cast repeated glances toward the parlor.

"I expect they'll be engaged for some time," Christopher stated, slipping into his redingote. As Silas glanced at him, he tipped his head to indicate the two in the parlor. "A strong rum might help settle your stomach. Or perhaps you would care to join me for a bite to eat at the inn? You can return here later if you wish."

"Why . . . ah . . . I believe I . . ." Silas's eyes widened as a jumbled bellow came from the parlor, and he made a hasty decision. "I believe I shall, sir. Thank you." He jerked on his tricorn, suddenly grateful for any excuse to be gone from this place.

Hiding an amused smile, Christopher opened the door and allowed the man to precede him. As the chill wind and pelting rain struck them, Silas shivered and hurriedly pulled up the collar of his coat. His nose reddened abruptly and seemed to stand out like a large, glowing beacon. He drew on a pair of tattered gloves and stuffed a frayed scarf into his collar, causing Christopher to raise a skeptical brow. If the man had wealth, there was not a great lot of visible evidence to substantiate the fact. His appearance was that of some hardworking accountant whose employer miserly doled out his wages. It would be interesting indeed to see just how deep the man would dig in his purse should a contest evolve for the fair hand of Erienne Fleming.

Two

The front door closed gently but with the same effect as a sudden crack of thunder. The unexpected sound startled Avery from his tirade, and he faced the hallway with sagging jaw, realizing that not only had Christopher Seton left, but also that Silas Chambers had gone with him. With a groan of despair, Avery turned to his daughter again and threw up his hands.

"Ye see what ye've done! We've lost another one because o' yer blamed foolishness! Dammit, girl! Ye'd best tell me why ye let that rascal in me house, or I'll set me whip to yer back."

Erienne rubbed the still stinging spot above her elbow where her father had held her arm. She could see the empty pegs beside the door and experienced a sense of elation that she had at least ordered that overbearing knave from the cottage. She was also abundantly relieved that Silas had seen fit to leave with him. Yet she felt a strange sense of loss too, as if something briefly seen and delightfully pleasant was forever gone from her life. She spoke with careful emphasis as she again tried to explain. "I have never met Christopher Seton before, Father, and whenever either you or Farrell described him, it was in less than accurate terms. You told me a Silas Chambers was on his way here, and when a man arrived, I assumed it was he." Turning away, she fumed silently to herself. And a vile beast he was too, leading me on like that and letting me believe he was another man!

Avery spoke in a half-weeping tone. "Me daughter escorts me blood enemy ter the bedchambers o' me own house, and only the good saints know what went on. And she tells me 'twas a mistake. A mere mistake."

Erienne stamped her foot in frustration. " 'Twas Farrell, Father! He stumbled in here drunk and passed out on the floor. Right there where you stand! And Mr. Cham . . . I mean Mr. Seton was kind enough to carry him upstairs to his bed."

Avery fairly roared, and his eyes flared, "You let 'at blighter lay hands on poor helpless Farrell again?"

"He didn't hurt him." Erienne scuffed her foot against the thread-bare carpet in embarrassment, mumbling to herself, " 'Twas me he abused."

Her reply did not soften Avery's rage. "Me lord! Ye make him sound like a bloody saint! He didn't hurt him," he mimed in a squeaky voice and thrust an accusing finger toward the door. " 'Twas 'at devil who laid me poor Farrell down in the first place. The very same one ye was consortin' with!"

Erienne gasped at the slur. "Consorting! Father! We put Farrell to bed, and when I started down the stairs, I stumbled. He caught me! He saved me from a fall! And that, Father, was all that happened."

" 'Twas enough!" Avery threw up his hands again, then folding them behind his back, began to pace in front of the hearth. " 'Twas enough," he repeated over his shoulder, "ter give 'at fine Mr. Chambers a clear view o' his own intended a-twistin' in the arms of another man. Why, he's probably halfway back ter York by now."

Erienne sighed in frustration. "Father, Silas Chambers was never my intended. He was only another one of your precious prospects."

Avery shook his head sadly and groaned. "Only another one. And they're gettin' fewer by the day. Without a dowry 'tis nigh impossible ter convince 'em ye'll be a fittin' bride." His anger found new fuel. "What with yer highfalutin ideas on marriage an' all. Gotta respect and like the bloke ye marry, ye say. Bah! 'Tis only an excuse ter reject 'em all. I've brought ye the best, and still ye turn 'em away."

"The best?" Erienne scoffed. "You brought the best, you say? You brought a wheezing, fat glutton; a stumbling, half-blind old man; a bone-thin pinchpenny with hairy warts on his cheeks. And you say you've brought me the best?"

Avery halted and stared at her in hurt reproof. "They were all single men, o' good report, o' good lineage, and each and every one was the bearer o' a wealthy purse."

"Father," Erienne took on a pleading tone, "bring me a young and handsome gentleman, one with a good purse, and I will love you and tend your needs and wants till your dying day."

He fixed her with a jaundiced eye and drew himself up, assuming his best lecturing posture. "Now, daughter, it becomes apparent ter me 'at ye've an error in yer way o' thinkin'."

Had Erienne been near a chair, she might have sank into it in sheer despair. As it was, she could only favor her father with a blank stare.

"Now mind ye, girl. I'm givin' ye a bit o' pure wisdom." He waggled a finger at her to emphasize his point. " 'Ere be more ter a man than a handsome face or a pair o' broad, square shoulders. Look at yer precious Mr. Seton, for instance."

Erienne flinched at the sound of the name and ground her teeth to keep back a flood of heated verbiage. The cad! He had deliberately tricked her!

"Now, 'ere's a cagey one for ye. Always schemin' ter get the upper hand."

Erienne almost nodded before she caught herself. The man had played upon her confusion for his own amusement, and her pride stung beneath the suspicion that he had been a step ahead of her all the time.

"Him being such a rich dandy, I s'pose those doxies on the waterfront would be proud to be on his arm, but no decent lady better take up with his sort. He'd fill their bellies with babes without so much as a promise o' marriage. And even if ye did get him ter say the vows with ye, which I doubt, he'd leave ye for one reason or another when he grew tired o' ye. 'Tis the way o' those handsome cocks. They seem just as proud o' what's in their britches as their own fine fair looks."

Blushing to the roots of her hair, Erienne recalled where her own gaze had briefly dwelt, with just as much curiosity perhaps as any other smitten virgin.

" 'Tis true enough 'at Seton's a handsome one, if ye go for 'em hard, bony jowls." Avery rubbed his knuckles against his own sagging dewlaps. "But ter those who know, he's a cold one, he is. A man can see it in his eyes."

Erienne remembered the warmth of those crystal-clear orbs and doubted the truth of her father's observation. There was a vibrant life and an intensity in those green eyes that no one could deny.

Avery ranted on, "With his arrogant and deceitful ways, I pity the wench who weds him."

Even if she detested the man, Erienne had to disagree again with her sire. Surely the wife of Christopher Seton would be far more envied than pitied.

"You needn't be concerned, Father." She smiled somewhat ruefully. "I shall never again be taken in by Mr. Seton's wiles."

Excusing herself, Erienne made her way up the stairs and paused briefly outside Farrell's door. The snores continued undisturbed. No doubt he would sleep the day away, then come the night rouse himself for another drinking bout.

She frowned slightly and glanced around. There was a faint scent in the hall, of a mild, manly cologne, and for an elusive moment the green eyes highlighted with light gray flicked through her mind and hinted at what the strong, straight lips had not been wont to speak. She shook her head to banish the vision, and the top step caught her eye. The memory of the way he had lifted her back and held her to him sent a dizzying thrill through her. She could almost feel the rock-hard arms clasped about her, and the smooth, sleek firmness of his well-muscled chest pressed against her bosom.

Erienne's face flamed at the meanderings of her mind, and she ran to her room, where she fell across the bed and lay staring out a rain-spattered window. His silken jibes echoed through her mind.

Cast down! Cross over! *Bovine!*

Suddenly her eyes flew wide as she realized the full import of what he had said. She could not find the slightest pleasure in being informed that he would not step over her to get to a cow. She cursed his glib tongue and herself for not seeing his meaning immediately. With an agonized groan, she rolled onto her back to stare at the cracked plaster of the ceiling, which gave her mind no gentler balm than the water-streaked glass had.

Downstairs in the parlor, Avery continued to pace in distraught agitation. Trying to find a wealthy husband for his daughter was proving to be the most difficult task he had ever set himself upon. It was true irony that just when Silas Chambers was getting into a heated froth at the idea of having a young and beauteous maid for a wife, that rapscallion Seton appeared to disrupt the whole affair, as if he had not done enough harm to the Fleming family.

"Damn!" Avery struck his fist into his palm, then sought a strong draught to assuage the pain of both hand and spirit. Restlessly he began to roam the room again, cursing his luck. "Hell and damnation!"

He had been well on his way in His Majesty's service when he had inadvertently saved one Baron Rothsman from certain capture during a confrontation with Irish rebels. The baron had proved effusive in his gratitude and urged the aging captain to retire and join his entourage in the London Court. Sheltered by the influence of the baron, he had progressed rapidly through several levels of the politico.

Avery's eyes grew distant, and he sampled a second share of the fiery brew.

It was a blissful time in his memory, an endless whirl of high-minded conferences and meetings and, in the evenings, the balls and social affairs. There had come into it all a pale-haired, newly widowed beauty of exceptional breeding, and though her eyes were always sad, she had not rejected the attention of the slightly graying Fleming. Avery discovered that her first husband had been an Irish rebel and that his final act had been to test a length of rope on one of His Majesty's prison barges shortly after the wedding. By then, Avery was well infatuated and cared naught that she had loved such a hated foe, but pressed her into marriage with him.

A child was born, a girl with locks as dark as her mother was fair, then two years later a son of the same mouse-brown hair and ruddy complexion as his father. A year after the boy arrived, Avery Fleming was elevated in position again. This one carried responsibilities far beyond his level of competence, but it introduced Avery to the private clubs of the London elite and to the high-stakes games of chance that flourished within the velvet walls. An awestruck Fleming took to the latter like a duck is gorged for the roasting platter, oblivious of the end that awaited him. Despite the worried warnings of his wife, he wagered heavily and even invested in a horse that seemed addicted to the sight of many other horses clearing the way well ahead of him.

His debauchery at play and ineptitude at work caused so much embarrassment for Rothsman that the baron soon refused to accept his calls. Angela Fleming suffered in her own way. She had to watch her personal fortune dwindle until the only dowry she could give her daughter was one which could never be taken from her, an education and as much preparation as possible for life as a wife on whatever level the girl would seek.

"Damn 'at foolishness!" Avery growled. "With the coin 'at woman wasted on 'at simple twit . . . Why, I could've still been livin' in London."

Dismissed from his position in that city a thrice of years ago, he had been banished to the North of England, where he was appointed mayor of Mawbry and carefully directed through his simple and limited duties by Lord Talbot. On leaving London he had left his debts unpaid, seeing no need to worry about debtors' prison, for in the northern climes he would be reasonably safe from discovery. It was a chance to start over again with a clean slate and prove himself to be a man of high intelligence.

Then Angela died, and he went through a brief period of mourning. A lively game of cards seemed to help him over his loss, and shortly thereafter it became his habit to take weekend jaunts with Farrell to Wirkinton or meet with the cronies at the Mawbry Inn for a game or two during the week. In his unquenchable quest for games of chance he often visited the waterfront, where he could be assured of finding a fresh face and a full purse. A few tars might have suspected that his skill with cards was more through the dexterity of his fingers than with luck, but a common seaman dared not speak out against an official. As it was, he had enlisted his talents only when the stakes were high or when he needed the purse. He was not so selfish that he was against sharing portions of the prize money by buying a round or two of ale or rum, but seamen were generally poor losers, especially that brawling, treacherous breed of Yankees, and he suspected that more than a few complained to their captains. He cursed himself for not being more cautious when Christopher Seton had asked to join his game, but sea captains were usually easy to spot, and Seton had not been of that ilk. Rather, he had given the appearance of being a gentleman of leisure or a nattily dressed dandy. His speech had been as precise and refined as any lord at court and his manners impeccable. There had been little evidence to indicate the man owned the vessel in port and a whole bloody fleet of others.

The size of the Yankee's purse had astounded him, and Avery

had purposed to take him for a substantial sum. His blood had rushed with the excitement and the challenge of besting a moneyed gentleman. Whatever the outcome, it had promised to be an exciting game even for those who watched. Sailors and their doxies had gathered close about the table. For a time Avery had played the cards straight, letting fate ply its erratic favor where it would, then as the stakes mounted he began to lay out his ploy, holding back the cards he needed. Across the table from him those hooded eyes never flickered even once, nor had the bland smile wavered far from that bronze visage. Thus, when Seton had reached across the table to flick open his coat, spilling the carefully hoarded cards in front of everyone, Avery was taken completely by surprise. Trying to think of how best to deny the accusation, he had gawked and sputtered. His blustering denials had placated no one, and though he could recall glancing about for reinforcement, there had been none until Farrell entered and rushed forward to defend his sire's honor. Never being one to indulge in good judgment, the younger Fleming had hotly issued a challenge to the stranger.

Avery's features grew grim. His carelessness had been the direct cause of his son losing the use of his arm, but how could he admit that to anyone but himself? He had hoped that Farrell would kill the fellow, thereby canceling the debt. Two thousand pounds he owed the blighter! Why couldn't things have gone his way just once? Why couldn't Farrell have killed him? Even if Seton owned a fleet of ships, no one in England would have mourned his loss. The man was a foreigner. A worthless Yankee!

A snarl transformed Avery's face as he remembered the sailors from the Yankee ship, *Cristina*, chortling after the game and patting the man on the back while they respectfully called him Mr. Seton. Why, they had rejoiced so heartily over his victory, Avery was of the firm belief they would have been ready to start a brawl in his defense. Everything had gone well for the Yankee, but nothing was left for the Flemings to be proud of. Word had spread faster than the plague that he had been called out as a cheat, and with that, creditors had started to hound him for their money and to close his accounts.

Avery's thick, rounded shoulders slumped wearily. "What's a poor beleaguered father ter do now? A crippled son! An arrogantly selective daughter! How will we make ends meet?"

His mind slowly churned as he debated his next course of action in getting his daughter married. A rich merchant near Wirkinton had seemed eager to meet Erienne after hearing him boast of her beauty and many talents. Though quite ancient himself, Smedley Goodfield was deeply appreciative of the young ladies and was sure to find the girl to his liking. The one fault Avery saw in him was that he was extremely tight with a coin, only parting with a shilling when he was forced to. However, with a sweet young thing to warm his blood and his bed, Smedley might prove to be a lot more generous. And, of course, as old as he was, he couldn't live much longer. Avery held a vision of Erienne widowed and wealthy. Were such an event to occur, he could enjoy life's abundant treasures once again.

Avery scratched a bristled jowl as a leering smile spread over his lips. He would do it! Come morning he would travel to Wirkinton and set the proposition to the aging merchant. Avery was certain the old man would accept. Then he would announce the news to his daughter, and the pair of them would be off to see Smedley Good-field. Of course, Avery knew Erienne would not be pleased with his selection, but she would have to bear up under her disappointment. After all, her mother had.

His spirits much brightened by the prospect, Avery quaffed an-other brew to celebrate his decision, then he rose and settled his hat firmly on his broad brow. A bunch of his friends were wagering on the droves of stock that would soon be coming to market at Mawbry, whether the first would be sheep, geese, or the like. With the antici-pation of Smedley Goodfield being in the family, he could now afford to lay odds on his preference.

A casual meeting ground for traveler and villager alike, the com-mon room of the Boar's Inn at Mawbry was rarely without at least a patron or two. Huge, rough-hewn wooden columns supported the upper floors of the establishment and provided a meager semblance of privacy for those who entered the lower room. The acrid odor of strong ale and the appetizing aroma of the roasting meats pervaded even the darkest corner. Kegs of rum and ale lined one wall, and in front of these the innkeeper swabbed his well-worn planks with a damp cloth. He cast an occasional eye toward a souse who dozed in the shadows at the end of the bar, while a serving wench bustled about to slide trenchers of food and tankards of ale before a pair of men who bent their heads close together across a trestle table near the hearth.

Seated at a table in front of the window, Christopher Seton tossed several coins onto the pitted surface to pay for the fare he and Silas Chambers had shared, then leaned back in the chair to sip the remainder of his ale leisurely. The barking of dogs on the street outside announced the hasty departure of Mr. Chambers and his rather nondescript carriage. Christopher smiled in amusement as he watched through the glass panes. The man had obviously been disturbed by the argument that had ensued between the Flemings, and with another to buy him a libation, he had readily confessed that he was somewhat hesitant about taking the maid to wife. It seemed the mayor had boasted of his daughter being as meek as she was comely, and though her beauty had certainly been proven, Mr. Chambers confided that the quality of meekness was most heartily strained. The girl had displayed a bit more fire than he thought he could handle. He was a most peaceable man, painstakingly cautious, and rather set in his ways. To be able to feast on such loveliness and to think of her as his own would no doubt be joy without peer, but her display of temper sorely worried him.

Christopher was not dissatisfied with Silas Chambers' decision to leave. Indeed, he was most comfortable with it. It had not been necessary to issue dire warnings or morose insinuations in order to dissuade Silas from returning to the Fleming cottage. All it had taken was a few understanding nods, noncommittal shrugs, and a sympathetic countenance to convince the man that he should approach this matter of marriage with a great deal of caution. Silas had appeared almost eager to heed this sage advice. After all, he had rationalized aloud, he had his small fortune to protect, and one could not be too careful about choosing a wife.

Christopher felt a presence beside his table, and raising his gaze, he found the short, straggly-haired sot anxiously eyeing the half-filled tankard that Silas had left.

"Ye be a stranger 'ere, gov'na?" the drunk asked.

It was not hard to guess what had lured the man, but Christopher was curious about Mawbry and its mayor and was not unwilling to listen to the babblings of a village alehound. Christopher gave an affirmative nod, and the man smiled broadly, showing badly rotted teeth, before his gaze darted to the cup again.

"May ol' Ben join ye, gov'na?"

As an invitation Christopher indicated the chair Silas had vacated.

As soon as the man flumped down into the seat, he caught up the tankard and greedily drained off the contents.

Christopher caught the eye of the serving wench and beckoned to her. "Bring my friend here another ale," he directed, "and perhaps some meat to fill his belly."

"Ye're a bleedin' saint, gov'na!" the man chortled, setting his heavy dewlaps to trembling and his fleshy red nose to jiggling ponderously. Purplish veins lined his face, and the left one of those dull blue eyes was slightly coated with a whitish film. He glanced nervously about, awaiting the fare. The woman slid the ale and a wooden trencher of meats before him, and leaning forward to take up the coins on the table, she smiled at Christopher, inviting him to view her voluptuous endowments as the blouse sagged away from her bosom. In an unexpected movement Ben slapped a gnarled hand over hers, startling both his patron and the serving maid.

"Mind ye take no more'n yer rightful due, Molly," he snarled. " 'Tis tenpence fer each o' them stouts and a wee tuppence more fer the meats, so count it out carefully. I'm not o' a mind ter see ye gits a tuppence or two extra. Ye been short o' charity fer ol' Ben, and I won't see ye thievin' from me gentleman friend 'ere."

While Christopher coughed to hide his humor, Molly bent a menacing glare on the salt. Still, she carefully counted out the necessary coin and departed. Satisfied, Ben lent his attention to his meal and his ale.

" 'Tis good o' ye ter look aftah ol' Ben, gov'na," he finally mumbled, dragging his ragged sleeve across his greasy mouth. He took a long pull from the tankard, then sighed deeply. "Ain't enough kind folk here about 'at'll give me the time o' day, much less a feast o' this sort. Ol' Ben's beholden ter ye."

"Have you need of employment?" Christopher queried.

The man shrugged his shabby shoulders. "Ain' a body what'll trust ol' Ben wit' a pinch o' salt, much less wit' chores ter be done. H'it ain't always been 'at way. Ol' Ben, he served in 'is Majesty's tubs fer better'n twenty years." Thoughtfully rubbing his bristly chin, he peered at the well-garbed gentleman. "I seen by yer walk ye've been on a deck yerself a time or two."

"A time or two perhaps," Christopher replied. "But I'm bound to the land now. At least for a while."

"Ye be stayin' 'ere at the inn?" At the other's nod, Ben was quick with another inquiry. "Ye be lookin' fer a place to make a home?"

"Would you have any suggestions if I were?" Christopher countered.

Ben fixed a bleary eye on Christopher and leaning back, folded his hands over his paunch. "I 'spect a gent like yerself would be wantin' a fancy 'ouse and yards. More's the pity! Lord Talbot claims most o' what's 'ere and about. 'Tain't likely he'll give ye a chance at any o' it, lest ye take a fancy ter his daughter and marry up wit' her. Course, it ain't quite 'at simple. His lordship gots ter see a man worth bein' his kin first, an' from what I hears, 'tis a wee mite hard ter please him. Not her, mind ye!" He chortled. "She'll like ye, all right. She's gots an eye fer the men."

Christopher declined with a chuckle. "I'm not really considering marriage at this time."

"Well, if'n ye were, seein's as ye're me friend an' all, I'd tell ye ter hie yerself over ter the mayor's and look over his girl. She be the only one in Mawbry what'll have a pity on ol' Ben and slip me a bite ter eat out the back door when I comes around." He snickered behind the hand that he rubbed his nose with. "O' course, the mayor'd come a cropper if'n he knowed about it."

"Should I decide to become seriously interested in acquiring a wife, I'll keep your suggestion in mind." The green eyes twinkled above the rim of his mug as Christopher sipped the brew.

"Now, mind ye, ye'd not be gettin' a dowry," Ben warned. "The mayor can't afford it. And there ain't no chance o' gettin' yerself lands like maybe ye would if'n ye set yer sights on ol' Talbot's snippet." His red-rimmed eyes took in the costly attire of the other. " 'Course, maybe ye'd not have a need for another's wealth. But even if ye could afford it, ain't no lands what's ter be 'ad around 'ere." He paused and raised a crooked finger to correct himself. " 'Ceptin' maybe 'at ol' place what burned a few years back. Saxton Hall it be, gov'na, but it be partly rubble now, not a fittin' port in any storm."

"Why is that?"

"All 'em Saxtons were murdered or run off. Some blame the Scots, some say not. More'n a score years back the ol' lord was dragged out in the middle o' night and run through with a claymore. His wife and boys managed ter escape, and nothin' was ever heard from any of 'em till . . . oh . . . long 'bout three . . . four years back one o' the sons come back ter claim it all. Oh, he were a proud-lookin' one, he were. Tall like yerself, with eyes what'd fix a body through when he blew hot an' mad. Then, when he barely had his feet firm

on the sod o' the place, the manor caught fire, and he burned ter death. Some say 'twas the Scots again." Ben slowly shook his shabby head. "Some say not."

Christopher's curiosity was piqued. "Are you saying you think it wasn't the Scots?"

Ben's head wagged from side to side. "There be 'ems what know, gov'na, and 'ems what don't. 'Tain't safe ter be ones what do."

"But you do," Christopher pressed. "Anyone with your quick mind has got to know."

Ben leered at his companion. "Aye, ye're a sharp one there, gov'na. I gots me wits 'bout me, 'tis true, an' in better times ol' Ben has ridden wid the wildest of 'em. Most folk think ol' Ben is a witless, half-blind ol' rummy. But I tells ye, gov'na, ol' Ben, he 'as a fine eye an' ear fer seein' and hearin' what goes on." He bent closer and lowered his voice to barely above a whisper. "I can tell ye tales 'bout some folks what'll stiffen the hairs on yer head. Why, they'd laugh ter see a man burn, they would." He shook his head as if suddenly troubled. "I'd best not ter talk of it. 'Tain't healthy."

Christopher beckoned to Molly and threw out another coin when she brought a replacement for Ben's empty tankard. She was all warmth and smiles for him, but when she glanced at the old tar, her lip curled sneeringly, and with a toss of her head, she pranced off to serve the men who sat near the hearth.

Ben drank deeply from the new mug, then leaned back in his seat. "Ye're a true friend, gov'na. I'd swear by me mother's grave ye are."

A robust fellow, with a fiery red mop of straggly hair tied in a queue beneath a tricorn, came through the door, stomping the mud from his boots and brushing the raindrops off his coat. Close behind him, almost trotting on his heels, was a fellow of seemingly like comportment, whose left ear appeared to twitch of its own will.

Ben hunched his shoulders as if he desired to escape being noticed by the newcomers and anxiously gulped down the remainder of his drink before he sidled out of his chair. "I gots ter be goin' now, gov'na."

The newcomers crossed the room to the bar as Ben slipped through the doorway and scurried down the street with ragged coattails flying, briefly glancing over his shoulder before disappearing around a corner.

"Timmy Sears!" the innkeeper hailed and chortled, " 'tis been such a while since I seen ye, I was wonderin' if the earth had opened and swallowed ye up."

"It did, Jamie!" the red-haired man roared back. "But the divil spewed me out again!"

"Ah, ye're a red-haired demon yerself, Timmy me boy."

The barkeep snatched up a couple of mugs and filled them from the spigot of the ale barrel. He set the mugs upon the slick surface of the bar and with a practiced hand sent one sliding down toward the pair. The seedy, dark-haired man with the restless ear intercepted it and, gleefully licking his lips, brought it toward them, almost making contact before his arm was rudely seized by his companion.

" 'Od's blood, Haggie. Ever since ye fell from yer horse and banged yer head, ye ain't got the manners ye was born with. Ye never go takin' what was meant for me. Now that ye'll be workin' 'round here, ye remember that, ye hear?"

The man nodded readily, and with rich enjoyment, Timmy Sears sank his own lips into the head of foam. Haggie watched with puckered mouth until the second mug passed, then eagerly caught it up and joined in a like refreshment.

"What are the two o' ye doin' here on a day like this?" the innkeeper inquired.

Sears laughed as he lowered his mug and slapped the flat of his hand down on the planks. " 'Tis the only place I can escape from me harpin' wife."

Sauntering close, Molly caressed his chest and smiled into his eyes. "I thought maybe ye'd come ter see me, Timmy."

The man took the maid into a great bear hug and swung her about until she fairly squealed with delight. When he set her to her feet again, he searched inside his coat pocket for a moment, then leering, slowly withdrew a coin, which he flipped before her gleaming eyes. She laughed with excited glee, and quickly grabbing the piece, she dropped it into her blouse. She danced away from him and, looking over her shoulder, smiled seductively. The promise was in her eyes, and she had no need to speak, for when she fled up the stairs, he came after her in eager haste. Haggard Bentworth slammed down his own mug and stumbled after them, but he came up smartly against his companion's heels as the red-haired man paused on the bottom step. Sears was nearly knocked face downward against the stairs by the force of the other's impact but managed to regain his balance. He came around with fire in his eye.

"Not up here, Haggie," he barked. "Ye can't follow me here. Go have yerself another ale." He shoved the man back and hastened after the swinging hips that by now had proceeded well up the stairway.

Christopher chuckled in his ale, then once again noted a shadow beside his table. His brow raised in mute question as he glanced up. The dark-haired man from the trestle table stood with a hand poised on the back of the chair Ben had vacated. He had the bearing of a military man, although his garb did not support that supposition. Over a stocky, muscular build, he wore a sleeveless leather jerkin, a thick, soft shirt, and snug breeches tucked into tall black boots.

"May I join you for a moment, sir?" He did not wait on an answer but spun the chair about and straddled the seat, facing Christopher. The man opened his jerkin and twitched a pair of pistols to a more comfortable position in his belt, then leaned forward, his forearms braced on the back of the chair.

"Old Ben waggled a drink or two from you, eh?"

Christopher eyed the other without comment, wondering why the man had approached him. His lack of a reply should have angered the intruder. Instead, the other gave a quick, disarming smile.

"Forgive me, sir." He reached out a friendly hand. "I am Allan Parker, the sheriff of Mawbry, appointed by Lord Talbot to protect the peace of these lands."

Christopher took the other's proffered hand and, introducing himself, watched the man for a reaction. There was no outward show that he had heard the name before, yet Christopher found it hard to believe that the story of his duel with Farrell had not reached the sheriff's ears.

"I believe 'tis part of my duty to warn strangers about Ben. Depending on the quality of whatever he drinks, he usually has a headful of ghosts, demons, and other hellish creatures. He should not be taken too seriously."

Christopher smiled. "Of course not."

The sheriff pondered him. "I don't remember ever seeing you here before. Are you from around these parts?"

"I have a town house in London, but one of my ships is in port at Wirkinton, and that is how I came to be here." Christopher supplied the information with no hesitation. "I'll be staying in Mawbry until I have concluded my business here."

"What business is that, if you don't mind me asking?"

"I came to collect a debt, and since the man seems to be lacking the wherewithal to pay, I might stay here a while as an added incentive for him to find it. In fact, the way it looks, I might have to take up temporary residence here."

The sheriff leaned his head back and laughed. "You'd probably do better taking something else in lieu of coin."

A lopsided grin twisted Christopher's lips. "My aspirations exactly, but I fear the man is stubbornly opposed to giving me what I want."

"Well, if you're seriously planning on taking up residence here, I should warn you there's no place but the inn for you to stay."

"Ben mentioned a manor house that was burned a few years back. He said the lord of the house was killed and that he knows of no kin who've come to claim the lands."

The man rubbed a hand nervously through his thick black hair. "I went out there myself soon after I arrived here, and though I've heard the rumor of a man being caught in the flames, I found no trace of a body. As for the manor, most of it still exists. Only the newer wing burned, as it was the only part built of wood. The stone of the old hall withstood the flames. Since the fire, the house has remained empty . . . unless, as some of the locals say, two ghosts roam the place, the old lord with a claymore spitting his breastbone, and the other one horribly burned and maimed." He frowned and shook his head slightly, as if confused. "Yet the tenants go about their labors as if they fully expect one of the Saxtons to return, and when Lord Talbot inquired about the lands, he was informed that the family has yet to relinquish title to it and that the taxes are still being paid."

"Who collects the rents?"

Allan stared at him thoughtfully for a moment. "Where did you say you came from?"

"What does that have to do with my question?" Christopher softened the query with a smile.

"I was just curious," Allan replied pleasantly.

"I'm from Boston, here to seek ports of trade for my ships." He arched a brow at the sheriff expectantly.

Allan shrugged and complied. "For the present I believe Lord Talbot collects the rents. He does it more or less as a favor for the family until something else is done about the ownership of the lands."

"Then he's not the one who pays the taxes?"

"Not when he desires to have the land. Why, 'twould be foolish of him to do so."

"Then perhaps this Lord Saxton isn't dead," Christopher responded. He rose to his feet and donned his long coat.

"I've been sheriff here for three years, and I've not seen any evidence that he's alive," Allan commented. He glanced around as a large carriage passed in front of the window, and quickly got to his feet. "That's Lord Talbot's coach now. He knows more about Saxton Hall than anyone around here. Come, I'll introduce you to him." Allan flashed him a smile. "If you're lucky, he'll have his daughter, Claudia, with him."

Settling his hat on his head, Christopher followed the man through the doorway and crossed the cobbled lane. A large, ornate carriage had halted a short distance from the inn, and the coachmen climbed down to hastily place a small stool before the door, which bore a lavish coat of arms. The decorative elements formed the larger part of the arms, and the shield itself was smallish and confused, thus making the three bars sinister it contained less obvious. The richness of the conveyance might have challenged those of royalty, and when Lord Talbot stepped out, his appearance proved to be just as overwhelming, for he was dressed in the brocades, laces, and silks of a bygone era. He was a man of middling years, yet well preserved. He faced the door and offered up his hand as a slim, dark-haired woman came into view. Her attire was more subdued, and from a distance she bore a striking resemblance to Erienne Fleming, yet on closer inspection Christopher discovered that she fell far short of the other's beauty. Her dark eyes narrowed too quickly in the outer corners and lacked the heaviness of lashes that fringed the pools of amethyst. Though her features could not be termed coarse, they were not as fine and delicate as those of the mayor's daughter, nor was her skin as fair. But then, it would be hard for any maid to equal or surpass the comeliness of the one he had already met.

Claudia Talbot paused beside her father, carefully pulling up the velvet hood of her cloak to protect her coiffure from the misting rain before slipping her gloved hand through the arm her father presented. Her eyes measured Christopher in a slow, exacting way that gave him every assurance that she was carefully assessing his physical attributes.

"Why, Allan," she purred when they neared, "I never thought you'd chase me down the street just to present another man to me. Aren't you the least bit jealous?"

The sheriff laughed and responded with like flirtation. "Claudia,

I have every faith that you'll remain true to me even though confronting a full regiment of men." He swept his hand about to indicate the man at his side. "May I present Christopher Seton from Boston? A gentleman by the cut of his clothes, and if he's not careful, another one to be smitten by your charms."

"I am honored, Miss Talbot," Christopher responded, bowing gallantly over her gloved hand.

"My goodness, you are a tall one," she observed coyly.

Christopher was well acquainted with the antics of forward women and recognized the bold gleam in the dark eyes. If he wanted feminine companionship, then here was an open invitation.

"And this worthy gentleman is Lord Nigel Talbot," Allan said, concluding the introductions.

"Seton . . . Seton . . ." Lord Talbot repeated thoughtfully. "I've heard that name before."

"Perhaps you remember it from the misunderstanding I had with your mayor a few weeks ago," Christopher suggested.

Lord Talbot looked at him curiously. "So you're the one who dueled with Farrell, eh? Well, I can't hold that against you. That young whelp brews trouble wherever he goes."

"Mr. Seton is here in Mawbry on business," Allan stated. "He might be interested in acquiring a country estate close by."

Lord Talbot chuckled. "Then I wish you good fortune, sir. 'Tis a great undertaking to establish lands and tenants, but in the long run it does have its rewards if you manage to accumulate the desired power. One must have wealth, however, to proceed."

Christopher met the man's deliberate stare. "I was wondering about Saxton Hall."

"Oh, you don't want that place," Claudia advised sweetly. "'Tis half burned and full of ghosts. Why, anyone around here can tell you the place has been plagued by disaster."

"I really can't imagine the possibility of a foreigner acquiring either the lands or the hall." Lord Talbot perused the Yankee speculatively. "Are you a man of occupation, or a gentleman of leisure?"

"Actually I'm a little of both." Christopher flashed white teeth in a quick grin. "I own several vessels that trade in ports around the world, but I'm also very much a man of leisure."

Claudia's dark eyes took on a new gleam. "You must be very rich."

Christopher shrugged casually. "I manage a few creature comforts."

"Saxton Hall would be a worthy estate with its holdings of lands, but I'm afraid it's not available." Lord Talbot gave him a brief smile. "If it were, I would have had it myself some time ago."

"Papa, you'd own all of England if the King would let you," Claudia teased, patting his arm.

His lordship turned a rueful smile on her. "I need it to keep you in the finery you demand."

Claudia giggled. "Which reminds me, Papa. I promised the dressmaker that I would come by to select material for a new gown. Since you have business with the mayor, I shall have to find my own escort." The corners of her lips lifted impishly as she met Christopher's gaze. "Can I be so bold as to ask you to accompany me, Mr. Seton?"

"Claudia!" her father spoke in shocked reproof. "You just met the man!"

"Papa, all the eligible young men around here are frightened to death of you," Claudia protested as if it were an old argument. "If I don't take the initiative, I'll die an old spinster."

Christopher's lips twitched in amusement as he glanced at her father. The man seemed appalled by his daughter's gall. "With your permission, sir."

Lord Talbot reluctantly nodded his head, and a chuckle came from Allan as Christopher decorously presented his arm. With a self-satisfied nod, Claudia took it and strolled along beside him, holding her head high in triumph. With this man as her escort, she would once again enjoy the envy of every woman in Mawbry. When she noticed a lone feminine figure standing at an upper window of the mayor's cottage, she experienced a special thrill at being spied upon by that one. Claudia loathed the comparisons that were constantly made between the two of them and that left her the one wanting in regard to beauty. Indeed, she felt a delicious glee whenever anyone spoke of the sorry suitors the mayor had enticed to his daughter. Claudia's fondest wish was to see the other woman bound in wedlock to a horrible beast of a man.

" 'Twould seem that Claudia has found another one to occupy her for a spell," Allan observed with humor.

Lord Talbot groaned in mock pain. "I almost find myself wishing her mother might have survived a few years longer. Considering that nagging carp, you know my desperation."

The sheriff laughed and jerked his head toward the mayor's cottage. "Claudia said you have business with Avery. Shall I accompany you?"

Lord Talbot declined. "Nay. This matter is of a personal nature." He gestured toward the departing couple. "What you may do for me is to keep an eye on that brazen twit. I don't relish the idea of having a Yankee as kin."

Allan smiled. "I shall try my best, my lord."

"Then I'll leave you to be about it."

Lord Talbot strode purposefully to the mayor's cottage and rapped on the door with the silver head of his ornate walking stick. His knock was not answered immediately, and he was beginning to wonder if it would be, when the portal was opened a crack. Erienne peered through the opening and might have been relieved to find it was not Silas Chambers if his lordship had been more to her liking. He was not.

Lord Talbot pushed the door wider with his cane, forcing Erienne to retreat a step.

"Don't peek at me through cracks, Erienne." He smiled appreciatively as his eyes roamed freely over her. "I like to see people when I talk to them. Is your father home?"

Confused and suddenly nervous, Erienne bobbed a quick curtsy and hastily replied, "Oh, no, sir. He's abroad in the village somewhere. Though I can't be sure, I do expect him home any moment."

"Well then, with your permission I'll wait inside by the fire. 'Tis a most miserable day."

Lord Talbot brushed past her and paused to shrug out of his cloak and doff his tricorn, handing both to her before passing on to the parlor and leaving a chagrined Erienne to close the door and hang the dampened garments on a peg. When she entered the parlor, she found him already seated in a tall-backed chair in front of the fireplace. He had crossed his leg and, where the long frock coat fell aside, displayed a masculine length of limb covered with fine gray silk breeches and stockings. His eyes warmed as she came into his vision, and he gave her what he hoped was a most fatherly smile.

"My dear Erienne, you have done a most magnificent task of managing this house since your mother passed on. I trust you have been happy here. Your father certainly seems to have taken well to his duties. Why, just the other day . . ."

He continued with a stream of chatter, eyeing the girl as she moved about. He rambled on without interruption, not that he was the least bit ill at ease, but seeking rather to allay her tension, for she appeared quite unsettled with his presence. She was, after all, a most desirable wench, and he found it amazing that a man like Avery Fleming could sire such a one.

Erienne listened with half an ear as his voice droned on. She was well aware of the reputation of Nigel Talbot. His exploits had been bantered among the gossips several times since the Flemings had moved to Mawbry. Thus she made a point to pass the front windows often so that any watchers (and she knew there would be at least several) could see and be witness to her continued innocence.

"I'll make some tea while we wait," she said hesitantly. She stirred the fire, placing a fresh block of peat on it, then hung a kettle of water on the hook above it.

Nigel Talbot regarded Erienne with growing ardor. Several weeks had passed since he had been to London and there was entertained by some rather lusty, lace-bedecked acquaintances in their richly appointed apartments. It was truly amazing that he had overlooked such rare fine fruit in his own orchard, but considering Erienne's subdued, ladylike composure, it was easy to understand why he had not really noticed her before. The bold ones drew immediate attention, yet it was not always the case that they were also the choice ones. Erienne Fleming was of prime quality and no doubt unspoiled.

His mind formed a vision of her in petticoats and stays, with bosom overflowing and tiny waist cinched to fit a man's hands. He imagined her black hair flowing loosely about her creamy soft shoulders, and his eyes widened as he realized the possibilities before him. Of course, this was delicate and must be broached with care. He did not intend to offer marriage, but surely Avery would not be foolish enough to turn down a substantial sum for her.

Lord Talbot rose to his feet and assumed his best heroic pose, his left hand on the casually braced cane, his right clasping the lapel of his brocaded coat so she might admire his manly form. A more experienced wench might have stared openly at what he was eager to display instead of trying to keep busy with inconsequential matters.

"My dear, dear Erienne . . ."

His wakening passion made his voice more forceful than he intended, and the suddenness and volume of his address made Erienne start. The cup and saucer she was placing on the sideboard rattled in her fingers, almost falling to the floor. Nervously she set them down and, clasping her still trembling hands together, faced him.

Nigel Talbot was a wise man beyond the impetuous years of youth. He retreated and tried again, this time more cordially. "My apologies, Erienne. I did not mean to startle you. 'Tis just that it comes to me that I have never really looked at you before." As he spoke, he closed the distance to her. "Never really seen your beauty."

He laid a long, slim, well-manicured hand upon her lower arm, and Erienne found no retreat with the sideboard to her back.

"Why, my dear, you're trembling." He looked down in the wide, frightened eyes and smiled tenderly. "Poor Erienne. Do not be afraid, my dear. I would not harm you for the world. Indeed, 'tis my fondest wish that we should come to know each other . . . much . . . much better." His fingers lightly squeezed her arm in gentle reassurance.

Suddenly a loud curse from the upper floor interrupted, and an uneven thumping and pounding was heard on the stairs. Lord Talbot stepped away from Erienne just as Farrell came stumbling past the open doorway. He almost went to his knees but managed to teeter to a halt. His eyes rolled several times past comprehensive vision as he straightened. He had managed to don a shirt, which now hung open to the waist. The breeches were loose almost to the point of embarrassment, and his stockinged toes curled away from the cold boards of the floor. When he managed to focus on the occupants of the parlor, his jaw dropped in surprise.

"Lor! Lord Talbot!" He rubbed his good hand against his temple as if to still a pounding there and raked his fingers through his tumbled mop of hair. "Yer lordship . . ." The "P" was oddly stressed. He mumbled an unsure apology and began to fumble with the buttons of his breeches. "I didn' know you were here . . ."

Lord Talbot struggled to appear an understanding guest. A slight tic at the corner of his moustache was the only betrayal of his true feelings. "I trust you are feeling well, Farrell."

The young man licked his lips as if an abiding dryness burned his mouth, and he grasped his shirt together over his sagging breeches when he caught Erienne's glare. "I just came down for a drink . . ." He cleared his throat as her eyes narrowed warningly and added, "of water." He saw the steaming pot in the fireplace. "Or maybe some tea."

He was gaining some degree of control and knew full well the duties of a host. "Erienne," he assumed an instructive tone, "would you be so kind as to pour us some tea? I'm sure Lord Talbot has been dying of thirst." His own thick swallow added his unspoken endorsement to the statement. He started to clear his throat but ended in a hacking cough. "A man needs a good warm brew to clear his gullet on a cold morning."

For once the sister was grateful for her brother's presence. "Farrell," Erienne said, smiling sweetly as she obeyed, " 'tis well past the noon hour."

Lord Talbot's irritation with Farrell was supreme, but he could hardly order the young man from the room so he could feast his eyes on the sister. It was obvious the brother intended to stay and impress his guest with his manners, but knowing the limits of his temper, Lord Talbot decided a tactful retreat at the present moment would be wise. After all, he had a great deal of thinking to do about the mayor's daughter before he launched into any positive action.

"I shan't be staying for tea," he announced, his voice curt and agitated. "My daughter will no doubt be wondering what is keeping me. Since I must leave for London in the morning, I will see your father when I return. I'm sure the matter will keep."

Three

Fodder would be anything but plentiful in the approaching months of winter, thus herds and flocks of sheep, pigs, geese, and the like began to flow into the cities and hamlets, where they would be sold at markets or fairs. Drovers prodded the animals onward, while dust roiled up in clouds around them. Though on a considerably lesser scale, the sight was as familiar in Mawbry as it was in York or London, for only a fool ignored the need for storing provender for the frigid weather ahead.

Erienne sought to bolster the family larder with the purchase of a small pig, the best her meager coins would buy. She could not bring herself to slaughter it, but she scratched out a few more shillings for the wandering pigsticker. The evening before he came, Avery grumpily declared the preparation of food to be woman's work and, fearful that his lot might fall to labor, took himself and Farrell off to Wirkinton for a day of "meetings," as Avery put it.

The busy butcher arrived with the dawn, and Erienne fled into the house until he had accomplished his work. She had readied the hot grains to make black pudding, but since it was not one of her favorite dishes, it was a laborious task requiring a stern stomach. She found stripping the intestine for sausage casings no less trying. Long slabs and larger portions of meat were packed in a barrel with layers of salt while she continued to cut away the fat from other pieces. Once the meat was trimmed, it was weighted down in the barrel with a stone, and the whole filled to the brim with a salty brine for the curing.

Behind the cottage in an open-sided hut used for like purposes, she built a fire, hung a kettle, and began trying down the fat for lard. The tiny bits of meat that clung to the chunks of fat floated to the top and had to be skimmed off, lest a scum form with them and spoil the lard. But when cooled on a cloth, the cracklings provided a tasty, crunchy tidbit to chew.

The hound from the neighboring cottage eyed her wistfully and, when her back was turned, wiggled under the fence and boldly approached. Flopping down close by, he raised his wet nose high in the air to sample the wafting aroma and then lowered his massive head until it rested forlornly on his paws. His brows twitched as his eyes followed her every movement. Whenever the opportunity presented itself, he'd sneak forward and grab a scrap in his large jowls, then take off like a shot when she ran after him with a broom, threatening to fetch the pigsticker after him. Undoubtedly he was not intimidated by her warning, for soon he came lumbering back to a spot where he could watch her again and sniff the tantalizing odors.

The air was crisp, but Erienne hardly felt its chill as she worked. Indeed, she had rolled up the sleeves of her faded dress, and with only a light chemise beneath her gown, she gave welcome to the cool breezes that now and then stirred the curling tendrils of hair escaping from beneath her kerchief. She was in a frenzy to have the task done before nightfall, and she wanted nothing to distract her or set her from her purpose. Intent on her labors and with watching the sizzling fat and the encroaching dog, she failed to notice that in the shadows near the corner of the house a man had come to stand and observe.

Christopher Seton's eyes passed over the shapely figure with warm admiration. The light breezes teased the dark curls, and she paused to tuck the stray wisps beneath her kerchief. Her arms reached forward as she turned away to another chore, and for a moment the bodice of her gown stretched tight across the slim back, reassuring him of the fact that the waist was naturally narrow and had no need to be shaped by the tight cinching of stays. In his far-reaching travels he had seen his share of women and been most selective of those he had chosen to sample. His experience could not truthfully be termed lacking, yet it was hard in his mind that this delectable bit whom he scrutinized so carefully far exceeded anything he could call to mind, whether here or halfway across an ocean or two.

In the past three years he had taken his four ships to the far eastern shores, sounding out fresh ports and seeking goods to trade. He had become much a man of the sea and ofttimes had been confined to a ship for long periods while under sail. Since arriving in England other matters had commanded his attention, and he had casually abstained from taking up a relationship until he met a companion worthy to be considered. Thus he was not unstirred by what he saw before him. There was a graceful naïveté about Erienne Fleming that totally intrigued him, and he thought he would greatly enjoy instructing her in the ways of love and lovers.

Erienne reached to thrust a log into the fire and caught sight of the dog sneaking toward the raw fat that had been piled on a nearby table. Shouting a warning, she came upright with the stick in her hand and, as the dog skittered off toward the hole in the fence, turned to throw it after him. Doing so, she finally caught sight of the tall, nattily garbed onlooker, and the shock that went through her made her catch her breath. She stared at him as if stunned, distressed that he should be a witness to her undignified actions and dowdy appearance when he looked so dapper in royal blue coat and gray breeches and waistcoat. As if through a haze it came to her that she should be angry at his intrusion, but before that urging took some direction, the man stepped across the low fence and came toward her in long, hasty strides. Her eyes flew open in fear, and a scream built slowly in her breast. Though she knew she was about to be cruelly ravished, her legs seemed numbed and her feet firmly rooted to the spot where she stood.

Then he was there before her, but instead of crushing her to earth, he bent aside and snatched the hem of her skirt from the blazing hearth. With quick swipes of his hat, he slashed the flames out, then lifting the smoldering cloth, rubbed it together until no wisp of smoke strayed forth. As she stared at him, he straightened and held up a handful of charred hem for her inspection.

"I believe, my dear Erienne," he began solicitously, the humor in his voice disguised by a disapproving frown, "that you either have a penchant for self-destruction . . . or you are somehow testing me . . . or my ability to protect you. I think this may bear further investigation."

It dawned on Erienne, as his gaze dropped, that he was far more interested in the considerable length of leg the raised skirt exposed. Catching the garment free of his grasp, she cast a sidelong glare at the man and moved a step away from him, then eyed him quizzically as he set aside his hat and removed his coat to lay it across a plank. The hearth radiated a fair amount of heat, warranting the shedding of the garment, but for a man who had been banned from the cottage, Christopher Seton seemed quite at ease.

"I suppose I must thank you for what you did," Erienne reluctantly conceded, "but if you hadn't been standing there, this would never have happened."

His brows gathered in a lopsided query while a smile touched his lips. "My apologies. I didn't mean to startle you."

"What were you doing spying on me?" she asked bluntly as she flounced down on a bench to inspect her charred skirts.

The lean, hard muscles of his thighs flexed beneath the tight-fitting breeches as he half sat, half leaned on a high stool nearby. "I grew bored with viewing the ladies who meander about the markets, and I came to see if the sights were better here at the mayor's cottage." The corners of his lips twitched with amusement, and his eyes gleamed into hers as he added, 'I am happy to report, they are!"

Erienne got to her feet in a huff. "Have you nothing better to do than go about ogling the women?"

"I suppose I could find something else to occupy me," he replied easily, "but I can't think of anything that's nearly as enjoyable, except, of course, being in a lady's company."

"Besides the fact that you're a scoundrel at the gaming tables," she responded tartly, "I'm beginning to suspect that you're a womanizing rake."

Christopher grinned leisurely as his perusal swept her. "I've been a long time at sea. However, I doubt that in your case my reaction would vary had I just left the London Court."

Erienne's eyes flared with poorly suppressed ire. The insufferable egotist! Did he dare think he could find a willing wench at the back door of the mayor's cottage? "I'm sure that Claudia Talbot would welcome your company, sir. Why don't you ride on over to see her? I hear his lordship traveled off to London this morning."

He laughed softly at her sneering tones. "I'd rather be courting you."

"Why?" she scoffed. "Because you want to thwart my father?"

His smiling eyes captured hers and held them prisoner until she felt a warmth suffuse her cheeks. He answered with slow deliberation. "Because you are the prettiest maid I've ever seen, and I'd like to get to know you better. And of course, we should delve into this matter of your accidents more thoroughly, too."

Twin spots of color grew in her cheeks, but the deepening dusk did much to hide her blush. Lifting her nose primly in the air, Erienne turned aside, tossing him a cool glance askance. "How many women have you told that to, Mr. Seton?"

A crooked smile accompanied his reply. "Several, I suppose, but I've never lied. Each had their place in time, and to this date, you *are* the best I've seen." He reached out and taking a handful of the cracklings, he chewed the crisp morsels as he awaited her reaction.

A flush of anger spread to the delicate tips of her ears, and icy fire smoldered in the deep blue-violet pools. "You conceited, unmitigated boor!" Her voice was as cold and as flat as the Russian steppes. "Do you think to add me to your long string of conquests?"

Her chilled contempt met him face to face until he rose and towered above her. His eyes grew distant, and he reached out a finger to flip a curl that had strayed from beneath the kerchief.

"Conquest?" His voice was soft and deeply resonant. "You mistake me, Erienne. In the rush of a moment's lust, there are purchased favors, and these are for the greater part forgotten. The times that are cherished and remembered are not taken, are not given, but shared, and are thus treasured as a most blissful event." He lifted his coat on his fingertips and slung it over his shoulder. "I do not ask that you yield to me, nor do I desire to conquer you. All I plead is that you grant me moments now and then that I might present my case, to the end that we could share a tender moment at some distant time."

Her face gave no sign of softening. Even so, its beauty fed his gaze and created in his being a sweet, hungering ache that could neither be easily put aside nor sated with anything less than what he desired.

"The harm you have done us all stands between us." Her tone was bitter. "And I must honor those who have honored me."

He considered her for a space, then slid his hat onto his head.

"I could promise ease and comfort for all of you." He paused and tipped his head without releasing her gaze. "Would that be a kindness or a curse?"

"Kindness or curse?" Erienne scoffed sneeringly. "Your wisdom escapes me, sir. I only know my father frets anxiously because of your accusation, and my brother whimpers painfully through his dreams because of your deed. With each passing day my own lot grows more wearisome, and that, too, because of you."

Christopher slipped an arm into the coat and shrugged it across those broad shoulders. "You have set your verdict against me before I can voice a plea. There is no argument for a closed mind."

"Begone with you!" she snapped. "Take your saws and bend them on some willing ear. I will not listen to your excuses, nor will I tolerate your mincing inanities! I want no part of you! Ever!"

He contemplated her with a half smile. "Be wary, Erienne. 'Tis a fact I've learned all too well that words cast out in the light of day, like doves, oft come home to roost in the darkest hours."

Incensed, Erienne searched about for a club and, finding none, snatched up the hearth broom, drawing it back over her shoulder as she advanced on him. "You lopheaded, caterwauling cock! Are you so boorish that I must drive you away like the hound? Begone from here!"

The green eyes sparkled with humor until she swung the improvised weapon. He sidestepped gracefully, then grinned in the face of her rage. Before she could come around again with another stroke, he retreated rapidly and stepped spryly over the fence. She glared at him across the barrier as he turned about, well out of her reach.

"Good evening, Miss Fleming." Christopher swept his hat to his breast, gave her a debonair bow, and set the hat jauntily onto his head again. His eyes briefly caressed her heaving bosom before raising to smile into her glare. "Please try to stay out of trouble, my sweet. I may not be around the next time."

The broom sailed through the air, but he dodged it easily and, giving her a last leer, sauntered off. It was a long moment later that Erienne calmed enough to realize that the sense of loss she had experienced before was even stronger now.

Disgruntled, she flounced back to the hearth and stared angrily into the flames until a small leather object on the brick floor caught her eye. Bending down, she realized it was a man's purse, and a weighty one at that. She turned it over in her hands and stared at the initials CS scored in the surface of it. Ire prickled along her spine, and the desire to throw it far away from her was paramount. Yet caution prevailed. If it was a rich purse, as she suspected, he'd be back to fetch it, and if she could not produce it, he might charge her for its loss or even accuse her of thieving. Perhaps it had not dropped out of his coat by accident, and his intent was to cause her some form of embarrassment. She was, after all, the only member of her family who was as yet unsullied by him.

Erienne glanced around, wondering where she might hide it until he came back. She had no wish for her father to find it, not when the initials clearly marked its owner. She could hear the accusations now. Her father would never believe she had not won the purse with the ultimate betrayal. The thought grated like sand against her peace of mind that Mr. Seton's return might come at an inconvenient moment and make matters worse. She winced as she imagined the results of such a meeting with her father and brother. It seemed preferable that she should return it, but until she could find a free moment, it had to be hidden.

The lean-to where her brother's less-than-magnificent gelding, Socrates, was stabled caught her eye, and she smiled to herself. It was the best place she knew of to store something that belonged to a braying ass.

Erienne used the back door of the inn to gain entrance to the place. A narrow stairway just inside the postern led upward to the second floor, and with Christopher Seton's purse hidden beneath her shawl, she made her way carefully up the steps. He had not come for the purse as she had feared, and rather than allow an occasion to arise where he could accuse her of being a thief, she would bring it to him and thus forestall an unpleasant scene.

The hour was early in the morning, the light of dawn still dim and misty. She was dressed simply in a neat blue dress with a prim collar, having left the cottage with only a shawl for warmth on the frosty morn. The well-worn soles of her black shoes barely made a sound on the bare wood floor of the upper hall as she hurried along. Her intention was to find his room, knock on his door, and give the purse to him, hopefully before she was seen prowling in the hall.

She had heard that the best rooms were on the east side of the inn, and she could not rightfully imagine the arrogant fellow accepting anything less. Most of the doors were closed, making her search for his room more difficult. At the portals of those chambers facing east, she paused to knock and chewed her lip worriedly as she waited for some response. When none came, she moved on to the third, pausing for a moment with her ear to the plank before she raised her knuckles and rapped.

In a moment the door was jerked open, and Erienne stumbled back with a gasp as the Yankee appeared with only a towel wrapped about his hips and an angry scowl on his face.

"I told you . . ." Christopher began harshly, then realizing his mistake, halted. His brows arched in surprise, and a slow grin spread across his lips. He seemed casually unconcerned with his state of undress.

"Erienne . . . I wasn't expecting you."

Obviously!

Erienne's face flamed. The sight of those brown shoulders and broad, furred chest increased her discomfiture, and she didn't dare look lower than that. Nervously she drew forth the purse and opened her mouth to explain her reason for coming when the sound of footsteps hurrying up the back stairs made her start. The fear of discovery paralyzed her, and she forgot her mission. To be found in the hall with a near-naked man was the end of whatever shreds of reputation she had remaining. Her father would be privy to the fact before the morning was out, and his tirade would challenge the broad side of a ship of the line for smoke and thunder.

Anxiously Erienne glanced up and down the corridor. She must fly, and the only other way was down the front stairs and through the common room. She had taken the first step in that direction when her arm was seized. Before she could resist, Christopher snatched her into his room. She stumbled in a short, quick circle, but the stout panel was already closed and locked when she returned to it. Her mouth flew open, but his hand clamped tightly over it to silence her protest. A frown and a quick shake of his head warned her. His other arm slipped about her waist, catching her close against him. Then she was lifted and moved away from the door until they stood near the bed.

The footsteps paused outside the portal, and a light scratching came against the wood. Erienne's eyes were wide and displayed her worry as she gazed up into the bronze visage and silently pleaded her case.

Christopher cleared his throat, as if just rousing from sleep, and called, "Who is it?"

" 'Tis me, Mr. Seton," a feminine voice replied. "Molly Harper, the servin' maid. The chore boy's taken with the sniffles this morn'n', so I thought I'd fetch water for yer bath meself. I brung it all the way up ter ye. Will ye open up so's I can come in?"

Christopher cocked a brow down at Erienne, as if seriously tempted by what the maid proposed. Seeing the workings of his mind, Erienne shook her head frantically.

"A moment please," he answered.

The fear tore through Erienne that he wanted to humiliate her just as he had her father. She began to struggle and became irate when he did not immediately release her from his grasp. He bent and whispered against her ear.

"Stay close, Erienne. The towel has come loose. If you step away, it is at your own risk."

Clenching her eyes tightly shut, she buried her face against his shoulder to hide the crimson tides that swept over her and clung to him with a panic born of desperation. Unable to see his face, she missed the smile that widened his lips.

"Come on, lovey, open up. These buckets is heavy." The plea accompanied another tapping.

"Patience, Molly." Christopher paused for a brief moment, gathering the towel about him again. Then his muscles flexed, and if she had found the breath, Erienne would have shrieked as he lifted her and dumped her onto the bed. She half raised with her mouth open to hotly voice her objection to whatever he had in mind, but he flung the bedcovers over her head, squelching comment.

"Lie still." His whisper bore a tone of command that could prompt immediate obedience from even the most reluctant. Erienne froze, and with a smile Christopher reached across to turn down the other side of the bed to make it seem as if he had just left it.

Frantic visions involving her possible fate flew through Erienne's mind. She considered the horrible humiliation she would suffer if she were discovered in the man's bed. Her fears burgeoned, her rage peaked, and she threw back the covers, intending to escape the trap he laid for her. In the next brief second she caught her breath sharply and snatched the covers back over her head again, for the sight of him standing stark naked beside the chair where his clothes were draped was too much for her virgin eyes to bear. It had been no more than a glimpse, but the vision of his tall, tanned, wide-shoul-dered form bathed in the pinkish light of the rising sun was forever branded in her brain.

Christopher chuckled softly as Erienne curled into the bed and finally obeyed his warning. He slipped on his breeches, secured them, and moved across the room to unlock the door.

Molly knew her trade and her competition, and the village of Mawbry suited her well, since there was an absolute lack of the latter. When Christopher opened the portal, she was through it in a trice and shrugging out of the yoke that bore the pails. Pressing herself tightly against the male form, she rubbed her fingers through the hair on his chest and fluttered her lashes.

"Oh, lovey, ye are a wondrous sight for any girl to behold."

"I've already told you, Molly. I have no need of yer services," Christopher stated bluntly. "I only want the water."

"Ah, come now, lovey," she crooned. "I knows ye've been away ter sea and needs a li'l tussle in bed. Why, with such a man as yerself, I'd be more'n willin' ter give ye all ye need without a hint o' a coin."

Christopher swept his hand toward the mentioned furnishing, drawing the maid's eyes to it. "I already have all I desire. Now be along with you."

Molly's dark eyes widened in surprise as she turned to stare at the bed. Unable to mistake the curvaceous form hidden beneath the quilt, she straightened indignantly and with a swish of her skirts was gone from the room, slamming the door behind her. Erienne waited, not daring to come out from beneath the covering until Christopher tapped her on the shoulder.

" 'Tis safe now. You can come out."

"Are you dressed?" she asked cautiously, her voice muffled beneath the covers.

Christopher chuckled. "I've got my breeches on, if that's what you're worried about. And I'm putting on my shirt." He reached for the garment and shrugged into it as the blankets lowered cautiously.

Erienne peered out over her wraps with the same wariness of a nervous hare until she saw Christopher's amused visage. The levity in those clear grayish-green eyes was hard to ignore. With an angry jerk, she tore off the covering and scrambled to her feet, trying to keep her skirts down to prevent any further embarrassment.

"You grinning buffoon!" she snapped and tossed the purse at him. "You did this to me deliberately."

The weighted purse hit him in the chest, and he caught it deftly as he laughed. "Did what?"

Irately she jerked down her skirts and smoothed back the curling wisps of hair that had escaped the sober knot at her nape. "I came here to return your purse, which I thought was gracious of me considering what you've done to my family, and then you haul me through your doorway and embarrass me in this manner!"

"I thought you didn't want to be seen, and to this moment I see no embarrassment for you. I was only trying to help." His grin had not dwindled in the least.

"Ha!" she scoffed and marched toward the door. As she reached it, she faced about and glared at him. "I don't like being made sport of, Mr. Seton, but you obviously enjoy causing discomfort in any manner. I only hope that someday you will meet one who is as skilled with weapons as you purportedly are. I should like to see such a contest. Good day to you, sir!"

Stalking out, she slammed the door behind her, enjoying the deafening sound it made. It bore evidence to the rage she felt. Indeed, she hoped she had made a lasting impression on that scoundrel.

A woman's scorn has been the downfall of a goodly number of men and the cause of many a conflict. In the case of Timmy Sears, Molly Harper's infatuation with Christopher Seton created a stumbling block the size of a mammoth boulder. Molly was certainly not what a person would call a "one-man woman," not that Timmy cared. After all, a girl had to make a living somehow. It was just that he had become used to "moving to the head of the line," so to speak, whenever he visited the Boar's Inn. It was a small honor but one he had come to see as his special right, being the meanest bruiser around and all.

Timmy, himself, was a blustery chap with a mop of copious red hair that usually jutted willy-nilly from under his tricorn. He had a ready though somewhat shallow wit, and as long as he had a wench to please his one hand and a mug of ale to occupy the other, his mood was generally liberal and boisterously jovial. He was large, broad, and squarely built, with a noticeable penchant to seize upon any excuse for a brawl, the more so if several lesser men were available to serve as opponents. It was firm in his mind that he had not been in a good fight for several weeks, since most of the stolid lads here and about had become ill disposed to broken heads or limbs and studiously avoided his overbearing overtures to mayhem.

Recently, however, there had come into Timmy's world a man of a type that, simply put, set him on edge. He was of a kind that made Timmy uncomfortable. To start with, the stranger was taller than Timmy, with shoulders every bit as broad, though two or three stone lighter in the girth perhaps. If that wasn't enough, the man was a smooth sort who was always neat as a pin and who obviously took a bath at least two or three times a month. To make matters worse, the bloke had an enviable reputation with firearms and moved with a sort of careless ease that gave one pause about resorting to any kind of foolishness.

Herein lay Timmy's quandary: Molly had started acting as if he didn't exist, while she doted and fawned over this Seton fellow, the very one who made Timmy's knuckles itch and who had moved into his favorite drinking place, it being of course the only one in all of Mawbry. The same wench, when bidden to serve the one who supplied her with trinkets, hurriedly slid trencher and tankard before him in her haste to be at the other's beck and call. A bauble did much to lighten her eyes, but payment for it was usually rushed and though temporarily satisfying, it left him with the gnawing suspicion that the wench made him pay dearly for what she would have freely given to the Yankee.

The worst of it was that this Mr. Seton clearly ignored her fawning attentions, denying Timmy a cause to call him out. Even though Timmy watched with the eyes of a sea eagle, the man did not so much as pinch those fine plump buttocks that oscillated ever so near to him, or reach out to fondle that full, ripe bosom, which was lowered for his gaze whenever she served him. She wore blouses so low that Timmy groaned in agony, and still the Yankee gave her no heed. It made the insult twofold in Timmy's mind. To reject that maid who stirred the jealousy was to carry the killing thrust home.

Timmy's spirit was sorely vexed, and his rage built, fed by the stranger's total lack of regard for his reputation as the village brute. When nearly every stout and worthy fellow in the North country scurried to get out of the way of Timmy Sears, the man calmly waited for the red-haired man to get out of his. It was enough to draw Timmy's insides in a knot, and in his mind he began to imagine ways he could shatter the Yankee's arrogance. Timmy would not be content until there was a fine knock-down-and-drag-out brawl to soothe his self-esteem.

Much gaiety was intertwined with the serious business of buying and selling while the seasonal markets of Mawbry were open. Musicians played their lutes and pipes for the high-stepping dancers while hands clapped in time to the music, tempting those who hung back to try their skills. Erienne watched them with eager attention, wanting to join but unable to convince Farrell to be her partner. He had agreed to tour the markets with her and had not argued against pausing to admire the dancing since Molly Harper was prancing through the steps and swinging her skirts with carefree abandon. However, he refused to leave himself open to the ridicule of those who might poke fun at him if he were to partake. After all, he was not a whole man.

Erienne understood and did not press, yet she hardly approved of the wall he was building around himself. Still, it was a day for merrymaking, and the smiles and laughter were infectious. Her toes tapped and her eyes sparkled. Her hands met in a rhythmic clapping until she saw the tall figure of a man leaning indolently against a nearby tree. She recognized him at once and realized he was regarding her with an amused smile. In the grayish-green eyes there was a glowing intensity, and the slow, thoroughly brazen scrutiny that followed brought the color mounting to her cheeks and ire burning through her being. He was deliberately trying to antagonize her, she was sure of it! No gentleman would look at a lady in such a manner.

Raising her nose to a lofty elevation, she turned a cool shoulder to the man. To her surprise, she found that Farrell had left her to her own ends and was wandering off with Molly in the direction of the inn. The serving wench had spent a triplet of hours trying to catch the Yankee's eye and now sought to stir a bit of jealousy. Never had she tried so hard to lure a man into her bed and never had she failed so miserably. It was enough to shatter a poor maid's confidence the way the man ignored her.

As Erienne ground her teeth in irritation, a hand came upon her arm, bringing her about with a start, wondering how Christopher Seton had crossed the distance between them so swiftly. She was much relieved to find that it was Allan Parker and not the Yankee.

Allan pressed a hand to his vested breast in a brief but gallant bow and stated the obvious with a pleased smile. "Your brother has left you in need of escort, Miss Fleming. One can never be sure when that dastardly band of Scots might choose to raid our village and sweep away our beauteous maidens. Thus I have come to offer my protection."

Erienne laughed brightly, hoping that obnoxious wretch of a Yankee was a witness to the man's manners. At least someone in the village knew how to comport himself like a gentleman.

"Would you care to join the dancing?" Allan invited.

She smiled, tossed her shawl over a bush, and laid her hand into the one he presented, casting a surreptitious glance toward the tree where the rakish fellow stood as the sheriff led her into the circle of dancers. The Yankee was grinning like a mindless jackanapes, and the suspicion that he was amused by it all pricked her pleasure for the moment.

The lively rigadoon, however, took her mind away from the watcher as she lent her talent to the dance. Christopher moved to stand at the fore of the spectators, and with his arms folded across his chest, his long legs braced slightly apart, he gave the impression of some king of old standing head and shoulders above the common folk, as if he had come with his magical sword to rescue them from the cruel oppressor. The fact that he was a most uncommon man in appearance was readily evident to young maid and old alike. Flirtatious glances, inviting smiles, and outright leers were tossed his way, but he seemed oblivious as his eyes followed the slender, dark-haired maid in the plum gown. He watched her feet fly in time with the music, and the display of trim, shapely ankles was anything but displeasing. Indeed, his steadfast perusal of Erienne Fleming became obvious to nearly every woman there, which caused a dull thud of disappointment to trip many a heart.

A large conveyance, recognizable as the Talbots' carriage, halted nearby, and Christopher used the excuse to intrude upon the sheriff. Christopher sidestepped the dancers, and reaching the man, tapped him lightly on the shoulder.

"Your pardon, Allan, but I thought you should be aware of Miss Talbot's arrival."

Allan glanced around and, seeing the coach, frowned slightly. Reluctantly he made his excuses to his partner before hurrying off. Erienne lifted a cool-eyed glare to the man who remained at her side, while the crowd eyed the two of them with wide-spreading grins. Nudging elbows brought the attention of others, and giggling, whispering conjectures ran wild.

"Shall we continue the dance, Miss Fleming?" Christopher queried with a debonair smile.

"Certainly not!" Erienne snapped and strode through the gaping bystanders with her head held high. Angrily she wound a way through the tents and the makeshift hovels that served the seasonal merchants, trying to ignore the man who seemed inclined to bedevil her with his presence. She could not gain any distance on his long-legged stride, and she tossed a command over her shoulder as he neared. "Go away! You're annoying me!"

"Come now, Erienne," he cajoled. "I'm only trying to return your shawl."

She stopped, realizing she had left the garment behind, and faced him. Her eyes blazed beneath his mocking gaze, and in a temper she reached to snatch the shawl from his hand, but it was soundly held in a firm grasp. She glared up into the grayish-green, sparkling eyes, but the heated words that were ready on her tongue were squelched by the interruption of a feminine voice calling, "Ya-hoo, Christopher."

Claudia hastened toward them, leaving Allan to follow close behind. Erienne felt a sharp and sudden irritation when she saw the woman, but she laid the blame to her own sorely vexed mood. Claudia was dressed out in a coral silk gown and a matching wide-brimmed hat, which all seemed rather overstated for the country market, but considering her intense greed for attention, one could hardly expect a less flamboyant arrival.

Claudia gave Erienne a derisive sneer as she joined them and, without otherwise acknowledging her presence, turned to Christopher.

"I'm so delighted to see you still in Mawbry, Christopher," she warbled. "I was afraid I would miss meeting you again."

"My business in Mawbry is not finished yet, and the way it looks, I might be here for some time yet." He drew a quick, challenging glare from Erienne and grinned lazily in the face of it.

Claudia saw the exchange and seethed to think that the other woman shared some secret with the Yankee. Thinking of a way to lead the man away, Claudia swept a hand about to indicate the inn. "During the fair, the innkeeper usually lays out a feast worthy of a king. I was wondering if you would care to sup with me?" She didn't wait for a denial but gave the sheriff a coy smile. "And of course you will accompany us, Allan."

"I shall be delighted." The sheriff gallantly turned to Erienne with an invitation. "Would you care to join us?"

The urge to kick Allan's shins had to be suppressed, and it was all Claudia could do to keep her glare off him and on Erienne. Beneath the shelter of her wide-brimmed hat, Claudia's eyes narrowed menacingly until the other could not miss the bold threat.

"I . . . can't." Erienne watched a smug smile grow on the woman's lips and wished she could wipe it away with a different reply, but she had not the coin to spare. Letting the woman believe she was being successful in frightening her off, however, was a bitter rue for her pride to swallow. "I really must be getting back. My family will be waiting for me."

"But your brother is at the inn now," Allan pointed out. "You must join us."

"No . . . no, really I can't." As the men waited expectantly for some plausible excuse, Erienne admitted with an embarrassed shrug, "I fear I am without coin."

Christopher quickly dismissed the problem. "I shall be more than happy to bear the expense, Miss Fleming." As she shot him an angry look his eyes gleamed their challenge, daring her to accept. "Please allow me."

Claudia was wise enough to know that she would be painted in a less than generous light if she protested aloud. She tried the glare again, silently demanding Erienne take the hint, and did not fathom that it was her glower that really settled the matter for the other woman.

"Thank you," Erienne murmured, coming to a firm decision. "I should like to join you very much."

Both men stepped forward to offer their arms, turning Claudia's surprise into outrage. The woman straightened indignantly but was totally reconciled when Erienne pointedly ignored Christopher's arm and slipped her hand through Allan's.

Erienne was not at all certain she wanted Farrell to see her in Christopher's company and was almost relieved to find him absent from the common room until she remembered Molly coming to the Yankee's room to serve him pleasure. Chewing her lip, she looked wonderingly toward the stairs, afraid that the woman was doing a like service for Farrell.

Erienne became aware that Christopher was watching her, and when her eyes came around to meet his, the depths of the North Sea could not have been colder than those eyes of blue-violet. She expected a mocking leer. Instead his smile bore a trace of compassion. Yet the idea that he could be pitying her or any of her family infuriated her. Mutely fuming, she slid into the chair Allan held for her.

Christopher assisted Claudia into the seat on the other side of him, and Erienne grew extremely vexed when he took for himself the one next to her own. To be within close proximity of the man was agonizingly distasteful to her past, present, and no doubt future state of mind.

In the manner of one accustomed to taking authority, Christopher ordered food to be set before them and a light wine poured for the ladies. He tossed down payment, and Allan seemed content to let him have the honors. When the feast was presented, Claudia condescended to doff her hat but carefully patted her hair in place before delicately sampling the fare.

The door opened, and Erienne blanched as her father strolled in. She had her back to him and didn't dare glance around as he swaggered to the bar. He slapped down coin for ale, then having received a tankard, leaned against the planks to glance about the room as he sipped. He spewed out the contents of his mouth in a rush when his eyes came upon Erienne and Christopher sitting at the same table. With stumbling gait, he half ran across the room, drawing all eyes to him. Erienne heard him coming and her heart leapt for fear. Avery was past the point of caution and failed to see anything beyond the fact that his daughter was willingly accepting the attentions of his fiercest foe. He rudely clasped her arm and hauled her out of the chair, while Claudia smirked behind a glass of wine.

"Ye evil little wench! Goin' behind my back again wit' this Yankee bastard!" Avery loudly berated. "I swear to ye 'twill be the last time ye do!"

The mayor brought his fist around with enough force to break his daughter's jaw, and Erienne tried to brace herself, certain the blow would fall with brutal force, but once again her faithful protector was there close at hand. With a flare of rage, Christopher shot out of his chair and caught Avery's wrist in a painfully tight grip, jerking him away from his daughter.

"Take yer filthy hands off me!" the portly man bellowed, attempting to gain his freedom, but the strong, broad hand held him fast.

Christopher's tone was deadly calm. "I beg you to consider your actions, Mayor. Your daughter came here with the sheriff and Miss Talbot. Would you insult them by such a display?"

As if coming from a fog, Avery became aware of the other two who also sat at the table. Red-faced, he hurriedly stuttered an apology, and Christopher released his hold, curbing the urge to give a short, backward thrust as he did so. He would have enjoyed seeing the man sprawl on his backside.

Avery caught hold of his daughter's arm again and hastened her toward the door. "Ye go on home now and cook me some vittles. I'll be home after I've had me one or two."

The door slammed behind her. Turning, Avery hitched up his breeches, glared about at those who still stared, and returned to the bar.

With tears of humiliation stinging her eyes and streaming down her cheeks, Erienne ran home. She wished now that she would not have allowed herself to be goaded by Claudia's glowering threat. The disgrace she had suffered in the inn would make it extremely difficult to hold her head up in front of the haughty woman.

Then there was the other matter. Claudia was almost vicious in her ambition to be the unrivaled and heralded beauty of the North country, and to gain that end she used her tongue to slander, abuse, or destroy without the least regard for truth. Like a whip, her tongue had the ability to make one writhe in agony. Erienne had no doubt the woman would well flay her reputation in her absence, and Claudia would paint a wildly distorted vision for the Yankee's eyes.

"What do I care?" Erienne mumbled miserably. "Claudia and Mr. Seton were most certainly made for each other."

Four

In the eastern sky, shafts of vibrant color radiated from the dawning sun and thrust through the mottled clouds, bathing the white-faced cottages of Mawbry with a rosy hue. Morning's blushing light penetrated the crystal panes of Erienne's chamber windows, rousing her from a restless sleep. She groaned and snuggled her head beneath the pillow, deriving no pleasure form the prospect that they must seek out another suitor in Wirkinton. She knew her father could not be swayed from his goal, especially since he had found her dining with the Yankee at the inn, and it was useless to delay.

Morosely she dragged herself from the bed and wandered down to the kitchen. Shivering in a threadbare robe, she stoked the fire in the hearth and swung the large, water-filled kettle over the growing flames. From a corner of the room, she pulled forth a copper tub that had been her mother's and found the last remaining sliver of soap that Farrell had given her. Once he had been thoughtful enough to bring home small gifts from Wirkinton for her, but that seemed ages ago. With each progressing day he took on more of his sire's qualities and remembered less the wise counseling of his mother.

It was a rare occasion indeed when she was allowed to travel beyond Mawbry or its surrounding countryside, and though the reason for going was definitely unappealing, she still groomed herself carefully and wore her best attire. At least no one in the port city could have grown bored with seeing the plum velvet gown.

Like any man of gentility, Avery left his daughter outside in front of the inn, there to await the coach while he himself entered the common room. Ensconced in his favorite place and with an ale to sip, he struck up a conversation with the innkeeper, making no effort to lower his tone as he spoke of his intentions to travel to the port city with his girl. Aside from gambling and drinking, exercising his vocal cords seemed Avery's greatest delight. Engrossed in doing so this morning, he failed to notice the tall figure rising from the shadows behind a massive pillar. The front door opened and closed, but Avery gave it no mind as he avidly quenched his thirst.

The crisp wind flirted with the cluster of soft ringlets cascading from the crown of Erienne's head and played with the hem of her skirts while it brought a fresh blush to her cheeks. Ramrod prim and bandbox polished, she was a most fetching sight for any man, many of whom paused after passing and openly glanced back for a second taste of her beauty. The one who was denied her company halted a moment outside the door of the inn and admired the trim, unbustled form. The fact that she had become a forbidden fruit for him only spiced his interest.

Christopher moved forward to stand close behind the young lady's right elbow. Erienne sensed his presence but, thinking it was her father, was slow to respond. As she glanced around, her gaze caught sight of the tall, expensive black boots, and her wonder became questioning surprise. Her head snapped up, and she found herself staring into the handsome and pleasantly smiling face of that one who haunted her.

Christopher tipped his hat and grinned down at her, then clasping his hands behind his back, he gazed up at the sky, where fitful flocks of fleecy clouds gamboled restlessly along on a nor'westerly breeze. "A fairly pleasant day for a ride," he commented. "Though I suspect we might be in for a bit of rain later on."

Erienne ground her teeth, holding a tight rein on her temper. "Out to ogle more women, Mr. Seton?"

"Actually, that isn't my prime purpose this morning," he answered smoothly. "Although I'd be a fool to ignore the sights, such as they are."

She did not miss the meaningful sparkle in his eyes and asked crisply, "Then what is your prime purpose?"

"Why, I am waiting for the coach to Wirkinton."

Erienne clenched her lips against a heated reply. She was appalled that such a coincidence should occur, but since he was well within his rights, she could say nothing. Glancing past his arm, she caught sight of his bay stallion tethered at the hitching post, which suggested that his mode of travel was undergoing a most recent change. Knowing that he had just left the common room where her father had gone, she could assume that Christopher had heard some exchange that had prompted his decision to travel by coach. She flung out a hand to indicate the animal. "You have a mount. Why don't you ride him?"

Christopher's grin was mockingly congenial. "I much prefer the comfort of a coach when I journey afar."

She scoffed. "No doubt you overheard my father say we're on our way to Wirkinton and intend to pester us all the way there."

"My dear Miss Fleming, I assure you that I have a matter of great importance to attend to in Wirkinton." He did not explain that anything to do with her was of primary importance to him. "Of course, your solution is simple," he offered pleasantly. "If you cannot abide my company, you can always stay home. I have no way of forcing you to go."

"We also have business in Wirkinton," she stated, lifting her chin primly.

"Another suitor?" he questioned amiably.

"You . . . Oh!" Her deep blush, having naught to do with the wind, gave him quick answer. "Why can't you leave us alone?"

"I have an investment in your family. I seek only what is mine, or at least some recompense should the debt remain unpaid."

"Ah, yes, the debt," she said, sneering. "The money you rooked from my father."

"My dear, I have no need to cheat anyone."

Erienne stamped her foot in protest. "Mr. Seton, whatever else I am, I am not *your* dear!"

A soft chuckle conveyed his delight. "You're the dearest thing I've seen for some time." His gaze swept downward, gliding effortlessly over her rounded bosom and slim waist until it reached the narrow black shoes peeking out from beneath her hem. Erienne immediately wished she had borne the prickly discomfort of her coarse woolen cloak instead of leaving it lay across her satchel, for his careful scrutiny left no curve untouched. Indeed, his close attention seemed to peel the very cloth away. When his eyes returned to meet hers, her cheeks were hot with indignation. "Aye." He smiled into her glare. "You are a sweet, dear thing indeed."

"Do you always undress a woman with your eyes?" she inquired sharply.

"Only those I have a yearning for."

In an irritated huff, Erienne flounced around and tried to ignore him but found the task beyond her means. He was about as easily dismissed from mind as a black panther at heel. There was, however, a way to protect herself from his relentless regard. Taking up the cloak, she spread it about her shoulders and warned him off by a wordless glower when he reached a hand toward her to lend assistance.

Giving a lazy shrug of his wide shoulders, Christopher smiled and withdrew his hand. Erienne concentrated on tying the cords at her throat and was not aware that he had drawn much nearer until his whisper brushed close against her ear, sending a warm, tingling shiver through her.

"You smell as sweet as jasmine on a summer's night."

Erienne snatched the hood up over her head, afraid he would notice the gooseflesh he had raised. Totally aware of his presence, she remained cautiously silent until the coach halted before the inn. The driver climbed down, and wiping his dry lips, he announced to the occupants of the coach that there would be a short delay, then turning, strode purposefully toward the common room. A portly fellow and his tall, thin companion plowed their way between the waiting couple, forcing them to step quickly aside or be trodden down underfoot.

When Erienne could reach her satchel again, it was already clasped in her adversary's hand. She raised a stern brow of disapproval, but Christopher awaited her with an amused patience that made resistance a simple, threadbare sham. Pointedly ignoring him, she lifted her skirts to step aboard and immediately felt his hand beneath her elbow aiding her ascent. He tossed her valise into the boot as she settled in the interior, then strode off, making Erienne crane her neck in an effort to see where he was going until he came back leading his horse. Quickly she pressed back in the seat, regaining her lofty air before he could take note of her interest. After securing the animal's reins to the rear of the boot, he climbed in and took the seat directly opposite her.

The other passengers, having satisfied their thirst and their various needs, came trooping back to the coach. Avery was the last to emerge from the inn, and being in high spirits, stepped sprightly to the carriage door. However, when he caught sight of their traveling companion, his jaw plummeted. Blustering in indecision, he stamped and fumed until finally, having no other choice, he joined them. Taking a place beside his daughter, he gave her a withering glare, making it obvious that he suspected her of inviting the man.

The wheels splashed through a large puddle as the coach swung onto the road, and Erienne leaned back, bracing herself against the jolting ride. The countryside along the way failed to hold her interest, for the presence of Christopher Seton wiped everything else from her mind. His gaze was persistent and touched her warmly. A smile was in his eyes and on his lips. Even in her father's company, he was completely at ease, not caring that the older man's scowl darkened progressively at the close attention he gave to the daughter.

The other travelers were openly delighted with Christopher's company, for he talked and laughed with them freely. He related stories and experiences gleaned from his many voyages and showed animal-white teeth against the warm bronze of his skin as he recounted more humorous tales. He had the portly man holding his sides with mirth, but Avery's rage grew with each passing mile.

Forced to observe, Erienne reluctantly admitted, but only to herself, that the Yankee had the charm, wit, and manners to handle himself well in any company. His manners were those of one born to wealth and position. Indeed, he acted the part of gentleman so well he could have authored the rule book. Yet Erienne sensed he could be equally at home with a crew of bawdy, fun-loving tars. He appeared to enjoy every facet of life.

Beneath the shadow of long lashes, Erienne's eyes passed carefully over the man. His broad shoulders filled a finely tailored coat of dark blue, and the breeches, of a light taupe hue that matched the vest, were close-fitting to display a superb length of firmly muscled limbs. It was obvious at a mere glance that he was boldly a man, even with all his clothes on. Much to her aggravation, Erienne realized he would be the standard by which she measured every suitor who vied for her hand.

The ride progressed southward, and Erienne could feel herself relaxing, almost enjoying the easy ways and casual banter of Mr. Seton. What she had feared would be a tense, stilted journey was becoming a pleasant outing, and she even experienced a mild disappointment when they reached their destination.

A small sign, identifying the inn as the Lion's Paw, swung on its hinges above the doorway, squeaking and flapping like a distraught bird in the stiff breezes. Avery kept his daughter to her place while Christopher and the other passengers alighted, then after hastily climbing down, he beckoned impatiently to her.

"Don't dally, girl," he snapped. Yanking his tricorn down against the wind, he cast a wary eye about to find Christopher untethering his stallion from the back of the coach. Remembering the incident in the inn at Mawbry, he lowered his voice a cautious degree to continue. "Mr. Goodfield's carriage is here awaitin' us, but I'll be havin' ter find rooms 'ere at the inn 'fore we leave. So hurry with ye."

Erienne's lack of enthusiasm greatly annoyed him, and as soon as her feet touched ground, he caught her arm in a fierce, painful grip and hustled her off to a waiting landau. He ignored her pleas to be allowed time to freshen herself, fearful of what that Yankee rascal might do if they delayed. Perhaps Avery had cause to worry. Christopher observed the happenings closely as he idly gathered the reins over the stallion's neck. He particularly noted the girl's reluctance to be prodded aboard the conveyance.

The coachman stepped to the boot and hauled back the canvas cover that protected the baggage. With a gesture and a question Christopher directed the man's attention to the landau.

"Why, 'at rig belongs to Mr. Goodfield. Oldest an' richest merchant 'round these parts," the coachman replied. "Ye follow this 'ere road a bit, then turn north at the crossroads. Ye can't miss the place. Biggest 'ouse ye ever seen."

Christopher flipped a coin into the driver's hand to display his gratitude, bidding the man to take a draught of ale on him. Chortling, the coachman thanked him profusely and hurried off toward the inn.

Erienne hesitated on the carriage step and looked back, finding the grayish-green eyes fastened on her. Christopher gave her a slow grin and cordially tipped his hat. Avery followed his daughter's gaze and glared when he found the object of her attention. Gripping her arm, he pushed her in, then hurried back to the coach to claim their baggage.

"Keep yer eyes to yerself," he warned Christopher direly. "I have me friends here, and a word from me, and they'll see ye done in good. Ye won't be any use to any woman when they finishes wit' ye."

The younger man returned a tolerant smile to the threat. "You don't learn very quickly, do you, Mayor? First you sent your son, and now you think to frighten me with your friends? Perhaps you've forgotten that I have a ship in port with a crew who've honed their teeth fighting pirates and privateers. Would you care to meet them again?"

"Leave me girl alone!" Avery spat the words out through his teeth.

"Why?" Christopher chuckled derisively. "So you can marry her off for a purse? I've got a purse. How much will you take for her?"

"I've told ye!" Avery thundered. "She ain't for ye, no matter how weighty yer purse!"

"Then you'd best pay up your debt, Mayor, because I won't be satisfied until it is done." Christopher swung into the saddle and with a nudge of his heel set his mount into an easy canter, leaving the mayor glaring after him.

An overwhelming feeling of depression came over Erienne at her first glimpse of Smedley Goodfield. He was old and wrinkled, with much the size and looks of a wizened elf. His hunched back and distorted shoulders were painful reminders of the taunt she had hurled at Christopher. Whatever she had said then, she was positive now that Smedley Goodfield would be her *very* last choice as a husband.

Shortly after their arrival, her father was bluntly invited to look over the gardens without being given much choice in the matter. She, on the other hand, was beckoned to sit on the settee beside Smedley. Erienne declined, taking a bench before the hearth, but she soon found this was only an invitation for the merchant to join her. From the first moment he sat beside her, she had to fight to keep his hands from invading the privacy of her clothes. In his fumbling eagerness he ripped her bodice, and considering her modest collar, his actions had no pretense of the accidental. With an outraged gasp Erienne threw off his bony hands and came to her feet, clutching the torn bodice together and snatching up her cloak.

"I am leaving, Mr. Goodfield!" She strained not to shout. "Good day to you!"

Her father was pacing nervously about the entry hall when she stormed out, and a brief argument ensued when he tried to urge her back to the drawing room.

"I'll have none of yer damned impertinence! *I'll* decide when we'll be leaving!" he snarled as he jabbed his thumb against his chest. "An' it won't be 'til we've settled on this matter o' marriage."

Erienne's face was a stiff mask as she fought the anger that churned within her. Slowly but emphatically she answered her parent. "The matter is already settled!" She took several deep breaths in an attempt to calm the raging tides that swept through her being. "The only way you can keep me here is to bind me hand and foot, then you'd best find a way to silence me, for I'll scream enough insults at that filthy old man that he'll throw us both out. I have had enough of that lecher's pawing hands." She threw open her cloak and displayed her torn gown. "See what he's done! My best gown, and he's ruined it."

"He'll buy ye ten more!" Avery cried in desperation. He couldn't allow her to go, not with his freedom at stake. What did a torn gown matter when the man wanted to marry her? The little twit was just being difficult. "If ye leave this house, I warn ye 'twill be by foot. Mr. Goodfield was kind enough to see us here in his carriage, and we've no other way to return."

Erienne held her chin high as she stalked toward the door. "Perhaps you are not yet ready to leave, Father, but I am."

"Where are ye going?" Avery demanded.

"As I said," she flung over her shoulder, "I'm leaving!"

Avery was in a quandary. He hadn't thought she would go off without him, not in a strange place. The suspicion grew in his mind that she was only testing him and really had no intention of leaving on her own. He gave a derisive snort. He would show her that he was a man of his word. "Ye'll see yerself back to the inn without me, girl. I'll be stayin' with Mr. Goodfield . . ."

The door slammed in his face, leaving him sputtering in astonishment. He started to charge after her, intending to drag her back, but Smedley's cane thumped imperiously in the drawing room, demanding attention. Worriedly Avery hurried toward the sound as he sought to find some excuse that would explain his daughter's actions and soothe the merchant's outraged vanity. Never had Avery's thoughts churned so frantically in so short a time.

Erienne stalked down the path that led away from the merchant's mansion. Her mind was in a turmoil, and her whole body was rigid with the anger she felt. It was enough that she was forced to bear the attentions of a seemingly endless procession of overly eligible men from every corner of England. It was enough that the only qualifications her father recognized in the suitors was the size of their purses and their readiness to defray his debts. It was enough that her own father had to use her as a tool to placate the creditors who had become anxious about their money. But now! Being commanded to please a doddering ancient lest he become offended . . . It was just too much!

Her skin crawled as she remembered the pawing hands of the many eager candidates, and their oh-so-endless ploys: the accidental brush of her bosom, the stealthy caress of her thigh beneath a table, the bold press of heated loins against her derrière, and the simpering leers that knowingly answered her questioning glares of anger.

Halting, she stood with clenched fists and grinding teeth. She knew all too well what the evening would bring if she returned to the Lion's Paw. Her father would come mewling in with Smedley Goodfield at his side, and he would press her to reach some compatible arrangement with the merchant. Of course, Smedley would sit fidgeting at her side, seizing every opportunity to lean against her, to caress her hip, or to bend close with his crooked, gap-toothed grin and whisper some lewd or vulgar comment or story in her ear, then cackle in glee when she reacted in horror, or if she didn't, to take her calmness as encouragement for more.

A spasm of pure disgust wrenched through her and caught her stomach into a tight knot. She was aware that her father feared debtors' prison, and it was the last place she wanted him to go. But she also had come to the realization that she could not bear to debase herself in the manner he proposed.

Erienne's panic was born small but rapidly grew as she thought of the aged merchant waiting at the inn with his nervous, ingratiating smile. She saw again the narrow face, the red-rimmed eyes that moved quickly like a rat's, the bone-thin, clawlike hand that had ripped her gown in his fevered haste . . .

A stone obelisk carved with an arrow pointing north to Mawbry caught her eye, and an idea began to flit through her mind. Wirkinton and the Lion's Paw lay to the south only a few miles away. The path to Mawbry presented a longer walk, a journey that would take the rest of the day and some of the night to complete. The wind was brisk and the air was growing increasingly chilly, but she wore her warmest cloak, and there was naught at the inn that she needed.

Indeed, anything there would only be a burden, and if she returned, she'd only be tender bait for the likes of Smedley Goodfield.

Erienne made her decision, and her desire to reach Mawbry before midnight gave impetus to her haste. Her slippers were ill suited to the pebble-strewn lane, and she had to stop often to remove the invading stones. Still, an hour on the road saw her fairly well along, and she felt no regret at having avoided another meeting with Smedley. It was only when clouds began to darken and churn close overhead that the first twinge of doubt pricked her. An occasional droplet of rain struck her face, and with the pressure of the ever-building wind, her cloak wrapped about her legs and seemed determined to impede her progress.

Stubbornly Erienne labored up another hill but paused at its brow when she saw a pair of roads joining together and each stretching out endlessly before her, one trailing off in one direction, the other lane winding off in another. Nothing was familiar, and the worry that she might take the wrong road greatly undermined her confidence. The lowering clouds were becoming a tumbling, indistinct mass, snuffing out the sunlight and lending no hint of the direction she should take.

The wind whipped the hilltop with an ever-deepening chill that made her shiver, but its icy breath gave her a small measure of assurance that it came from the north. Clenching her gloveless fingers against its frosty nip, she set her jaw in grim determination and struck out again on what she dearly hoped was a northerly trek.

"Marriage!" she scoffed beneath her breath. She was beginning to detest the word.

She bent to pick another pebble from her shoe, but when she glanced casually over her shoulder, she stopped and slowly began to straighten. Paused on the hill behind her, silhouetted like some evil wizard against the black, turbulent vapors that seethed behind him, a man sat astride a dark horse. The wind whipped his cloak out wide about him, lending wings to his form, and staring at him, Erienne knew a sudden, bone-chilling fear. She had heard innumerable tales of murder and ravishment done along the roads and byways of North England, of highwaymen stripping their victims of valuables, virtue, or life, and she was sure this man posed a threat to her.

She began to back away, and the rider urged his steed forward. Fighting the bit, the animal pranced sideways for a moment, giving her a good view of the pair. Erienne caught her breath, and her trepidations rapidly vanished as she recognized that magnificent, glistening stallion and the man sitting astride him.

Christopher Seton! The very name scalded her being with hot indignation. She felt an urge to scream in utter rage. Of all the people who could have come over that hill, why did it have to be him?

Her attempt to scramble from the road made him kick his horse. The stallion was long-legged and quickly closed the distance between them, flinging up clods of dirt as he followed her into the soft, rock-strewn turf beside the road. Grinding her teeth in frustration, Erienne dodged the pursuit, lifting her skirts well above her knees as she darted in the opposite direction. Christopher was not to be outdone, for he flung himself from the stallion, and in two long strides was upon her, swooping her up in his arms.

"Put me down, you pompous oaf! Put me down!" Erienne kicked her legs and pushed at the broad chest in a frenzied effort to gain her release.

"Be still, little minx, and listen!" he demanded, his voice sounding harsh and angry in her ear. "Do you not understand what could happen to you on this road? The bands of thieves and miscreants who roam this countryside would see you as a most tempting morsel. You'd be sport for them for a night or two . . . if you lasted that long. Did you give a thought to that?"

Coldly rejecting the logic of his warning, Erienne jerked her face aside. "I insist you put me down, sir."

"Only when you're willing to listen to reason."

Mutinously she glared up at him. "How did you know where I was?"

The green eyes sparkled with unbridled humor. "Your father and that twisted excuse for a man with him came back to the inn looking for you. The mayor raised quite a furor when he couldn't find you." Christopher laughed shortly. "After seeing Smedley, I decided you would run off before facing him again, and I was right. You left a clear set of tracks in your haste to flee."

"You're conceited, Mr. Seton, if you think I welcome your protection, or your company."

"You needn't be so formal, Erienne," he teased with a devilishly wicked grin. "You may call me Christopher, or my dear, or my love, or any endearment of your choice."

Erienne's eyes struck sparks of fiery indignation. "My desire," she said flatly, "is to be put to the ground immediately."

"As you wish, milady." Christopher withdrew his arm from beneath her knees, letting her limbs slide against him until her toes barely touched the moss-covered slope. The full shock of his firm, hard body went through Erienne with the effect of a searing bolt of lightning. Almost as quickly, a vision was conjured up, one bathed by the pinkish rays of the dawning sun with a lone figure of a naked man silhouetted against its light.

"Unhand me!" she commanded, trying to hide her burning cheeks with rage. No proper lady would allow such a vision to take root and flourish in her mind. "I am quite capable of standing on my own feet."

Placing his hands about her slender waist, Christopher lifted her onto a boulder that formed a small, flat plateau beside the road. "Stay here," he enjoined, "until I return with my horse."

"I'm not a child you can order about," she protested. "I'm a grown woman!"

He cocked a handsome brow as he gave her a lengthy inspection. Even through the cloak, his eyes seemed to burn her. "Now, that's the first real truth I've heard you say."

Erienne blushed profusely and pulled the garment tighter about her. "Has anyone ever told you how detestable you are?"

His white teeth gleamed behind a lopsided grin. "Thus far, my dear, every member of your family."

"Then why don't you leave us alone?" she snapped.

Laughing, he stepped away to fetch his mount and commented over his shoulder as he gathered the reins. "The way things are going, Erienne, I'm beginning to think your father will never get you married off." He led the stallion back to her. "I just would like some assurance that I'm not going to lose out completely on my investment."

"Do you honestly think you have some claim to me?" she jeered. "Some right to annoy and bore me with your presence?"

His shoulders moved in a careless shrug. "As much as your other suitors do. Indeed, with the two thousand pounds your father owes me, perhaps more. I wonder which of your gallant beaux will want to part with such a sum." His laughter mocked her. "You might as well be put on the block and let them bid for you. 'Twould save your father considerable time and effort in his attempt to find you a generous husband."

Erienne opened her mouth to voice her objection to such a suggestion, but she was abruptly silenced when he swept her up and placed her onto the back of his horse. Swinging up behind her, he gave her no choice but to accept his company.

"This is outrageous, Mr. Seton!" she stormed. "Put me down!"

"If you're not aware of it, my sweet, we're about to get soaked." Even as he spoke, raindrops began to pelt them. "Since I can't leave you here alone, you'll have to come with me."

"I'm not going anywhere with you!" she cried.

"Well, I'm not going to sit here in the rain and argue with you." He kicked the stallion, squelching her protest as the animal leapt forward into a full gallop. She was flung back hard against the stalwart chest, and for safety's sake, she had to submit to the arm he laid about her. Though she would have openly denied it, she was grateful for its security and for the nestling seat his thighs provided her.

Whipped by the wind, the rain rapidly soaked through her cloak and ran in cold runnels down the front of her torn bodice. Erienne squinted upward toward the frenzied sky, but the large, splashing droplets forced her to turn her face away and seek shelter against his chest. Looking down at her, Christopher pulled his cloak about her to provide more protection, but in the next moments it seemed that a whole torrent of water was unleashed upon them. Icy sheets slashed down upon them, wetting their garments until they became dead weights that hindered movement. The wind and frigid rain were relentless, assaulting them from every angle.

Through the heavy downpour the vague shape of a structure became visible in the distance. Urging the steed off the road, Christopher rode through the trees toward it. The barren limbs provided no protection from the storm but snatched at them, snaring their clothing as if seeking to prevent their passage.

As they neared, the building became recognizable as an old, abandoned stable. A tumbledown cottage stood beside it, but without a roof it left serious doubt that any but the smallest creatures would find shelter within its crumbling walls. The doors of the stable gaped wide, though one hung askew on a lone stiff, rusty hinge. Leafless vines entangled the edifice, and a decaying log lay on the ground across the entrance. Despite its dilapidated state, the barn offered considerably more protection than the cottage.

Christopher dismounted in front of the doors and reached up to lift Erienne from her place. The wind billowed beneath her wet cloak, sending a piercing chill through her as its frigid breath touched her soaked gown. She shivered uncontrollably as Christopher carried her across the log and into the dark interior. He set her to her feet, then peered about into the shadows.

"Not as cozy as the Lion's Paw, but at least it will give us some shelter from the storm," he stated. Discarding his sodden cloak, he glanced down at her and arched a dubious brow. "You look like a drowned rabbit."

Erienne's trembling chin raised to a lofty level as she eyed him coolly. A violent shuddering made it difficult to retort with effective rancor, but she tried. "I s-suppose you t-think Claudia would look b-better at a t-time like this."

Christopher laughed at a mental vision of Claudia trying to look elegant in a wide hat that flopped dripping wet about her ears. "You needn't be jealous of her," he responded glibly. " 'Twas you I followed to Wirkinton."

"Aha! S-so you d-do admit it."

"Of course."

Erienne stared at him blankly, finding her argument suddenly deflated by his acknowledgment.

Christopher chuckled and went back to lead the stallion through the doorway. Erienne huddled in her dripping clothes as he untied a covered roll behind the saddle. Producing his redingote, he tossed it to her and turned back to strip the saddle from the back of the steed, advising over his shoulder, "You'd better put that on before you take a chill."

She gripped her own water-weighted cloak about her and turned her face away, not wishing to shred her pride by removing the outer garment and revealing her torn gown. "Keep your gallant offering for yourself, Mr. Seton. I have no use for it."

Christopher arched a brow as he peered at her over his shoulder. "Are you trying to convince me how foolish you are?"

"Foolish or n-not, I won't wear it."

"You'll wear it," he stated flatly, giving her cause to wonder if he threatened her. Doffing his own sodden coat and vest, he flung the garments over the boards of a stall. "I'll try to make a fire so we can get dried out a bit."

He prowled about the stable, contemplating the several large holes in the roof. Without a doubt he had his choice of chimneys and a good supply of kindling; it would just be a matter of getting the fire started. Toward that end the tinderbox he carried with him would suffice.

Erienne's shaking limbs gave way beneath her, and she slowly crumpled to her knees. She was aware of Christopher moving about the stables gathering and breaking wood from the stalls, but the idea of a warming fire seemed so distant. She sat in abject misery with her hair hanging in wet strands down her back. Her cheeks and hands were numb and icy, her nose red and cold. Even her shoes were soaked.

When she saw the first small flickering flames begin to glow in the deepening darkness, she found herself too cold and stiff to move to its warmth. She shivered in her wet garb until Christopher came to stand above her. She kept her eyes downcast, too tired to fight with him any longer, and perhaps more pertinently not willing to raise her gaze along the wetly clinging breeches that flaunted his manhood.

"Will you come by the fire?" he questioned softly.

Drawing herself into a tight, miserable knot, Erienne shook her head, so tense with the cold she could not answer him. She had her pride, and it was better to be thought stubborn than weak. She failed to consider that Christopher Seton was a man who took matters into his own hands. Reaching down, he pulled her to her feet, then swept her up in his arms. She gritted a denial through clenched teeth, afraid she would be reduced to one shivering, shaking mass if she tried to speak. Despite her feeble protest, Christopher's arms remained warm and secure about her. He set her to her feet near the fire and began to pluck at the ties of her cloak. In a sudden panic, Erienne caught the garment together and tried to pull away, shaking her head.

"N-no! Leave me alone!"

"If you won't help yourself, Erienne, then someone else must do it."

Prying her hands free, he slipped the cloak from her shoulders and let it fall to a sodden heap at her feet. Surprise swept his visage as he glimpsed the tattered shreds of her gown and soft, creamy breasts barely covered by a soaked chemise. Anxiously Erienne gathered the torn pieces of her bodice together and refused to meet his inquiring frown.

"I can understand Smedley becoming eager." His tone was sharp and derisive. "But did he hurt you?"

"W-would it be any of your business if he h-had?" she questioned, puzzled by his anger.

"It might," he answered brusquely. "It all depends on whether your father can pay off his debts or not. Besides, I've gotten in the habit of coming to your rescue, and since you seem in great need of my services, I am reluctant to stop at this early date."

Without pardon or preamble, he turned her about and much to her horror began to unfasten her gown. Shivering violently, Erienne fought to hold the soaked bodice in place over her bosom while trying to pull away from him. The corset pushed her breasts upward until she nearly overflowed the thin chemise, and she knew without the gown, she would have no protection against those probing grayish-green eyes.

Christopher was more determined . . . and stronger. The gown, the corset, and the layers of petticoats soon lay at her feet. Only then did Erienne gain her freedom.

"Leave me alone!" she gasped, stumbling away from the fire. She tried to cover herself with her arms, for the dampened shift had molded itself in a transparent film to her body.

Christopher came after her and enfolded her quaking form in the redingote. "If you could see past that pretty little nose of yours, you'd realize I'm only trying to help you." He swept her up into his arms. "For a very fiery vixen, you're about as cold and pale as an icicle." His eyes gleamed into hers. "And as I've told you before, I have to protect my investments."

"You brute! Knave!" she railed.

His laughing breath touched her brow. "Your endearments intrigue me, my sweet."

He sat her beside the fire, then knelt to pull off her slippers. Erienne gasped in shock when his hands went up her shift to unfasten the garters at her knees. Against her struggling efforts, he slipped the stockings down and placed them on a stone beside the fire.

"My pleasure would be to take the shift from you as well," he stated with a wicked grin. "So be thankful I've let you retain some of your modesty."

"Don't get any high-minded ideas that you're any better than Mr. Goodfield," she stated hotly. Although she was already beginning to feel warmer and could speak with more clarity, her outrage at being forcefully disrobed prevented her from experiencing the smallest grain of gratitude. "You accost me here in this deserted place and force your will on me. Believe me, sir, my father will hear of this!"

"That will be as you desire, Erienne, but take a warning. I don't run from your family's threats and what I'm doing now is for your own good. If you want someone hurt because of your own stubborn pride, then the consequences will be on your head, not mine."

"I suppose when you wounded my brother, 'twas for his good, too."

Christopher laughed shortly. "Your brother knows what happened. Let him tell you. Or you can ask some of the witnesses who were at the duel. I don't need to defend myself to you or your family."

"And, of course, you're the poor innocent." She chuckled derisively. "For the sake of me, Mr. Seton, I just can't believe that."

His eyes glowed in the warm light of the fire as he gave her a lazy smile. "I never claimed to be an innocent, my sweet, but neither am I your blackhearted villain."

"I would hardly expect you to admit it if you were," she retorted crisply.

"I'm a fairly honest person." The tantalizing grin returned and grew wider when she gave him a doubtful stare. "Then there are times when it becomes expedient to hold back the truth."

"What you're trying to say is that you're a liar when it meets your mood."

"That's not what I'm saying at all."

"Then explain what you mean," she urged, eyeing him coolly.

"Why should I?" he mocked with a smile twitching at the corner of his mouth. "You wouldn't believe me anyway."

"You're right, of course. I wouldn't believe a word you said."

"Then you might as well sleep if you can. We'll be staying the night here, and I see no reason to bore you further with any more lies."

"I won't stay here! Not with you!" She shook her head passionately. "Never!"

Half frowning, half smiling, he peered at her. "Do you want to go back out into the storm?"

Turning aside, Erienne refused to answer him. She was not yet ready to leave the comfort of their haven, but she couldn't trust him either. The sight of him was enough to make any maid wary. All he needed was a ring in his ear to be a swashbuckling pirate. The white shirt, open to the waist, revealed the firm, muscular chest with its crisp matting of hair. Broad-shouldered and narrow-waisted, he even had the torso of a pirate, or at least those of fanciful dreams, and with his wicked smile and his wet hair curling darkly about his face, he would have made a most handsome buccaneer.

"If you refuse to answer me, then I must presume you see the logic in staying here. Good!" His amusement deepened as she tossed him a glare. "If the rain stops during the night, I'll see that you're home before sunup. Since your father is still in Wirkinton and your brother is probably sleeping off another drunk," he refrained from making any mention of Molly, "no one need know that you spent the night here with me."

"How dare you cast aspersions on Farrell!" Sparks of indignation flashed in her eyes. "How dare you!"

"You needn't feel insulted, my sweet," he said and grinned. "I don't judge you by your brother's antics."

"Oh, you cad! You utter cad! He wouldn't be like that if you hadn't shot him!"

"Really?" Christopher gazed at her dubiously. "The way the rumors have it, your brother was cutting a wide swath before we ever met."

He picked up her clothes and began spreading them before the fire. Any further retort Erienne might have made was squelched by his actions, for he seemed quite familiar with the intricate detail of the garments. Embarrassed, she rolled into a knot, facing away from him and jerking the redingote up close about her neck in what she hoped was a pointed dismissal. It was a long time before the seething irritation calmed. Exhausted, she lay still and watched the snapping, crackling fire until eyelids sagged and her resistance gave way to sleep.

Erienne was jolted awake by the intruding suspicion that she was being watched, and a mild panic grew when she failed to recognize her surroundings. A tallow lantern bathed the small area around her in a soft, golden light, and she felt the warmth of a fire on her cheek. Beyond the light, deep shadows wavered into an impenetrable wall of intense darkness. Huge, rough timbers formed an unfamiliar pattern above her head, too low and dark to be part of her own bedchamber. Beneath the prickly covering she felt a cloying dampness against her skin, and when she searched with a hand, she recalled it was the shift she wore . . . the single garment Christopher Seton had left when he had stripped her of the rest.

Everything came back to her in a rush, and she sat up with a gasp, her eyes flying in search of the knave. He was far too close for her peace of mind, for he sat with his back braced against a nearby post, a knee drawn up, and an arm dangling across it. His gaze never wavered from her, but when it dipped downward, she saw the light that flared in his eyes, making her conscious of her lack of modesty. The redingote had dropped away, and when she glanced quickly down, her fears were realized, for no detail was left to the imagination. Her skin glowed in the firelight, and the soft, rosy peaks of her bosom strained against the delicate fabric. With a shocked gasp, she snatched the woolen garment to her.

"How long have you been sitting there watching me sleep?" she demanded.

A slow smile touched his lips. "Long enough."

She was in no mood for games. "Long enough for what?"

His smoldering gaze passed over her. "Long enough to come to the determination that you're worth far more than any debt."

Erienne's mouth sagged slightly, and she stared at him in surprise, unconscious of the vision she presented as her hair tumbled about her shoulders in loose array. Mr. Seton, you can hardly think of me as compensation for an unpaid debt. If you do, you've taken leave of a goodly portion of your senses."

"If your father has his way, 'tis exactly what you'll become. You'll be bought and sold for a mere pittance."

"I wouldn't exactly call two thousand pounds a mere pittance," she scoffed. "And besides, if it weren't for you, I wouldn't have to marry at all. At least, not for wealth."

Christopher shrugged his shoulders carelessly. "Your father need not consider finding you a rich husband. Your companionship in exchange for two thousand pounds seems a fair enough trade to me."

"My companionship!" She laughed caustically. "You mean your paid paramour, don't you?"

"Only if you would feel so inclined, my sweet. I have never yet forced a lady."

"And no doubt you've had many to sample from."

His smile was as smooth as his voice. "A gentleman never tells, my sweet."

Erienne tossed her head. "You rate yourself too highly."

"My mother did her best, but I have a mind of my own." His grin widened. "I've always held myself adaptable to the circumstances."

"You mean you're a self-made cad," she said with firm conviction.

"Aye, Erienne, but with me you'll never be bored. I promise you that."

The warmth in his tone brought the heat creeping into her cheeks. As if instructing an errant student slow to learn, she pronounced her words carefully. "Mr. Seton, I would prefer it immensely if you call me Miss Fleming."

His chuckle sounded low and deep. "I think after sharing a bed and spending the night together, we should progress to something more intimate, at least while we're alone. Now, my love, I should like you to consider the advantages of letting me become your suitor. I am not as ancient as my predecessors. A full score, ten, and three I be. I am strong and have clean habits. I have never been an abuser of women." He ignored her light scoff. "And I have wealth to see you richly garbed, as your beauty demands. As to my appearance . . ." He swept a hand before him. "You can determine that for yourself."

"I have the distinct feeling you're propositioning me, Mr. Seton," she replied brittlely.

"Only trying to convince you of my merits, my love."

"You needn't try. 'Twould be a waste. I shall always hate you."

"Will you, my dear?" His brows crinkled inquiringly. "Do you hate me more than Silas Chambers, perhaps? Or even Smedley Goodfield?"

She faced away, not daring to answer his question.

"I think not." He answered his own inquiry. " 'Tis my suspicion that you'd prefer a real man to warm your bed rather than one of those doddering fools your father would have you wed. They've passed their prime, and though they'd struggle mightily to perform the intimate duties of a husband, 'tis questionable whether they would be able to do anything more than drool in helpless lust."

His statements brought a bright hue creeping into Erienne's cheeks. "How dare you insult me with your half-witted proposals, as if you were some grand gift to womankind. As I've already stated, Mr. Seton, I'd sooner wed an ogre than bed down with the likes of you!"

His answer, though spoken in a hushed voice, tore through her with more force than her father's bellowing threats could ever do. "Shall I show you how thinly guarded your insults are?"

Erienne scrambled up, desperately clutching the redingote about her. She was suddenly leery of being alone with him and of what he could do if he set his mind to having her. Still, she made up her mind that she would not give him the pleasure of seeing her daunted by this threat. "You're arrogant, sir, if you believe I'd ever fall swooning at your feet."

Christopher came to his feet in one quick, effortless motion, drawing a gasp from her. His taunting grin and the broad, half-naked chest made her realize the folly in baiting him. He had all but stated he was no gentleman and did exactly what he chose to do. He could choose to take her.

Gripping the coat around her shoulders, she stumbled back as he advanced on her with slow, deliberate strides and a devilishly wayward smile. As he neared, his booted foot trod on the end of the redingote, abruptly halting her retreat. Erienne fought to snatch it free, but he continued forward until she dropped it and fled with a strangled cry to the far side of the stable. The crumbling wall offered no haven from his approach, and she searched for a weapon, finding none close at hand.

"Stay away from me!" She glanced wildly about but quickly dismissed the idea of bolting past him. As evidenced on prior occasions, he was as quick as he was strong. He halted before her, his wide shoulders narrowing her world to a dark, limited space. Angrily she shoved at his chest, but her attempt to thrust him away only succeeded in pulling his shirt apart. His long fingers closed around her wrist.

"Pride and foolishness," he mocked while his eyes burned into hers.

Erienne tried to wrench her hand away, but his free arm slipped about her waist and brought her full against his hardened frame. In the next instant his lips were on hers, and his fiery kiss warmed her to the core of her being, twisting, bruising, demanding. His mouth moved hungrily over hers, forcing hers to open beneath his mounting ardor. His tongue played upon her lips, then slipped within to taste leisurely the full sweetness of her mouth, shocking Erienne's sense of propriety. She tried to turn her face aside, afraid that her will and her hatred would crumble beneath the onslaught of his fervor. She was held in an unyielding vise, her waist clamped beneath his arm, and her soft breasts crushed against his chest. His hand slid downward over her buttock, pressing her to him until she could not ignore the evidence of his burning passion.

His mouth left hers and slid down her throat, and her senses erupted in a ball of flame that followed his lips downward. She could not draw a deep breath or free herself from those hot, sultry kisses.

She shook her head lamely in a denial, wanting him to stop before she was consumed. Then his mouth came upon her breast, and her breath caught as the wet, white heat of it scalded her through the thin cloth, bringing her nipple to a taut peak. With outraged modesty, she sought to push him away, sure that she would swoon if he did not stop.

"Christopher . . . don't!"

With a soft chuckle he released her, and Erienne's mind went reeling as he stepped away from her. She leaned weakly against the wall, gasping for breath. Holding a hand over her throbbing breast, she could only stare at him as if she, he, and the world had gone mad. No virginal platitudes could erase the astonished look of wonder from her face, nor soften the chaotic pounding of her heart.

"Be satisfied with your ancient suitors if you can, Erienne Fleming. Or face the truth of what I've said."

Almost in a daze, Erienne watched him as he turned and moved toward the stallion who had begun to snort and stamp nervously. She was much confused by her own emotions. Her newfound knowledge of Christopher Seton was like a mouse nibbling inside a wall, boding of trouble yet to come, and yet unstoppable at the moment.

Stepping out into the misty darkness, Christopher moved away from the stable and for a long moment waited in silence. He turned his head from side to side to catch the slightest murmur, then it came, a low, muffled sound in the distance, like a shadowed intruder flitting across the stillness of the night or like slow, plodding hoofbeats, only much softer, as if . . .

He ran back into the stables and began gathering the clothes from about the fire. "Get dressed. We'll have to leave. There are riders coming, mayhaps a score or more, and the horses are traveling with muffled hooves." He tossed her clothes to her. "I doubt they are honest men going about at this hour in that fashion."

Erienne hastily complied and was tugging at the laces of her stays when he returned and brushed her hands aside. Hurriedly he accomplished the task for her.

" 'Tis the least I can do, milady," he whispered close to her ear.

Erienne fumed in ungrateful silence as she yanked on her petticoats and gown. "Are you certain you heard someone coming?"

Christopher threw his redingote about her, giving her no time to fasten the gown, and pulled her toward the horse. "If you doubt me, stay here! You'll find out soon enough."

Erienne accepted his answer for the moment and stepped aside as he grabbed the old wooden bucket he had used to water his horse. He ran back to the fire and immediately doused it, then kicked dirt over the hissing, smoking pile of ashes until it was smothered beneath a heavy layer, and darkness once again reigned unchallenged in the dilapidated barn. He took the reins, throwing their cloaks and his vest and frockcoat over the saddle. He led the horse from the stable and into a thicket some distance away from the road. Erienne held onto the tail of the steed as they felt their way through the stygian gloom. They waited in the deepest shadow as the sound of muffled hooves drew nearer. A low voice called out in the night, bringing the band to a halt on the road, and soon a trio of riders pushed through the brush toward the stable.

"I tell ye I smell smoke," one of the men argued in a hushed voice. "An' I've ridden this road 'nough to know this be the only place it could come from."

"Yer man's gone, lad, and 'ere ain't no need fer ye to be snoopin' in every nook an' cranny fer 'im. Ye let 'im slip through yer fingers, ye did."

The horseman who had ridden to the fore left his mount and entered the stables, stopping just inside the door to look around. Returning to his steed, he swung into the saddle. "If anyone was here, they've gone."

"Ye can rest easy now, Timmy," one of the mounted men crowed. " 'Ere ain't nobody gonna pounce on ye from the dark."

"Shut yer bloomin' trap, ye blighter. I've lived as long as I 'ave by bein' careful, I 'ave."

"Let's get back to the others," the first man said. "We've a long ride ahead of us."

When the men returned to the road, Erienne released her breath in a long, slow gasp, until then unaware that she had been holding it. She was supremely thankful that her instincts had prodded her to accompany Christopher rather than remain in the barn. As they waited for the band of riders to move on, the thought crossed her mind that she would have indeed been caught at the mercy of those men had Christopher Seton not come along.

The ride to Mawbry was cloaked in wet, grayish mists that hung close over the moors and rocky slopes. It twined about gnarled, twisted trunks of ancient oaks and blanketed the winding road until it seemed as if they swam amid a sea of thick, wispish vapors set apart from reality.

Uncomfortably aware of the man who rode behind her, Erienne tried to sit stiffly erect, but the journey was long and she was weary. His redingote kept her warm, and despite her resolve to remain aloof, she found herself sagging repeatedly against him. The shock of meeting that wide, hard chest immediately jerked her upright again, and once more she'd try again to bolster her flagging spirit.

"Relax, Erienne," Christopher admonished at last. "You'll be rid of me soon enough."

His words brought back a remembrance of the haunting sense of loss she had experienced when he had walked out of the cottage and also when he had strolled away from the backyard. The memory of his kiss made her plight all the more unbearable. With other men she had known only a shivering revulsion when they tried to steal even the smallest peck. Such had not been the case with Christopher, and she feared that she was destined to remember his ardent embrace for the rest of her life.

Dawn was invading the mists by the time they reached Mawbry. Christopher wound his way around the small hamlet to the mayor's cottage, leaned down to open the gate at the back of the cottage, and halted the animal near the rear portal. No loud snores emitted from the open window of Farrell's room, reassuring her that he had not yet come home. Braced by the steady support of Christopher's arm, she slid to the ground. She doffed the redingote, tossed it back to him, then would have rapidly departed from his presence, but his inquiry halted her.

"Aren't you going to invite me in?"

Erienne whirled with a flare of rage, and found, as she suspected, the amused and mocking grin challenging her. "Certainly not!"

Christopher sighed in feigned disappointment. "Such is the gratitude of a fickle wench!"

"Fickle!" she gasped. "You call me fickle? Why, you overconceited . . . buffoon! You . . . you . . ."

He kicked his horse into motion and cleared the fence with a graceful arc, his laughter trailing behind him. Erienne stamped her foot and glared after him, mumbling dire threats under her breath. She had never known a man who delighted in riling her as much as he did, and it nettled her sorely to consider his flawless success.

* * *

Midafternoon marked the time of Avery's return, and when she saw him coming down the road with long, outraged strides, Erienne wrung her hands in anxious worry. Farrell had not seen fit to come home from his escapades and thankfully could relate nothing of her return. Still, she had kept a nervous vigil through the day, fearing what her father's reaction would be. She grimaced when he came storming through the door, slamming it behind him. Seeing her in the parlor doorway, he glowered and yanked off his coat.

"So! Ye're home, are ye? And me worryin' all the way that some blackguard might have taken ye to his lair."

Erienne dared not reveal how closely he came to the truth. Since their parting, Christopher had played too much on her mind, and she would have greatly relished the pleasure of forgetting him.

" 'Pon me soul, girl. I don't know what takes yer mind. Ye rant and rave about Smedley Goodfield pawin' ye when ye know good enough he'd have the right to it if ye married him."

Her stomach knotted in revulsion. "That's exactly why I left. I couldn't bear the thought of it."

"Aaah!" He looked at her, narrowing his eyes. "Ye got yer druthers, do ye? That blighter Seton was pawin' ye, and ye never hawked a word. But come along a good man with marriage on his mind, and ye're suddenly squeamish about where he puts his hands. Seems to me with yer high-flyin' ideals, ye'd take into account that Mr. Seton ain't wantin' ter marry ye." He chortled as if amused. "Oh, he'd be willing enough to lay his bold self 'pon ye and have his pleasure fine and good. O' course, if ye should take his seed in ye and nurture it, ye can expect from the likes o' him to be left with a wee babe in yer belly and nary a husband on yer arm."

Erienne's cheeks warmed at the crudity of her father's words. Not wanting to face his gleeful sneer, she turned aside and spoke in a low voice. "You needn't worry yourself about Mr. Seton. He's the last man I'd choose."

The repetition with which she issued that statement was beginning to ring a note of insincerity in her own mind.

"Hah!" Avery scoffed in disbelief. "First maybe! But not last! I'd wager ol' Smedley would rank at least a choice or two below yer fancy Mr. Seton."

Five

If there could be such a thing as a gray albino, then surely the next suitor to ply for Erienne's hand was just that. With mouse-gray hair, a grayish hue to his face, watery gray eyes, and a bluish tinge around his lips, Harford Newton could hardly be described as anything else. His pudgy gray hands were sweaty, and he carried a kerchief which he constantly plied to his thick lips or to his ever-drizzling nose. Despite his bulk, he seemed to suffer unduly from the chills of winter, for though the day was mild and not overly crisp, his collar was pulled up snugly about his indistinct neck and a scarf laid about it. His shape and posture were generally reminiscent of an overripe melon which had gone soft, not quite fat but rather loose and flabby. His manner resembled that of a pampered house cat, demanding and arrogant. Yet unlike the cat, his eyes, when they were met by a direct gaze, seemed to retreat into the roundness of his face.

The thought of those hot, moist hands pawing her while he squirmed eagerly beside her in bed brought a sharp sense of panic to Erienne. She recalled a time when as a child she had raced too hard across the moors and suffered a threatening sickness in her stomach, something not too different from what she felt when she looked at Harford Newton. The realization that she could not stand this one whatever the cause congealed on the surface of her mind like ice on a small pond, and in the midst of it all Christopher's words came back to haunt her. He had been arrogant in his belief that she could abide him better than any of her suitors, and it vexed her to think that he might be perfectly correct in his assumption.

By dint of will Erienne managed to maintain a guise of cool politeness with the man. She turned aside his eager advances, hoping beyond hope that he would soon grasp the meaning of her refusals, for her stomach tightened progressively with each passing moment. His arm brushed her bosom, and his hand eagerly sought her thigh as if he had already founded his claim upon her. She was afraid to test her father's patience again, and it was nearly in desperation that she excused herself. Flying in hasty retreat to her bedchamber, she refused to heed his threats and return to the parlor until she was assured that Harford Newton was clear of the house and unlikely to come back. When she saw her erstwhile suitor's carriage move away from the house, she heaved a long sigh of relief. Yet knowledge that she would have to contend with her father's rage quickly diminished any feelings of contentment. Venturing back to the parlor she found him pouring a hearty libation and she braced herself as he turned an ominous eye toward her.

"I nearly had ter put a ring in this one's nose ter get him here, girl, and I swear his eyes lit up when he saw ye. I was sure we had found the one. But ye!" He flung up a hand contemptuously. "Ye and yer high-minded ways! Ye won't have any o' 'em!"

Erienne tossed her head with an uneasy laugh. "Well, there is always Mr. Seton's offer."

Avery slammed his fist down on the table and glowered at her. "I'd sooner the both of ye burned in hell than see him get his hands on ye!"

Erienne laughed again to hide the hurt in her voice. "Really, Father! Your concern is touching, and your value of me, at least in the Crown's sterling, is almost surprising."

He glared at her for a moment, his eyes piercing her through. "An' what do ye think I'll do for the preservation o' yer damned purity, girl? Spend the last o' me days in debtors' prison?" He sneered. "Oh, I've taken me share o' coin for a little fun in cards now an' then, but I've spent as much on ye an' yer brother. I'd not think it unkind if ye paid me back a bit an' found yerself a man with a bit o' gold in his purse who could overlook the lack o' same in yers. 'Tain't askin' too much. You're overage as 'tis. But nay, ye'd see me sent ter Newgate for the sake o' yer bloody virginity!"

Erienne faced away to hide a quickening tear. " 'Tis mine to give or mine to hold and dear enough to keep from those you would bring here. But what do you care? You chortle like a lusty hound and leave your own daughter to fight off the beasts."

"Beasts is it, eh?" He drained the last of his drink with a quick toss of his head and frowned into his glass as if he wished there were more. " 'Tis a fine fare-thee-well when a man's only daughter gets so highfalutin she can no longer abide his will." He caught her arm and jerked her around, demanding her attention. "Do ye think there's any other way?" His eyes grew wide and harried. He clasped his gnarled fist in front of his gut. "I have a gnawin' fear down here when I think o' a cold, wet cell for me final restin' place. I'm forced upon the rocks, girl, and I have no other way ter turn. I tell ye, I will seek out another an' another 'til I find one who meets even yer high-flown taste!"

"You know I would not see you put in a cell," Erienne argued. "But I have a bit of pride, too. When it comes to the truth of the matter, I'd be selling myself to one of those simpering toms for two thousand pounds. Isn't a wife worth more than that, Father?"

"Two!" Avery threw his head back and guffawed. "Try doublin' that, girl. Why, 'tis two I owe to that struttin' cock himself, and as much ter those preyin' merchants in Wirkinton."

"Four? Four thousand?" Erienne stared at her father, appalled. "You mean you wagered two thousand pounds against Christopher Seton when you already owed that much?"

Avery would not meet her eyes but examined the back of his short, stumpy fingers. "Well, it seemed a worthy bet. 'Twould have paid me debts had not that scoundrel been so quick with his eye."

A sudden coldness crept up Erienne's spine. "You mean . . . you cheated?"

" 'Twas too much money ter lose. Do ye ken? I had ter do somethin'!"

She was numb with shock. Christopher Seton was right! Her father had cheated! And Farrell? He had defended their father's honor when all the time there was none.

Her stomach heaved, and she faced away, unable to look at her parent. He had let Farrell challenge Christopher, when all the while he must have known that one of them could be killed. Of course! He had hoped it would be Christopher Seton. He would have done murder to save himself from the shame he was guilty of. But it was Farrell who had paid the price for his cheating, and now it was her turn to be used, just as he had used her brother and their mother.

Her voice was frayed and cracked as she spoke with undisguised sarcasm. "Why don't you just put me on the block and have done with it? Sell me into bondage for perhaps ten or so years. Why, I'd only be a little past a score and ten when the debt is paid. As long as your notes are taken care of, what does it matter whether I'm married or just a slave?"

Erienne paused, expecting a hasty denial, then in the ensuing silence she turned slowly to stare in burgeoning horror at her father. He leaned an elbow on the back of a chair and returned her gaze with a half-wild light in his eyes.

"On the block, ye say?" he mused aloud and rubbed his hands together in glee. "On the block? Ye may have hit upon an idea, girl."

"Father!" The full realization of what she had done hit her. Unconsciously she had repeated Christopher's sarcasm, and it had come tumbling back on her like an avalanche. She tried to explain. "I spoke in jest, Father. Surely you cannot consider it."

Avery gave no evidence of having heard her. "That should bring a fair enough flurry of 'em. The highest bidder . . . for a bright and comely wife."

"Wife?" Erienne repeated in a pained whisper.

"A wife who can cipher and write might bring a goodly sum, maybe a bit more'n two thousand pounds. And after 'tis done, she can't say nay to his pawin'."

Erienne closed her eyes, trying to calm her reeling mind. What had she done?

"O' course, there's got ter be a way ter keep that Seton bastard from havin' her. Hot in his britches for her, he is. I seen the way he eyed her in the coach, as if he'd 'ave taken her then and there. Aye, there's got ter be a way."

"Father, I beg you," Erienne pleaded. "Please don't do this to me."

Avery chortled suddenly, giving her no mind. "I'll post it, that's what I'll do. I'll have Farrell write it out for me. Ter wit!" He held up a finger, noting his would-be quotation. "One Christopher Seton will not be permitted to take part in the roup."

Chuckling like a mischievous imp, Avery sank onto the edge of a chair and, rocking to and fro in glee, slapped a hand down on a knee. His eyes gleamed as he already savored the revenge he would heap on his foe. He hardly noticed when his daughter ran from the room.

By midmorning of the next day the handbills were posted, and they proclaimed that a most unusual happening would occur ten days hence. The maid, Erienne Fleming, would be sold as a bride to the highest bidder. The roup was to be held in front of the inn, or if the weather posed a problem, inside in the common room. The bill beckoned all eligible men to count the number of coins in their purse, for a minimum bid would be set for the likes of such a talented and fair maid. At the bottom of the script, in bolder lettering, a clear note was written to one Christopher Seton, warning that he would not be allowed to take part.

Ben stumbled from the inn when he saw the tall Yankee sitting astride the dark stallion in front of the posting board. With his black-toothed grin, he peered up at Christopher and thumped the parchment. "Hears ye're banned from the roup, gov'na. The word's spreadin' faster'n I can spit 'bout this 'ere sport. Seein's as how ye said ye weren't in no marryin' mood, ol' Ben's been wonderin' what ye be up ter. Maybe the mayor gotta 'nother reason 'sides his boy for holdin' ye away from his girl."

"Not yet." The answer was blunt.

The ancient one cackled in glee. " 'At sounds like a threat ter me, gov'na."

Christopher gave a crisp, affirmative nod, and reining his horse away, rode off at a leisurely trot. Ben watched for a moment, then hearing a clatter of hooves rapidly approaching from behind, he hastily dove aside, narrowly avoiding the threshing hooves as Timmy Sears rode past on his steed. The red-haired man gave the souse no heed as Ben jumped up to shake a threatening fist at his back. It was only after Timmy had passed a stride or two beyond earshot that Ben gave voice to several insults. In an outraged dither, the old man failed to notice that another rider was quickly closing in from the rear.

Haggard saw the rumpled form in his path and hauled back franti-cally on the reins, attempting to stop his shaggy, long-haired mount before he trod upon the man. The steed had a mind of his own, having been gelded far too late in life, and was still inclined to be of a stallion's stubborn temperament. The horse ignored his rider's command, failing to see the reason until the last possible moment, then he halted with a single stiff-legged bound. Haggie bounced twice in the saddle, coming down slowly after the last with a low, teeth-grinding moan and with his face tightly balled up in a grimace. Ben looked around and hurriedly stumbled aside, allowing the man a clear path to continue on his way. Haggard's style of horsemanship from that point on was a rather stilted one, with his body rigidly erect in the saddle and his legs clamped firmly about the barrel of his mount. It was the only way he could pursue his companion down the winding roads with any degree of comfort.

Christopher Seton bade farewell to the mate and stepped from the pilot's boat to climb the ladder onto the dock. He dusted his hands, settled his hat against the shifting afternoon breezes, and made his way with leisured stride to the Crimson Hind, a waterfront tavern known for its frosty ale, which was cooled in an ice cellar deep between its pilings. His mind was busy as he strolled along through the narrow streets that crowded close upon the waterfront.

Captain Daniels had returned from London with the ship, bringing back several purchases Christopher had made there. At morning's first light, he would set sail again and proceed to a spot Christopher had noted on the charts. There the captain would deposit the lot ashore, then return to Wirkinton for a space before sailing on to London and then plying the waters along the coasts. Until the hook was hauled, a rotation ashore for the crew had been arranged, giving many of them a few hours at the pubs while others manned and secured the vessel.

The Hind was empty this late afternoon, and a bored barkeep seemed to welcome Christopher's presence. The barkeep sent a boy for a fresh jug from the cellar and chatted endlessly until the customer was served with a frothy mug of the cool brew. Christopher took the tankard and chose a comfortable seat near the huge hearth that warmed the common room, there propping his feet on a low stool. He stared into the shifting flames while the fire danced and snapped in a mesmerizing ballet, but his mind was wandering far afield as a tumbling mass of black hair swirled through his thoughts. Beneath its fullness, dark-fringed violet-blue eyes glowed with their own light, the color in their depths shifting like a richly hued gemstone. A frown gathered the brows in anger, and the eyes grew cold and piercing. He searched his memory and selected a moment when they were bright and full of laughter, then held the vision in his mind.

A nose was added. Slim, straight, finely boned, yet ever so slightly pert, just short of stilted perfection. The features were delicate, the shape of the face neither narrow and pinched, nor wide and moonish, but softly oval, with gently rising cheekbones that were touched with a light blush of color.

A pair of lips formed in his imagination. Not the pouting rosebuds of the simpering *femmes* at Court, but gently curving and just wide enough to be expressive and alive. The corners deepened with a quirk as she scowled, and once more he sought until he found in his recollection a time when they had turned upward and the lips parted with laughter. There, his mind stayed and burned with the memory of their incredible softness beneath his own.

The rest of her came to him in a rush. The long, slender limbs and the body that possessed the trim, sleek grace of a cat and was neither rolling in folds of fat like the soft ladies of the evening, nor thin and bony, but with a subdued strength and honesty that lent her an easy, almost naïve elegance. In all, she seemed totally unaware of her own beauty, and was simply Erienne, one apart and above all the others who dwelt in the depths of his memories.

She promised, in fact, to be that one who would neither lag behind nor charge ahead, but would rather stand beside or walk along with the man of her choice. It chastened him sorely that he was prevented from enjoying her company. It was also firm in his mind that she would be far better off removed from the tender care of her father and the good influence of her brother. It touched his mind that the roup would accomplish that. However, the odds of her leaping from the pan only to land in the fire were oppressive. He had seen enough of her suitors to rank them all in the category of fire and was sure at least several would be present and actively bidding.

Her taunt came back to haunt him. Hunchback! Scarred! Cripple! Her chances of winning a man with at least one of those qualifications were great. In fact, it began to appear as if she could hardly avoid it.

Christopher's reverie was shattered as a group of men came boisterously through the front door of the inn. There were some dozen of the chaps, and it soon became apparent that this was not the first pub they had visited. A loud, raucous voice rose above the rest, and Christopher turned his head to find Timmy Sears in the center of the mob and acting very much as if he were their leader.

" 'Ere, lads," he bellowed in rare good humor. "Belly up, and 'ave a stout on Timmy."

A chorus of rowdy cheers indicated the readiness of the others to accept the largess as Mr. Sears plunked down a hefty purse on the planks. A highly relieved barkeep hastened to set out his largest mugs and filled them with a like portion of ale. The crude jests and brutish repartee were silenced for a while as the eager fellows noisily worked their gullets to down the brew. Even the ever-present Haggard buried his nose in the foam and greedily slurped the stout while the overflow ran past the brim and down his cheeks and neck. Once the aching thirsts were satisfied, the conversations returned.

"Aargh!" Timmy cleared his throat loudly. "Even good bitters lose the flavor when 'ey're cooled too much. Should be warm as the day is, then a man can enjoy the taste." His wisdom was not lost on his companions as the round of nodding heads and murmured assents gave witness.

"Hey, Timmy!" a coarse voice crowed. A set of scarred knuckles rapped the plank near his purse. "Ye got yerself a good boodle here. Ye gonna get inter ol' Avery's roup?"

"Aye!" Sears braced his hands on the bar and swelled his chests. "An' I has set meself ter go as 'igh as . . . oh . . . maybe a hun'erd pounds or so."

"Oiiee!" Another shook a limp hand in feigned amazement. "A hun'erd quid fer just a wench?"

Timmy scowled at the scoffer. "H'aint just a wench! H'it's fer a wife."

"But ye gots a wife," the other protested.

Timmy drew himself up and squinted at the ceiling reflectively. "An' just maybe if'n I gets this 'un, I'll have me a roup o' me own fer the old 'un."

"Haw!" Haggard barked out. "That 'un ain't worth ten bob, let alone a hun'erd quid."

Timmy's eyes narrowed as he glared at his hanger-on. " 'Tis too!" he declared trying to bolster the prospective value. "Why, she's got a lot 'o good nights left in 'er."

"If that's so," another chimed in, "why ye want this one?"

" 'Cause I gots meself all 'ot fer her," Timmy gritted out with a broad grin. " 'At's why."

"I'll say ye 'ave!" an unidentified member guffawed. "Ever since ol'

Molly tossed ye ov . . . uh!" An elbow in the ribs warned the man, but too much had gotten out.

"What's 'is?" Timmy glared around, his brows beetling menacingly. "What's 'is I hear? Do ye say Molly tossed me over?"

"Ahh," the man tried to soften Timmy with pity. "We all knows she's got 'erself all softheaded over 'at Yankee feller."

Timmy's lowered head swung in the manner of a bull setting for a charge as he tried to identify the bold one who taunted him so harshly. "Yankee?" he ground between clenched teeth. "Molly? Tossed me over, ye sez?"

"Aw, Timmy," the foolish one gave himself away. "Ain't yer fau—"

His word was interrupted by a meaty "thunk" as a broad fist slammed into his chin. The man staggered backward, flailing wildly as his numbed brain fought for balance until he sprawled across the low table beside that very one whom they had been discussing.

Christopher had seen him coming and seizing his mug, rose and quickly stepped out of the way. The abused one tumbled to the floor and rolled about, moaning. Christopher surveyed the damage and then calmly stepped over the man, moving out of the shadows where he had sat unnoticed.

Sears nearly choked as he recognized the Yankee, seeing him through a red haze. "'Ere now, lads . . ." he swaggered about in front of his comrades while trying to find a clear path between the tables to his enemy, the one he blamed for most of his woes, ". . . is the very Yankee we was speakin' o'. Ye can see the cut o' him clear now. Sort o' foppy an' dandy, as if he can't dress himself like the rest o' us."

Haggard leaned forward to see better until he caught Timmy's smartly sweeping arm alongside his head. He shook the offended member, then dug a finger in his ear to clear a persistent ringing.

"Mr. Sears," Christopher softly but firmly addressed the red-haired man in the sudden hush that filled the room, "I have heard enough of your foolish drivel in the past few moments to last me a lifetime." He had not been in the best of moods when the group entered. His temper had been well tested in the past days, and he trod very near to the edge of losing it entirely. He was not inclined to tolerate more inanity.

Timmy was not a complete fool. Considering the way the Yankee moved, he decided it was best to employ a bit of aid on his own behalf. He could get his own licks in after the others had softened the man up a mite.

"Ye see, lads," he challenged them, "this 'ere is 'at same rebel who come ter our Mawbry town and 'as all the womenfolk goin' around in a froth. Why, the way they's been battin' his name about ye can just bet he's been sneakin' from bed ter bed. Even Molly is all upset wid him, an' ye can see he ain't up ter payin' her price wid all 'at free stuff hangin' on his arm."

Timmy gave no notice to the fact that while he spoke other men had entered the place and spread out behind his group to listen. Haggard was the only one who worried over the fact that the sun had sunk, that the tars from the ships were coming ashore, and that the newcomers were strangely garbed for English seamen. Nervously he tugged at Timmy's sleeve to get his attention.

"Not now, Haggie." Timmy brushed him away without a glance and continued, trying to rouse his rabble. "We gots us Mr. Yankee Seton 'ere, who's fondled the mayor's daughter once too often and got hisself banned from the roup. He's too fancy for good ol' Molly, and she a right proper doxy, too. Why, no matter how many times she's comforted us lads, she takes a good bath every Saturday, regular as a clock, and he just looks down his cocky long nose at her."

An angry murmur rose from his companions at this obvious affront against the gentle one they all knew so well. Christopher casually sipped his ale as the door swung open and several more sailors entered, one of them a tall, gray-haired man in a long blue coat, the sort that captains were prone to wear. He hung back with the rest of the tars while he surveyed the scene.

Haggard sidled close to Timmy and made another plea for attention, tugging at the man's sleeve as he glanced nervously about.

"Back off!" Sears commanded, roughly shrugging the man away. "Ye see how he simpers in his ale, men? He's afraid ter come out with what he thinks o' Mawbry men."

"If you really want to know what I think, Mr. Sears," Christopher replied gently but loud enough to be heard clearly over the angry grumbles of Sears' cronies, "I am of the opinion that *you* are a fool. The mayor can hardly accept your niggardly hundred quid when he owes me better than twenty times that amount. I further doubt the girl would favor you. I've heard"—a grin spread across his face—"the only way she takes pork is well salted."

"Pork?" Timmy puzzled a moment before the meaning dawned. "Pig! Ye heard him, lads!" he bellowed. "He called me a pig!" He took a step forward, motioning for his men to follow. "Let's see the ruddy beggar giggle his way out o' this one! Let's get him, lads."

After a brief surge forward, his companions halted and peered warily at the meaty fists that clasped their shoulders. Their gazes raised to the leering grins that seemed to form an endless wall behind them, and they quickly gave up the idea of joining Timmy.

Worriedly Haggard grasped the red-haired man's arm, attempting to turn him around, and finally managed to get his eye. "Th . . . they . . . they're . . . !!" Haggard failed to form the words as he repeatedly jabbed a finger toward the men. Timmy conceded to look and his jaw slowly descended as he stared at the twenty-odd men who stood in several silent ranks behind his men. Haggard jerked his thumb over his own shoulder at Christopher and choked, "His men!"

The man in the long blue coat pressed to the fore. "Any difficulty, Mr. Seton?"

"No, Captain Daniels," Christopher replied. "No difficulty. At least, nothing that I can't handle."

Handle! The word stuck in Timmy's craw. As if he were some animal to be handled! He faced his foe again.

Christopher smiled lazily. "A simple apology will do, Mr. Sears."

"Apology!"

The smile did not waver. "I really have no penchant to abuse a drunkard."

"Speak English, man!" Timmy shook his head. "I don't care how many penchan's ye ain't got."

Christopher sipped again and set his mug aside. "You did understand 'drunkard,' though."

Timmy gave a long, careful look over his shoulder. " 'Tis just ye and me then, Mr. Seton?"

"Just you and me, Mr. Sears." Christopher answered with a brief nod and doffed his coat.

Sears spit into his hands and rubbed them together. A gleam came into his eye, and he gloated as he considered the slimmer man before him. He lowered his head and, with a roar of pure glee, charged.

Timmy crossed the room before he realized his arms were still empty. He caught himself against the wall and spun about to see where the Yankee devil had gone to. The man was standing to one side halfway back, his smile still neatly in place. Snorting, Timmy plowed his way toward his target again. Christopher stepped aside again, but this time slammed a fist into the thick belly, driving the wind from the man. As Sears came about to grapple, a solid right cross spun him about in the other direction.

Sears careened into the wall again and this time was a trifle slower to turn. Shaking his head to clear the cobwebs, he waited until the multiple visions dwindled to the singular and he could focus properly on his adversary. Sears spread his arms and with a bellow of rage lurched across the room, then deftly sailed on past his opponent as a booted foot was applied to his rear, giving him impetus.

When the red haze cleared away, Timmy found he had engulfed only a pair of tables and three or four chairs. It was hard to tell from all the pieces. As he clawed his way free of the splintered furnishings, he cast about for the devil Seton, finding him but a few paces away, as yet untouched. Sears came to his feet and launched himself in silence this time. Christopher stood his ground, burying a fist into Timmy's stomach and straightening him with another to his jaw, then with quick thrusts repeating the blows. The red head bobbed with each strike, but Timmy stayed close, reaching out to encircle the other with his massive arms. Those meaty members had cracked the ribs of many an opponent, and the bloodshot eyes shone with the expected victory as he sought to close and lock the vise.

With the heel of his hand Christopher forced the broad chin up and back. Timmy was surprised to find himself being slowly turned. He was forced back until his heels touched the bar and he felt the edge of the plank press into the small of his back. Just when he thought his spine would snap, Christopher released his hold. The Yankee stepped back, catching his hands in Timmy's collar, and hauled the man around, sweeping him wide, then letting go. Timmy spun across the room, then sprawled, rolling and banging his head and shins until he came to rest against the hearth. Gasping for breath, he was slow to pick himself up. When he did, he stared at Christopher and then slowly sank into a chair that stood behind him. That damned Seton had a way of taking the fun out of brawling, and Timmy had lost his appetite for mayhem.

The barkeep had spread Timmy's purse open on the bar, and at each splintering crash had lifted an appropriate coin. He grinned at Timmy as he dropped a handful in his strongbox.

"Take some out o' his, too!" the red-haired man barked, glowing and jerking a thumb at Christopher.

The barkeep shrugged and countered, "He ain't smashed nothin', not even his bloomin' mug."

Timmy lurched across the room and snatched up the slim remainder of his purse. He tucked it away as Christopher placed his cup intact upon the plank. The Yankee picked up his frock coat and turned to his captain as he donned it.

"Care for a stroll, John?" he asked. "I feel a need to cool off some."

The captain smiled and puffed his pipe alight, and the two left the tavern. Haggard lent an arm to Timmy and sought to smooth his ruffled feathers.

"Don't give him no mind, mate. Why, ye were so fast he hardly laid a hand on ye."

Her father's words burned in Erienne's memory with the bitter gall of betrayal. The fact that he could have been so crass as to take her flippant suggestion seriously flawed his character in her mind. Her thoughts traced slowly over the events that had led up to her present predicament, seeking to find that exact moment when all had gone astray. Yesterday she would have been ready to blame Christopher Seton for their troubles, but what she had heard from her father's own lips changed much of that. She was seeing her parent's true character much more clearly now, and it shamed her to the core.

Born in the back of her mind, where it persisted like a stubborn seed caught between one's teeth, was the thought that the cottage where they lived had ceased to be her home. It was a realization of which she was becoming increasingly aware. Yet there was no place else to go. She had no kin that she knew of, no other haven to seek out. If she left, her fortune would be what she would make herself.

Erienne's dilemma seethed, and its solution hid itself in the chaotic frenzy of her thoughts. She was like a raft set adrift in a turbulent sea—having no security where she was, but finding no escape from it either.

When darkness descended, she withdrew to her bedchamber. Beyond the protection of the cottage's walls, the wind howled, and the low clouds made the night sky a dense black ether that devoured any struggling light. She laid a large block of peat on the fire and sank in a chair before the hearth, draping her hands listlessly over the wooden arms. Smoke welled up around the dried turf, and then slowly the tongues of flickering fire began to lick upward to consume the block. While the twisting, dancing flames held her eye, her mind roamed far afield.

There was, of course, Christopher's proposal. Erienne leaned back against the wooden frame of the chair and imagined herself on his arm, dressed in a rich gown, with twinkling jewels twined about her throat. He could show her the sights of the world and, when they were alone, the secrets of love. Her mind and heart could become hopelessly entangled with fulfilling his every desire until . . .

Her mind formed a vision of herself standing with a swollen belly before her stalwart lover. His arm was raised in a silent command for her to depart, and there was a frown of displeasure on his face.

Erienne angrily shook her head to thrust the image from her mind. What Christopher Seton proposed was quite out of the question. If she gave herself to him, there would always be the gnawing fear that she'd be just another one of his light-of-loves, cherished today but forgotten tomorrow.

The house grew still as her father and brother retired for the night. Farrell had seemed somewhat abashed by his part in the preparations for the roup. As his father had bade, he had penned the wording and delivered the parchments to the posting boards, but then he had grown glum and distant with the passing of hours. He had been abnormally polite to her, even remaining sober, yet Erienne held no hope that he would help her, for that would mean going against their father, and he had always held the elder in the highest esteem.

The fire flamed high, then died back. The peat glowed and snapped as if with a stoic purpose to consume itself. Erienne stared into its softly burning light until the clock chimed twice. She glanced around her in surprise and rubbed her suddenly chilled hands together. The room was icy cold, and on the small stand beside the bed the flaming wick of a candle sputtered feebly in a puddle of melted wax. She flinched as her feet struck the cold floor, and she eagerly sought out the cozy warmth beneath the heavy quilts of her bed. As she huddled under them, a firm conviction settled down within her thoughts. On the morrow she would fly. Somewhere, someone would have need of her neat, well-formed penmanship or her quick, easy way with numbers, and they might be moved to pay her a stipend for the proper application of both or either. Perhaps a widowed duchess or a countess in London would have need of a companion. With such a hope burning in her, Erienne relaxed and freed her mind so it could at last seek out that sweet, numb bliss of Morpheus.

Sleet plagued the morning sky, coming down in a fine mist, and quickly formed a thin, crusty layer of ice over the roads. Avery paused in the Boar's Inn, where he ordered a draught of bitters. " 'Tis medicinal in nature," he was wont to excuse if anyone raised a brow and questioned. After massaging his dewlaps and loudly clearing his throat, he would further explain, "Clears the soots and tars from me pipes, it does. Aye, and I needs it for the ripeness of me age."

On this frosty morn, Jamie slid a scupper of bitters to him with a comment. "Thought ye might not be comin' out on a day like this, Mayor."

"Argh, on a day like this more'n any other." Avery's voice was hoarse and gravely after the brief walk in the chill weather. He rubbed his belly as if to soothe a pain and pushed the scupper back. "Put a finger o' solid brandy in it, Jamie. A man needs a bit o' fire in his innards to bring him alive on a chill morn'n."

When the innkeeper complied, Avery seized the fortified bitters and took a liberal draught. "Aaarrgh," he bellowed, lowering the cup. He hammered his breastbone with a closed fist. "Brings a man to life. Aye! That it does. Quickens the mind." He leaned an elbow on the wooden planks and took on the manner of a man expounding a deep, hidden truth. "And ye know, Jamie, 'tis a grave need for a man in me delicate position ter keep his mind as quick as it can be. 'Tis a rare night we can feel safe in our beds, what wit' bein' at the shims and schemes o' them Scots who come down wit' their clans and do war agin' us. We need our wits about us, Jamie. That we do."

The innkeeper interjected with an appropriate nod and busied himself scrubbing pewter mugs. The subject was clearly a favored one in Avery's heart, and he rambled on, content with the other's feigned interest. Avery did not realize that at the moment the revolt was much closer to home.

Erienne's plan did not extend beyond the immediate moment of escape. It was enough that she had decided in what direction to go. London was not unfamiliar to her, and it was a likely place to start her search for employment.

She dressed herself warmly for the trip that would take her from her home. Farrell's snores continued to fill the silence even as she crept downstairs to the back door. The satchel she carried held the sum total of her possessions. It was not much, but it would have to do.

Settling her hood over her head as protection against the frigid weather, she lifted her skirts and ran quickly across the yard to the lean-to where the gelding was kept. Since Farrell no longer tended the animal and she had taken over the stable duties to see it properly cared for, she would lay claim to it now. She was determined to see herself better prepared than when she had set out on foot from Wirkinton.

The sidesaddle was hers, given to her by her mother, but hardly rich enough to be worth selling, which no doubt was the reason it was still in her possession. Her father would have confiscated it long ago had he thought there would have been some gain in doing so.

The horse was tall, and even with the aid of a step, she had to jump, half dragging herself across the sidesaddle. Stabbing blindly with her foot until she found the stirrup, she twisted about clumsily to arrange herself and her skirts, all the while keeping a tight rein on the prancing steed.

"Walk softly if you care for my hide, Socrates," she admonished, rubbing his neck. "I have a need for stealth this morning, and I do not wish to rouse the town."

The horse nickered and tossed its head, displaying its desire to be gone. Erienne saw no need to delay him. Having made up her mind, she was just as eager as he to be on her way.

She urged him from the lean-to, then caught her breath and bent her face away from a pelting gust of sleet. She loathed the prospect of another uncomfortable ride, but there was nothing short of a horrific disaster that would keep her from it.

Inside the inn, Avery's voice droned on while the innkeeper neared the front window to nudge Ben from his loud snoring. " 'Ere now, find yerself another place ter bed down. I'm tired o' hearin' 'at noise." He paused to look out the panes and gave a short grunt. "Now 'ere's one wit' a stiff craw," he observed, gesturing in the direction of the horse and rider coming down the road. "She'll be chilled ter her bones 'fore too long. I wonder who . . ." He stared at the figure more intently, then his jaw dropped as recognition came. " 'Od's bodken! Get yerself over 'ere, Mayor. Ain' that yer daughter?"

Avery waved an arm in dismissal. "Goin' out ter market, no doubt." He jerked his thumb to the handbill displayed on the opposite wall. "We've had a bit of a tiff over that, we have. Ain't hardly said two words ter me since me boy posted 'em. Gets a little uppity when things go agin' the way she wants. Goin' out on a day like this an' leavin' a good, warm fire shows she ain't got a brain in her head.

Why . . ." He began to show a bit of concern and stepped toward the window, hitching up his breeches over his belly. "She could catch her death out there in the wet, and she'd fairly knocked the bottom out o' the biddin' if she had ter stand up wit' a drippin' nose and a case o' the sniffles."

"Goin' ter market, ha!" Jamie scoffed. "She gots her a mount and a big bundle on behind her." He suppressed his rising laughter at the sight of Avery's darkening scowl and suddenly crimson face. His voice was almost small as he continued. "I think she's havin' none o' it, Mayor. I think . . . she's leavin' ye."

Avery launched himself toward the portal and jerked it open as his daughter rode past. He ran out onto the street, bellowing her name, but Erienne, recognizing his voice, slashed Socrates's flanks to send the animal into a full-out gallop down the road.

"Erienne!" Avery called again, then cupped his hands and shouted at the rapidly fleeing figure. "Erienne Fleming! Come back here, ye little twit! There's no place from here ter London where ye can hide from me! Come back! Come back, I say!"

A sense of panic seized Erienne. Perhaps it had only been a wild guess her father made, but his threat set her plans awry. He would follow. He would rouse Farrell, and they would soon be after her on whatever conveyance they could find. If she kept to the road south, they might overtake her, or if she reached London, he would give the word to his friends to keep an eye out for her, no doubt promising a healthy reward if they brought her back.

A sudden thought dawned. If she rode on until she was out of sight of the hamlet, then cut westward for a space and picked up the old coast road going north, she might yet escape them all. She smiled at her own wisdom and the accompanying vision of her father riding south at breakneck speed. He would be furious when he could not find her.

A short distance past Mawbry, Erienne slowed the horse to a walk and began to watch for a rocky place where her departure from the road could not be later noted. Leaving the lane, she wove a serpentine path through a wooded copse for a time, and farther on prodded Socrates over a rocky slope and through a small, shallow stream. By the time she was headed north, she was fairly confident that her trail could not be followed.

Once she had made the wide sweep around Mawbry, she let Socrates go at his own speed. The gelding was not in condition for extended runs and tired easily when she prodded him into the faster gaits. At the slower pace, she felt the chill more and clutched the heavy woolen cloak about her in an attempt to find as much warmth as possible.

The ground grew considerably more broken and hilly as she progressed northward. Undulating moors spotted with gray tarns swept out before her, fading into obscurity as the leaden sky came down to touch the horizon.

Around noon, she paused to take food and rest, finding shelter beneath a tree. Huddling in her cloak, she chewed on a piece of cold meat and tore off a small chunk of bread, then shared water with the gelding, who grazed nearby. She tried to rest, but the persistent presence of grayish-green eyes staring at her from the back of her mind thwarted her effort. It irritated her that even in his absence he could annoy her.

In the saddle again, she was forced to concentrate on the terrain. The going was becoming steadily more difficult, with gullies and washouts cutting her path now and again. The knolls and hills were barren and windswept with a few gnarled trees. In the deeper, sheltered valleys, the oaks were tall and ancient, spreading their limbs far over her head, having left a twisted jumble of fallen, moss-bedecked branches and brushwood for her to guide her mount through.

By late afternoon, a great weariness took hold of her, and she began to entertain the idea of finding shelter. Coming upon a narrow path in a wooded copse, she paused a moment to survey the land. Somewhere ahead of her the baying of hounds blended with the soft sounds of the falling mists. It was a welcoming sound, for it promised of civilization nearby.

Suddenly in the silence a rock tumbled behind her, startling her. With her heart thumping in her bosom she gazed over her shoulder and peered through the oncoming gloom, searching for the source. Nothing stirred, yet she could not shake the feeling that something was out there. Uneasy now, she urged Socrates forward into his loose-jointed canter and crossed a rise in the path where she pulled the horse up in the shelter of a large tree, turning him about so she could view the trail behind her without being seen. She waited tensely, remembering Christopher's dire warnings about traveling alone. At the moment she thought she might welcome the sight of him. At least he was no friend of her father.

The clatter of horse's hooves and tumbling stones again startled her from her thoughts. Whirling Socrates about, she kicked him into a full run, keeping him to the side of the path, where the ground was soft and the hoofbeats echoed less. She raced headlong down the narrow, winding lane. Beyond the gnarled roots of a twisted tree, the path dipped down, then turned hard, almost back upon itself. Socrates slipped but managed to keep his feet beneath him, and with wild abandon flung himself around the bend, charging full bore into a large pack of yelping, scattering hounds that were hot on the trail of a fleeing hind. Their blood was up, and they snapped at the flashing hooves as the frightened horse jumped and reared. The reins were jerked from Erienne's hands, and in desperation she gripped the flying mane with both hands, fighting to keep her slippery seat. One hound drew blood, and the warm, wet taste in his mouth was all it took. As the horse dashed on past in a wild-eyed frenzy, the dog threw back his head and gave vent to a hunting call. It sent the pack in quick pursuit of his new quarry that raced on down the trail.

The path angled across a swift-flowing brook. Only the open way of the stream could be seen, and without guidance the horse swerved to follow it. He sped along the rock-strewn bed against the current, sending a spray of water wide on either side. She cried out for him to stop and tried to turn his head as she saw ahead of them a rising hill over which the stream tumbled in burbling abandon. As he struck the first upslope, the gelding went to his knees, and Erienne fought to stay in the saddle. Then he lunged upward, trying to climb the rocky streambed. He slid and stumbled backward, then slowly clawed the air with his forefeet before he began to topple over.

Erienne's cry of alarm was silenced abruptly when she hit the rock-littered bank. Her head slammed against a moss-covered stone, and a white flash of pain burst in her brain. Slowly the brightness ebbed, and a deepening dusk descended. She saw the dark shapes of the trees above her, wavering and indistinct as if through a sheet of water. Fighting the darkening shrouds of oblivion, she rolled and tried to rise to her feet. The glade swam and dipped with a sudden lurch. She caught herself against the icy bank, struggling against the current that would drag her in deeper while her legs grew numb in the cold, rippling stream.

The baying had changed to a snarling, yelping mélange, and she could see a confusion of roiling white and brown at the vale's edge and realized the pack was nearly upon her. One charged closer, snarling and snapping, and in desperation, Erienne lashed out weakly with the riding crop that was still clutched in her fist. The dog yelped and leapt away as it struck. Another tried, and for his effort got the same treatment, but Erienne's arms were growing weary, her vision blurred. The pain in the back of her head was spreading down her neck and across her shoulders. It tore at every nerve in her being, sapping her strength and her will. The hounds sensed her weakness and gathered eagerly closer. Erienne fought to clear her vision and waved the crop feebly in front of her.

The hounds saw before them a wounded beast, and the heat of the chase filled them. They snarled and snapped at each other, working up courage for the kill. Erienne slipped, sliding deeper in the water, and the icy coldness of it made her gasp. The wet chill crept upward through her bodice, while its frigid touch numbed her lower body. She lashed out with the quirt again, but her strength was rapidly fleeing, and though she caught the hip of a hound who had ventured too close, she knew it would only be a matter of time before they would win.

Suddenly a sharp shout rent the air, followed by the crack of a whip. The rattling crash of hooves came along the streambed, and a long-legged black horse raced into view, sending geysers of water spraying up around him. His rider lashed out with a long whip as they plunged into the pack, drawing blood from one hound after another until they tucked their tails and fled, yelping.

Erienne clutched the tangle of roots with both hands, and her head sagged wearily against her outstretched arms. She saw the man as if through a long tunnel. He came to ground with a single bound, his cloak flying wide behind him until he resembled a great bird swooping down toward her. Erienne smiled with detached amusement and closed her eyes, hearing him splash across the stream toward her. His arm slipped beneath her shoulders, and a hoarse voice murmured words that failed to penetrate her confusion as he pried her fingers loose from the roots. Strong, steel-sinewed arms lifted her and held her close against a broad chest. Her head lolled limply on his shoulder, and even the fear that she might be in the clutches of some dreaded winged beast could not rouse her from her darkening world.

Six

A yellowish-red glow became her sun, a light shining through the darkness, warming her pleasantly and giving her comfort. It was the focal point of her reality, a nurturing sphere of fire and flame, a sun that refused to die. Its energy burst in tiny, flaring sparks that arched and fell, hissing into oblivion, only to be followed again and again by the same crackling display of colored fire. Green, blue, red, yellow fanned upward in an undulating array of hues, expanding from a base of white-hot heat. Yet beyond the glow there was blackness, deep and impenetrable, and she was held within it, like a solitary planet bound in orbit by a force too powerful to resist, feeling the warmth of the sun but unable to draw closer.

Erienne fought her way upward through shreds of sticky, clinging slumber and became distantly aware that her sun was nothing more than a fire blazing in a huge stone hearth. Her eyelids were heavy, her vision blurred. There was a dull, throbbing ache in the back of her head and a great weariness in her limbs. Her bruised body, stripped of its wet garments, was wrapped in soft, furry comfort. Velvet draperies hung from the canopy of the bed and were pulled shut on three sides to shield her from the cold drafts of the room, while the side facing the hearth remained opened to catch the warmth. With the fire, the enveloping velvet tent, and the soft fur coverings she was well protected from that dreadful icy chill that haunted her from an earlier time.

She rolled her head against a pillowy softness, and her nostrils caught an evasive half-sweet, leathery man-smell from the fur throws that enveloped her. The scent stirred a memory of strong arms holding her close and of her cheek resting against a stalwart shoulder. And was there . . . was there a moment when warm lips touched her own?

Without fear or panic the realization drifted down upon her that as long as she had been awake, she had unconsciously heard the deep, even breathing of someone else in the room. She listened until she determined the sound came from the shadows near the hearth. A tall armchair stood facing the bed, partially silhouetted against the warm glow of the firelight, and within it a man sat oddly hunched, his face and torso lost in darkness. The flickering light danced across his legs, and the shadow of one appeared twisted and misshapen.

She must have gasped, for the heavy breathing stopped and a towering black form rose from the chair. He came toward the bed, and against the firelight, his huge cloaked form seemed to shift and grow and broaden in a cold, disjointed way. Hidden in the shadows, the face was devoid of features. Fingers that seemed more like the taloned claws of an eagle reached out, and weakly Erienne tried to move away. The effort proved too much, and she did not struggle as reality, such as it was, slipped from her tenuous grasp.

Erienne's mind wandered restlessly through a mirage of flame and shadow, fleeing from one and finding no comfort in the other. The fire was intense, holding her mind and body in a sweltering heat that made her toss and turn. Broken words spilled from her lips as she fought the torment. Then darkness blew its chilly breath upon her, sending a shiver through her. Out of the night emerged a winged creature that perched at the end of the bed. Tilting its grotesque head from side to side, it carefully watched her with eyes that glowed red in the meager light. She whimpered as it drew nearer, and her muffled cries echoed her fear.

Feverish and witless, she slipped through the grayish fog of days and the deeper shroud of nights, pliant beneath the hands that swabbed wet cloths along her burning skin as she raged in delirium, or when she grew chilled and shivery, tugged the fur robe close about her. A sturdy arm braced her shoulders as a cup was forced between her parched lips, and a rasping whisper touched her ear, commanding her to drink. Then the dark creature retreated from the bed to sit crouched in the shadows beside the glowing ball of flame. The eyes seemed to feed on her movements, awaiting that moment when she could cease her ravings and face him, and she dared not consider what price the strange beast would ask for its care.

Erienne's eyelids fluttered slowly open as the warm morning light intruded upon her sleep and roused her to awareness. The bed hangings had been tied back to the heavy posts, allowing the sun to penetrate into her world. Reality had come to stay, yet her mind was in a tangle of confusion, and she could make no sense of where she was. It seemed ages ago since she had left her father's cottage, but from the moment of her rescue to the present, her memory could recall little beyond bits and parts of nightmarish dreams.

The dark green velvet of the canopy above her head drew her attention, and she stared at the subtle-hued crest embroidered in the fabric there, wondering how she had come to be in these chambers and in such a grand bed. A pair of stags, worked with crimson, brown, and gold threads, rose on hind legs to form an arch above the crest that bore a broken antler clasped in a mailed fist. The thought dawned that this was no commoner's bed, but a massive piece fit for a noble lord and his lady.

The chambers were huge and old and smelled of musty disuse. Some effort had been made to sweep and clean away the dust that had accumulated with time, but the attempt had been taken only to the degree that the room was now bearable. Cobwebs still clung to the dark, heavy beams that supported the ceiling. A few faded tapestries hung from the walls, ancient relics of a bygone era. They, too, bore a coating of dirt and cobwebs that had remained undisturbed for some time. Sunlight filtered through the dingy glass of tall, narrow, castlelike windows and fell in a similar pattern on the stone floor, which had been swept but remained in dire need of a scrubbing.

The hearth was stained and blackened from much use, and in its depths a cheerful fire crackled and danced. Beside it, a large, ornately carved chair sat askew across from a slightly smaller replica. To the right of the bed, more velvet hangings partially hid a small bathing closet and privy, a luxury well beyond that of a simple cottage.

Erienne rose slowly to an elbow and waited for the room to settle down before carefully tucking the pillows behind her back. Her eyes strayed about the room and returned to trace along the fur robe that was wrapped snugly about her. She ran a hand admiringly over its silky softness, then lifted it, feeling its touch against her bare skin. The sight of her own nakedness stirred a mixture of visions both fleeting and confused. Images of a large, black shape framed by a red sun drifted through her mind, blending with rasping, indistinct whispers. Unable to take a firm grasp on the haunting impressions and sort them out in the full light of reality, she experienced a growing unease that what had happened here was better left forgotten.

A rattle of dishes came from just outside the door, and Erienne clutched the robe beneath her chin as a rather pert, gray-haired woman entered the chamber carrying a covered tray. The woman halted in surprise when her eyes fell on the bed and found its occupant sitting up against the pillows.

"Oh, ye're awake." The sparkle in her voice was as lively as those in her eyes and smile. "The master said he thought the fever had left ye and that ye might be feelin' better this morn'n'. I'm glad ter see ye are, mum."

"The master?" Erienne did not miss the significance of the word.

"Aye, mum. Lord Saxton, he be." The woman brought the tray to the bed and uncovered it to reveal a pot of tea and a cup of broth. "Now that ye're yerself again, ye'll probably be wantin' heartier fare than this." She chuckled. "I'll see if the cook can stir up somethin' 'sides dust in the kitchen."

Erienne's curiosity plagued her more than hunger. "Where am I?"

"Why, Saxton Hall, mum." The elder tilted her head and looked at the younger woman wonderingly, finding the question rather strange, since Lord Saxton had volunteered only a minimum of information. "Don't ye be knowin' where ye are?"

"I hit my head, and I didn't know where I had been taken."

"Taken? Ye mean the master brought ye here, mum?"

Erienne managed a puzzled nod. "At least I think he did. I fell from my horse, and that's as much as I can remember. Weren't you here?"

"Oh, no, mum. After the east wing burned a few years ago, we all—the servants, I mean—went ter work for the Marquess Leicester, him being a friend o' the old lord and all. 'Twas only this week that the master arranged for our return. We had ter travel all the way from London, and so we just arrived this morn'n.' 'Twas only himself here with ye when we came."

Erienne could feel the heat creeping up her neck and into her cheeks. Whoever this Lord Saxton was, he had not left even a shred of clothing that she could assuage her modesty with. "This is the master's chambers?" she questioned carefully. "Lord Saxton's bed?"

"Aye, mum." The woman poured a cup of tea and set it on the tray. "He's been livin' here no more'n a week or two himself."

"Was he out hunting yesterday?" Erienne queried.

The elder frowned slightly. "Nay, mum. He said he was here with ye."

Erienne's mind tumbled in an eddy of confusion. It seemed that only a night had passed since she had fallen from Socrates, but having no awareness of what really happened, she could not be sure. Trembling fingers took up the cup of tea, and she almost held her breath as she asked, "Did he say how long I'd been here?"

"This be the fourth day, mum."

Four days! Four days she had been here alone with Lord Saxton, with no one to care for her but him. She wanted to writhe beneath the agony of embarrassment.

"The master said ye were real sick, mum."

"I must have been," Erienne whispered miserably. "I can't remember anything."

"Ye've had a fever, and with hittin' yer head, I can understand 'at ye might be somewhat confused." She laid a spoon beside the bowl of broth. "Why did ye ask if the master was out huntin'? Did ye meet him then?"

"I was attacked by a pack of hounds. I thought perhaps they were his." The memory of those sharp-fanged beasts sent a shiver through her.

"Oh, 'em beasts most likely belonged ter someone else scrubbin' 'round his lordship's lands. There's usually a lot o' poachers here'bouts. We was havin' trouble with 'em even before the manor burned, especially with that rascal, Timmy Sears. Seems I recall he had a pack o' hounds even then, and they were just as likely ter sink their fangs into a man as any o' the game they were chasin'."

"I fear they mistook me for something wild," Erienne murmured. She sipped from the porcelain cup and managed a smile. "Thank you for the tea . . . Madam . . . ah . . ."

"Mrs. Kendall it be, mum. Aggie Kendall. I be the housekeeper.

Most o' me kin is hired on as help here, and I'll be tellin' ye the truth when I say there's a fine lot o' us. Me sisters and her daughters along with me own girls, and me husband and his brother. The other ones here are the stablemaster and his sons. They be the outside help. They come from the master's lands."

Erienne tried to summon some vision of the master from her confused dreams but failed to put a face to the black shape in her mind. "Where is Lord Saxton now?"

"Oh, he's gone for a while, mum. He left right after we got here. He said for us ter look after ye until ye were feelin' better, then ter have the carriage take ye back to her father."

Erienne set the cup down as a sudden feeling of dread washed over her. "I'd rather not go back to Mawbry. If it wouldn't be too much trouble, I . . . I would prefer being taken elsewhere. It doesn't matter where."

"Oh, no, mum. The master was most firm 'bout gettin' ye back ter yer father. When ye're ready, ye're ter be put in the coach and delivered directly ter him."

Erienne stared at the woman, wondering if she or this Lord Saxton knew what they were sending her back to. "Are you sure your master wanted me returned to my father? Could there not be some mistake?"

"I'm sorry, mum. His lordship was quite clear 'bout instructin' us. Ye're ter be returned ter yer father."

Biting despair seized Erienne, and she slumped against the pillows. It was a dismal thought indeed that after having successfully escaped her sire, she would be taken back at the mere whim of a man whom she had never met. Surely it was cruel fate that had brought her here. Indeed, if Socrates had not charged full bore into the midst of the hounds and stirred up their baying voices, Lord Saxton might not have been drawn to her at all. It was not likely that she would have survived, but then, at the present moment she thought death would be preferable over marriage to either Harford Newton or Smedley Goodfield.

Aggie Kendall found no words to reconcile the lass to her master's orders and quietly took herself from the room. Erienne was deeply concerned about her state of circumstances and hardly noticed the woman's departure. Exhausted from her ordeal and suffering from an overwhelming depression, Erienne spent the rest of the morning weeping and sleeping.

A tray was brought to her at noon, and though her appetite was seriously lacking, she forced herself to eat. The food helped to revive some of her lagging spirit, and she approached Aggie on the possibility of having the water pitcher filled so she might bathe herself.

"I'll be happy ter fetch it meself, mum," the housekeeper replied cheerily. Anxious to please, she opened the armoire doors and laid out a threadbare dressing gown that Erienne recognized. Glancing past the housekeeper, she was surprised to see that her own clothes had been placed inside. Aggie followed her gaze and answered her unspoken question. "The master must o' put 'em away, mum."

"He gave up these chambers for me?" Erienne posed the inquiry, curious as to whether he would press to share the rooms with her before he sent her back to her father. She had not forgotten her meeting with Smedley Goodfield, and she knew that if Lord Saxton was of that ilk, she would not be safe for very long in his chambers.

" 'Tis not really a matter o' givin' 'em up, mum. Since the master just come here, he hasn't settled himself in any room yet, though these are the lord's chambers. As ye may have noticed"—Aggie swept a hand to indicate the room—"it has been a while since anyone occupied it." She glanced about thoughtfully and released a pensive sigh. "I was here when the master was born, when the old lord and his lady occupied these rooms. Since then there's been a lot what's happened, and 'tis sad ter see how time an' neglect have misused the manor." She stared wistfully toward the windows for a moment, and then seeming to take a firm grip on her straying thoughts, she smiled brightly and gazed at Erienne again, blinking away the tears that had come into her eyes. "We're here ter stay this time, mum. The master has said so. We'll see the manor cleaned an' scrubbed an' shinin' bright as never before. They won't drive us out again."

As if embarrassed by her own verbosity, Aggie turned and hurried out of the chamber, leaving Erienne much bemused. About the time her family moved to Mawbry, many stories were floating around about the manor and the Saxton family. Very much a stranger to the North country then, she had let the comments drift by without a great deal of notice, and she was somewhat at a loss now to remember all the details beyond the fact that they had blamed the burning on the raiding bands of Scots.

Water was brought for a bath, and fresh linens and soap were provided. Aggie bustled about to set everything within reach of the bed, though Erienne assured her that she was feeling much stronger.

But the woman was most eager to do the master's bidding and quickly declared that his orders were for the servants to take special care of his guest.

Timid about coming out of her fur cocoon and revealing her naked state, Erienne waited until the housekeeper had left before attempting to bathe herself. Maneuvering to the edge of the bed, she gingerly raised herself to her feet. Her legs trembled weakly beneath her, and her head throbbed, and it was a long time before the room stopped swaying. She realized she had misjudged her strength, but she was determined to dress herself, and if Lord Saxton had returned, seek him out and state her case to him.

In mulling over her situation, Erienne had come to the conclusion that her only hope was to plead for her freedom. Perhaps Lord Saxton was not aware of what her father planned for her and was of the opinion that he was doing the honorable thing by sending her back. If she presented the facts to him, he might take pity on her and allow her to continue her journey toward freedom. It was her most heartfelt desire that he would.

The bath refreshed her, yet as she rubbed the wet cloth along her skin, she was haunted by a strange feeling that this had been done very recently by hands that were clawlike and gnarled. Her spine prickled at the idea. Yet the thought was so outlandish, she could make no sense of it. She dismissed the impression as being part of a nightmare she had dreamt, and she donned her chemise.

She found her brush and comb in the armoire, and though she tired quickly and had to pause often to rest, she diligently worked the snarls out of her hair and caught the tresses into a woven knot at the nape of her neck. This gone, she slipped on the blue gown that now had to be considered her best, and carefully made her way from the room.

Beyond the bedchamber, it was readily apparent that many months or even years had passed without the care and attention of servants in the house. Cobwebs formed intricate patterns across the arched ceilings of the halls, and what furnishings she passed had been covered long ago by wide cloths that now bore a grayish accumulation of dust. She pressed on, eventually finding herself at the top of stairs that turned in broad flights around a square newel decorated with shell-arched alcoves. Her descent brought her into what appeared to be the interior of a large, round tower. To her left, a heavy wooden door with a massive lock marked the entrance to the manor. A small, crystal-paned inset overlooked the wide, curving lane that swept beside the entry.

In the opposite direction, a short, arched passageway opened onto a great chamber or the common room of the manor. A young woman was there, busily scrubbing the stone floor. She rose as Erienne came slowly across the room and at her inquiry, bobbed a polite curtsy, holding an arm out to indicate the rear of the manse.

Following the maid's directions and the muted sound of voices, Erienne pushed open a heavy door to find the housekeeper and three other women busily restoring the ancient kitchen to a state of usefulness. A young lad was kneeling beside the fireplace, scraping away long-dead ashes and cakes of soot, while an older man applied his cleaning efforts to a large copper kettle. The cook had already cleared a table and was preparing venison and vegetables for the evening meal.

"Good afternoon, mum," the effervescent housekeeper greeted, wiping her hands on a long white apron. " 'Tis a pleasure to see ye up and about. Be ye feelin' a bit more chipper?"

"Better now, thank you." Erienne glanced about, hardly expecting to find the master in the kitchen but hoping just the same for some indication of his whereabouts. "Has Lord Saxton returned yet?"

"Oh, no, mum." The woman came slowly across the stone floor. "The master said he'd be gone for several days."

"Oh." Erienne frowned in rushing disappointment. There would be no chance to argue her case before his servants returned her to her father.

"Mum?"

Erienne looked up. "What is it?"

"Be ye needin' anythin'?"

She released a wavering sigh. "No, nothing at the moment. If you don't mind, I'll wander around the manor a bit and look around."

"Oh, certainly, mum," Aggie replied. "Should ye need anythin', ye let me know. I'll be busy here for a while."

Erienne nodded in distraction and returned to the great chamber. The maid and the wooden bucket were gone, but the scrub brush had been left on the floor in a pool of water, indicating that the girl would soon return. From the state of the manor, it was easy to assess that the servants would be occupied for some time with their labors. In fact—the sudden thought struck Erienne—they were so busy, they might not even notice if she slipped away.

It was an idea that formed out of desperation, but Erienne dismissed her weakness and the harsh reminder of her sore muscles with the thought that if she didn't escape now, she might yet find herself espoused to Harford Newton, the gray mouse, or Smedley Goodfield, the lascivious elf. She eased open the portal, and a low, betraying squeak of hinges made her grimace. She waited with thumping heart until she was assured that no one was coming to investigate. Peering out, she saw that the stables were just in sight beyond the west end of the house. The rear of a large black carriage jutted out through the widespread doors. From where she stood, it seemed a simple enough matter to enter the stables to see if Socrates was inside.

She was about to slip through the portal when a youth emerged from the stables carrying a wooden bucket and a long-handled brush. While she waited, he began to scrub mud and grime from the back parts of the coach. Erienne glanced around but realized there was no time to think of another course of action, for the cleaning maid was coming around the end of the manor with her wooden pail, slopping water over its brim. As the girl hurried toward the front door, Erienne stood back and quickly pushed the portal closed. Weaker than she had been a moment before, she climbed the stairs and reached the second level before the door swung open again.

Seeking another way to escape, she roamed the halls of the upper story, opening doors and following passageways, but her search proved futile, for they only led to more chambers or halls. Her strength was ebbing, but the thought of Harford Newton urged her on until she found herself in a wide gallery. Here, as in the other rooms, the cleaning had yet to be done, and her attention was drawn to a trail of manly footprints left in the dust. A set led to the far end of the hall, where a stout door had been boarded up with planks. Other footprints returned, giving her little hope that she would find a way of escape from this passage. Still, her curiosity was piqued. She could not fathom why an inside door should be bolted in such a fashion and could determine only that something was hidden beyond it.

Erienne seriously debated the wisdom of testing the door. If there was something behind it that needed to be kept under lock and key, then she might be foolish to open it. She had heard passing comments about Saxton Hall being haunted, and though she had never put much store in ghostly tales, she did not wish to press her luck when she was too weak to flee.

Smedley and Harford came to mind, spurring her forward until she stood at the portal. Shaking fingers tested the planks that barred the door, and to her surprise she found them loose enough to allow easy removal. Yet she was cautious, not knowing what lay beyond the portal. She rapped lightly on the smooth surface of the door and leaned her ear against it, calling out in a low voice, "Is anyone there?"

No mournful wail or hideous shriek answered her, but she felt only mildly reassured. She knocked louder, and again no answer came. Holding visions of the elf and the mouse in mind, she gathered what courage she could muster and pulled away the planks.

The door itself seemed fairly new, as if it were a recent replacement for what had been there before. A large key jutted from the lock, and when she tried it, there was a slow, rusty grinding and laborious click. She twisted the latch and pulled. To her amazement sunlight spilled into the gallery, and she saw that she was standing at the opening of a balcony. It was black and charred-looking, as if it had been scorched. Moving toward the edge, Erienne gasped in shock, for there below her lay the tumbled, burned ruins of what had been a fairly sizable wing.

Suddenly Erienne felt the stones beneath her feet start to give way, and with a grating noise begin to pull away from their mooring. Pieces of the stone rail tumbled toward the ash heap far below, and for a frightening moment Erienne thought she would follow their descent. In a panic she threw herself toward the door, gaining the safety of the interior as the stones near the edge plummeted downward. Breathless and shaken, she slammed the portal and turned the key firmly in the lock. She leaned weakly against the wall, feeling her limbs trembling beneath her. She realized now why the door had been boarded up. The original door had no doubt been burned or warped by the heat, and when it was replaced, the planks were added to bar the passage of an unsuspecting intruder. Erienne was of the sudden and firm belief that some measure should have been taken to dissuade the curious ones, too.

With a grist of questions grinding in the turning mill of her mind, she returned to the bedchamber. She had not the strength to continue her search even with the combined faces of Smedley and Harford haunting her. She sank wearily into bed and fully clothed, pulled the fur robe close about her. She could only hope that sometime during the night she could slip out to the stables, free Socrates, and be on her way. But for now, she had to rest and try to renew some measure of her energy.

A tray of food was brought toward evening, and when Aggie returned later to help Erienne into her bedclothes, she carried with her a warm toddy, which she encouraged the younger woman to drink. " 'Twill ease the aches and give ye a bit of strength. By morn'n, mum, ye should be feelin' more like yer old self again."

Erienne sampled the spiced brew, finding it flavorsome and warmly soothing. Hopefully it would do all that it was purported to do. "I suppose," she began almost hesitantly, "that it's absolutely out of the question that I be taken somewhere else besides Mawbry. You see," she shrugged slightly, "my father and I have had a disagreement of sorts, and I would rather avoid being taken back."

"I'm sorry, mum, but Lord Saxton was most clear on that point." Aggie's tone was genuinely sympathetic.

"I understand," Erienne heaved a ragged sigh. "You must do as your master has directed."

"Aye, mum. I have no other choice. I'm sorry."

Erienne tasted from the cup again before inquiring, "Can you tell me about the east wing that burned?"

Aggie's face was carefully blank as she replied, "Lord Saxton would be the one to ask, mum. He bade me say nothing of it to anyone."

The younger woman slowly nodded. "And of course you cannot go against his wishes."

"No, mum," the housekeeper murmured.

"You seem very loyal to him," Erienne observed wryly.

"Aye, that I am." It was a soft answer but firm with conviction.

After such a reply, Erienne saw no advantage in pressing the woman further. Erienne tilted the cup to drain the last of its contents and set it aside, yawning in earnest behind a slender hand.

Aggie chuckled and folded aside the fur robe on the bed. "Ye should have a good sleep now, mum. The toddy'll make sure o' that. 'Tis been known ter cure many a sleepless night and a weary body."

Erienne curled into the inviting softness and was amazed to find the tenseness ebbing from her aching muscles. She almost purred in contentment and vaguely wondered why she had wanted to resist the sleep that was quickly overtaking her.

Cold, blustery winds swept fluffy clouds across the morning sky as Erienne glumly waited for the coachman to climb to his seat. No one could deny that she was traveling back to Mawbry in grand style. The large black coach was rather ancient in vintage but lacked neither comfort nor luxury. Dark green velvet lined the interior in subdued richness, and on the exterior of the doors was the same crest she had seen above the master's bed. It all bespoke a family's ancient heritage.

The housekeeper's bubbling comments at how well and fit she looked confirmed in Erienne's mind that Aggie Kendall had only sought to be helpful when she encouraged her to drink the toddy. The cheerful woman did not seem capable of deceit, and Erienne had not the heart to crush her enthusiasm by displaying any annoyance at having been given the potion. Whether she could have escaped or not was a question that would remain unanswered.

"Good-bye, mum," Aggie called from the stone path that led to the tower entry. "Godspeed to ye."

Erienne leaned forward to wave a hand in farewell. "Thank you for your kindness, Mrs. Kendall. If I caused you any bother, I'm sorry."

"Oh, no bother, mum. No bother at all. Indeed, 'twas a pleasure ter serve a bright young lass such as yerself. It helped ter ease the gloom o' this place, it bein' empty for so long and all, I mean."

Erienne nodded, letting her gaze range over the face of the manor. It was a rather austere Jacobean structure built solidly behind the front tower, the peak of which rose to a height equaling the tall chimneys. The burned wing was barely visible from where she sat and was overgrown now with dry and withered weeds. Thick groves of trees covered the hillside to the side and back of the manor and were clustered close around a portion of the lane which ended at the manse. It was the same road that wandered over the rolling hills, taking one to Mawbry and beyond. To the north, the firth stretched like a narrow stream across the horizon, sometimes glistening blue beneath the sun, other times hidden beneath low-lying clouds.

The carriage dipped as the coachman's weight came upon it, and Erienne leaned back in the velvet cushions, heaving a sigh. Her cloak, having been dried and cleaned, warmed her against the chill of the day, but it failed miserably to lessen the coldness gripping her heart.

The sight of Socrates trailing behind the coach brought the townspeople of Mawbry running. The carriage itself roused their curiosity, for the large, elegantly appointed conveyance with its tightly wrought crest was not entirely unknown to them, though it had been a thrice of years since they had seen it.

By the time the coach halted before the mayor's cottage, a crowd was already gathering, and her father, hurrying from the inn, had to push his way through the gaping villagers to gain the inner circle. Farrell stepped from the house in time to receive Socrates' reins and stood somewhat in awe when the footman opened the carriage door and Erienne emerged. Seeing his daughter, Avery Fleming planted his feet firmly apart and set his arms akimbo. He made no attempt to soften his sharp tones.

"So! Ye wicked little twit! Ye've come back ter me, ye have. And I'm supposin' ye've got a fine tale ter tell me 'bout where ye've been for a better part o' a week."

Erienne's manner was cool and distant. She resented being insulted in front of the villagers. Her father knew full well why she had left, and her answer to him was simple, almost curt. "I took Socrates out for a long ride."

"A long ride! Five days ye been gone, and ye tell me that! Har! Ye run off, ye did!" He peered at her suspiciously. "What I'm wonderin' is why ye come back. I never thought to see ye again, and here ye are arrivin' in a grand coach, as if ye were some blooded princess come ter pay us commoners a call."

Erienne's ire showed a little as she made her reply. "I wouldn't have come back at all if I had been given a choice in the matter. Lord Saxton took matters into his own hands and had his servants bring me back." Meeting her father's gaze, she raised a delicately shaped brow. "No doubt a friend of yours, Father."

"There ain't been a Lord Saxton since he burned ter death," he blustered. "Ye're lyin', ye are!"

"You are mistaken, Father." She managed a wan smile. "Lord Saxton is not dead, but alive."

"There are those who saw him at the windows with the fire eatin' at his back!" Avery argued. "He can't be alive!"

"Undoubtedly he is," Erienne replied calmly. "He's living at Saxton Hall with a staff of servants . . ."

"Then it must be his ghost!" her father scoffed. "Or someone playin' tricks on ye! What did he look like?"

"I never really saw him clearly. His face was in the shadows . . . or was covered by something." A quick and fleeting vision of a dark shape silhouetted against the light prompted her to add, "He seemed lame or deformed . . ." A murmur went through the townspeople, and some crossed themselves. Erienne hurried to explain. "I can't be sure about what I saw. I hit my head, and it was dark. I might have imagined it."

"Ye tell me that for the better part o' a week ye couldn't see the man?" Avery laughed in derision. "Ye must think me daft, girl, if ye would have me believe that."

"I have no reason to lie," Erienne argued.

The footman placed her satchel and saddle near the front portal of the cottage, then came back to close the carriage door.

"Ye there!" Avery jabbed a forefinger at him and leered about at the villagers, thinking he would put quick death to this preposterous claim. "Can you tell us what yer . . . ah . . . master looks like?"

"I'm not rightly sure, sir."

Avery was taken aback. "Eh?"

"I haven't seen him for three years."

"How is it that ye haven't seen him? Ye work for him, don't ye?"

"I haven't had the opportunity to see Lord Saxton for myself since I retuned to Saxton Hall."

"Then how do ye know it be Lord Saxton ye're workin' for?"

"Mrs. Kendall said as much, sir, and she saw him."

"Mrs. Kendall?" Avery frowned.

Erienne supplied the information. "Lord Saxton's housekeeper."

Avery's brows gathered in an angry frown. He could make no sense of what they were claiming, and he suspected they were seeking to play him for a fool. He waved his hand sharply, sending Erienne into the cottage. As she went, he spoke again to the footman.

"I don't know yer master, and I don't know his reasons, but ye can thank him, whoe'er he might be, for returnin' me girl ter me. He'll be welcomed here ter me home whene'er he ventures ter Mawbry."

The coach pulled around and headed back north. The villagers drifted away, having a story to relate and enlarge upon. The burning of Saxton Hall had dimmed in their memories. Details had been forgotten, but that would not stop them from recounting the happening as they now remembered it.

The mayor frowned at his son as he stood holding Socrates' reins. "Ye put that animal where yer sister can't get her hands on it again, or I'll see it fed to the dogs."

Avery strode into the cottage, slammed the door behind him, and faced Erienne, who waited near the stairs. Folding his arms across his chest like a ponderous monarch, he demanded, "Now, me fine little lass, I'll be hearin' whatever explanation ye have for leavin' here."

Erienne turned away slightly, lifting her own chin as she answered him. "I had set my mind that I would not bend to your whim anymore. I intended to seek out employment wherever I could find it and make my own way in the world. I would never have returned if Lord Saxton hadn't made arrangements to send me back."

Avery's eyes grew piercing. "Well, girl, since ye've chosen ter disobey me, yer own good father, ye know I have no choice but ter take me trust from ye. I had a worry, I did, what with the roup bein' only a couple o' days away and half the town an' all the men wonderin' if I be playin' some game with them."

Erienne answered him boldly. "Your worries were indeed great, Father, but unlike mine they were what you brought upon yourself. Mine are those which another has imposed upon me."

"Imposed upon ye! Imposed upon ye, indeed!" Avery snarled, redfaced and irate. "Why, here I've tended ye these many months since yer ma passed on. Gave ye the best I could, food ter fill yer belly and a roof over yer head, and maybe a new gown now and then just to make ye happy." He ignored her light scoff, adding, "And I did me best ter find ye a fittin' husband."

"Fitting husband? A frail bag of bones, or one too plump to count his toes? A drooling, slobbery mouse of a man with clammy hands? Or a spinster too ancient to seek a wife on his own? Fitting husband, you say?" She laughed in contempt. "More like a fitting purse for a man with a desperate need."

"Be that as it may," her father ground through his teeth, "but until ye leave this house, ye'll find yer chamber door locked through the night. Ye'll go no place on the morrow but with Farrell and meself . . . then come the roup, we'll see what high price ye'll bring."

"I'll go to my room now." Erienne spoke in a flat, emotionless tone. "I'll stay there whether you lock the door or not, and I'll go to your roup. But I warn you now to make all the arrangements beforehand. The marriage must take place the day following the roup, for I will stay in this house only one night after you've sold me, and when I leave, I will no longer recognize that you have any authority over me."

Seven

For half an hour before the appointed time, Farrell stood before the inn and hawked to any and all who passed, "Hear ye! Hear ye! The roup for the mayor's daughter, Erienne, is about to commence. Hear ye! Hear ye! Gather round one and all. 'Twill be her hand in marriage ye'll be biddin' for."

Erienne shuddered as her brother's plaintive call drifted in through the open bedroom window. In another few moments she would be on the platform with him, and there would be no choice for her but to endure the probing stares of the men. The crowd was growing steadily larger in front of the inn. No doubt many were coming out of curiosity rather than with plans to participate. After today, it would be hard for the townfolk to forget the Flemings. Her father had certainly done nothing else to warrant fame, for he had spent most of his time seeking after his own pleasures and very little establishing himself as a memorable mayor.

Erienne closed the window and turned the latch. Today she would be sold, tomorrow wedded. She had settled herself to that fact. Whether she would be able to abide her husband or not was yet to be determined, but she fervently prayed it would not be either Smedley Goodfield or Harford Newton.

Absently she smoothed a stray wisp of a curl from her temple. In outright defiance of her father's command to let her hair fall freely, she had twisted the heavy black tresses in the usual large knot at the nape of her neck. It suited her mood to portray the aging spinster, but she failed miserably in that quest. Hers was a soft and rare beauty that would remain ageless for many years to come, and with her dark hair pulled back, the perfection of the delicate features and oval contour of her face was readily evident.

Erienne glanced about the small bedchamber, seeing it with the eyes of a stranger. The low ceiling, the bare wood floor, the tiny windows that had let in a minimum of light . . . seemed totally different now. Beyond tomorrow, the details would be like ashes in her mind, easily swept away. She would have a new home, hopefully happier than this one had been of late, and she would be a wife, perhaps even a mother. Necessity would never allow her to think again of the girlish hopes and dreams that had been born in this room. She left the room and slowly made her way down the stairs to where her father waited.

"Here ye are," he snorted. "Thought I might have ter come fetch ye."

"There was no need to fret, Father," she answered in a soft tone. "I said I would go to your roup."

Avery peered at her closely, confused by her calm manner. He had expected outright mutiny and had prepared himself to be firm. Seeing her quiet and submissive made him uneasy. He was reminded of her mother and knew she would not have tolerated this treatment of her daughter.

"Let's be off," he ordered gruffly, thrusting the twinge of conscience from him. He drew out his timepiece and noted the hour. "We've just time enough ter let the gentlemen look ye over before the biddin' begins. Might raise it a mite. 'Tain't every day there's a roup such as this with one so comely ter be bartered off."

"No, 'tis rare indeed that a father sells his daughter," Erienne responded, unable to resist the sarcasm.

Avery chortled. "I have ye ter thank, miss, for givin' me the idea."

Resolutely Erienne drew on her woolen cloak and lifted the deep hood to cover her head, choosing to protect herself as much from the curious stares as to hide her pale face. Her pride ached, but the fear of what lay in store for her was reducing her to a trembling, shaking coward. She had given her word that she would go to the roup and marry the man who bought her, yet her promise did not eliminate her anxieties and fears.

Lord Talbot's carriage was pulled to the side of the road a short distance from the cottage, and when Avery craned his neck to see within, Claudia leaned forward to the window. She looked Erienne over with a condescending smile.

"My dear Erienne, I do wish you good fortune with finding a husband among that gathering of wayward souls. You seem to have stirred the attention of all the wealthy wretches of our society. I'm just glad it's not me."

Without nod or reply, Erienne continued on her way. The woman's chiding laughter stiffened her resolve to accept what was being done to her with as much dignity as she could muster. What else could she do when she knew no amount of pleading would have any effect?

The usual gathering of townfolk was present in the crowd, and she saw several strangers crowded among them. The men looked her over carefully as she approached, and the grins that spread across their faces made her think that their minds were running far afield. If she had once felt unclothed beneath Christopher's gaze, then the ogling stares of these men made her feel unclean.

Farrell had made a small platform before the inn, and as the crowd parted for her, she fastened her gaze on the structure rather than recognize those faces that she feared would be there. She had no wish to see Harford, Smedley, or any of the other suitors she had rejected.

Almost in a daze, she moved to mount the steps, and in her narrowed vision she found a hand ready to assist. It was strong, lean, well manicured, showing darkly tanned against the crisp white cuff of his sleeve. The sight of it set her heart to fluttering, and she knew even before she glanced up that she would find Christopher Seton standing beside her. She was right, and he looked so handsome it nearly took her breath away.

Avery thrust his way rudely between them. "If ye've read the notice, Mr. Seton, ye ought ter know ye won't be allowed ter bid."

With a mocking smile lightly curving his lips, Christopher inclined his head briefly to indicate his acknowledgment of the declaration. "You've made yourself abundantly clear, sir."

"Then what be ye here for?"

Christopher laughed as if amused. "Why, I have a financial interest in the proceedings. If you'll remember, there is a matter of a gambling debt you promised to pay?"

"I told ye!" Avery barked. "Ye'll get yer money!"

Christopher reached inside his coat and withdrew a light bundle of neatly tied papers. "If your memory serves you with this also, Mayor, you should recognize these as the debts you left London without paying."

Avery stared at him in shock, unable to voice a reply or denial.

Christopher casually unfolded the parchments and drew his attention to the name carefully penned across them. "Your signature, I believe."

After a quick, hesitant glance, Avery grew red and outraged. "And what if 'tis? What concern be it o' yers?"

"The debts are very much my concern," Christopher replied pleasantly. "I have redeemed them from the London merchants and increased your indebtedness to me."

Avery was clearly bemused. "Why would ye do such a thing?"

"Oh, I realize that you are unable to reimburse me at the present moment, but I am prepared to be generous. I am not usually a man of hasty decision when it concerns a lasting relationship, but you have forced my hand. In exchange for your daughter's hand in marriage, I will give you a certificate of payment for these debts."

"Never!" Farrell railed, drowning out Erienne's surprised gasp. He had come to stand on the platform near the top of the steps and now shook his fist at Christopher. "I won't have a sister of mine married to the likes of ye!"

Christopher raised his gaze to consider the younger man in open mockery. "Why not ask your sister what her pleasure might be?"

"I'll kill ye meself before I'd let her marry ye!" Farrell growled. "So take the warning, Mr. Seton."

Christopher gave a derisive laugh. "You should be careful with your threats, sir. I don't think you could bear the loss of another arm."

"Ye were lucky then. Ye won't be again," Farrell snarled savagely.

"With your record, I really don't think I have much to worry about."

Christopher turned back to Avery, abruptly dismissing the brother. "Think on my offer carefully, Mayor. You'll either have to turn a fair profit from the sale of your daughter today, or give her over to me now in full payment of your debts."

Erienne remembered the nights she had sat beside Farrell's bed while he lay twisting and writhing in torment. She had craved revenge for what the Yankee had done to her brother, and now that same one was demanding either her hand in marriage or payment for a debt, as if he really didn't care which he got. How could he be so arrogant to believe that she would fall at his feet in gratitude after all he had done and when he had never wasted a moment's breath to ply her with a promise of love or devotion? In an unsteady tone she questioned, "You would take a bride who loathes you?"

Christopher considered her a moment before making an inquiry of his own. "You would prefer marrying the sort I see here?"

Erienne's eyes fell from his, for he had struck smartly to the root of her distress.

"She'll take her chances on the block," Avery snarled. "There are those here who might be willin' ter pay the bride price for such a comely lass. Besides, I'd have a bit of a tiff on me hands if I disappointed any o' these here lads by givin' her over ter ye before they had a chance at her. Seein's as how some o' 'em are me friends, that would be hard fer me ter do." He nodded his head in self-agreement. "Can't rightly do that ter me friends."

Christopher stuffed the papers back into his coat. "You have made your decision, and I will await the outcome. Be assured that I will expect full reimbursement of my money before I will consider the matter settled." He touched the brim of his hat briefly. "Until later then."

Avery prodded his stunned daughter, urging her up the steps. It was a difficult moment for Erienne. She wanted to maintain an air of cool disdain, to face them all in calm defiance, but her mauled pride and an aching distrust of the future assailed her senses. Momentarily blinded by a rush of tears, she stumbled on the hem of her gown. Once again she found a supportive hand coming to her aid. Long fingers grasped her elbow and held her firmly until she regained her balance. Furious with herself that she should display such weakness, Erienne lifted her chin and found the grayish-green eyes resting on her with something akin to compassion or pity. It was too much for her to bear.

"Please . . . don't . . . don't touch me," she whispered.

His hand slipped away, and he gave a short, scornful laugh. "When you say that to your husband, my sweet, remember to be more commanding. Perhaps you'll be more effective."

He strode away and Erienne watched through welling tears as

the Talbots' carriage drew up beside him and Claudia's face again appeared at the window.

"Why, Christopher, what are you doing here?" Claudia presented an injured mien as he stepped to the carriage. "Don't tell me you're going to bid for a wife. Surely a man of your wealth and stature can do better than Erienne Fleming."

Christopher could well guess who she had in mind. "I am here to collect a debt."

Claudia laughed in relief. "Well, that I can understand. 'Twas the other I was worried about. I thought surely you had taken leave of your senses."

A bland smile touched his lips. "Not quite."

"Come now, gentlemen," Avery hawked. "Gather 'round now and feast yer eyes on this lovely. Ye won't see another to compare with her after she's taken. Come and look. The roup will be startin' a mere moment from now."

Avery took hold of Erienne's cloak, and when she tried to resist its removal, chortled and with a mocking bow, swept it from her. A loud roar of approval came from the audience as the men feasted their eyes on the prize. Spurred on, Avery caught his fingers in the thick knot of hair and spilled it from its mooring, draping it over Erienne's shoulder and breast.

"See for yerselves, gentlemen. Is she not worth a fortune?"

Erienne's jaw was clamped tight as she stared down into a sea of gaping leers. She felt her skin crawl and had to steady herself against a moment of panic. She raised her head, and her breath halted as she found Christopher's attention fully upon her. Of a sudden she wished she would not have been so proud and foolish to dismiss his offer, for she had seen none in the crowd who did not cause a cold feeling of dread to knot in the pit of her stomach.

Claudia's eyes narrowed as she also noticed where Christopher's gaze was directed. She cleared her throat and smiled prettily as he turned back. "I'd like to invite you for a ride about the countryside, Christopher, but you seem unduly interested in the proceedings. Perhaps you would rather stay here." Her eyes were bright as she awaited a denial.

"Forgive me, Miss Talbot." A brief smile touched his lips. "The debt is for a considerable sum, and it may be my only chance to collect it."

"Oh, I see." She was annoyed by his refusal but managed to

disguise the fact. "I shall leave you to your business, then." She couldn't resist a hopeful question. "Will I be seeing you later?"

"I'll be leaving Mawbry this evening. My business will be finished here, and I don't know when I'll be coming back."

"Oh, but you have to!" she exclaimed. "When will I see you again if you don't?"

Christopher hid his amusement at the woman's lack of coyness. "I'll be keeping my room here at the inn. It shouldn't be too long before I return."

Claudia sighed in relief. "Do let me know when you come, Christopher. We shall be giving a ball during the winter season, and I wouldn't want you to miss it." Her lips tightened at the corners as he glanced over his shoulder without answering. She was beginning to suspect that his business centered very much around the mayor's daughter. "I must be off, Christopher, but should you have a change of plans about tonight, I'll be home alone all evening." A faint smile curved her lips. "Father is still in London, and is likely to be gone for some time yet."

"I shall remember," Christopher replied and tipped his hat. "Good day."

Claudia inclined her bonneted head briefly in a farewell gesture, irritated that he made no effort to delay her. She consoled herself with the thought that if he had some interest in Erienne, it was a wasted effort. At least after the roup she would be someone else's wife and well out of reach.

The carriage swung onto the road, and Christopher gave his full attention to the proceedings, casually leaning against a post while his eyes rested on Erienne.

"Gentlemen, ye've come here in hopes o' finding yerself a wife, and a wife she shall be . . . ter one o' ye!" Avery chortled, directing a finger toward those who were pressing in for a closer look. He took on a serious mien as he caught hold of the lapels of his coat. "Now, I gave her me word that it be marriage ye gentlemen had in mind, nothin' less, and I'll be expectin' ye ter follow through accordin'ly. I'll be a witness ter the nuptials meself and will tolerate no shenanigans. Do I make meself clear?"

A shiver of revulsion went through Erienne as her eyes found the man whom she had dubbed the gray mouse. He had moved to stand near the front, and his smug smile made her all too aware that he would be one of the serious participants. If he made the high bid, he might seek retribution for having been rejected when he first came to call, and she might never again know a peaceful day or a restful night.

Erienne cast her eyes surreptitiously over the faces in the crowd. Smedley Goodfield, at least, was not among them, but Silas Chambers was present. His modest carriage was pulled up nearby, and the old, wizened driver shivered in a threadbare coat.

For the most part, the men who had gathered around the platform seemed a wayward lot, having no obvious redeemable qualities. She had their full attention, all except a white-haired, wealthily garbed individual who had brought along a small collapsible seat on which he sat busily attending the book folded out across his knee. From all outward appearances, he was totally absorbed with the figures in the ledger.

Avery held up his arms widespread for silence and attention from the crowd. "Now, gentlemen, as ye've no doubt heard, I am sorely set upon by me creditors, or I'd have never considered this action. But they press 'pon me at every turn, and even this one"—he gestured briefly in the direction of Christopher Seton—"came ter me very home ter demand payment. Have pity on a man and on this young wench who has never known a man. She's been a fair good blessin' ter Farrell and meself these past years since her poor mother died, but she's reached a time when she should take herself a husband and get away from this worrisome labor o' carin' for her kin. So I urge ye, gentlemen, ter loosen yer purse strings. Come forward, those o' ye who've come ter this affair in a serious manner. Come forward. Here, let 'em gather close."

He consulted the huge turnip-size watch he carried in his waistcoat and held the timepiece high before his audience. "The time is nigh, and now it'll begin. What do I hear from ye gentlemen? What do I hear now? Is it a thousand pounds I hear? A thousand pounds?"

It was Silas Chambers who first responded to the prompting by tentatively raising a hand. In a rather hesitant tone he replied, "Aye . . . Aye, one thousand pounds."

Standing in the background, Christopher unfolded the packet of papers and took out a pair of bills. He waved them to gain Avery's attention and silently mouthed the words, "A mere pittance."

Avery reddened and redoubled his efforts. "Ah, gentlemen, take a look at the prize ye'd be winnin'. Me own fair daughter, beautiful ter a fault. Intelligent. Able ter read and write. A good head with ciphers. A credit to any man she comes ter."

"Fifteen hundred," came a crude voice from the gathering. "Fifteen hundred for the wench."

"A wench it be now." Avery grew a trifle ruffled. "Do ye understand that this sale is final upon the conclusion of wedlock only? And 'twill be wedlock, I vow. So do not be thinkin' ye'll buy me daughter for addin' ter some unseemly harem. 'Tis wedlock only, and wedlock I'm talking o'. There be no hanky-panky, and I will make sure o' that. Now come ye, gentlemen. Come ye. Loosen yer purse strings, I beg ye. Ye see the man standin' there awaitin' and agloatin'. Be out with it now. Certainly more than a thousand pounds. Certainly more than fifteen hundred."

The man sitting on the collapsible seat raised his quill and spoke in a flat, disinterested tone. "Two thousand.'"

Avery took heart at the bid. "Two thousand! Two thousand to this gentleman. Do I hear twenty-five? Do I hear twenty-five?"

"Ah, twenty-one hundred pounds," Silas Chambers lightly bade. "Twenty-one. Aye, twenty-one, I'll go."

"Twenty-one it is then! Twenty-one! Do I hear anythin' else?"

"Twenty-three!" Harford Newton joined in, dabbing his thick lips with a handkerchief. "Twenty-three!"

"Twenty-three it is then! Twenty-three hundred! Come, gentlemen. Ye're not even close ter me debts, and I would see a bit for meself now and me good fair son with his crippled arm. Dig deep into yer purses. Dig out the last bit o' coin. Twenty-three it is now."

"Twenty-four!" the same crude voice in the back shouted. "Twenty-four hundred pounds!" There was a slight blurring of syllables, as if the man had imbibed a trifle too much before attending the auction.

In a worried frenzy Silas hastened to reaffirm his own position. "Twenty-five hundred! Twenty-five hundred pounds!" He was becoming almost breathless with the risk that was involved in this bidding and with the hope that the others would stop once and for all. He was, after all, of goodly means, but not overly wealthy.

"Twenty-five hundred 'tis!" Avery chimed out. "Twenty-five! Ah, gentlemen, I implore ye. Be kind ter an old man and his crippled son. Here ye see before ye a fine example o' womanhood. Indeed, I've said it before and say again, a credit ter any man. A helpmate as it were ter ease yer burdens and see ye kindly through life and bear ye many children."

Erienne turned slightly away from her father at his last comment. She was aware of Christopher's unrelenting stare, and when she lifted her gaze she saw he had now removed perhaps half the bills from the bulk and stood casually dangling them from his fingers, as if he too were imploring the others to bid more to make his time worthwhile. An ache grew in her chest and tightened until it restricted her breathing. He had amazed her with his offer of marriage, but now he appeared to have totally dismissed the idea, as if his first consideration had only been compensation for the debts he held.

"Twenty-five hundred! Do I hear twenty-six?" Avery urged. "Twenty-seven? Ah, come, gentlemen. Why, we've hardly warmed up ter the biddin', and the man is still standin' there with his debts. I implore ye ter reach into those purses. She'll not go for a pittance such as this when the man is waitin' ter collect his due. Twenty-eight hundred! Twenty-eight hundred! Do I hear twenty-eight hundred?"

"Three thousand!" the gray mouse chimed in.

A murmur went through the crowd, and Erienne's knees began to tremble beneath her. Silas Chambers quickly sought out his purse and began to count its contents. There was a jumble of voices from the back as the tipsy contender consulted his friends. Avery's smile broadened slightly until Christopher shook out another bill and added it to the rest.

"Three thousand!" Avery called and lifted a hand. "Who'll make it more? Thirty-five? Thirty-five? Who'll say thirty-five?"

Silence answered his plea as Silas continued to count, and the others conversed among themselves. The gleam in the eyes of the gray mouse grew brighter.

"Thirty-one? Before it's too late, gentlemen, I beg ye consider the prize."

The man on the folding stool slammed his book closed, placed the quill firmly into his case, and rose from the rather questionable comfort of his seat. "Five thousand pounds!" he said bluntly and coldly. "Five thousand, I say."

A sudden silence fell over the crowd. Silas Chambers stopped counting; he could not muster another bid. The gray mouse's face fell in disappointed defeat. Even the tippler from the back knew that the bid was well past his means. Five thousand pounds was a sum that could not be readily challenged.

Christopher's expression was one of disbelief. He looked Erienne over carefully, as if to judge her for her worth, and appeared dubious as he crinkled his brows. At that precise moment Erienne was certain that if he had been near enough for her to reach, she would have tried clawing his eyes out.

"Five thousand it is then!" Avery declared cheerily. "Five thousand! I say it once. Yer last chance, gentlemen. Five thousand twice!" He glanced about but found no takers. "Five thousand it be then! Ter this gentleman here." He clapped his hands together and pointed to the dapperly garbed man. "Ye've purchased a rare prize for yerself, sir."

"Oh, I'm not buying her for myself," the man explained.

Avery's brows shot up in surprise. "Ye were biddin' for another?" At the man's stilted nod, he queried, "And who might that be, sir?"

"Why, Lord Saxton."

Erienne gasped and stared at the man in surprise. Beyond a nightmarish form that flitted like a shapeless ghost through her memory she had no face, no shape to give to the man who had tended her through her illness.

Avery was not completely convinced. "Have ye some proof that ye come in his name? I did hear at one time his lordship was dead."

The man withdrew a letter marked with a wax seal and handed it up to Avery for his consideration. "I am Thornton Jagger," he explained. "As the letter will attest, I have been a barrister for the Saxton family a number of years. If you have doubts, I am sure there are those here who can confirm that the seal is authentic."

A buzz of voices rose from the crowd and quickly became a confused medley of gossip, conjectures, and some truths indistinguishable one from another. Erienne caught the words, "burned," "scarred," "hideous" among the jargon and a slow feeling of horror began to send cold shivers of apprehension through her. She fought to remain calm as the barrister mounted the steps. The man dropped a bag of money onto a small table that served as a desk and began scratching his name across the bottom of the banns, identifying himself as agent of Lord Saxton.

Christopher pushed his way through the crowd and climbed to the platform. He waggled the packet of bills beneath Avery's nose. "I claim it all but fifty pounds, and that I leave for your own convenience. Four thousand, nine hundred fifty pounds is my price for these. Any objections?"

Avery gaped up at the man who towered over him, wishing there were some way he could keep a larger part of the fortune for himself, but he knew with what he had left unpaid in London and the settlement of the gambling debt he had with Christopher, it added up to well over five thousand. It was at the very least a fair deal, and he could do nothing but nod and give his mute consent to the matter.

Christopher picked up the pouch, quickly counted out fifty pounds, and dropped the coins on the table. He tucked the remainder inside his coat and thumped a finger against the bundle of debts. "I never thought you would come near to matching these, but you have, and I am satisfied. From this day forth we are finished with the debts between us, Mayor."

"A pox on you!" Erienne snarled near Christopher's shoulder. His banal dismissal of the affair provoked her beyond the anger she felt toward her father. Before any could stop her, she jerked the packet from his hand and grabbed up several of the coins. She fled from their presence, never wanting to see any of them again.

Avery made to follow her but was delayed as he had to sidestep Christopher several times. "Get out o' me way!" he cried. "The twit's taken me money!"

Christopher condescended and stepped aside. As Avery departed in haste, Farrell grabbed Christopher's sleeve and angrily accused, "Ye did that on purpose! I saw ye!"

The Yankee lifted his shoulders in a casual manner. "Your sister has a right to whatever she took and more. I only made sure she had a head start."

The younger man could find no further argument in the face of the statement. He picked up the rest of the coins and stuffed them in his coat pocket, then holding his lame arm, sneered, "At least we'll be free of ye."

Christopher looked at him with the same tolerant smile until Farrell's gaze dropped. Brushing rudely past, Farrell descended the steps and hurried after his family.

Avery chased after Erienne with coattails flying, anxious to get back the coins she had taken. By the time he reached the cottage, he was sweating and gasping for breath. Slamming the door, he found her in front of the parlor hearth, staring into the growing flames that licked greedily around the packet of bills.

"Here, girl! What do ye think ye're doin'?" he demanded. "Those papers are important. They're me only proof that I paid that rascal. And what have ye done with me money?"

" 'Tis mine now," Erienne stated coldly. "My dowry! My share of the bride money! A small pittance of worth that I'm taking from here. You would do well to see that all matters are arranged for tomorrow, because this will be the last night I spend in this house. Do you understand, Father?" She stressed the title with an acid smile of contempt. "I will never be back."

Eight

The rickety livery from Mawbry was hired to deliver the Fleming family to a church on the outskirts of Carlisle, for it was there that the services would be conducted. The day had dawned crisp and cold, with a bone-chilling wind buffeting the trees into a wild frenzy of motion. The aging of the hours lent no hope for a warming, for noon had passed and still the air was frigid, much like the silence that filled the coach.

The conveyance bumped and jolted along, adding greatly to Farrell's discomfort. He held his aching head in his hand and closed his eyes, but he could find no part of that sleep he had lost during the previous night's revelry. Avery was no better off, for it was not every day a family gained a lord into their fold, and he had spent until the wee hours of the morning drinking and boasting about their good fortune. It was the opinion of his friends that Lord Saxton was a generous soul, having wasted an extravagant sum to purchase the chit, and it was probably just as well that she was marrying him. After her stay at Saxton Hall, rumors and conjectures had been bandied about, and more than a few wondered if his lordship had taken some liberties with the girl. But if he had, at least he was correcting the matter by speaking the vows with her. Of course, the gossips were still wont to make much ado over the whole affair, and they seized and savored every tidbit that drifted their way, wringing it for whatever sweetness it might produce.

For the duration of the ride, Erienne kept her thoughts to herself, having no wish to appear amiable to her father. She held to the corner of the carriage, where she huddled in her cloak, trying to find a bit of warmth in the drafty conveyance. In preparation for the day, she had dressed herself in what had become her best gown. She had no bridal garb. In fact, she preferred a dowdy appearance, since it expressed her lack of joy. Still, it was the day of her wedding, and she had carefully bathed herself and brushed her hair to its best luster. It was the least she could do.

The carriage rattled through the narrow streets of Carlisle. Leaning out, Avery shouted up to the driver, giving directions that in a few moments took them to the small stone church on the outskirts. When they arrived, Lord Saxton's coach was already in the lane in front. The coachman and footman, dressed out in white stockings and matching coats and breeches of a deep forest green trimmed with black, were waiting near the team of silky blacks. The conveyance itself was empty, and since there was no evidence of his lordship's presence in the yard, the mayor was quick to assume that the man was awaiting his bride inside.

Avery plowed through the doors, abruptly gaining the attention of Thornton Jagger and the good parson who stood together near a tall, narrow desk at one end of the pews near the front. Just inside the front portal, a barrel-chested man dressed in a black coat and breeches had taken up a waiting stance, having braced his feet apart and folded his arms across his chest. There was no one else in the chapel. Though the man's attire was certainly more somber than Lord Talbot's, Avery allowed that there was no accounting for the varying tastes of the gentry. He cleared his throat.

"Er . . . yer lordship . . ." he began.

The fellow raised his brows in mild surprise. "If ye be talkin' ter me, sir, me name's Bundy. I be Lord Saxton's servant . . . his man, sir."

Avery blushed at his mistake and chortled to hide his embarrassment. "O' course . . . ah . . . his man." He glanced about the interior of the church, finding no other whom he could lay the title to. "Where is his lordship?"

"Me master is in the rectory, sir. He'll join ye when it's time."

Avery straightened himself, wondering if he should take offense, for the servant's tone was tinged with a bluntness that dismissed the possibility of the future father-in-law joining his lordship. The mayor would clearly have to bide his time if he wanted his curiosity appeased.

The front door came slowly open, and Farrell made his way inside, holding his head carefully upright, as if he feared it would fall off. He eased himself into one of the back pews and closed his eyes. There he would remain, hopefully undisturbed, until the service was over.

Erienne moved on to the front bench, her own back ramrod stiff. Her life, as she knew it, was about to come to an end, and she felt very much like a felon who was readying himself for the final event at Triple Tree and wondering if the noose would be the end of his sufferings or if there were truly a hell beyond. With trembling limbs, she sank to the seat and sat quietly alone in his misery, having no doubt that her father would inform her when the affair was to begin.

The Reverend Miller seemed unconcerned with the groom's absence as he prepared the documents, inspected the wording, and placed his seal and signature on the banns. Thornton Jagger scrawled his name with a flair, identifying himself as a witness, then her father bent low over the parchment and carefully penned his own beneath the barrister's. Beckoned to the fore and handed the quill, Erienne endured the moment and masked her trepidations by an extreme effort of will. Though the documents blurred before her eyes, the only hint of her agitation was a rapidly pulsing vein that throbbed in her neck just below a finely shaped ear.

The proceedings dragged to a halt when the prospective bridegroom failed to join them. Avery grew vexed with the waiting and questioned sharply, "Well, is his lordship comin' out o' his hole? Or did he intend for his barrister ter conduct the affair again?"

Reverend Miller hastened to allay his fears. "I'm sure Lord Saxton will want to speak the vows for himself, sir. I'll send his man for him now."

The clergyman gestured to Bundy, and the servant hurried along a dark hall through an alcove at its end. He disappeared through the arched opening, and an eternity meandered past before footsteps were heard again in the corridor. This time they were odd ones. A thump, and then a scrape, like the sound of a step and then something being pulled or dragged. As Erienne listened, the words of the crowd tore through her memory.

Crippled! Hideously scarred!

The haunting echo of the footsteps died away as Lord Saxton's form came partly into view, at first only a black shape with a flowing cloak covering most of his body. The upper part of his body remained obscured in the darkness of the hall, but when he passed where the light was better, Erienne gasped as she saw the reason why he moved with an odd, twisting motion. The boot of his right leg bore a thick, heavy, wedge-shaped sole, as if for the purpose of straightening a clubbed or twisted foot. After each step he took, the weighted foot was dragged sideways to meet the other.

Erienne's mind froze, and she stared in congealed horror. She was so cold and scared and so utterly unnerved that she knew she could not have moved a muscle to flee had the opportunity presented itself. She waited as one transfixed, not knowing what to expect of the rest of him. Almost reluctantly she raised her gaze, and when the candlelight finally touched his full form, Erienne's knees nearly buckled beneath her. What she saw was more frightening than anything she had ever imagined or even tried to prepare herself for.

Lord Saxton's face and head were completely covered by a black leather helm. Two slitted holes had been cut for the eyes, two tiny ones for his nostrils, and a row of small, square openings formed a mouth for the mask. It was a neatly stitched creation that had been shaped to fit over his head without giving any hint of the features beneath. Even the eyes were hidden in the shadowed depth of the slashed openings.

Erienne's shock was great, and it was through a numbed sense of awareness that she noticed other details about him. Except for a white shirt, he was dressed entirely in black. Leather gloves of the same hue covered his hands, and he gripped a heavy, silver-handled cane. Beneath the cloak his shoulders seemed thick and broad. The left one rose slightly higher than the other, whether from deformity or because of the unbalanced gait she could not rightly determine. In all, he presented a most fearsome mien for a young bride seeing her future husband for the first time.

He halted before them and bowed stiffly. "Miss Fleming." His voice sounded hollow and distant, while his breath hissed eerily through the openings of the mask. He half turned to acknowledge her father with a brief nod of greeting. "Mayor."

Avery managed to close his mouth and gave an indistinct nod. "Lor . . . Lord Saxton."

The masked one returned his full attention to Erienne. "I must beg your pardon for my appearance. Once I was like any other man, straight and strong, but I fell to misfortune when a fire scarred me. Now dogs bark at my heels, and I frighten children, thus I wear the mask. The rest of me is as you see it. Perhaps you can understand why I have preferred to remain unseen and why I have conducted my affairs through an agent. However, this was one occasion that I could hardly ignore. Having seen you in my home and being presented with the opportunity to make you my wife, I hastened to make the arrangements. Now it is your choice to make." He eyed her closely as he waited for comment, but none came. "Do you stand by your father's words? Will you accept me as your husband?"

Erienne was reminded of the notice she had given her father, vowing to leave his house for good. She did not believe he would welcome her back if it meant that he had to return the funds to Lord Saxton. It seemed that she had no other option, and her voice was ragged and strained as she replied, "Aye, my lord. I stand by my father's words."

"Well then, let's be about it." Avery had recovered his aplomb and was impatient to be on with the affair before the man changed his mind. "We've wasted precious time as it is."

Her father's fawning eagerness tore at Erienne like the knotted ends of a cat-o'-nine, destroying the last vestige of respect she had for him. The fact that he could so casually commit her to what promised to be a life of horror seethed like a slavering fiend within her bosom. She resolved to give him no more than the barest homage due a parent, and if it should be that she would never see him again, then that too she could accept. He had used her and Farrell ruthlessly for his own purpose and shown no compassion when it had become apparent that she would be bound in wedlock to this twisted, misshapen caricature of a man who waited at her side. Henceforth, he would be hardly more than a stranger to her.

As the ceremony was conducted, Erienne stood beside the cripple, feeling dwarfed by his presence. In muted, trembling tones, she replied to the questions Reverend Miller presented to her. The hollow-voiced answer of Lord Saxton echoed hauntingly in the stillness as he, too, was asked in rote if he would give his troth toward this marriage. The last tremulous ray of hope that she would somehow be saved from this nightmare was snuffed out as the vows were finalized. A heavy black gloom closed tightly about her, stifling her very breath. She stared at the well-worn stone of the chapel floor until gloved fingers brushed her arm, breaking her trance and drawing a small, startled gasp from her. She lifted her head to look with widened eyes into the mask.

"The ring, Erienne! Take the ring!" her father urged from behind her, and numbly Erienne gazed down to see that the black-leathered fingers were holding a massive, jeweled ring, the value of which she could not even imagine. Avery was nearly panting in eagerness as he watched the ring being placed on her finger, but Erienne was too deeply distracted by the almost reptilian coolness of the hands that performed the deed to notice or even care about her new possession.

In too brief a time it was done. She had become the wife of the dreadful Lord Saxton, yet she wondered how she could bear to live when every moment of her life would be a nightmare. How could it not be when she would be bound to a being who looked like he had crawled from the pits of hell?

In a great show of affection, Avery turned his daughter to face him and kissed her on the cheek, then enthusiastically took her hand to view the costly bauble. Pure greed glittered in his eyes almost as brightly as the stones that encrusted the ring, and for a naked moment his smile betrayed the workings of his grasping mind. If somehow he could entice Erienne back home and weave a story to tell his lordship about how she was grieving about leaving her kin, there would be more of a chance that her husband would invite the whole family to live at the manor. Once in the home, it was only a step farther into the man's coffer.

Avery smoothed his manner and put a worrisome frown on his face before sidling toward his new son-in-law. "I'm thinkin' me daughter will be wantin' ter come home for the last o' her belongin's, milord."

"There'll be no need for that." The rasping syllables sighed from the mask. "She will have everything she needs at the manor."

"But the girl has packed precious few o' her clothes." Avery indicated her small satchel as he told the lie. "Hardly a token ter wear."

"Clothes will be provided for her at Saxton Hall. Others may be purchased as she desires them."

"Ye'll deny me a last few hours with me daughter?" Avery pressed on foolishly. "I've been a right good father, ye know, not likin' what

I've had ter do for her own good, but still committed ter seein' her properly wed ter a man what'll take care o' her . . . and her family."

The blank, featureless face of leather turned squarely toward Avery, and the glimmer behind the eyeholes bore into him with a hard, penetrating coldness. The mayor's spine prickled as tiny barbs of fear set themselves against it, and his bravado dwindled swiftly.

"You have been paid well for your daughter." The sibilant voice was curt and frigid. "There'll be no more haggling. The bargain has been struck, and you'll get nothing more from me. Now begone with you before I decide the bargain has been ill met."

Avery stumbled back with slackened jaw at being so boldly threatened and wasted no moment departing. Snatching up his tricorn and jamming it on his head, he hurried up the aisle and in a loud voice roused his son from his dozing. Oblivious to everything that had occurred, Farrell stumbled after him, and the mayor made his exit without so much as a word of farewell to his daughter.

The slamming of the heavy door reverberated through Erienne's consciousness. It clearly marked the ending of a way of life she had known since her mother died, yet at the present moment she felt no loss or grief, only an aching dread of what tomorrow would bring.

Rousing to awareness, she saw the large, dark shape of her husband limping away from her up the aisle. Thornton Jagger stood beside her, plucking at her sleeve.

"Lord Saxton wishes to leave now, madam. Are you ready?"

Erienne gave a brief, indifferent nod, donned her cloak, and allowed the barrister to escort her on his arm. She was outwardly meek but inwardly so torn with despair and hopelessness that she could set herself to no path of resistance. The servant, Bundy, trailed them, and when they reached the carriage, she found Lord Saxton already seated within. She was relieved that he had not provided room for her beside him. He sat in the middle of the seat, his hands braced on the head of his cane, his knees spread, and the grotesque boot with the thick sole stretched out to the side in full view.

Accepting Mr. Jagger's assistance, Erienne climbed into the velvet-lined interior. Wary of her new husband's awesome presence, she sank to the cushioned seat opposite him and for a moment adjusted her skirts and cloak in an effort to avoid meeting his gaze.

Bundy hauled himself to the top of the coach and settled beside the driver. The carriage began to move away from the church, and Erienne gave a last, uncertain glance toward the small stone edifice.

Thornton Jagger stood where she had left him, and the sight of his solitary figure reminded her of her own feelings of dejection. Despite her husband's presence, she was completely alone and forlorn.

Her despair must have shown, for Lord Saxton deemed to break his stoical silence.

"Take heart, madam. Reverend Miller has enough experience to know the difference between the last rites and a wedding ceremony. This coach is not taking you to hell . . ." He gave the smallest of shrugs as he added, "Or to heaven, for that matter."

The leather helm lent his voice a lisping, unnatural quality, and only the occasional glint of reflected light deep within the eyeholes assured her that there was indeed a man inside the mask. By his statement she could guess that he was aware of his appearance and perhaps understood to some degree her trepidation, if not her revulsion.

The ride from the church dragged on in painful, unbroken silence. Erienne could not trust herself to speak for fear she would give way to her emotions and sob out her anguish. She was utterly terrified of this masked man who was now her husband, and she was not at all sure their destination was not to some hellish place. The chiding thought kept running through her mind. How could she have been so haughty to reject Christopher Seton or even the other suitors who had offered her marriage? However detestable he was or unhandsome they had been, any of them would have been more acceptable to her than this hooded creature who watched her like a hungry hawk. He was the epitome of her worst nightmare, and having been snared in his sharp talons, she was tender bait for the devouring.

The carriage bumped along a winding stretch of rutted road, and for a brief time Erienne's plight was pushed to the back of her mind as she struggled to keep her seat and thus maintain her dignity. Lord Saxton swayed easily with the rocking motion of the conveyance and seemed undisturbed by the rough going. She envied him his poise as she braced against the sudden dips and plunges. The hood of her cloak fell away, and her hair tumbled free of its simple ties, falling around her shoulders in shimmering dark waves, but she had no calm moment wherein she could repair her appearance.

Finally the jostling eased, and she reached up to recoil her hair, but with a flick of his hand Lord Saxton halted her. Slowly Erienne lowered her arms, and for the rest of the journey sat tense and ill at ease beneath that unwavering perusal. The unblinking mask gave her no hint of just how closely her husband watched her. It was an endless ride to the unknown, and time dragged by in painful agony.

As they neared Saxton Hall the road traced the crest of a hill for a space of time, and Erienne gazed out upon the land she would soon come to know. An aura of rosy light had settled upon the western sky with the advent of dusk, and in the distance the dark silhouette of the manor stood in stark contrast against the soft, billowing pink clouds that clustered close over the horizon. Well beyond it, a narrow strip of the sea gleamed like a sapphire jewel wedged between the hills.

The conveyance dipped down into the valley, carrying them closer to that crypt which was certain to become her prison. Her head formed into an icy lump in the pit of her stomach, and no amount of prayerful entreaties could ease her trepidations. She was locked in the grip of total horror, and there was no escape.

All too quickly for her peace of mind the carriage was pulling to a halt before the tower entry. Erienne waited in apprehension as Lord Saxton climbed down. She could not bear the thought of being touched by those smoothly gloved and impersonal hands again, yet she could think of no tactical way of refusing his assistance from the carriage. When he turned back, a cold, shivering shudder swept through her, and she tried to brace herself. The gloved hand raised but it was to make a quick gesture to the footman. The young man hastened to the door and offered up his hand. Erienne almost sighed with relief as she accepted the substitution. She was confused at the clemency shown by her husband and wondered if he actually knew how she loathed his touch. Or was this just a glimpse of a coldly calculating character?

Stepping to the ground, she paused beside him while the footman ran ahead to open the front door. As much as she dared, Erienne kept her gaze averted from her husband until he spoke.

"Not being light of foot, madam, I would prefer to follow you." He lifted a hand in an invitation for her to precede him.

Erienne needed no other encouragement to hurry up the path away from him. She tried to ignore the sound of his dragging foot, but the thunder of a stampeding horde could not have drowned out that fearsome scrape . . . clop . . . scrape . . . clop.

Mrs. Kendall waited with the butler, Paine, inside the door, and her beaming face momentarily quelled Erienne's anxieties. Enthusiastically beckoned in, Erienne moved past the footman and butler and followed the housekeeper across the tower entry while Paine held the door for his master. Upon entering the great hall, Erienne paused in surprise. Absent were the dust-laden, grayish shrouds that had covered the furnishings. The hall had undergone a thorough cleaning from the stone floor to the higher arches of the oaken beams that bridged the ceiling. For the first time Erienne realized the towering walls were hung with tapestries, shields, and other trappings of ancient chivalry. A crackling fire burned in the huge stone hearth, casting a warm glow about the room. A small grouping of chairs sat before it on a large area rug. Nearer the kitchen, massive, straight-backed chairs, their seats cushioned and covered with deep green velvet, were gathered in precise order around a long trestle table. In the darker corners, stout candles burned on the branches of candelabrums that stood to the floor on their own heavy bases. Their tiny, flickering flames combined with the firelight to provide a welcoming warmth while holding back the ever-deepening shadows of night.

"We did our best ter see it cleaned for ye, mum," Aggie stated and glanced about with smiling satisfaction at their accomplishments. "I suppose 'twas hard for a stranger ter imagine that underneath all them coverin's and grime there was a room so grand. I was here meself as a young woman so I knew what a foin place it was when the old lord ruled the manor."

A hollow voice sounded from the entry, calling the housekeeper's name and bringing both women around with a start. Aggie recovered her composure quickly and seemed not the least bit timid as she faced the ominously hooded master of the house.

"Did you want me, milord?"

Paine took his master's cloak and stepped aside as Lord Saxton addressed the woman.

"You may show your mistress to her chambers. Perhaps she would care to freshen up before dinner."

"Aye, milord." The housekeeper bobbed a curtsy. Taking Erienne's small valise from the footman, she faced her mistress with a cheery smile. "Come along, mum. There be a nice warm fire just waitin' for ye."

Erienne moved toward the tower, feeling her husband's gaze following her across the room. His stare set a deeper fear burgeoning within her. How could she bear what was yet to come? How could she endure the long, dark hours in his arms and not reveal her revulsion when his rasping breath or his scarred hands touched her skin?

The housekeeper led the way down a dimly lit hallway of the upper floor, and even in the gloom it was readily apparent that the corridor had been carefully cleaned. Candles provided the light and cast a softly glowing sheen over the marble floors.

" 'Twill be the lord's chambers ye'll be havin', mum, just like before," Aggie announced. "We've tidied them for ye, and they're lookin' fit for a king"—she grinned aside at Erienne as she added—"or maybe his queen."

"The manor certainly looks different," Erienne commented in a low tone that might have betrayed her lack of enthusiasm for being there, but Aggie did not notice as she trilled on.

"Just wait till ye see what the master has bought for ye, mum. The loveliest gowns ye'll ever be wantin' ter see. Why, they must o' cost him a fair penny ter see them done in such a short time." Her eyes twinkled as she looked at Erienne. "He seems to be mightily taken with ye, mum."

Aye! Erienne's mind laconically agreed. And with enough wealth to beat the other hagglers!

They paused before the large, paneled door that Erienne remembered from her first visit, and after a brief curtsy, Aggie pushed the portal wide. Erienne moved through the entry and was immediately assailed with the memories of the nights spent here. The scrubbing and tidying had progressed near a point of perfection, making the room appear totally different. Yet the image of a dark shape slumped in a chair and surrounded by shadows was as clear as the window-panes now were. Her mind completed the indistinct figure of her fevered dreams, with the hooded head, the heavily booted foot, and the broad-shouldered bulk of her husband.

Erienne shuddered in nightmarish horror, and panic threatened to send her fleeing from the room. It took tremendous restraint to await its fading. She did so as one who rides out a tumultuous storm on the sea, knowing it would end but gritting her teeth and hanging on for dear life until it did.

Aggie hurried across the room to the armoire and pulled open its doors to reveal the variety of clothing it contained. She brought out several rich gowns for Erienne's inspection and displayed the sheer fragile lace of the delicately worked chemises and nightgowns. Slippers with tall, curving heels and small, fancy embellishments were eagerly shown, and there were bonnets with feathers or laces, any of which would have made Claudia Talbot suffer a twinge or two of envy.

Erienne roused from her daze, realizing the kindly woman was awaiting her reaction. There was expectant hope in the wrinkled, rosy-cheeked face, and Erienne could not deny the gentlehearted woman.

"Everything is lovely, Aggie," she murmured with a smile. Indeed, few brides were gifted with such finery on the day marking their wedding. Usually it was the husband who received what his bride brought as a dowry. Erienne knew only too well that it was her lack of one that had brought her to this fate.

"The master thought o' everything, he did," the housekeeper said as she pulled back the draperies to reveal the small bathing chamber. "He was anxious ter see ye made comfortable."

In the now immaculate dressing room, there were lace-edged linens ready for her toilette, a tall mirror in the corner, and crystal bottles of scented oils and vials of perfume that had been added to the dressing table since her last visit. Everything was ready for her merest whim or comfort.

Yet even in the face of all the gifts, Erienne could not resist turning the discussion to the man himself. "You seem to know Lord Saxton better than anyone, Aggie. What sort of man is he?"

The housekeeper considered the younger woman for a moment and, reading the agony in her face, understood something of the battle that raged in her mind. Even though she felt pity for the girl, she was also bound by loyalty to Lord Saxton. Hoping to make her new mistress understand a small measure of the misfortunes that had befallen the members of the Saxton family, Aggie spoke quite out of her usual ebullient character.

"I know the master well enough ter understand why he feels pressed ter do the things he does, mum. His family suffered much from the hands o' murderers and from those who'd place themselves in high authority. The old lord was called out in the dead of night by a band of cutthroats and was slain before the eyes of his kin. Mary Saxton feared the rest o' them would be killed, so she fled with her children. About three years back her eldest son come ter claim the title and the lands." Aggie inclined her head in an easterly direction. "Ye've seen the charred ruins o' the newer wing. Some say 'twas deliberately torched by those same ones who killed the old lord and knowin'ly at a time when the son occupied it . . ."

"The burns he mentioned . . ." Erienne pressed. "Was he caught in the fire?"

Aggie turned to stare pensively into the hearth, watching the shifting colors of the flames. "Me master has suffered much in his own way, but he bade me say nothing at all ter ye about him. I only sought ter ease yer fear o' him, I did."

Erienne's shoulders slumped as disappointment and an overwhelming feeling of fatigue drained away her strength. The day's events had exacted a heavy toll on her brain and her body, and the housekeeper's revelation only increased her apprehensions. "If you don't mind, Aggie," she murmured listlessly, "I feel greatly in need of a moment to myself."

Sympathetic to her plight, the woman offered, "Would ye be wantin' me to turn down the bed so ye can rest, mum? Or perhaps lay out some clothes for ye?"

Erienne shook her head. "Not now. Later."

Aggie nodded and went to the door, then paused there with her hand on the knob until Erienne looked up to see if something were needed. "Mum, I know 'tis none o' me business," she began hesitantly, "but if ye will just have a bit o' faith. Lord Saxton is . . . well, like I said, he bade me say nothin' about him, but I will give ye this much. When ye come ter know him, ye will be amazed at the man ye find beneath the robes. And if ye can trust me at all, mum, I do not think ye'll be the least bit disappointed. Thank ye, mum."

Before Erienne had a chance to question her, the woman slipped out and closed the door behind her. Alone for the first time since she had left her father's cottage, Erienne stood in the middle of the room and stared dully about. Bride of Saxton Hall, she thought morosely. Mistress of a manor which, like a chameleon, was changing before her very eyes. She smiled wryly to herself. If only such a feat could be accomplished in her husband, that beneath that austere garb he might prove to be an acceptable husband.

Erienne thrust the thought from her mind and reprimanded herself for such foolish dreaming. She had to deal with the reality of being married to Lord Saxton just as he was. It was too late to turn back now.

More than an hour had passed before Erienne roused herself from her doldrums enough to sort through the gowns in the armoire, yet the soft velvets and fine linens could not sway her from her conviction that she was doomed. She stared dismally at the clothes Lord Saxton had purchased for her, finding no fault with them but knowing no joy in possessing them either. She saw before her eyes luxuries every woman dreams of, yet she knew that in a twinkling of an eye she would have traded them to another if that same one would have also taken her place as bride of Lord Saxton. The hour was quickly approaching when she would have to submit herself to her husband, and at the present moment the thought of death held no greater fear for her.

Having no particular preference in mind, she withdrew a pink satin gown trimmed with green satin cording and tossed it on the bed. The prospect of joining her husband downstairs for their wedding supper filled her with distress, but if she remained in the chambers, he might come that much sooner to dispense with the formalities between them. She had no wish to appear anxious for his lovemaking, and she began to hurry.

At her summons, Aggie came with a young woman named Tessie, who had been brought from London to serve as personal maid for the new mistress, and Erienne was left in her care. A scented bath was prepared and enjoyed. Her skin was gently patted dry, and a light, perfumed oil rubbed into it. The corset strings were tightened, and a bustle pad was applied over her petticoats. Then she sat while Tessie dressed her dark hair in an elegant, upswept coiffure, weaving narrow pink and green satin ribbons through the raven tresses and coiling them about a long, curling strand that was left to fall against her throat and the beginning swell of her bosom. Then the gown was donned, and Erienne had second thoughts about her selection.

The bodice of the gown fit closely to her cinched waist. The sleeves were long and narrow, ending in a design of scrolled green cording sewn to the fabric at the wrists. The same decorative application was added to the décolletage, and this was where Erienne had most of her difficulty. The deep neckline bared her bosom in what seemed to her a most shocking display, barely rising above the blushing peaks of her breasts. Considering her aversion to her husband, the gown was a poor choice. He had, of course, during her illness, seen far more than what the gown revealed, and judging by the fine fit of the garments, he had not been the least bit bashful about her nudity. Still, she was not of a mind to tease him now with an extravagant showing of her bosom. With Tessie in attendance, however, she could not put it aside for another, not when the girl had taken such care to coil the same colored ribbons through her hair. She fretted, wondering how to approach the matter tactfully, and her dilemma was complicated by Aggie's return.

"Oh, mum, ye look as radiant as the mornin' sun," the woman exclaimed.

"The gown is very lovely," Erienne responded after winning a battle to steady her voice. "Yet it seemed a trifle chilly downstairs. I think perhaps I will be more comfortable wearing something else."

"No need for ye ter worry, mum. I'll fetch ye a shawl." The housekeeper went eagerly to search the armoire until she found one of black lace. She brought it to Erienne with a shrug. "I fear there's no other, mum, and this one is so thin 'twill hardly keep ye warm."

"It will do, I suppose," Erienne replied none too eagerly and slipped it about her shoulders, purposefully pulling it high over her bosom. Even a kerchief would have been an improvement.

"Lord Sax—" Erienne paused to reform her question. "My husband, where is he?"

"Down below in the common room, mum," Aggie informed her kindly. "He's waitin' for ye."

The woman's answer was enough to start Erienne's insides churning with cold dread again. She drew in a long, slow breath and, gathering what courage she could, left the room. The high heels of her slippers echoed through the silent hall and marked her descent down the winding stairs. The rhythmic tap of her heels was much like a death roll drumming out a warning of impending disaster, yet as she came around the last turn of the newel and caught the slow scrape-clop of her husband's footsteps coming into the tower, she was sure that doom was there and waiting.

When she stepped past the bend, he was there at the bottom of the stairs. Her eyes could not penetrate the mask, but she felt his gaze glide leisurely over her, taking in every detail of her appearance. Her heart refused to stop its wild thudding, and the last few descending steps became a test of nerve. She halted on the first elevation in front of him and found that with the added height of the step, it was barely enough to match his. Her eyes had to raise slightly to meet the shining glimmer behind the eyeholes.

"Madam, I compliment you on your beauty." His hands raised and slowly lifted the shawl away from her shoulders. "However, since your beauty needs no other adornment, I prefer the simplicity of the gown."

He laid the lace over the balustrade, and Erienne saw the glint of his eyes as they dipped downward toward her bosom. It took an extreme effort not to react and shield the bare curves from his perusal. Her heart beat so heavily, she wondered if he would notice how her breasts quivered. In the next moment she was sure he did.

"Come near the fire, Erienne," he bade gently. "You're trembling."

He stood aside, not making any attempt to touch her, and Erienne moved past him into the great hall. Near the hearth she perched rigidly on the edge of a chair, poised like a bird ready to flee at the first sign of threat. Considering her, Lord Saxton poured wine into a silver goblet and handed it to her.

"This will help."

Erienne felt in dire need of something that would stiffen her quaking knees and quell her trembling. She sipped the wine, carefully keeping her attention on the fire until the silence between them began to grow stilted and tense. Whenever her gaze moved to where he stood, she found the blank, featureless mask regarding her in mute appraisal. It was too much for her to bear. Nervously she took the glass and rose to meander about the room, pretending to admire or inspect a painting or a carving here and a tapestry there, yet deliberately seeking an area safe from his regard. There was none.

Though the leather hood was blank, unsmiling, unfrowning, always void of expression, a thing that any bride would fear, she realized the greater fear by far was the unknown horror of what lay beneath it. Once long ago she had glimpsed an old tar whose face was half destroyed by shot. Now her imagination ran rampant when she thought of the scars a fire could leave, and she wondered if she would find a smooth, featureless mask of seared flesh, or a twisted, ravaged snarl frozen forever on his face.

The awareness of his presence in the room was enough to unravel Erienne's composure. Even his smallest movement made her start. Her legs continued to shake beneath her, threatening to give way under the strain of her fear. Having found no place where she could be safe from his scrutiny, she returned to the hearth and sank into her chair.

"Do you find your rooms suitable?" the hoarse voice inquired as he refilled her glass.

Erienne released a halting breath, trying to relieve her tension, but knew she had failed when her voice quavered. "They are . . . very nice. Thank you."

The sound of his breathing was magnified as it came through the tiny openings, and when he spoke, the words sounded strange and eerie. "Aggie has done a most remarkable feat in setting the manor aright. 'Twill be some time before it is finished, but at least we can enjoy a few of its comforts now. I must apologize for its earlier state. I was staying here alone at the time of your mishap."

She dared not raise her gaze as she answered in a low, murmuring tone. "I . . . I must thank you for taking care of me."

"My pleasure, madam." The rasping voice was unmistakably warm.

Erienne's eyes met briefly the unseen ones behind the mask, then fled again as her cheeks blazed with color. She had no need to be told what was on his mind, for the memory of her own nakedness and vulnerability caused her such excruciating shame she wondered if she would ever forget it. A long moment passed before she could subdue her embarrassment and make a reply. "I don't remember too much about what happened . . . how you found me . . . or my illness."

He lowered himself stiffly into his chair. "I heard the hounds and realized someone was hunting on my lands. I followed the sound of their barking and found you. I brought you back here, stayed with you until Aggie arrived. By then the fever had gone, and I knew you were better."

"And so you proposed to buy me as a wife?"

"I assure you, madam, it was a temptation that I could not resist."

Paine came across the room and paused at the edge of the rug to announce with stilted dignity that dinner was about to be served. Lord Saxton rose and stood beside her chair, again not touching but comporting himself with the manners of a gentleman. Moving ahead of him at his invitation, Erienne went to the table and there became aware that only one service had been set at the end closest to the fire.

"My lord, there is only one place," she stated the obvious with some surprise.

"I shall be taking my dinner later, madam," he explained.

His reasons for abstaining became clear, and she gratefully accepted the decision, since she had no wish to witness the doffing of his mask. It would be hard enough to face him in the bedchamber without enduring the sight of his scarred visage across the table.

Sweeping aside the longer train of her gown, she moved to take her place. Her husband held her chair and after moving it forward, he paused for a long, endless moment behind her. Erienne was held frozen by his nearness and by the suspicion that his eyes were upon her. She dared not glance down to her bosom or turn to look at him, for she was fearful of where his gaze was directed. The pulse throbbed in her throat until he finally moved away, dragging his cumbersome foot to a seat at the head of the table. With a quick, nervous glance downward, Erienne inspected her gaping neckline and was shocked to see a rosy crest partially visible above her chemise. In heated embarrassment she pressed the gown against her bosom and could not resist a comment.

"Is it your intention for me to display myself with equal impartiality to everyone who may care to look, or should I place the fault with the gown?"

His laughter hissed through the openings of the mask. "I would rather you select your gowns with more care when we have guests and reserve such sights for my pleasure, madam. I am not an overly generous man in that regard. In fact, I could not abide the thought of another man having what I had claimed for myself, and since you appeared to have no preference in mind as to your suitors, I sought to bring my desires into fruition." He paused a moment as he looked at her. "You had no one you preferred, did you?"

Erienne averted her gaze as the image of Christopher Seton bloomed in her mind, but she banished it as quickly as it came. She hated the man. For all of his glib proposals, he had been content to see her sold to someone else and had eagerly claimed his money when it was all done. She answered in a glum whisper. "Nay, milord. I had no preference."

"Good! Then I have no reason to feel any qualms about snatching you from beneath the noses of the others." A sibilant chuckle sounded. " 'Twas either them or me, and I think, madam, you are better off with me." His gloved hand rose briefly to make his point. "Take for instance Harford Newton."

"The gray mouse?"

"An appropriate appellation, my dear."

"What about him?"

"Did your father inform you that his wife of thirty-odd years fell to her death on the stairs? Some speculate Harford Newton pushed her. If I had not given Mr. Jagger instructions to top all bids, you would have been dining with him tonight as his bride."

Erienne stared at him as his words penetrated her consciousness. Life with Harford Newton might have been more despicable than she had first realized, but it was no guarantee that marriage to Lord Saxton would be all that much better.

"You have obviously taken some time to learn what you could about my suitors. Why?"

"I simply wished to be aware of your options, at least the ones your father presented to you, madam, and came to the conclusion that I was probably your best choice."

"Had you not instructed your servants to return me to my father, I might have been able to find employment and lead a quiet, modest life in other climes."

"Madam, the likelihood of that was most improbable. As a gentleman, I felt responsible for your welfare. I could not have let you go unescorted where the whims of life were so unpredictable."

"You could have found employment for me, or given me a position here. I am not unskilled at scrubbing floors or cooking a meal."

"That may well be true, my love, but think on this carefully. With you close under my hand, my restraint might have found its limits. Were you then willing to become my mistress?"

"No, of course not, but . . ."

"Then I see no reason for further discussion on the matter." The subject was dismissed abruptly with his statement.

Though the cook was one of exceptional ability, Erienne barely tasted the food. She ate slowly, knowing that however distant, the end of the meal would come far too soon for her comfort. The wine was sipped more liberally, yet it failed to dull her senses or her qualms. She delayed as much as she could, but all too quickly it came to an end.

"I have some matters that demand my attention," Lord Saxton announced as they left the table. "I will need a few moments to take care of them. You may await me in your chambers."

The slow beat of drums in the back of her mind began again, boding her doom, and her heart took up the ponderous rhythm. Her limbs felt like dead weights, and any motion was an effort. Her spirit became a numb lump within her body as she made her way to the tower and slowly climbed the stairs. In the bedchamber she stared at the huge, velvet-draped bed wherein her virginity would shortly find its tomb. It was, for all of its ominous presence, a lordly bed. The hangings could hold in the warmth and provide all the privacy a married couple would need on a cold winter's night . . . or muffle the terrified cries of a woman trapped in the arms of a bestial husband . . .

The grains of time were sifting much too rapidly through the narrowed waist of the glass. Tessie came to help her into her nightgarments and folded down the bedcovers to reveal wide lace on the sheets and comforters. The maid was discreet and left as silently as she had come. Left truly alone in her misery, Erienne paced the floor, praying desperately for the strength and fortitude that was required to face whatever lay before her, and perhaps even to be able to escape some small part of the horror she expected.

"Erienne . . ."

With a small gasp Erienne whirled to face the intruder who spoke her name. It gave her no comfort to find her husband standing just inside the door. She had not heard him enter, and the strangeness of that was lost in the depth of her turmoil.

"You startled me." The tremor in her voice could not be controlled.

"My apology, madam. You seemed engrossed in your thoughts."

Remembering the gossamer thinness of her attire, Erienne gathered the dressing gown more closely about her and turned aside as her husband crossed to the hearth. She heard the chair creak slightly beneath his weight and experienced a mild relief that he did not immediately press her. Still, she was very near the precipice of hysteria and realized that she must get a firm grip on herself before she collapsed completely.

"I thought you would be later, milord," she murmured with candor. "I need more time to prepare myself."

"You are beautiful just as you are, my love."

She moved to stand beside the chair across from his. "I think you know what I mean, milord." When he made no comment, she took a deep breath to steady herself and plunged on. "I have heard something of the evils suffered by your family, and you make me wonder why you took me as your bride. You dress me in rich gowns and talk glibly of beauty when there has been so much bitterness in your own life."

He leaned forward, resting an arm across his thigh as he peered up at her. "Do you think it odd, madam, that I take pleasure in your beauty? Do you think me some perverted soul who would garb you in finery to torment myself . . . or you? Believe me, I have no such intention in mind. Just as one bereft of talents can enjoy the masterpiece of a genius, the perfection of your appearance pleases me. I may be scarred, madam, but I am not blind." He sat back in his chair and examined the head of his cane, adding, "There is also a certain pride in the possession of a worthy piece."

She was fearful of rousing whatever dark angers there might be lying dormant in the man. With such a fierce-looking appearance, his temper could prove to be more violent than anything she could handle, yet she couldn't resist a twist of sarcasm. "You seem well able to afford whatever you wish, milord."

"I have enough to meet my needs," he replied.

"With all that has happened to your family, would not revenge be the sweeter nectar? Have you wealth to gain that, too?"

"Be not misled, madam." His voice was quiet, subdued. "There is revenge, then there is justice. Sometimes the two are met as one."

The cold logic of his statement made her shudder. Almost fearfully she inquired, "And your revenge . . . or justice . . . is it directed toward me . . . or my kin?"

He countered her question with one of his own. "Have you done ill against me?"

"How could I? I never knew you before today."

He again considered the twisted head of his cane. "The innocent have nothing to fear from me."

Erienne moved to the hearth to warm her icy fingers, replying in a taut, desperate whisper, "I feel like a fox snared in a trap. If you have naught against me, then why have you committed this act? Why did you purchase me?"

The masked head tilted upward until she was sure the eyes behind the small openings rested on her. "Because I wanted you."

Her quaking knees threatened to give way, and she sought the safety of the chair. It was a long moment before she conquered her violent trembling and regained her composure. Her dressing robe afforded her little protection from the hearth's heat or the twin black holes that watched her. She vividly remembered the morning she had awakened in this same chamber to find herself void of clothing and in the master's bed. However unplanned and innocent that event had been, this marriage was the result of her accident, and despite what he said, Erienne was sure that the union had been the quirk of an evil mind intent on her complete debasement.

She spoke in a barely audible voice. "I believe you sent me back to my father because you intended to purchase me. It was your plan all along."

His gloved hand moved in a casual gesture as he admitted the fact. "It seemed the simplest thing to do. My man was given his instructions. He was to give the highest bid whatever the cost. You see, my love, your value to me is unlimited."

Her knuckles whitened as she clutched the ornately carved arm of the chair. She felt the heat of the fire on her cheek, but it failed to halt the coldness spreading within her. "Were you so certain, then, that you wanted me?" She made a feeble attempt to laugh. "After all, you know nothing of me. I may prove to be a purchase you will regret."

"Whatever your failings, I doubt they will change the fact that I want you." His hollow chuckle held a note of mockery. "You see, I have become hopelessly entangled in my desire. You have captured my dreams, my thoughts, my fancy."

"But why?" she wailed in confusion. "Why me?"

His answer was spoken in wonder. "Are you so casual of your beauty that you are not aware of its effect?"

She shook her head in frantic denial. "I would hardly term the bidding at the roup eager or frenzied. Consider Silas Chambers. Was not his money dearer to him than the possession of my hand?"

Lord Saxton's echoing chuckle filled the chambers of her mind. "Men have been known to hoard wealth and make of themselves paupers. Tell me, my dear, what good is gold if it cannot buy what a man desires?"

She was beset by his blunt honesty. "As your wealth has purchased a bride for you?"

"Not just a bride, my dearest Erienne, but one of my choosing . . . you!" He nodded his black-hooded head slowly. "I could never have won you any other way. You would have refused my proposals as certainly as you rejected those who answered your father's call. Will you berate me for using my wits and wealth to obtain that which I desire?"

In a mild display of bravado she raised her chin a notch. "And what do you expect of a purchased bride?"

He gave the slightest of shrugs. "What does any man expect of his wife . . . to give him ease and comfort, to hear him out and give him counsel when she can, to bear his children in due season."

Her eyes widened, and she stared at him, unable to hide her amazement.

"Do you doubt my ability to sire offspring, my dear?" he asked chidingly.

Blushing furiously, Erienne glanced away. "I . . . I . . . didn't think you would want children, that is all."

"On the contrary, Erienne. My self-esteem has need of a balm of sorts, and I can think of no greater succor than for you to bear the fruit of my seed."

As quickly as it rose, the color drained from her face, leaving it ashen. "You ask much of me, milord," she replied unsteadily. "Before I was put on the block, I wondered whether I could yield to a man who, at best, was a stranger to me." She clenched her hands tightly to control their shaking. "I know I am bound by my word, but 'twill be hard for me, for you are much more than a stranger to me." She raised her eyes to the blank staring holes in his mask, and her voice was a husky whisper as she stated, "You are everything I fear."

He came to his feet, and in the shifting firelight loomed large and menacing over his surroundings. His awesome presence filled the room, and Erienne watched him with the same rapt attention a trapped mouse gives a stalking cat. Feeling his unswerving gaze, she clutched the dressing gown close about her throat and shrank back in the chair until finally he turned away from her. He moved to a table beneath the windows and taking up one of the decanters that sat on the tray there, splashed an ample draught of wine into a goblet. The halting gait brought him back to her.

"Drink this," his eerie voice bade with a tired note when he held the goblet out to her." " 'Twill take the edge from your fear."

Though the wine at dinner had failed to ease her distress, Erienne obediently took the glass and raised it to her lips, glancing up at him as he waited. It blazed in her mind that the time to consummate their marriage was near at hand, and she was being made ready for the event. Seeking to delay that deadly moment, she sipped the wine slowly, stretching its life in the glass. Lord Saxton was patient to the last and finally no drop of liquid remained to mark her stay of execution. He took the glass from her trembling hand, set it aside, and reached out to draw her from the chair. The wine, however, had not been entirely wasted on Erienne. It lent strength and impetus to her less than steady nerves. She slipped sideways out of the chair, avoiding the gloved assistance much as she would a coiled snake.

His massive form made her achingly aware of her own helplessness and the futility of trying to resist him, yet she moved back a step, poised to fly if he came after her.

The hand dropped, and she relaxed slightly. She was wary of angering him and bringing him to a level of violence that would destroy her. Rape was no beginning for any marriage, but she could not bring herself to yield either. Her mind sought some rationale that would hold him off in a peaceful fashion.

She looked up at him in desperate appeal, wishing she could see behind the black barrier of his mask, yet at the same time grateful that she couldn't. "Lord Saxton, if you will allow me some time to know you and still my fears. Please understand," she pleaded. "I have every intention of fulfilling my part of the vows. Only I need time."

"I know mine is not the most desirable of appearances, madam." His tone was openly sardonic. "But despite what you may think, I am not the brute beast to trap you in a corner and force myself upon you."

Erienne found no encouragement in his statement. After all, they were just words, and she had learned long ago that a man's actions displayed his truer nature more than the things he said.

"I am as other men, with much the same desires. The very sight of you here in these chambers and the knowledge that you are my wife wrenches my vitals in a painful knot. My body aches to release the passion you have aroused in me. Yet I must accept the fact that your shock has been great and that you are bemused by the detail of your much altered circumstances." He released a long, halting sigh as if reluctant to continue, and there was no humor in his voice when he spoke. "As long as I have strength to control what you stir in me, you need only make known to me your desires, and I shall seek to honor them. There is but one warning I would give you. Though the mare I have purchased cannot be ridden, I would view her grace and beauty and thus salve my needs until she is ready to receive my hand and yield me the full rights of her mate. Madam," his darkly gloved hand indicated the heavy oaken portal of her chamber where a brass key brightly shone in the latch, "I bid you never turn that lock or otherwise bar the door against me. As you will have the freedom of this house and grounds, I too will come and go as I please. Do you understand?"

"Yes, milord," she murmured, willing to yield anything if it would hasten his departure.

He limped closer, and Erienne felt the soft caress of his gaze. Fearing what might follow, she held her breath. His gloved hands reached out, and she steeled herself as his fingers plucked at the ties of her robe. He slipped it from her shoulders, and it fell in billowing waves to the floor, leaving the gossamer mist of her gown to provide modesty. It failed miserably in the firelight. The thin lawn clung like a translucent vapor, revealing the sleek curves of her hips and thighs and molding itself with greedy delight to the tantalizing fullness of her bosom.

"You needn't fear," his voice hoarsely rasped, "but I would see you as my bride before I leave. Loosen the gown, and let me look at you."

Time ceased to exist as Erienne hesitated. She wanted to deny the request but knew that she would be foolish to test him after he had committed himself to such restrictions. Her fingers shook as she unfastened the opening, and she stood in quaking silence as the gown slid to her feet. She could not meet the blank, inhuman gaze of the mask as it ranged with deliberate slowness over the full detail of her, pausing at length on the pale-hued breasts and the slender curve of her hips. She fastened her gaze on a distant point and struggled to quell the shriek of utter panic that was building deep within her. If he touched her again, she knew she would break and crumble until she groveled and begged for mercy at his feet.

When it came, his hollow whisper was enough to make her flinch and stare in wide-eyed fear at the stark, emotionless mask.

"Get into bed before you catch a chill."

His command penetrated her paralyzed thoughts. Erienne eagerly sought the covering of her gown and fled like a startled doe to the haven of the quilts. Sinking into the downy softness of the bed, she pulled the comforters up close about her chin. Lord Saxton stood where she had left him, as if he fought some greater battle within himself. Cautiously she watched until he swung his heavily booted foot about and went to the door, dragging his foot behind him. The panel closed as he left, and silence filled the room. Only the fading sound of his passage remained, but it was enough to shred the young bride's emotions. In total relief and absolute misery, she sobbed into the pillow, paying no heed to the passing of the moon or darkness creeping over her room as the fire dwindled to a dull glow in the hearth.

Nine

Glistening bright sunlight filled the bedchamber in rich abundance as Aggie threw back the heavy drapes. Rousing slowly, Erienne blinked and shaded her tear-swollen eyes from the blinding brilliance, then huddled deeper into the soft warmth of the comforters, not yet ready to face another day as wife of Lord Saxton.

"The master be comin' up ter see ya, mum," the housekeeper announced with gentle but unmistakable urgency. "And I know ye'll be wantin' ter look yer best for him."

Erienne groaned her rebellion and passionately shook her head beneath the covers. At the moment, crooked teeth and a large wart on the end of her nose would have better suited her needs, since winning Lord Saxton's approval was the farthermost thing from her desire. Indeed, she would rather not have attracted him at all, and she could see no need in rousing his interest beyond what it already was.

"Come now, mum," Aggie coaxed. "Ye've too fair a face ter be hidin' it, especially from the master. Mark me words, mum. Ye'll come ter rue the day ye were less than kindly."

Erienne threw off the covers and sat up, turning a worried countenance to the woman. "I don't suppose you'd know," she began in an anxious rush, "if Lord Saxton has ever displayed a tendency toward violence?"

Jovial laughter bubbled from the woman as she moved her head slowly from side to side. "The Saxtons have always been most gentle with their womenfolk. Ye needn't fear anything from him, mum. But if ye're *wise*"—she raised a brow and looked directly into the wide, amethyst-blue eyes as she stressed the word—"ye'll treat him with the reasonable regard and have a care for his pleasure. He's a wealthy man . . . beyond most lords . . and . . ."

"Pah!" Erienne flounced back on the bed in disgust. "I care not a whit for his wealth. All I ever wanted was a reasonable, gentle husband, a man I could show some fondness for. Not one who frightens me with his mere presence."

She didn't care if this was just a servant and she was being indiscreet with her emotions. Considering the circumstances, her feelings had to be obvious to everyone, and if it was a folly to be frank with this woman, then it was better to know one's enemies from the beginning than to live a lifetime of deception.

"The fear will pass, mum," Aggie Kendall encouraged gently. "Until then, 'tis a good thing ter look yer best in every situation, lest one day ye regret it." She poured water into the washbasin, dipped a cloth into it, and after wringing it out, handed it to her young mistress. "For yer eyes, mum, ter take the sleep from 'em."

A few moments later, when the master of Saxton Hall entered the chamber with his ponderous gait, no evidence of Erienne's restless night remained. Hair brushed to a lustrous sheen, a deep red velvet dressing robe donned, and temples and wrists touched with an attar of rose, she was ready to solicit any man's approval. Erienne laid the blame to Aggie's gentle but unwavering insistence, for the housekeeper had hovered over Tessie's shoulder to see that the toilette was accomplished without delay, lest they keep the master waiting. Pleased with the results, Aggie gave a last glance toward the couple before hurriedly making her departure, pushing Tessie ahead of her, and leaving Lord Saxton alone with his young bride.

"Good morning, madam," the voice sighed through the opening of the mask.

A stiff-necked nod gave evidence of Erienne's unflagging wariness. "Milord."

His tone was softened with humor. "You seem to have suffered no ill effects from your first night here as mistress of the manor."

A brief shrug lifted her slender shoulders. "Tessie is quite talented . . . and Aggie *very* persistent."

"You must forgive Aggie, my dear. She is absolutely loyal to the family, and she sees in you a hope for its continuation. Indeed, she's anxious for us to produce an heir."

Erienne had the feeling he was laughing at her, but she could find no cause for his amusement. The subject was one she wished most dearly to avoid. Her silence spoke for itself as she maintained a cool disinterest. Lord Saxton was undismayed.

"I have no preference myself. A girl with her mother's eyes would suit me just as well."

Moving to stand near the dressing table, Erienne cast a cautious glance back at him as she rearranged the crystal vials. "And what of a son, milord? If he were to resemble his father, what would he look like?"

"You need have no fear, my dear. A man's scars do not carry to his offspring."

She released her breath haltingly and looked about, feeling the cage of despair closing in about her. "Is that why you bought me? To carry on the line?"

"As I've told you before, madam, I purchased you because I wanted you. Everything else is of secondary importance. The children you bear will undoubtedly be treasured because you will be their mother. Offspring by another woman might not be so dear. You are, my lovely Erienne, the one who has haunted my thoughts and dreams."

"Am I, then, to be your prisoner here?"

"You'll be nothing of the sort, madam. I assure you of that. If you desire an outing, you have only to inform me or one of our servants, and the coach will be provided for you. If you enjoy riding, there is a fine mare with white stockings and a good temperament in the stables. Keats will be happy to saddle her for you. There is, however, a thing I would caution you about. Without proper escort 'twould not be advisable to wander any distance. I plead caution in traveling beyond the immediate area of the manor. For your own safety, madam, I urge this."

"I have heard tales of miscreants roaming this North country, but I have yet to face any more villainous than those who attempt to warn me of them." Erienne dismissed the occurrence that had driven her and Christopher from the tumbledown stable. After all, it was not certain whether those men had been highwaymen.

" 'Tis my wish, madam, that you never meet the ones who prey upon the countryside."

Erienne looked pointedly at him. "Have you met them, milord?"

" 'Twas not the Scots who torched Saxton Hall, I assure you. Since my life may depend upon my caution, I have learned to be wary of many."

Beneath the blank stare of the mask, she lowered her gaze and spoke in a low voice. "I am curious to know why the manor was burned. If it was deliberate, can you tell me the reason?"

"Madam, there is not much I know about the ones responsible, but I do know that their instinct for survival is great. Like a pack of wolves, they strike out at anything that threatens them."

"Did you threaten their existence?"

"My very presence is a threat to them."

Her brow puckered slightly. "Then surely they'll try again."

He nodded in cold agreement. "Aye, but they'll not catch me unaware."

"You seem quite certain of that."

"Madam, of all people, you should be the one to realize that I leave as little as possible to chance."

The next several days dragged by as if they were weighted with heavy chains, and Erienne found no ease for her fear of Lord Saxton. When he walked the dark halls of the manor with that halting gait, her attention froze as she waited and listened. Yet as threatening as that sound was to her serenity, she had learned to be leery of the silence even more. For one so obviously hampered, Lord Saxton seemed able to move about at times without the slightest whisper of movement, like a ghost or a shadow in the night. And it was indeed at night when her trembling disquiet burgeoned, for she would sudd- denly find him in the room, that blank, expressionless mask turned toward her with not even a slight glimmer visible behind its gruesome half smile.

Though the door to her bedchamber had a stout and sturdy lock, she had not found the courage to test it or his command, lest her blatant refusal of his entry arouse his wrath and bring some terrible dark vengeance down upon her. Thus, in whatever state of dishabille she happened to be, whether bereft of clothes, meagerly garbed, or thankfully robed, she had no choice but to accept his company. She quickly learned that having Tessie in attendance was no deterrent either, for with a slight gesture of his gloved hand he would dismiss the girl, and in quick obedience the maid would abandon her mistress to whatever fate the master intended.

While he was in the room, Erienne was tormented by uncertainty. He had given his word only to the limit of his restraint. If he were pressed beyond that, she could find herself reluctantly easing his desires. In her mind was formed a haunting vision of herself cowering and quivering with hysterical pleas tumbling from her trembling lips. The vision frightened her, for she realized it could very well become a reality if he tried to take her.

When the moment came when she found him gone, no longer standing in the shadows, no longer sitting in his chair, a feeling of great relief swept over her. She had survived another night; she would see another day. Yet, like a thief in the back of her mind, there was a thought that robbed her of peace. It was the sure knowledge that at some time, one day, one night, one moment the debt would be called due, and she would be required to pay in full.

A week had not yet aged to maturity when Aggie came to fetch the morning tray, bringing with her a summons from Lord Saxton bidding the mistress to join him in the great chamber. Erienne accepted the directive with a low, inarticulate murmur of acknowledgment, but inwardly she quaked. She was certain he intended to bring up the matter of their relationship, to ridicule her for not being the loving wife she had promised to be, and she was horrified at the prospect of the confrontation.

While Tessie helped her into her dressing gown and brushed her hair, Erienne strived to control her quaking. She fervently hoped that something would divert her husband's attention so she might avoid the session with him, but the idea was only a wish and had no basis in fact. The moment swiftly came for her to face her husband.

Pausing a moment at the entry to the great chamber, she drew a deep breath and tried to collect herself. She was not at all sure she had succeeded when she passed through the arched portal and stepped into the beast's lair. Lord Saxton was standing before the hearth with an arm braced across the back of a chair. Erienne attributed it to her fear of the moment that he appeared to stand half again as tall as normal. His towering height did not diminish as she neared.

Though its cloth was velvet and the neckline high, the robe seemed inadequate beneath his close regard, but she had learned in their brief marriage that he did not miss an opportunity to watch her or to admire what he had claimed as his. She sank into the chair that faced him, feeling a need to relieve her trembling limbs. Whatever courage she had mustered had dwindled to little more than a troubled apprehension. She made a play of smoothing her robe to keep from looking at him, but he was patient, and finally there was nothing left to do but raise her gaze to the blank, staring mask.

"There are some things that need to be purchased from Wirkinton, madam," he stated in his strange, low, whispery voice, "and I thought you might enjoy the outing. I have asked Aggie to go with you."

"Will you not be going also, milord?" Erienne asked, barely managing to control the note of hope in her voice.

"I have other business to attend. I shall not be able to accompany you."

"What am I supposed to do?"

"Why, madam, I expect you to spend the day shopping for whatever you will," he answered in a tone of mild surprise. He tossed a small leather purse onto the table beside her, where it landed with a solid "thunk" that betrayed its wealth. "This should suffice for the day. If there is something of greater value you desire, inform Tanner so he might mark it and return for it later."

"I'm sure this will be more than enough, milord," Erienne assured him softly, taking up the pouch.

"Then I will let you be on your way. Aggie is no doubt eager to get started." He paused a long moment before adding, "I will assume that you will be considerate of the woman and give her no anxious moments . . ."

"Milord?" Erienne's tone was one of confusion.

"Aggie will feel remiss in her duties should something go awry."

Erienne felt his pointed stare and lowered her eyes as a blush deepened the hue of her cheeks. The fact that the notion of flight had flitted more than once through her thoughts made it difficult to meet his gaze and pretend innocence. She nodded slightly in submission. "She'll have no reason to worry, milord. I shall not stray of my own accord."

" 'Tis good then." He moved with his awkward gait to the fireplace and stood staring down into the flames a long moment before he faced her again. From behind the slashes in the mask his eyes seemed to glimmer at her as he spoke. "I will be awaiting your return, madam."

Hesitantly she rose to her feet. "Then I am free to go?"

He dipped his hooded head in assent. "Of course, madam."

The thrill of being set free for a day surged through Erienne, and it was hard to hold her steps to a dignified walk. Her feet carried her quickly across the room, leaving the master of Saxton Hall staring silently after her.

With something akin to a child's eagerness, Erienne settled back against the plush carriage seats and snuggled her velvet cloak close about her smiling face. Aggie's presence reminded her that she was not entirely free, but the woman's happy chatter helped to liven the journey. After almost a week of marriage, to be allowed to escape, however briefly, was like a reprieve from hell. Not that Lord Saxton had treated her unkindly. Indeed, despite his terrifying appearance, he had been most gentlemanly. Still, there had been times when she had almost felt as if she had been confined to a dungeon and was only waiting for the torture to begin. It had been a strained, tense week, but now, at least for a few hours, she could relax without the threat of his presence.

The coach eased through the narrow streets of Wirkinton, winding its way to Farthingale Inn, where it halted. There, while the ladies enjoyed a light repast and visited the nearby shops, Tanner would remain and await their pleasure or need.

Once fortified with the warming tea and nourishment, Erienne inspected the list of goods that were to be purchased, then with Aggie at her side promptly set to the task. In the confident manner of a mistress of a great house, she went to the different stalls and shops, inspected the items, and bargained for the best prices until the merchants begged for mercy. She listened patiently as they praised their goods. Then unmoved, she declared that unless the price were fair, she would have to go elsewhere, after which they heaved disappointed sighs and gave in, unwilling to see even the smallest profit slip through their fingers. The housekeeper stood back with a pleased smile, assured that this was indeed a mistress who would do her husband proud.

The thought of escape was far from Erienne's mind when she bade Aggie to buy fresh fruit at the market down the street while she looked for a coppersmith from whom she might acquire a pot for the kitchen. Aggie did not hesitate but hastened off. Erienne readjusted the several packages she carried before setting off on her errand.

She was not immediately successful in her quest and was contemplating a return to the coach to rid herself of her burdens when from a nearby shop several overdressed and overexposed strumpets bustled onto the cobbled thoroughfare. Erienne struggled with her packages to avoid the oversize skirts and petticoats and the dangerous ribs and tips of the parasols that seemed to jab her from every hand. Before the women could move on, a group of seamen descended upon them, and to her horror Erienne found herself seized from behind. The bundles of merchandise fell to the cobblestones, and she was hauled around to face a bearded tar whose shape and size resembled that of a walrus.

"Oooiiee, girlie! Ye're a fine one, ye are. Ain't never seen such a doxie like ye before."

"Let me go!" Erienne gasped. She struggled in earnest to preserve her dignity while avoiding the ruddy, puckered lips that eagerly sought her mouth. His breath, sour with the stench of strong ale, emitted from a gaping leer that grew wider as his brawny hands rudely pawed her back and brought her ever nearer to that broad, whiskered face.

"Unhand me!" Erienne shrieked and braced her arm against the man's throat, trying to get some leverage in order to gain her freedom. The man howled with laughter and easily swept her arm aside. His embrace tightened about her, squeezing the breath from her, and Erienne shivered in revulsion as his slobbering wet lips touched her cheek and slid downward along her throat.

"Ye smell as sweet as sin, girlie," he chortled.

Suddenly a large presence loomed close beside them, and Erienne looked up to find Christopher Seton standing at the man's elbow. At her gasp, the seaman glanced around.

" 'Oo's this now?" the tar questioned sneeringly. "Some dandy what's got his eye on me girlie? Go on an' get yer own, mate. This one's mine."

A mildly tolerant smile touched the handsome visage, but the glint in the green eyes was hard as steel. "If you do not choose to make mourners of your friends today, my good man, I suggest you promptly release the lady," he warned in a mild tone of reproof. "The

master of Saxton Hall would take it much amiss if you did ill by his lady."

The seaman's jaw slowly sagged, betraying his confusion. He stared at the other as if wondering whether to take him seriously or not.

"The master of Saxton Hall? Have you not heard of him?" Christopher questioned in chiding amazement.

"Naugh!" the great lummox replied roughly.

"The ghost of Saxton Hall, some call him," Christopher obligingly explained. "Burned to a crisp, others have said, but still he lives. The way the rumors have been flying about, you're either deaf or a stranger to these parts if you've not heard of him. Were I you, I would take extreme care to treat his lady gently else you might shortly regret it."

The tar hastened to excuse his error. "I didn't know the lil' filly was someone's missus. The boys and me were only 'avin' a bit o' fun." He set Erienne from him and in an anxious scramble restored her packages to her. "No harm done, ye see."

"If that is the case, perhaps Lord Saxton will be lenient with you." Christopher raised a wondering brow to Erienne, who reddened deeply beneath his bold inspection. "None the worse for wear, it seems." He presented his arm gallantly. "Madam, may I escort you from this rowdy bunch and see you safely away?"

Erienne ignored his offer and walked stiffly through the gawking tars and tarts, who opened a path for her. Christopher followed, slapping his riding crop casually against his leg as he observed the indignant swing of her skirts. He grinned broadly and quickened his pace, catching up with her and matching his long stride to her brisk, angry step.

"You have your nerve," she snapped, casting an indignant glare at him.

"My lady?" His tone questioned her statement while his eyes shone with suppressed humor.

"Mindlessly spilling tales about my husband that aren't true!" she accused, then paused to rearrange several of the parcels she carried.

"May I lend you some assistance with those things?" he inquired solicitously.

"Indeed not!" she answered sharply, then gasped in dismay when a smaller one slipped from her grasp.

Deftly Christopher caught the package in midair. Curious, he brought it to his nose to sample its scent, then cocked a dubious brow at her. "Perfume for my lady?"

Erienne snatched it from him. "Spices for the kitchen . . . *if* you must know, Mr. Seton."

"That's reassuring," he replied. "The scent was rather pungent, nothing like your usual sweet fragrance."

"We were discussing my husband," Erienne reminded him pertly.

"And so is everybody else. Indeed, the merest mention of him is likely to send a shiver of fear through the stoutest of hearts."

"You do much to fan the flames with such foolish talk of ghosts and devils."

"I only meant to convince the seaman to free you so there need be no shedding of blood. I gained your disfavor by defending myself against your brother. To avoid any further wounding of my reputation, I simply plied gentle words and warnings. Did I err? Would you have seen me give the man his due and deal him a death blow?"

"Of course not!" Erienne exclaimed in frustration.

Amused by her irritation, Christopher teased, "Pardon me for not playing the smitten suitor and defending you with blade in hand." He glanced about him as if searching for someone. "I'd have thought your husband would still be panting about your skirts. Where is the chap, anyway?"

"He . . . didn't come with me," Erienne answered haltingly.

"Indeed?" Christopher's tone held a strong, undisguised note of hope as he turned to gaze down at her expectantly.

"He had business elsewhere," she hurried to explain.

"And do I dare hope that you've come here unescorted?" he asked eagerly.

"Aggie . . . I mean, our housekeeper came with me." Erienne glanced down the street, not wanting to meet the warm, humorous glint in those gray-flecked green eyes. "She should be here somewhere."

"You mean you are not yet ready to leave Saxton Hall?"

Erienne's head snapped up in surprise, and her eyes searched his.

Christopher smiled pleasantly. "Lord Saxton is well known to me, hardly the sort a beautiful young woman would enjoy having as her husband." He saw the flash of fire in the blue-violet depths, but he continued, undisturbed. "Despite your avowed hatred of me, Erienne, would you not find my company more enjoyable than that twisted excuse for a man? My apartments in London are certainly more comfortable than a cold and drafty manor house."

"And what, pray, would be the rents on such an establishment?" she queried with icy sarcasm.

He disregarded the sardonic edge to her voice. Indeed, his smile would have been one of great compassion except for the leer in his eyes. "That question could be settled with almost no discussion at all. Though words tumble prettily from your lips, my sweet, to talk with you is not what I have in mind."

Erienne turned and stalked away with an abruptness that gave him cause to quicken his step as he followed her. When he took a place beside her again, she gave him a glare that should have shriveled his heart to a nub. "You amaze me, sir! You truly amaze me! I've not been a wife a full week, scarce enough to know my husband well . . ."

"If at all," he scoffed in muted tone.

"And yet," she raged on, ignoring his interruption, "you insult the man, knowing him not at all, I'd wager. I must firmly tell you that there is more to him than others see. He has been kind and courteous to me, providing for my every comfort, and has never stooped to rudeness, unlike others I might mention." She gave her head a toss reminiscent of a high-spirited filly. "He has been most civilized and gentlemanly."

"Pray tell, sweet lady," the unquenchable rake chortled close to her ear, "what else could he be? Has he taken you in his arms and proven his manhood?"

Erienne faced him squarely, her mouth agape at his crude affront. A half smile twisted a corner of his mouth as his eyes warmly caressed her.

"I assure you, my love," he murmured softly, "I would not have wasted the time. By now, you would have had no doubt as to the readiness of my passion."

Erienne gasped and felt a scalding hotness creeping up from her bosom. "You . . . you . . . insufferable, boorish knave!" she stammered in angry amazement. "In the last few moments you have proposed that I take a place as your mistress, and now you confront me with your open lust. Can you honestly believe that I take my vows lightly? Indeed, I do not! I am firmly bound by my word! But if you would do me honor, however small, then take yourself from my sight and henceforth restrict me from your company."

"I fear 'tis met that I cannot," he sighed in overstated apology. "You have boldly captured my deepest desire, and with that, most probably my heart."

"Most probably! Most probably! Ohhh!"

Erienne swung a daintily slippered foot with dire intent, but he lightly stepped aside and laughingly saved his shin from the blow.

"Such a temper," he chided.

"Depart from me, you cloddish lout! Leave me before I retch at the very sight of you!"

Christopher grinned broadly and swept her a low bow. "As you wish, milady. Since I perceive that Aggie is that one over there craning her neck in an effort to find you, I shall leave you and be about my business."

Erienne caught a glimpse of the housekeeper down the lane, doing much as he had described. Grinding her teeth in vexation, Erienne strode away from him and fairly seethed with hot anger as she heard his last comment.

"If my lady should change her mind, my ship will be here or in London. Captain Daniels will know where to find me."

Erienne refused to gratify him with a retort, but it was a dire struggle she made for composure as the housekeeper joined her.

"Mum? Are ye all right?" Aggie questioned in anxious worry when she saw her mistress' reddened countenance. Her next statement was almost an understatement. "Ye look a bit flushed."

"Yes, of course. I'm fine," Erienne answered stiffly. "There are just too many scalawags abroad for a decent woman to be straying off alone." She cast a glance back down the street but could see no sign of her detractor. With his absence some semblance of sanity returned, and she relaxed, but only a trifle. Her temper was too badly frayed to allow her to devote too much attention to shopping. "After we find a kettle, I should like to return home."

"But mum, ye haven't bought anythin' for yerself yet."

"Lord Saxton has been generous. I can think of nothing I lack."

"Very well, mum."

A pot was found and purchased a short time later, and when they came from the shop, Erienne was astonished to find the coach waiting for them a short distance away. It seemed that with its presence the street had filled with a multitude of gaping bystanders who were trying to stare without really appearing to do so. Several groups of whispering women bent their heads together, but when her gaze came upon them, they quickly straightened and began to peruse the wares of a nearby peddler. Erienne's bemusement vanished abruptly when the carriage door swung open and the cloaked form of her husband descended to await her. Acutely aware of the sudden silence on the street and the weight of many stares, she hurried toward him. Bundy stepped to meet her and, taking the packages, carried them to the boot. She released a trembling breath as she faced Lord Saxton.

"My lord," her voice quavered only slightly, "I was not expecting to see you here."

"I had business with Mr. Jagger, and since he was leaving for London, I begged a ride from him." He contemplated her a moment. "Have you finished here, madam?"

"Aye, milord."

He raised his arm, half blocking the entrance to the carriage as he offered his assistance. Erienne stared, unable to move.

"Take my arm, madam," he urged softly. " 'Tis unseemly that you should embarrass me before so many."

She quelled a shudder and reluctantly placed her hand on the proffered arm. She was surprised to find it well formed and firmly muscled beneath the cloth of his coat, not at all unpleasant to touch. The strength she had feared but never doubted was evident. Yet strangely, touching him made it all seem less sinister, as if for the first time she was able to think of him as a flesh-and-blood man and not some cold, scarred creature from the nether world. His other hand, briefly resting on her waist, helped brace her ascent into the carriage.

Aided by Bundy, Aggie climbed to the top of the coach and settled herself beside Tanner, purposefully leaving the privacy of the interior to the wedded couple. Bundy squeezed his bulk in beside the woman. Caught between the two hulking men, Aggie displayed a momentary distress before she gave first one and then the other a sharp jab with her elbows.

"Keep ter yer places now," she warned. "I won't be crushed ter smithereens by the likes o' both o' ye."

A buzz of voices rose along the street as Lord Saxton made his entry into the carriage. He braced his weighted foot on the step, grasped the sides of the door with his gloved hands, and hoisted himself into the interior. He settled into the seat across from Erienne, and the conveyance lurched into motion. When they had passed from the cobbled thoroughfare onto the dirt road leading from the

173

city, a softly echoing chuckle came from Lord Saxton. Erienne stared at him, curious to know what had amused him.

"You see, madam?" His oddly half-whispering, half-rasping voice won her full attention. "Touching me is not at all like taking hold of a serpent."

In sudden embarrassment Erienne glanced away. It was as if he had read her mind from the beginning, for the very words had flitted through her thoughts. She had never considered him to be a man, but rather something diabolical.

"I am a man, Erienne," he assured her, the laughter gone from his voice, and once again he seemed to read her thoughts. "With all the needs and desires of a man. And you, my darling Erienne, are so beautiful it tortures me."

Though she felt the eyes behind the mask resting heavily upon her, she could not look at the leather visage. Her answer was barely audible. "I struggle with myself, milord. My imaginings run rampant, and I think it eases my fears no more to see your mask than to glimpse whatever lies beneath it. Perhaps if I could see your face . . ."

"You would recoil in rage and horror," he interrupted her curtly. "Wild imaginings might one day be conquered by a dream, but the surest knowledge of my face would forever bar the door between us. I would rather let darkness and uncertainty be your wooer than have sure knowledge of the fact haunt you. If I have to, I will bide my time, but even you must see there is a worth beneath the meanest of exteriors, that even a scratched and worn carriage may yet yield a comfortable ride."

Erienne kept her silence, bracing herself against the sway of the carriage. His words haunted her. He wanted her, and someday she must submit. But for now, the fear of what lay behind the mask was still too much for her.

They were yet a goodly distance from Mawbry when gunshots sounded from behind them, startling the occupants of the coach. Bundy opened the small compartment above the forward seat and urgently announced, "Highwaymen, milord! A full dozen of 'em! Comin' up behind!"

Lord Saxton leaned out the window to see the oncoming band of thieves but quickly ducked back in when a shot splintered the wood of the door near his head. He flung a command in the direction of the compartment. "Tell Tanner to keep them at a good distance.

I'll see what I can do to dissuade the beggars. And Bundy . . . get Aggie down."

"Aye, sir!" the man responded almost cheerfully and slammed the small door. An outraged squawk was heard as he shoved Aggie down into the boot beneath his feet. In angry protest the woman sputtered a stream of curt insults but ceased the invective abruptly when a stray ball whined off a roadside boulder. Without so much as another snort, she scrunched deeply into the boot.

Lord Saxton faced his young wife with an apology. "Madam, I am sorry to inconvenience you, but I must ask you to move here to the forward seat."

Erienne hurriedly obeyed as Tanner urged the horses into a faster pace and Bundy fired a few wild shots from the top of the carriage. As soon as she had cleared the rear seat, Lord Saxton grabbed the front part of the cushion and pulled up. To her amazement, a trunk-like compartment was revealed. Within it was a neat stack of over a dozen muskets and a box of premeasured charges in silk tubes. Her husband hefted a flintlock out and reached across to the top of the seat, flipping a pair of latches that held a short, wide panel over the seat closed. He cocked the flint and checked the priming pan, then sat forward so that he was free of the swaying sides of the coach. A long moment passed as he waited, then he lifted the gun to his shoulder. It seemed it had no more than touched in place than a cloud of smoke, accompanied by a deep-throated bark, filled the coach. Erienne jumped at the ear-wrenching explosion, and a brief second later she saw one of the highwaymen swept off his mount as if by a puppeteer's string. Lord Saxton set aside the fired piece and took another. The musket came up and, before Erienne could brace herself, the hammer fell, filling the coach with another deafening roar. Again the charging brigands suffered a loss as another rider sprawled in the dust.

Taking up another musket, he glanced Erienne's way briefly and rasped out a command, "Madam, stay behind me."

The hatch above their seats was pulled open, and Bundy's voice called down, "Almost to the bridge, milord."

Lord Saxton debated the statement briefly before he nodded and replied, "Good! Just to the other side then."

The small door was snapped shut without further comment from above. Lord Saxton tucked two of the muskets beneath his arm and took hold of the door latch with the other hand.

"Brace yourself, my dear," he calmly informed Erienne.

Glancing through the rear portal, she could see that one of the riders, bolder than the rest, had spurred his horse to the fore and now raced a good length ahead of his more cautious fellows. He was beginning to gain on the speeding carriage when the conveyance careened around a sharp curve, and he was momentarily lost from sight. Erienne struggled to maintain her balance through the wildly lurching swing, but no sooner had it ceased than a sustained hollow roar assailed her already ringing ears, and she realized they were crossing a narrow wooden bridge with low post rails on either side.

The roar ceased, and another lurching and heaving began as the driver stood on the brake lever and hauled at the reins to bring the team to a halt. Before they were at a full stop, Lord Saxton threw open the door and with a hand on the sill, swung himself out and down, skidding to a halt in the middle of the road. Going to one knee, he laid one of the muskets beside him and casually checked the pan on the other before he pulled back the heavy snap lock. He waited in the sudden stillness as the thunder of hooves in the distance drew nearer.

The lead rider came around the bend into view, and Lord Saxton bided his time until the horse's hooves struck the bridge floor, then he flipped the gun to his shoulder and fired. The heavy ball took the horse square in the chest. The animal's forelegs collapsed beneath him, and he fell nose downward toward the dirt, then somersaulted hooves over head through the air, sending his rider hurtling in a high arc. The man landed with a bellow of pain, then rolled along the bridge for a short space while his dying horse threshed in the dust.

The highwayman struggled to his feet and shook his head as if dazed. He was slow to look around, but when he did, he gave another loud bellow as he saw the rest of the charging band being funneled onto the bridge by their speeding steeds. The unseated one dove toward the rail and cleared it in an ungainly leap just ahead of the racing group, landing a fraction of a moment later flat on his face in the icy water below. The last that was seen of him, he was struggling to stay afloat as his heavy clothes dragged him down and the swift current tumbled him over and over in the shallow bed.

His companions gave no thought to helping him as the first one plowed into the dying horse and was rapidly followed by the others. The last rider avoided the tangle on the bridge, but his mount took the bit and raced off into a growth of briars. The horse screamed and bucked as the thorns raked his legs. On the third energetic leap, the steed and rider parted company, and the latter sailed high into the air before coming down with flailing limbs and, as he disappeared into the briar bushes, a crescendoing shriek.

Chuckling, Lord Saxton came to his feet and discharged the second musket into the air. The brigands completely lost heart for the charge and redoubled their efforts to extricate themselves from the chaos on the bridge.

A loud, cackling laugh came from the top of the carriage, and Bundy hooted, "Ye did it, milord! Ye upsot every one of 'em! Ain' nobody what gots an eye for a shot like ye, milord."

"Are you all right up there?" his lordship questioned.

Bundy chortled. "All except Aggie, who's in bit o' a tiff 'bout her squashed bonnet."

Another brief chuckle came from Lord Saxton. Dragging his lame foot back to the carriage, he slid the muskets onto the floor and looked up at his young wife. "And you, madam? How have you fared?"

Erienne smiled. "I am quite well, milord, thanks to you."

Lord Saxton swung himself into the interior and closed the door behind him. When he had seated himself, he rapped once with his cane on the small upper hatch, and the coach lurched into motion. As Erienne watched, he reloaded the four emptied muskets, laid them in their places inside the compartment, then closed the cushioned lid. He felt his wife's stare as he leaned back in the seat and looked at her.

"You would stare at a cripple, madam?" Humor was heavy in his whispered voice.

"You amaze me, milord." Erienne shook her head with a quick, negative movement. "You seem to be ill at ease in this world, and yet you deal with its difficulties so remarkably well. I get the feeling that in spite of your handicaps you are a step or two ahead of most people."

"I will take that as a compliment, my love."

Erienne pressed her curiosity farther and couched her statement as a half question. "You handled the guns with unusual skill."

"The result of long practice, dear Erienne."

"You have no doubt heard of Christopher Seton and his purported skill at dueling. Do you think you could best him?"

Her husband's answer was preceded by a derisive laugh. "Such an event would prove most fascinating, even to me, but I do not tempt fate, my dear, by dwelling on such remote possibilities."

"I did not mean to imply a possibility, milord," Erienne apologized. "I only meant to learn where you would place a man of such skill."

"By my side, had I the choice. 'Tis not wise to foolishly antagonize a man adept with weapons."

"My father and brother," she said slowly. "Are they fools in your eyes?"

"Your father? I hesitate to judge." He laughed easily and dusted the knee of his breeches. "I am sure that before I would yield you up, I would prove myself a fool several times over." He paused and considered his wife, who sat erect, eyes averted, while she tried to subdue a blush. "Your brother? He failed to consider his choices and rashly chose wrong. The hasty spirit of youth perhaps, but he suffers much from his own making."

"You are truthful and honest, milord," Erienne assured him, still unable to meet his unflinching gaze. "I cannot fault you for that."

"If you think me so honorable, my love, hear me out. I do not hold with dueling, yet I have never stepped away from a contest of arms. If I could secure your love for myself with such an event, I would challenge all those who would come against me."

Erienne was completely unprepared to deal with his statement. When she had given voice to the wedding vows, it had been with a bitter, acrid taste of betrayal in her mouth. The week of marriage that had gone by had brought her no closer to an attitude of yielding. She was perpetually impaled on the horns of her dilemma.

Turning her face aside, she stared out of the window and could think of no worthy comment. Lord Saxton's eyes moved along the delicate profile, then dipped lower, to where the parted cloak revealed the full shape of her breast. His gaze lingered there for a pleasurable moment before gliding downward to where her gloved hands lay primly folded in her lap. He mentally sighed.

"Do you wish to stop in Mawbry to visit your family?" he asked after a moment.

"I have nothing to say to them, milord," she murmured. "I would rather continue on to Saxton Hall."

Lord Saxton braced his palms against the head of his cane while he mused on her answer. If she entertained some fears about what he might demand of her when they reached Saxton Hall, then she was not willing to spare herself by delaying it with a visit to her relatives.

The sun began to sink behind the horizon, bathing her face and bosom in the soft, golden light. Erienne knew he watched her, for she felt the heat of his gaze more firmly than the warmth of the sun. A time later she was relieved when the light faded from the heavens and darkness shielded her from that unswerving attention, but even then there was that strange quality about her husband that made her wonder if he were something more than human, if his eyes could penetrate the ebony shadows, and if she would ever cease to feel the unsettling timidity she experienced in his presence.

When Erienne awoke the next morning, she found that Lord Saxton had taken his leave of the manor and left word that he might be gone for several days. She considered his absence as something of a reprieve, but her conscience was not totally free. Rolling up her sleeves, she set out to prove that she was a capable mistress of the house, if not yet a wife. She organized the servants, and while some were given the task of maintaining the living quarters of the manse, others were set to cleaning areas that were still bound by dust and time.

Though some of the tenants paid their rents in edible items, there were always spices and other precious and rare condiments to be purchased, and the kitchen had to be restocked with supplies. She compiled a list of necessities that warranted another trip to market, this one to be undertaken by Paine.

Curious about the tenants themselves, Erienne bade Tanner to bring the coach around. Armed with healing herbs, teas, and medicinal salves, she took Tessie and began visiting the cottages to see if there was a need that she could fill. There were grins aplenty to welcome her, and their bubbling laughter and beaming faces were visible proof that, despite his frightening appearance, they were thankful for Lord Saxton's return. She was amazed by their fierce loyalty to the family, and she did not miss how their mouths tightened when Lord Talbot's name was mentioned. The last years had not been easy for them, but with the rightful lord in his place, they were quick to express a new hope for their future.

Erienne came away with a newly sprouted seedling of respect growing within her for her husband, for in the brief visit she had learned that he was already easing their plight by reducing their rents and had done away with the laws imposed upon them by Lord Talbot, and in their stead had presented statutes that were fair and easy to live with. He had also imported a pair of bulls and nearly a dozen rams from Scotland, all of which promised to produce healthier, sturdier stock for the tenants. In more ways than one, she began to understand why the people welcomed her husband's coming.

Ten

Lord Saxton's insistent rap on the door of the mayor's cottage was answered by an impatient shout. After a brief stumbling sound, the portal was swung open to reveal a badly disheveled Farrell. The young man had his eyes downcast and was obviously not feeling his best. His face was ashen, and sagging red pouches underscored his eyes. When he raised his gaze, he stared in mute surprise at the darkly clothed one, seeming to forget his present malady.

"I have something to discuss with the mayor," Lord Saxton announced bluntly. "Is he home?"

Farrell gave a lame nod and stepped back from the door, pulling it wider to admit the forbidding presence into the cottage. Farrell caught sight of the waiting landau and hesitantly gestured to the driver.

"Would yer man care to come in and wait by the fire in the kitchen? 'Tis a brutal day to be sittin' out."

"My business here will be brief," Lord Saxton answered. "And Bundy seems to prefer the cold."

"I'll get my father," the younger man offered. "He's tryin' to cook up somethin' to eat."

"Either that, or burning something," Lord Saxton remarked dryly as he caught a whiff of scorched grease that wafted from the rear of the house on a brown haze.

Farrell glanced toward the kitchen in chagrin. "'Tis a rare day that we have a decent meal. I think Father is only now beginnin' to consider Erienne's real worth."

A harsh laugh came from the mask. "A late hour for that."

The muscles in Farrell's cheeks tensed, and he massaged his crippled arm as he turned slightly away from the other man. "I guess now that ye've got her, we won't be seein' her anymore."

"That's entirely up to my wife."

Farrell gave him a challenging look, daring to lift his gaze to that black mask. "Ye mean ye'll let us come and see her?"

"There are no chains on the doors of Saxton Hall."

Farrell scoffed. "Well, there must be some reason why she's not runnin'. She did here quickly enough. And ye're not exactly"—he gulped as he realized the insult he had been about to give—"I mean . . ."

"Fetch your father," Lord Saxton bade tersely. Sweeping his cumbered foot about, he entered the parlor, where he lowered his large frame into the chair beside the fireplace. Bracing a hand on the head of his cane and glancing about, he saw that the cottage was in a sad, untidy state. Clothes were scattered helter-skelter, and dirty dishes were piled on tables. It was readily evident that the two men who occupied the cottage were lacking not only Erienne's cooking skills but her penchant for neatness as well.

Avery hesitated outside the parlor, hopefully composing his face in such a manner that his fear of his son-in-law would not be noted. "Ahhh, milord," he greeted in a guise of enthusiasm as he came into the parlor. "I see ye've made yerself ter home."

"Hardly!" The statement was curt.

The mayor stared at him in confusion, not knowing how to react. "I s'pose ye come here ter complain 'bout me girl." He held up a hand as if to declare his innocence. "Whate'er she's done, it weren't me fault. Her mother's ter blame. Filled the twit's head with rubbish, she did. All that learnin' and cipherin' . . . 'tain't good for a girl ter know all that stuff."

Lord Saxton's voice was like a breath of winter's north wind as he spoke. "You sold her too cheaply, mayor. The sum of five thousand pounds was but a mere pittance of what I was willing to pay."

The brief chuckle that came held no humor. "But then, that is your loss. The matter is done with, and I have what I want."

Avery slowly sank into the chair behind him and closed his gaping mouth. "Ye mean . . . ye would o' . . . paid more for the twit?"

"I would easily have doubled the amount."

The mayor cast a glance about the room, feeling suddenly miserable. "Why . . . I'da been a rich man."

"I wouldn't feel too badly if I were you. It probably would not have lasted too long."

Avery peered at him closely, unable to mark the insult clearly. "If ye weren't intendin' ter bend me ear with complaints, why'd ye come?"

"I wanted to report an attack on my carriage." Lord Saxton saw the surprise of the other and further explained. "I was returning from Wirkinton with my wife when highwaymen tried to overtake us. Fortunately I was prepared for them."

"Yer coach, milord?"

"Aye! My coach."

"Ye say ye were expectin' 'em?"

"Not at that moment, but I had guessed that sooner or later they would try to take my coach."

"Seein's as how ye're here ter tell about it, I s'pect ye did 'em some damage."

"Two of the highwaymen were killed, and I would guess the rest were badly shaken."

"I ain't heard a word about it."

"For a mayor, you're not very well informed."

Avery blustered in hot anger until he felt the cold, unfaltering stare that seemed to pierce him through, and he promptly lost courage. " 'Tis the sheriff's duty ter tell me what happens here."

"Then perhaps I should have sought the sheriff out instead." Lord Saxton's voice had grown no warmer. "But I thought you might be interested in learning that Erienne is safe."

"Ah . . . well, she always seems ter do all right for herself. I never worry much about her. She's strong . . . and willful."

The glove hand tightened on the handle of the cane long before Lord Saxton chose to reply. " 'Tis a rare father who shows such confidence in his daughter." He issued a brief, derisive laugh. "Why, one could easily mistake it for lack of concern."

"Huh?" Avery was momentarily perplexed.

"Never mind." Lord Saxton rose to his feet. "I shall be going now. I have business to attend to in York."

"Ah . . . gov'na," Avery began and cleared his throat sharply. "I was wonderin' if maybe, seein's as ye're me girl's husband and all, ye could spare a few quid for her poor family. We've been down on our luck, the boy and me, and we narrowly have a coin ter our name. We had ter sell ol' Socrates . . . and since ye said ye were willin' ter pay more . . ."

"I have set aside an allowance for your daughter." His lordship's tone was harsh. "If she chooses to help you, she may, but I will give nothing more to you without her approval."

"Ye let a woman run yer affairs?" Avery blurted in surprise.

"Her family is her affair," Lord Saxton answered brusquely.

"She's got a powerful mean heart toward me since I sold her."

"That, Mayor, is your problem, not mine."

Barely an hour after Lord Saxton's landau departed on the eastern road leading to York, the travel-worn Christopher Seton entered town on the south road from Wirkinton. He led his equally road-weary horse to the stable at the rear of the inn, where he bade the boy take extra care with the animal and for a reward tossed him a bright tuppence.

Christopher had no more than stepped out from the stable doorway when he felt fingers plucking at his sleeve. He glanced aside to find Ben scuttling along beside him, a wide and partly toothless grin on his ruddy face.

" 'Hain't seen ye in a week or so, gov'na," the old tar chortled. "Ol' Ben was afeared ye'd met wit' yer Maker. Ye been keepin' yerself busy?"

"I had to see to my ship in Wirkinton." Christopher did not halt or slow his pace but laughed as he pushed open the back door of the inn. "Only the good die young, Ben. You and I will be around after many suns have set."

They navigated the short hall that led into the common room and moved toward the table near the window. Molly's eyes lit up when she recognized the tall form. She shrugged her blouse off her shoulders, letting it sag low over her bosom, and gave Christopher a coy smile as he motioned for two mugs. In a moment she was there, sliding the brimming tankards onto the table.

"Thought ye might o' left ol' Mawbry for good, gov'na," she

crooned as she braced her hands on the table and leaned forward, giving him a very personal review of her ripe bosom. "I'da been mighty sad if ye hadn't come back."

Christopher glanced up, briefly noting the immodest display that bared her large nipples. He leaned back in his chair and tossed down several coins. "Just the ale, Molly. Nothing else."

Miffed, she straightened and flounced away. She didn't know whose petticoats he was getting beneath, but whoever the woman was, she had to be sapping his strength with her demands. Why else would such a stalwart, virile-looking man deny a generous offer when it was placed before his naked eyes?

Ben licked his lips in eager anticipation as he took up his tankard. "Govna, ye're as good as me own muther, God rest her soul." He dispatched a goodly share of the brew before he lowered it again. With a deep sigh of appreciation, he wiped his sleeve across his mouth. "So! Ye've been away, ye 'ave, an' ye gone an' missed all the 'appenin's 'ereabouts."

"Happenings?" Christopher leisurely quaffed his ale as he regarded his companion with patient expectation.

"Aye, gov'na." Ben relished the opportunity to brief his benefactor. " 'At Lord Saxton, he's up and married the mayor's daughter, and just yesterday almost got hisself waylaid by a bunch o' bloody pirates, he did."

Christopher's brows came together in a worried frown. "Was anyone hurt?"

"Oh, his missus was with him, all right." Ben snickered knowingly and leaned closer. "But ye needn't concern yerself 'bout her. It were only 'em thieves what got hurt. His lordship killed a couple an' set the rest ter their heels." Ben's voice lowered to a hoarse whisper. "I hears as how there ain't a one o' 'em ken walk without a hitch."

Christopher digested the information in silence until a drum of hoofbeats broke into his musings. Ben rose and peeked out the front window. Just as quickly he was back.

"I'll . . . uh . . . see ye later, gov'na."

Ben guzzled the contents of his mug before fading back into the shadows at the rear of the room. He propped a chair against the wall and seemed to doze almost as soon as he settled into it.

A moment later the door burst open, and Timmy Sears stomped into the inn. Treading on his heels, Haggard glanced happily about, then almost jumped out of his shoes when he saw Christopher at the table near the window. He caught Timmy's arm and frantically gestured, seeming to have difficulty finding the words to speak. His companion turned to see what was troubling him, and the red brows shot up as he found the reason for Haggard's dither.

"I'm wounded," Timmy declared, hastily sweeping his cloak aside to reveal an arm hanging in a sling.

"So I see," Christopher calmly replied while he further appraised the man's condition. Timmy's woolen coat was short in sleeves and length and was stretched taut across the broad shoulders. His clothes were wrinkled, as if he had put them on too soon after a washing, while his boots had a slightly dampish look and were turned up at the toes.

Molly was curious and beat a hasty path to his side. " 'Ere now, Timmy dear. Ye look like ye were trampled by a herd o' swine."

"Almost was, Molly." He slipped his good arm about her shoulders and mumbled beneath his breath. "Bunch o' witless fools." He cleared his throat and spoke so all could hear. "Nah! Me crazy ol' nag took a cropper on a patch o' ice and sent me sailin'."

Keeping a wary eye on the Yankee, Haggard sidled to the bar and chortled nervously. "Wish I'da seen ye."

Timmy glared at his companion, then dismissed him from mind as he lifted the bandaged wing. " 'Tain't broke, just a bit stiff. Hah, busted me mount, though. Had ter put another shot into him."

"Another shot?" Molly looked up at him innocently.

"I mean as how he busted his leg, and I had ter finish him off."

"How'd ye get here, then, if ye plinked him?"

"Got me another one." Timmy drew himself up. "A better one than that old nag."

"Hah, I'll bet!" Molly said, laughing. "An' who'd ye steal it from this time?"

Timmy's face took on a dark look, and he scowled at her. "If ye thinks I'd stoop ter thievery . . . Why, here . . ." He fished with two fingers into the pocket of his waistcoat. "Look what I brought ye."

He held a pair of gold earrings and dangled them in front of her eyes, which immediately grew large and soft. Molly forgot all about teasing him and even put Christopher Seton out of mind for the moment.

"Ohhh, Timmy, ye're too good ter me. Always bringin' me trinkets an' whatnots." She took one from him and held it to her ear.

"Want ter come up," she indicated the stairs with a tilt of her head, "an' . . . uh . . . see how they look on me?"

"Don't know," Timmy replied casually. "Where'd ye have it in mind to wear 'em?"

"Why, in me room, o' course." Molly stared at him with a puzzled frown, then thumped his shoulder with a light blow, eliciting a wince of pain. "Awwwh, Timmy, yer allays funnin'. Come on."

Molly hitched up her skirt and took the stairs in a prim gallop. Timmy needed no further urging to lope at her heels.

The night was dark, and Timmy Sears was restless. His life had not been much fun lately. He had been well battered and bruised. He had been shamed in front of his friends. And if that was not enough, his wife had begun making demands on him. One of his companions, maybe that blundering lickspittle Haggard, had made a casual comment comparing his hundred quid to the five thousand laid out at the roup. His wife had quickly seized upon the fact that he had money. There followed a verbal listing of nigh unto a thousand things they needed. New tiles for the roof. new dishes for the table. Indeed, a new table and chairs to replace the good, sturdy bench they had shared these many years. A bolt of cloth, threads, needles. Some of this and a little of that. A new pot for the hearth, since the old one was perilously thin at the bottom. And on . . . and on . . . and on . . .

Timmy sat up in bed and ran his hands through his shaggy hair. What did the woman think he was made of, anyway, that he could support her in the lap of luxury like some . . . some . . . *Christopher Seton!* The name surged through his mind, and around it his woes seethed.

"Sneakin' around and disturbin' the peace o' Mawbry homes," he mumbled. "Woundin' young lads and accusin' the mayor hisself o' cheatin', then snatchin' the money for the girl right from under the old man's nose. Why, Avery didn't even have enough left for a good toot."

Sears chuckled to himself and sucked his teeth in sheer envy. "How'd the Yankee do it? The way he sports about, one might get the idea he has as much power as Lord Talbot, or that highfalutin Saxton . . ."

Timmy's chin jutted, and his brows beetled in ponderous thought. "Now, that's another one." He rubbed his arm as the memory of his plunge into the icy water was brought painfully to mind. He had been so close to dealing a blow to the rumors that the man was a ghost, but his plan had been rudely cheated. Now he felt a need for revenge. "One way or the other, he'll pay."

Timmy climbed from the bed carefully so as not to rouse his spouse. She had grown most amorous of late, and he was a bit weary of her unwarranted attention. Besides, she had lost another tooth just that morning, and he was not used to her lopsided smile yet.

His stomach rumbled as the greasy stew from supper changed its angle of attack and shifted across his belly. He eased open the back door and made his way toward the privy, being careful where he placed his bare feet. His hounds had a way of littering the country-side with all manner of debris, and he'd just as soon avoid getting his toes tangled in something.

The distance of the privy from the cottage compromised convenience with comfort in the form of the prevailing breezes. He made his way unhindered and swung open the creaky door. He settled himself inside, and a few moments later sank into a dreamy half-awake state. Something stirred outside, and he blinked himself to attention until he caught the sound again. It was like a horse stamping an impatient hoof. He stood up and leaned forward to push the door wide, then peered out.

The night's depth of darkness was impenetrable, then a breeze stirred, and the clouds allowed a shaft of moonlight to sweep across the yard. Sears' breath sucked in with a ragged, wheezing sound, but a shriek of pure terror caught in his throat. There, standing in the silvered light, was a huge black horse whose eyes seemed to blaze with white fire, and on his back was a shadowed being with great wings spread out from his shoulders, as if he were making ready to launch himself from the steed's back.

A hoarse, squawking scream tore itself from Timmy's throat, and he whirled, leaping. His foot struck upon the seat, and he hardly paused as with the strength of three men he burst through the thin boards that sheathed the rear of the privy. Before his feet touched earth, his legs were already driving in a fearsome pace. They carried him without hesitation toward a mass of thornbushes several rods away.

A peal of terrifying laughter rang out behind him, and he redoubled his pounding progress. He did not halt as he plunged deep in the protection of the thicket, hardly aware of the thorns that shredded his nightshirt and hide.

Later he swore that he had heard the beat of ghostly hooves close behind him, and his wife smiled and noddingly commented that he had run so fast it took him until nearly four in the morning to reach the cottage again. His friends at the Boar's Inn who knew of Timmy's bent toward brawling buried their laughter in mugs before agreeing in strained, stentorian tones that his bravery had been stouthearted in the face of the winged creature.

The days of Lord Saxton's absence numbered four, and though she had kept busy with her duties as mistress of the manor, Erienne grew restive within the stone walls. She remembered her husband's statement that if she desired an outing, she was free to ride the mare from the stables. Taking him at his word, she garbed herself in riding habit and went down to present her plea to Keats.

Since her arrival at Saxton Hall, she had not ventured to the stables, though the idea of escape had nibbled at her thoughts and she had wondered how far she would get taking one of her husband's horses. The overriding fear that he would come after her and she would then have to deal with his wrath put quick death to such meanderings of the mind. The only place where she could even hope to find safety was with Christopher Seton, but her pride would never yield that victory to him. If he had truly cared about her as he had claimed, he could have at least presented some form of protest about the roup. Instead, he had readily accepted payment for the debts and voiced no objection to her being bought by another man. When last she saw him, he had seemed most content with his freedom, and if she ran to him now, ready to give all he demanded of her, then surely she would only be feeding his arrogance. She had no doubt that an affair with him would be wildly exciting, but one day she would have to face the fact that he was just using her for a time. When another woman came along whom he liked better, it would be the end. It was better that she saved herself such grief before falling hopelessly in love with him.

When she entered the stables, Erienne saw a youth about her size and near an age of ten and five cleaning a far stall. He straightened as the door squeaked behind her, then his eyes widened as he caught sight of her. He came at a run to meet her, and snatching off his hat, halted before her. He bobbed his head forward several times in what might have been a hesitant bow, and the grin that split his face made her smile.

"Are you Keats?" she inquired.

"Aye, mum," he replied eagerly and gave another jerky bow.

"I don't think we've met. I'm . . ."

"Oh, I know who you are, mum. I've seen ye comin' and goin', and . . . beggin' yer pardon, mum . . . I'd have ter be blind not ter notice a mistress as comely as yerself."

Erienne laughed. "Why, thank you, Keats."

His face took on a deeper hue of red, and slightly befuddled by his boldness, he gestured toward a dark mare with white stockings that stood in a nearby stall. "The master said ye might be comin' ter fetch Morgana. Would ye be wantin' me ter saddle her for ye, mum?"

"I would like that immensely."

If it were possible, the grin widened, and he slapped his hat against his flanks as he spun joyfully about. He led the mare from her stall and held her for Erienne's inspection. The animal seemed of a calm, friendly spirit as she nuzzled the lad's arm, yet she was of a class that would have made Socrates shrivel in dismayed embarrassment. She was nearly black and silky smooth with a long-flowing mane and tail.

Erienne scratched the dark neck. "She's beautiful."

"Aye, that she is, mum, and she's yers. The master said so."

Erienne was overwhelmed. She had never owned a horse before and certainly had never considered that she would possess an animal of Morgana's beauty. The gift pleased her and made her even more aware of her husband's generosity. Though she had not yielded as she had promised, the presents still continued to flow. Whatever the depths of his scars, he seemed to be several steps above Smedley Goodfield and the host of other suitors who would have stopped the gifts at the first hint of her rejection.

"Would ye be wantin' me ter go with ye, mum?" Keats asked when the mare stood ready.

"No, that won't be necessary. I shan't be gone long, and I plan to stay in sight of the manor."

Keats locked his hands together to accept the slender booted foot and was amazed at the agility his mistress displayed as she was boosted into the saddle. Indeed, she was like a feather briefly touching his hands. As she rode away, he stood at the door of the stables and stared after her until he felt assured that she could handle the mount, then he turned back to his labors, whistling an airy tune. He had already come to the conclusion that the master was as gifted at choosing a wife as he was at selecting horses. They certainly were a right fine lot to look at, every last one of them.

Erienne avoided the black rubble of the east wing as she passed the manor, for it reminded her of her husband's stark mask and her own inability to conform to a wifely state. The air was cold against her face as she raced over the moors, yet she found it exhilarating, and she inhaled its freshness. The mare was swift and agile, quick to respond to her hand. Erienne felt in unison with it, and the tension that had chained her the past two weeks began to slip away.

Nearly an hour later she was in a valley to the east of the manor, in an opening that was banked by a wooded area on three sides. She had slowed the horse's gait to a walk when the distant sound of baying hounds caught her attention. Her heart doubled its beat as the memory of snarling jowls and sharp fangs flashed through her mind. A sudden foreboding descended upon her, and though she could see the manor on the hill behind her, it was too far away to lend any comforting thoughts of protection.

She had to fight an overriding panic as she turned the mare about and retraced her path across the valley. Her fears were diminishing as she neared the wooded copse. In another few moments she would be safe at the manor, and she began to relax, unaware of the eyes that watched her from the woods.

Timmy Sears chortled to himself and rubbed his bruised arm. Vengeance on this so-called Lord Saxton would taste sweet as he took his pleasure on the girl. Seeing as how the Yankee had wanted her too, the revenge would be twofold.

He kicked his horse, sending it thrashing from the trees and onto the lane in front of Erienne, startling a cry from her. The mare danced away at this unexpected confrontation, and she had to fight to keep her control over the animal. Timmy's broad hand reached out for the reins, but Erienne was incensed at his boldness and brought the quirt slashing down across his wrist.

"Get away from me, you lout!" She swung the mare around until the reins were well out of Timmy's reach, then glared at him over the steed's neck. "Poachers and their mongrels are not welcome on these lands. Get off!"

Timmy sucked his lacerated hand as his eyes bore into her. "For a wench 'oo was sold on the block, ye've gotten high-minded since ye married his lordship."

"Whatever my circumstances have been, Timothy Sears," she retorted, "it has always been well above your kind. 'Tis your wont to trod ruthlessly over people, and you have trespassed on my husband's lands far too often."

" 'Twill be more'n his lands I'll be havin' me fun on this time, yer ladyship."

Tiny shards of fear pricked Erienne's spine while a coldness congealed in the pit of her stomach. She had heard enough tales about Timmy Sears to know that he could be a dangerous, unruly scamp. Driven by self-preservation, she spun the mare around. Timmy was prepared for her attempt. He kicked his mount forward and was beside her before she could flee. He seized the bridle, preventing her escape, but the quirt was still in Erienne's hand, and she used it with vicious intent, bringing it down across his arm and slashing his face.

Howling a curse, Timmy swung his arm back in violent reaction, landing a blow across her shoulders. The breath was nearly driven from Erienne, but she fought to stay in the saddle as the mare danced away. Timmy reached out to grab her, tearing her sleeve at the shoulder as he tried to pull her from the saddle. Erienne struck out with the whip again, now more enraged than she was afraid. She was determined not to be bested by this boorish fellow. The quirt caught his cheek, and as she drew her arm back, she brought the whip down hard on the mare's flanks, making her rear. Timmy was nearly torn from his saddle before the bridle was jerked from his hand. As his grip loosened, Erienne drove her heel into her mount's side, sending her into a full-out run.

"Ye bitch!" he roared, charging after her. "I'll see 'at ye pay!"

Suddenly a shot rang out, filling the air with a deafening crack. Startled, Erienne leaned low in the saddle, thinking that Timmy was firing at her. Then, out of the corner of her eye, she saw another horse and rider racing from the woods into the clearing, and she recognized Bundy. He was loading his musket as he came.

"Come on, ye bastard!" he shouted. "Come on, and let me fill yer hide with shot!"

Timmy Sears saw the man jerk the ramrod from the barrel and knew the weapon was almost ready to be fired again. He did not pause. Turning tail, he leaned low over the saddle and whipped his horse's flanks with his hat in a frenzied effort to escape the shot that he knew would be forthcoming. Another loud crack pierced the air, and Timmy was relieved a second later when he heard the echoing boom. He cackled in glee as a loud curse was bellowed after him, but knowing that the man would be quickly reloading, he did not waste a moment throwing back a jeer. There'd be another time when he could spend his lust upon the wench, and he vowed he would make her pay dearly.

Erienne reined her mount about to observe Timmy Sears' flight. The last she saw of him was his coattails flying out behind him as he passed over the top of a hill. She sagged in relief, taking air into her lungs in small gasps.

Bundy halted his horse beside hers and urgently questioned, "Are ye all right, mum? Did he harm ye?"

She had begun to shake in nervous reaction and could only nod.

"He's an evil man, that Timmy Sears," he stated, then glared off toward the hill over which the red-haired man had disappeared. Bundy let out his breath in a disappointed sigh. "His lordship would-na missed."

Erienne was unable to form a question with her trembling lips.

" 'Tis a good thing the master and me came back when we did, mum."

"Lord Saxton is back?" she finally managed.

"Aye, and when he found ye gone, he sent me lookin' fer ye. He won't like it when I tell him what happened. He won't like it at all."

Eleven

The high, bright moon cast a silver halo around the ebony clouds and sent a fleeting, whimsical ever-changing array of shadow and light across the hills. A seaborne breeze wafted over the land, rustling treetops and swooping with an airy rush over the moors. A few meager cottages huddled here and yonder, fading to blots of darkness as lamps were snuffed and shutters were barred for the night. There was a sleepy stillness beneath the sighing wind, a quiet assurance that all was well. None heard the thundering hooves of the fierce black stallion or saw the ominously cloaked and hooded rider who guided the steed on its breakneck race. The animal sped along, matching the wind over the narrow road that trailed through the valley. His hooves flashed like quicksilver in a brief spot of light, and his coat glistened as the muscles beneath it rolled and heaved. Flared nostrils and blazing eyes gave him the look of some dragon beast closing in for the kill, and the silent figure on his back added to the illusion that this foray was a hunt to the death. The flying cloak gave wings to the image, yet bound to the earth they were, and ever onward did they ride, never slacking the pace, never slowing for the sake of man or beast.

Some distance away, the oversized mistress of a small cottage stumbled from her sagging bed, unable to sleep beside her loudly snoring husband. She tossed a few clumps of dried peat onto the fire and stood back to watch the progress of the flames. Disturbed by the anxiety that filled her, she shivered and glanced about. There was a coldness within her stout belly, a churning of apprehension that something dreadful was about to befall them. She crossed the dirt floor, her slippers flapping loosely at her heels, and poured herself a draught of strong ale, then returned to the hearth to settle her bulk beside a rough-hewn table, laying a flabby arm upon the planks as she sipped the brew and stared into the golden flames.

Half the contents remained in the mug when she canted her head to listen, confused by the low, distant rumble. Was it thunder she heard? Or just the wind?

She lifted the mug to drink again but paused, this time to concentrate intently on the sound. It was growing louder and more consistent . . . and regular . . . like the drum of a horse's hooves.

The tankard was slammed down, and as fast as her generous frame could move, she ran to the window to throw open the shutters. A small, trembling cry came from her throat as she saw the black apparition skimming along the shadows of the trees. The cloak flapped out behind him, and horse and rider appeared to swoop down upon the cottage. Her mind was frozen with fear, and she gaped in slackjawed awe as the horse was reined to an abrupt halt before their door. The black reared in a terrible display of temper, pawing the air with flashing hooves as he shattered the stillness of the night with an angry whinny.

The woman sobbed and stumbled back from the window, her hand clutched to her throat, her face a mask of terror. The deep hood of the cloak hid the face of the rider, but she was sure she had seen a grinning skull and that this was the angel of death come to take them.

"Timmy! He's back! Timmy, wake up!" she blubbered. "Oh, Timmy love! I never doubted ye fer a moment."

Timmy Sears struggled up from the pillow, blinking his bleary eyes until he found his wife. The look of horror on her face brought him to full awareness. Grabbing his breeches, he stuffed his legs and the tail of his nightshirt into them before scrambling to the window to see what had given her such a fright. His heart jumped as he viewed the object of her fear.

"Timmy Sears!" The eerie voice sent cold shivers down the man's spine. "Come forth and die! Ye're a murderer, and hell waits for you!"

"That's what I saw!" Timmy cried. "But what is it?"

"Death!" his wife replied with conviction. "He's come after us!"

"Bolt the shutters! We can't let him in!"

"Timmy Sears," the droning voice called. "Come forth and die!"

"I ain't comin'!" Timmy bellowed and slammed the shutters closed.

An horrendous laugh tore through the night. "Then stay and burn! Stay and burn, ye devil!"

"He means ter set a torch ter us!" Timmy's voice hit a high pitch.

"He wants ye! Not me!" his wife screamed. She threw open the door, and before her husband could stop her, she fled the dwelling, shouting back over her shoulder, "I ain't burnin' fer no murderer!"

Timmy seized an ax and bolted through the door, considering the torment of fire far worse than a quick slaying. He had seen a man die in flames once, and though it had amused him at the time, he would just as soon avoid that same end. But then, death had to catch him first, and he had always been rather handy in a fight.

"Stand yer ground, ye blackhearted whoreson!" he roared. "I ain't dyin' easy!"

Booming laughter rang through the valley. "Timmy Sears! For murder I've come to avenge! Ye've killed more than once, and 'tis only fair that yer dyin' be slow."

A sword sang from its scabbard and whipped the air, flashing with a cold glint of steel beneath the moonlight, then death dismounted with the easy grace of a nightborne shade.

"What be ye after?" Timmy demanded in a squeaky croak. "I've done naught ter ye!"

"Aye, but ye have, Timmy. Ye've killed and laid the finest low, and ye shall pay yer due."

"Who are ye? Who are ye?"

"Remember the torch ye laid to the manor, Timmy? Remember the man ye saw burned?"

"Ye're not him!" Timmy shook his head in terrified disbelief. "He's dead! He's dead, I tell ye! I saw him die meself! Burned he was! Screamin' as he fell into the flames. There were others who saw him, too!"

"And who were they, Timmy, that ye can say they saw me, too? Am I not here standin' before ye and claimin' that ye were the man who did the deed?"

"Only a ghost could've escaped those flames."

"Now ye know, Timmy. Now ye know."

"Good Lord, ye are him! Ye even sound like him!"

"I've come to take ye, Timmy, down into hell with me."

"Ye've no right ter single me out! I can name ye a full dozen and more who were there!"

"Aye, and I'll be hearin' from ye now while I sharpen my sword on yer ax."

Timmy cringed and sobbed as the blade flicked all around him, nicking him here and there, and he could not meet or halt it with the clumsy ax.

"Tell me now, Timmy, before it's too late. Ye've not much time here on earth."

Death was all around him in a swirling black cloak, filling the night with laughter, and though the air was chilled, Timmy could already feel the tongues of branding fire that would scorch him in hell. He fell to his knees and began to blubber, pleading for his life and saying things he had never dared recall before.

The fragrance of roses pervaded the chamber as steam from the scented bath drifted up and dissipated in the air. The water was warm and soothing to Erienne's sore muscles, and she relaxed in the tub, leaning her back against the rim as she dribbled droplets from a sponge across her shoulders, those same that Timmy Sears had bruised only the day before. Her mind drifted back to that moment when she had entered the manor and found her husband waiting anxiously before the hearth. On hearing her approach, he had faced about to greet her with her name on his lips, but the syllables had died as he took in her torn habit. Bundy had been a step or two behind her, and it was the servant who had answered while Erienne watched the gloved hands tighten into taut fists. Lord Saxton had muttered a low, savage curse, vowing that Timmy Sears would be dealt with, and when he turned to her again, she had braced herself to hear all manner of chiding accusations. Amazingly none came. Instead, he had shown a gentle concern for her welfare and bade her take a chair while he poured a dainty draught of brandy. As she sipped the calming brew, he had hovered close, speaking in muted tones of inconsequential matters until she began to relax. Later he had come to her chambers as she was preparing for bed, but his visit was brief, and he had left with a casual promise to return in the morning.

The chamber door opened, causing Erienne considerable consternation until she recognized the quick, energetic footsteps of Tessie, then Erienne relaxed, thankful that the hour of his visit was not at hand. The footfalls were muffled as the girl came across the rug that had been recently placed in the room, and the arras swayed as she entered the small bathing chamber. A light bundle of clean, fresh-scented towels was carried in over her arm, and she placed them beside the tub before setting out a light perfumed oil in preparation for the grooming.

Erienne yielded to Tessie's penchant for methodical orderliness and rose from the bath. The maid was there immediately to pat her skin dry, using several of the linen cloths and tossing them away as they became slightly damp. Tessie began to lightly massage the attar into her back, and Erienne lifted her arms to secure her fallen tresses lest they become saturated with the oil. Her pale body, still rosy from the brisk toweling, gleamed with a soft luster in the morning light. The perfection of the slender limbs and full, ripe bosom was not lost on the one who watched.

Suddenly Tessie gasped, and Erienne looked around to see what had startled the girl and found the dark form of her husband filling the opening provided by the velvet hangings. His unheralded entry never failed to unnerve her, and her heart began a quick, solid thumping.

"Good morning, my love." A subtle hint of humor was evident in the rasping whisper.

Erienne gave an indistinct nod as she cast a surreptitious glance about for covering. The towels lay in a discarded heap near his feet on the floor, and her robe had been left on the bench in front of her dressing table, well out of her immediate grasp.

Casually Lord Saxton entered, crossing to that same bench and lowered his weight to the cushion, entrapping the garment beneath his hip. Erienne quickly gave up the idea of retrieving it and attempted to appear unaffected as Tessie sought equally as hard to continue with her task. An increasing nervousness overtook the girl when the featureless mask turned directly to face her. The master's awesome presence contrasted sharply with the stark nakedness of his mistress, and it proved too much for the young maid to bear. Murmuring a flustered, indistinct excuse, she hurried from the room.

Soft laughter echoed from the mask as the door slammed, and then the overwhelming gaze came to rest on Erienne. Her modesty chafed beneath the bold spur of his unrelenting regard. A deepening scarlet crept downward to the delicate pink of her breasts, yet her attempt to cover herself with her arms was met with another chuckle.

"Actually, my love, until you blushed, I was watching your face."

Not really knowing what to do with her hands, Erienne stared at him, fighting a deepening embarrassment. It was impossible to see behind the mask, but the heat of his gaze burned her to the core.

"Not that I would ignore everything else you seek to hide." Amusement softened the harsh edge of his voice. "Indeed, madam, were you to crook your finger in the slightest of welcome signs, I would in avid lust bear you to the bed and fulfill the requirements of a husband."

"Milord, you . . . you jest with me," she stammered, clasping her hands together lest he take some minor gesture for a sign.

"Would you test me?" He half rose from the bench. "A simple yes will do." He waited until Erienne forgot her modesty and spread both hands in front of her as if to ward him off.

"Milord, I . . ." The words of denial caught in her throat.

"I thought not." Sweeping her robe aside, he sank to the seat again and tossed the garment to her.

Clutching it close in grateful relief, Erienne looked at him hesitantly, feeling as if she had just betrayed a friend. "My lord," she murmured softly, seeking to assuage her own guilt, "I rest myself on your patience and understanding."

"Madam, have you considered that a thing dreaded is better done and put behind you?"

She managed a meager nod. "I know that, milord, but . . ."

He swept a hand to dismiss her statement. "I know! 'Tis hard for you to face that moment." He braced an elbow on his knee and leaned forward, and Erienne caught the hard, gleaming light behind the eyeholes as he regarded her. "Are you sure you can ever face that moment, madam?"

"I . . . I will . . ."

"If you had been able to choose," he interrupted, "can you name me a man whom you might have wished to marry? If there is such a one, then perhaps I could go to him . . ."

"There is no one, milord," she murmured, forcing the image of Christopher Seton from mind. She was certain that what she felt for him was only a passing fascination, and in a short time she would forget he ever existed. At least she hoped she would.

"Very well, madam." He straightened as he continued. "I did in fact come here on another matter. I have business in London with the Marquess Leicester, and I have made arrangements to take you with me."

"The Marquess Leicester?"

"An old acquaintance of the family, my dear. I'm sure you will enjoy meeting him and his charming wife. We shall be staying with them for several days, so you'll be needing clothes packed for you. I would suggest something for social affairs."

"And would you have a preference for what I wear today, milord?"

"You seem to have a fine knowledge for what is appropriate, madam. 'Twill be your choice, since my preference would not be in the realm of practicality."

Her dark, delicately shaped brows arched with an unspoken question.

"You are very lovely as you are," he explained. "But I fear you would draw more attention than I prefer."

Erienne glanced away from those hidden eyes, not knowing what to answer. By every turn of a conversation, he made it obvious that he desired her and was impatient to claim his due as husband.

"Dress yourself, madam." He rose and moved to the edge of the arras, where he announced, "For the sake of my own comportment, I shall await you downstairs."

Erienne found the preparation for the journey unexciting and the grooming tedious and without merit. If her husband chose to cast her off for another woman, she would be greatly relieved. She did not wish to be presented at her best. Yet Tessie worked diligently toward that end and left no detail wanting. The raven tresses were curled into a sedate cluster of ringlets that was secured at the nape of her neck. Frilly garters were donned to hold the knee-length silk stockings in place. A corset was tightened over the delicate chemise, and then a traveling dress of deep, rich peacock velvet was eased in place. The lower half of the sleeves and the standing collar of the garment were ornately stitched with silken threads. Froths of delicately pleated pink lace lay against her throat and filled the slashed and flared cuffs. A small, padded, false rump supported the fullness and longer length of the skirt at the back. Lastly, a pert hat with a sweeping plume was placed at a saucy angle over the carefully con-

structed coiffure, and it was here that Erienne made a protest. Though the hat was in excellent taste, she did not wish to give the slightest impression that she was competing with Claudia Talbot for the most extravagant millinery.

"But mum, ye're the wife of a lord now," Aggie argued. " 'Tis yer duty ter dress yerself accordin'ly. Ye would not have folk whisper that the master is tightfisted with ye, now would ye? Especially when he's spent such a fortune for yer garments. See for yerself how grand ye look in the clothes he bought ye. 'Twould be a waste not to indulge yerself in the luxuries he's provided. Go on. Take a look." She urged Erienne to the long pane of silvered glass and waited while her young mistress contemplated her reflection. "Well? Do ye look like some milkmaid's daughter, or a grand lady?"

Erienne had to admit that Tessie had done wonders for her appearance. No one could call her dowdy by any stretch of the imagination. She could even understand to some degree why Lord Saxton thought her pretty. She had good features, clear skin, a nice long neck, and thick, shining hair. Though slender and slightly taller than average, she had no need of padding to fill the top of her chemise or round out her hips.

A bit of mutiny still showed in her countenance as she considered what her husband's reaction might be to her appearance. With the long trip to London still ahead of her, and not knowing what the sleeping arrangements would be while they were en route and after they arrived, she was very cautious about soliciting any more of his attention.

Aggie lightly pinched her cheeks to bring forth the color. " 'Tis a rare sight ye are, mum, and anyone can see why ye've taken the master's fancy. Ye're lovely. Just lovely. And it wouldn't harm nothin' if ye were ter add a bit o' a smile."

Erienne managed a lame, uninterested grimace.

In return the housekeeper gave her a shaming look. "Mum, if ye allow me ter say it, I've seen better on a steamin' clam."

Tessie clapped a hand over her mouth to muffle a giggle, while a deeper color rose in Erienne's cheeks. She gritted out another smile until Aggie sighed in resignation and went to the door.

"If that be the best ye can muster, I suppose 'twill have ter do."

Erienne felt somewhat harassed. Since Aggie's main objective seemed to be offspring for the Saxton family, Erienne was beginning to suspect that the woman was entirely unsympathetic to her plight and was prodding her into pleasing Lord Saxton.

A short time later, she was confronted with even more evidence that the housekeeper was striving to bring about an intimate and congenial relationship between master and mistress. The coach was loaded with their baggage at the front door, and Lord Saxton had paused beside it to discuss the route with Tanner. When Erienne emerged from the manor, she won her husband's immediate regard, and from his lack of response to the driver's question, made it obvious that she had his undivided attention. However, it was not his actions that led to her assurance that Aggie was trying to guide affairs, but the appearance of Tessie and her quick ascent to the driver's seat. Settling a heavy woolen cloak about her shoulders, the maid took a place beside Bundy.

Erienne lifted an inquiring gaze to her husband, thinking he had ordered the maid to ride on top.

Mistaking her unspoken question, he stated, "You'll be needing Tessie's assistance while we're at the Leicesters." A mocking chuckle came from the mask. "Unless, of course, you can abide my assistance at your bath."

Erienne would not give him the satisfaction of seeing her blush and was quick to suggest, "Surely, milord, the girl could share the comfort of the coach with us."

"Oh, no mum." Tessie shook her head, and her round face displayed her brimming excitement as she gathered the cloak about her. "Aggie made me promise that I would ride up here with Tanner."

The quirk in Erienne's brow deepened as her suspicions about Aggie were further confirmed. Erienne made a silent pledge to thwart this matchmaking arrangement after their first stop. No doubt the girl would be more willing to accept her offer after she had had some experience at being crushed between the two men.

This time when Erienne climbed into the coach, she had her choice of seats, and after making her selection, her husband doffed his cloak and joined her there. Leaning back, he relaxed against the cushions, stretching his twisted foot out toward the side while resting his left leg casually against her own. Furtively she glanced toward the offending limb and saw the shape of it was long and leanly muscular. No difference could be noted in the other thigh. His boots came to his knees, hiding any defect there, and though the skirt of his coat had been drawn back, his hips were concealed beneath a long waistcoat.

Attempting to avoid the contact, Erienne braced herself in the corner, but with every bump and lurch of the carriage, she slipped against him again. He made no effort to move away, and they traveled along for some distance as she fought in vain to keep her place.

" 'Tis foolishness you know," the low, rough voice finally broke the silence and gained her immediate attention.

"Foolishness, milord?" He had not deemed even to glance her way, and she looked in bemusement at his stark profile.

"This continuous effort to avoid touching me. 'Tis foolishness."

Any denial was stricken from her tongue by the truth of his words. She was his wife, and one day she must bear his children, however distasteful the idea appeared to her now. Resisting the inevitable was no better than swimming upstream against a mighty torrent of water. Someday she would have to abandon her resistance and let the mighty rushing force take her where it would.

In their brief marriage she had become aware that wisdom was essential when dealing with Lord Saxton. However gross his appearance was, his mind was not lame, and he read her with unerring ease, which placed her at a great disadvantage, for she knew absolutely nothing about him. The thought came to her that if she wanted to survive this marriage with her sanity intact, she must first begin to accept him as a man, and perhaps then she could come to know him as her husband.

Her gaze lightly touched his frame. She had so much to learn about him, and to gain the knowledge, she had to rely upon a more pragmatic form of learning and to make inquiries, since she was not adept at guessing his thoughts. Much as it frightened her, she took a deep breath to steady her trembling nerves and broached the subject that most intrigued her.

"I have been wondering, milord, how it was possible for you to survive the fire. There is nothing left of the manor's east wing but rubble, which seems to indicate that it was no small blaze. I have tried but I cannot imagine how you managed to escape . . ."

"I am no ghost, madam," he replied bluntly.

"I have never believed in ghosts, milord," she murmured softly.

"Neither do you believe me a flesh-and-blood man." A long silence ensued before he asked, "Are you afraid I'll prove to be some deformed monster in your bed, madam?"

Erienne's cheeks burned with the heat of her embarrassment. Her gaze dropped to the thinly gloved hand clenched tightly in her lap, and she spoke in a small voice. "I did not mean to rouse your ire, milord."

He gave an odd shrug. "All brides are curious about their husbands. You have more reason than most."

"I am curious . . ." she began unsteadily, "not because I'm concerned about going to bed with you, but . . ." Suddenly realizing how her words could be misconstrued, she bit her lip worriedly and awaited his reaction.

It was as she suspected. He pounced on her statement with zeal. "If that be the case, madam, then perhaps you will welcome me in your chambers tonight. I will be more than happy to prove myself a capable husband. I can request only a single room for us at the inn, and we can warm each other through the night."

"I . . . would rather not, milord," she replied in a strained whisper.

His hooded head dipped briefly. "As you wish, my love. I shall await your pleasure."

Though her relief was great, Erienne dared not release an audible sigh. Sometimes there was safety in ignorance, and she was content to let the silence continue undisturbed for however long he chose.

When they approached the bridge at Mawbry, Erienne directed her interest to the crowd of people gathered on it. They were leaning over the side to view something in the stream. As the prancing team came toward them, the villagers stepped out of the way, but a small cart blocked the far end of the bridge, making it impossible for the coach to pass. Wondering what had attracted the onlookers, Erienne sat forward in her seat. She scanned the passing faces for those familiar to her, then her gaze went beyond them to the bank on the far side of the stream, where several men were standing. Her eyes widened as she found the object of their concern. A man was sprawled head downward beside the stream, his arms flung wide in a grotesque fashion. The middle and upper part of his body and head were covered with blood, while the eyes stared unblinkingly at the leaden skies above. Even through the macabre mask, Erienne could see the shriek of horror stillborn on the twisted lips.

She shrank back in the seat, closing her eyes to shut out the horrid sight and pressing a trembling hand against her lips as she struggled against a sudden wave of nausea. Lord Saxton took note of her ashen face and leaned forward to see what had upset her, then finding the reason, immediately rapped on the carriage roof with his cane. The small door behind the driver's seat opened and the face of Bundy appeared.

"Aye, milord?"

"See if you can find out what has happened down there and who that poor devil is," he ordered.

"Right away, milord."

After an exchange with several people on the bridge, Bundy called to Ben, who ambled forth to supply the information. " 'Tis Timmy Sears. Some'un stuck him, then slit his throat ter finish 'im off. His poor widder is at the inn now, and she's swearin' the last she saw o' Timmy, he were gittin' ready ter fight an angel o' death way up by their place. A night rider dressed all in black."

"Damn!"

The oath was barely heard, even by Erienne, who turned to her husband in surprise. He gripped the handle of his cane with such intensity that his fingers stood out like talons beneath the soft hide. She remembered his assurances concerning the man and wondered if this was his method of handling unruly rowdies. Whether his reaction was sincere anger over Timmy's death or a ruse to hide an act of murder, she could not say.

"Tell them to send for the sheriff," Lord Saxton called up to Bundy brusquely. "Then find someone to get that cart moved out of our way."

"Aye, milord," the servant replied and snapped the small portal closed.

Lord Saxton braced both hands on the handle of the cane and leaned back in the seat. Though the featureless mask gave no hint, Erienne sensed his tension and could not bring herself to question him until the cart was muscled aside and the carriage was moving again. Plucking up her courage, she managed to ask, "Are you angry because Timmy was killed?"

"Uhm!" The grunt was noncommittal.

Erienne could not decide if his answer was an aye or a nay. In trembling disquiet, she tried again, knowing she would be haunted by too many suspicions if she did not pursue the matter. "Did you talk with Timmy . . . about what happened yesterday?"

The face of the mask came around, and she was impaled by those piercing eyes.

"Murder has no hand in justice, madam. I did not kill him."

The answer was curt and final, and Erienne pressed back against the seat, daring no further word, not even an apology. She had braved too much as it was.

The hooded head turned away from her until the leather visage faced the window. She had no choice but to join her husband in silent observation of the countryside they passed.

Nightfall was threatening when the coach was halted before an inn. Erienne's hesitation became obvious as Lord Saxton offered up his hand to aid her descent, and when she could not quell her qualms enough to accept, the iron-thewed fingers closed with gentle care about her own. When she stepped to the ground, he made no attempt to release her hand, and a long moment passed as he stared down at her. Unable to control the quaking that had seized her, she searched the fearsome mask for some hint of his intent, but the deepening dusk forbade any glimpse of the eyes. He drew in a breath as if to speak, but as she waited, he released it again in a heavy sigh and shook his leather-garbed head. His hand dropped away from her own and swept aside in an invitation for her to follow Bundy.

Only a few patrons were in the common room, and those grew suddenly silent as Lord Saxton followed his lady in. A deathlike stillness fell over the room until a garishly garbed fop who had imbibed too much banged his empty tankard on the table and loudly called for a refill. When none came, he lifted himself from his chair, snatched his vest down with a jerk, and after several sidesteps managed to turn about, just in time to see Erienne moving toward the stairway that stood behind him. He forgot about his mission to the barkeep as his gaze ranged the full length of her. His eyes took on a brightness that betrayed the wayward path of his mind, while his smile closely compared to a lecherous leer. He swept her a low, clumsy bow that from his point of view was nothing short of graceful and flamboyant.

"My fair lady . . ." he declared gallantly, then sought to rise. His limbs refused to respond adequately, and disturbing his balance by his attempt, he teetered precariously on one foot before falling into a nearby chair. After a moment he raised his gaze, but seeing only the back of Lord Saxton's flowing cloak where the daintier form had been a moment before, he blinked until finally his flicking eyelids slowed their movement and rested undisturbed against his paunchy cheeks. Almost as quickly as they settled, a high-pitched, whistling snore issued from his lips.

Dinner was brought to Erienne's room, and Lord Saxton joined her for a short time until Tessie began to lay out her bedclothes. To Erienne's relief, he excused himself for the evening. His ponderous footfalls echoed in the empty hall, and for a brief moment later, she heard the door across the hall open and close, shutting off the sound. Long after Tessie had left, Erienne sat beside the fireplace in her room and stared into the flames, trying to convince herself that there was no reason to fear her husband. If somehow, by dint of will, she could overcome her trepidations and give herself as she had vowed, perhaps with the first hurdle past her, her apprehensions would recede. Yet now the gory vision of Timmy Sears intruded into her thoughts, and she knew it would be some time before she could dismiss that from memory.

The inn grew quiet as the guests retired for the night. As she slipped between the downy comforters, Erienne detected a distant thump and a scrape, but when nothing more was heard, she finally relaxed and allowed sleep to overtake her troubled thoughts.

The night aged, and the sound came again. A thump and a scrape in the hall, then a light rapping on her door. For a moment Erienne's wits were scattered. She had been roused from a deep sleep, and the tightly woven threads of slumber refused to free her mind. The tapping was repeated, and with a start Erienne came fully awake, realizing it had to be Lord Saxton at her door. She could think of only one reason for his coming, and that was to share her bed.

Her whole body quaked as she rose from the bed. Willing herself to accept her fate, she hurriedly slipped into her robe, but her hands were shaking when she lit a candle from the fireplace, and the wavering flame of the candle gave ready evidence of her nervousness. Needing no reminder of how frightened she was, she left the candlestand on a table. Her nerves stretched taut as she crossed the room, and her mind raced with wild imaginings that tore at her resolve. The rapping came again, and biting a trembling lip, she paused at the portal to summon whatever courage she could muster.

The key had barely turned in the lock before the door was shoved roughly open and she was flung back. She gasped in shock as she saw her mistake. It was not her husband at all, but the sodden roué from the common room. Garbed in breeches, stockings, and a loose-sleeved shirt that hung open to reveal a flabby chest, he leaned with insolent boldness against the doorjamb and held up a flagon of wine.

"Here, missy." He waved the bottle to tempt her. "I brought ye a little somethin' ter enjoy afore we gets down ter serious matters." Laughing, he lazily sauntered inside and kicked the door shut behind him.

Erienne had regained her spunk as soon as she realized her hour of doom was not at hand, but for caution's sake, she retreated, giving the man a crisp warning. "I'm not alone here. My husband is in the room across the hall."

"Aye, I saw the gimp, and I figured ye'd be needin' some good company tonight." The fop chortled and flexed his arms. "If I can't whip the likes o' him, I should be layin' in me grave."

"If you don't forsake this foolishness," she retorted, "he will accommodate you. He is considered a marksman . . ."

"Bah! I'll be well gone before he drags himself from bed." The drunk set the bottle aside, and his eyes fastened on her in burning lust. He lifted his chest to lessen the girth of the soft paunch that overran the top of his breeches and pulled his shirt free. "You know, if yer husband were any kind o' man at all, he'd be here with you. I wouldn't leave a pretty little thing like you alone, no indeed."

"I will most certainly scream if you don't leave," she cried, outraged at the audacity of the man.

"Aw, c'mon, duckie." The fellow was unabashed by her threat. He was sure she would enjoy what he had to offer. "No need ter get yerself up in a ruffle. I'll just have me due and be off. No harm done ter ye 'cept a touch o' wear and tear."

He lunged at her, but Erienne had avoided many a grasping plunge and stepped nimbly from his path. Before he came around, she snatched up the fireplace poker and laid if firmly across his backside, eliciting a muffled yowl from the man. He came up hard against the panels of the wall and whirled, rubbing his posterior where the poker had cruelly bruised him.

"Ho! So's ye want ter play it mean, do ye?" He glared at her. "Well, ol' Gyles can be just as rough as milady wants."

Spreading his arms, he came after her. His eyes spoke of vengeance as strongly as his voice had, but Erienne was undaunted. The fire of defiance snapped in her own eyes, and she faced him, weaving the poker in front of her as she fell back until, much to her dismay, she came up against the side of the bed and was trapped there by the advancing debauchee. Seeing his goal near, Gyles chortled in glee and dove at her. Erienne was quicker. She ducked low and spun to one side, avoiding his far-flung reach, but the poker was swept away before she could strike. Gyles collided with the bed and bounced once on the mattress, then came to his feet again as she started toward the door. His arm stretched out and he seized her by the scruff of the neck. Erienne wasted no moment fighting over the loose robe. She jerked free of its flowing sleeves, leaving it in his grasp.

Raising his bewildered gaze from the empty garment, Gyles saw the sleek body barely concealed by the diaphanous gown fleeing toward the door. The lust flared brighter in his eyes, and he plowed after her, disregarding the sheet that twined about his foot until it was snared tight. Erienne heard the solid crash of the heavy body against the floor, and in a quick movement, she turned and flipped the blankets over him. His muffled curses filled the room as he twisted and roiled in an effort to get free. Erienne did not stay to help him but flew toward the door. When Gyles managed to free his head, he saw only the hem of her gown flit through the open portal. Muttering a lewd promise, he struggled up and staggered after her.

Pausing in the hall, Erienne glanced about in indecision. Though she feared the man himself, Lord Saxton was the only one who might provide some haven for her. She heard the plodding gait of the man behind her and, making up her mind, ran across the hall. After a quick rap on the door, she twisted the latch and bolted into her husband's room. The room was shaded in deep shadows, with only a dull shaft of moonlight streaming in through the window. It was enough to outline dimly the shape of the man who rose naked from the bed. Seeing him thus, Erienne halted in sudden confusion, not knowing whether to stay or go. The fop took the choice from her. Plunging through the doorway behind her, he saw her silhouette framed against the window and eagerly sought to throw his arms about her. He failed to see the larger shadow that moved in the darkness. As Gyles swooped to take her, Erienne spun about to avoid his reach but stumbled to her knees as his hand caught the back of her gown. The delicate fabric split down the front, and before the rending tear was complete a savage growl came, bringing the lusting roué upright with a start of surprise.

Gyles gasped as another's hand gripped his wrist in a painful vise, and in the next instant he felt a solid jolt of a hard fist in his belly. He doubled over, holding his middle, and as he moaned in pain, a bare knee came upward, striking his chin and flipping him backward onto the floor. He rolled and blindly scrambled for the door, crawling on his hands, belly, and knees until he gained the safety of the hall, and there sobbed in relief at having escaped that ill-tempered demon in the room. The door was slammed behind him, and Erienne clutched her gown together as her husband limped back to her. The indistinct glow of the moon cast more shadow than light, but a dull, silvery-hued ray slanted down across his body from midwaist to upper thigh, showing more detail than Erienne cared to view. She saw no deformity. The hips were slim, the belly flat and taut, and despite her innocence, she was inclined to believe he was as much of a man as any could hope to be.

He must have felt her gaze, for his reaction brought a sudden hotness flooding into Erienne's cheeks. Quickly dropping her gaze, she pushed herself up from the floor, thankful for the fall of long hair that formed a blanketing shield about her hot face. He stepped to lend his assistance, slipping a hand to her waist as she rose. Though she braced herself for the contact, the warmth of his touch penetrated the thin cloth.

"Are you all right?" His whisper no longer bore the lisping quality the mask lent to his voice, but still it seemed oddly strained.

Erienne kept her gaze carefully averted. "I'm sorry for the intrusion, milord. I heard a knock on my door, and as I thought it was you, I opened it."

"No need for your apology, madam," his rasping whisper assured her. "I can well understand why the man made the attempt. You are a rare prize indeed, and I cannot be offended by your willingness to admit me into your chambers." His hand lightly caressed her back through the fragile fabric, and though she stood unmoving, every nerve in her body tightened. "Will you stay in here with me?"

She bit her lip. The moment to put aside all refusal was at hand, yet for the life of her she could not say the word. Even after seeing him unclothed and being assured that he was at least partly unscarred, the sure certainty of the hideousness that remained held her at bay. "I . . . I would rather go back to my room, milord . . . if you don't mind."

His hand dropped away. "If you will then wait a moment, madam, I will see that the innkeeper is informed about this man's penchant for attacking his guests."

He reached for the robe lying across the end of the bed and shrugged into it. Erienne's gaze lifted, but the darkness cloaked his form, and her curiosity, as uncertain as it was, was not appeased. She came quickly to the determination that it was just as well, for she might regret seeing his scarred face. He pulled on his mask, boots, and gloves before entering the meager pool of light shining through the window. Moving to the bed, he tossed back the bedcovers.

"You might as well stay warm while you wait," he said, and as Erienne hesitated, his mockery surfaced as a gentle jibe. "You're not opposed to sharing my bed after I leave it, are you?"

Daring no comment, she crawled into the warm softness of it and was at once reminded by the lingering essence of the time she had awakened in Saxton Hall to find herself in his bed. That same pleasant but elusive scent had teased her senses then, just as it did now. There was some strange quality about it that she could not quite lay a finger to, a hauntingly vague memory of another time and place. Yet she could not quite bring the moment into focus. It was beyond her grasp.

Twelve

When the carriage turned up the lane leading to the sprawling country estate of the Leicesters, Erienne realized that her husband was not without influential friends. Here the grounds were well tended and orderly, a far cry from the wildness and rugged terrain surrounding Saxton Hall. The mansion reigned in stately splendor, and at her first glimpse of it, Erienne became immensely thankful that Tessie had enticed her to wear a rich costume of deep red velvet.

Lord Saxton spoke without preamble as they neared the house. "Though you may abhor and detest the form that is thrust upon me, madam, I assure you the Leicesters are exceptional people. They are indeed old friends of my family, and I greatly savor their friendship. There are several things I must set aright, and they have given me invaluable advice and assistance toward those ends."

A butler, grandly outfitted in white wig, red coat, and white breeches, met them at the door and took their wraps. They were promptly escorted to a drawing room, where the marquess and his lady were waiting to receive them. Erienne was somewhat over-whelmed by the wealthy decor, but when the marquess crossed the room, eagerly extending a bony hand in greeting to Lord Saxton, her attention turned to him and the small, trim woman who hung back, seeming reluctant to come forward as she glanced hesitantly toward the masked one.

White of hair, narrow of frame, and slightly stooped, the marquess gave the physical impression of age, yet his rosy cheeks, twinkling blue eyes, and ever-willing smile were the epitome of eternal youth.

"So kind of you to come this soon after your marriage, Stuart," he said warmly. "I was hoping I would be able to meet your young bride, and now that I see her, I can understand what has driven you in such a fever lately."

Lord Saxton slipped his gloved hand beneath his wife's arm. "The fever must be contagious. We had to fight off at least one smitten swain en route."

The marquess' eyes twinkled as he gallantly bestowed a kiss on Erienne's hand. "I suppose Stuart has been completely neglectful of telling you anything about us."

"Stuart?" She glanced at her husband with wide uncertainty. " 'Twould seem there is much he has failed to tell me."

"You must forgive him, child," the marquess begged with a chuckle. "His manners have been much afflicted by his enchantment with you. I'm sure his mother is as horrified as you are."

Erienne's surprise deepened. This was the first hint she had had of any living Saxton kin, and she lifted a wondering brow at her husband. "Your mother?"

Lord Saxton gave her arm a gentle squeeze. "You will meet her in good time, my love."

"His father and I were as close as brothers," the marquess interjected. "His death was a most dreadful thing, simply dreadful. And of course, the burning of the manse . . . vicious! I shall not rest until we find the culprits responsible for the deeds." He shook his head, for a moment seeming troubled, then suddenly he brightened and patted her hand. "You are a lovely little thing. As lovely as my own Anne."

His wife laughed chidingly as he held out a hand to her. She came to stand beside him and rested a long, slender hand on his arm. "Oh, Phillip, your eyes deceive you. I have never been as beautiful as this child."

She took Erienne's hand in her own. "I hope we shall be the best of friends, my dear."

For the most part Anne kept her gaze averted from Lord Saxton, but whenever she did deem to glance at him, she almost frowned. Her distress did not escape his notice.

"Have you come to hate me in my absence, Anne?" he questioned.

Angrily she flipped a hand toward his mask and stated quite brusquely, "I hate that thing!"

Erienne was amazed by the woman's reaction but had little time to dwell on the reply as Lord Saxton pulled her arm through his. He patted her hand gently while holding it firmly in place against her attempts to withdraw it.

"Believe me, Anne, when I say that my own wife hates what is beneath it even more than you do the mask." Turning, he bowed over the hand he had entrapped. "We shall return to you as soon as our affairs permit. Until then, my love, I leave you in the tender care of our gracious hostess."

He straightened and with his halting gait followed Phillip from the room. Anne seemed to grit her teeth and flinch at each thump of the thick-soled boot. When the door closed behind the men, she glared at it a long moment. Erienne could not be sure, but she thought she heard the woman mutter beneath her breath, "Stubborn whelp!"

"Madam? Did you speak?" Erienne asked in surprise.

Anne faced her with wide, innocent eyes and a bright smile. " 'Twas nothing, my dear. Nothing at all. I was only murmuring to myself. It comes with age, you know . . . talking to oneself."

She put a gentle arm around the younger woman. "My dear, you must be simply famished after that long ride, and those men have completely abandoned us for the sake of their dreadful business. We'll have a bite to eat together, and then we'll take a carriage ride about town. The day is simply gorgeous, and it would be a shame for us to waste it waiting for our husbands. Why, if we plan it right, we could be gone the whole afternoon."

They were indeed, and Erienne was entertained throughout in a manner she had not thought possible by a stranger. Anne Leicester was as gracious and kind as she was witty and warm. Her lighthearted charm was infectious, and Erienne felt the tension melt away with the laughter.

The evening swept past in a relaxed and congenial atmosphere. In the presence of the older couple Lord Saxton seemed a little less frightening. While dining, Erienne even managed to remain calm beneath his unwavering stare. As was his habit, he abstained from food and drink, choosing to eat in privacy at a later hour, and bestowed upon her his full attention.

It was late before they retired, and Erienne glided effortlessly to her room, pleasantly warmed with the wine she had sipped. She was aware of her husband following at his awkward pace, but the sharp edge of her fear had been blunted since their arrival at the Leicesters, and the sound failed to send the usual shiver running through her.

Lord Saxton was the one who felt the bite of discomfort as he admired the gentle, swaying hips and the incredibly narrow curve of her waist. His restraint was tested far beyond any limit he had ever considered, and fully aware that another disrobing might see the end of it, he took refuge in the adjoining chambers.

As she snuggled in bed, Erienne gave a great deal of thought to the proximity of her fearsome husband, for that awkward pacing continued until her eyes sagged with sleep. Her dreams were widespread and fleeting, like the clouds that chased the moon beyond the terrace doors. At times she floated in a vague, half-awake awareness or sank deep in the nether realms of Morpheus and was never quite sure through which she wandered. Shadows flitted across her bed as streams of silvery light flooded through the crystal panes, casting images that intertwined with her slumbering ventures.

A more manly form took shape in the thickening fog of her mind, and she strove to find the detail of him in the darkness. He stood tall and silent at the end of her bed, his furred chest and broad shoulders void of shirt, with a thumb hooked casually in the waistband of his breeches while his other arm hung relaxed at his side. His dark hair was short and tousled, his jaw lean and firm, and she imagined grayish-green eyes glowing at her from the shadows. The presence stayed with her, unmoving, unchanging, always staring. With a sigh, she turned her head on the pillow and in her dreams she saw him move close. His fingers plucked at the fastenings of her gown, and she felt the hot, licking flames of desire sweep through her as a warm mouth caressed the soft crest of her breast. The pulsing heat throbbed in her loins and spread like flaming oil through her veins. The face loomed above her, and sudden recognition of the man she had conjured brought her upright with a startled gasp.

"Christopher!"

Erienne glanced about her, peering into the shadows and dark recesses of the room. They were empty. Nothing stirred in the night-shaded stillness, and with a trembling sigh, she sagged back against the pillows, bemused and . . . disappointed?

He had only been a figment of her imagination, and yet her young body had been aroused by the imagined kisses and the bold caresses. Her clamoring heart refused to soften its deafening beat, and she pressed an unsteady hand over her bosom as if to slow its frantic pounding. It was a long hour before the pulse in her throat quieted, and she again relaxed in the embrace of sleep.

Shimmering rays of light streamed through the bedroom doors, filling the chamber with a rich abundance. Erienne stretched in the luxurious comfort of the bed, pulling up her long hair to spread it in thick waves across the pillows, then her brows creased in a troubled frown as she remembered the path her mind had wandered while she slept. Even in her dreams she could not escape the Yankee.

Disturbed by the betrayal of her subconscious mind, she donned a velvet robe and slippers and stepped out onto the terrace. The fresh scent of a frosty morn wafted on a gentle breeze that swirled through the trees and shrubs. She inhaled deeply of its fragrance, then watching her breath cloud before her eyes, blew long streamers of white into the chilled air. The cold penetrated her wrap, yet she was thankful for its crispness, for it cleared her mind of the haunting memory of her dreams.

The distant sound of muted voices drifted to her on a gentle rush of wind, making her pause. Peering through the trees, she recognized the dark shape of her husband moving through the carefully tended garden. At his side was a woman garbed in a long, hooded cloak. She was taller than Anne and moved with the confident grace of one well assured of her station in life. Erienne could not hear what was being said, but the woman seemed to be pleading with him as she walked along. Now and then she held an arm out in plaintive supplication, and Lord Saxton would answer with a slow shake of his head. After a time, the woman paused and faced the dark figure, laying a hand on his arm as she spoke intently for some time. The masked one turned away slightly, as if reluctant to listen, and waited in silence until she finished. He explained briefly, and again the woman made an appeal. He gave another small, negative shake of his head, and with a brief bow of farewell, he swung his heavily shod foot about and left her. The woman made as if to stop him but apparently thought better of it. After a moment she turned, and with head lowered, slowly walked into the house.

Confused by what she had seen, Erienne returned to her chambers. It was none of her business, of course, what her husband discussed with anyone. She had gained no right to question him, nor had she the nerve to do so. Still, the scene she had just witnessed left her curious. The woman had obviously felt no fear of Lord Saxton, for she had touched him freely, something his wife could not do.

A short time later Erienne joined the Leicesters for the morning meal, and her bemusement deepened when she was informed that Lord Saxton had left. Since they had connecting rooms, she thought it rather strange that he had refrained from visiting her in her chambers and delivering the message himself.

"Did he say when he would be back?" she inquired.

"No, my dear," Anne replied kindly. "But I assure you, you'll have no time to miss him. We shall be attending an assembly this evening, and you'll be too busy enjoying yourself even to think of your husband."

Erienne doubted the possibility of the woman's statement. Stuart Saxton was not a figure one could easily forget. His dreadful appearance burdened her mind like an oppressive weight every hour of the day.

That evening when she was dressing for the affair, a small silk box was delivered to her bedchamber, and the meticulously garbed servant who brought it decorously announced that the gift was from Lord Saxton. A note written in a bold hand and signed with the single initial "S" accompanied the box and bade her to honor the Saxton family by wearing the gift to the assembly. Erienne was puzzled by the aloof manner in which her husband was conveying messages and presents. She did not believe he had grown shy of late and worried that his absence might have stemmed from a growing vexation with her.

When she lifted the lid and beheld the triple-strand pearl choker resting on the bed of royal blue silk, her apprehensions ceased to exist. It seemed unlikely that her husband would bestow such an expensive piece of jewelry on her when he was angry with her.

Small diamonds and a large sapphire adorned the clasp, and more of the same precious gems embellished the pair of pearl earrings that completed the set. The gift was far better than she deserved, she mused as the dreams of the night past came back to accuse her. It would be much more beneficial to their marriage if she kept her fantasies to a more wifely path.

Seeking to fulfill Lord Saxton's request and present herself in a regal manner, Erienne chose a pale blue satin gown to complement the jewelry. A white fichu trimmed with a delicate lace sewn with tiny seed pearls was draped to bare her shoulders coyly. Tiny clusters of seed pearls nested in the tufts of the satin skirt. Tessie swept her hair back from her face and painstakingly curled it in a mass of ringlets that fell in soft tiers from the crown of her head and ended at the nape of her neck. The necklace and earrings were donned, and her reflection bore out the fact that she would at least do the Saxton name no harm.

She had only heard stories from her mother of the social gatherings of the elite and was rather nervous over what was to be her first experience. When they arrived, Anne introduced her about to the different lords and their ladies as the new mistress of Saxton Hall, gaily explaining that the manor was just as far north in England as London was south. By keeping up a stream of vivacious chatter, the woman gave little time for serious questions, and if any were overly curious, she laughingly swept her guest on to the next group.

It seemed as if the Leicesters knew nearly everyone present, for the circle around them widened. Erienne soon began to wonder if there would ever be an end to the formalities. Intertwined with the introductions were comments on the happenings in France. Everyone was aghast at the massacres of political prisoners in the streets of Paris and quickly agreed that such a thing could not happen in England. The fact that the French King had been taken prisoner was shocking, and what was even more disruptive to the orderly English mind was that many expected him to be executed before too much time elapsed.

Several ladies, anxious to speak with Anne, wedged their way in front of Erienne, separating her from the older couple. Left more or less to herself for the moment, she took the opportunity to look through the hall. The rooms, though elegant, were a trifle stuffy, and feeling in need of a breath of fresh air, she moved toward the tall French doors that led out onto the narrow balconies. She had almost gained her goal when a satin-garbed gentleman seized her arm. Surprised, she looked around and found herself staring into Lord Talbot's smirking grin.

"Why, 'tis Erienne! Sweet, little Erienne!" He was astounded at his good fortune and made only a small effort to subdue the lust that shone in his eyes as he warmly appraised her. "My dear, you are simply ravishing. 'Tis amazing what the proper clothes will do for one."

Erienne tried politely to disengage her arm, but he glanced about imperiously, appearing not to notice as he arched a darkened eyebrow.

"You came . . . unescorted?"

"Oh, no, milord," she rushed to assure him. "I am here with the Leicesters. We . . . ah . . . were separated . . ."

"You mean your husband didn't . . . ?" He let the incomplete question hang with heavy innuendo.

"N-no," Erienne stammered, feeling the full weight of the implied neglect. "I mean . . . he had pressing business elsewhere."

"Tsk! Tsk!" Lord Talbot twitched the ends of his thin, waxed moustache as he pursed his lips in mild disdain. "The idea! Leaving such a lovely wife to fend for herself. Well, from what I hear of him, I can well understand his reluctance to appear in public and why he chooses to wear that hideous mask. Poor devil!"

Erienne's spine stiffened, and she was rather amazed at the hot indignation she experienced at this slur against her husband. After all, the statements had been very much a part of her own thinking. "I have seen no evidence that Lord Saxton is anything but human, milord."

Nigel Talbot pulled back his coat and, resting a hand on his hip, flexed a knee and leaned close, in the process gaining a clear downward view of the upper curves of her bosom underneath the fichu. "Tell me, my dear," he half whispered, "what does he really look like beneath that mask? Is he the horribly scarred wretch everyone thinks he is?"

Erienne stood rigid, stunned by the affront. "If he wanted people to know, milord, I'm sure he would give up wearing the mask."

"Is it possible"—Talbot straightened and glanced quickly to either side, then pressed a heavily scented lace handkerchief to his lips as if to squelch a threatening giggle—"that even *you* don't know what he looks like?"

"I have seen him in the dark," she stated, chafing under his snickering arrogance. It was one time she wished Lord Saxton would appear. She had no doubt that by his mere presence he could silence the muffled chortles and pale even the painted blush on the man's cheeks.

"In the dark, you say?" His eyes gleamed knowingly.

Lifting her slim nose to a lofty height, she refused to answer him. She would not gratify the man's salacious bent by explaining that the moment to which she was referring had naught to do with the intimacies of marriage.

Talbot was undaunted. His gaze was slow and pointedly bold as he perused her soft and exquisite radiance. "There is something about marriage that always enhances the beauty of a woman. I must compliment your husband on his excellent taste, at least in choosing a wife. However, I will chide him on his neglect of such a fair creature."

Turning slightly away from her, he scanned the crowded room. "I came here with several friends, all gentlemen of good account, of course." He drew himself up as if the association enhanced his own importance. "When last I saw them, they had obtained companionship for the evening and were preparing to leave, but I can hardly ignore my duty to Avery and leave his daughter unattended amid strangers. I see no help for it, my dear. You will have to come with me."

"I assure you, milord, I am quite well escorted," she insisted. "You needn't have a care."

"Nonsense, child." He dismissed her statement with a wave of his lacy handkerchief. "If you were being looked after, you'd not be standing here alone. Why, any disreputable scoundrel could whisk you off, and no one would ever know."

"How true!" Erienne mused derisively.

Suddenly Talbot waved to someone across the room, and Erienne spotted three richly garbed men, each with a lavishly gowned woman on his arm. One of them returned Nigel's gesture and pointed toward the entrance with a leering, knowing grin; then as a body the three couples moved in that direction.

"Come, my dear," Nigel commanded, assuming Erienne's assent. She opened her mouth to protest, but a waggled finger in front of her nose silenced her. "I really must have a care for Avery's daughter. I will hear no more of you staying here alone."

"Lord Talbot, I am not alone!" she cried in desperation.

"Most assuredly not while I'm with you, my dear." He tucked her hand beneath his elbow and held it firmly in place as he half dragged her through the crowd. "You know, I was really quite miffed that your father chose to put you on the block without consulting me. I am sure we could have arrived at some equitable arrangement."

Erienne tried to give him as much resistance as she could without creating a scene. "I don't think my father was aware that you were seeking a wife."

"Heaven forbid!" Lord Talbot chortled. "The thought of marriage never entered my mind."

" 'Twas a condition of the roup," Erienne panted as she was towed rudely along.

"Tish, tosh!" Talbot sneered airily. "A few hundred pounds would have settled your father on that score."

They were in the foyer, and as they passed a slim column, she hooked her arm around it. With that anchor, she snatched her other arm free and immediately feared that she had left some skin behind.

Talbot faced her with a brow raised in surprise and, at her glare, hurried to explain in a conciliatory manner. "I only meant, my dear child, that you might have occupied a quite . . . ah . . . special place in my household. I'm sure you would have preferred it above your present situation. Avery should never have forced you to wed that scarred beast of a man."

A deepening pink hue was creeping upward from the top of Erienne's gown. "My husband may be scarred, sir, but he is not a beast."

"My dear girl." His eyelids lowered as he savored the beauty her anger roused. "I only wish to assure you that should the horror of your bondage become more pressing than you can bear, such a position in my household could still be arranged. I, for one, do not consider marriage to be a blemish, as many do."

He snapped his fingers loudly, winning the attention of the butler away from several guests who were just entering. "My cloak and hat," he demanded arrogantly, "and fetch the Lady Saxton's too."

"Really, Lord Talbot!" Erienne protested vehemently. "I cannot go with you! I am here with the Leicesters, and they will be most distraught if they cannot find me."

"Calm your fears, child," Lord Talbot soothed. "I shall leave a message informing them that you have departed with me and"—he smiled down at her sanguinely—"that you are receiving only the best of care. Now come, my dear, my friends are waiting in the carriage."

He caught her arm as she tried to turn away, and he ignored her attempts to pry his fingers away.

"Please!" she gritted out in an anxious whisper. She tried to twist her arm free, fearful of rousing the ire of such a powerful man, but also determined to stay where she was. "You are hurting me!"

A man detached himself from the new arrivals and approached the butler, who was in the process of handing the cloaks, cane, and hat to Lord Talbot. As the man neared, his own cloak slipped from his arm, falling at his lordship's feet. He bent to scoop up the garment, and when he straightened, his head struck Talbot's forearm with enough force to break his grip on Erienne. She was thrust away by the intruding body and, seeing the opportunity granted her, lifted her skirts and fled without a backward glance. The man's plunge continued upward, his shoulder striking Talbot in the ribs, then his arm caught solidly beneath the sagging chin. With a loud "clop" Talbot's mouth closed, and he staggered backward on high gilt heels to slam against the wall. He clapped a hand over his bruised mouth and hopped forward, teetering on one foot as he strove to regain his balance until the other man caught his arm with almost undue force; then he was held in check with one foot clear of the floor and one shoulder strained high.

"My apologies, sir," his assailant cajoled.

Lord Talbot looked in horror at the blood in his palm. "I bi' my ton', you damn foo'!"

The man released his grasp, and his lordship nearly fell at the sudden lack of support. He was caught again, this time a bit more gently. "I really am sorry, Lord Talbot. I hope you are not seriously injured."

Talbot's head snapped up, and his eyes widened as he recognized the tall form. "Seton! I thought it was some country oaf!" A quick vision of Farrell Fleming's half-cocked arm crossed his mind, and he dispensed with the possibility of an outright challenge.

Christopher faced the butler, laying his cloak over Erienne's, which the man still held, and nodding to the man to put them both away. Christopher grinned ruefully as he turned back to his lordship. "Again my apology, Lord Talbot. I must admit my eyes were on the lady you were with."

" 'Twas the mayor's daughter." Talbot's tone was brusque and curt. After searching the room and failing to catch any glimpse of her, he grunted in derision. "Or should I say, the Lady Saxton?"

"She is very lovely. But then, I expect Lord Saxton is more aware of that than anyone else."

" 'Twould seem that wealth agrees with the wench." He missed the slight lowering of the lids over the grayish-green eyes, and with a brief sigh he resigned himself to a momentary defeat. "For a man who can't even mount a horse, how can he do justice to that little filly?"

"Mount a horse?" Christopher repeated with a query.

"Aye! 'Tis rumored the man is too clumsy even to ride." Talbot gingerly tested a rib, worrying that it might be cracked. "If you will excuse me, Seton. I must repair my appearance."

"Of course, my lord." Christopher raised a hand to indicate to the butler, who held out a satin cloak. "If you're leaving, you'll no doubt be needing this."

Talbot loftily waved the servant away. "I've changed my mind. I shall be staying for a while." He smirked. "The filly has spirit. She should prove highly entertaining in a chase."

A corner of Christopher's mouth lifted in a meager smile. "I've heard Lord Saxton is quite adept with firearms. Be careful that you don't get clipped."

"Pah!" Talbot dabbed his handkerchief to his lips. "The man is so clumsy, he'd sound a warning a mile away."

Erienne anxiously searched until she found Anne seated with a couple at one of the small tables provided for the playing of cards. The older woman's face brightened when she saw her, and she patted the seat of the chair beside her invitingly.

"Sit here, my dear. You were gone so long, we were beginning to worry about you. I sent Phillip to find you, and now that you're here, you can join us."

Erienne disliked the reminder of what had ruined her father, yet after her recent experience with Lord Talbot, she was eager to accept the security of the woman's nearness. "I'm afraid I know nothing about the game."

"Triumph is quite simple, my dear," Anne assured her gaily. " 'Twill take you only a moment or two to learn, then you'll never want to stop."

The statement did not ease Erienne's qualms about the wickedness of cards, but considering them a lesser evil than what Lord Talbot had planned for her, she agreed to play. They entered the game, and though Erienne tried to concentrate on learning the rules, she was wary of those who paused to watch, until she was certain that none wore the silver satin that readily identified his haughty lordship. After playing a few hands, she was quite surprised to find that she was actually enjoying the game. She suffered a twinge of uncertainty, however, when Phillip returned to their table and requested a private word with his wife. Assurances were made of their quick return, and Erienne forced herself to relax as Anne excused herself. A new hand was dealt as another woman took the vacant seat.

The newcomer laughed apologetically. "I'm not very good at this."

Erienne smiled at the elegantly attired woman. "If you were, I'd be in trouble."

The two who completed the foursome exchanged confident nods. This promised to be an easy game for them.

"I am the Countess Ashford, my dear," the woman murmured with a gracious smile. "And you are . . . ?"

"Erienne, my lady. Erienne Saxton."

"You are very young," the countess observed, studying the creamy visage. "And very lovely."

"May I return the compliment?" Erienne replied without guile. Though perhaps between an age two score ten and three score, the countess possessed a serene beauty that the oncoming years could not tarnish.

"Shall we get started?" the man in their group suggested.

"Of course," the countess readily agreed, collecting her cards.

Erienne took the first bid and studied her cards intently until she sensed a presence at her back. Cautiously she paused, but out of the corner of her eye she saw a lean, darkly garbed leg and a black shoe. Her qualms eased. As long as it was not Lord Talbot, she was free to concentrate on the game. Not overly confident with it, she was worried over making the right play and thoughtfully fingered the knave of diamonds in her hand as she considered the possible repercussions for playing it.

"You'll do better with the king, my lady," the man behind her advised.

Erienne froze for an instant of time as the familiar voice scattered her thoughts. Her heart began to hammer wildly in her bosom, and her cheeks grew flushed. She had no need to see the man's face to know who stood at her back. She now felt his presence with every fiber of her being, and despite her shock, a growing, comforting warmth suffused her, thawing her stilted wariness. She quickly attributed the sensation to a feeling of security with him close at hand, though the idea was contrary to her earlier experiences with the worldly Christopher Seton.

She glanced up to see if any of her companions had taken note of her discomposure. The gently smiling eyes of the countess rested on her, and in a soft voice, she reminded, "Your play, my dear."

Erienne dropped her gaze to her cards. Her family could attest to the fact that Christopher was knowledgeable at cards, and his advice could be trusted. With sudden decision she thrust the knave back into the hand and played the king. A queen fell, and when all the cards were down, she had won the round and the tokens.

The Countess Ashford chuckled. "I think I would do well, sir, if I let you play this game. I have always preferred to watch people matching wits against each other and not against me."

"Thank you, madam," Christopher flashed the woman a charming grin as he dragged up a chair beside Erienne. "I hope I shall prove worthy of your confidence."

"I have no doubt that you will, sir."

Erienne sent a cool glance skimming over him as he took the seat beside her. The memory of his intrusion in her dreams was not dimmed when she saw how crisply tailored and handsome he was in the dark blue silk and flawless white shirt.

Christopher's eyes gleamed as they lightly caressed her in return, and he gave a brief nod of greeting. "Good evening, my lady."

Erienne stiffly inclined her head. "Sir."

He introduced himself to the others and, taking up the pack, began to shuffle the cards. His lean, brown fingers worked with dexterity, giving Erienne cause to believe that her father was either blind or a fool not to have recognized the man's skill. But then, perhaps Avery had been too intent on cheating to notice anything.

"What are you doing here in London?" she asked, carefully guarding her tone so it might sound gracious. "I thought you would be in Mawbry, or Wirkinton . . . or some such place."

Christopher began to deal, but his attention never strayed far from her. She was quite lovely in her finery, and his gaze eagerly feasted on the beauteous fare. "I saw no reason to stay when you weren't there."

Erienne's eyes swept about the table surreptitiously, finding the two other players occupied with their cards. The countess calmly sipped a sherry that had been brought to her and for the moment seemed distracted, allowing Erienne the opportunity to frown a warning at Christopher. He smiled leisurely in reply, showing incredibly white teeth, and gestured to her cards.

"I believe 'tis your bid, my lady."

Erienne tried to concentrate on the cards, but the effort proved futile. She decided no bid at all was better than making a fool of herself.

"Pass."

"Are you sure?" Christopher asked solicitously.

"Quite sure." She pointedly ignored the mocking gleam in his eyes.

"You're not going to win that way," he chided. "Besides, I expected more of a challenge from you."

"Why don't you bid?" She arched a lovely brow, daring him in return.

"I thought I would," he replied easily and spoke his choice to the other couple. "Three."

"Four," the man responded with a sly grin.

The woman shook her head, and the bid came back to Christopher.

"You don't make it easy for me, sir," he stated with a chuckle. "Five it is!"

"You're very bold with your bidding," Erienne pointed out.

"When I'm allowed to be," Christopher agreed, dulling her meagerly veiled barb. "I am not easily dissuaded, and I usually take the initiative if I think I can win."

"So 'twould seem with cards."

His eyes glowed as he smiled at her. "With everything, my lady."

Erienne did not dare contradict his statement. Had they been alone she might have reminded him that after he had asked for her hand in marriage, he had accepted the outcome of the roup quite congenially. He had been like a passive church mouse who had lost a coveted portion of cheese to a more determined rodent and then had blandly continued on his own way, content in recouping his debt.

Seeking some way to undermine his ambitious bid, she watched the game carefully. He led out with an ace of spades and waited for the other cards to fall. The other man slammed down a king and groaned in mock frustration.

" 'Tis your good fortune that I have no other spades."

In his next play Christopher won her knave with his queen. His ten of spades saw the last of theirs, but he played a nine in the same suit for good measure. Erienne held the ace of diamonds to the last, hoping she would find a flaw in his strategy. As he laid out his last card, he grinned at her.

"An ace of hearts, my lady. Have you anything better?"

Declining comment, she tossed out the solitary diamond with a slight show of irritation. He seemed in jovial spirits as he gathered up the cards. He accepted the tokens from the couple and as the two turned to speak with the countess, he faced Erienne with a hint of a mischievous smile.

"I believe you owe me a token, my lady. Or do you wish me to extend credit?"

"What, and have you claim I owe you some further recompense?" she declined with a scornful laugh as she flipped him a wooden chip. "Definitely not!"

Christopher sighed in exaggerated disappointment. "Too bad. I was looking forward to collecting."

"You always are," she murmured as he leaned forward to pick up the chip.

"You can hardly fault me there." His tone was equally soft as his eyes caressed her warmly. "You sorely test my restraints, my lady."

"Restraints?" She raised a delicate brow in disbelief. "I have seen no evidence of such."

"Madam, if you really knew, you'd think me a scoundrel."

"I already do."

"I don't suppose your husband has let you come unescorted." He waited expectantly for a reply.

"You may relax, sir. I've come with the Leicesters this time."

"I was hoping for a turn of fate, but I suppose I must accept the fact." He came to his feet and extended his hand to her. "I should like to treat these wealthy peasants to a taste of real beauty. The Leicesters can hardly protest if you enjoy yourself, and the music is most entrancing. Will you pleasure me with this dance, my lady?"

A piquant denial was ready on her lips, but the swiftly flowing strains of the music drifting from the ballroom made her want to move to its rhythm. For a breathless moment she envisioned herself following the steps of the *contredanse* on his arm. The tutoring she had received from the schools and her mother had included many hours of instruction on the dances. Until now, she had found little opportunity to put her skill to practice. A thrill went through her, returning the spots of color to her cheeks, and she could no more deny the moment than the arm her erstwhile tormentor offered.

She rose to her feet and laid her hand lightly upon his sleeve. Christopher smiled into her eyes and made their excuses to the others, giving a brief nod of farewell to the countess. Slipping a hand beneath Erienne's bare arm, he escorted her to the hall where the guests were gathering. As they entered the *contredanse*, he showed a leg, and when he straightened, the warm, glowing light in his eyes made her heartbeat quicken all the more. She sank into a deep curtsy, feeling positively wicked. She was a married woman, newly wedded at that, and here she was with a man who had to be the most envied rake in all of London. She suffered a momentary twinge of conscience when Lord Saxton's darkly masked face loomed up in her mind, and she wondered what he would say of a wife who cavorted like a mindless maiden on the ballroom floor with such a man as Christopher Seton.

"You dance divinely, my lady," he observed in passing her. "May I ask who was your instructor? Some handsome suitor, perhaps?"

Erienne's lashes lowered as she gave him a sidelong glance. How he liked to tease her about the poor assortment of petitioners who had plied for her hand. "In the main, my mother, sir."

"A great lady, no doubt. Did you inherit your beauty from her?"

"I'm something of a curiosity in the family." She waited until he came near again before continuing. "My mother was quite fair."

His mouth tilted upward in a roguish grin. "You certainly bear no resemblance to your father."

Her laughter bubbled to the surface like a fountain of crystal-clear water, fresh and sparkling, light and airy. The sound flowed as subtly as a gently flowing stream through Christopher's mind, yet its eroding effect was devastating, washing away every thought but one. The fact that he wanted her was becoming a hard-pressing reality, and he found no way to ease his goading desires.

When the *contredanse* was ended, Lord Talbot appeared beside them almost magically and postured grandly before Erienne as he offered an apology, pointedly ignoring Christopher.

"If I offended you, my lady, I'm sorry. Your beauty makes me careless and, I fear, something of a boorish knave. Am I forgiven?"

The desire to reject his pompous excuse was strong within her, but the consequences to the Fleming and Saxton families had to be considered. The man's power in the North country had been felt much too often not to give serious deliberation to it now. Stiffly she nodded the concession.

"Then you will allow me the pleasure of this next dance." He stretched out his hand expectantly.

Though Christopher's manner remained stoic, Erienne could sense his growing agitation with the man, for his eyes rested on the dandified lord with a total lack of charity. She knew Lord Talbot would not be above pressing the matter if she refused him, and she was just as aware that Christopher was not swayed by the man's importance. Hoping to avoid an angry confrontation, she accepted the proffered hand.

Having won her, Lord Talbot raised a hand and motioned for the musicians to begin a waltz, a scandalous dance which had its beginning nearly a century before in the Austrian Court but still managed to raise more than a few brows in England. It caused Erienne some consternation when the man placed a hand on her waist and took her fingers into a firm grasp. She was stiff and mechanical for the first few sweeping circles until the graceful rhythm eased some of her tension.

"You are a very gracious and lovely lady," Talbot commented. His eyes briefly marked Christopher, who stood watching them with his arms folded across his chest. Talbot had the distinct impression that the Yankee would not let the wench out of his sight, not even for a moment. "How well do you know Mr. Seton?"

Erienne did not trust Talbot, even when it concerned the one whom she had so often professed hatred for. "Why do you ask?"

"I was wondering how he came to be here. Does he hold a title?"

"Not that I'm aware of," she answered uneasily as his hand crept up her side.

"Usually these affairs are only for titled gentlemen and landed lords," Talbot stated with a lofty air. "He must be the guest of some erring soul."

She pointedly replaced his hand on her waist as she gave answer. "The Leicesters said the assemblies are becoming more relaxed, that any gentleman of credible manners and means can attend with proper invitation."

"Aye, 'tis so, and I am appalled that we must allow commoners to attend. They lack so many of the social graces. Why, the way that fellow came striding into the place and knocked me around, I shall be sore for a week."

"Christopher?"

"Aye! That bumbling buffoon," Talbot sneered, then flinched as he tested his still-tender tongue.

Erienne glanced between the two men in amazement and remembered the glimpse she had had of deep russet hair and broad shoulders just before she had been thrust free. An amused giggle threatened to burst forth as the identity of her protector dawned.

"The man should be grateful that I chose not to call him out."

She refrained from comment, considering he had made a wise decision for the sake of his own health.

"Look at him," Talbot jeered in derision. "He's like a stallion straining at the bit." Intentionally Talbot waltzed her around in front of the mentioned one before sweeping her away again. He derived a certain pleasure at dangling the delectable sweetmeat before the other's gaze, perhaps for the same reason one teases a youngling by holding a treasured bauble just out of hand's reach.

Lord Talbot's statement was not far from the truth, Erienne realized. Christopher's brows were gathered in a harsh frown as he closely observed their flight about the room, as if he had some special right to be jealous when she danced with another man. Before the last note of the music quivered and died, he was there beside them.

"I claim the next dance." His voice was flat, his statement blunt.

Lord Talbot was the one left frowning as the younger man led Erienne away. Much in the manner of his lordship, Christopher gestured to the musicians, and another waltz began. Laying his hand on her waist, he faced her, and his eyes shone with a purposeful light as he swirled her about in wide, graceful circles. Like the man himself, his movements were bold and sweeping, with none of the mincing steps his lordship had demonstrated. Erienne was very much aware of his arm about her waist and of the strength and power of the shoulder that flexed beneath her hand. As they glided across the floor with seemingly effortless ease, others paused to watch in admiration. They were an uncommonly handsome couple, and muted whispers rose as the onlookers exchanged questions and conjectures about them. Between the pair, however, there was almost a stilted silence. Erienne would no longer meet his gaze and resisted being held too close, much too conscious of the magnetism of his powerful frame and the uneven beat of her heart.

"My lady is displeased over something?" he finally queried with a slight twist of a grin.

For a turn or two she debated her answer. For the sake of pride, she could not tell him how well he disrupted her thoughts and that the calm serenity she displayed hid emotions that were well roiled by the fact of his nearness. Shielding herself against his mockery, she chose to attack rather than reveal her weakness. "You treated Lord Talbot most rudely."

"Rudely?" Christopher laughed in sharp derision. "The man was ready to drag you off, and I assure you, my lady, he had nothing honorable in mind."

She lifted her chin, displaying the long, graceful throat with its jeweled adornment, and leaned back against his arm. "He apologized and for the most part was a gentleman in the dance."

" 'Tis obvious you need serious counseling on the definition of gentleman, madam. Lord Talbot is a rake of the first water, and I caution you to be wary of his attention."

Miffed, she turned her face aside and answered loftily, "He is probably no worse than others I know."

"Would you explain the same to Lord Saxton if he were here to warn you of the man?"

Erienne almost halted as she glanced up at Christopher, feeling a trifle hurt by his barb. "I have always been as truthful and honest as I can be to my husband."

"And of course," he smiled lazily, "you have told him all about us."

This time Erienne did stop, her ire rising. It was bad enough to be plagued by her own thoughts and dreams, but to have him taunt her . . . it was too much! She would see his suspicions put to quick death. "Us? Pray tell, sir. Just what is there to say about us?"

He leaned close and spoke in a low voice. "If you'll remember, madam, you were not exactly cool to my kisses."

"Oh!" The single syllable escaped her lips while other words failed her. Abruptly she turned and started to leave the floor, but he seized her wrist and half guided, half dragged her through the open doors that led to a dimly lit, foliage-bedecked gallery. Once they had passed from sight of the other dancers, Erienne snatched her wrist free and rubbed the smarting member, groaning through gritted teeth, "Men!"

She presented her back as he stepped near, and though she could not dismiss him from any part of her awareness, she managed an attitude of cool disdain. Christopher's mood softened as his eyes feasted on the beauty of the long, shining ringlets and the soft, delicate creaminess of her shoulders. The fragrance of her perfume drifted through his senses, and the throbbing hunger began anew. He was seized by a strong yearning to hold her against him, a desire that burned through him and cauterized his very mind with his need. He slipped an arm about her slender waist, pulling her back against him as he bent to murmur close to her ear.

"Erienne, my love . . ."

"Don't touch me!" she gasped and jerked away as his whisper stabbed to the roots of her being, tearing holes in the thin façade of her composure. Shaking, she faced him, holding up both wrists accusingly. "You see? They are both bruised. You are no better than he is. For most of this evening I have been dragged hither and fro by men who declare they only wish to protect me."

Christopher recognized her anger and gave a brief, mocking bow. "Your pardon, my lady. I only sought to tell you about a man whose intentions are less than honorable."

"And what of yours, sir?" she scoffed. "If we should venture to the warmth of yonder stable, would you, then, withhold yourself? Or see my virtue to an end?"

He moved close but carefully refrained from contact, though his eyes devoured with ravenous hunger all that he saw. "You have guessed the truth, madam." His voice was husky and warm. " 'Tis my dearest yearning to take you in my arms and have done with this damned virginity. If your husband cannot do the thing, then in mercy let it fall to me, but do not waste yourself on that strutting cock, Talbot. He would use you to the limits of his boredom, than hand you to his friends for whatever end they could conceive."

Erienne stared up at him, and when she spoke it was almost in awe. "And what of you, Christopher? If I were to yield myself to you, would you, then, honor me?"

"Honor you?" he breathed. "Sweetest Erienne, how could I not? You are ever in my thoughts, bending me, twisting me, plucking at the fibers of my mind. The man inside me trembles whenever you're near, and I groan in agony for the touch of your hand laid upon me in a soft caress. I am beset with my desire for you, and if I thought for one moment that you would not loathe me forever, I would ease my lusts this very night, be you willing or nay. But I'd rather hear my name fall from your lips with words of love than snarled in tones of hate. 'Tis the one thing that keeps you safe from me, Erienne. 'Tis the only thing."

She could only gaze at him, her lips parted as a tumult of emotions coursed through her bosom. There raged within her a memory of a night in an abandoned stable, when his kisses had seared through her resistance and left her shaken with the realization of her own passion. The feelings came back, and she was seized by a biting, raging fear that if she delayed a moment longer, she could dishonor herself, her husband, and her house. She whirled and fled, afraid that he would press for an answer and was just as frightened of the one she would give.

Thirteen

The jamb of the window was cool against Erienne's temple as she stared out through the crystal panes. Before night had settled over the land, clouds had gathered and now formed a gossamer veil that hid the face of a bashful, waning moon. Far off to the south a multitude of London lamps cast an amber glow against the lowering mass. Even as she watched, a soft, misting rain began to fall, and the distant lights faded until only the gnarled, naked arms of the ancient oaks twisted up into the darkness, their forms dimly lit by the stable lanterns. Beyond the grounds of the manse, no detail, no hint of habitation could be seen.

Erienne rubbed her brow against the smooth wood, as if to soothe the confusion that churned inside her head. She was thankful that Lord Saxton had not returned from his business, for she was skeptical of how well she could hide her agitation from him.

Her breath clouded the diamond-shaped panes, shutting off her view of the world beyond. With a half-angry discontent, she moved away from the window and gathered the soft, velvet robe close about her against the chill of the room. Seeking warmth, she went to the fireplace and sat on a low stool in front of it. The lamps had been doused in the chamber except for a single candle on the bedside commode. Blending with its meager light, the leaping flames threw a soft, golden illumination into the room, elongating and distorting shadows.

Though a deep weariness had come upon her after the rush of the long day had ebbed, her thoughts continued to tumble in a crashing, tumultuous surf and refused to give her rest. Christopher's words would not remain interred in the back of her mind, where she wished to bury them. Instead, they crept forward like gray, thin ghouls to torment her and maul her peace of mind.

"That rakish Yankee attacks me from every side," she moaned and shook her head in abject frustration, setting the long tresses swaying with fluid motion. "His boldness knows no bounds! Why won't he leave me alone?"

No answer came from the dancing flames, and she shifted to another rationale in a desperate attempt to bring her roiling discontent to heel.

" 'Twas the music," she excused. "The rhythm and the dance which excited me."

Even as she spoke them, the words sounded hollow and without substance. It was *his* arms that had warmed her! *His* voice that had shot tiny little bursting shards of delight through her! *His* nearness that had sent her senses reeling!

She fought against the whirlpool of unwelcome emotions that threatened to drag her down to a new depth of despair. There was a tremor in her breast that would not obey the command of her will. Then slowly a darker shape took form, and the ghosts dissipated before its threat. The featureless leather mask, though unchanged, stared at her with an accusing glare.

Erienne's head came up with a jerk, and her eyes were wide as they searched the room for the one whose stealth had oftentimes brought him in unheeded. Though the chamber was empty, she rose to her feet and began to pace nervously, her restless strides measuring the width and breadth of the bedroom. There seemed to be no escape from her plight. The more she tried to find some reason and logic in her feelings, the more confused she became, until finally with a moan of hopeless frustration, she tossed aside her robe and fell back upon the bed. She lay without moving, letting the cool air seep through the thin gown and touch her body. Her shaking eased by slow degrees, and her mind was lulled by the serene stillness of the room. Her eyelids sagged as her mind drifted where it would, swirling through the dances and the moments when sparkling grayish-green eyes had held hers prisoner. The shadowed form came back to stand at the end of her bed, but this time she could conjure no manly features in the gloom. The thing stared at her with a fixed smile and red, glowing eyes that pierced the darkness, paralyzing her with a sudden fear. Then a log fell in the fireplace, and in the flare of light, her eyes caught the broad shoulders, the black garments, and the smooth mask of her husband.

With a startled gasp, she sat upright. The smile and the red eyes were nothing more than dark holes in his leather visage, yet her terror did not wane as she thought of what he might have seen in her.

"My pardon, Erienne," he rasped. "You were so still, I thought you were asleep. 'Twas not my intent to frighten you."

The frantic throbbing of her heart would not be calmed by his assurance. She sought to steady her voice as she answered, "You've been gone so long, milord, I was beginning to think you had either forgotten or deserted me."

Wheezing laughter came from the mask. "Unlikely, madam."

She felt the bold touch of his hungry gaze, and inwardly she shivered. His gloved hand reached out, and she froze as it pushed aside her tumbling hair. His fingers moved in one long, slow, unending caress along her arm, and even through the light covering of her gown she was sure she could feel the inhuman coolness of his touch. Her pulse quickened when he stepped nearer, and in one scrambling leap she was out of the bed. Flying across the room, she fetched a small jeweled box that Anne had presented her earlier in the evening.

"Look at this, milord," she bade, bringing it back to him and giving no mind to the transparency of her nightgown as she stood before him with the box resting on outstretched palms. Her only thought was to avoid his caresses and, if she could, to placate his temper. "Isn't it lovely?"

Lord Saxton opened the velvet-lined box, momentarily displaying an interest in it, then without looking up he startled her with a hoarsely murmured inquiry. "Do you realize how much I want you, Erienne?"

She lowered the box, then stared helplessly into the eyeholes of the mask when he raised his head. Tears filled her eyes as she struggled with the turmoil that writhed within her. She knew she had no right to deny him, but neither could she bring herself to the point of yielding. The fear of what lay beneath the mask could not be easily set aside.

His breath sighed through the openings in the leather. "Never mind. I can see you're not ready to become my wife."

She raised a hand to him in plaintive appeal, but as hard as she tried, she could not make herself touch him. She could not think of him as a husband.

Lord Saxton rose and made his laborious way to the door, where he paused and spoke over his shoulder. "I have more business to attend on the morrow. I will be gone before you waken."

With that, he left and closed the door behind him, leaving Erienne to stare in rampant misery at the portal. Her shoulders began to shake as muted sobs welled up within her and tears streamed down her face.

When she joined the Leicesters for the morning meal, Erienne was surprised to find them already in the drawing room with another visitor, one who managed immediately to turn her emotions into a jangled knot of sensations. When she first saw him, standing tall and dashing beside the window, her heart quickened and she had to squelch a surge of excitement. Then anger and resentment began to well up in her breast as she thought of the man's audacity in presenting himself to her husband's friends.

Anne came across the room where Erienne had halted beside the door and took her arm. "Come, my dear. I have someone I'd like you to meet."

Erienne resisted being drawn forward and, avoiding Christopher's amused gaze, replied in a muted tone, "Your pardon, my lady, but Mr. Seton and I are already acquainted."

"Acquainted perhaps, Erienne," Anne responded pleasantly, "but I'll wager never properly introduced." She led the reluctant young woman across the space and halted before the man. "Lady Saxton, may I present Mr. Christopher Seton, a kinsman of yours, I believe."

Erienne looked at her hostess in astonishment, not quite sure she had heard her correctly. She gingerly repeated the word that had caused her distress. "Kinsman?"

"Oh, yes! Let me see now. The Setons and Saxtons are related in several ways." Anne pondered the matter for a moment, then waved a hand as if to dismiss it all. "Well, no matter. The latest was by marriage, and I believe there was a common ancestor back there somewhere. That would make you at least cousins."

"Cousins?" Erienne's dismay leaked through in her voice, and she felt as if someone had just closed a heavy gate to bar her escape.

"At the very least," Anne assured her earnestly. "And quite possibly something else as well."

"But he's a Yankee!" Erienne protested. Humor shone brighter in the translucent orbs, and a warming ire at his effrontery stirred in her.

"Really, my dear," Anne reproached the young wife gently, "we cannot all be so fortunate as to live out our lives on good, English soil, but one can hardly ignore the ties of blood. I, for one, have completely forgiven my sister—"

"Harrumph!" The marquess interrupted his wife's chatter abruptly. "Let's not get into a detailed review of the family tree, my dear. I'm sure Christopher can explain it all in simpler terms." He turned to his guest expectantly.

"Actually"—Christopher's shoulders lifted in a lazy shrug—"Stuart's mother was a Seton before marriage. I have always been considered something of an outcast by the family, so they usually strive to disallow whatever claim I may have."

"I believe I understand their reasoning," Erienne quipped in subtle sarcasm.

Grinning roguishly, he inclined his head. "Thank you, cousin."

"I am not your cousin!" she corrected crisply. "Indeed, had I known *you* were kin, I would *never* have consented to this marriage."

"You mean you haven't fallen madly in love with Stuart yet?" he chided. His eyes gleamed with mischief, and when she opened her mouth to retort, he put up a hand to halt her. "No need to explain, cousin. I have no great love for him myself. We tolerate each other only because the situation demands it. In fact, we seem to exist only to antagonize the other. I envy him his newly acquired bride, and he is jealous of my good looks, which"—he shrugged—"simply makes us both quite incompatible."

Phillip turned to his wife, seeking to ease the tension of the moment. "We'd better have breakfast, my dear, if we are to be about our affairs."

"Christopher, will you bring Erienne along?" Anne urged sweetly as she took her husband's arm and moved toward the dining room.

"Of course, madam." Christopher gallantly presented his arm to the dark-haired beauty, at the same time catching her hand and pulling it through the crook of his elbow, not giving her a chance to deny him.

Erienne yielded rather than make a scene, but behind Anne's back she glared up at him and hissed, "You're outrageous!"

"Has anyone told you this morning," he breathed, blithely ignoring her irritation as he bent his head near hers, "how beautiful you are?"

She lifted her slim nose to a higher elevation, avoiding any reply. Still, she could not quite quell the stirring of pleasure his words aroused.

Christopher pondered her silence for a moment as his gaze lightly caressed her. "Anne tells me that my cousin is quite smitten with you, but since he lacks the appearance that would make him socially acceptable, he is reluctant to appear in public with you." His smile widened into a grin as she looked at him in surprise. "I am therefore considering offering my services as your escort."

A crisp, cool smile was briefly bestowed upon him. "You seem to have it well planned . . . except for one thing. I have no intention of going anywhere with you."

"But you'll have need of a capable chaperon," he argued.

"Thank you for your offer, but I think I would rather take my chances alone. I believe I would be safer."

"The Leicesters have an appointment this morning, and since Stuart is not here, I've asked if I might take you for a ride about the city."

Her mouth came open with her surprise, and she searched the tanned visage, taken aback by his nerve. She greatly suspected that he was setting a trap for her but fully intended to avoid it. "I should like to decline, sir."

He seemed undismayed. "I thought you might enjoy the outing, but if you would rather stay here with me, I'm sure we can find something to do while the Leicesters are away." Peering at her askance, he awaited her reaction.

Irate sparks flashed in the blue-violet eyes as Erienne became aware that she had been snared. She knew the folly of remaining in the manse alone with the Yankee rake. By the time the Leicesters returned, there would be serious doubt as to the continued state of her virtue. Cousin or not, she would be hard pressed to avoid his amorous bent.

"Your persistence amazes me, sir."

"I simply know what I want, that's all," he answered warmly.

"I am a married woman!" she gritted.

"How well I know!"

At the table Christopher held her chair as she slipped into it, and then he went around the table to take a place opposite her. For Erienne, his presence caused as much distress as when her husband sat across from her. With those glowing eyes constantly on her, she felt as if she were being devoured instead of the excellent fare.

Shortly after the morning meal, the Leicesters made their apologies and hurried on their way, leaving Erienne no choice but to let Christopher escort her to the waiting coach. It was evident that he had expended a goodly amount of coin in the hiring of such a fine livery, and he was most gallant as he handed her into its plush interior.

"Since I favor your company, madam, I shall try to be on my best behavior," he said as he settled into the seat beside her.

"If you are not, my husband will hear of it, sir," she warned direly.

He chuckled. "I shall try to remember everything my mother taught me about proper decorum."

Erienne rolled her eyes in wide disbelief. "This should prove to be an interesting day."

Relaxing back in his seat, Christopher smiled at her. "Might I start off by saying that I am honored by this privilege, madam? You are an exceptional-looking woman, and 'tis a joy to see you appropriately gowned. At least Stuart is not stingy with you."

He was right, of course. Lord Saxton was generous beyond the measure of most husbands. It made her even more cognizant of the fact that she had never given him anything in return, not even his rightful due as a man or as a husband.

Erienne smoothed the cream-colored skirt of watered silk, feeling very much a lady of worth. The emerald-green velvet bodice was cut in the manner of a short vest but with a stiff, standing collar and long, fitted sleeves. Puffs of silk adorned the velvet hat that Tessie had encouraged her to wear, and a long streamer of creamy silk swept gracefully beneath her chin and over her shoulder. The creation combined rich, stylish flair with discriminatingly good taste, something both the Talbots lacked but which was applied with almost casual ease in everything her companion assayed. He had completely destroyed the low opinion she had previously held of Yankees, and yet at the same time he had also confirmed her suspicions that their gall was beyond measure.

"Would it be improper for me to ask where you are taking me?" Her question carried more than a hint of satire.

"Anywhere my lady wishes. Vauxhall Gardens might do to begin."

" 'Tis really not the best season for it," she commented.

Christopher glanced at her in surprise. "You have seen it?"

"My mother took me there several times."

He tried again. "We might have tea at the Rotunda."

"I wonder if it's changed much."

"You've been there, too," he stated with deflated enthusiasm.

"Why, Christopher," she said and laughed, detecting his disappointment, "I used to live in London. I really can't name a sight that I haven't seen."

He mulled over her reply for a moment, then a slow smile came upon his face. "There is at least one thing in London you haven't seen."

Erienne could only stare at him in bemusement as he opened the small door behind the driver and spoke with the man. Then with a confident grin, he leaned back in the seat.

" 'Twill be a few moments before we get there, my lady. You might as well relax and enjoy the ride."

His suggestion was hard to follow, and she swiftly came to the conclusion that he was about as easily dismissed from mind as her husband. She could no more feel at ease with him than she could the other, though the contrast between the pair was like night and day.

"How well do you know Stuart?" she asked, determining that conversation was better than silence. Though he had promised to conduct himself in an orderly fashion, he was taking the opportunity to study her in detail.

"As well as anyone, I guess," he replied easily. "But then, no one knows him very well at all."

"Are you aware that Timmy Sears is dead?"

He gave a brief nod. "I had heard as much."

"Stuart seemed . . . ah . . . distressed over the man's death."

Christopher's answer was slow in coming. "Perhaps Stuart realizes the possibility of someone accusing him of the killing. A few of your husband's tenants voiced their suspicions that it was Timmy Sears who torched Saxton Hall, mainly out of spite because of the many times he had been chased off the lands. Nothing could be proven, of course, but the man was into constant mischief. Stuart lost a great deal because of that fire."

"Do you really think Timmy set fire to the manse?"

A shrug conveyed his indecision, and he replied with care. "I have heard a wide variety of tales about that. One as acceptable as any is that perhaps Lord Saxton inadvertently rode into a high-waymen's camp and recognized some of them. The marquess received a message to that effect, but before the authorities could arrive, the new wing wherein Lord Saxton had made his chambers was torched." Christopher glanced out the window as he added, "He had often complained of the drafts of the old house, and now I suppose he has to endure the cold."

Erienne sensed a poignant sadness in him in that moment of silence but could find no reason for it, except that he sympathized with his cousin. The mood seemed completely out of character for the man himself. "But if Stuart knows who was responsible for the torching of the hall, surely he could call them before the courts to make them pay their due."

Again there was a long pause before an answer came. "Lord Sax-ton is not the same man he once was. He thinks differently. He saw his father slain, and he remembers hiding beside his mother, afraid to let out a frightened whimper for fear the men would find and kill them, too. The burning of the manor brought it all home to him. 'Tis possible to see a long series of apparently unrelated events in the happenings, from the slaying of the old lord and the driving of his family away from the hall, to the burning and even the piracy that has laid hold of Cumberland. Perhaps Stuart sees a single hand behind it all and seeks a meticulous justice that can extend to the leaders and the highest one involved."

Erienne gave serious thought to his answer and was uncertain as to what part she played in all of it. Was her husband a man bent solely on revenge? Or was he seeking out a broader sweep of his vengeance? If she dallied too long, would she someday find his anger turned to her?

"Do you know why his father was slain?" she asked quietly.

A long sigh slipped from her companion. " 'Tis difficult to say, Erienne. Several harsh accusations were thrust upon his name when he tried to bring about a peaceful settlement with the Scots over the bordering lands, and some lords at court took it upon themselves to question his loyalty because he had married the daughter of a High-land chieftain. At the same time a band of highwaymen began to range through the North country, thieving and murdering. Many accused the Scots, but Stuart's father argued that it was some of the locals who had banded together. He set about to prove his suspicions, but he was killed before he could. Of course, the blame for that also fell to the Scots."

"If this is all true, I don't understand why Stuart went back to Saxton Hall."

"Why does any man go back to his heritage? To clear the family name. To take his rightful place as lord of his lands. To avenge the murder and destruction of his family and bring to task those who were responsible."

"You seem to know a great deal about my husband after all," Erienne pointed out.

Christopher smiled wryly. "As much as I hate to admit it, my lady, I'm kin to the man, and I've learned all the family secrets."

"What of his mother? Where is she?"

"After the death of her husband, Mary Saxton took what remained of her family and left the North country. She spent many years a widow, then married an old friend of the family. She will no doubt arrange a visit to Saxton Hall after her son puts his house in order. She does not wish to intrude until then."

"She must have been greatly saddened by what happened to her son."

"She is quite a woman. I think you'll like her."

"But will she like me? A wife bought on the block?"

"I can assure you, my lady, you have naught to fear. She despaired that Stuart would marry at all, and since you're such a fine choice for her son, she can't help but like you." His grin broadened. "If she doesn't, I hope she makes Stuart give you up so I can have you. After being married to such a beast, perhaps you could tolerate me a little better."

"Stuart is not a beast!" Erienne protested impatiently. "And I dislike the fact that everyone calls him one."

"You rise quickly to his defense." He regarded her closely as he teased, "I hope you're not falling in love with the man."

"From what I've heard, he needs someone to love him, and what better person to do that than his wife?"

"You distress me, Erienne." His mouth twisted in a lightly mocking grin. "You give me no cause to hope for myself."

"Nor should I," she retorted pertly. "I am a married woman."

He laughed briefly. "You seem to take special delight in reminding me."

"If you hadn't been so fond of your precious debt, you might have . . ." She halted abruptly, aghast at what she had been about to say. She had her pride, and she could not bear to let him perceive her disappointments or the reasons behind them.

Christopher peered at her closely and took note of her sudden uneasiness. "I might have what, my lady?"

Erienne held her silence. She had not meant to chide him openly, but she was firm in the belief that if he had truly wanted her, he would have done something more at the roup than just casually accept the outcome.

"Bought you for a wife?" he pressed.

"Don't be absurd!" Her slim nose tilted upward as she turned it in profile to him.

"Have you so quickly forgotten, my lady? Your father prevented me from taking part in the bidding." His eyes never wavered from her face. "Did you expect something more of me?"

"Pray tell, what more could you have done?" Her sarcasm came through clearly. "You goaded my father until he was forced to seek a higher bid." She flung out a hand. "And you came eagerly enough for your payment when the coins were being counted."

"Madam, can it be that you resent me because I failed to snatch you away from your father and carry you off to some hidden valley?" His tone was one of amazement.

Indignant color stained Erienne's cheeks. "You're right, of course. I do resent you, but not for the reasons you state."

"Might I remind you that I proposed marriage, and you were the one who rejected my offer? In no uncertain terms, you let me know how you loathed me. Was that a lie?"

"No!" The word was lashed out in anger.

"You seem to be content with Stuart," he began slowly and saw a frown flicker across her lovely brow. "Do you, indeed, prefer the cripple above me?"

The tiny nod she gave was stiff and difficult. "Stuart has been very kind."

"Useless as a man," he muttered scornfully.

"That's not fair!" she cried.

He stared at her curiously. "The statement is fair unless you're the one who keeps him at bay."

A livid blush swept into her cheeks, and she quickly directed her attention out the window, unable to meet his probing gaze.

"How you managed that, madam, is quite beyond me," he stated, taking a cue from her silence. "By now, the man must be in torment, knowing that you are his but forbidden to touch you. I can well understand his plight."

"Please!" She cast him a quick glare. "This is not a proper discussion, even for cousins!"

Christopher relented, at least for the moment, and allowed her ire to cool. When she was able to take note of her surroundings again, Erienne became aware that the coach was winding its way down to the waterfront. She was relieved when it soon halted, for the confines of the carriage had provided no escape from his unwavering contemplation. Glancing about, she saw that they had stopped near a huge three-masted ship docked close against the quay. A figurehead of a woman with flowing red tresses graced the head of the ship, and the name *Christina* was carved into the stern.

Christopher opened the door and stepped out. She laid a gloved hand into the one he offered up and descended to the cobbled wharf. Though a smile was in his eyes, he remained silent beneath her quizzical gaze and took her arm through his, leading her past kegs, barrels, and bales of hemp toward the gangplank of the vessel. Other ships were in dock, but none compared to the lady, *Christina*. Like a proud queen, she stood tall and serene amid her consorts. On board, a man in a blue coat came to where the gangplank touched the ship. When he espied the couple, he smiled and waved a greeting that was immediately returned by Christopher.

"Captain Daniels, have we permission to come aboard?" he called.

The man gave a throaty chuckle and beckoned them aboard. "At your pleasure, Mr. Seton."

The wind ruffled the dark russet hair as Christopher swept off his hat and gave her a rueful grin. "Madam, may I entice you aboard?"

Her gaze flicked over the faces of the men who had come to the rail to appease their curiosity. She could not hear what was being said as they murmured and chuckled together, but she sensed that she and Christopher were the topic of their animated conversation.

"With so many to come to my aid should you prove incapable of continuing your gentlemanly performance, I suppose I shall be safe enough," she quipped.

An amused chuckle came with his reply. "Madam, if we were cast upon a lonely isle with these same men, I'm sure the stress of your beauty would soon overwhelm them, and you would have to depend upon me to provide protection for you. There is not always safety in numbers, my sweet, and sometimes circumstances play a heavy hand upon the actions of men."

Finding no appropriate retort, she accepted the arm he offered and allowed him to escort her across the plank. When she glanced down and saw how far they were above the water, she tightened her grip and tried to dismiss the fact that his arm pressed casually against her breast.

The captain greeted Christopher with a broad smile and hearty handshake. "Welcome aboard, sir."

Christopher kept her near as he made the introductions. "Erienne, may I present Captain John Daniels, a man I have often sailed the seas with? John, this is the Lady Saxton. I believe you have heard me mention her."

Captain Daniels took the slender, gloved hand between his own and spoke with jovial warmth. "I thought Christopher had lost his senses when he talked about how lovely you were. I am relieved to see that his claims are quite well founded."

Erienne was not displeased with the compliment and murmured her gratitude before she met Christopher's steadfast gaze.

"This is your ship?" she queried and raised her gaze along the tallest mast to where it seemed to touch the underbelly of the sky. The mast rose to a staggering, dizzying height, and she had to look down quickly to set her swaying world aright and was glad for the support of her escort's arm.

"Aye, my lady," Christopher replied. "This one is the largest of the five ships I own."

"Would you care to see her?" the captain offered.

She sensed the man's pride for his ship and laughed gaily. "I was hoping I could."

Captain Daniels walked beside the couple as they moved toward the quarterdeck. Only a brief glance about was enough to assure Erienne that the vessel was well tended and everything was in its place. Christopher held his silence as they descended to the lower decks, allowing the captain the sole privilege of showing off the ship. No more than a third of the hands were aboard, and some of them stared outright as the lady passed, while others cast surreptitious glances in her direction, but each in his fashion paused to admire her beauty.

When the tour of the lower decks was complete, the captain led Erienne and Christopher to his cabin, where he poured a light cordial. He gave a nod to each of the two bedrooms that lay at either end of the main cabin and made a casual comment.

"The quarters might seem a bit cramped, madam, but this is where Mr. Seton and I have passed many an hour on the high seas."

"Do you have a voyage planned for the near future?" she asked and hoped she was successful in disguising her interest in whether Christopher would soon be leaving England or not.

"I am at Mr. Seton's disposal while we're here. When we leave will be up to him."

Erienne was somewhat astonished by the man's statement. To think that a whole vessel and its crew catered to the whims of one man seemed most extravagant, and she could only wonder at the wealth that could afford such luxury.

The three of them shared lunch on the ship. Captain Daniels had as many amusing yarns and stories as he had accounts of actual happenings at sea. Erienne was entertained thoroughly by the deft humor of the men, and despite her earlier qualms could not think of a specific time of relaxed conversation that she had enjoyed more.

In comparison, the rest of the afternoon passed quite serenely. Vauxhall Gardens was for a summer stroll, but the quietness of it on a wintry day could not be denied. Erienne was content to let her escort lead her through the baroque pavilions and the tree-lined lanes. As promised, Christopher lent himself to a most gentlemanly comportment and treated her in a grand style, making her feel as if she were the only woman in the world. In the Rotunda's "enchanted palace," tea was served in arched alcoves around the perimeter, while an orchestra provided soft music as a background for a congenial conversation.

In all, it proved to be a most enchanting day, and Erienne experienced a tinge of regret when it came to an end. She knew on the morrow she would be journeying back to Saxton Hall with her husband, and it left her in a melancholy mood as she watched the rented livery pull away from the Leicester mansion, carrying her escort with it. Christopher had held her hand briefly at the door and brushed a cousinly kiss against her cheek before making his departure. It was a simple contact, but the memory of it lingered far too long for her to be able to discount its effect on her.

The mists hung stubbornly in the low spots as the Saxtons' coach departed the Leicester mansion and ventured northward in the chill, brisk morning air. The sun, barely piercing the day with its light, was heavily swathed in fuchsia clouds that hung close over the horizon. The carriage rattled past farms that lay north of the Thames and crossed stone bridges where thickly curling vapors hovered over streams and marshes. As the day aged, the skies became gray and bleak, the air decidedly crisp. Tessie had relented to her mistress' pleas to take shelter inside the coach. Though Erienne understood the girl's timidity in the presence of Lord Saxton, not even the bulk of the two men who rode above could provide enough warmth to equal the interior. The young maid avoided glancing in the master's direction and was content to nap in her corner while her mistress chose to do the same in the seat beside her.

At noon they paused at an inn, and though the place had several guests, the common room fell deathly quiet as Lord Saxton guided his young wife to a table. His presence never failed to quicken the service, for all were wary of inciting his wrath. As usual, he declined to sample the fare, and after escorting Erienne back to the coach, excused himself briefly from her company.

They were on the road again and settling themselves for another long jaunt when there was a shout in the distance and the small hatch behind the driver's seat opened.

"A coach comin' up from behind, milord," Bundy called down. "A big 'un with a small troop o' riders."

Lord Saxton gave him a quick reply. "Be wary of them, and at the next wide place in the road, let them pass."

"Aye, milord." Bundy closed the port.

Erienne could see nothing from her seat at the rear, but the drum of heavy hooves coming toward them from behind was growing more distinct. Their own coach slowed and the ride became rough as Tanner edged it onto the extreme side of the road. A whip cracked with a loud report, and the jangle of harness grew louder. Erienne saw the horses first, and a carefully matched, magnificent team they were. The coach itself was large and black, with velvet curtains drawn tightly over the window. A driver and guard shared the front seat, while a pair of footmen were at the rear. Eight horsemen followed and were as well armed as any of the King's men. Though the richness of the hurrying entourage was obvious, a newer-looking patch on the door showed where a coat of arms had once been.

Erienne could not understand why such a high house should choose to travel with their coat of arms concealed. It was certainly not done with the intention of deterring the interest of thieves, not when there was so much evidence of wealth.

Lord Saxton observed the passing of the conveyance without comment. His only reaction was to consult his small pocket watch after the coach had gone on ahead. Then he leaned in the corner of his seat and folded his arms as if he would nap, but an occasional glint of light reflected from within the eyeholes assured her that she was closely watched.

They halted at another inn toward evening, and the place was abuzz with speculation about the mysterious black coach that had swept past without pausing. A few guests, unheedful of the one who kept to the shadows, boasted of having heard of a scarred and crippled lord of the North country who wore a strange helm and was reluctant to be named. They made odds that he was the one who traveled behind closely drawn curtains. Then finally catching sight of Lord Saxton's awesome visage, those same ones gaped . . . paled . . . and sputtered in confusion. They murmured with as much amazement at his lady's equally stunning beauty. Erienne had the vague impression that her husband enjoyed the difference in reactions and had a bent to play on it. But he also boldly made his claim on her, so none would overstep the bounds as the foolish roué had done on their trip south. One of those large, gloved hands lingering possessively on the small of her back readily conveyed the message.

The black coach was apparently traveling the same route as the Saxtons', for reports of it continued throughout the next day. The first white, downy flakes that settled over the road gave witness to its passing, but as they traveled farther north, no further hint could be seen in the deepening snow. The frosty mantling of white slowed their progress, and it was the following evening before they put Mawbry behind them. The gray bulk of Saxton Hall was a welcome sight even to Erienne, whose weariness forbade more than a nibble at dinner. The security of her own bed beneath her was a balm that brought her to the edge of sleep. There she hung for a space while her mind rooted through the rich loam of recent events. The vision of a smiling Christopher dissipated as the blank, staring mask of Lord

Saxton pushed to the fore. The black leather visage stayed until she sank into an exhausted slumber whose depths brooked no invasion of frivolity.

The number of days since their return had not fully aged into a week, and yet it seemed that hardly an evening passed without some claim that a night rider was seen roaming the northern hills. Doors of cottages, formerly left unbarred while the occupants slumbered in their beds, were now bolted hard and fast against any intrusion, casual or otherwise.

Haggard was one who came panting to the sheriff and breathlessly told about the thing that had chased him in the night. His eager declaration that he was ready to bear arms against the creature, should he be so fortunate as to be gifted with a weapon, won him a position as one of the sheriff's men. From then on, it seemed that Allan Parker could not move or turn without stumbling over the loyal man. Having lost Timmy, Haggard was eager for companionship, and he liberally displayed that readiness toward Allan. Haggard's constant presence wore at the patience of the sheriff. Only a harsh command to "stay put" seemed to penetrate the thick skull.

Christopher Seton came back to Mawbry, and word of the Yankee's return filtered to the hall. Though Lord Saxton was not wont to talk of the man, the young maids of the household were most eager to gossip when the subject concerned him, sometimes within hearing range of their mistress. Molly had begun to prattle about the wench she had caught him with in the inn several weeks past but refused to reveal the woman's identity. As a result Claudia's name was linked with his, since she had been seen in his company once or twice. By the time Erienne heard the rumors, they were well steeped with the indiscretions of the two. The stories left a sickening ache around her heart, a feeling she could not readily dismiss with arguments that she actually loathed the man.

Lord Saxton made a request of his wife on that Friday afternoon following their return, and in compliance Erienne came down to dinner dressed in the same gown she had worn the night of her wedding. She understood why her husband favored the dress. Its décolletage was most revealing, and his reaction to it this evening was no different from the first time she had worn it. He waited at the bottom of the stairs, holding one arm behind his back as he watched her descent with close attention.

"Madam," he rasped in his hoarse voice, "you are a rare jewel, a rose among the briars, and with each day's passing you grow more beautiful."

Erienne halted before him and saw his eyes flicker downward, giving her cause to wonder if the gown fully displayed her bosom as it had when he had stood behind her chair on their wedding night. She remained pliable beneath his regard, knowing that any attempt to cover herself would only stir his mockery.

"I once said your beauty needs no adornment, madam, and though I am still of that mind, I think a small bauble would not detract overmuch." He withdrew his arm from behind his back and dangled a heavily jeweled necklace before her eyes. "You would honor me if you would wear it, my love."

He looked up expectantly, holding the magnificent piece, and Erienne realized he was waiting for permission to put it on her. She nodded hesitantly, uncertain as to how long she could bear his touch against her bare skin. His hands slipped behind her neck, dragging the emerald and diamond necklace around the slender column. Inclining her head toward him, she waited with thumping heart as he tried to secure the clasp.

"Can you fasten it with your gloves on?" she murmured.

"Hold still a moment," he bade huskily and behind her back drew off first one glove and then the other. Erienne held her breath until his bare fingers touched her, then she almost sagged against him in relief. They were warm, human, masculinely firm.

A faint essence of a clean, manly scent wafted up from his clothing, stirring forth confused memories from the back of her mind and touching her with a strange sense of pleasure. Her mind groped feebly from the logic of the sensation, but the only memory she could recall with any clarity was that first moment when she had found herself in his bed after her fall from Socrates.

The clasp of the necklace was fastened with a barely audible clink, and Erienne, expecting him to step away, was startled to feel his fingers on her back again, this time caressing her bare skin with soft strokes. Slowly she turned her head to look up into his masked face, and the eyes behind the small openings met her inquiring gaze.

"My hands have trembled at the thought of touching you," he whispered raggedly. "But I may have erred in doing so."

Delicately shaped brows lifted in mute question.

"From this moment on, the temptation may prove too hard to

resist. Having touched you, I only want you more." He paused, then sighed heavily, seeming to fight an inner battle within himself. When he continued, his words were strained and halting. "Have I been a fool in taking you to wife, Erienne? Perhaps you will only continue to hate me or find another you prefer. Maybe I've been unfair to both of us and it was my own brand of cruel jealousy that could not bear to let you go."

"I entered into the vows with full knowledge and a will to see them out, milord. You are my husband, and I only beg some time to bring my mind to full harness. You understand well enough that there is a barrier between us. My fears are as difficult to me as your scars are to you, but in time perhaps both will cease to be the obstacles that keep us apart. If you will wait upon my adjustment, I have it in my heart and mind to be nothing less than a good wife to you . . . in every way."

His hand, as if on its own volition, came upward from her back and hovered out of range of her vision, as if he yearned to caress her cheek but fought against the urge. After a moment's pause, he dropped it over her shoulder again. Behind her back, she could feel him jerking on his gloves, and on impulse she laid a palm against his chest, finding it firmly muscled beneath the crispness of his shirt.

"You see, milord? I can touch you now, and it does not cause me to shudder."

Carefully, so as not to alarm her, he raised his gloved hand and gently rubbed his knuckles along her cheek. "My dear Erienne, beneath this twisted exterior there beats a human heart quite warmed by your beauty. 'Tis painful for me to wait, but I will endure anything knowing there is hope."

He straightened, and in a courtly gesture offered his arm. "Madam, you must be famished, and I have a great need of a chilly hall to take my mind from the craving lusts that gnaw at me."

With a laugh, Erienne dropped a slim hand on the dark sleeve. "Perhaps I should be the one to wear the mask, milord, or at least a few more clothes."

"If I had my way, there'd be less of the latter," he replied as his eyes dipped to where the largest of the emeralds nestled coyly between the ripely swelling breasts. "But I should keep in mind that there are servants to consider."

Self-consciously she fingered the heavy necklace, aware of his devouring gaze. "When you look at me like that, I feel as if there is a definite dearth of the latter."

Her husband responded with a wry chuckle. "Madam, if looking is a hanging offense, then I'd rather fulfill every facet of my desire and be strung up for a lion than a lamb. I am most anxious to claim my husbandly rights, so if I misread your distaste of me and overwait the moment, be sure to inform me of that fact, and I shall most eagerly respond."

She sensed the smile that must have touched his lips as he stared down at her, and her cheeks grew flushed beneath his unwavering regard. She glanced away, drawing a soft laugh from the dark mask, and his other hand, coming to rest upon her own, squeezed her fingers affectionately.

Erienne knew she was dreaming. She saw her own dark curls as she knelt in rapt attention beside her mother, who was seated at the harpsichord, playing, as was her wont, for the children. The impossibility of this awakened Erienne, and she lay without moving, totally confused, for the twanging tones of a harpsichord still floated eerily through the manse, drifting up from below. The instrument was out of tune, and the notes were struck with such force and intensity that the back of her neck crawled. She could almost feel the rage conveyed in the music.

Several moments passed before she recognized the melody. It was an olden aire, and the words taunted her with their bitter poignancy, drifting through her mind with the haunting refrain, "Alas, my love, you do me wrong to cast me off so discourteously."

Erienne rose from the bed and quickly donned her dressing gown. She could not remember having seen a harpsichord in the house, but there were many rooms still unused, and she had not yet lifted every dust cover to view its treasure.

Following the sound of the violent chords, she was led to a wing where the house had not yet been made habitable. Once in the hall, a soft light guided her to where a door stood ajar, and she carefully pushed it wide. A tall candelabrum sat on a small table in the middle of the room, its yellowed stumps of candles providing the light that had drawn her. The nape of her neck crawled again. The furniture was still draped with the heavy dust cloths, except for one piece sitting across the room, and there the covering had been thrown back. Seated before the keyboard half facing her, head and shoulders mercifully masked in shadows, was the silhouette of a man. The leather helm and black gloves were cast aside on the mantel of the harpsichord, and she could see the wildly tossed hair that must have grown in patchwork locks between scars. He almost attacked the instrument, seeming to rip the notes from it as he vented his frustration with the world at large and, Erienne feared, with her in particular.

As if with a will of their own, her feet moved forward, slowly, haltingly, then of a sudden the music stopped, dying off in an unmelodious chord as the man's head jerked up. The eyes, she thought, gleamed with a half-mad feral glint.

"Lord Saxton?" she queried in a breathless whisper.

"Stand back!" The command was coarse and harsh. "Come no closer lest your sanity depart you, woman."

Erienne halted as his tone brooked no disobedience and realized for the first time that she had left her slippers upstairs. The stone floor was cold beneath her feet, and it sent a chill creeping up her limbs.

Lord Saxton snatched the gloves and hid his hands while he donned them, then he grasped the leather helm and tugged it down, pulling the collar of his robe snug around the base, ignoring the laces that tightened the mask. He braced his hands wide apart on the mantel as he asked, "Do you play?"

Erienne laughed. "Once upon a time, milord, but then only a few simple pieces, certainly nothing with the emotion you display."

With a heavy sigh, he waved a hand in a gesture of impatience. "I can't seem to make it come out right anymore."

"You have too much anger in you," she said softly.

He scoffed. "Are you in addition to your beauty a seer of the ages that you can read me so openly?"

For the first time Erienne felt as if she could understand a small part of him. "No, milord, but I have known grief and anger and hatred, and I have seen them in others around me. Indeed . . . Stuart"—his name did not come easily in his presence—"I have known precious little else these past couple of years. My mother was the only one to express love to me, and she is many months gone. Though you wear the mask, I can see in you many of those emotions . . . and they frighten me."

"They needn't. I mean no harm to you."

Her gaze lowered, and she half turned to stare into the darkness.

"However scarred your body might be, I realize that your soul suffers far more, and because of this, I pity you."

He gave a snort of derision. "I urge you to save your pity for a more deserving soul, madam. 'Tis the last thing I want from you."

"Stuart . . ."

"And I would urge you, madam, to have a care when addressing me. The use of my given name in public could bring about your widowhood in a most untimely manner."

"I will be careful, milord." She moved forward, glancing about the room in curiosity. "Would this be the music room?"

" 'Twas my father's study. He doted on his lady's skill with this."

"You seem to know the manor well."

"Why do you say that, my love?"

"I have wandered about this place for several days," she answered softly, "but I found no harpsichord."

"I am a normal man in the guise of a beast. While you dream upon your pillows, madam, I am pierced with visions of the one my heart would have, and I roam this house in agony. Whatever distractions I find here, I welcome."

"I do not begrudge you anything, Stuart," she said gently.

He rose and with that odd hitching gait, came to stand close before her. "Madam, you would hide in your chambers, trembling with fear, if you knew the full weight of that emotion I now hold in check."

Slowly he lifted a hand, and Erienne fought the urge to flee as he reached out to cup her breast. Her whole body trembled beneath his touch, and it took all of her resolve to stand quietly while his thumb caressed the soft peak. Then his arm slipped about her slender waist as if to draw her toward him, and she broke, twisting out of his embrace, and was gone, flying in sudden panic through the house, never pausing until she was again in her chamber. Gasping for breath and with weak knees trembling beneath her, she rested her back against that solid-paneled door which, though unbolted, had protected her thus far, and from far below came the hollow echo of rasping, mocking laughter.

Fourteen

The night was cold and crystal clear. The stars twinkled with a brilliance of their own. With the crisp air, the light snow cover squeaked beneath the feet, and one had to tread softly to pass through the night unheard.

In a small valley near the top of a swelling moor, a camp had been laid, and it bore a feeling of permanency. Lanterns were lit, and a half-score tents were banked with straw and dead leaves as added protection against the cold. At the far end of the valley a shallow cave was stacked with powder kegs, wooden boxes, and other supplies. Near one side of it, a series of rope stalls held more than a dozen horses. In the center of the camp a pair of heavily garbed men half squatted on logs beside a fire.

"Poor ol' Timmy," one sighed. "'At night rider took him, he did. Skewered him right through the gizzard, then slit his throat."

"Aye," the other agreed, nodding his head before he sucked at a small earthen cup of ale. "'At blackhearted whelp o' the devil's runnin' too close for comfort. 'At ol' widder woman, she says as how she saw the night rider not more'n two or three miles south o' here."

"The cap'n better be findin' us another hideout. In a trade the likes o' this, Luddie, 'tain't wise ter keep chambers too long in one spot."

"Aye, we've got enough fer a foin spree. Even figgerin' what Timmy took ter lay off on his doxie, 'twould fetch us a high time in Carlisle. Remember, Orton, 'at low street tavern? An' 'at sweet plumpy, red-haired wench what serviced the rooms?"

Orton surveyed the high stone cliffs that surrounded them, then stood up and stamped his numb feet. He jerked his head toward the dark-shadowed opening that marked the entrance to the hidden vale. " 'Oo's on lookout?"

Luddie huddled beneath his dark cloak. "John Turner's out there. He'll be comin' in near midnight and wake ol' Clyde."

"Then I'll be turnin' in," Orton stated, tossing a large log on the fire. Stomping off, he entered one of the tents and soon doused the light.

Luddie watched for a while, then shivered and went to his own tent. The camp grew quiet. The lamps went out one by one, and soon the only light came from the dimmed lantern hanging from the stable cave and the flickering fire. The multitude of snores grew loud, and no one heard the distant grunt as John Turner was struck from behind. A rope swished in the still night air as it sailed over a stout branch of a tall tree. The limp form was dragged up feet first, and in the gentle breezes he swung like a pendulum with the creaking of the branch to mark the passing of time.

A vague movement came near the entrance, and an indistinct black form materialized from the darkness. The shape paused at the very edge of the firelight where the dancing flames cast a dim glow over the black, shrouded figure and the huge ebony stallion he rode. Like the eerie quiet before a raging storm, the ghost rider waited with deathlike stillness.

His arm came forward, swinging a dark shape on the end of a long rope so that it landed in the fire. There was a crackling and a snapping, and in a moment a dead yew, perhaps the height of a man, was ablaze with white-hot flames. The nighthawk reined the horse around, careless now of sound. He jerked the rope, and the blazing tree soared. With a thunderous bellow, he set spurs to his heavy-muscled steed, swinging him a wide circle and dragging the tree behind. The thing bounced, twisted, crashed, bounced again, as if it were a wild creature at the end of a tether. Burning brands flew in every direction, and the canvas shelters burst readily into flame. The rider made a wide sweep of the tents, igniting them all.

The camp dissolved into a screaming melee. Men burst from the burning tents and rushed about in mindless confusion, screaming and shouting, slapping at the bits of charred or flaming canvas that clung to them while frantically trying to salvage their hides and hair or whatever unscorched portions remained of them.

The night rider spurred his mount toward the cave and hurled his brand atop the small kegs that were neatly stacked against the back wall. The horses shrieked in panic and broke their ties to race out and plow, jumping and kicking, through the already dazed men of the camp.

Old Clyde was on his way toward the entrance when he came upright in sudden fear. He screamed, and the snow melted about his shuffling feet as he tried to put some direction to them. The black stallion reared before him, its rider garbed in flowing cloak and with a length of pale blue steel in his hand. The apparition laughed, and Clyde would later swear the rider's eyes flashed fire as he shouted for all who would listen.

"Cutthroats and the likes of ye shall find no haven in these hills! I will search ye out wherever ye go until ye scatter and flee for yer lives!"

Clyde waited, clenching his eyes tightly shut. He was certain that his end would come and was almost as sure that the flashing steel had already sapped his life without his knowledge. After a moment he lowered his arms from off his head and opened his eyes. His raised foot sagged until his toe tentatively touched the ground, and his jaw hung slack, nearly meeting it.

The vision was gone. What remained was only a peal of laughter echoing above the din in the vale.

Clyde turned and found two others gaping behind him. His hand shook as he gestured over his shoulder. "Did ye see?" His fear-trebled voice broke, and he tried again. "Did ye see him? I fought him off."

His hand searched wildly for a weapon to support his claim. A broken tent pole seemed to fill it magically, and he brandished it in gleeful relief that he was still alive.

Someone in the camp fired a musket, and the ball ricocheted from a cliff to whine harmlessly off in the night. Then a voice gabbled in growing fear. "The fire! The powder kegs! They're on fire!"

As if to support the statement, a bright flash filled the stable cave, and a score or so of small flaming casks went bounding through the vale. Horses ran everywhere, and the blazing tents and clothes were pounded into a snowy wet rubble amid the tumbled rocks. Men leapt for shelter or sought with bare hands to scratch shallow trenches in the icy earth where they lay, anything to escape the burning kegs and the flaring gunpowder that with a vengeance sought them out.

A mile or so away a black-clad rider paused in crossing a low bridge to look back at the havoc he had wrought. A rapid series of flashes lit the night sky. Flaming brands etched neat, fiery arcs and fell sputtering through the air while a herd of horses fled at breakneck speed across a distant rise. Even from where he was, he could still hear the bellows of rage and screams of pain.

The night rider chuckled to himself. It was better than five miles to the nearest shelter, and a lightly clad walk on a cold winter's night should give them all something to think about.

Lord Saxton's rooms were at the front of the manse, and from the diamond-paned windows one had a clear view of the road that wound its way across the valley toward the tower entry. Erienne had ventured to the chambers with Aggie to judge the need for further furnishings, and for the first time Erienne surveyed the rooms, which were slightly smaller than her own. A small, separate alcove provided privacy for baths and grooming, and as in the larger room, everything was neatly in place. The foot of the heavily draped, canopied bed opened toward the hearth, where a pair of Elizabethan chairs sat at a small table. Nearer the windows and on the adjoining walls, two tall armoires, locked against intrusion, faced each other from opposite sides of the room. A wide desk was placed beneath the windows where it could catch the light, and a thick, leather-bound book lay on its polished planks near an oil lamp.

Aggie gestured to the volume and stated matter-of-factly, "The master keeps a record o' his tenants here. Ye'll find an account o' all the births and deaths o' those who've ever lived here on the Saxton lands. Someday, mum, the births o' yer wee ones will be noted here in his lordship's own hand."

Erienne was not sure if she appreciated the reminder of what her duties entailed, but she could hardly fault the woman for the enthusiasm she displayed when the subject concerned the family's continuance. She was accepting the fact that Aggie was uncommonly fond of her master, and like a doting mother, seemed blind to his fear-some appearance.

That fact was not true of his wife, however, and even as she stood in his bedchamber, well aware that he had left the manor a full hour before, she could not feel totally at ease. He had startled her so many times by appearing without warning, she could never be sure where he was. She had come to his rooms almost reluctantly, not wanting to intrude, yet knowing she could not continue to avoid them without arousing the servants' curiosity.

"There's a coach comin', mum," Aggie called from the window.

Erienne joined the housekeeper at the crystal panes. Apprehension settled in as Erienne recognized the conveyance, and she was more than a little curious as to what manner of business Lord Talbot was about today and who he would be wanting to see.

She waited beside the window until the coach halted, not in the mood to humor the man by rushing down to meet him. She remembered his conduct at the assembly far too well to look forward to entertaining him in the absence of Lord Saxton.

"Why, mum"—Aggie leaned forward as a billowing skirt appeared in the door of the coach—" 'tis Miss Talbot. Goodness, I wonder what brings her here."

Surprise etched the lovely features of her mistress and was quickly replaced by a look of dismay. Self-consciously Erienne smoothed her gown. Since she had dressed for warmth and work, it was not her best, yet she rejected the idea of changing into one of the fine gowns Lord Saxton had given her, just to impress the woman. Somehow that seemed vain and pretentious.

Erienne cast a last glance about her and determined that a rug in front of the hearth would greatly improve the comfort of the room. As she descended the stairs to meet the woman, it dawned on her that she was just as reluctant to meet Claudia as she was Lord Talbot. Neither was very endearing as a friend.

Claudia had been shown into the great hall and was sitting in Lord Saxton's chair near the fireplace when Erienne entered. Claudia glanced around as she came across the room, and then Claudia smiled in derisive amusement as her gaze flickered over the plain woolen gown of her hostess.

"How fit you look, Erienne," she observed. "I'd have thought you'd have aged at least a score since your marriage."

Feigning her own amusement, Erienne inquired, "Whatever made you think that, Claudia?"

"Why, I've heard that Lord Saxton is no less than a beast, that he is simply ghastly to look at."

Erienne managed a benevolent smile. "Did you come out of curiosity?"

"My dear Erienne, I came to offer my condolences."

"How kind of you, Claudia," Erienne responded sweetly. "But you have made a dreadful mistake. My husband is very much alive."

"Poor Erienne," Claudie sighed in exaggerated concern. "You try so hard to be brave." Eagerly she leaned forward in her chair as she asked, "Tell me, does he beat you? Is he mean to you?"

Laughter dispelled the idea. "Oh, Claudia, do I look as if I've been beaten?"

"Is he as ugly as the rumors make him out to be?"

"I really cannot answer that," Erienne replied with a shrug and casually gestured to the table beside her as Aggie brought in tea.

Claudia's countenance displayed amazement. "My goodness, Erienne, why not?"

"Because I've never seen my husband's face." The answer came simply. "He wears a mask."

"Even to bed?"

The teacups clattered on their saucers as Aggie nearly dropped the tray. Regaining her composure, she set the service on the table where her mistress had indicated and asked, "Will that be all, mum?"

Erienne welcomed the distraction, however brief. It gave her a moment to soothe the bristling ire she felt at Claudia's rude interrogation. "Yes, Aggie. Thank you."

Only Erienne saw the dubious glance the housekeeper cast toward the guest before Aggie hurriedly took her leave. When Erienne faced Claudia again, her own smile of amusement was genuine.

"I have never seen my husband's face at any time," she stated, pouring tea. "He prefers it that way."

Claudia took the proffered cup and wiggled back in her chair. "It must be dreadfully disturbing not to be able to see what your husband looks like." She giggled. "Why, even in broad daylight you'd never be able to recognize him without his mask."

"On the contrary, I believe I would know my husband anywhere. He walks with a definite limp."

"Oh, dear, 'tis more horrible than I had imagined. A beast of a man! Does he lap his food, or must you feed him?"

Irate sparks of indignation flared through Erienne, and she struggled mightily to speak in a calm tone. "My husband is a gentleman, Claudia, not a beast."

The woman laughed scornfully. "A gentleman? My dear Erienne, do you know the meaning of the word?"

"Perhaps more than you, Claudia. I've seen the worst of men, and dealing with them has taught me to judge a man by his comportment and not by the shape of his nose. My husband may not have the pampered looks of a milk-fed weasel, but he is, in truth, far more of a gentleman than most I've met."

"If you're so proud of him, Erienne, perhaps you would like to show him off at a ball we're having. No doubt he would feel more at home at a masque, but this will be a much more regal affair. Papa has asked me to extend an invitation to you and your . . . ah . . . husband." Her eyes passed lightly over Erienne. "I hope you can find something appropriate to wear."

A door closed behind Erienne, and the scrape-clop of Lord Saxton's footsteps came across the room. Claudia's eyes widened as her gaze went past her hostess and found the large, dark shape approaching them.

Erienne glanced around as her husband halted beside her chair. "My lord, I wasn't expecting you back so soon."

"We have a guest," he stated, his voice strong but rasping as he awaited an introduction.

Erienne quickly obliged as Claudia still stared with sagging jaw, seeming for once to be at a complete loss for words. "We have just been invited to a ball, my lord."

"Oh?" The hooded eyes fell upon the woman, who gulped. "Is this affair in the near future?"

Claudia nodded nervously. "Why . . . ah . . . yes . . . two weeks hence."

Lord Saxton looked down at his young wife. "And have you a suitable gown to wear?"

Erienne smiled. "Yes, any one of several, my lord."

"Then I see no reason why you shouldn't go to the Talbots' ball."

Claudia rose to her feet and with a delicately manicured hand at her throat, spoke unsteadily. "I . . . I really must be going now, but I shall inform my father that you'll be coming." She felt as if the eyes behind the unblinking holes could see to the most private depths of her being, and there was much there she did not want to yield. The almost overpowering urge to scream already made her voice tremble, and she dared nothing more than the meekest farewell. "Good day to you both."

The woman hastened toward the door, not even tossing back a glance.

"Do come back again, Claudia," Erienne called pleasantly. "Perhaps when you can stay longer." She curbed her threatening laughter until she heard the coach pull away from the drive, then she leaned back in her chair and giggled in glee. "My dear Stuart, did you see the look on her face when you came in? She was absolutely terrified of you."

"My dear Stuart," he mimed with a chuckle. "Now, that is a phrase my heart has longed to hear. Dare I hope that you're growing fond of me?"

Erienne gave him a timid answer. "At least I don't fear you as much as I did."

"Then perhaps I should be grateful to your friend for improving my circumstance with you."

Erienne's slim nose wrinkled in distaste. "I beg your pardon, my lord, but she is no friend of mine. She came here because she heard rumors about you, and she needs a curiosity to liven her ball. People say that she and I resemble each other, and I believe she resents me for that reason."

Lord Saxton leaned forward, bracing his hands on his cane as he looked down at her. "Madam, before I took this encumbrance upon myself, I was considered by no few to be something of a rake. 'Tis therefore my expert opinion that the young woman feels much envy and thus a more than significant jealousy?"

"But Claudia has everything," Erienne argued.

"Not everything, my love, and she will need far more than beauty to make her happy." He paused a moment until Erienne met the blank stare. "And you, my love? What more would you need to make you happy?"

She lowered her gaze in confusion as a hot flush crept into her cheeks. The words she had once bravely voiced to Aggie now hid themselves behind a wall of trepidation and fear. She had stated that she wanted a plain, ordinary man whom she could show some affection for, but there was no use dreaming for the impossible. She had to be content in the fact that she could now look at her husband without feeling the hair crawl on the back of her neck.

The visit of Claudia was not even dismissed from mind before another coach was seen coming toward the manse. It was shortly before midday of the following morn when Aggie came puffing into the old lord's study, where Erienne was carefully cleaning the gilded harpsichord. Two maids had been set to dusting the other artifacts and furnishings of the room, and among the three of them the chamber was taking on a look of elegance.

"If me eyes don't deceive me, mum, the hired livery from Mawbry is comin' up the lane. I've seen it a time or two, and I can tell ye truthfully, 'tis a miracle it goes anywhere at all."

"Mawbry?" Erienne rubbed the back of her hand across her brow, inadvertently smearing the black smudge that was there into a long streak. "Who could be coming to see us from Mawbry?"

Aggie lifted her plump shoulders in a shrug. "Yer father perhaps? Maybe he's lonesome for ye."

More likely out of coin, Erienne mused as she wiped her hands on her apron. "I'll go down and meet him."

"Beggin' yer pardon, mum, but wouldn't ye rather tidy yerself? Ye wouldn't be wantin' folks ter think ye're just a hirelin' here."

Erienne glanced down at herself and discovered that her gown and apron were quite soiled. Immediately she began pulling at the ties of her apron as she hurried toward the door. "Have you seen Lord Saxton?"

"The master and Bundy were gone 'fore I rose this morn'n', mum, and there's been no sign of 'em since."

"If Lord Saxton should return, please inform him that we have another guest."

"Aye, mum. That I will."

Erienne had mounted the stairs and was hurrying toward her bedchamber when a large form recognizable as her husband stepped from the hall leading from the east wing. She was almost past when the realization of his presence struck her, but before she could turn, he stepped near and reached a long arm out, catching her at the waist and pulling her around to face him.

"Madam, where do you go in such a flurry?" The amusement was evident in his voice as he chided, "And looking for all the world like you've just crawled from a dustbin."

"I can say the same for you, milord," she returned, brushing off

his coatsleeve, where dirt and a tangled mass of cobwebs clung. She glanced down the shadowed corridor, wondering how he had managed to return to the manse without being seen and then be in a wing where there were no outside doors. "Have you grown wings of late that you can swoop in and out unobserved? Aggie said you were out."

"Did she now? And as busy as she is, is it any wonder that she missed seeing me return? Were you looking for me?"

"We have a visitor approaching . . . and I . . . I think it may be my father."

"Your father, eh? And do you think he's finally come to his senses and wants you back with him?"

"I doubt that, my lord. More likely he comes to cure a lightness of his purse."

"And do you think I should aid him in that regard?"

"I fear he would only lose it at the gaming tables or let Farrell drink down what it would buy. They are probably both better off without it."

She took her hand from his arm, blushing as she realized how familiar and wifely the gesture seemed. Confused by her own manner, she stood away, giving a lame excuse. "I'd better go tidy myself."

Lord Saxton followed her into her chambers and leaned an arm against the windowsill while she took fresh clothing from the armoire. The gown she wore fastened down the back, and without Tessie's aid she could not undo it. She glanced his way, hesitant about making such a wifely request when she was reluctant to commit herself to any familiarity beyond what had already been established. He watched her closely in return, and it dawned on her that he knew exactly what was going through her mind. Releasing a trembling sigh, she went to him and lifted her hair aside as she presented her back to him. The task was delayed as he doffed his gloves, and she stood quietly, not daring to look over her shoulder until the gown was loosened and he had drawn on the gloves again. She stepped away, hunching her shoulders forward until the bodice dropped down over her arms, then wiggled out of the garment.

"Madam, have you noticed that it's snowing?" he asked, admiring the gentle swing of her hips before she disappeared behind the arras. " 'Tis most likely we'll be having an overnight guest if this continues."

"I'm hurrying," she called, taking his statement as a warning. After a quick swipe of a wet cloth across her face and a few yanks of a brush through her hair, she reappeared in her shift. In her haste, she was oblivious to the sight she presented him when she stepped into the gown and bent over to pull it up over her petticoats. The shallow bodice of the shift gapped away from the creamy flesh, baring the delicately hued peaks and sending a surging hotness flooding into his loins. Thrusting her arms through the long sleeves, she hurried to him, unaware of his discomfort, and again turned her back, this time glancing over her shoulder with a timid smile.

Lord Saxton released his breath in slow degrees as he pulled off the gloves. The urge to do more than this simple service savaged his restraint, and by the time he had completed the torturous task, he was of the firm opinion that he was a man who had made his own hell.

Escorted down the stairs on her husband's arm, Erienne felt her nerves tense with each descending step. Her father's loud voice boomed through the manse as he addressed Farrell, boasting of all that he had once had in London and of the many lords who had lent an ear to his wisdom.

"Ahh, there I had it all, and someday I will have it again, me boy. Ye just watch. We'll live in a place as grand as this and have servants ter wait on us hand and foot. Oh, 'twill be fine, Farrell. Fine indeed."

The heavy thud of Lord Saxton's weighted shoe brought Avery around to face the couple as they entered the great chamber. His eyes quickly flitted over them, and his face displayed a momentary tightening at sight of his daughter's gown. Even though it was simple and modest, both cut and cloth were well beyond what he could afford. It was not right that the chit should enjoy such luxury and not share with her kin.

"Well, good day, Erienne!" His voice seemed overloud. "The passage of time appears ter have done ye well."

Erienne passed him with cool dignity and nodded briefly to Farrell before slipping into the chair her husband pulled around for her. Avery cleared his throat and perched on the long bench that sat in front of the hearth.

"I guess ye both be wonderin' why I've come. Well, I brought ye some news, I did. Bad news, I fear. And seein's as how ye're now kin, milord, I thought 'twould be best ter warn ye."

"Warn us about what?" Lord Saxton questioned.

"Me and Allan Parker . . . he bein' the sheriff of Mawbry, ye know . . . well, we were up ter Lord Talbot's the other day, and I overheard the two o' 'em talkin' . . . Allan and his lordship, I mean. 'Twas just a quick exchange, ye understand, 'fore they seen me listenin'." He peered up at his host as he made his point.

"Well?" The word was issued in a tone of impatience.

Avery released a long sigh. "They were talkin' 'bout ye, milord, and sayin' as how they think ye could be the night rider."

Erienne gasped and glanced up at her husband, who after a moment began to chuckle.

"I thought it funny too, milord," Avery chortled. "Why, ter me knowledge ye don't even sit a horse, and ye seem kind o' slow. . . ." He waved his hand to negate his statement and gestured to his head. "Not slow here, mind ye, but with ye bein' a cripple an' all . . . Well, it all seems a mite farfetched ter think o' ye ridin' across the moors like some lunatic." He nodded his head vigorously. "I said as much ter his lordship, but then he asked me who I thought it was, and I couldn't rightly say."

Lord Saxton's voice bore traces of humor as he asked, "And were you able to convince Talbot of my innocence?"

"I cannot rightly say, but if ye've proof o' yer whereabouts last night maybe I ought ter hear 'bout it."

"Why last night?" his host inquired.

" 'At night rider struck again durin' the night, this time leavin' ol' Ben crumpled dead against the back door o' the inn."

Erienne caught her hand to her throat in shock, but only a deadly silence came from Lord Saxton. Almost calmly he asked, "How can you be sure it was the night rider who murdered Ben? Did anyone see him?"

Avery drew himself up in an authoritative manner. "The bloody blighter did ol' Ben in just like he did Timmy Sears. Spitted 'im right through the chest and slit his throat, 'e did, and left 'im 'ere. . . ."

Erienne shuddered and turned her face aside.

"Spare us the details, man," Lord Saxton bade sharply. He splashed some sherry into a glass and pressed it into his wife's hand. "Here, this will help you."

"Must o' been some'in' she ate," Avery declared with a chuckle. "I didn't bring her up ter be a weak-kneed twit." He peered at the lord with a twisted smile of amusement. "Unless, o' course, ye've started yerself a wee one growin' in her belly."

Lord Saxton spun around to face his father-in-law, and somehow the blank mask seemed to take on a threatening frown. Ducking his head beneath that fearsome stare, Avery cleared his throat again and lowered his gaze to where his foot nervously shuffled against the stone floor.

Erienne struggled against the horrible vision of Ben sprawled limp and bloody. Though pale and trembling, she faced her father and spoke with care. "Lord Saxton . . . was with me . . . last night. He . . . could not . . . be . . . the night rider."

Avery lifted his shoulders in a manner of indifference. "I wasn't the one what thought it. But I'll be tellin' the sheriff what ye said, that his lordship here was with ye all night."

Erienne opened her mouth to correct the statement, then slowly closed it again. Her husband looked around as if expecting her to speak, and was amazed when she did not.

In rapt attention, Farrell had watched the hypnotic sway of the sherry as it sloshed back and forth against the sides of the crystal decanter. At times his tongue had followed the motion, moving over his parched lips as he savored the brew in his mind. The trip from Mawbry had been overlong and unduly rough, as he had developed quite a thirst on the way. Of late, he had lacked the coin to buy anything more than the cheapest ale, and he dearly needed something to take the chill from his bones.

"Ah . . . Lord Saxton . . . if I might impose upon you to fill another glass there . . ."

Stuart's gaze came around to the younger man, who hesitantly motioned to the decanter. The eyes behind the mask flicked over the rumpled clothes and the soiled shirt, then clouded with pity. With a flagging reluctance, he poured a shallow draught into a glass and noted the unsteadiness of the hand that accepted it from his grasp. The low, sibilant voice seemed to echo in the room as he spoke. "I understand that you were an accurate shot before your arm was injured, Mr. Fleming."

Farrell paused with the glass half raised to his lips and stared mutely into the mask.

"Have you considered developing your skill with your left hand? It might prove difficult, but if you're persistent, 'tis possible to learn to handle a weapon just as well with it."

"That arm's 'bout as useless as the other," Avery sneered. " 'Tain't good for nothin' more 'an bringin' a glass to his lips. Why, he's a cripple, can't ye see that?"

Farrell downed the drink in a gulp and then slowly held out the glass as if hoping for a refill. Lord Saxton ignored the silent plea, took the glass from him, and set it aside.

"He'll be as much of a cripple as he wants to be," Stuart stated firmly. "Or he can be his own man."

Avery momentarily displayed his contempt for his host. "Like ye, milord?"

"Father!" Erienne gasped.

"Never mind, my love," Stuart murmured over his shoulder.

"Well! Will ye listen to that now? Love she is," Avery chortled. "I never thought I'd see the day when a man would be sayin' 'at ter her." He jabbed a finger at his daughter as he cast an eye toward his son-in-law. "I tell ye that chit caused me a barrelful o' sorrow, the likes o' which I ain't got over yet. I was a poor, bereaved man. I lost me wife. Me boy was crippled, and this girl thought she had ter have a man what she could admire. And here she is now, defendin' the likes o' yerself, sir, as if ye were the grandest-lookin' man what's come along since the dawnin' o' time. If she ain't so particular now, why couldn't she have set aside her foolishness long ago and married a kindly man what woulda taken pity on me in me old age?" He shook his head in bemusement. "I'll never understand her. Never!"

A moment of weighty silence passed as Erienne, Lord Saxton, and even Farrell stared in astonishment at the blustering man. Then the lord of the manor contemplated his lady, and when the blue-violet eyes raised to his, they were wide with uncertainty.

Stuart felt a need to clear his own throat. "I believe we were discussing Farrell's shooting ability." He faced the younger man as he continued. "I know something about firearms myself, and I think you'd be interested in my collection. After we've taken some nourishment, I'll show you a few pieces I have. About ten or twelve years ago, Waters made a bell-muzzle pistol with a spring-operated bayonet. 'Tis a most remarkable weapon."

Farrell displayed more enthusiasm than he had in the past two months as he replied, "Do you think I could shoot something like that?"

"It might set you back on your heels today, but if you worked at strengthening your arm, in time you might be able to handle it. Of course, you will need a clear head and a steady hand."

The day aged, and the winter winds blew across the moors, sweeping the snow into sculptured drifts that resembled frozen waves in a sea of white and preventing the passage of the coach. Fires were fed to warm the manor as night approached, and oil lamps provided light as the guests were directed to their chambers. When the manor grew still, Erienne pulled a thin wrapper over her gown and went to rap lightly on Lord Saxton's door.

"Milord, 'tis Erienne," she called softly through the thick, wooden plank. "Might I come in?"

"A moment please, my love," he answered.

After a while the slow, ponderous footsteps drew near the door. It was opened to reveal her husband in a long, red velvet dressing robe. The collar was pulled up close about his neck. The mask and gloves were in place, and the heavily shod boot was visible beneath the hem.

"Am I disturbing you, milord?" she asked timidly.

"Aye, madam, but not in the manner you mean."

Though his statement bewildered her, she went on to explain her reason for coming. "I wanted to thank you for what you did for Farrell today."

Lord Saxton stepped back and swept his arm inward in a silent invitation for her to enter. Erienne complied and went to stand before the fireplace. Unaware of how clearly the light silhouetted her body through her garments, she stretched forth her hands to the blazing warmth. Her husband took a chair in the shadows, where he could enjoy the long-limbed, full-bosomed beauty of her without compromising his stoic demeanor.

Erienne spoke softly over her shoulder, knowing he was there but unable to see him. "I saw a spark of life in Farrell today that I was afraid would never be seen again. Why, he actually laughed at dinner."

"Your father is blind to your brother's needs."

"You put it kindly, Stuart, and if Father persists in undermining Farrell's confidence, my brother will be no better than Ben was." She shook her head sadly and blinked at the tears blurring her vision. "Poor Ben, he was such a pitiful old man." She sniffed and quickly brushed at the wetness on her cheek. "Some of the people in Mawbry will miss him."

A question came from the shadows. "Why did you let your father believe I was with you all night?"

Erienne gave a tiny shrug. "I saw no need in explaining our . . . our arrangement. I know you didn't murder Ben, just as I have come to the determination that you didn't kill Timmy Sears. Those were deeds done by a coward, and if I've learned one thing about you since our marriage, milord, it is the fact that you are no coward." She laughed. "If there is a coward in this family 'tis I."

He spoke in a soft, rasping whisper. "Thank you for your trust, madam, and I will take heart in your use of the word 'family.' Perhaps sometime in the near future we'll become a family in truth."

Dubiously Erienne faced her husband, whose breath halted as the outline of her was boldly betrayed through the diaphanous clothing. His gaze fell to where the inward curve of her thighs joined, and in fascination he watched the play of firelight through her limbs as she moved toward him.

"Stuart?" Erienne stopped before him, and he dragged his eyes upward to meet her smiling face. "Thank you, Stuart."

Leaning forward, she pressed her cheek briefly against the side of the leather mask and then fled the room in anxious haste. It was a long time before his lordship could regulate his breathing and cool the fire in his loins.

The snow left as quickly as it came, and Avery Fleming went back to his cottage the following day, no richer than he had come. He had found no opportunity to approach either his daughter or her husband on the matter of a loan. Thus he glumly took his leave of the hall. Farrell, however, was much taken with his host's skill with weapons and stayed to end out the week. He felt no inclination to indulge himself with strong drink as he practiced with the firearms. Though loading proved difficult, with the aid of his teeth, the clamp of his thighs, and a hand that he had heretofore considered useless, he managed to do it without aid, mainly because Lord Saxton refused to give it.

By the time he was ready to depart, Farrell had taken on the appearance of a new man. At Erienne's insistence, he soaked in a steaming hot tub while his clothes were washed and tidied. He sat in front of the hearth clutching a sheet around him while she trimmed his hair, shaved the light but unsightly fuzz from his chin, and blithely ignored his protests. His shirt and stock came back to him crisply starched and neatly mended, and for the first time in several weeks his boots were blacked and polished.

On his return to the village, there were many in Mawbry who didn't recognize him when he stepped down from the Saxton carriage. His drinking cronies whistled in jovial admiration but loudly groaned their disappointment when they found he had no coin to spend. He won hoots of disbelief at his declaration that he would be seeking work to occupy himself, and then he astounded them further when he announced that in about a thrice of weeks he would be visiting Saxton Hall again at the invitation of Lord Saxton himself.

A trio of days remained before the Talbots' ball, and Erienne was still much in a quandary over her final selection of attire. She longed to wear the emeralds, but the gown that set the massive necklace off at its best was also the one that liberally displayed her bosom. The idea of entertaining Nigel Talbot and his guests with such an exhibition was, of course, unthinkable. Her other gowns were rich enough, but they were either the wrong color, or the neckline made the jeweled piece look clumsy. Disheartening as it was to put aside the idea of wearing the necklace, it seemed the only choice left to her.

Summoned to Lord Saxton's bedchamber, she was more than a little nervous as she knocked on his door. Immediately his voice came from within, bidding her enter. Drawing in a ragged breath, she turned the knob and braved the lion's den.

The first thing that met her eye was a huge dressmaker's box tied with ribbons on the bed. Lord Saxton was just rising from his desk. He had obviously been working at his accounts, for a ledger was open in front of him, and he was tugging a last glove into place.

"Come in, my dear. I have something for you."

The tension ebbed from her body, and she managed a more relaxed smile as she closed the door behind her.

He swept a hand toward the box. "Bundy went to Mawbry to meet the coach from London and brought this back. Anne sent it . . . at my request."

"But what . . ."

"Open it." His voice was soft despite its roughness.

Erienne felt no different than a child surprised with a gift. It was a warm, suspenseful, pleasant experience, and she prolonged it as much as she could as she carefully undid the ribbons and lifted the lid. Then she stared in stunned amazement at what lay beneath, afraid to reach out and touch the fragile lace or the rich ivory satin that made up the gown.

" 'Tis beautiful, milord." She looked up at her husband, her eyes soft and tender, and slowly shook her head. "You have given me so much, how can I accept more when I have failed . . ."

"I do what pleases me, madam," he interrupted, "and it pleases me to see my wife in clothes equal to her beauty. Do you like it?"

Erienne smiled and reached out ever so carefully to lift the garment from the box. "My lord, you know a woman's mind too well and what pleases one even more. How could I not? 'Tis the loveliest gown I've ever seen, much less owned."

She held the dress before her and went to assay the effect in the tall mirror that stood in the dressing room. The satin bodice was covered with lace, the scallops of which overlapped onto the bosom. The lace sleeves were massively full, ending just below the elbow, and were attached to the bodice beneath the arms to leave the shoulders bare. A wide sash of fresh green was tied about the waist and trailed in streamers down the back of the lace and ivory satin skirt, falling to the short train.

Lord Saxton spoke from behind her. "I left the details to Anne, and as usual she has not disappointed me." He leaned on his cane and inclined his head back toward the bed as his wife faced him. "There is something else in the box I thought you might need."

Erienne laid the gown aside and went to look inside the box. On a voluminous cloak of green velvet lay a pair of white silk stockings, the sheerest of shifts, and a pair of cream satin slippers adorned with silver-filigreed buckles.

"You've thought of everything, milord."

His answer came after a brief nod. "I tried to, madam."

Fifteen

The afternoon of the grand affair Erienne sat at her dressing table as Tessie painstakingly arranged her hair in an elegant coiffure. Her corset had been cinched tightly over the shift, pushing her bosom upward until its fullness strained against the gossamer cloth. The transparency of the chemise made no pretense at hiding the softly veiled peaks with a bit of lace or intricate embroidery. Indeed, the garment seemed intent on displaying every detail of her woman's body, more so than any she had previously owned.

The gown had been carefully spread upon the bed to await its donning, while the necklace lay closer at hand on the table. All was in readiness, and equally blended portions of tension and excitement grew in Erienne's breast as the hours dwindled rapidly away. She greatly distrusted Claudia Talbot to treat her husband in a credible manner, and scenes of imagined confrontations formed in her mind. She did not doubt Lord Saxton's ability to handle the ridicule that was sure to come. Rather, it was her own temper that worried her.

With a question, Tessie drew her notice to a matter more pertinent to the moment. The two of them were intent upon discussing how the last curl should lay in the intricately coiled mass and once again failed to note Lord Saxton's entry into the chamber.

"Are you almost finished?" the haunting, husky voice asked, startling them both and bringing their attention around to where he stood just beyond the arras.

Tessie quickly fastened the curl and patted it in place, then curtsied. "Aye, milord."

His gloved hand flicked in a gesture of silent dismissal, and the girl hurried from the chamber. Leaning on the cane, he laboriously entered the bathing alcove and stepped behind his wife. The blank mask considered her image in the mirror, and though Erienne could not see his eyes, she felt the bold touch of his gaze against her thinly veiled bosom.

Reaching out, Lord Saxton slowly ran a gloved finger along her spine, moving it from her nape downward to the top of her shift, then upward again until his hand rested on her shoulder.

"Madam, if some doddering ancient viewed you this moment, 'twould surely send his heart into its final palpitations."

The corners of her mouth lifted in a soft smile. "You tease, Stuart. I am just a simple maid."

A low chuckle came from the leather helm. "Aye, so simple that when that darling, pampered child, Claudia, first sets eyes on you, she will be seized with such an apoplectic shade of jealousy that all the froggies in the marsh will groan in envy."

His wife laughed and reached up to her shoulder to squeeze his hand in gratitude. "Milord, you are either far too gracious, or the stress of your infirmities has weakened your mind. If anyone should admire me tonight, 'twill only be because of the finery I wear."

She rose to her feet, and he followed her to the fireplace, where she sat and lifted the hem of her shift high above her knees. From the secrecy of the mask he admired the long, sleek trimness of her limbs as she donned her stockings. When she leaned over to smooth the silk leggings, he caught his breath, for she allowed him a most tantalizing view of her bosom.

"I have decided, madam, that you shall not be shirked in this hour but rather be presented as a single, perfect bloom that would set them all to shame. That brings me to the reason I have sought a word with you."

The muted half whisper bore a note that made Erienne halt and look up at him in close attention.

"It has been heavy on my mind that from what should be an affair of gaiety, you may receive much abuse because of me and what others see of me." Though strongly spoken, the words came slowly, as if he chose them carefully. "I have therefore come upon a manner wherein the viper's fangs are drawn and the somewhat macabre intentions of Miss Talbot and her retinue are set awry. I have arranged an escort for you, a man of such formidable reputation that on his arm, no one will dare harass you." He held up a hand to silence her protest. "In this matter I am firm, and as your husband, I bid you see my cause as I explain it. I will countenance no argument. The man should be arriving forthwith, and though you may have fears, and I surely understand that you might, he has assured me that he will escort you with every care that I myself would give."

The expressionless mask considered her with a sternness that brooked no refusal. Erienne was subdued by its blank regard, and she could only murmur in a small voice, "I have no wish to displease, milord."

Lord Saxton returned to her dressing table and scooped up the costly chain of emeralds and diamonds. When he beckoned, Erienne came to him and presented her back. In a moment his warm, naked fingers laid the strand about her throat. The task done, the hands caressed the soft curve of her shoulder and moved downward until they rested at her waist. After a strained clearing of his throat, he withdrew his touch and spoke brusquely.

"I bid you enjoy yourself, madam. I shall not see you again before you leave." He traversed a labored path to the door, there pausing for a last look. "I shall send Tessie back so you can complete your toilet. Aggie will inform you when the gentleman is here. Good night, my love."

The preparations were completed, and when the summons came, Tessie followed her mistress, carefully holding the heavy velvet cloak across her arms so it would not sweep the floor. Erienne was most wary of the identity of her escort and made her way down the stairs with as much stealth as she could manage herself and could encourage from the girl. Erienne mulled over the limited choices Stuart had, and she had fleeting visions of some of Talbot's friends offering their services, for the benefit of their host, of course. She had not taken Christopher's warning lightly, despite her rather flippant dismissal of it at the time.

At the entrance of the great hall, Erienne halted and clutched a hand over her suddenly pounding heart as she saw the one who awaited her. She found it hard to believe that her husband would be so foolish as to trust the Yankee to protect and uphold her virtue.

He stood in front of the hearth, staring into the flames. A tall, slender-hipped, broad-shouldered man, Christopher Seton was as handsome of physique as he was of face. Garbed in silver-gray silk and white shirt and stock, he looked the part of some landed gentry. His chiseled profile was touched by the warm light of the fire, and the growing ache in her bosom attested to the degree of its handsomeness.

In an attempt to regain her serenity, Erienne let out a slow, steadying breath and entered the room, bringing him about to face her as her heels tapped against the stone floor. Smiling, he came across to meet her while his eyes plumbed the depths of her beauty. When he halted before her, he bowed with a grand, sweeping gesture.

"Lady Saxton, I am honored."

"Christopher Seton." She forced a strong note of sarcasm in order to hide the shakiness of her voice. "You are beneath contempt."

"Madam?" He straightened with a look of bemused surprise.

"You have somehow convinced my husband that the fox should watch over the hen house."

A slow grin came with his answer. "Lady Saxton, your husband's skill with weapons is widely known, and I do not doubt that he would take up arms against any man who would abuse you. You have my word that while we're in public, I shall comport myself with such dignity and propriety that you need have no fear of your reputation."

She regarded him with a widely skeptical frown. "And Lord Talbot? Will he admit you?"

"Set aside your fears, madam. I would not be here unless assured of that fact."

"I have promised my husband that I will abide by his wishes in this matter," she stated. "I shall therefore propose a truce. For this evening alone, you shall respect me as a lady, and I will try to regard you as a gentleman, just as we did at our last meeting."

Christopher gave her a shallow nod. "Until the ball is over then, my lady."

"Agreed."

There was something subtle in the way his smile changed that made Erienne uneasy, but in London he had restrained himself to her satisfaction, and with Tanner driving the coach and Bundy going along as added protection against the thieves, she had only to call out for assistance, and she would have it. Thus assured, she turned to Tessie.

"You needn't wait up for me. It might be quite late before we return."

The maid dipped in a quick curtsy. "Yes, mum."

Erienne reached for her cloak, but Christopher took it from the waiting maid.

"Allow me, my lady," he offered.

Scarcely breathing, Erienne waited as those lean, strong hands arranged the cloak over her shoulders, then with solicitous care he ushered her out to the waiting coach. Once within the interior, Erienne snuggled beneath the fur throw on the rear seat and placed her feet near the warming pan. Velvet curtains were drawn snugly over the small windows, providing more privacy than Erienne thought she wanted. She cast an apprehensive eye toward Christopher as he climbed in, but much to her relief, he settled across from her. As he caught her gaze, he smiled.

"I fear the nearness of you would completely destroy my good intentions, my lady. 'Tis safer if I sit here."

Erienne relaxed back in the seat. The evening was off to a good beginning. She could only hope that his restraint would continue and her resistance would not be tested. Just the memory of his kiss could sap the strength from her limbs and leave her breasts tingling for the want of his caress.

Small interior lanterns gave off a weak light, softly illuminating his handsome face and making her aware of his casual gaze, but she was soon placated by his warm, masculine voice. He knew how to entertain with vivid stories, and she listened with avid interest, laughing now and then at his humor. The two of them, content to be in each other's company, hardly noticed when less than an hour later, the coach turned up the drive to the Talbot mansion. As the coach came to a halt before the elaborate manse, Erienne sat forward in the seat, immediately tense and nervous. Christopher caught her brief, anxious glance and reached out to take hold of her hand. He gave her fingers a gentle squeeze of reassurance.

"You'll likely set them all agog, Erienne," he whispered.

A smile wavered on her lips, and she watched as he brought her fingers to his lips to kiss their pale tips slowly. The gentleness of his gesture plucked at the strings of her heart and set a seed of bittersweet yearning growing deep within her. Then his head raised and his gaze softly caressed the delicate visage.

"I think we'd better go in before I forget my promise and make love to you here and now."

Erienne waited as he stepped lightly to the ground, then he turned back, offering up a hand. Though touching him sent the pulse leaping through her veins, she accepted his assistance to the door of the manse. Within the elaborate foyer, he drew the wrap from her shoulders, and though his touch was brief, it was like a soft caress. A maid received their cloaks, and they were led to the entry of the great hall. There the majordomo stepped ahead of them and decorously announced:

"Lady Saxton . . ."

A sudden hush settled over the guests as those present immediately turned, anxious to appease their curiosity about this woman and her husband, the purported beast of Saxton Hall. What they saw confused them, for the nightmare they had been prepared for was truly a vision in white standing on the threshold of the room with a tall, handsome gentleman at her side.

"And Mr. Seton."

Almost as quickly as the silence fell, a confused medley of inquiries filled the room. Those who stood nearest Claudia heard her gasp, and they stared, baffled, as she hurried toward the couple. When she neared, she cast an eye in Christopher's direction before scowling darkly at Erienne. What she blurted was not exactly what she had meant to say, but she could not think rationally when the sharp talons of rage clawed at her savagely.

"What are you doing here?"

Christopher stepped forward in a protective manner, half shielding Erienne with his bulk. "You invited me, remember? I have the invitation right here." He thrust his hand in his coat. "Written in your own hand, I believe."

"I know I invited you!" she replied impatiently. "But you were supposed to come alone!"

He smiled pleasantly. "My apologies, Claudia. Lord Saxton was otherwise occupied, and he desired that I should escort his lady."

Claudia's mouth tightened, and an icy coldness hardened the dark eyes. This was not what she had planned, not at all. She sorely regretted not being able to send the Lady Saxton home to her beastly husband. It was what the snip deserved for daring to come without him.

"You look positively divine, Erienne." She made no attempt to hide the cool smirk in her smile. "I'm really surprised. Who would have thought that the mayor's daughter could do so well in outfitting herself with jewels and all? Tell me, dear, are those baubles real?"

Christopher chuckled and answered the barb himself. "I understand they've been in Lord Saxton's family for some time, and I suspect that they're real enough. Of course, it would take an eye well acquainted with precious gems to recognize their worth, wouldn't it?"

Claudia cast him an oblique glance. "Tell me, Christopher, why would Lord Saxton trust you to look after his lady? I would think the man would be most fearful of you."

Laughter twinkled in his gray-green eyes as he waved a hand casually around the room. "Are we not well chaperoned, Claudia? Then there is Bundy and the coachman, Tanner. You no doubt have heard how Lord Saxton put the thieves to rout? I'm certain he would give short shrift to any man who would try to take his lady from him."

Claudia smiled blandly. "Then I hope you intend to be extremely careful, Christopher. I would hate to see such a handsome and charming man laid in his grave because he became enamored with his charge."

"Thank you, Claudia. Your concern is touching." He clicked his heels and bent forward in a shallow bow. "I shall take care."

The woman was completely disarmed by his soft-spoken defense and with a last blazing glare at Erienne, Claudia moved away. Allan Parker stood talking with two other men near the corner of the room, and she strode purposely to him.

The sheriff was nearly as resplendent as his surroundings. His dark blue-and-gray garb was richly decorated with silver, giving it an almost military appearance, yet it was conspicuously void of either honors or rank. The bare shoulders of his coat seemed to cry out for epaulets, and the barren breast for medals of valor and badges of campaigns.

Slipping her arm through his, Claudia brought his rather skeptical gaze around to her. He seemed somewhat confused by her attention until he glanced toward the entry and saw Christopher with Erienne. The sight of the couple ended his puzzlement and brought a smile of amusement to his lips. But when his eyes flicked over Erienne in warm appreciation, his ribs received a quick, sharp jab from Claudia's elbow. She was not about to let another man amend his favor because of an infatuation with her rival's beauty.

"My lady," Christopher murmured aside to Erienne, "I fear you have quite astounded everyone by your beauty."

"They're disappointed because Stuart didn't come," she whispered back. "But if they thought to make a laughingstock of him, they're mightily mistaken. He is no one's fool."

"You sound as if you admire the man," Christopher remarked.

"I do."

He arched his brow as he contemplated her. "You do baffle me, Erienne. I had all hopes of you fleeing after a fortnight of wedlock with Stuart. I was waiting to welcome you with open arms. Now I am bemused as to what to do. Am I really to believe that you prefer a scarred cripple above me?"

Erienne glanced around at the lily-white faces that wore hopeful smiles and the eyes that watched Christopher in eager anticipation. She could have lost herself in deep reverie in that moment, having such a handsome man at her side, but the memory of Lord Saxton standing behind her in the silvered glass jolted her back to reality. "I have no second choice," she stated bluntly. "What is done is done. I am honor-bound, and there can never be a turning back."

Christopher's eyes flicked about the room, in his turn taking note of the men who were still eyeing her. He guessed their thoughts were not so different from his own. Little did they know how strong-minded and determined the lady was. But then, he had always had a rather persistent nature himself, and he was not as easily daunted as other men.

Decorously he presented his arm. "Come, my sweet. People are staring, and I would have this dance before I find you swept away by some overzealous swain."

He led Erienne forward on his arm, and the guests opened a corridor to the ballroom, where the musicians struck up a quick, lively tune. Before he could lead her onto the floor to join the rest of the couples, however, they were intercepted by a richly garbed servant. Indeed, his attire rivaled that of the royal house.

"Lord Talbot requests the presence of Lady Saxton in his study," he loftily announced in monotone. He gave her a stiff bow. "If you will please follow me, my lady."

Erienne looked worriedly toward Christopher, but he was already reaching to take her arm.

"Lead the way," he bade the servant.

That one's brows raised at the man's audacity to invite himself. "I believe Lord Talbot requested only the lady's presence, sir."

A lazy grin drew up a corner of Christopher's mouth. "Then he will be getting more than he bargained for, or nothing at all. I promised Lord Saxton that I would not let his lady out of my sight."

The servant seemed momentarily perplexed as to what to do and finally decided to leave the matter up to his master. "This way, sir."

Christopher guided her leisurely along in the wake of the impatient servant. They were taken through a door and down a long, wide corridor until they reached a pair of gilt-trimmed doors. Bidding them to wait, the servant rapped lightly and then entered. When he returned, he held open a door for their admittance.

Dressed out in white and gold satin liberally adorned with golden braid, Nigel Talbot rose from an ornate desk as they came in. He stepped around the end of the desk and moved to meet Erienne while his eyes eagerly devoured her beauty. They briefly touched the necklace before dropping to her bosom.

Erienne sank into a polite curtsy. "Lord Talbot."

"My dear child, 'tis so good to see you again," he said. As she straightened, he took both her hands into his and bestowed a kiss on each before raising his heated gaze once again. "You look absolutely ravishing," he murmured, then glanced about. He had not been able to persuade his daughter to change her mind about inviting the Yankee and pointedly chose to ignore his presence. "But where is your husband? I thought he would be here with you."

"Lord Saxton could not come," she replied. "He addressed Mr. Seton to accompany me in his stead."

Taking a pinch of snuff, Talbot looked Christopher over with a haughtily cocked brow, well aware that the younger man had not deemed to pay homage to him.

"The favor Lord Saxton asked of me was twofold, sir," Christopher explained, withdrawing a packet from inside his coat and presenting it to the man. A slow smile touched his lips. "His lordship also asked me to bring this letter to you."

Nigel's eyes flicked over the Yankee with open distaste. Talbot broke the seal of the document and briefly scanned the contents. After a moment he raised a tightly controlled and carefully blank stare to Christopher, who was still smiling pleasantly. With a flick of his wrist, Talbot tossed the letter aside on a low table.

"There's time enough for business at a later date." His grand air had fled, and he faced Erienne, trying to force the stiff muscles of his face into some semblance of a smile. "Tonight we will enjoy the festivities. We have many guests from London and York, and they've come here to have a rare good time. I hope that is your intention, my lady."

Within reason, Erienne mused, but managed a gracious reply. "Of course, my lord."

"You may expect me to claim a dance or two later," he stated, his expression easing somewhat. "I shall insist upon it. What with your newly acquired status and your husband barely known among the blooded classes, I'm sure you have need of someone to teach you the proper decorum of these affairs. I shall be most eager to lend my assistance in tutoring you."

"Perhaps you mistake the Saxtons' heritage," Christopher responded smoothly. "If you're unaware of it, they're quite an old family, possibly older than your own."

Lord Talbot slanted a questioning look toward the man. "You seem to know a lot about them, young man. As for myself, I was not that well acquainted with them. I met the old lord only briefly before he was murdered by those cutthroats. The present lord has remained rather reclusive."

Christopher's grin deepened. "Can you blame him?"

Lord Talbot gave a low snort. "I suppose if I were scarred to the degree he is, I would be loath to present myself in public, too. But the man should learn to trust someone, and 'tis certain I mean him no harm."

"I have always found Lord Saxton to be a reasonable man, not unwilling to trust those who deserve it," Christopher replied and slipped a hand beneath Erienne's elbow. "If you will excuse us now, my lord, Lady Saxton promised me a dance."

Talbot straightened himself indignantly. He was sure the fellow had completely lost his senses or lacked knowledge of the correct etiquette with a titled lord. Why, no one dared walk away from him before they were dismissed.

Christopher opened the door and with a crisp nod to the gawking man, drew Erienne out ahead of him. They were in the hall before she dared release her breath.

"Lord Talbot will never forgive you for that," she whispered worriedly.

A low chuckle preceded his reply. "I don't think I'll miss his affection."

"You should be more careful," she warned. "He's a man of much influence."

"He's a man of much arrogance, and I could not resist deflating him a bit." Christopher looked down at her, and his eyes danced with green lights as he searched her face. "Do I actually detect some concern for me in your admonition, my sweet?"

"When you're so reckless, someone needs to try to get you to listen to reason," she said impatiently.

"I take heart that you care."

"There's really no reason for you to feel conceit," she responded dryly.

"Ah, milady pricks me with her thorns and wounds me to the quick."

"Your hide is thicker than an oxen's," she scoffed. "And your skull just as dense."

"Don't be mean, my love," he coaxed. "Give me a warm smile to soothe this heart that beats only for you."

"I've heard stories that convince me that your heart is quite fickle, sir."

"Madam?" His brows raised in surprise. "Do you give credence to gossip?"

"Perhaps I should ask Claudia if it is true that you are wont to visit her while her father is away." Erienne stared at him in open suspicion.

His amused laughter took the sting from her charge. "When I have expended so much energy on you, madam, how can you believe that I have any interest in another woman?"

Erienne glanced around to see if anyone stood near enough to overhear his words, then, assured that they were alone in the hall, leaned forward to whisper accusingly, "You have managed to accumulate a following of twittering females in Mawbry. Why shouldn't I believe the rumors?"

"And why should you care if they are true?" He returned a question back at her. "You're a married woman."

"I know that!" she snapped.

His lips twitched with ill-suppressed amusement. "I thought you needed reminding, my love."

"I am not your love!" she protested, as much to squelch the sudden sweet pang of pleasure his endearment caused as to discourage him.

"Oh, but you are," he murmured warmly.

Those glowing eyes burned into hers, suffusing her with a growing aura of warmth. The trembling began again, and the strength in her limbs ebbed. How could she claim disinterest in the man when the very words from his mouth could so effectively stir her senses?

His gaze lowered and lightly caressed her bosom, dipping to where the green gem twinkled between her creamy breasts. Her breath halted as the kindling fire flared brighter in those grayish-green orbs, and then they caught and held her own.

"If you're not aware of it yet, madam, I'm rather single-minded in my pursuits. You're the woman I want, and I'll not be satisfied until I have you."

"Christopher, Christopher," she groaned. "When will you ever accept the fact that I'm a married woman?"

"Only when I can claim you as my wife." He lifted his head and thoughtfully listened to the strings of their violins as they began another melody. "Lord Talbot has a penchant for waltzes," he mused aloud, "and if I know the man at all, he'll soon be here requesting your hand." Purposefully he took her arm and led her onto the dance floor.

"Perhaps I have misjudged you, Christopher," Erienne commented as he whirled her about in a wide sweep of the ballroom.

"How so, my love?" He searched her face for some hint of her meaning.

"You watch over me as closely as Stuart," she stated and grew thoughtful. "Perhaps more so."

"I have not given up hope that you will someday become mine, madam, and I choose to safeguard against those who would take you from me."

"What of Stuart?" She raised a lovely brow as she awaited his answer.

It was a long moment before he gave a reply. "In the ways of love, I do not consider Stuart as much a threat as an inconvenience."

"An inconvenience?" she queried.

"I shall have to deal with him in time, and that will be the difficult part. I cannot dismiss the man without rousing your hatred again. 'Tis a most perplexing problem."

"You amaze me, Christopher." Erienne shook her head, somewhat shocked by his casual disregard of her husband. "You truly amaze me."

"The feeling is mutual, my love." His voice came as a soft caress and sent an eddy of sensations spiraling down through the core of her being.

Lord Talbot frowned in sharp displeasure as he watched the two and grew annoyed when he heard the whispers that praised the good looks and talent of the couple. Catching the sheriff's eye, Nigel Talbot jerked his head sharply toward the direction of his study and returned there to await the man.

Claudia had also observed the blissful flight of the handsome pair about the ballroom floor, and her hatred of Erienne seethed to even greater heights. She caught sight of Allan Parker and hurried to claim him for the dance, wanting to show that milkweed daughter of the mayor a thing or two about waltzing.

"I'm sorry, Claudia." Allan gave his excuses. "Your father wants to see me."

Fire shot through the dark eyes, and she flounced from the room ahead of the sheriff, muttering beneath her breath and not caring how many stares she attracted because of her angry exit. This was her ball! And she would be damned before she would let Erienne Saxton ruin it!

She threw open the door of her father's study, and as she marched in, Talbot gave an impatient snort. His daughter would be difficult to deal with, as usual.

"Papa, you have no right to summon Allan just when he was going to dance with me!" she complained.

"There's a matter of business I wished to discuss with him," he explained.

In a huff, Claudia dropped in the nearest chair and flung up her hand. "Well, hurry up! I'm not going to wait all evening."

Talbot curbed his irritation and spoke coaxingly, "Claudia, dearest child, would you please go to my chambers and get my gold-headed cane for me? My old wound is acting up."

"Send one of the servants, Papa. I'm tired."

"Be a good girl, my dear, and do as I asked." His smile was forced.

She heaved an exasperated sigh and flounced from the room, slamming the door behind her.

The echo of its closing had barely died when Nigel Talbot caught up the letter from the table and slapped it irately with the back of his hand. "That damned Saxton! He summons me to Saxton Hall, as if I were some commoner, to discuss the rents collected while the family was not in residence."

Allan half sat on the corner of the massive desk and propped a foot on a seat of a silk brocade chair as he plucked a sweet from a nearby tray. Considering the bonbon, he commented without concern. "That should add up to a pretty penny."

" 'Tis more than a few coppers!" Talbot tossed the letter on the table and began to pace angrily. "Why, I've been collecting the rents for almost a score of years."

The sheriff chewed for a moment. "Am I to understand that you consider this Lord Saxton a threat?"

Talbot glared about the room. "I wish he would have come himself instead of sending that impertinent Yankee in his place. We would have seen, then, if he's the one."

"The rumors have it that he can't even sit a horse," Allan interjected.

"I've heard them, too, but where else can we look? The only other stranger in the area is Christopher Seton, and he's just too convenient."

Allan lifted his shoulders briefly. "So far, that one is just who he claims to be. He owns some ships, and one, the *Christina*, has been in and out of Wirkinton several times these past few months. It always seems to have a bit of new cargo to trade or sell."

"Just the same, we should be kept aware of the man." Talbot smirked. "Who knows? Perhaps he'll get tangled up with the night rider, and we'll find him in a bloody heap somewhere."

A smile turned the sheriff's lips. "If that should happen, do you suppose Lord Saxton would allow either of us to escort his lady?"

His lordship gave a short, sneering laugh. "The man must be naïve to trust Seton. It makes me wonder if he has his wits about him."

The sheriff nodded as he selected another candy. "He set Sears and his bunch to rout easily enough."

"That peabrained lout!" Talbot waved a hand angrily. "Who knows what harm he might have done?"

Allan dusted his hands and stood to his feet. "Have you heard anything from your man in the London Court?"

Lord Talbot paced fretfully again. "Nothing. Nothing at all. Just the usual."

The sheriff pursed his lips but was prevented further comment as Claudia threw open the doors. She crossed the room in haste and handed her father a heavy silver-headed walking stick.

"This was the only one I could find. Are you sure you didn't . . ." She paused as she took note of the cane leaning beside the fireplace. "Why, there's the gold one. You had it all the time." She giggled as she hugged her father's arm. "You've been so forgetful lately, Papa. I do believe you're getting old."

She gave an airy laugh and turned away, missing the angry glare her sire bent upon her.

"Come, Allan." She coyly minced her way to the door. "I insist you forget about business and come dance with me. After all, it's my ball!"

Lord Talbot ignored both canes and followed the pair out of the room, tugging at the loose skin beneath his chin.

The festivities continued in grand style, and though the night aged for some, for Erienne it might have been nurtured by a perpetual fountain of youth. The quick music, the fast dances, the thrill and excitement of being swept along on a handsome man's arm and being almost openly courted filled her with a fresh gaiety she had never experienced before. She felt totally alive, and even Claudia's icy glowers could not penetrate the aura of bliss that surrounded her. Other men eagerly presented themselves for her attention, and the glow dimmed somewhat as she was taken from Christopher's side.

Lord Talbot came to claim his tithe of the dances and swung her away in a swirling waltz. Claudia felt no concern leaving the sheriff's side and went immediately to Christopher, coyly demanding a dance as payment for the invitation. As if by prearrangement, the musicians coursed through a lengthy medley of tunes, and Claudia warmed to the heady feel of his arms about her. She pressed her lightly clad bosom to him whenever the dance allowed and moved so close that her hips caressed his loins. If his eyes lowered to her, a pouting smile was ready beneath hooded eyes, as if she understood and only awaited his proposal.

Lord Talbot, for his part, began as a gentleman, concentrating on matching the bold, sweeping motions of the Yankee, but the light grace of the lady warmed him, and Erienne was forced ever to be wary in order to protect her modesty.

When the last notes of the music were struck, Christopher drew away from his partner, convinced that he had just suffered the most wanton assaults on his person he had ever experienced in public. He had, of course, a higher goal in mind and was not inclined to be dragged off to the lady's bedchamber, though she firmly looped an arm through his. Catching the eye of Allan Parker, he approached the man with a greeting and a moment later effectively disengaged himself, murmuring his excuse. Claudia's mouth came open to vent her objection, but he was already moving away and purposefully striding toward his destination.

Erienne had avoided the final pat of Lord Talbot and left the flushed and overexcited elder stewing in frustration. She was most happy to welcome the return of her appointed escort and to entrust her virtue to their truce. They met in the maze of guests, and from then on Christopher kept the larger part of the dance floor between them and their host while Talbot stood at the sidelines and, like an anxious stork, craned his neck for a sight of the one who eluded him.

"You're being obvious," Erienne cautioned her partner.

"So is he," Christopher replied, "and if he persists, he'll be lucky if I don't lengthen his stride by a boot in the rear."

"Why are you so determined to harass Lord Talbot?"

"You know my reasons for disliking the man."

"Me?" she asked incredulously.

"What little time I have with you, I am loath to share with him."

"Why, Christopher," the blue-violet eyes flashed with puckish humor, and the barest hint of a smile curved her lips to mock him. "Methinks thou dost protest the man overmuch."

He went mechanically through the steps of the dance while his mind plunged to a depth beyond her insight. When his attention returned to her, he nodded and agreed. "Aye, the man! Him, I do protest. I protest his arrogance, his careless flaunting of his power. I protest the wealth he wallows in while his tenants grub for a meager subsistence. Aye, I protest the man, and I decry the possibility that anything entrusted to my care should fall to him."

The dark frown that accompanied his outburst surprised Erienne. She leaned back against his arm to see his face clearly. She had never guessed that the frivolous and capricious Christopher Seton had such a deeply serious vein in his otherwise lighthearted character.

The black side of his mood was as fleeting as the leap of a trout in a stream, a surprise in that no warning of its presence had preceded it, then it was gone, with not even the fading ripples to evidence its passing. Again he was the smiling rake, poised, sure, sweeping her across the room in a swirling rhythm that dazzled her and made other couples seem ploddishly clumsy. He swung her past Lord Talbot, but before that worthy could as much as raise a hand to stop them, they were lost in the crowd again. Near the far doorway Christopher paused and, taking Erienne's arm, led her through it.

"Some refreshment, my lady?" He met her questioning gaze and grinned. "Lord Talbot was near a state of apoplexy. He'll no doubt halt the music and seek you out."

They neared the lavishly covered tables, and he took up a small china plate.

"A tidbit? Some other morsel, perhaps?" He did not wait for an answer but laid several samples on the dish. When he had filled it, he pressed it into her hand.

"Really, Christopher, I'm not hungry," Erienne insisted.

"Then just hold the plate, my love," he whispered. "I will fetch you a glass also, and if Nigel appears you will have a case to present."

In the ballroom the music stopped as Christopher had predicted, and a murmur rose from the bemused dancers as Talbot pushed his way through them in his search for Erienne and her escort. The murmur grew louder as the host persisted in making several circuits of the room until he espied his goal in the adjoining chamber.

He charged hence, leaving his guests to their own ends, and it was Claudia who waved the musicians into motion once more. Talbot fought to control his irritation as he approached his quarry. Erienne quaked inside but took her cue from Christopher, who returned to press a glass of champagne into her hand. She sipped the sparkling, amber liquid, borrowing her bravado from his presence.

"There you are, my dear child," Talbot simpered, though his moustache quivered with suppressed ire. He struck a lordly pose as he paused before them. "I have been searching everywhere for you. You will, of course, be merciful and grant me another dance."

Erienne laughed as she showed him her plate. "Your table is so splendidly provided, I fear 'twill take me a full hour to finish what I have here. Besides, I am feeling a bit faint from the dancing."

"In that case, my dear . . ." He took the plate from her and set it aside, then interposed himself between the couple, taking Erienne by the arm. A note of victory crept into his voice as he continued. "I deem it necessary, in view of your plight, that you should retire with me to my parlor to rest."

"Your parlor?" Christopher questioned with a bland smile.

Talbot cast a haughty glare of supremacy to challenge that one's interference. He cocked a silk-stockinged leg in a kingly posture and reached a hand to brace himself on the table. It came down in the middle of Erienne's discarded plate. Feeling the ooze of caviar between his fingers, he jerked the member away. The plate flipped neatly upward and scattered its remnants on the length of his sleeve, then came down with a crash to the floor, speckling his white shoes with the black roe and splinters of china.

He twisted about, and the stiffened tails of his satin coat swept the table, tipping a carafe of fruity wine. He gasped as the snow-cooled brew soaked through his breeches and stood rigid until the chill passed. His breeches and stockings took on a bluish-violet hue as the wine trickled down his legs. Caviar mottled his right sleeve with a widening pattern, and a deep red canape perched like a trained snail atop his shoulder.

A twitter of laughter began nearby but retreated like a receding ripple as he cast a stony glare about him. Erienne sipped from her glass, then coughed delicately into a kerchief. Christopher's smile had not changed, while others seized the moment to admire the painted ceiling, the walls, or the baroque woodwork of the room.

Lord Talbot's fists were clenched at his sides as he took himself with squishing gait from the further consideration of gawking fools. In a few moments, whispers ran rampant as to how the lord of the manor had stormed up the stairway to his apartments, cursing the ball, his daughter, the cook, the servants, his manservant, who skittered anxiously in his wake, and above all, that damned Yankee!

The grand clock in the hall had chimed the twelfth hour, and the number of guests had diminished to barely a fourth. Claudia had found no chance to press her suit with Christopher but still seemed confident as she joined her father to bid farewell to a pair of their departing guests.

"I do hope you enjoyed yourselves." She smiled and nodded as the couple answered, then turned a brief sneer to their backs as they moved on. "Margaret is really getting plump, don't you agree, Papa? We'll have to enlarge the doors if she doesn't stop eating."

Talbot sighed as a memory assailed him. He could remember a time when the lady had been most tender to the touch and plump in all the right places. "She was such a pretty little thing when she was younger. As eager to please as anyone I've ever seen."

"That had to be at least a score of years ago, Papa. Neither one of you are spring birds anymore."

Talbot's dream burst like a bubble. Had it been that long ago?

He cleared his throat and paid her back full measure for her bold reminder. "I'm sure you're disappointed with the evening, my dear. That pretty little Erienne stole both it and the Yankee from beneath your nose."

Claudia tossed her head flippantly. "Huh, Christopher was only being nice because he felt responsible for her. Once she's abed, she'll be out of our hair, and I'll have plenty of time to assure him that I'm not angry."

"If your intention is that they spend the night, my dear, then you'd best hurry." He inclined his head toward the entry hall. "They said their farewells a few moments ago."

Claudia gasped as she followed his gaze and saw Christopher receiving their cloaks from the butler. She wasted no time reaching the foyer and making her protest known. "You're not leaving, are you? Why, I simply cannot hear of it. We've had rooms prepared for the both of you." She leaned toward Christopher, smiling suggestively. "Separately, of course."

Erienne hastened to allay the possibility. "I shall, of course, release Mr. Seton to whatever decision he might make. As for myself, I shall return to Saxton Hall."

"How sweet of you, my dear," Claudia almost cooed, but her hopes were quickly dashed as Christopher withdrew his arm.

"I am not released from my bond," he replied. "I gave my word that I would see the lady home. Lord Saxton will expect it."

"But you can't!" Claudia grasped at any excuse in an effort to win his company. "Look! 'Tis snowing outside. A storm is upon us."

Christopher turned with a questioning smile to Erienne.

"I must!" she stated simply.

He faced the other woman with a shrug. "I must."

Claudia stared at him and could find no further plea, though her lips parted several times as she searched for one.

"Good night, Claudia," he said, assisting Erienne with her cloak. "Thank you for inviting me."

"Yes," Erienne chimed in, deepening Claudia's confusion. " 'Twas a most delightful affair. Thank you."

The woman clamped her mouth tightly shut. With so many others about, she could not trust herself to make a decent farewell. The heat of her angry glare was felt by Erienne as she tucked her hand through her escort's arm. She smiled pleasantly.

"Good night, Claudia."

The impressively handsome couple made their way out to the waiting coach. Tanner had already mounted to the driver's seat, while Bundy waited beside the door of the conveyance and anxiously shifted his weight from foot to foot. When the couple were settled within, the man climbed to the top and, cradling a heavy blunderbuss in his arm, wrapped a heavy blanket about himself to ward off the piercing chill; then Tanner clucked to the horses, shook the reins, and the coach moved away.

The night was quiet, as it often is when the snow falls soft and gentle. The hushed, blanketed world of dark and virgin white enclosed them in a silken void where the only sounds were the muffled hoofbeats and the slight creaking and groaning of the carriage as it progressed through the deepening snow. The lanterns cast dim orbs of light into the night on either side of the coach, barely penetrating the heavy snowfall.

Inside, another pair of twin lanterns gave off their own fragile light as Erienne huddled in the corner of the rear seat, bracing herself against the sway. In the opposite seat Christopher pulled his cloak close about him and turned up the collar to ward off the chill. Avoiding his gaze, Erienne sat forward and pushed aside the velvet curtain for a moment to observe the downward flight of the huge, gold-washed crystal flakes that drifted through the pale lantern light. Settling back, she spread the thick fur robe over her skirts, channeling the heat of the warming pan upon her.

It was not long before Christopher gave up his struggle to find some warmth, and with a low grunt of dissension, left his place and his cloak and moved into the seat beside her. He lifted the robe and pulled it over his legs. After tucking it securely about them, he leaned back and silently dared his companion to object.

Erienne was uneasy with his boldness, and it passed through her mind that if Lord Saxton had given thought to the night's chill, he would have planned better and sent along another robe. Her worries burgeoned when Christopher placed his arm along the back of the seat. He met her wary gaze until she turned away, then he leisurely admired the soft blush on the creamy skin of her cheeks, the slim, straight nose, and the delicately formed lips, which seemed to beckon the touch of his own. He watched her as one might observe a trembling, dew-laden rose, awed by its delicate beauty.

The dark, heavy lashes fluttered downward self-consciously as he continued to stare, and Erienne knew a pleasure in the moment that was truly strange in her world. He had played the gentleman throughout most of the evening, and the thoughts of his gallantry burned like a well-banked fire at the core of her contentment. The night was hushed and still around them, and she was snug and safe from the world outside. No threat seemed imminent.

The coach jolted, and Christopher's hand fell to her shoulder. She glanced at him and found nothing more intimidating than a slightly perplexed and thoughtful frown on his face. The warmth and comfort of her place made her drowsy, and she leaned her head back in the crook of his elbow. It lay there naturally, like a bird that had found its nest. With half-closed eyes, she saw him reach to turn down the wick of the lantern closest to her, and in a dreamlike state viewed the ebbing flame until it went out.

His long fingers came back to lay alongside her jaw, and slowly turn her face to his. His shadow, cast by the far lamp, covered her, and then his lips were upon hers, moving slowly and fanning fires that she had never guessed were even kindled. Her hand crept up to caress his corded neck above the stock, then as some semblance of reality returned, it pressed against his chest, pushing him away. As she gasped for breath, it was he who turned away and sat frowning angrily at the other wall of the coach. The pounding of her heart refused to slow, and she reviewed the condition of her mind as if from a distance. If not held in check by her struggling will, her trembling hands might have urged him back. Such a simple kiss it was. Surely no great disaster could have come of it, but she knew the ice was thin, and must be tenderly trod lest she find herself adrift in a raging sea of no return.

Erienne tried to raise herself upright, but her shoulders were still entrapped by his arm. It tightened about her, and he came back to her without hesitation. His mouth was suddenly there upon hers, insisting, stirring, demanding that she answer yea or nay. And yet she could not say yea, for she was bound to another. Neither could she speak the word nay, for this was the very moment she had yearned would come.

Her reply came as light as the touch of dew in spring. Neither yea nor nay, but her mind cried with agonized yearning, Oh, my love, please don't go away.

Christopher saw the answer, middle ground as it was, felt it in the almost indistinct turning of her lips beneath his, the slightest yielding of the hand that rested on his chest. He slipped an arm about her waist, bringing her closer to him as his knees deepened. Her cloak fell away, tumbling unnoticed to the seat behind her.

She shivered as his mouth left hers and traced a molten path over her cheek, her brow, and then paused to press gently against the fragile eyelids, which flickered downward and waited for his touch. He nuzzled aside the sweet-scented tresses and, finding her ear, touched it lightly with his tongue.

A throbbing pressure grew in the man's loins. He had played out his hand with patience, but now it was waning before the tumult of his passions. His concern for her timidity dwindled apace with his growing need, and his hand came up to cup the fullness of her breast.

A shocked gasp caught in Erienne's throat, and she came upright, pushing at his chest with both hands and striking away the brand that seared her. She held him at arm's length and confronted him in a breathless whisper, "You press yourself beyond the bounds of propriety, sir! You gave your word!"

"Aye, madam, that I did," he whispered back. "But listen well, my love, and mark the bounds." He leaned closer. "Sweet Erienne, the ball is over."

His arm cradled her head as she stared at him aghast, and then his lips smothered hers. Her flurry of protests diminished to a moan of despair. Or was it rapture?

His hand came back, and this time her arms were entrapped by his enveloping embrace. Beneath the silken confines of her bodice, her nipple grew taut beneath his stroking thumb. The heat of his caress flared through her, setting fire to every nerve. The top of the sleeve bit into her shoulder, and she gave to ease the pressure. There was a slight tugging behind her back and her bodice fell loose. Her eyes flew wide as he freed the swelling fullness of her breasts, and then her senses erupted in a fiery blaze as his hand brushed away the chemise and moved upon her naked flesh. She turned away in a feeble attempt to escape his passion and to cool her own inflamed desires, but he followed, drawing her back and half lifting her against him. The cry that came to her throat became another moan that was taken from her by his kiss. His parted lips slanted across hers and devoured their sweetness with a ferocity that gave evidence of his starved senses. The kiss was relentless in its demand, searching out the dark, honeyed cavern of her mouth, stroking her nerves awake with each flick of his tongue, and setting her whole being aflame with its warmth.

"Sweet, darling love," he breathed, pressing ardent kisses upon her trembling mouth, "I want you so. Yield to me, Erienne."

"Nay, Christopher, I cannot!"

He pulled back and looked down at her, letting his eyes sweep the flushed cheeks and the golden orbs of her breasts. "Then speak a lie, madam, and say you want no part of me."

Though her mouth opened, no words formed, and she could only stare up at him, helplessly caught in the web of her own desires. Slowly he leaned forward and replaced his lips upon hers to possess their softness leisurely and languidly. He met no resistance, and with a sighing moan Erienne let him press her back upon the fur robe crumpled beneath her shoulders. Their mouths melded in warm communion, turning, twisting, devouring, until their needs became a greedy search for more. Passions flared, and their hunger grew, mounting on soaring wings. He muttered hoarse, unintelligible words as he pressed fevered kisses along her throat, sending her world toppling into a chaos of sensation. The white-hot heat of his mouth on a rose-hued peak was a sudden shock that made her catch her breath. Her lips parted, but she did not call out as the licking fires consumed her. Beyond her will, her hands caressed his shoulder, and her fingers threaded through the darkly burnished hair that ended in wispy waves at his nape.

His arm slipped around her knees and lifted her legs across his. She gave a small gasp as his hand found its way unerringly beneath her skirts and stroked upward along a bare thigh.

"Christopher, you cannot do this," she whispered in desperation. "I belong to another."

"You belong to me, Erienne. From the first, you have been mine."

"I belong to him," she protested weakly, but Christopher's lips came back to hover over hers. A tremor went through her as his hand claimed the softness of her, touching her where no other had ever dared. The eyes above her own glowed intently as his caresses grew purposefully bolder. She caught her breath and stared at him in surprise as the strange sensations leapt through her, setting her whole being on fire, and she writhed, unable to stop her cartwheeling world. A shivering shudder went through her as she curled against him, and she felt his lips against her hair, heard her name hoarsely whispered.

A thump on the top of the carriage made them start. Christopher pulled away slightly, reaching out to turn down the wick in the lantern, then his hand moved to push aside the velvet curtain. Through the falling flakes, the wan glow of the tower lights of Saxton Hall could be seen on a distant hill. Dropping the shade, he released his breath in a halting sigh and straightened, pulling her up with him.

" 'Twould seem, madam, that we must continue this at another time," he stated. "We're almost home."

Shaken to the core of her being, Erienne would not meet his eyes as she hurriedly fumbled with her bodice. She turned aside to hide her nakedness from him, but his hands came to assist, fastening the catches of her gown.

"I'll be staying the night at the hall," he breathed, dropping a kiss upon her nape.

She gasped and moved away, casting a quick, nervous glance at him as she pleaded, "Go away, Christopher. I beg you. Please go away."

"I have a matter to discuss with you, madam, and it must be said tonight. I will come to your chamber . . ."

"No!" She shook her head passionately, fearful of what might happen if he came to her again. She had escaped this moment, not entirely unscathed, but nevertheless a virgin. That state, however, was most tenuous and could not withstand another full-fledged attack of his ardor. "I will not let you in, Christopher! Go away!"

"Very well, madam." He seemed to measure his words carefully. "I shall try to restrain myself until the morrow, then we will have this matter out, and you will be mine before the day is done."

She stared at him aghast, realizing he meant every word he said. The coach gave a last shudder as it came to a halt, seeming to mirror the one that went through her. He would have no pity on her, and he would damn anyone who stood in his way. She could not let it happen!

Sixteen

Bundy opened the carriage door, and Erienne did not wait for the step to be set in place before she scrambled out, unaided by both men. It was as if a demon with spurs of pure panic rode astride her shoulders and drove her on. She fairly flew toward the stalwart portal of Saxton Hall, heedless of the snow that covered her low slippers. Her skirts leveled a wide path marked only by the tiny imprint of her flying feet.

The slamming of the massive portal reverberated through the hushed night, and in the dying echoes Bundy cast a cautious glance inside the coach at Christopher, who gave him a wry, lopsided grin as he folded the lap robe and placed it on the front seat. Taking up his cloak and the lady's, he stepped down and stood gazing about, letting the cold night air cool his brain and body.

Erienne raced past an astounded Paine, who had heard the coach and was there to see about his duties. She did not care how she rocked the aging man back on his heels with her rapid flight. She took to the stairs and, gaining the safety of her chamber, slammed that oaken panel as well, locking it with a quick twist of her wrist. Only then did she dare pause to catch her breath. Whether it was from relief at having escaped the Yankee, the exertion of her flight, or plain, simple fear, her heart thudded in her breast, seeming to jolt her entire body with every beat.

Her mind raced beneath the impact of the evening's events. For the first time since her marriage she had locked the door to her chamber, and she was afraid that Lord Saxton might attempt a visit and find the portal barred against him. But a greater fear gnawed at her that Christopher might find his way to her chamber and seek to finish what he had started. She was absolutely certain that she could not withstand that rake's persuasive, unrelenting assault. He dogged her heels at every turn, and she had the distinct feeling that if she were to board a ship for the farthest corner of the world, it would not be long before she would see the tall, raked masts of the frigate-size *Cristina* on the horizon racing after her.

Erienne held her breath as she heard slow footsteps come down the hall, pause a long moment by her door, then fade away in the direction of the guest room. She was dismayed that he was to be a guest in Saxton Hall for the night and she would have to face him come the morningtide. In the coach she had been ready to yield to him, and she was frightened of his promise to continue his pursuit. Her whole being burned with the fire that he had torched. His hands on her body, her lips on hers, his forceful persuasiveness had been her downfall. She had not been able to withstand his ardor, and her pride had toppled beneath his deliberate attack on her senses. He had brought her to that moment of sweet ecstasy, knowing full well what he was doing to her, and now she would forever hunger for that same devastating bliss.

A ragged sob escaped her, and she flung herself away from the door. Pressing trembling fingers against her temples, she began to pace restlessly about the room. She had given sacred vows in a church, and even though her marriage was unconsummated, she was bound by her word to be a proper wife. She could not betray her husband in such a despicable manner. He wanted her too, and yet he had held himself in restraint. And now if he came, he would see that something was amiss, and what would she tell him? That she had almost given herself to another man?

A violent trembling seized her. Her emotions were torn asunder, and she could find no peace in the depths of her thoughts. What her heart yearned for went against everything she deemed honorable, and yet what honor demanded, she could not bring herself to do.

Be Lord Saxton's wife in more than name? Submit herself to passions? She could not bear it.

Erienne paused beside the huge chair where Lord Saxton often sat and laid an unsteady hand along its back. She remembered her surprise when first she touched him. Expecting an overwhelming sense of revulsion to seize her, she had been amazed to find no evidence of distortion or weakness. Beneath her fingers she had felt the warmth, the quickness of life, the rippling bulges of firmly toned muscles.

Somehow before meeting her husband, she had to calm herself. She could not let him see the flush of passion on her cheeks, or the warm light of desire in her eyes. She was frightened of rousing some conflict between the two men. Each was fully capable of violence, and if one of them were wounded or killed, she would be forever tormented by guilt and sadness.

The house was deathly still, and only the chimes of a distant clock tolling the second hour broke the silence. No boldly striding footfalls, no shuffling steps came to her door; no light rapping on the planks, no thump of a cane was heard in the night. Relief came in slow degrees as she realized that neither Christopher nor Lord Saxton were bound for her chamber.

She sponged away the last traces that remained of the ball and garbed herself in gown and robe. The garments were the usual diaphanous frills that were hardly worthy of any name, let alone the actuality, but they were typical of those selected by Lord Saxton. Sinking to the bench at her dressing table, she picked up the brush and idly stroked her hair as she mused on the evening. A thousand images flitted through her mind: the ball, the grandeur of the Talbot mansion, the man's persistence, Claudia's sneering smiles; and her own thoughts came back to Christopher. She remembered when first she met him. She had been so anxious for a handsome suitor, she had readily welcomed him into the cottage. Though her father had been much at fault in the affairs between the two, he could not yet hear Christopher's name without turning a livid red. It still bemused her that Avery could be so nonchalant about all that he had done, as if he were the innocent one.

She laid down the brush and pressed her hair flat against the sides of her head, letting the long tresses fall in rippling dark waves down her back. "Am I in truth my father's daughter?" she whispered softly. "Is it my brow that bears a resemblance?" She leaned forward and peered intently at the image. "Perhaps the eyes are his, or the nose." She moved the chimneyed candle to shift the light to see her image better, then lifted her chin and turned her head from side to side, tracing the pouting lower lip with a questing fingertip. "Where is the likeness? Is it outward?" Her eyes widened as a slow horror dawned. " 'Tis not outward, but inward! 'Tis here!" Her clenched fist flew to her bosom and pressed over her heart as she stared at the slack-jawed image that gaped back in distaste. "I have denied my husband the rights of my own vows, and yet there is within me this disabling desire to yield the same to another. My father yielded to his own greed and gaming lusts and sold me in the bargain. 'Tis the same. My father's blood is mine!"

She came to her feet and braced her hands on the table, leaning close to deny what her reflection accused her of. "I shan't let it be! My husband shall have what I have promised him!"

She was in the hall without consciously willing it so, and then at the door of Lord Saxton's chambers. Before she could dwell on the horror that awaited her, she opened the heavily carved portal, stepped inside and closed it, reaching behind her to turn the latch.

A low fire snapped and crackled in the hearth, and though the velvet drapes were pulled around the sides of the canopied bed, the foot was open to the warmth of the fire. Within the shadows of its interior, there was a hurried movement and then a hoarse, muffled whisper that sounded loud in the still room.

"Who comes to me?"

Erienne's heart fluttered in her breast, but she could no more retreat from her course than the gallant Joan of Arc. Erienne moved slowly forward until she reached the end of the bed, her shadow lengthening and joining the deeper ones. In the shifting firelight, she could see the huddled, twisted form of her husband beneath the cover and saw that he had hastily wrapped a light silk cloth about his head.

" 'Tis Erienne, milord." She loosed the belt and dropped her robe, then leaned a knee upon the bed. The waiting silence continued, and drawing up her other knee and climbing onto the mattress, she sat back on her heels. Her voice trembled as she spoke her reason for coming. "My lord, I am less afraid of what you are than what I might become if you do not make me your wife in full. 'Tis my plea that you take me to you so no further questions might be involved in our marriage."

She leaned forward, reaching out to take the silken mask away, but his hand caught her wrist and held it from its goal. Even close Erienne could see only the dark shadow of his eyes and nothing more.

Lord Saxton shook his head and whispered softly, "In truth, my love, this face is still the one that will set you to flight."

Erienne turned her hand to hold his, and his head bowed over it. Through the cloth his lips caressed her hand, and Erienne was moved by the infinite gentleness of his kiss. After a moment he straightened, and when he spoke, his whisper was tender and held an odd note of pity, as if he knew full well the conflict that raged within her.

"Erienne, my love . . . pull the drapes."

She raised up on her knees, and her arms stretched wide to grasp the curtains. The firelight betrayed her beauty through the filmy gown, showing the slender curves of her body in silhouette, then the weak light was shut out and the darkness of the bed was unbroken. For Erienne, it was like having a door close behind her with the finality of one never to be opened again. She had come, bound with honor to carry out her commitments as wife, yet now that she was on the threshold of that fulfillment, she could not bring herself to make the last move. She waited, struggling with her fears and the almost overwhelming desire to flee.

The bed dipped as Lord Saxton rose to kneel before her. Like a feather floating to the ground his hands slipped down her lightly clad arms, and then the token armor of her gown was lifted over her head. As the garment floated away, the whipcord arms came slowly around her, and the warmth of his body pressed full against the coolness of her own. Erienne silenced the gasp that was born in her throat. The jolt of surprise she experienced had naught to do with revulsion, but rather with the bold, manly touch of him. The alien hardness was a hot brand against her thighs. In the back of her mind there bloomed a vision of him as he had appeared to her at the inn in that moment when he had been aroused by her presence. The shock to her innocence, then, had been no less than what it was now.

His strength was unexpected. He lifted her easily, turning her and taking her down with him. Though the cloth still pressed to her ear and separated the scarred face from her, his naked lips caressed her throat and ventured downward until they were hot and moist upon her breast, rousing her to a warmth she had not thought possible with him. A word came to her lips, but she squelched it cruelly, for it was the name of another. The realization of where her mind strayed made her all the more determined in this quest. She moved against him in an attitude of eager response, and her hand, slipping about his neck, found a long, wrinkled scar that traced along the rippling muscles of his back. It helped convince her that it was Lord Saxton making love to her. Her husband was the scarred one, not Christopher Seton.

She held fast to that security as his caresses grew bolder, exploring the secrets of her body with the sureness of a knowledgeable lover. She was distantly surprised, for she had half expected a fumbling eagerness and a rough uncertainty. But he was gentle . . . so infinitely gentle. His hand wandered with deliberate slowness over every detail of her, as if savoring what he found, and she trembled beneath his lightest touch.

He moved between her thighs, and she gasped as the fiery brand intruded into the delicate softness of her. A sudden, quicksilver pain flashed through her as the resisting flesh split beneath the mounting pressure. His manhood penetrated deep within her, and Erienne bit her lip to keep from crying out, hiding her face against the base of his throat. Her nails dug into the flesh of his back, but he seemed not to notice as his lips touched her ear and brow. His breathing was harsh and ragged, sounding hoarse in her ear, and she could feel the solid beat of his heart against her naked breast. With utmost care he began to move, slowly at first, and the sharp, tingling pain faded. The soft, rosy peaks were teased beneath the crisp furring that covered his chest. She began to answer his thrusting hips, and a frenzied wildness swept them on and upward to dizzying heights. The expanding pleasure, that same which she had so recently experienced, made her writhe and arch her hips against his. They soared onward in a hurtling, twisting flight, climbing together until the ether was thin and heady. Erienne gasped for breath, wanting more, and he gave it. It was a common goal they sought as their bodies strained together, muscles flexing, limbs entwined.

A small cry broke from Erienne's lips as the blissful aura burst around them, bathing them in pulsating waves of pleasure that seemed destined never to die. Slowly, ever so slowly, they drifted back to earth, spent and exhausted but completely content in the union of their bodies.

In the aftermath of their passion, Erienne curled against her husband, firm in her belief that Stuart Saxton was no empty shell but a man of extraordinarily skill and prowess. Like the manse, though scarred and charred on the outside, he bore within him a wealth of qualities above the common man. Her hand caressed the furred chest, and almost without guidance, it drifted down toward the twisted leg he carefully held away from her. Again she was stopped as his fingers became a gentle band of steel around her narrow wrist.

"Remember what you have, Erienne," his whisper warned softly. "All I can give you in this world. Do not tempt fate beyond this moment, for 'twould grieve me sorely to see this night turned into a time of hatred."

Erienne started to protest, but his finger came across her lips and shushed her.

"You may be ready, my love, but I am not." He reached across to carefully tuck the quilt in close about her against a chance chill. "I like the feel of you close within my arms, and 'tis my wont to have you sleep beside me until I wake at morningtide. Will you stay?"

"Aye, milord." She snuggled close to him, but his low, wheezing laughter made her draw back again to try to see the eyes that were only a dark shadow behind the silken cloth. "Something amuses you?"

"Sleep! 'Twill be impossible with you in my arms."

"Shall I go?" she questioned, resting a hand on his chest.

"Never!" He caught her to him in a fierce embrace, burying his face against her throat. "I have waited an eternity for this," he rasped, "and though I may be damned on the morrow, I will not let it end so quickly."

"Damned, milord? How so?"

"I will explain later, my love. Now I would savor once again the delights that you have brought within my grasp."

Sunlight softly penetrated Erienne's sleep, and her eyes fluttered slowly open as she sensed a presence at the edge of the canopied bed. The large, black-garbed form of her husband half filled the opening where the velvet hangings had been pulled aside. Beyond him, the light of a new day filled the chamber, and with the contrast she saw not so much the shape of a beast but a man with wide shoulders wearing a dark leather mask and dressed in somber attire. Surely after such a sweetly blissful night, it was only a trick of her mind that he seemed taller and straighter. She felt his gaze upon her and blinked the lingering slumber from her eyes.

"Good morning, milord," she murmured with a smile gently curving her lips.

"An excellent morning, my love, and you have made it so," he rasped.

At his gentle reminder of the intimacy they had shared, a rosy hue crept into her cheeks and spread downward along the ivory-white throat. The night had held many exceptional and unexpected pleasures for them both, and she was still much in awe of what had transpired.

Clutching the sheet to her, she accepted the gloved hand he extended and sat up, swinging her long legs over the side of the bed. Lord Saxton enjoyed the view of the silken limbs and, where the sheet sagged, the enticing fullness of her bosom. He reached out to smooth the tumbled locks over her shoulder, and with a finger traced the creamy throat downward from her ear. Erienne rubbed her cheek against the darkly gloved hand, amazing him with the softly glowing warmth in her eyes.

"You no longer fear me, madam?" he hoarsely questioned.

It came with a slow dawning that all of her apprehensions had fled. Though the mask was still a barrier between them, it no longer bothered her and would eventually be removed.

"I am content to be your wife in every way, milord," she murmured.

Lord Saxton was stunned by the commitment she voiced and could find no worthy reply. He had never expected her to yield her loveliness to an ugly beast, and now she was tearing down all the boundaries between them. What was he to think of her? Did she love the beast? Had he won the game, or lost it?

Erienne laid a tentative hand upon his arm. "We have much to learn about each other, and we have a lifetime to do it in. It troubles me that I have never seen your face, and I wonder if you might relent . . ."

"Nay, I cannot." He swung away from her and dragged his heavily booted foot across the expanse of the rug. Halting before the fireplace, he stared for a long, troubled moment into the undulating flames, then he leaned his head back, rolling it across his shoulders as if plagued by some pain there. Now that she had given herself to him, he found it even more difficult to rid himself of the mask. She would only hate him the more, and he'd lose everything.

"As you gave me time," she said softly, intruding into his thoughts, "I shall wait for you, my lord."

He half turned to look at her and found a gentle smile awaiting him. An urge swept over him in that moment, and it was all he could do to keep from taking her in his arms, ridding himself of the mask and gloves, and kissing those tender lips until they throbbed beneath his. Yet common sense ruled. He had to bide his time, or lose the perfect rose that he had held so carefully in his grasp.

"I must be gone for a time this morning," he stated with measured words. "Mr. Seton will be joining you in the hall for breakfast. I doubt that I'll return before he leaves. Will you give him my apologies?"

Erienne glanced away from the expressionless, staring mask, feeling the heat of a blush creep back into her cheeks. Christopher was the last person she wanted to face this morning, but she could find no adequate excuse to deny her husband's request. When it came, her nod of acquiescence was barely noticeable.

It was the housekeeper's gentle persistence that hastened Erienne on her way and brought her downstairs to the hall before too much time had elapsed. She had dallied in her morning bath, hoping Christopher would lose patience and leave, but beyond the velvet drapes of the alcove, Aggie had bustled about the bedchamber in high good spirits, spreading up the bedcovers that had been folded down but left undisturbed through the night. Between Aggie and Tessie, a crisp, pale pink silk with a delicately trimmed white lawn fichu was selected. The housekeeper's haste infected the maid, whose hands flew as she plied the brush enthusiastically to her mistress' glistening black locks. In hardly any time at all Erienne's hair was dressed in a soft, charming coiffure that was swept off her nape, and she was ready to meet the one who turned her life inside out.

Despite the enthusiastic compliments of the two women, Erienne felt utterly unprepared for her meeting with Christopher. She desperately wanted to be secure in her fully acquired status of wife, but there was a nagging memory that worried her and made her reluctant to face him. Even in the heat of her passion, when everything was coming together from the ends of the earth toward that moment of bliss, an elusive scent had wafted through her head, filling her mind with brief glimpses of his chiseled profile.

She paused in the tower to gather her composure, though nothing seemed to slow the outrageous beat of her heart. Numbly she stared at a puddle of water that remained after some careless foot had tracked snow into the entry. It was as if she were blind to its presence, for her mind was bound up with the man who waited in the common room. She was atremble at the idea of confronting him, and her consternation would have been no worse if their passion had ended in the yielding of her virginity. The blush of shame was hot on her cheeks, and no comforting thought came to relieve her of the memory of their moments together in the coach.

When she entered the common room, she found him seated before the fire in Lord Saxton's chair, his long legs stretched out before him. She moved toward him, and he quickly rose to stand and watch her. There was a small quirk of a puzzled smile on his lips, and though his gaze ranged the full length of her, it lacked the roguish gleam that had at other times brought a vivid hue to her cheeks.

"I had . . . hoped you would be gone by now," she commented unsteadily.

"I waited to see you, my lady," he murmured.

Erienne glanced away in nervous apprehension. His warm, masculine voice never failed to bring her senses alive. "There was no need for you to, Christopher. The night past has ended, and nothing more will come of it. I am . . . I am distressed that I might have somehow encouraged you to forget yourself, but you have my promise that it won't happen again."

"Is it truly the beast you prefer, Erienne?" he asked soberly.

"I care for Lord Saxton," she said in desperation, tears welling up in her eyes. Fists clenched against the silken folds of her skirt, she faced him and spoke almost pleadingly. "He is my husband. I will not bring shame to bear upon him or the Saxton name!"

Choking off a sob, she pressed the back of her hand against her quivering mouth and turned aside. He moved to stand close behind her and leaned over her shoulder, speaking in a hushed tone as she angrily wiped at the dampened lashes.

"Don't cry, my sweet," he entreated. "I cannot bear to see you distressed."

"Then go away," she begged. "Go away and leave me alone."

His brows came together in a troubled frown. "For the life of me, my love, I can't do that."

"Why not?" She faced him with the question.

His gaze dropped and he stared at the floor in thoughtful concentration for a long moment. When he looked at her again, his gaze was direct and unflinching. "Because I have fallen in love with you."

Jolted by his words, Erienne stared at him in stunned silence. How could it be? He was a man of the world, well acquainted with conquests and easy victories. He was no unseasoned lad who gave his heart to the first fair damsel who smiled at him. What had she done to gain this distinction? For the most part she had been stubborn and willful, suspicious of his intentions. How could he love her?

"We will not speak of it," she murmured in ragged desperation.

"Will not speaking of it soothe the hurt?" he asked. He began to pace the room in growing vexation. "Dammit, Erienne, I have followed you from one end of this country to the other, played every hand I could just to get you to consider me as a man, but my efforts have all been for naught. You still regard me as some evil monster who has cruelly abused your family. You'd rather take a beast to your breast and nurture him with the sweet joys of wedlock than consider me as a fit husband. Am I mad? Can you tell me why a sane man would tag upon your skirts, hoping to garner the smallest crumb of affection while you feed the cake to that most unsightly of men? If you think I am not jealous of your husband, let me assure you, madam, you are wrong! I hate that mask! I hate that twisted leg! I hate that heavy cane! He has what I want, and silence on the matter will *not* make that vetch any sweeter!"

A rattle of dishes warned of a servant's entry into the hall, but Christopher was incensed, and half turning with a growl, he gestured Paine back.

"Get out of here, man!"

"Christopher!" Erienne gasped and took two halting steps to follow the befuddled servant, but Christopher came around to face her with a glare.

"Stay where you are, madam! I am not finished with you."

"You have no right to give orders here," she protested, her own ire growing. "This is my husband's house!"

"I'll give orders when and where I damn well please, and for once, you will stand and listen until I'm through!"

More than a trifle outraged herself, Erienne hurled back her answer. "You may command the men on your ship to your will, *Mister* Seton, but you have no such authority here! Good day to you!"

Catching up her skirts, she whirled and stalked toward the tower until she heard the sound of rapid footsteps coming behind her, then a sudden panic seized her that he would make such a scene that she would not be able to face the servants . . . or her husband. She raced into the entry, stepping over the puddle, and took to the stairs, forcing every bit of strength she could into her limbs. She had barely gained the fourth step when she heard sliding feet, a loud thump, and then a painful grunt followed by an angry curse. When she whirled, Christopher was just coming to rest in a heap against the wall after sliding across the floor, partway on his back. For a moment she stared aghast at the dignified man sprawled in a most undignified manner, but when he raised his head to look at her with barely contained rage, she was struck by the humor of it all. Bubbling laughter broke forth, winning from him a dark scowl of exasperation.

"Are you hurt, Christopher?" she asked sweetly.

"Aye! My pride has been mightily bruised!"

"Oh, that will mend, sir," she chuckled, spreading her skirts to perch primly on the step above him. Her eyes danced with a lively light that was simply dazzling to behold. "But you should take care. If such a modest spot of water can bring you down so abruptly, I would not advise sailing beyond these shores."

" 'Tis not a spot of water that's brought me down, but a waspish wench who sets her barbs against me at every turn."

"You dare accuse me when you come in here huffing and snorting like a raging bull?" She gave a throaty, skeptical laugh. "Really, Christopher, you ought to be ashamed of yourself. You frightened Paine and nearly made me swallow my heart."

"That's an impossibility, madam, for that thing is surely made of cold, hard steel."

"You're pouting," she chided flippantly, "because I have not fallen swooning at your feet."

"I'm angry because you continually deny the fact that you should be my wife!" he stated emphatically.

Footsteps on the stairs behind Erienne made them glance up. Aggie came nonchalantly down the steps, seeming unaware of Christopher's storm-dark frown. Excusing herself, she stepped past her mistress. Finally, on reaching level footing, she contemplated the man, a twinkle of mischief in her eye. "Aren't ye a wee bit old ter be takin' yer leisure on the floor, sir?"

He raised a brow at Erienne as that one smothered a giggle, and with a snort, got to his feet and brushed off his breeches and coatsleeve. "I see that I gather no sympathy here, so I shall leave you both to fare as you might with Lord Saxton."

"Don't go away angry, sir," Aggie cajoled. "Ye haven't eaten yer meal. Stay and dine with the lovely mistress here."

Christopher gave a low grunt of derision. "No doubt I will find warmer companionship at the Boar's Inn."

Erienne raised her head. The idea that he might seek out solace from Molly's arms upset her and filled her with a roweling jealousy. An image of his long, muscular form entrapped by the twining limbs of that lusty wench made Erienne's heart sink sickeningly. She could not bear the thought of him making love to another woman, even though only a few hours ago she had given herself to her husband. Her cheeks grew flushed at the conflict that raged within her, and she struck out in anger.

"Then go!" she cried. "And be quick about it! Hopefully I will forget that you even exist!"

Christopher frowned at her sharply as Aggie slipped away quickly and discreetly. "Is that what you really want?" he demanded. "Never to see me again?"

"Aye, Mr. Seton!" The words burst out in bitter ire, and she felt no urge to halt them. "That is the way of it!"

He swore silently before he growled, "If that is what the lady desires, then that is exactly what she shall have!"

He yanked open the door and in two strides he was out, slamming it behind him. Tears welled in Erienne's eyes, and she muffled a sob as she flew up the stairs to her room, there to copy his manner by flinging shut the portal.

Erienne's rare fit of temper left the servants exchanging worried glances. The mistress had never raised so much as a brow in reprimand to any of them. Whenever a problem arose, she had always addressed the matter with quiet yet unmistakable authority. Thus, when the word got around that she had ordered the gentleman, Mr. Seton, from the house, it caused more than a few mouths to gape. Paine served her the noon meal with a questioning uncertainty, not daring to encourage her to taste the fare that she readily pushed aside. Even Aggie seemed dismayed, though in the morning she had appeared quite cheery after cleaning the master's chambers. The maids who usually did that particular chore had been shooed off without explanation to some other portion of the house. Though the housekeeper gave the servants little time to discuss these happenings, worried conjectures still began to flit about the manor. The presence of such a man as Christopher Seton in the manse was certainly something to talk about, especially when he had sent Paine fleeing from the hall. And, of course, they could only wonder what he had done to cause Lady Saxton's vexation.

That particular spur drove Erienne to seek a walk in the cool air beyond the dark and silent walls of the manse. The sun had made a rare and brilliant appearance, dispensing with much of the snow that had fallen during the night as it continued its flight across the sky. Though large patches of white remained huddled behind protecting walls and shrubs, stepping-stones were now visible, bordering a small, overgrown garden that lay between the main house and the tumbled eastern wing.

Erienne paused on the path to take in deep gulps of the icy breeze that stung her cheeks. She needed its bracing coolness to clear her head and perhaps mend the tattered shreds of her emotions. She was distressed that she could not discipline her thoughts and banish Christopher from her mind. She wanted desperately to hold fast to the bliss she had shared with Lord Saxton, but invading images, combining the moments in her husband's bed with those in the coach, kept flashing through her consciousness, viciously attacking the goal of faithfulness she had set for herself. The impossible yearnings of her heart clashed against her will, and the battle raged in a desperate but fruitless struggle.

Sadly she recognized the path that was laid out for her in life, that one of honor, and though it would mean a severe wounding of that vital organ that throbbed achingly in her chest, she would do what was right. The die was cast. She was Lord Saxton's wife. She had made a commitment.

Petulantly Erienne kicked at a small pebble in front of her. It bounced along, leading her gaze to a spot near the wall where a bit of color broke the monotony of the snow and the dull grays and dead browns of a tangle of brush. There, trembling forlornly in the breeze, was a tiny blood-red rose. The bush was small and weak, bearing a single blossom that by some miracle had brought its beauty into winter's midst.

Almost in awe Erienne cupped the fragile bloom between her hands and bent low to catch the delicate fragrance that wafted from its crimson-hued petals. From a time long ago, when her dreams had held such grand illusions of a prince offering a single rose to vow his love to his lady fair, she recalled a legend that a rose found in winter brought the promise of true love found.

Erienne touched the delicate petals, and for a moment she held a vision of a silver-helmed knight who bore beneath his gleaming visor an all too familiar face. In the illusion he fought with singular purpose to rescue her from her fate and in so doing became her victor, her only love. He leaned near to take her in his arms, then the silver-helmed knight was gone, dissipated in the chill breeze that swept the garden, forever banished from her sight.

A long, wavering sigh slipped from her. Her heart seemed weighted with lead, and it yearned for a lightening of its burden. Yet no succor came. No dawning brightness lit her gloom. Christopher was gone and might never be back.

'Twas Lord Saxton's standing order that none of the servants were to wait up if he failed to come home before the household was ready to retire. None did so this night, and the halls grew quiet and still as each found his bed. Candles were left burning to relieve the gloom that pervaded the darkened halls, and by their meager light the master passed like a ghost through the house. With painfully silenced tread, he climbed the stairs and moved down the corridor toward Erienne's room. Pushing the portal gently ajar, he leaned against the jamb and fed his hungry gaze on the form within the bed. Her gentle, even breathing marked her depth of slumber as she lay on her side facing the hearth with a hand tucked beneath her pillow. Her long hair streamed out into the darkness beyond, and he knew if he gathered her close the luxuriant mass would spill about him and fill his head with an intoxicating scent. The sight of her fulfilled the vision he had kept of her throughout the day, that of a stirringly beautiful woman who warmed his blood more than he could bear.

Careful to make no sound that would betray his presence, he crossed to the bed and pulled the velvet hangings closed to darken the interior. Moving to the far side, he doffed his gloves and mask. Soon he was a pale shadow in the night, slipping beneath the covers. Surrounded by the velvet hangings, he became only a movement in the blackness. A soft sigh escaped Erienne's lips as he pressed close against her back. He inhaled the delicate fragrance of her hair and brushed aside the silken strands to kiss the tender nape. His hand found its way beneath her gown and searched out the womanly softness of her.

Wavering between fantasy and awareness, Erienne lay pliant beneath the roaming hand while elusive grayish-green eyes flickered at the edge of her consciousness. An essence, not unlike brandy, filled her head as the warmth of the firm body penetrated her gown. She stirred against him, and his whisper filled her mind.

"I can't leave you alone." He touched his lips to the smoothly rising slope of her shoulder. "The thought of you stumbles the beat of my heart and arouses such a hunger in me that I must seek you out or groan beneath the torture of it. You have chained me to you, Erienne. The beast is your slave."

The gown was drawn over her head and banished to the darkness, with only a whisper of a sound evidencing its fall to the floor. Erienne's mind broke to the surface of full awareness as he pulled her close to the hard, naked heat of him. He was a man, fully aroused against the coolness of her buttocks. Her breasts warmed beneath his caress, and the slow, languid strokes of his fingers upon their throbbing peaks plucked at the strings of her passion, sending bursting shards of excitement hurtling through her until her loins awakened with a hunger of their own. His caresses continued, following the curving arch of her hip, and her heart quickened its pace beneath his questing search. A husky moan escaped her as he became bolder, intruding into the privacy of her woman's flesh and setting her senses aquiver with expectant eagerness. She melted against his warmth, arching her neck as his teeth nibbled at the slim column.

With a hand on her shoulder, he pressed her back upon the bed, and Erienne caught her breath as his tongue moved slowly over a soft crest of a breast, setting her whole body ashiver. His kisses slipped downward to caress her waist and belly, leaving in their wake a fiery trail that fairly threatened to consume her. She lay willing and eager as he rose above her in the darkness. She welcomed his weight with open limbs, then gasped as the plunging hotness penetrated. Her hands slipped over his shoulders, finding the scar that helped to banish Christopher's countenance from mind. Then with hypnotic motion his loins caressed hers, slow and sure, sheathing the flaming blade and drawing away until it became sweet, ecstatic torture. In blissful response she arched her hips against him, and the grayish-green eyes came back as her hands slipped downward over the hard, flexing buttocks. In her mind the shining orbs gleamed in triumph, but she was past the point of chiding her will into obedience, and she did not care at the moment what image her thoughts conjured in the dark.

In the softly glowing aftermath of their passion, Erienne was content to nestle in the warmth of the large manly form that curled against her. He lay on his side facing her, his legs drawn up beneath her buttocks, with the right foot extended well beyond the silken limbs that rested across his thighs. The only sound that intruded into the silence was the muted ticking of a distant clock. The heavy bed hanging forbade the smallest glimmer to shine through, cloaking them in intimate darkness. Even so, Erienne was haunted by faint and fleeting impressions of a chiseled profile and warm gray-green eyes.

"You've been drinking," she murmured softly.

"Aye," he answered in a rasping whisper and kissed her brow. "I fear I was quite besotted with desire for you."

She smiled in the dark. "Your desire has the smell of strong drink."

"My plight would not ease with a cup or two. The brew only sharpened my cravings."

"Why didn't you come home? I was waiting for you."

He responded with a low chuckle. "Aye, and to have returned to you in the light of day would have been disastrous indeed. Do you not ken how much of a temptation you are, madam?"

"I don't understand," she replied in confusion.

"I am trapped in darkness, Erienne. I can only come to you when the night will hide my face, and yet there grows in me a craving to take you in my arms while the sun is high, when I can see you flushed and warm with passion. 'Tis my hell that I must be a beast of the night."

It was much later when Erienne roused to the unfamiliar presence beside her in bed. Her husband's deep, even breathing assured her that he was asleep, and like thistledown wavering on a breeze her hand slipped hesitantly along his side, reaching his hip and sliding downward, ever so carefully, until she was halted by the feel of a raised, smooth scar, such as a burn would make, on her husband's thigh. How far it extended down his leg, she had no way of knowing, but the welt discouraged further exploring. She drew her hand away as a slight shudder went through her, and she wondered if she would ever come to the place where she would totally abandon her qualms.

*　　*　　*

Lord Talbot's ornate personal carriage drew up before the Saxton manse after a space of a week following the grand ball. The two footmen leapt to the ground, and while one ran to hold the horses, the other hastily placed a small stepping-stool beneath the door before opening it. A gold-buckled shoe reached out and felt cautiously for the step, then the richly brocaded form of Lord Talbot followed. Stepping to the ground, he looked about arrogantly and adjusted his equally elaborate cloak with a shrug of his shoulders. The footman ran ahead to thump the large door knocker as his lordship fastidiously picked his way toward the tower entry with a silk-wrapped packet carried daintily in his gloved left hand.

Paine answered the summons and received from the footman the curt announcement of his lordship's presence. The butler seemed unaffected by the lord's arrival and handled himself with the usual dignified efficiency. After accepting the gloves, the tricorn, and the heavy cloak, he ushered Lord Talbot into the great hall, there bidding him to wait until the master was informed of his visit.

Though considerably less grand than Lord Talbot's manor, the hall of the Saxton estate clearly bespoke of its age and heritage. The high-arched, crudely carved trusses and the tapestries hanging from the plastered and timbered walls whispered of a time when chivalry and honor ruled the land. The chamber sharply contrasted with the grandiosity of the man's attire. Each would have been well suited to a score and ten years past, but now, while the manor remained undated, the lavish raiment of the lord appeared quite outmoded and ostentatious.

Paine came back to escort Talbot to the chamber beyond the common room, where Lord Saxton and his lady would receive their guest. The fancified gentleman marked his progress across the stone floors with a sharp rap of high heels. The butler stepped before him to open the door, then moved back, allowing the man to enter the withdrawing room. The masked one rose as Talbot pranced into his presence, and though the latter waited an appropriate length of time, there was no hint of a bow or even a nod of that stern, helmeted pate. Erienne sat rigid and unmoving, as her husband had bade her. As he had explained, the law ordained that the two lords were equal, and Lord Saxton would have it no other way. Indeed, if their individual worth were accountable by wealth of land, as it so often was, Lord Talbot might well be the one found lacking.

Talbot was piqued because the other did not accept a lesser status, but he managed to control his irritation to only a mild furrowing of his brow and a light twitching of his moustache. With a directness characteristic of the trained diplomat, he plunged into the matter that had brought him to the hall.

"I must apologize for the tardiness of our meeting. I can only plead the press of other business and a lack of cooperation from the weather."

The hollow, whispering voice replied with equal forthrightness. "Welcome to Saxton Hall." The gloved hand indicated a chair near his own. "Will you join us here by the fire?"

As Nigel Talbot accepted the proffered seat, his eyes settled on Erienne and warmed considerably, having such a wealth of beauty to feast upon. " 'Tis good to see you again, Lady Saxton. I trust you've been well."

"Very well, thank you." She nodded stiffly as she returned the greeting.

Talbot's gaze lingered overlong on the soft swell of her bosom displayed above her gown, and when he finally remembered himself and looked to the lord of the manor, he found that one facing him in the stilted silence of the room. Though the leather visage remained void of any human expression, he had the distinct impression that he had just foolishly trespassed where he should not have. It caused him to wonder how the Yankee could manage to escort the lady about the countryside when her husband seemed so possessive of her.

"I have brought some records of the rents I collected in your absence," he stated, bringing forth the ledger. "Of course, you must understand that there have been expenses we've had to deduct, and they amount to a goodly sum. We've had to elect some officers for the protection of your lands and properties. The scavengers would have torn this place apart stone by stone, and then, too, there are not many folk who fancy having traitors in their midst."

The masked head snapped up, and the rasping voice sounded sharp as Lord Saxton questioned, "Traitors? What do you mean?"

"Why, everyone knows your father sold his favors to Scotland. He married that old chieftain's daughter . . ." Talbot waved his hand as he tried to recall. "What was her name? 'Twas so long ago, I fear I've forgotten."

"Seton," Lord Saxton answered bluntly. "Mary Seton."

Nigel Talbot's jaw sagged slightly in surprise. "Seton? You mean the same as Christopher Seton?"

"Aye." The master of the house inclined his head. "The same. Kin by blood, they are."

"Are?" Nigel caught the significance of the word. "You mean your mother is still alive?" He closed his mouth as the other nodded and tried to recollect his thinking, murmuring distantly, "I'm sorry, I thought the lady was dead."

Lord Saxton leaned on his sturdy cane, commanding the other's attention with his awesome appearance. "Though the miscreants sought to find and kill us all, we managed to escape. My mother lives."

Talbot frowned slightly. "And the sons? What of them?"

Erienne's interest perked, heightened by the singular word, sons. She had been under the impression there was only the one son, and now, once again, she was aware of how little her husband had told her of his family. He seemed most secretive about it, as if reluctant to share with her that part of his life. Though she continued to sit quietly through the exchange, she hung to every word of their discussion, hoping to glean some knowledge that she might otherwise not hear.

Lord Saxton answered the inquiry as he turned aside. "They escaped with her."

"I must assume you are the oldest since you are the titled lord," Talbot replied. "But what of the younger? Does he still live?"

The shadowed eyes flicked over the man. "I believe him to be in fine health. You will have the opportunity of meeting him face to face at a later date."

Nigel Talbot managed a nod. "Of course, I would enjoy that."

Lord Saxton waved a gloved hand to the ledger. "We were talking about the rents you collected. If that is your accounting of them, I shall look it over at my leisure."

Talbot seemed reluctant to hand it over. "There are some expenses I should explain."

"No doubt I'll have many questions to ask after I study your figures," his host responded. "My steward has kept his own accounting of the sum the tenants said were paid. 'Twill be interesting to see how well the two compare. 'Tis not often that a royal decree is handed down giving authority for one lord to collect rents for another. If you still have the dispatches issuing that directive, I should like to inspect the various seals and signatures. My steward has been unable to find a record of such a writ, and 'twill be helpful if he had the names of those who issued it." Lord Saxton reached out a hand expectantly. "The ledger please."

Erienne observed Lord Talbot's struggle for control in the tensing muscles in his face. The man was obviously incensed, but his host left no options open to him. His nostrils were pinched, his mouth downturned as he grudgingly handed over the book.

"I shall take into account that there were moneys expended in the protection of my lands," Lord Saxton stated as he set the book aside on the table. "And if I have any questions, you will be the first I ask. In the meantime, I shall send my man to fetch the dispatches . . ."

"I've . . . they've been misplaced." Nigel Talbot's face reddened as he struggled for an explanation. "After such a long time, you can hardly expect me to remember where they are."

"I am a patient man," Lord Saxton assured him almost pleasantly, despite the roughness of his voice. "Would a fortnight be enough time for you to find them?"

Talbot stammered a reply. "I'm . . . not sure."

"A month then? We'll say a month and see what comes of it. I'll send my steward around about this time next month. That should be more than enough time." The gloved hand clasped the other's arm almost in a gesture of familiarity as Lord Saxton led the flamboyant man to the door. " 'Twill take some time to look over the accounts, but I wish to assure you that our home is open to visitors whenever you and your charming daughter wish an outing. 'Twas good of you to answer my summons, and you may expect that I will be very thorough when estimating what your value has been toward these lands. I'm at your disposal whenever you wish an audience . . . except, of course, this Friday. I shall be going to Carlisle to attend some business."

Lord Talbot was so enraged by the man's audacity, he dared no comment. In the hall he gathered his outer garments and left with a stiff nod of farewell. Smiling behind the mask, Lord Saxton stood at the window and watched the carriage depart. He could almost feel pity for anyone living under Talbot's roof, for surely the days ahead would not be pleasant for them.

"Stuart?"

He turned as he heard the questioning tone in his wife's voice and the rhythmic tap of her heels as she came toward him. "Aye, my love?"

The expression on her face showed bemusement. "Why didn't you tell me you had a younger brother?"

He took her hand into his. " 'Twould frighten you, my love, if you knew all the secrets of the Saxtons. For now, the less you know, the better."

"Then you are hiding something from me," she pressed.

"In time, madam, you will learn all there is to know about me and my family. Until then, I beg you to trust me."

" 'Tis a dangerous game you play with Lord Talbot," she warned. "You make me afraid when you deliberately taunt the man."

Laughter wheezed from the mask. "I'm merely offering him a little meat to chew. 'Tis the best way I know to determine whether he's really a lamb or a wolf under all that fancy fleece."

Erienne smiled ruefully. "He does look a bit overdressed."

Lord Saxton leaned both hands on his cane, and his voice came in a sibilant whisper. "Aye, madam, and though the act would not prove as delightful as undressing you, I intend to strip the man bare."

Seventeen

On that following Friday, Lord Saxton's personal landau pulled up in front of a rather nondescript town house in Carlisle. The darkly garbed figure stepped down and half turned as he spoke to Bundy, who remained in the driver's seat.

"I shall be here several hours. Return for me near dusk." He thrust a finger into his waistcoat pocket and tossed up a couple of gold coins. "Here, have yourself an ale or two and take your ease, but mind you don't spend too much in any one place."

Bundy grinned back. "Do ye expect an accounting, milord?"

His lordship responded with a low, amused grunt. "See that it's well spent, Bundy."

"Aye, that I will, milord."

Lord Saxton turned and made his way to the door of the town house, there to rap boldly upon its planks, while Bundy slapped the reins and guided the four-in-hand through the narrow streets, keeping them at a prancing trot that made bystanders turn and stare. He knew precisely where he was going and did not slacken the display of the magnificent steeds until he reached the first of the waterfront taverns. By the time he scrambled down from the high seat, he had gathered a worthy audience. The coat of arms on the carriage door attracted nearly as much attention as the team, and when a tankard of good, cool ale made its way from the tavern into his hand by way of a generous soul, Bundy carefully explained that both team and carriage belonged to the lord of Saxton Hall, who was at that very moment attending to some important business a few streets away. There was little enough to be said about his lordship, except that he would be returning to the manse come eveningfall. He allowed those who would to admire the animals before making his departure with the two gold coins still secure in his purse.

Minding well his master's words, Bundy passed on to the next inn, the next pub, the next tavern, where with almost boring repetition the carriage and team always drew notice, and he was put to pains to explain them. At each place he was the recipient of an offering of an ale or two, and with an alacrity that betrayed his thirst, he showed his appreciation for the gifts and his delight to boast of his master's fine steeds.

It was almost a relief when the appointed hour finally drew nigh, and the afternoon of tippling and sipping was broken off. He returned to the simple town house and was admiring the gold coins when the front door opened and the crippled one appeared.

"This one didn't even cost ye a mite, milord," Bundy said, chuckling. He displayed the gleaming coins and made as if to toss them down, but a gloved hand raised to halt him.

"The next ones will be on me."

Bundy smiled and pocketed the pair. "Thank ye kindly, milord."

When Lord Saxton stood ready to mount, he glanced back toward the town house. A drapery on a higher floor was drawn aside, and the dainty kerchief of a woman could be seen waving good-bye. He raised his own hand briefly, then climbed inside, pulling the door shut behind him. A moment later his cane rapped sharply on the carriage roof, and Bundy clucked to the horses, setting them into their high-stepping action.

They left Carlisle and a few miles down the road wandered through the small village of Wrae. Once clear of the town, Bundy roused the team to a swifter gait, and by the time full night was upon them, they were several miles into their journey home.

The road wound through the broken foothills and down into the narrow coastal plains that would return them back to Saxton Hall. The black shapes of great oaks were pillared with stately grace on either side of the ancient road. Rock walls bordered small farms where a dim candle or a lantern marked a cottage, and here and there they rattled over the hand-hewn slabs that Roman legions had laid.

The hours waned, and across the velvet expanse of the bejeweled night sky the coy half moon played tag with chasing clouds. The lamps of the carriage cast dancing shadows on either side, and at times it seemed that they were pursued by a strange, elusive flock. They swept by a denser copse of trees some distance down the road, and with their passing, another noise joined the rumble of the wheels, a sound of many hooves. Nervously Bundy glanced back over his shoulders and saw behind them a group of dark-clad horsemen leaving the copse. He rapped the butt of his whip sharply on the roof of the coach, then cracked the long tail of it over the backs of the team, urging them into a pace that far exceeded the showy trot. Though comfortable, the landau was light and built for speed, and the four beasts that drew it were powerful in their stride. Each animal knew its place and was well matched to the ability of the others. They stretched out, and the following horsemen were hard pressed even to maintain their distance. A few wild shots were fired, falling well short of their mark, and then the pursuers settled down to the chase, frenziedly whipping their horses to a greater effort.

Horsemen will argue for years to come the merits of a man on a horse or in a cart behind, but here the race was well laid out, and the four straining beasts in their gleaming leather harnesses set a wicked pace indeed. Those behind were bent on reaching the conveyance and bringing it to a halt. But always the landau remained just out of their reach.

A sweeping curve that would take the quarry out of sight appeared in the road ahead of them, and the huntsmen raced the faster, not wishing to give the prey time to turn aside and hide. They thundered around the bend, and for a moment broke their stride, confused. The carriage still raced in the distance, but in its wake a single man stood high in the stirrups with a hooded cloak flaring wide in the night breeze. His horse gleamed moonstone black, and its long mane and tail flew like ebon gonfalons in the wind. Their puzzlement was replaced with a grinding determination to see this one ridden down, and they had no mind to swerve as they spurred their mounts on. The apparition raised an arm, and at its end a great bore of a pistol stared back at them. A flash, a roar, and with a half-screaming grunt, one of the charging pack was flung from his saddle and fell crashing to the ground. The other arm of the ghostly one raised, and it, too, bore a weapon. Another flash, another roar, and another one crumpled and, after a pace or two, slid quietly from his steed to roll beneath the following hooves.

The single rider jammed the pistols into the saddle holsters, and with a keening cry, lifted high a wickedly shining saber. He set spur to the stallion he rode and charged headlong into their midst, sending the flock scattering in wild flight as he whipped the saber back and forth among them. Before the highwaymen gathered their wits, another fell, slashed fatally from shoulder to hip. The blade flashed again in the moonlight and hid itself momentarily in the chest of another.

The brigands could not face this specter from the night. Their minds were full of terrifying memories of an exploding cave, burning tents from which they had fled, and of that same black, glistening steed rearing high and echoing his master's cry with a piercing whinny. Their low-bred mounts pitched and balked as the stallion whirled in their midst, snorting and lashing out with flashing hooves. A man screamed as the thirsty, blood-reddened blade laid open his arm to the bone. The reins dropped from his numbed hand, and his horse took flight, bouncing and leaping across the rock-strewn sod until it crashed into a low stone wall. Upended in its terror, the steed spilled its rider onto the rocks. Then the ravaging banshee spurred his demon steed at the three who were as yet untouched, but they spun their mounts about and fled, lest his vengeance take them too.

Behind the rock wall, the wounded man cowered and tried to crawl away as the ghostly form rode toward him. The man sobbed for pity, and the night rider halted his mount for a moment, contemplating the miserable coward. Like a bird alighting from flight, the nighthawk came to ground, his cloak spreading wide and then settling around him in the manner of folding wings. He leaned down, his face still hidden in the long, cowled hood, and seized the neck of the man's shirt. The garment was ripped clear in a single stroke, and to the wounded one's bemusement, the other bound his arm and stanched the bleeding, tying the bandage tight. The specter stood back and, drawing the saber, rested its tip in the turf.

"Ye may live." The voice was harsh and full of anger. "A sorry plight for a niggardly coward as yerself, but that will also depend on what ye tell me in the next few moments."

The highwayman glanced about in roweling trepidation. The carriage had halted a distance down the road, but the driver appeared loath to come back and held his distance warily.

"You have a camp?" the night rider demanded.

"Aye, a small one." The man's voice quavered as he answered. At any moment the blade might lift and flash, taking his life from him as it had Timmy Sears'. " 'Ere's no more big ones now. We're all over now, an' only the captain knows where the supplies are kept. And the booty, too," he eagerly volunteered. "They won't let us 'ave any 'til ye're caught, they said." His information spent, he huddled close against the rocks, awaiting the probability of his fate.

"If ye're of a mind, ye might hie yerself back to yer captain," the eerie voice sneered, "but I've heard the price of failure for yer kind is more often death. I will give ye life. If ye spend it cheaply, 'tis yer account. My advice would be to catch a horse and see yerself well into the South of England and hope yer captain's spies do not find ye out."

The man trembled and shrank, squeezing his eyelids shut and bobbing his head while a small, squeaking sound issued from his throat. When he opened his eyes again, he was alone. Even the carriage was gone. A saddled horse grazed nearby, and he needed no second prompting. What the demon rider said was true. 'Twas whispered well among his companions that those who failed the captain's bidding were never found to have a second chance.

The tiny candle flame sputtered against the draft that flowed through the room as Erienne moved toward the enclosed bookshelves that lined the far wall. She had come to the small library in search of a volume she had seen several days earlier while browsing through the closed wing. A superficial cleaning had been done, but for the most part, the room was just as it had been when she first came to Saxton Hall. The ghostly shapes of the cloth-draped furnishings enhanced the tomblike atmosphere, while the flickering light cast eerie shadows on the walls and ceilings. It was not a comfortable room to be in, especially with the deathly chill that moved like an invisible spirit through it.

Erienne drew the collar of her dressing gown up close about her neck as her gaze flitted about the room in search of an opening where the air was entering. Moving toward the windows, she found each tightly shut against a wayward breeze. It puzzled her, for the walls were sturdy and thick, not allowing for any possible penetration. Then she realized that the tiny flame at the end of the candle she was holding had stopped wavering.

She whirled to face the bookcase, a tingling creeping along her spine. The case was built against an inside wall, and she knew another room lay beyond. It seemed impossible for a draft to be flowing around the cases, yet strangely the light had fluttered the most when she stood next to them.

Watching the glowing light carefully, she moved slowly forward. As she neared, the tiny flame began to dip and dance on the wick. Her heart took up a frantic beating as she stepped in front of a case and felt an airy rush swirl the bottom of her nightgown, touching on her bare limbs. She held the candle close to the section from where the air flowed, and the light was almost snuffed out in the waft. A wire mesh was inserted in the doors, and shielding the light, she peered through, noticing that the shelves in this particular section were canted back ever so slightly to one side. Opening the door, she pushed at the side of a shelf that was leaning inward, and as if it were on a well-oiled hinge, the whole inside case slipped backward, allowing a greater current of air to channel through. Erienne's heart began to pound, for the draft was as cold as a frigid breath of winter from outside.

Quelling her first instinct to flee to her chamber, she pushed at the edge of the shelves again. The case swung farther, exposing a small, barren cubicle where total darkness reigned beyond the meager glow of her candle. Her nerves stretched taut as she stepped past the case of shelves, through the door, and into the narrow corridor on the other side. She held the candle high and glanced about. A stairway led downward, and with some reservations, she set her feet to the steps, shivering as the current of air swept beneath the hem of her gown. Her heart fluttered within her bosom, and her breath came in trembling gasps with the tension that filled her.

She crept down the stairs until she reached level footing and there held the candle high to inspect her surroundings. It seemed she was in some kind of long, narrow cave that extended toward a vague, dim light some distance away. The chill of the breeze invaded her clothing, but she was scarcely aware of it as she moved toward the faint glow, shielding the candle flame from the strengthening draft. As she neared the end, she realized the passage continued on around a bend, and it was from this area that the source of illumination was coming.

Shaking with the cold and her own apprehensions, she snuffed her candle and stepped around the corner, then halted, not daring to breathe. The tall, black-clad figure of a man was moving beyond the lantern that hung from a peg on the wall halfway between them. She could see only his back, but she took careful note that he was dressed entirely in black, from his full-sleeved shirt to the high, trim boots he wore. He moved with an ease that was familiar to her, but only when he faced the light did she realize how well she knew him.

"Christopher!" The gasp came unbidden from her throat.

His head snapped up, and he squinted against the light of the lantern as he tried to see beyond it. He moved toward her with a question. "Erienne?"

"Aye, 'tis Erienne," she stated, experiencing a rush of emotions, first relief, pleasure, fear, and then anger. She settled on anger to hide the softer feelings. "What are you doing down here?"

His eyes roamed slowly down the length of her as she came into the circle of light, glowing warmly in appreciation of what they beheld. When he raised his gaze, he grinned and gave a simple answer. "Exploring."

"Exploring? In my husband's house? How dare you, Christopher! Have you no propriety?" She could not quite escape the fact that she had to struggle hard to maintain her show of outrage. The knowledge that she had been afraid she would never see him again was too blatant in her memory to be dismissed readily.

"He knows I'm here," he answered casually. "Ask him when he comes back."

"I intend to."

He returned a question to her. "How did you find your way down here?"

She lifted her shoulders in a tiny shrug, turning away. "I couldn't sleep, and I went to the old library in search of a book. When I felt a draft coming from the bookcase, I found this passage."

"I should have closed the case better the last time I used it," he mused aloud.

Her eyes came back to him, wide with surprise. "You mean you entered some other way tonight?"

He grinned leisurely. "Did you think I would chance the temptation of passing near your chamber? I entered from outside."

Though a light blush suffused her, she could not resist the query. "And did you also resist the temptation of passing Molly's chamber?"

Christopher's brows crinkled dubiously as he met her hesitant gaze. "Molly? Please, madam. I am more discriminating than that."

A sudden happiness welled up within her, but she hid it behind another inquiry, waving a hand to indicate their surroundings. "What is this passage used for?"

"Whatever use it serves. Your husband's mother fled this way with her sons when the old lord was slain."

"But what are you using it for now? Why are you here?"

"You are better off not knowing the answer to that." His brow arched as he peered at her. "And I trust you will not speak of this to anyone but Stuart?" He waited expectantly.

"Are you a thief?" she inquired bluntly.

His answer came with a curt laugh. "Hardly!"

Erienne was disappointed by his refusal to answer her, and her frustration was obvious in her tone. "I wish someone would explain what's going on around here!"

"'Tis part of an old struggle," he sighed, "and the details are not always clear."

"I would like to hear them, Christopher," she pressed. "Even Stuart will not confide in me, and I have a right to know. I am not a child."

His grin broadened as his eyes swept her. "You're right in that, madam." Then his smile faded, and he grew serious. "But there is also a dire need for caution. My life depends on it."

"Do you think I would tell anyone when it might mean your death?" she questioned in amazement.

"You have stated your hatred of me, my lady," he pointed out, "and you have given me no reason to trust you with my life."

She met his stare with an unwavering gaze. "I wish no harm to come to you, Christopher."

He mused on her answer for a long moment, then queried abruptly, "Your father? What loyalty do you owe him?"

"I owe him nothing more than what has passed behind me."

"You're cold," he observed.

Erienne was confused by his abrupt change of topic and struggled to return to the same path she had started on. "My father deserves nothing . . . !" Then she saw where his gaze was directed and, glancing down, realized the twin peaks of her breasts were standing taut and high beneath her robe. Her cheeks grew suddenly hot with embarrassment, and she whirled, folding her arms across her chest and groaning her frustration with the man.

Christopher laughed and, picking up his coat, came to wrap it around her. "I prefer you unbound and soft," he murmured warmly against her ear, "with your hair flowing free."

Erienne felt suffocated by his nearness. Her whole being throbbed with an awareness of him, but she knew that if she gave any hint of her weakness, it would lead only to disaster. Over her shoulder, she reminded him pertly, "You were going to explain about this cave."

He chuckled and stepped away, rubbing his palms together as he paced about. "I suppose I should give you a brief history of the old lord first. Broderick Saxton was a peacemaker, a learned man, caught in the crossfire between the English and the Scots." Thoughtfully he moved to the far end of the cave to close the heavy door, shutting off the draft, and then returned to stand before her. "There was a Jacobite uprising some fifty years ago. Some Scots, mostly Lowlanders, sided with the English Crown, while the Highlanders, smitten with Bonnie Charlie, lifted their swords and vowed to set free their lands. The border shifted many times, and Saxton Hall was caught in that tug-of-war. The lord of the manor sought a peaceful settlement between his kinsmen and the English. His own father was English, his mother of the Highland clans. For his loyalty, he was allowed to keep these lands when the strife came to an end and Cumberland was firmly a part of England. There were some who resented him and said all manner of evil things against him. He married Mary Seton, also of a Highland clan, and she bore him two sons. More than a score of years back, when the youngest had yet to reach his tenth year, a band of men called the old lord from the manor after the family had retired for the night, and when he came forth in good faith, the leader slew him before he could lay hand to his claymore. Some claim it was the Highlanders who came to carry out their vengeance."

Christopher paused for a long moment in deep thought, then as he continued his story, he strode back and forth in front of her. "There are others who say 'twas not the marauding bands from the North, but men of English blood who hated Scots by any name and who were jealous of the lord's power and fortune. At any end, they murdered him and attacked the manor, seeking to slay all who might have witnessed the murder. The unarmed servants fled, and Mary Saxton hid here in this passage before she managed to escape with her sons."

"What happened to them?" Erienne asked quietly.

He seemed reluctant to answer. He lifted a cup from a pail of water and drank from it before finally relenting. "The marquess had a small cottage in the South of Wales, and there it was deemed that Mary and her sons could reside safely for a while. After a few months passed, an abortive attempt was made to kidnap or murder the sons. She gathered her family and remaining wealth and went elsewhere, breathing not a word about their heritage to anyone. When the boys came of an age, circumstances forbade the immediate return of the elder. But when he could, he petitioned the high court to bestow title to the family lands upon him, and armed with his memories and a respectable fortune of his own, he came to Saxton Hall to claim his heritage."

"And someone tried to murder him." Erienne raised her gaze in question. "How could the same men have killed the old lord and torched the manor too, Christopher? The first event happened so many years ago. If any of them are still living, surely their hatred has mellowed by now."

"Hatred. Greed. Jealousy. Who knows whether time mellows or whets the passions? But this Lord Saxton is intent on finding those responsible, whether they've passed on to hell or not." The look that came on his face gave Erienne a chill, but it was briefly seen, for he turned away abruptly.

"Justice must be paid sooner or later," she murmured.

He nodded in agreement. "I believe Mary Saxton has come to that conclusion also. She has lost too much to stand and take it any longer."

"I would like to meet her someday."

"God willing, you shall." He reached to take her hand and bestowed a kiss on the chilled fingers, then lifted his head to gaze into her eyes.

For a moment Erienne was held in a space of frozen time, unable to drag her eyes from the ones that commanded her attention. It was as if he searched out her very soul, and he had a way of making her feel consumed by that heated regard. With an effort, she freed herself from those mesmerizing orbs and whispered nervously, "I'd better go back upstairs now. I've been gone too long as it is."

"Your husband should be returning shortly," he murmured.

She looked at him, perplexed. "How do you know that?"

"I passed his coach some miles down the road. Unless he has found some other lady love, I imagine he intends to be with you shortly." His grin came back. "At least, that would be my intent if I were your husband."

The warmth of his voice touched a quickness in her that left her fingers trembling as she raised the candle. "Will you light this please? I need it to find my way back."

He ignored her request and reached to take the lantern from the wall. "I'll take you upstairs."

"It isn't necessary," she was quick to insist, afraid for more reasons than one.

"I'd never forgive myself if some harm came to you down here," he responded lightly.

He lifted the lantern, casting its glow before them, and waited on her pleasure with amused patience. Erienne saw the challenge in his eyes and groaned inwardly. How could she refuse to pick up the gauntlet when she knew he would taunt her with his chiding humor if she did not? Adjusting the oversize coat about her shoulders, she rose to the bait against her better judgment and moved with him along the stony corridor. They were well past the bend when a sudden scurrying accompanied by strident squeaking came from the darkness. At the sound, Erienne stumbled back with a gasp, having an intense aversion for the rodents. In the next instant, the heel of her slipper caught on a rock lip, twisting her ankle and nearly sending her sprawling. Almost before the cry of pain was wrenched from her lips, Christopher's arms were about her, and he used the excuse to bring her snugly against his own hard body.

Embarrassed by the contact that brought bosom to chest and thigh to thigh and made her excruciatingly aware of his masculinity, Erienne pushed hurriedly away. She tried to walk again, anxious to be away, but when her weight came down on her ankle, a quick grimace touched her features. Christopher caught her reaction and, without so much as a murmured pardon, took the coat from her shoulders, pressed the lantern in her hand, and lifted her up in his arms.

"You can't take me upstairs!" she protested. "What if you're seen?"

The lights danced in his eyes as he met her astonished stare. "I'm beginning to think, madam, that you worry more about propriety than yourself. Most of the servants are in bed asleep."

"But what if Stuart comes?" she argued. "You said he's on his way."

Christopher chuckled. "Meeting him now would be most interesting. He might even challenge me to a duel over your honor." He raised a brow at her. "Would you be grieved if he wounded me?"

"Don't you realize a thing like that could happen?" she questioned, angry because he dismissed the possibility with flippant ease.

"Don't fret, my love," he cajoled with a smile twitching at the corners of his mouth. "If I hear him coming, I'll run, and as clumsy as he is, he'll never be able to catch me." He shifted her weight closer against him and smiled into her chiding stare. "I like the way you feel in my arms."

"Remember yourself, sir," she admonished crisply, ignoring her leaping pulse.

"I'm trying, madam. I'm really trying."

Tentatively she curled an arm around his neck and relaxed against him as she held the lantern to light their way. He was silent as he climbed the stairs with her, and though she kept her gaze averted, she could feel his eyes on her. In a few moments they were in the corridor leading from the wing, and with unerring direction, he turned down the hall toward her bedchamber.

Erienne was most observant of that fact and remembered the night he had paused outside her door. "You seem to know your way quite well through this house. Even the way to my chamber."

"I know where the lord's chambers are and that you're using them," he replied, meeting her gaze.

"I don't think I'll ever feel safe in this house again," she replied with more truth than sarcasm.

A devilish grin gleamed back at her. "I would never dream of forcing my attentions on you, my lady."

"I have defended myself much too often to believe that," she declared.

He halted at her door, turned the latch, and nudged the portal wide with a shoulder. Carrying her inside, he paused near a table to let her deposit the lantern on its surface, then continued on to the four-poster. "I am but a man with no more than a common vigor," he stated. "Can I be faulted if I admire a woman of uncommon beauty?"

The bedcovers were turned down, and he lowered her to the softness of the feather ticks. His eyes searched the amethyst depths and saw in them a wide uncertainty that both bemused and fascinated him. It was this that made him pull away, though he yearned to speak his mind. He was goaded by a desire to press his lips upon that sweetly parted mouth and ease his passions while the tiny candle flame lent its soft illumination to those wide, liquid pools he gazed into. But there was much to be lost too if he moved unwisely, and he was not willing to test the moment just yet.

Gallantly he brought her fingertips to his lips and pressed a soft kiss to them, then he turned and, taking up the lantern, quickly departed from the chamber, leaving no echoing sound to follow him. It was a long, long time before Erienne managed to subdue her trembling and relax back in the bed.

The chimes of the clock in the hall marked a half hour's passage of time before Erienne heard her husband's halting footsteps coming down the hall. She watched the door until his dark shape appeared, and she wondered at the sudden guilt that rose up within her. Not willing to yield to the idea that she was succumbing to the Yankee's persistent wooing, she patted the bed in an invitation for Lord Saxton to sit beside her and, when he complied, rose on her knees to embrace him, laying her cheek against his shoulder.

"Will you be angry with me if I told you I found a way through to the cave downstairs?" she whispered.

His hooded head half turned, as if he were surprised at her statement. "Then I beg for your discretion, madam. 'Twould be folly for anyone else to know about it."

"The secret is safe with me, my lord."

"You're a loyal wife, Erienne. No doubt better than I deserve."

"Will you come to bed?" she coaxed, wanting to push aside the unrelenting memory of that moment when Christopher had stared down into her eyes and her emotions had raged a terrible war.

"Aye, my love. Let me douse the candles."

"Will you not leave them burning that I may know you better?" If she had light, perhaps she would not be haunted by the other's visage. She was growing more afraid of her imagination than of what her husband hid from her.

"In time, my sweet. In time."

Much later she lay against his broad chest, completely fulfilled yet more tormented than she cared to be. The impression of Christopher Seton had been stronger this time, plaguing her relentlessly as Stuart made love to her. The fleeting invasions of Christopher's face into the private moments with her husband made her prey for an accusing conscience.

"Stuart?"

"Aye, my love?" His rasping whisper came in the dark.

"Farrell is coming tomorrow, and you promised to help him with using the pistols again. Would you have an aversion to teaching me also?"

Her husband drew back with the question, "Whatever for, my love?"

"I would like to know how to shoot . . . in case there should ever come a time when you are taken from this hall by force. If I can, I want to be able to defend you."

"If that is your wish, madam. I see no harm in it. You'll at least be able to protect yourself if anything should happen."

"Can you teach me to shoot as well as you do?" she asked with enthusiasm.

Grating laughter filled the velvet enclosure of their bed. "What, and have you turn the sights on me when you grow vexed with sight of me?" He paused and realized she was serious. "That skill, madam, comes with years of practice and the dire need to defend one's life. I can teach you only the use and care of the gun. The other comes with time." He pressed his lips against her throat. " 'Tis much like love. It only improves with careful practice."

In the next several days, Erienne's ears rang nearly continuously from the loud explosions of shot, while her arm and shoulder suffered from the weight and recoil of the flintlock and the smaller pistol. Each morning and afternoon she was taken through the drill of loading, aiming, and firing. Farrell's progress was no better than her own, for he had to overcome the unaccustomed use of his left hand in the matter of priming and steadying the flintlocks.

Though Erienne was eager to learn, she found it difficult to sight the weapons properly so she could hit the targets. It was only when Lord Saxton stood at her back with his arms bracing hers that she began to understand the position of the weapon in relationship to her body and the necessity of a firm grip.

By the end of the third week, she was putting the shot within a fairly close proximity of the targets. Farrell had returned to Mawbry on the Monday of the week previous, and for the next days she had her husband's full and undivided attention, which was handed out with generous familiarity. A press of an arm across her bosom as he helped her take aim, the brush of his loins against her buttocks, or a gloved hand fitting the butt of the flintlock against her shoulder while his palm rested casually on her breast. This intimate handling of her person was a fair indication of the pleasure he derived in claiming her as his own, and when those gloved hands paused to caress her softer parts, no hint of fear or revulsion remained to shake her composure. It was only that haunting image in the back of her mind that would not give her rest.

Her curiosity about the cave escalated. She couldn't quite set it from mind, nor had she been sufficiently appeased by Christopher's explanation about its use, for in the days following the discovery of it, she dwelt on the fact that he had given only a brief historical sketch of the family and had avoided answering her inquiry concerning the cave's present function. When she attempted to ask Lord Saxton about it, he only shrugged and assured her that her questions would be satisfied in a short time.

He was gone for a day, and the servants were cleaning in another part of the manor when the thought of the cave drew her once more to the old library. This time she came better prepared for an exploration, having claimed a lantern from the stable and a heavier shawl from her armoire. She slipped quickly through the bookcase opening and took care to close it behind her.

Despite the fact that the hour was a little past two in the afternoon, darkness held the interior of the passage in a firm grip. Beyond the circle of light cast by the lantern there was only a black void filled with uncertainties. A distant skittering cooled her boldness, yet she knew that if she wanted to see where the passage led, she would have to overcome her qualms.

The narrow stairs led her to the lower level, and she continued on, passing the bend and coming to the area where she had discovered Christopher. The corridor was empty now, and looking about, she found nothing more interesting than several sets of reins hanging from a bar, a wooden chair, a locked chest, and a pair of black boots sitting neatly beside it. She moved beyond the meager furnishings and went to test the door that she had seen Christopher close. It was made of heavy planks and bore no other security than a bar that could be lifted from both sides. A thin, dim thread of sunlight filtered in from beneath the door, tempting her to drag the portal open.

At first, what she saw bemused her, for the only thing that met her eye was a large heap of tangled brush. Barely enough room existed to slip past, but pressing close to the side, she made her way through the thick growth and found herself at the edge of a wooded copse on the side of a hill that gradually sloped away from the manor house. Above the mass of trees that clustered close together against the hillside she could see several of the towering chimneys that rose above the high-pitched roofs. Low-growing brush filled the area beneath the trees, hiding to the casual eye any hint of a trail or pathway that might have wandered through the woods. She had had no thought of going beyond the end of the passageway, but in a long patch of melting snow the recent impression of a man's footprints gave evidence that someone had passed this way only a short time before. The tracks were too short and wide for Christopher to have made them, and since they did not belong to her husband either, she could only determine that someone else knew of the hidden passageway.

Curious, Erienne raised her head and searched the countryside, letting her gaze range far and wide. She saw nothing out of the ordinary, a hillside covered with trees, a small, trickling brook wandering through the valley, jagged rock protruding from the incline. She was about to turn away when at the edge of her vision, a quick, furtive movement caught her eye. She stared hard through the trees, wondering if it might have been her imagination, then she saw it again, a man in dull-hued clothes sprinting from bush to shrub, nearly hidden in the dense shadows of the copse.

Her heart began to thump faster. For some reason that short, squarish figure hit a strong chord of familiarity, spurring her curiosity to know just who it was. Lifting her skirts, she hurried along the slope, never pausing as her feet slipped and slid on the wet turf. The chill breeze penetrated her woolen shawl and brought a deeper color to her cheeks. Twigs plucked at her garments and smoothly coiffured hair, dragging free several strands as she brushed past. The man continued his careful pace, oblivious to her presence. At the outskirts of a denser thicket, Erienne paused, hiding herself behind a tall shrub as he stopped to cast a glance about. He looked over his shoulder in her direction, and Erienne caught her breath as she saw the face of Bundy through the tangled web of twigs. She pressed a hand over her mouth and sank lower, wondering what furtive affair he was about and why he was not with her husband. She could have sworn the two of them had departed by coach together.

Continuing on his way, Bundy splashed across a stream that meandered through the trees, and Erienne saw where he was going. A tiny cottage lay at the foot of a hill, nestled so tightly in the trees it was barely visible. A tall, overgrown hedge grew out to the side of it, and at the far end, the wheels of a carriage could be seen jutting out from behind it. A small lane entered through the trees, halting near the carriage.

Bundy slipped through the hedge that jutted out past the cottage, but the growth was so thick it forbade any glimpse of what lay beyond it. Erienne was startled to hear a high whinny and a sudden pounding of hooves, as if a horse had been startled by the man's appearance. She heard Bundy's chuckle and then a squeak of a hinge, the same which a gate or a door might make when opened. Bemused, she left her haven and hurried toward the stream. It formed a momentary barrier in her path until she found a place where several stones provided a way across it.

Growing more cautious as she neared the hedge, she slowed her pace and took care where she set her feet. Even so, the snorting and high, piercing shriek of a horse indicated that the animal had sensed her presence.

"What be the matter with ye, Saracen!" Bundy questioned. "Settle yerself down now."

The horse whinnied again and, by the sound of its thumping hooves, nervously cantered to and fro.

"Ahh, I know what's eatin' at yer pride. The master left ye behind and took yer rival, eh? Well, ye needn't be feelin' so rejected, me fine, handsome stallion. He saves ye for the best, he does. There be no denyin' that."

Erienne peered through the hedge and caught a stirring view of an animal she would not soon forget. In nervous agitation, a glistening black stallion tossed his head and pranced back and forth along the inside of a small paddock. He was majestic in appearance, with a proud look about him that few steeds could match. His mane and tail flowed like the sweeping train of a black-garbed prince, and he set down his flashing hooves with precise motion as he made a wide sweep of the area. When he paused for a moment, his ears remained perked, and his nostrils flared as his large, alert eyes searched in her direction. Then with a snort, he took up the pace again, flinging high his long tail.

Dragging her gaze away from the magnificent beast, she surveyed the area sheltered by the hedge. Two different paddocks existed and were separated by a walk. Six enclosed stalls were built next to the cottage, two of which opened by way of a gate into each of the paddocks. Four carefully matched steeds stood in the smaller stalls, while the larger stall and paddock opposite Saracen's stood empty.

Erienne's brows puckered in thoughtful bemusement. She knew this was her husband's land she stood upon, but before today she had had no idea this cottage even existed. Bundy, however, seemed quite familiar with it and also with the animals stabled here. Like the cottage, he was a most secretive man, except with Lord Saxton.

Drawing away from the shrubs, Erienne headed back toward the stream. Since Bundy's loyalty to her husband was most evident, he could not mean them any harm. Lord Saxton undoubtedly knew about the place, and she had to trust that whatever he and Christopher Seton were doing was within the law.

It took some searching to find the opening to the passageway, and she had to retrace her steps twice before she found the particular shrubs that covered it. Several moments later she was in her bedchamber stripping off the soiled gown. She made herself presentable again, and a thrice of hours later, informed that her husband's landau was approaching, she went to greet him at the front portal. She stood outside the tower entry and watched the four-in-hand draw near. The closer they came, the more surprised she became, for the four prancing steeds looked very much like the ones she had seen in the stalls next to the cottage. Though she had not inspected the carriage that had been there, her husband's landau seemed a close match.

Erienne's eyes flew to the coachman, and a sudden prickling went along her spine. Bundy was driving! Her mind began to churn in a restless frenzy, grasping for some logical explanation but finding none. Lord Saxton had been gone all afternoon. So how could Bundy be with him?

The smile that she had prepared for her husband was only a shallow reflection of its former self. Dismay dimmed the light in her eyes, and knowing she would have trouble meeting the gaze behind the slitted holes, she turned toward the tower as he came near, letting him slip an arm about her waist. She could hardly suspect him of being involved in a clandestine affair of the heart, yet something was not right here. The pieces did not join neatly together, and she could only wonder at the mystery that involved him, Bundy, and Christopher Seton.

Eighteen

A festival was held at Saxton Hall to lure the warmer winds of spring to their clime. It was a time of gaiety, feasting, and dancing, when lord and lady, servant and peasant alike joined in the merry-making. It was also a time for a fair of sorts, when the tenants could gather their handiwork of the winter months for the purpose of selling or bartering it away to the visitors who were wont to come. Crude and temporary stands and fancier pavilions and tents were erected for the display of merchandise. Woolens, laces, and miscellaneous wares were to be had for a tuppence or two.

'Twas decreed that the day would be fair of weather, for no cloud would dare cast its shadow over such festivities, and indeed it was. The sun's presence added warmth to the snaggletoothed grins of eager young faces and those of the very ancient as well. Hands gnarled by hard work clapped in enthusiasm while the quick-stepping feet of dancers flew in time with the music. Small crowds formed here and there to watch the various sights. Jugglers and acrobats performed their feats for pennies, while jesters garbed themselves like the knights of yore and, equipped with clever horse shapes strapped about their waists, acted out inane jousts to amuse the people.

Lord Saxton and his lady toured the grounds, pausing now and then at the stands or in the open to watch the minstrels or the dances. The crowds gave way before them but seemed to fill in close behind. Whenever they did pause, the gaiety soon grew subdued, as many were wont to stand with half-quaffed mug in hand and simply stare at this terrible-looking lord. With spry alertness, children sought out the shelter of their mothers' skirts and peered out as that ominous ogre approached with his blank-staring mask and fearsome gait. Though the tenants spoke in respectful tones of him, for the most part they were inclined to speculate at what horror the helm did hide and the courage of the lady who had to face him each night. Exaggerated tales of how he had set a band of thieves to rout were bantered about. It was said that he had dealt with others of renown and gave no quarter. Yet he was also the one who had come among them with his steward to inquire of their welfare and whether the rents in the past had been fair or not. After the burden Lord Talbot had placed upon them, they were amazed and grateful when he had slashed the rates to less than half the mark.

After his coming, the word had quickly spread among them. The lord of Saxton Hall was home, and they began to hope that the ills that had beset them would be turned aright. A new sense of justice was established, and henceforth what was right was right, and what was wrong was wrong. There would be no shading of the till or a thumb upon the scale. Here was a justice stern but fair, one they could understand and live with. No whimsical quirk to tip the scales against them. No greedy palm stretched forth in bold demand while truth and fairness quaked. And somehow all of them were the happier for it.

In many ways Lord Saxton had ceased to be the unknown beast and in their eyes had taken on the manner of a worthy lord. They now scoffed at the wild tales that told of him flying in the night like a great winged bat. Indeed, he had become something of a hero to them all, and they began to take offense when one unduly criticized him.

Yet for all of their loyalty and respect, nothing had been effective in setting aside their reticence until they watched the lady at his side. They forgot that Erienne had once passed along as one of them and brushed their elbows in the marketplace. They saw her only as the mistress of the manor now, and her ease and comfort with the man who quietly escorted her did much to ease their trepidations.

They gaped in bemused awe as she laughed and chatted with him. The resting of her hand on his arm, her casual acceptance of his touch, and an intimate whispering between the two did much to dispell the lingering qualms.

To be sure, Erienne Saxton was as gracious a lady as any they had ever known. Mothers watched with pleased smiles as she touched this child and bent to kiss that one. She doled out bits of sweets to the gamins and often paused to coax the younger ones to come to her. The women were soon abuzz with how she actually held a wee babe in her arms and cradled it close against her. It was even told how the lord himself chuckled at the babe's delight and held out a black-gloved finger for the lad to play with.

Fears softened as the day wore on, and there grew out of it a pleasant feeling of contentment. Even if this present lord had the appearance of being born in the fires of hell rather than merely having been tested by them, the tenants were settled on the fact that they were far better off for having him as their lord and his lady as the mistress of their lands.

For some at least, that idea was reaffirmed when the mayor of Mawbry decided to join his son for a visit to Saxton Hall. While the younger Fleming's interest turned to a contest of skills with firearms, the elder displayed his relentless fascination with wagering. It took on many forms and aspects, from the hiding of a pebble beneath a thrice of cups, to a little game with cards. After all, it was only for a tuppence or two, and perhaps 'twas the best the tenants could afford, Avery reasoned, but come summer they could earn enough to make up for the loss. Still, he was careful to carry on his activities well out of eyesight of his host.

As the day wore on, the mayor became so completely engrossed with his purpose that he failed to notice his daughter eyeing him quizzically from nearby. He was surprised when he heard her calling him. Hastily gathering up his winnings and concealing them in his coat, he excused himself from the small collection of men and swaggered toward his daughter, as the idea of cheating had never so much as entered his mind.

Erienne tilted her head as she looked at him curiously. "Father, I hope you have remembered that you're a guest here and have not taken advantage of the fact that you are related . . . in some manner."

Avery drew himself up and flapped his wings in the manner of an outraged rooster. "What do ye mean, girl? Do ye think I don't know how to conduct meself at an outin' such as this? Here I am with most o' me life behind me, and ye tryin' ter give me counsel at this late date. Why, I've been with dukes and earls and higher lords than the Saxton name has borne. Now ye're worryin' about me conduct with a few simple peasants. A pox on ye now!"

"A pox on you," Erienne returned in an angry whisper, "if you've been cheating my husband's people. If I hear one word about you working your shifty ways here today, I'll see that you never bring your shadow on these lands again."

Avery's face took on a deep hue of vermilion. Leaning toward her, he spoke through gnashing teeth. "Why, ye little turntail snip. Ye'd rather take the word o' some mindless folk and condemn yer own father without allowin' him a word in his own defense. Just 'cause ye be wearin' fancy skirts now and ye got yerself a high title, ye don't need ter be actin' so grand with me. I know where ye really come from."

"One word! Remember it!" Erienne warned crisply. "I will not see you cheating these people."

Avery's eyes flared as he drew back his hand to threaten her. "Ye keep a civil tongue in yer head, girl! I'll not be called a cheat by the likes o' ye!"

In his rage, he was deaf to the shocked gasps of the peasants, and he never saw the black face of the mask turn their way, but of a sudden his raised hand was seized by the wrist in a grip that he could not break. He glanced to see who held him, and the bottom fell out of his stomach. He gulped, ready to run and hide, but his feet were frozen to the turf and wouldn't obey his urging. He stood with quaking limbs as he faced the masked countenance of his lordship, Saxton.

"Is there ought amiss here?" the harsh, rasping voice demanded. The cold, ebony shades of the eyeholes riveted the man where he stood.

The mayor's mouth opened spasmodically, but it was too dry to allow words to form. There was no possible way he could extract himself.

Erienne watched her father's futile attempts at speech and took pity on him, though she could not fully understand why. He had never been extravagant in his mercy toward her. "The argument is an old one, my lord," she answered for her kin. "It fairly vexed us both."

Lord Saxton's gaze never wavered from the man. "I suggest, Mayor, that henceforth you consider the delicacy of your mortal body before you again tempt the Fates this sorely. Your daughter now falls under my protection, and you have no further right to abuse her."

Words failed to come from Avery's throat as they were bidden, and he had to suffice with a hesitant nodding of his head.

"Good!" Lord Saxton released his hold. "Henceforth, I shall expect you to give my lady proper respect and to be careful when dealing on any of my lands. Otherwise, the consequences shall be laid at your feet."

Avery stood mute, rubbing his aching wrist as the master of the manor led Erienne away. He knew if word got back to either of them how he had cheated the peasants, he might lose far more than he had gained. Still, it was only a threepence or a farthing here and there, and even if he wanted to give the coins back, he had no idea who had actually lost to him.

Just before dusk of the following afternoon, Erienne stood at the tower entry and watched the landau pull away from the manor. She was curious to know just how far it would go in its journey and was as equally perplexed by the secrecy surrounding the cottage and the magnificent black steed that was kept concealed. Many questions had begun to plague her. The accusations of Lord Talbot and the sheriff concerning the night rider played on her mind. Despite her avowed trust, she could not fully escape the mental vision of Ben lying sprawled in his own blood with a masked, black-garbed form standing above him with bloodied knife. The thought frightened her and fairly shredded the faith she had laid to her husband.

An urge grew strong within her as the landau disappeared from sight. She had to see for herself if it would stop at the cottage. Perhaps if she found her husband there, he might tell her what game he was playing, and then hopefully her fears could be set to rest. She longed for assurance. In any form! Anything!

Once again, she fetched a lantern and her woolen shawl before entering the passageway. The different quirks and crannies of it were already becoming familiar to her, and she pressed on to the bend with more confidence. A light shone from the area where she had met Christopher, and becoming more cautious, she put out her own lantern and moved with more stealth around the corner. The passageway was empty, but just as she was stepping into the light she heard a low scrape outside the door and saw the handle begin to turn. Moving back into the shadows, she pressed close against the wall and held her breath as the portal swung open. She almost gasped as Christopher came striding in, dressed in the same dark clothes he had been wearing when she last saw him. He seemed sure of his purpose, for he went directly to the locked chest, knelt before it, and fit a key into the lock. Hardly daring to breathe, she watched as he drew forth a pair of pistols and a long saber enclosed in an elaborate sheath. He snugged the belt bearing the scabbard about his narrow hips, then tucked the pistols into the leather band. Almost as quickly, he locked the chest and disappeared through the doorway again, leaving Erienne to sag slowly against the wall in relief.

Her mind began to fly in a chaotic frenzy. No good could come of the weapons he had taken from the chest. Indeed, the sight of them was a portent of a dangerous conflict. But with whom? Another Timmy Sears? Or a doddering old drunk?

Then a sudden coldness gripped Erienne's heart. The night rider wore black and took to ground when it was dark, doing his murdering by way of a sword and leaving his victims' blood spilled upon the turf. Christopher had a saber, and he was dressed in black. Hidden below was a powerful black steed that could fly like the wind. The combination of man and beast could be a most formidable one.

Erienne stepped out of the shadows and set a flame to the wick of her lantern, then hurried back along the passageway. There was little time to waste if she wanted to see what Christopher was up to. If she went to the cottage by foot, he and the stallion might be gone by the time she got there, leaving her questions unanswered. She had to see for herself if her fears had any basis.

It was only when she had reached the interior of the stable and had led forth the mare Morgana that she realized to go venturing out at night dressed as a woman was most foolhardy. As she debated her next course of action, her gaze fell on several garments hanging over a short line stretched in front of a stall, undoubtedly spread to dry after a washing. A shirt, a short-cropped coat, and a pair of boy's breeches were among the brief assortment and near enough to her size to be serviceable. They obviously belonged to Keats, but in consideration of the fact that he would suffer as much embarrassment as she would if she asked to use them, she thought the best thing to do was to borrow them without his knowledge. Snatching them off the line, she ran into the corner of an empty stall and hurriedly doffed her gown and chemise. The cold air touched on her bare skin, sending shivers along her flesh, and in desperate haste she yanked on the clothes. She had no time to lace the shirtfront, though it gapped open well past her bosom. She covered it with the coat and took a silk sash from her gown, tying the sash about her waist to secure the breeches in place. They reached to just below her knees, leaving visible a shocking display of calves smoothly clad in white silk stockings. Her slippers had a reasonable heel and posed no problem, but her hair, having been left free to flow down her back, had to be tucked in a filthy tricorn she found. She grimaced as she tugged it on, wondering what kind of vermin she was inviting.

Ignoring her sidesaddle, she chose one fit for a man. With the help of an empty keg, she mounted to the seat and adjusted her position for a few moments. Being in almost direct contact with the saddle was an entirely new experience for her and not one she was sure she could long endure. Either she was too soft or the seat was too hard, but whatever the cause, it did not lend toward exceptional comfort.

Thumping her heels against the mare's side, she left the stables and cut a wide path away from the house, heading in the general direction of the cottage. Dusk had left the countryside bathed in a deep hue of magenta, but the oncoming shades of night were greedily nipping away at the dull light. It was only by chance that she caught sight of a dark-clad rider on a black horse already on the road and some distance ahead. Finding little doubt in her mind that it was Christopher Seton, Erienne gave chase. She had no thought of overtaking him, nor did she believe she could if it came to a race. Her intention was merely to see what he was up to and if she had any real reason to suspect that he was the fearsome night avenger.

The sphere of the moon severed its bond with earth and rose higher in the heavens to cast its silvery glow over the countryside, lending just enough light to show her the dark shape ahead. Over dale and hill, through brook and puddle, Erienne followed, sometimes only catching a glimpse of her quarry on a far-off rising. The distance between them extended, and when she lost sight of him, she began to worry that he had increased the lead. The road curved and wound its way around a shallow stream. Determining that the latter provided the straighter course, Erienne prodded the mare into the water, seeking to gain some ground. The hooves clattered along the rocky bed of the brook, echoing through the tunnel of trees that lined the way. It was an act of pure folly, for the one she followed had paused further ahead in the shadows.

Christopher's head came up as he heard the rattling hooves of an approaching horseman. He had been aware for some time that someone was behind him and decided the game had gone far enough. Whirling the black stallion about, he paralleled the road for a ways. He knew of a special place where he could properly greet the fellow.

Erienne guided the mare carefully up the slope from the stream, then urged it in a fast canter back to the road. She had lost sight of the dark rider, and the thought that he might have taken another direction make her push the steed even harder. She was passing a small embankment crowned with low trees when suddenly a black shape flew out at her from the brush. A scream was jolted from her as a hard body slammed into hers, and she was swept from the saddle.

Christopher realized his mistake on contact, for the one he carried with him was much too light and soft to be anything but a woman. He twisted in midair, taking the impact of the fall upon himself to save the frailer body. At the same time an angry whinny pierced the night air as the reins were jerked from Erienne's hand and the bit tore into the horse's mouth. Christopher had barely come to a halt in the dust of the road when he looked up to see the thrashing forefeet of the rearing mare. Recognition jolted through him at sight of the white stockings, and he knew at once who his unwilling guest was. Thinking the steed was bent upon some distraught vengeance, he threw himself across the twisting she-cat he held. The spritely mount leaped over them in a graceful arch, and in a rattle of hooves was gone, racing back in the direction she had come.

Christopher's attention was brought back abruptly to the little wild thing he had caught. In a frenzied effort to gain her release, she clawed his face with raking nails and sought to tear the hair from his head with grasping fists. He was hard pressed to defend himself until he caught the flailing arms firmly in his grasp and pressed them down, using his greater weight to subdue the Lady Saxton.

Erienne was trapped, held firmly in the middle of the dusty road. Her outraged struggles had loosened her hair and disarranged her clothes to the point that her modesty was savaged. Her coat had come open in the scuffle, and their shirts were twisted awry, leaving her bosom bare against a hard chest. The meager pair of breeches made her increasingly aware of the growing pressure against her loins. She was pinned almost face to face with her captor, and even though the visage was shadowed, she could hardly miss the fact of his identity or the half-leering grin that taunted her.

"Christopher! You beast! Let me go!" Angrily she struggled but could not influence him with her prowess.

His teeth gleamed in the dark as his grin widened. "Nay, madam. Not until you vow to control your passion. I fear before too long I would be somewhat frayed by your zealous attention."

"I shall turn that statement back to you, sir!" she retorted.

He responded with an exaggerated sigh of disappointment. "I was rather enjoying the moment."

"So I noticed!" she quipped before she thought, then bit her lip, hoping he might mistake her meaning.

He didn't. He was most aware of the effect her meagerly clad body had on him, and he replied with laughter in his voice. "Though you may choose to fault my passions, madam, they're quite honestly aroused."

"Aye!" she agreed jeeringly. "By every twitching skirt that saunters by!"

"I swear, 'tis not a skirt that attracts me now." Holding her wrists clasped in one hand, he moved his hand down along her flank and replied in a thoughtful tone, " 'Tis more like a pair of boy's breeches. What? Has my ambush yielded me a stable boy?"

Erienne's indignation found new fuel that he could so casually fondle her, as if he had a perfect right. "Get off, you . . . you . . . ass!" It was the most damaging insult she could think of at the moment. "Get off me!"

"An ass, you say?" he mocked. "Madam, may I point out that asses are to be ridden, and at the moment you are bearing my weight. Now, I know women are made to bear—usually their husbands or the seed they plant—but I would not suggest that you have the shape or looks even approaching an ass."

She ground her teeth in growing impatience at his wont to turn the simplest comment into an exercise of his wit. She could not bear the bold feel of him against her another moment. "Will you get off me?!"

"Certainly, my sweet." He complied as if her every wish was his command. Lifting her to her feet, he solicitously dusted her backside.

"Enough!" she cried. The breeches had lost much to old age and use and seemed far too light a layer to protect her from the familiarity of his hand.

He straightened, but his gaze did not raise to meet hers. Rather, it was directed downward, and her eyes followed quickly to find her breasts gleaming pale and bare between the gaping, plunging neckline of the shirt. With a shocked gasp, she snatched the wayward garments closed and struggled to secure the lacings. Then his attention dipped even farther, and he stared in rueful amazement at her lower half.

"Why are you wandering about in this outlandish garb, pray tell?"

Petulantly Erienne moved away from him and resumed dusting herself, having solved the problem of the shirt. "There are those," she answered sharply, "who would set upon a woman in the night, and 'twas my thought to pass unnoticed as a lad. I didn't know you were wont to leap out at passersby like a witless madman."

Christopher's eyes caressed the shapely backside and admired the way the breeches stretched tightly to her derrière when she knelt to retrieve the hat. "You weren't merely passing by, my lady," he pointed out. "You were following me. Why?"

Erienne whirled to face him. "Aye! That I was, and from what I see, someone should follow you to see what mischief you're up to!"

"Mischief?" His tone was one of innocence and surprise. "Now, why would you be thinking I'm up to mischief?"

She made a sweeping gesture with her hand, indicating the black garments he wore. "A black steed? Black clothes? Riding out at night? 'Twould appear that you have the same habits as the night rider."

Christopher smiled sardonically. "And, of course, you would have me murdering poor, simple folk while they sleep."

Erienne looked at him levelly. "I was going to ask you about that." She drew a deep breath to steady her voice. "If you were the night rider, why would you murder Ben?"

He returned the question to her. "If I were the night rider, why would I be so foolish as to murder a man who knew about my enemies? Do you call that wisdom, madam? Nay! I call that foolishness. But if I were one of those he could talk about, then I would have good reason to see him silenced before he told his tales."

Erienne dared not release a sigh of relief, for there were other names on the list of murder victims. "What of Timmy Sears?"

"What about him?" Christopher inquired. "A thief! A murderer!"

He shrugged. "Perhaps he was even one of those who set fire to the wing at Saxton Hall."

"Did you kill him?" she asked.

"If I were the night rider, why would I be so foolish as to murder a man who blubbered tales, places, and names of my enemies? Neither is that wisdom, madam. I believe Timmy's mistake was in confessing too much to his friends. Not having the saintliness of priests, they sent him to a higher judgment."

"And the others who were killed?" she pressed.

"If I were the night rider, madam, I would protect myself to the point of killing those who try to take my life. I do not count that as murder."

"You are the night rider, aren't you?" she said with conviction.

"Madam, if the sheriff comes to you and asks the same about me, what can you tell him of a certainty? Why should I confess and possibly make of you a liar?"

Erienne stared at him, feeling suddenly confused. She could not bear the thought of him being hanged. The idea frightened her as much as if her own life were threatened. Perhaps even more so.

"Mind you, I make no confessions, madam."

"Nor do you make any denials," she responded.

He grinned and spread his hands innocently. "I had business abroad and with so many tales of highwaymen roaming about, I took what precautions I could to pass unnoticed, and, of course, I chose a swift horse. What else can you say against me?"

"You needn't waste your breath further, Mr. Seton. I am convinced that you are the one the sheriff is looking for. I don't as yet understand your reasons, but I hope they are honorable." Though she waited, no assurances came, and she realized she would hear none. Dusting off the tricorn, she glanced about for her mount and failed to see any sign of it. "You frightened off my horse. How am I going to get back home?"

Christopher raised his head and gave a low, warbling whistle. In the waiting silence, hoofbeats were heard, and then Erienne gasped as she caught sight of the glistening black steed galloping toward them. Freed from restraint, the stallion's unswerving direction gave her cause to wonder if he would stop. For safety's sake she stepped behind Christopher, cautiously taking hold of his shirt as the beast came to a skidding halt beside them. Having little trust for stallions or their temperament, she held her breath as she was lifted onto the back of the steed and gratefully accepted the comforting presence of the Yankee behind her. She allowed him to hold her against his warm body, and at the moment it didn't matter that the threadbare breeches did not provide much protection between the two of them.

Still clutching the tricorn, she shook out her hair, preparing to bundle it beneath the hat, but at Christopher's exaggerated cough, she turned a questioning look over her shoulder to catch his rueful smile in the brightly gleaming moonlight.

"I believe, my lady," he choked, "that you have gathered a bit of dust from the road. I'm afraid we'll both need a bath after this."

Erienne raised a dubious brow, and his grin widened.

"Separate baths, of course. I wouldn't want to burden your virgin-minded purity with the sight of a naked man."

"I'm not a virgin!" Erienne protested, then cringed in chagrin as his chuckling laughter raked her composure. She sought to hide beneath the hat, but in her haste to don it, the thing went tumbling to the road.

"Then you wouldn't be appalled by bathing in a common tub?" he queried with humor. He leaned close to her ear, and warm shivers went through her as he whispered, "The idea fairly entraps my imagination."

The warmth that went through her could not be laid entirely to a hot blush. "You, sir, have a very evil imagination!"

"Nay, madam," he denied. "Vivid, aye! But nothing about you is evil, and that's all I think about."

" 'Tis obvious that you're easily . . ." She paused, searching for a more sarcastic and descriptive word than "encouraged."

"Aroused?" he queried.

Erienne gasped. "Certainly not!"

"Have you changed your mind? You said at a twitch of a skirt . . ."

"I know what I said!"

"The subject seems to be on your mind quite a bit, my lady."

"I wonder why," she retorted with unmistakable satire. It was impossible to ignore the manly feel of him against her.

"Because you lust after my body?" he asked, feigning innocence.

Erienne caught her breath in outrage. "I am a married woman, sir!"

He heaved a laborious sigh. "Here we go again!"

"Oh, you buffoon! Why don't you leave me alone?"

"Did I ask you to follow me?" he protested.

She groaned aloud in frustration. "I'm sorry I did!"

"Were you bruised?" He snuggled her closer against his body. "You feel all right to me."

"Christopher, if I weren't so afraid of this horse, I'd slap you," she threatened.

"Why? I only inquired of your health."

"Because you make free with your hands! Now, stop that!" She threw away the hand that had settled on her thigh. "Don't you ever get tired of playing the rake?"

"The sport warms and excites me, madam," he said, chuckling in her ear.

Erienne opened her mouth to give him a chiding comment but thought better of it, since he always seemed to have an answer ready for her. Though it was difficult, she refrained from further debate and let the ride continue in silence.

The moon poured out its silvered light over the hills and vales and lent to Christopher's gaze a most fascinating view. With increasing repetition, he glanced downward to where the loosening laces of her shirt revealed the soft, swelling fullness and the deep valley between. On a pretext, he shifted her weight with an arm about her waist and was satisfied with the results, which left her more fully exposed and lent enticing glimpses of a darker crest.

Erienne was too frustrated with her inability to move away from the rutting rake to give notice to her attire. He seemed to be well warmed by her nearness, and no amount of effort could put his presence from mind. They were approaching Saxton Hall before she dared to speak again.

"I left my gown in the stable," she confided. "I'll have to go back there to get dressed."

"I'll get your clothes," he offered. "Just tell me where they are."

Erienne found no real reason to argue and carefully explained where she had hidden her garments. "Leave them in the passageway," she directed. "I'll fetch them later."

In a seemingly short time she was in her chambers, soaking in a tub of warm, soothing water. Aggie had dismissed Tessie, letting the young maid retire for the evening, while she stayed to fold down the bedcovers, lay out a nightgown, and assist her young mistress. The housekeeper left two pails of fresh water beside the tub and, intending to return when Erienne began washing her hair, stepped out to fetch more towels.

Erienne heard the door close behind the woman, then almost as an echo the distant chiming of the clock heralded the hour of eleven. She sat up in surprise, for the evening had seemed incredibly short. Lord Saxton could return at any moment, and how would she explain this late bath? If she dared mention Christopher, he might see something in her eyes that would betray her fascination with the man.

Hurrying now, she wet her hair and applied the fragrant soap, then began to scrub the soggy mass. Her eyes stung as soapy trails dribbled down her brow, and she splashed water onto her face in an effort to relieve the caustic burning. Clenching her eyes tightly shut, she felt alongside the tub for the full pail, then heard the door open and close.

"Aggie, come help me, please," she called. "I've got soap in my eyes, and I can't find the pail of water to rinse my hair."

The large rug in her bedchamber muffled the sound of the footsteps, and Erienne felt a presence come near the tub. The bucket was lifted, and leaning her head forward, she waited for the liquid warmth to wash through her hair. It came as expected, and she spread the soapy tresses to catch the cleansing tide. The second bucket was emptied before she called for a towel. After wringing the wetness from her hair, she rose to await the linen, then receiving it, wrapped it tightly about her head. With a sigh, she flung back her head and finally opened her stinging eyes to find the grinning face of Christopher Seton before her.

"Christopher!" Her shocked gasp was followed by sheer panic, and she clutched an arm across her bosom, while the other hand tried to conceal her womanhood. "Get out! Get out of here!"

He reached for her robe. "You sounded as if you were in distress, my lady, and I thought you might have needed help." He casually held out the garment. "Do you need this?"

Though she had to sacrifice another view of her nakedness to claim the offering, Erienne snatched it without delay, clutching it to her bosom. Her eyes blazed as she thrust an arm out toward the door. "Out! Get out! Now!"

"But Aggie's in the hall," he argued with a hint of a smile. The mirror afforded him an enticing reflection of a most shapely back. "I brought your clothes up, but she came up the stairs, and I had to duck in here or be seen."

"I told you to leave them in the passageway!" she gritted.

"But there are rats and other vermin down there, madam." His eyes danced with devilish humor as he played on her squeamishness. "I didn't want them nesting in your clothes."

Erienne considered his excuse reasonable, since the merest thought of the rodents in her clothes made her shudder, but she was quick to demand, "What if Aggie finds you in here?"

His wide shoulders lifted in a languid gesture of unconcern. "I locked the door. She will no doubt think your husband has come back and leave."

"And what if Stuart should return?" she asked irately. "You're bound to find yourself facing him over the sights of dueling pistols yet."

He grinned and glanced toward the mirror again, admiring the narrow curve of her waist and the rounded buttocks. "I'll worry about that when the time comes."

Growing suspicious, Erienne looked around and then gasped at the sight of her own bare back reflected in the silvered glass. With a strangled cry of outrage, she came around with a doubled fist, but her arm was laughingly caught and held against her attempts to snatch it free.

"Now I have you, my lady." His eyes gleamed above a broadening smile. "And you will not escape me until I've had my say."

"You think you can come in here like a raging lunatic, with no regard for propriety, and make me listen to you?!" Her ire rose that he might think her easy prey to his whim. "Do you think because of what happened in the coach you have a right to accost me in my own chamber?! Indeed not, sir! I don't want to hear any of your confessions. I insist that you leave before Stuart finds you here!"

She stepped over the side of the tub, snatching on her robe in irate jerks, and would have left the bathing chamber to his disposal, but strong arms swept her off the floor and, despite her outraged gasp, lifted her up against a hard chest.

"Erienne, listen to me," he said, growing serious.

The blue-violet pools flashed with fire. She would not relent for fear that the happenings in the coach might be repeated and with more devastating results. "I shall scream if you don't leave this very minute! I swear I will, Christopher."

The muscles in his cheek tensed and flexed as their eyes clashed. Christopher realized what he had to say would be better presented in a calmer moment, but he had hoped to have it out at last. "I'll leave you to your saintly bed, madam," he growled, "but first there is something I want of you, and I will have it!"

His mouth lowered toward hers, opening as it neared, and Erienne's heart gave a sudden lurch as she became aware of his intention. She made a feeble attempt to turn her face away, knowing the weakening effect of his kiss, but his gaze bore into her, paralyzing her will. Then his lips came upon hers with a wet, hot heat that catapulted through her like a flaring comet, setting her whole being on fire. It was a wild, wanton kiss that uprooted every nerve in her body and cindered her meager resistance beneath the crushing weight of unquenched passion. His mouth slanted across hers, invading the dewy warmth until she felt consumed to the uttermost part of her being. A weak trembling began in her limbs, shaking her resolve and shredding her will, and yet he would not stop kissing her.

It seemed an eternity before he raised his head. Then his eyes burned into hers, and without a word he crossed to the bed with her. Erienne knew her vulnerability and seriously doubted that she could lift a hand to hold him off if he chose to take her. The grayish-green eyes stared into her very mind, and she was hardly aware of the moment he placed her on the bed. As he turned away, her feelings ranged from an apex of relief to the epitome of disappointment. She didn't want him to go, but neither could she ask him to stay. In another moment he was to the door, and then he was gone.

Erienne drew the bedcovers over her shoulder and curled in a tight, miserable knot beneath them. The evening had taken its toll on her emotions, and she could not stop shaking. Her body was like a taut bowstring that still twanged after the arrow had left it. She clenched her teeth and fought against the tumult of frayed emotions, but no effort of hers could bring about a calming.

With a cry of frustration, she sat up and snatched the towel from her head, sailing it to the floor. The chill of her damp hair lent to her shivering, and she ran to huddle on a stool before the hearth. There she hung her head over her knees, spreading the long tresses before the heat of the fire while she brushed them dry. Though the radiating warmth brought a blush to her skin, it failed to soothe her tensed nerves.

She returned to the bed and, by dint of determination, forced herself to think of something sobering. A dark shape became the focal point of her concentration, and she envisioned the large, limping form of her husband while she crushed the dreamy illusions of

Christopher beneath a stubborn will. The misshapen image tugged at the heart of her conscience, and gradually the trembling ceased. Encouraging the sobering thoughts to continue, she recounted the months and moments since her first meeting with Lord Saxton. The memories began to play with her consciousness, conjuring murky, indistinct visions and blending them until they were swept up in a confused jumble of events that lost touch with reality. As if through a murky haze she saw long-fanged, gaping jowls closing in for the kill, then geysers of water spraying upward from the path of churning black hooves. A cloaked figure swung down from the prancing steed and splashed through the stream toward her.

Erienne heaved a soft sigh as she settled in the sheltering arms of sleep. Having been set to their course by the willful determination of her mind, her dreams took up the pattern. She stood amid swirling draperies, lost in their never-ending lengths. In confusion she ran hither and yon, but the pastel shades of silken cloth held her prisoner. Then through the pale-hued mists a dark-cloaked shadow limped haltingly toward her. Though she fled, she found no escape, and it came ever nearer until her world became a blackened void. She drifted, helpless, numb, wanting to sit or stand or scream, but paralyzed in the nether land, unable to move.

Strong arms reached to anchor her and drew her back. She felt the vibrant heat of a man's body press close against her back. Her mind struggled to full awareness, for no dream had ever come so boldly to her. Though her eyes found only the same dark void of sleep, her senses confirmed the fact that reality had come to her in the shape of a man. Yet fantasy was still tightly woven through the warp of reason, and the two were inseparable, for he was darkness to her, warm and alive, but without a form or face she could recognize. She was seized by a sudden fear that the tormenting rogue had returned to lie in bed with her, and she started up with a gasp. A hand came to restrain her, and a rasping whisper calmed her.

"Nay, never fly from me, my love. Come here, and nest a while in my arms."

Erienne relaxed back against him and allowed him to turn her in his arms until they lay together, soft, curving flesh against smooth, hard, rippling thews. His head dipped downward, and her breath caught as a flaming tongue swirled over her breasts. It wandered with tantalizing slowness over them, leaving a fiery trail after its passing. Her senses reeled in a wild, giddy flight that left her panting and breathless. Reality ceased to matter. He became all things to her, a handsome lover, a scarred husband, a form in a black cloak that snatched her from the drooling fangs of the hunting hounds.

She felt him rise above her, and she quivered as his hands stroked slowly downward over the swell of her breasts and continued on to the curve of her hips, then upward along the inside of her thighs. A need began to grow in her, a hollow feeling that ached to be filled. She reached up to urge him down into her arms, and her hand brushed the crisp mat of hair on his chest. The muscles beneath her palm were firm and bulging, and much in wonder, she moved trembling fingers across the wide expanse, admiring the form that was ever concealed from her gaze. She rose on her knees to face him and moved slightly forward between his thighs, resting her hands on the lean, fleshed ribs. She reached to press her lips against his throat, while her breasts lightly caressed his chest. Pulling her wildly tumbling hair over his shoulders, she slipped her arms behind his neck and came full against him. His breath halted, and the sweet, pure bliss of it spurred his heart to a trip-hammer beat.

"Kiss me," she begged in a whisper. She longed for him to erase the brand of Christopher's kiss on her lips, to place his own there so no thought of the other man could intrude upon their intimacy.

His lips dipped to her shoulder, then he eased her back to the bed, and his mouth moved upon her breast. A mild disappointment grew that he avoided touching his lips to hers, but she could not long deny the sweeping excitement of the hot, sultry kisses that caressed her body. He moved above her, and with no trepidation about his scars, she welcomed him. Her arms and body ached with a desire to hold him close and bring him home full measure. Her head came hard against his chest as she felt him comply, and the heat of his fullness deep within her roused a throbbing need that built and grew to such an intensity she thought she could not bear it. Fingertips found the familiar scar, and her nails lightly raked his back as she softly mewled and lifted her hips to meet him. She breathed a name, and for a moment the universe stopped its motion. He drew away, but she raised herself against him, with her head arched back, her hair forming a torrent of tousled silk that flowed to the bed beneath her. He kissed that sweet throat, and began again, lifting her even higher to that blinding, pulsing moment of release until she gasped and caught her breath with the ecstasy of it.

Sanity returned in slow degrees, and Erienne settled back to earth.

There was a movement beside her, and her hand brushed his back as he left the cozy lair. She summoned the last dregs of her energy to roll to the firelit side of the bed, there pulling aside the drapes just as the door was closing.

"Stuart?" Her voice could only manage a whisper, and she stared into the shifting, dancing flames, wondering what had possessed him to leave. It was his usual wont to stay, and she sorely yearned for the warmth of him beside her. The intimacy between them had been most pleasant, and tonight no face had haunted her, no vision of . . .

Something cold gripped Erienne's heart, and a sudden horror filled her mind as she recalled the name she had whispered, and it was not Stuart.

In total misery she twisted around and buried her face in the pillow, feeling a flaming blush upon her cheeks.

"Oh, Stuart," she moaned, "what have I done?"

Nineteen

Morning came nigh, and Erienne bolstered her nerve with a careful grooming of her person. She would have preferred staying in her chamber until the morning was well spent but knew that would be the coward's way, and she had no wish to lend herself to such a judgment. She donned a pale blue frock that boasted a high neckband, and with ribbons twined in her hair, she presented a most charming vision to her husband as she came timidly across the great hall. He waited beside his chair near the hearth, and Erienne felt impending doom in his unswerving gaze. Slipping into the chair across from his, she gave him a small, unsteady smile and then stared into the warming fire, unable to meet his eyes.

If she had expected any explosive diatribes, they did not come. There was only the waiting silence, and knowing she must face what lay before her, she set herself firmly to her resolve. She took in a deep breath and lifted her gaze to await boldly and openly whatever question he might have.

"Good morning, my dear," the hoarse voice bade almost cheerily. "My apologies for leaving you so abruptly last night."

Erienne was taken aback by his good humor and could find no

cause for it. Surely he had heard her whisper his cousin's name and must realize she was, albeit unconsciously, yearning for another man while he made love to her.

"I thought you might enjoy an outing to Carlisle today. Would that be agreeable to you?"

"Of course, my lord."

"Good. Then after you've taken the morning meal, we'll be on our way."

"Will I need to change clothes?" she asked hesitantly.

"Nay, madam. You are quite charming as you are. A rare jewel for me to feast my eyes upon, and although there is someone I wish you to meet there, we'll have a chance to talk on the way. 'Tis time, madam, that I put my house in order."

Erienne tensed, for his statement boded ill. It would seem that he was not through with her yet.

Lord Saxton half turned toward the table, where a service had been set for her. "Come, Erienne. You must be nearly famished."

A denial came readily to her lips, but she silenced the words. The thought of facing Stuart had made her queasy, but there was no need to hasten her comeuppance for lack of an appetite, and a few morsels might help to settle her stomach.

The cook was one of rare talent, and Erienne could not lay the blame of her discontentment to the delectable fare that was placed before her. Still, she could not bring herself to taste more than a bite or two, and when Paine came to announce that Bundy was wanting to speak with his master in the drawing room, she was relieved that she could finally push her plate aside without inviting an inquiry. She returned to the hearth and slowly sipped her tea as she waited for her husband.

The chimes had struck a quarter-hour note before Lord Saxton came back to the great hall. He paused beside her chair to make his apologies.

"I'm sorry, madam, but I must delay our visit to Carlisle. A most urgent matter has been brought to my attention, and as much as it distresses me to leave you, I must. I'm not quite sure when I'll be back."

Erienne did not question the good fortune that had saved her from the expected confrontation. She continued sipping her tea, feeling the tension ebb. The landau was brought around. She heard it rumble away again, and she sat in the stillness that followed as one who had been reprieved from hell.

A drowsiness came over her as she began to relax, and realizing that she had slept very little during the night, she climbed the stairs and returned to her chamber. Doffing her gown, she struggled beneath the bedcovers and sank effortlessly into a much-needed slumber.

The first tinges of pink were beginning to streak the western sky when Erienne roused from her nap. She felt greatly refreshed and in an energetic mood that demanded some activity beyond the common duties of a mistress of the house. The mare Morgana came to mind, and though she had no intention of repeating the folly of chasing after Christopher, the thought of a ride appealed to her.

With no deliberation at all, she garbed herself in the proper riding attire of a lady. She had had enough of being a lad and much preferred to be treated with deference for her gender should she come upon that wily rogue again. Remembering her close encounter with Timmy Sears, however, she laid out a pair of flintlock pistols, just in case there were any more like him lurking about.

She tied a coin in the tail of the stableboy's shirt and took the garments with her when she went down to the stables, hiding them beneath the dark gray cloak she wore until she was sure she could return them without being seen. Keats was out fetching water at the well when she entered the barn, and she used the opportunity to hide the garments under a saddle, where they would not be overlooked. In the guise of complete innocence, she was admiring the mare when the lad returned, and she sweetly bade him to saddle the steed.

"Mum, the master gave the strictest orders that ye were not to go off unattended. Seein' as how I can't let ye go without answerin' to him, would ye be wantin' me to ride with ye?"

Erienne was about to agree when she caught sight of a man on horseback riding up the lane toward the manor. Stepping to the door, she watched until the form atop the steed became recognizable as kin. The sight of Farrell on horseback sent a happy thrill through her. He had bought the animal with coin he had earned himself, but the fact that he trusted himself to ride again gave her the greatest pleasure.

"My brother is here," she announced to Keats. "I'll ask him to ride with me for a while."

"Aye, mum. I'll saddle the mare right away."

When Farrell drew near the tower entry, Erienne called to him and waved an arm to catch his eye as he glanced about. Responding in kind, he prodded the animal on down the lane toward her.

"Good evening," she greeted cheerily. "I am in need of an escort, and since Lord Saxton is not at home, I was wondering if I might impose upon your good graces to ride with me for a spell."

"Lord Saxton is gone?" he inquired, his tone heavily tinged with disappointment. He had been in hopes that they could do some more shooting and had brought along his own small collection of firearms to practice with.

Erienne laughed as she took note of the long musket and the three pistols the saddle bore. "I know I'm only your sister, and for that reason a poor substitute for the one you have obviously come to see."

Farrell jerked his head toward the lane and chuckled in good humor. "Come on. 'Tis the least I can do for a sister."

She accepted a helping hand onto the back of the mare and adjusted her skirts and cloak before giving a nod to her brother. He led the way for a short time, choosing the direction, and then reined up, grinning back at her.

"You're becoming quite sure of yourself, aren't you?" she asked with a laugh. She realized her own pride in his accomplishments and knew she had Stuart to thank for bringing her brother out of his shell.

"Care to race?" he challenged with some of his old zest for life.

Erienne glanced around. She knew they were on the road that led south, but the night had snuffed the radiance of the sunset, and after the previous night's experience, she was somewhat leery of traveling so far from the manor without more protection. The highwaymen were known for their merciless attacks on the defenseless, and she had not the desire to become prey to violence of any form.

"We'd better go back," she replied. "I didn't realize it was getting so late."

"Let's race to the hilltop," her brother coaxed. "Then we'll go back."

Erienne thumped the mare's side with her heels, and laughter spilled over her shoulder as the horse took flight. Farrell let out a whoop as he charged after her, and the sound of their gaiety joined with that of the thundering hooves and the wind that whistled past their ears. She set herself wholeheartedly to the race, urging Morgana on with light slaps of the quirt. Farrell drew alongside, and he was half a length ahead as he came atop the hill.

Suddenly a shot cracked through the air, followed by several more discharges of gunpowder. Farrell jerked hard on the reins, pulling his steed to a jolting halt. Erienne was but a heartbeat slower in skidding to a stop. They sat stock still, straining to hear while their eyes searched through the gloom of late twilight for any hint of trouble. A scream of horror pierced the quiet, ending in a half-sobbed, pleading, "No!" and another shot rang out. This one echoed across the hill, and a thin, keening cry, weaker than the first, rose up to join it. It ended abruptly, as if a blow had silenced it.

Erienne's hair crawled on her scalp, and after a quick glance at Farrell they carefully urged their horses in the shadow of a line of oaks that bordered the road and moved forward to the brow of the hill. A dark-garbed man sat atop a horse on the next rise and from there watched the roadway. Farrell motioned with his hand, and Erienne paused with baited breath, but the lookout did not sound a warning. A moment passed and a distant voice called to the man, and after a brief exchange, he spurred his mount back toward his companion, leaving his post.

Their sighs of relief mingled in the stillness. Keeping to the shelter of darkness the trees provided, they crept forward until they reached the crest of the far hill and could gaze down into the vale. There, below them on the road, was a halted coach and several black-garbed men working by lanternlight around the conveyance. A horse lay dead near the tongue, and the rest of the team was being led away. The doors of the coach gaped wide, and Erienne gasped as the lamps cast their yellowish glow over the body of a wealthily garbed man hanging head downward from the interior of the coach. The driver and footman were sprawled in the road. The only survivor was a young woman who had been lashed, her arms spread wide, to the whippletree so that she straddled the grounded tongue. For the amusement of her captors she was being rudely pawed and relieved of her jewelry. Her sobbing pleas went unheard beneath the uproarious laughter of the men.

Farrell crowded Erienne farther back in the shadows, well away from the moonlight, and his whisper came with a note of urgency. "They will kill her . . . or do worse . . . I cannot wait for help!"

"There's more than a dozen of them, Farrell. What can we do?"

"Can you ride on and get the sheriff? I'll see if I can hold them off . . . somehow."

" 'Twould be madness to charge in there alone," Erienne protested.

"Hand me your pistols," he whispered and held out his hand to receive them, gesturing impatiently when she delayed. "Hurry!"

Erienne had a mind of her own and expressed it. "Farrell, perhaps we can hold them off together. See those trees on the hillside near the coach? We can take cover in them and get behind the thieves. If we can get close and hit two or three, the others might flee before the girl is harmed. You can't fire a pistol and rein your horse at the same time."

"You're right, of course," he muttered. "I'm not much use with only one arm."

"We don't have time for that, Farrell," she pleaded. "The girl needs us both."

"With all the commotion the thieves are making, a whole regiment could charge through the trees, and it wouldn't be heard." He gave a low chuckle. "Are you up to it, Erienne?"

"Aye!" she whispered back and coaxed the mare along behind the crest of the hill until they could get into the trees and brush.

They found a vantage point on a slightly higher bluff rising above the road near the coach and there dismounted to hide behind the cover of trees and boulders. Down below the muffled weeping of the girl blended with the laughter and shouts of the highwaymen. The thieves had left her for the moment while they ripped apart the baggage and crudely searched the bodies of the dead men.

"Erienne, can you hear me?" Farrell questioned in a low whisper.

"Aye."

"If we manage to frighten the thieves away, I'll ride down there and get the girl. You stay here and hold them at bay until I get her free, then ride like hell out of here. Do you understand?"

"Don't worry," she assured him dryly. "That's what I plan to do. Ride as if the very devil were after me. Do you have a knife to cut her free?"

"Aye, and be a good girl for once." Farrell's voice was barely audible, but she heard the laughter in it.

Erienne clenched her teeth to keep them from rattling as she carefully checked her weapons. She was thankful that her brother had brought the wherewithal to reload the pair. With his weapons, he could now offer an attack that might count for something in the defense of the girl. His plan was to move about and make it seem as if there were more than the two of them. Since she was hampered by her skirts, she had to hold to her place. Their supply of weapons was meager indeed compared to what the thieves carried, but with any luck they would set the murdering band to fight, and hopefully the three of them could escape unharmed.

Farrell crept away to take a temporary position behind a tree, and Erienne waited for the roar of his pistol to come as a signal. She was so tense that she wondered how she would be able to hit anything, even after her husband's careful tutoring. The horror she had seen within the last moments made her aware of what Christopher might be dealing with in his night rides. Though he had not admitted to being the dreaded nighthawk, she could not dismiss the evidence she had seen, and she vowed to be more understanding toward his cause in the future.

Her brother's shot rang out, and Erienne's fingers tightened as she settled her aim. She felt a nauseous quivering in her stomach when she saw two forms collapse abruptly near the lantern. A shout rang out from one of the thieves, and they scattered from the light, but not soon enough. Erienne gave herself no time to debate her actions; she knew the life of the girl depended on how quickly she could make the other pistol bark. This time she tried not to blink as the shot exploded, but it was all she could do to keep the weapon steady. Her surprise was so great when she saw another man fall that she almost looked around to see if Farrell had fired at the same time. Then she heard his rustling movements on the other side of her, and knew he was just settling into place again. Licking her parched lips, she began to reload. She was shaking as hard as she was praying, and she had to take a steadying grip on herself to be able to complete the task. The deafening roar of Farrell's musket rent the air, and the scream that followed sent a coldness coursing through her veins. She raised the sights of her weapon, finding the halo of light void of the fleeing thieves. Her eyes searched, and the moonlight showed her a hint of movement at the base of the bluff below. She kept her gaze fastened on the darkness until the shadow proved to be a man climbing up toward her. Coming slowly to her feet, she clutched the butt of the flintlock with both hands and set her sights on the moving body. The fellow raised his head to glance about, and this time she closed her eyes tightly as she squeezed the trigger. The report deafened her, but not enough to blot out the thumping, thudding sound of his body falling down the incline. She banished the gore from her thoughts as she saw Farrell scrambling toward his horse.

Quickly Erienne reloaded and then waited in the appalling silence, her eyes searching the shadows for any sign of a skulker. She heard the gelding thrash through the woods behind her, and after a moment her brother came into her range of vision. He plunged from the darkness, racing headlong toward the coach and, when he neared the girl, flung himself down from the steed, holding one of the reins in his left hand as he ran to her. Halting beside her, he began to saw at the tough cords that bound the girl.

Erienne watched carefully for any movement that would prove itself a target for her weapon. She was aware of no warning sound or movement, but of a sudden she was nearly engulfed from behind. A hand reached over her shoulder to seize the pistol, and the same arm swept her back against a rock hard frame. Before she could cry out, a gloved hand clapped across her mouth and a gruff voice, curt and hushed, filled her mind.

"You little minx, what are you trying to do? Get on that damned nag and get out of here before you get yourself killed!"

The arm spun her about, and she was set free. Her breath caught in her throat as she saw the huge form that stood before her. The enveloping cloak blended with ebony darkness, and though she tried to see into the deep shadow beneath the cowl, she found no proof that a face was even there.

"Christopher?" His name came in a tentative question.

"Go! Get out of here!" he commanded.

The hooded head turned slightly toward the glade. Two figures had left the darkness of the woods and were approaching Farrell from behind. He had half freed the girl and gave no sign of being aware of them.

"Damn!"

The expletive came from the deep cowl, then in a rush the night rider was gone. Erienne stumbled back as he appeared a brief second later on a huge black horse. The pair sailed out of the darkness, seeming to take flight as they went past. The stallion's hooves struck sparks from the rock-littered slope, and a low, keening moan sent shivers up her spine. From the extended arm of the flying dark figure there came a flash and a roar of a pistol. One of the thieves fell with a scream, clutching his chest, and the weapon lowered from sight. When the hand reappeared, it was filled with a long, gleaming length of steel. The saber swept high briefly, and the eerie battle cry was renewed. The horse rushed on as the second brigand dropped his knife and struggled to draw and cock his own flintlock. The saber dipped as the shadow dashed past him. The pistol fell, and the man staggered a few steps and slowly sank to the ground.

The black-cloaked rider made a sweep of the field, then approached Farrell, who halted in his task and stood back brandishing the ridiculously short blade in his good hand. The night rider gave him no heed, but with the tip of his saber flipped one of the lanterns onto the road, where it crashed and flickered out. Another one followed in a flaming arch, landing in the same spot and lighting the spilled oil. The hawk paused and stared down at Farrell briefly, then gestured to the girl, whose wrists were still bound to the coach.

"Get her free and get out of here!" The saber pointed up the hillside, and the voice, though low, bore an unmistakable tone of command. "And take that twit of a sister with you when you go!"

The black steed moved alongside the coach, and the saber swung low again. The last lantern sailed into the air and then broke apart on the road. The only light in the glade was provided by moonlight and by the small, greedy flames of the spilled oil, which failed to illuminate the figures near the coach.

In a moment Farrell had the girl free and labored to lift her to the back of the horse. After a fruitless effort, he stopped and hauled himself into the saddle, then freeing a stirrup for the girl, held his crippled arm down.

"My arm is useless. Take hold of it, and I will pull you up. Use the stirrup."

The girl complied, and in a trice was behind him on the horse. She had no need to be told to secure her position but clutched her arms tightly about his waist.

Farrell kicked the steed, and the horse lunged forward. A shot was fired from the woods as he raced off, but it whistled wide. He hauled back on the reins when he neared the slope where he had left Erienne and yelled up. The night rider followed him, and his terse bark rang out in a tone that brooked no disobedience.

"Go! Get out of here!"

Erienne had already retraced a few steps back into the woods and with the aid of a decaying stump, climbed atop the mare. She set the steed to flight, skimming along the shadows of the trees. The night rider spurred the stallion, keeping behind her fleeing form but holding to the moonlit road. He was there when Erienne cast a quick glance over her shoulder. When she disappeared over the hill, he halted and swung his horses sideways to prevent any possible pursuit. As he waited, he leisurely reloaded his pistol and let his gaze range over the clearing he had just left.

In the silence, small sounds of movement came from the brush as the highwaymen crept cautiously forth. A figure came to the edge of the firelight and then another. The night rider watched his quarry gather like a once-flushed flock of birds coming back to feed.

"Aye," he muttered to himself. "And they need to be flushed again."

He lifted the saber high and set heel to his mount, giving voice to the keening wail that was his war cry. The robbers needed only the sight of the apparition sweeping down upon them like a hunting hawk, the darkened gleam of the saber in the night, and the ominous thunder of the great hooves to abandon their bravado. One of the thieves bellowed a warning even as he took flight himself. The others scrambled over each other to get away and once more sought safety in the underbrush, all save one.

The undaunted highwayman drew his pistol with his left hand and his sword with the right and held them wide to either side as the specter flew toward him. Here was the experienced soldier who did not panic under adversity.

"Fools!" he roared. "He is but one! If you will not stand and fight, I will take this one myself!"

"He's yers, Cap'n!" a voice shouted back.

A short space away the huge black beast sat on his haunches and slid to a halt. The thief glanced away from the other's saber and saw the threatening bore of a horse pistol held in the opposite hand.

"Well, Mr. Phantom," the man challenged boldly, "will it be a test of lead?" The pistol lifted slightly. "Or of steel?" He saluted his adversary with a quick sweep of the blade.

Though the highwayman wore a cloth covering over his head, the night shadow recognized the curt phrases and subtle accent of the one he faced.

"Milord Sheriff, we meet at last."

"So! You know me, my friend." The sardonic tone turned to sneering laughter. "That knowledge will cost you your life. What shall it be? Your saber?"

"Nay, I have another weapon to match your own," the whispery voice replied.

First the saber and then the pistol were thrust back into their respective sheaths. Turning the horse sideways to shield against a shot, the night specter dismounted. He waited until Allan Parker tucked his pistol away before slapping the rump of the stallion to send him into the clearing a short distance away. He drew a slim rapier, whose naked length winked a silvery blue in the moonlight. Casually he returned the salute.

Parker bent slightly to drag a dagger from his boottop. The style of the duel was clear. It would be of the Burgundian cavalier, a forceful attack to close and bring both weapons into play, either to trap the single blade of the opponent or thrust the short blade into the ribs.

The black hawk reached his left arm behind his back, and catching the length of his cloak, wrapped some of its fullness around his arm to form a shield of sorts that could as easily entangle a blade. Parker recognized the ploy and realized he faced no simple opponent but one well versed in the art of arms. He also took note of the brace of smaller pistols the man carried in his waistband. This was indeed to be a test to the death.

The swords came together in a light play, but after the initial engagements, the sheriff grew more cautious. His first simple attacks were turned aside with ease, and the riposte was so swift and sure he was forced to labor in his own defense. He was left with no doubt as to the skill of the man he faced.

A brief chuckle came from the cowl, and the harsh, whispery voice lent no hint of its owner's identity. "Do you worry yet, Milord Sheriff?"

Allan laughed as he met his opponent's sudden attack with his long blade but slashed empty night air with the short one when the night rider faded lightly away from its threat. "I do not know you now, my friend, but I shall look upon your face soon enough."

He lunged into his own attack in the second quarter but had to quickly retreat as it was effectively parried and the other's blade threatened his groin.

"Not as easy as Timmy Sears, eh?" the hawk queried with a sneer.

Parker almost stumbled but recovered quickly. "How . . ."

"Who else would Timmy have gone to after I visited him that night? You are the thieves' captain, and naturally you would have been the one he went looking for to make his confessions. He was a fool to tell you what he had spilled. It cost him his life."

The blue blade began to weave a tighter pattern, and in spite of the sheriff's best efforts, which were considerable, its hungry tongue licked ever closer to his body. A sudden sharp pain stung his left forearm, then a tug sent the dagger sailing far into the high grass.

As he labored to protect himself, Parker was seized with the sudden belief that this relentless shadow could kill whenever the whim betook him. A light sweat glistened on Parker's face, and his upper lip trembled with stress of this new knowledge.

"Then there was Ben," the night rider continued. "Frail, no possible challenge to one of your skill."

Breathing heavily, Parker did not answer. An ache had begun to grow in his right shoulder as he beat down pass after pass.

"Did he put up much of a fight?" the hooded foe chided. "Or did you catch him in a nap?"

The sheriff panted, and sweat flew from his brow. For the first time in his life he knew he faced one who could kill him.

"You are too young to be the one I search for. There is another who keeps his silk trappings clean while you do his filthy deeds. Lord Talbot, perhaps?"

"You bas . . . bastard!" Parker gasped. "Fight like a man! Show your face!"

" 'Tis death to see it, Milord Sheriff. Didn't you know?" His chiding laughter mocked the other.

Parker's gaze shifted momentarily behind his opponent, and he almost smiled. He found new energy and set upon his adversary in a savage fury. His heavier blade chopped, hacked, and stabbed, but was ever met and found no fragile flesh to flay.

Of a sudden, there was a shout, and two thieves launched an attack from the shadows where they had crept, but the night rider ducked beneath their assault. One of the flailing arms pulled the hood from his head before the two brigands came together with a crunch in midair and fell half stunned behind him. He locked hilts with the sheriff, meeting his attack, and they stood face to face.

"You!" Allan cried.

Christopher Seton laughed in the sheriff's face. "Death, Milord Sheriff. But later."

He shoved hard, and the man stumbled back into a full charge of an onrushing four, sending them falling in a tangled heap as Christopher wickedly slashed the air with his sword. A sharp, piercing whistle rent the night, and the stallion charged forward. Christopher thrust his blade into its sheath, and as the steed came alongside, caught an arm across the saddle. His feet struck the ground, and with the impetus, he swung astride his fleeing mount.

The sheriff scrambled to his feet and, with a snarled curse, clawed the pistol from his belt. He lowered the sights of the weapon to send a leaden ball in thunderous pursuit of the flying night hawk, but to no effect. He cursed again and glanced around. Another man was kneeling in the dust, leveling a long musket at the target. Allan snatched it from him and took the shot himself.

Christopher felt a searing blow against his right side before he heard the roar of the musket. The reins fell from his numbed right hand, and he lurched aside. The ground was a dark blur beneath him, ready to consume him, but he sought to keep his senses. He twisted his left hand in the flying mane and, by sheer dint of will, pulled himself upright. The pace of his mount seemed to slow as he slumped low over its back.

The sheriff let out a caterwauling cry and, with a loud command, launched his men to their horses. "After him, you fools! Don't let him escape!"

"Go, Saracen! Go!" Christopher grunted as each flying pace shook him to the core. "Show them your heels, lad! Go!"

The stallion was running free, but he held to the road as the easier course. A shout came from somewhere behind, and a bullet whined by close at hand. Saracen stretched out and fairly flew as the sheriff led his men in a headlong chase through the moonlit night.

The road dipped after it came over the hill, then wound through the valley, bending to the left as it began to meander across the low hills. Once the pursuers were out of sight, Christopher spoke to the stallion and coaxed him into a slow trot. He leaned forward and managed to catch first one rein, then the other and regained a better degree of control. He slowed the steed to a walk, then sent him scrambling down the bank into a thicket below. There he halted in the cover of trees and carefully tucked the cloak beneath and around a warm and sticky right leg, lest the blood from his side leave a trail that could be followed in daylight.

Erienne had fallen behind deliberately and let Farrell lead the chase. Realizing that the cloaked form was no longer trailing her, she paused on a distant knoll and searched along the road where she had just come, hoping he would soon appear. She was certain this shade of the night was the one she thought him to be. Tonight he had set himself against the lawless, murdering band as one bent on a mission of justice, and she had seen enough to convince her that his intent was for good and not evil.

The mare had forded brooklets and traversed dew-laden fields and dusty roads until her white stockings were well begrimed. She pranced, worrying at the restraint that held her in place, but Erienne gave the impatient steed no mind as she fought a battle of indecision. A gunshot had echoed across the moors, and then a heavier boom of a musket had followed. The second report was what frightened her, for the night rider had not been equipped with such a weapon. The questions blazed through her mind. Should she return to help? Could she assist him? Or would it be better if she was gone, giving him the freedom he would need to see to himself?

She peered intently down the road and tried to sort out the shadows cast by low, fleeting clouds for any possible movement of man or beast. For a moment her eyes betrayed her, and she thought she saw a man coming on a horse, but when the moonlight swept the road a moment later, there was nothing. Her head came up as she caught the sound of a distant rumble, and she listened until it became the thunder of mounted horsemen coming full apace.

Erienne reined the mare about and kicked hard with her heel to send the steed leaping into a fast run. Her cloak billowed out behind, and when the lawless band came over the rising, they raised up a hue and cry at seeing the black-winged figure fleeing ahead of them. The air cracked with a report of a pistol, but the shot whined harmlessly past.

Farther up the road, Farrell drew the gelding up short and whirled him around, finding his sister nowhere in sight. The shot had come a fair distance away, but the low rumble of noise that followed made him pull back in the darkness. He looped the reins around his useless hand and checked the loading of his weapons. Then after a word of caution to the girl behind him, he waited.

Erienne came into view a long moment later, and Farrell raised his pistol as he saw the group of riders racing behind her. He squeezed off a shot, and the band came to a skidding halt, raising up a plume of dust in the road. Farrell thrust the pistol away and snatched up the long musket. Laying it across the upper part of his crippled arm, he carefully sighted his target. The shot exploded and struck home, jerking a thief around with a loud scream. The man teetered for a moment in the saddle, then managed to turn his horse about and send him galloping down the road. His companions gave up the chase just as quickly, all except the stalwart sheriff, who shouted after them.

"Come back, you fools! We might lose a man or two, but if we keep together we can take him! Come back, I say!"

A rude contradiction was thrown back at him over a shoulder. "Ye're the fool if ye think we'll stay an' take the first shot from the blighter! Take it yerself!"

Farrell had taken up the second pistol, and he let fly another report. The lead ball winged past Parker's ear, and deciding that discretion was the better part of valor, he struck out after his cohorts, determining that it would be folly indeed to try to catch the night rider when that one was well armed and there was no way of accounting for what weapons his confederates had. The odds were definitely against him tonight, yet there would again come a time when the two of them would meet. He promised himself that much.

Erienne saw the last of the thieves heading off into the night. A flood of relief came with the knowledge that they had given up the chase, but she was plagued by a greater anxiety, that of Christopher's whereabouts. If the murdering band had set out after him, where was he? Was he wounded somewhere? Did he need her help?

Farrell rode beside his sister until they reached the familiar lands of Saxton Hall, then Erienne waved him on.

"Get the girl to the manor," she bade. "Aggie will know what to do to help her. I'll come along in a moment."

"Will you be all right?" he demanded. "The night rider may still be around here somewhere."

"See to the girl, Farrell," Erienne directed, taking on a tone of sisterly authority. "Quickly!"

She waited until her brother was out of sight before turning the mare into the woods and urging her in the direction of the cottage. The moon cast its light through the barren limbs, creating dark, tangled images on the leaf-covered sod and confusing the path. Erienne eyed the shadows carefully, half expecting some movement to startle her, and did not realize her tension until she reached the cottage. The windows were tightly shuttered, and no light escaped from between the planks to give any assurance of occupancy. Nothing stirred, nothing moved. No evidence of her husband's landau was visible. For the most part the place seemed deserted.

Keeping to the sod to muffle the noise of the hooves, she rode past the front of the cottage on to the far side. A snuffling snort came from one of the paddocks behind the shrubs, pricking her curiosity. If Saracen was here, then Christopher had to be around somewhere, and her anxieties would be relieved. She slid from the mare and pushed her way through the greenery. The gate squeaked slightly as she opened it, and the sound brought up the ears of the steed who stood in the paddock across from Saracen's. The horse watched her in alert attention and gave a low neigh as it reached its nose out across the fence toward her. Erienne scratched the steed's neck, giving him the attention he sought. It was too dark to see his coloring, and she went in search of a lantern. One hung against the inside wall of the stable, and running her hand along the shelf beside it, she found flint to strike. In another moment a tiny flame flickered at the tip of the wick and grew stronger. By its light she proved the animal to be Christopher's own bay stallion. Saracen's yard and stable were empty, firming in her mind the identity of the night hawk, but it did not ease her trepidations. She wanted to be certain that wherever Christopher was, he was safe.

The stallion began to prance up and down his paddock, and on the other side of the shrubs the mare responded with a nervous stamping and snorting. Then the bay suddenly halted and stood facing the shrubs with his tail erect, his ears cocked, and his nostrils flared. Though his reaction might have been caused by the nearness of the mare, Erienne did not dismiss the possibility of someone or something else being out there.

She slipped through the shrubs with the lantern and found the mare staring toward the trees. The light cast a meager glow over the first stalwart trunks, but beyond them the darkness was dense. As Erienne neared, a black shape moved there, and a snort came from the ebon shadows. Behind her, the mare flagged her tail and pranced with a showy sidestep at the end of her tether.

Taking heart from the lack of a threat, Erienne approached the trees. "Christopher?" she called in a whisper. "Are you there?"

No answer came, and her skin crawled on her nape. Perhaps it wasn't Christopher at all. Perhaps he was lying wounded or dead somewhere, and it was one of the highwaymen who had turned and followed her.

Her fear for Christopher prodded her forward. Regardless of what or whom she met in the woods, she was going to search until she found him.

She had taken no more than a few steps into the trees when she stopped and gasped, clutching a hand to her throat in sudden dread. The black stallion came forward trustingly, carrying on his back a tall, cloaked form that swayed precariously in the saddle.

"Oh, no," she moaned. She had no need to see the blood to know he was hurt. The light of the lantern showed his face drawn and ashen. The lids sagged over eyes void of their usual sparkle.

Christopher smiled with difficulty and tried to allay her fears. "Good evening, mad—"

The effort sapped the last of his waning strength, and the world lurched in a slow tumble and grew dark. With a frightened cry, Erienne dropped the lantern and leapt forward as he began to topple from the saddle. She caught her arms about him, but his greater weight bore her to the ground beneath him. For an anxious, fear-filled moment she cradled his tousled head close against her breast and sobbed, "Oh, my darling Christopher, what have they done to you?"

Sanity returned out of dire necessity, and her trembling hands flew in frantic haste. She righted the lantern and began to search beneath the cloak for the wound, pulling the sticky shirt free of his breeches. The hard, cold blade of fear pierced through her as her gaze touched where the shot had left a gaping hole in his side. On further examination, she found where it had entered his back. Panic threatened, but she steeled herself against it, knowing it would do him no good if she broke beneath the lashing fear that assailed her. Her hands shook as she ripped a length of cloth from her petticoat. She pressed a wad of it against the torn flesh to stanch the flow of blood, then wrapped another piece tightly about his waist.

A low, creaking sound of an opening door came from the direction of the cottage, and Erienne glanced around as a man holding a lantern stepped from the doorway. He peered past his beacon toward the glow of her lamp, craning his neck to see through the trees that hid her. He called softly, "That you, master?"

"Bundy! Bundy, come help!" she cried, recognizing his voice. "Mr. Seton's been hurt. Hurry!"

Shifting rays of light flashed through the darkness as the servant ran toward her. He asked no questions when he saw the limp figure sprawled beside her but quickly knelt at Christopher's side. He lifted a limp eyelid, then briefly examined her handiwork before jumping to his feet again.

"We'd better get him up ter the big house, where Aggie can tend him," he said urgently. He caught Saracen's reins and then lifted Christopher in his arms and carefully eased him over the saddle. "I'll take him through the passageway so none o' the servants will see," he announced and glanced at her. "Will ye come with me, mum? Or will ye be ridin' yer horse to the stables? I can return later for it if ye wish."

"I'm coming with you," Erienne replied with no hesitation.

Bundy led the way through the trees toward the manse, and she followed, keeping an anxious watch over Christopher. When they reached the heavy door that marked the entry to the hidden passage, the servant transferred the unconscious man to his shoulder. She carefully guided him past the opening and held the lantern high to light the way as they hurried through the corridor. For Erienne, it seemed an eternity before they reached the bookcase at the far end.

"I'll see if the way is clear," she whispered and hurried toward the library door. She set aside the lantern, doffed her cloak, and smoothed her hair before entering the hallway. Though she heard a muffled weeping and other sounds coming from the guest rooms that lay beyond Lord Saxton's chambers, the upper-floor corridor leading from the eastern section was quiet and void of servants. Quickly retracing her steps to the library, Erienne motioned the man out.

"Hurry before someone comes this way."

"Get Aggie, mum," he bade. "She'll know what ter do for Mr. Seton, and she can be trusted."

Her feet fairly flew as she ran down the stairs. She came to a skidding halt in the doorway of the tower when she noticed Farrell standing beside the hearth in the great hall. Cautiously she slowed her pace but sought to pass him without stopping. It was not to be.

Bemused, Farrell glanced from her to the front entry. He had not heard the front door open, and he made his thoughts clear with a simple question. "How did you come in? I've been waiting for you, and when you didn't come back, I thought I would have to go out and find you. And now here you are. How did you get upstairs without me seeing you?"

Erienne would not trust him with her precious knowledge and

gave the excuse, "Perhaps you were with the girl. How is she, anyway?"

"Poor girl, they killed her father, and she can't seem to stop crying. Aggie has put her to bed with a toddy. She said it would help her sleep."

Erienne's mind flew. If Farrell found Christopher wounded in the house, he might take his news back to the sheriff. Aggie's toddy might provide the solution to her dilemma. With so much at stake, she saw the need for Farrell to be unaware of the happenings in the house. "You might want to try one of Aggie's toddies yourself, Farrell. 'Twill help you sleep, and it works wonders for rejuvenating one's spirits. Come the morningtide, you'll be refreshed and ready to meet the girl."

Farrell's face darkened with a blush, for he had not been blind to the girl's comeliness. Those wide, dark eyes and bountiful reddish locks curling tousled around her pale and delicate face had been a vision worth remembering.

"Her name's Juliana Becker," he murmured distantly. "She's only seventeen."

Erienne fretted at her delay in getting back to Christopher. "If you don't mind dining alone, Farrell, I'll have one of the servants bring a tray of food to your room. I fear I am too distressed to eat, and I'll probably retire as soon as I can." This last she threw back over her shoulder as she hurried to the kitchen.

"Has Lord Saxton returned?" Farrell called.

"I don't think so," she answered without passing. "At least, I haven't seen him."

"Should he return, tell him I would like to borrow the coach to take the girl back to her mother in the morning. They live in York."

"I'm sure that will be acceptable, Farrell. Just tell Paine, and he can have Tanner bring the carriage around whenever you're ready."

The kitchen door swung closed behind her, but when she could not find Aggie there, Erienne made her way back through the hall again, not caring how badly she confused Farrell with her haste. In the west wing, she found the housekeeper just leaving the guest room where the girl had been ensconced for the night.

"Miss Becker is resting much easier now, mum," Aggie announced. " 'Tis lucky she is—"

"Aggie, I need your help," Erienne interrupted anxiously. "Mr. Seton has been hurt, and Bundy said you would know what to do."

"How bad is he? Can ye tell, mum?" Aggie asked in fretful haste as she hurried down the corridor with her mistress.

"He's got an awful-looking hole in his side," the younger woman replied worriedly. "The shot went all the way through, and he seems to have lost a lot of blood."

Aggie did not waste another moment with inquiries. Lifting her skirts, she broke into a run, never relenting her puffing pace until she careened around the corner by Lord Saxton's bedchamber door. The portal was partially open, and Erienne halted in surprise when the woman swept through without pausing. To her further amazement she saw Bundy bending over Christopher, who lay on the bed. The covers had been turned down and towels were spread beneath the bandaged area. Except for a sheet that covered his lower half, he was devoid of clothing. The black cloak and garments lay in a heap on the floor beside the tall riding boots.

Bundy stood away as the housekeeper approached the bed, and as the woman cut away the makeshift bandage and examined the wound, Erienne hung back, cringing as the pain of the probing fingers penetrated his oblivion. A moan came from his pale lips as he writhed in agony, and she muffled a frightened sob beneath his hand. She had never known how deeply she cared for the Yankee until this moment when she saw him helpless and in need. He had always been so strong, so capable, never really seeming to need anyone. Her feelings ached to be expressed, and it was her torment that she could not touch him in a loving manner or whisper the words that would tell him of her love.

"The shot went through, all right," Aggie stated, "but it 'pears ter be a clean wound." She washed the blood from her hands and gestured to the hearth. "We'll need a kettle 'o water on the fire and some clean linen."

"Shouldn't we move Mr. Seton to another room?" Erienne asked fretfully. After whispering Christopher's name while her husband was making love to her, she was fearful of Stuart returning home and finding his rival ensconced in his bed. She could not be certain that Lord Saxton would not become violent and do his cousin more hurt.

Bundy glanced quickly at the housekeeper and then cleared his throat, choosing his words carefully. "Lord Saxton won't be returnin' for several days, mum, so I 'spect it'll be all right if Mr. Seton uses his room till then. He'll be safer here. The servants will think 'tis his lordship come down sick, and they won't likely be snoopin' about. 'Tis better to be safe and not rouse undue suspicion."

"But if Lord Saxton is gone, why are you not with him?" Erienne inquired in bemusement. "And where is the landau?"

"In the stables, mum. I brought it back a couple o' hours ago. The master'll be stayin' with friends now. They'll look after his wants, and he won't need the carriage."

The servant's statement did not relieve her worry, but she accepted Lord Saxton's absence as a blessing. Christopher needed care and attention, and she could give it more freely if her husband was not here to witness her concern. There was only Farrell to worry about now, but she determined to take care of that matter immediately.

"My brother has a great aversion to Mr. Seton," she stated. "If he finds the Yankee here, he might sound the warning that he is wounded. Under the circumstances, Aggie, I believe it is expedient that you prepare him a toddy."

The woman gave a quick nod. "I'll take care o' it right away, mum. Please see to Mr. Seton while I'm gone. I've gots me herbs and healin' potions ter fetch from the kitchen."

Bundy went off with the housekeeper to find an iron pot, leaving Erienne to sit with the wounded man. She busied herself tearing an old sheet into bandages, then she gently bathed the blood away from the area of the wound. Dipping the strong, lean hands separately in the basin, she carefully washed away the stains from the thin fingers. She kissed them, and tears welled in her eyes as she let his hand rest in hers. She understood her emotions more clearly now, though she couldn't exactly say when her love had started to bloom, but it came upon her with a solid certainty that she had loved Christopher Seton for some time now. And yet she had also grown to care for her husband with a deep, abiding affection.

It was disquieting to dwell on the knowledge that she could care for two men at the same time. In many ways she loved them differently. But then, there were also those moments when she was unable to separate one from the other. Christopher was dashing, charming, handsome, a man any woman could easily be enamored with. Lord Saxton, on the other hand, had gained her affection while having none of those traits.

Was her love for her husband, then, based on pity? Abruptly she rejected the idea. She had felt sorry for Ben but could hardly claim that she had loved him. Stuart Saxton made her feel very much the wife and undeniably a woman. And yet, strangely, it was at the heights of this mood that she had the most difficulty banishing Christopher from mind. Sometimes in her love play with her husband, she was assailed with such strong impressions of the other man, she had to reach out and touch the scarred back to affirm that it was Stuart and not Christopher with her. She could only reason that her desire for the Yankee was so strong she had put his face and name to the man who came to her only in darkness.

Aggie and Bundy returned, and Erienne stayed near as the woman tended the wound. The gore was cleaned away, and a soft, white salve was thickly applied before bandages were pressed first to his side and then to his back. The whole was tightly bound with several layers of linen that crossed his chest and was secured in place by a piece across his shoulder.

When the ordeal was finally over, Erienne sank weakly into a chair beside the bed, thankful to have it behind her. She refused the pleas of both servants to go to her own chambers and rest until the morning, stating resolutely, "I'll sleep here for the night."

Aggie saw no opening for argument and finally offered, "Mum, I'll watch him, while ye go and tidy yerself for bed, then ye can come back whenever ye're ready." She waved a hand to indicate the soiled riding habit her mistress wore. "Ye'll be much more comfortable in a fresh gown and wrapper than bound up in that."

"Are you sure . . . ?" Erienne began worriedly but was unable to put words to her fears.

"He'll be fine, mum," the housekeeper assured her, patting her arm affectionately. "He's a big, strong man, and with a little gentle care and rest, he'll be like new again in no time."

Relenting, Erienne allowed the woman to lead her to the door and there she promised, "I'll be back in a few moments."

As vowed, she did return, and she took a place in a chair near the bed to pass the long hours of the night. Curling her legs beneath her, she leaned her head and shoulders on the mattress of the bed and there slumbered, finding cozy warmth beneath a fur throw.

Dawn had broached the eastern sky when Christopher finally stirred. She came awake instantly and raised her head to find him watching her. Their eyes held for an eternity, and she could feel the slow pounding of her heart as he seemed to stare into her very soul.

"I'm thirsty," he said in a gravelly whisper.

She fetched a glassful of water and, bringing it back to the bed, placed an arm beneath his back and supported him with her own shoulder and strength while he quenched his thirst. As she set the glass aside, he raised his hand to caress her cheek, letting his fingers glide through the thick, curling tresses.

"I love you," he breathed. Their eyes held for a long, blissful moment, then with a sigh he lay back and closed his eyes. His fingers reached out to entwine hers in a weak grip that did much to bear out his words. Tears trembled on Erienne's lashes as her emotions were again tested to the limit, and she was grateful that her husband was not there, for he would have seen firsthand how she cared for this man.

Christopher wandered in and out through the depths of sleep as the day aged into night and the sun dawned afresh the next morning. He roused to awareness after the morning star had taken a place of dominance in the eastern heavens. Aggie came with a thick broth for the invalid and fluffed the pillows, bracing his back with their feather softness. When he refused to be fed, she provided a way for him to feed himself without undue stress, then set about to tidy the room. He sipped the soup from a mug while his gaze followed Erienne, who had remained to help the woman. He made no attempt to conceal his interest, giving cause for Erienne to worry at his lack of discretion. She did not lightly dismiss the fact that Aggie was fond of her master and had great hopes for the continuance of the family.

Christopher slept through most of the day and into the night, waking at intervals to take liquids and broth that either Aggie or Erienne pressed upon him. On the third day, a fever came upon him, and with it Erienne's fears mounted, but Aggie was quick to assure her that it was not an uncommon occurrence with a wounded man. The housekeeper bade her to bathe his skin with tepid water to reduce the fever and left her mistress to the chore, seeming undismayed that she had requested the lady of the manor to be that familiar with a man who was not her husband. While he slept Erienne found the task genuinely unsettling. With the freedom to peruse and touch his near-naked form, she became aghast at the frequency with which her gaze caressed the wide shoulders, the tapering, furred chest, the lean, hard waist, and the flat belly. She could not bring herself to uncover him below the hips, and the merest thought of doing so brought a livid blush to her cheeks, even in the privacy of the room.

Retaining a semblance of composure while he was awake was another ordeal, even though he was not quite lucid. His cheeks were flushed with the fever and his eyes somewhat glazed and overwarm as they rested on her. Still, she became excruciatingly aware of the effect of her ministering when her glance innocently strayed to where the sheet covered his loins. Of a sudden her own cheeks were flooded with color, but when her eyes flew upward, he met her stare calmly and without chagrin.

She fled the room in haste, and once in her chamber, she flung open a window and attempted to cool her burning cheeks in the crisp air. She struggled with a feeling of her own guilt, for in the last days she had been so painfully aware of him as a man, of his blatant sensuality, and of the wild, flowing current of excitement that lay just beneath the surface of every glance they exchanged, every touch, every spoken word.

Once she had hated him for causes she had thought were justi-fied, but the sting had been taken out of her ire in slow degrees. It could not be lightly discounted that he had risked his life to save Farrell and the Becker girl. The stabilizing force of hatred had flown, leaning her prey to the softer emotions, and love, that fearsome, dangerous, overpowering emotion, was nestling in like a tiger of the wilds, securing its lair deep in her mind and heart, where it would ever threaten her resolve.

She stayed away from the master's chambers for the rest of the day, letting Bundy and Aggie carry on without her. Between the two of them, they provided assurances that the wound was knitting amazingly well and that the fever had left. By nightfall, her mind was so frayed by the battle that raged within it, she numbly sought out her bed and prayed that her husband would soon return and establish himself even more firmly in her thoughts, rooting out the Yankee once and for all.

Lulled by the warming fire, she dallied through memories, clear and vague. A vision of a cloaked form and a prancing black steed was conjured from the events of the past few days, and then the darkly garbed figure became her husband bending down to lift her from the icy water of the creek. Behind him was the same black stallion, and of a sudden the leather mask was transformed into a deep cowl.

With a gasp, Erienne rolled back upon the bed and stared with widened eyes at the canopy, her mind caught in a sudden turmoil.

Was this another madness? Had her passion put a face to that which before had no face at all? Was this a dream? A wish born out of desire?

Her thoughts strained for clarity amid her confused memory. She could not pick a definite image or shape that identified the one who had taken her from the stream. The impression of a dark winged rider soaring from his rearing mount had stayed with her, but as she thought about it, she realized she had never seen Stuart on a horse. The suspicion that it was Christopher brought another question to mind. What had she seen by firelight that same evening? A misshapen form of a crippled man? Or just the distorted shape of a normal man? If Christopher proved to be the night rider as well as the one who had rescued her, then what else was he? Surely something more than the rutting roué he had always seemed to be.

A fear began to insinuate itself, but she cast off the idea as preposterous. Though Stuart had always come to her in darkness, she had nonetheless formed a vision of him, perhaps indistinct where her knowledge did not extend, but otherwise familiar to her. A twisted leg, a scarred back, a rasping voice were very much a part of that image and did not match the handsomer appearance of Christopher Seton.

The jumbled pieces of the puzzle turned over in her mind, but no fragment fit to another to provide a broader glimpse of the truth. The endless boredom of their passage allied with her fatigue, and she sank into an exhausted slumber. No nightmares lurked within her dreams, only the endless roiling of questions, fears, and doubts.

Twenty

Morning came as was its habit of many a year, bursting forth this day in the guise of a blustery spring day slashed with stinging spits of rain. The icy droplets beat against the crystal panes with the force of the wind, speckling the glass with tiny jewels of moisture, while on the roof, the tiles rattled and the eaves moaned as the playful gusts ran rampant.

Erienne rose refreshed and blithely went about her toilet until in the brushing of her hair, her thoughts came rushing back full force. Her hand halted halfway through a stroke as confusion sank its sharp, persistent talons into her mind, quickly setting the mood for her day.

A determination to get to the heart of the matter grew within her, and leaving her chambers, she set her direction toward the master's bedroom, where she intended to confront Christopher on the issue of her rescue from the stream. She had neared the door when she paused in brief bewilderment, hearing Aggie's voice through the thick panels. The woman's tone was low and indistinct, but urgent, half arguing, half pleading. Erienne was at once beset that she was cast in the role of eavesdropper and quickly put her hand to the door, rattling the latch loudly as she turned it.

When the portal swung wide, displaying the occupants of the chamber, she found Christopher propped up against the pillows with a trace of an amused smile on his lips, obviously much better than on the prior day, and Aggie standing at the foot of the bed, red of face and with her arms akimbo. At the sight of her, Christopher coughed lightly behind his hand, and the housekeeper busied herself removing the breakfast tray, though her lips remained tightly compressed and her cheeks oddly flushed. Erienne readily dismissed the matter from mind, for she could well imagine the woman berating the man for not taking proper care of himself or engaging in some unauthorized activity, which at least in Aggie's eyes would be unforgivable.

"I'll be goin' down now ter fetch some hot water from the kitchen ter tend the wound, Lady Saxton." The housekeeper stressed the title as she cast an imperious glance toward the man. "Will ye do me a favor and remove the old bandage while I'm gone?"

Erienne nodded in rising confusion. The woman's usual effervescence was most apparently in absence, and the cause could not be explained in any manner that courted rationality. If it was jealousy for Lord Saxton's sake, then why, Erienne mused, would she have laid such a task to her?

Aggie handed her a pair of small sewing scissors and, with a last smug nod of her head toward the invalid, was quickly gone. Even before the door closed behind her, Erienne felt Christopher's stare, and when she glanced around, she found a hunger in his eyes that had naught to do with the stomach. It touched off a quickness in her own pulse, one she strived hard to hide with a proper scolding.

"If you wish me to attend you, Mr. Seton, I insist that you exercise a finer degree of self-control, at least in the presence of others. Poor Aggie is fiercely loyal to Stuart and will not long abide your uninvited pandering."

Unmoved by her chiding, he plucked at the bandage. "Are you sure you have the stomach for this?"

Erienne seated herself on the edge of the bed near his left side. "I tended Farrell's arm long enough. I'll warrant I can handle this as well." A rueful smile brought up the corners of her lips. "However, I should warn you to hold yourself still, or I might be tempted to take some portion of your hide away as recompense."

"As you command, my lady." He spread his arms, completely surrendering himself to her ministering, and let his left hand fall casually upon her hip as she leaned forward to strip the strap that crossed his shoulder and held the bandage high. Feeling his fingers brush her backside, she paused and purposefully lifted his hand by the wrist, moving it to where it could rest harmlessly on the mattress.

"I will not stand for your shenanigans either, Mr. Seton," she admonished.

A slow smile curved his lips. "You're being terribly formal, my lady. Have you grown averse to my name of a sudden?"

"I don't wish to encourage you in your blatant disregard of my status as a married woman, that is all," she explained pertly. "You are being very forward in Aggie's presence, and 'tis obvious that she is peeved with you."

"Do you think calling me 'Mr. Seton' is going to stop me from wanting you?" he asked as his eyes caressed her. "You know very little about me . . . or men . . . if you think mere words can quench what I feel for you. 'Tis no simple lust that gnaws at me, Erienne, but an ever-raging desire to have you with me every moment, to feel your softness beneath my searching hand, and to claim you as my own. Nay, no stilted title can cool what burns in me."

She stared at him in speechless wonder. He had played the rutting stag so well, she had to consider his words as another ploy to break down the barrier between them and to add her to his list of conquests. Still, they were effective in bringing to mind a similar awareness of her own desires. He was there whenever she closed her eyelids, haunting her with his presence, and she yearned to have him hold her and kiss her without the restrictions between them.

His gaze now met hers without wavering, promising more than she, in good conscience, could accept. Despite her outward calm, her thoughts were put to rout, and she completely forgot what it was that she wanted to discuss with him. Her hands trembled as she bent her attention to her chore, and she had to use all her concentration to steady them as she inserted the tip of the scissors into the top of the wrappings. She snipped downward until the bandage was parted, and she carefully raised the cloth away. A mild shudder went through her as she found a cloying black and greenish matter bonding wound and cloth together. The fabric had to be painstakingly eased away from the skin lest the bleeding be started anew. Though she worked diligently and with caring patience to pry it from the pink, healthy flesh, she was aware that all the prodding and pulling were painful, yet he never twitched a muscle and whenever she glanced up, there was always that odd, inscrutable gaze that seemed to probe into her mind and an enigmatic smile playing about his lips.

"Roll toward me," she directed and leaned close to reach around him as he complied. Easing the bandage away from the wound on his back, she pushed it as far beneath him as she could before sponging the dried blood from his back. The basin of tepid water had been placed on the bed beside him, and as he lay flat she reached across to wring the cloth out. In the next moment his left hand rose and pressed lightly between her shoulders, causing her to fall toward him until he could capture her lips with his own. Off balance, she could not immediately withdraw and was held snared by a torrid kiss that torched her cool-minded resolve and cindered it beneath the heat of his demand. His open mouth moved upon hers with a hunger that greedily sought for a like response. The stirring rush of excitement flared through her, and the need was there to answer him, but the sudden intrusion of a black, staring mask into her mind made her push away with a sudden gasp. She came to her feet, her cheeks ablaze with the shame of her own ardor.

Christopher challenged her with a mocking grin. "You must have read my mind, madam. 'Twas the very gift I desired."

"You have your nerve taking such liberties in my husband's house," she panted breathlessly. "You will certainly destroy yourself if you continue to indulge in such foolery." Her rebuke only seemed to amuse him, for his grin deepened, making her doubt that she would ever be effective in discouraging his rutting tendencies. Regaining some measure of control, she gestured with a hand that still trembled. "Sir, if you will be so kind as to raise yourself on the other side, I will take away the bandage."

Christopher pressed his left palm against the mattress and lifted himself until she could reach beneath him. Even then, she was hard driven to ignore his nearness and the uneven beat of her heart. After a moment's fumbling she found the noisome bandage and withdrew it. As she deposited the rag in the basin for removal, a light rap came upon the door, and at her summons Bundy entered.

It was a cue for Erienne to excuse herself and leave her charge to the other's care. She was thankful for the interruption and sought the privacy of her bedchamber. As she closed the door behind her a gnawing disquiet descended, but she could not name a definite cause. Despite all of that which she had proposed, she had solved only one puzzle, the identity of the night rider. She was satisfied that Christopher's cause was just, yet she was haunted by the faceless shadow of that one who had flown to rescue her from the stream. She could no longer believe it had been her husband, and she feared even here a fantasy of Christopher was replacing Stuart, much as it had in those dark, enshrouded trysts in her husband's arms.

This was, of course, the place where she attended her husband in the night, there on yonder bed, and as her eyes slid over the velvet hangings, her mind took up a restless chase. Of late she had begun to fantasize about Christopher far too much while her husband made love to her. Something in those heated embraces had brought him to mind, and now those illusions were beginning to spill over in other areas of her marriage, muddling once-firm certainties and confusing images of both cousins. Was this the curse of the Fleming blood? Could she ever be true to one? Would her own desire continue to bring another to mind whenever her husband held her and brought her to a bliss that waxed to a numbing height in its intensity? She saw an image of that blank leather mask bending low as if to kiss her, and slowly, as before, it became the impassioned visage of that one who haunted her.

Erienne's mind rebelled and just as quickly was snatched by another thought, one that took her breath with the suddenness of its assault.

Seton! Saxton! Cousins? Or brothers? There had been two sons born of the Saxton family. Stuart was the elder, but what of the younger? Could he be in truth the one she knew as Christopher Seton? What better way to weave a trap for the rascals who had burned the manse than to let one take a place as lord while the other played out a masquerade? If they were brothers, perhaps they worked together to avenge the scarring of the one. Christopher, being the more mobile of the two, brandished his sword and pistol in the name of justice as the nighthawk, while the older brother established fear in the hearts of the brigands by his mere existence. The ones responsible for the burning of the manse had hoped to kill him but had to be frustrated by their failure.

A wry smile touched her lips as she grew firm in that newfound belief. Christopher had free access to the manor and knew it well, as if he had been born here.

She perched on the foot of the bed, and though she stared hard, she saw nothing. Her mind spun in an aimless, racing whirlwind. There was something else here, something that wavered just beyond her grasp. The suspicion that something was not quite right had not left her. She rubbed her hands, and almost as quickly a coldness began to grow in her as she remembered that moment when she had reached for the bandage. Her right hand caressed the palm of her left, gently, as if it were Christopher's back, and suddenly she knew what she had touched. A puckered scar on his shoulder. A night not too long past she had felt that scar on Stuart's back when he had brought her to a height of passion.

A strangled cry of denial escaped her lips as the full realization dawned on her. Her husband had sent another to her bed in his stead! In a slow-moving vision, she recounted the intimacies they had shared, when her hands had moved over his body to appease a wifely curiosity and when his knowledgeable caresses had brought sighs of pleasure from her lips, just as Christopher had done in the carriage.

Erienne could no longer face the mocking windows and, twisting about, buried her face into the coverlet of the bed. Her half-choked, wailing sobs were muffled in the bedding. The ache in her breast was unbearable, and there was no ease from the scalding shame she felt. She had been used! Duped! Agonizing hands, formed like clawed talons, gathered the fabric, and as she wept, she curled in a knot and slowly slipped to her knees on the floor. She clutched the coverlet over her ears as if to shut out the laughing voice that echoed in her head. She had been used! They had made a game of her! Fool! Fool! Fool!

Erienne could not shut out the ridicule that raked her, and then it came to her like a blast of winter air. She clutched the quilt in her belly and, as she rocked back upon her heels, raised her face to heaven and slowly scrubbed with the blanket as if to cleanse her loins, but there was that in her which had been given her and she could not rid herself of it. Their betrayal tore at her.

She huddled there and sobbed in the coverlet. What right had they to bargain for what was hers and hers alone to give? To pass her off from one to the other without any regard for her own desires and honor?

She came to her feet, a flare of rage heating her heart. She would face the rogue, and were her husband here, she would face him also and have the whole thing out and done with. The multitude of masquerades was done! Her gloom was forgotten. She had a task before her and held no doubt that she would perform it well.

With that resolve burning through her, she smoothed the bedcovers and, pouring water from the ewer into the basin, washed the bloodstains from her hands. The dirty water went into a bucket, and she poured afresh, this time wetting a cloth and laving her face. Beneath the cooling strokes, some meager understanding of her husband's reasoning dawned. If Stuart had been injured by the fire to such a degree as to be rendered incapable in the duties of a husband, then by letting his brother have her, he could at least have been assured that any offspring she bore would be in part his blood. Still, it was not enough to salve the pain she felt. They had not comported themselves with any compassion for her pride or feelings.

A sound came from the corridor, and she stepped close to the door to listen. It was Bundy and Aggie leaving the master's room, and their voices were subdued as they passed her chamber. The roué was alone now and could not flee, and she would not let him again evade the questions. She took the resolution upon her. This time would do as well as any.

She was down the hall in a trice and through the door of the master's chambers, locking it behind her to forbid interruption. Deliberately removing the key, she dropped it into her bodice as she turned to face the one she had come to confront.

Christopher was propped up in the bed sipping from a steaming mug of brandy and honey, a potion prescribed by Aggie to ease the discomfort of the new bandage. He had watched Erienne's entry over the rim of the cup and now lowered it as his amused gaze raked her.

"Do you think it safe there, madam?"

There was enough of a smirk in his question to spur Erienne's ire higher. Still, she forced herself to breathe calmly and, with leisured purpose, crossed the room to stand at the foot of his bed.

"I have a matter or two to settle with you, sir." Her tone was almost flat, and his brow raised at the lean seriousness of her manner.

"And I with you, madam." He smiled and lifted the glass for another sip of the heady brew.

"I know who you are," she stated bluntly.

His arm paused, and he looked up at her in surprise, his lips parted to receive the brim.

"I know you and Stuart are brothers." Now the subject was broached, she rushed into it headlong. "I cannot understand the why of it, but I know of you. You seem to be much more the creature of the night than even I had realized until this hour. For whatever his reasons, my husband has let you come to pleasure me in his stead. I don't understand why you were in this bed the first night, but since then, you have always come to me and, hidden in darkness, have put a bastard babe within my belly."

Christopher choked abruptly, and the cup twitched in his hand before he set it aside. He coughed to clear his throat and cocked a brow at her as he struggled to find his voice. "Madam, your news is most dear to my heart, but I urge you to be more gentle in the telling of it. You have nearly strangled me."

"*Gentle!*" she railed, forgetting her composure at his offhandish humor. "Were you gentle with me when you played your game with me?!"

"Now, Erienne, dearest love . . ."

"Don't you 'dearest love' me!" she flared. "You debaucher! You sneak thief of a woman's virtue! You used me! You took me when I thought you were another!"

"My love," he cajoled, "I can explain if you will just let me."

"You will indeed, sir! And that is why I have come! To hear your explanations! Go on! Tell me the reason you tricked me!"

He opened his mouth to speak again, but a thunder of feet in the hall and a heavy pounding on the door halted him.

" 'Tis urgent I speak with ye!" Bundy roared through the panel.

Erienne's brow darkened angrily, and a stubborn determination rose. "I will not let him in," she gritted.

Bundy's fist beat upon the panels again. "The sheriff is coming!"

Christopher began to slide toward the edge of the bed. "Erienne, my sweet, open the door. We will speak of this matter later . . . in private. You have my word on it."

Seeing the necessity for yielding, she fumbled in her bodice until she retrieved the key. Thrusting it in the lock, she opened the door.

Bundy swept past her with a half-mumbled apology. "Yer pardon, milady."

"Where are they?" Christopher questioned curtly.

Bundy halted by the bedside and panted, "Only a mile or so away. Keats was out exercisin' a horse and saw 'em comin'."

"Damn!" Christopher muttered and grimaced as he tried to move.

"You must hide him, Bundy," Erienne said urgently. "Take him to the passage."

"She's right. I cannot be taken," Christopher declared. "Parker would see that I didn't last out the week, and I doubt that even Lord Saxton could fetch help that fast. My clothes, Bundy. At once!"

He threw off the covers and stood to his feet with a grimace, ignoring the fact that below the bandage he was stark naked. Erienne could not. The sight of that tall, lean-hipped, broad-shouldered form brought a scalding hotness to her cheeks. Whirling on a heel, she ran from the room, slamming the door behind her. She was abashed that he could treat her so outrageously casually in front of a servant, and she could not halt the return of mortifying shame. Her thoughts again in a flurry, she entered the doubtful shelter of her chamber and paced about.

A mild panic seized her at the realization that in the absence of Lord Saxton she would have to meet the sheriff herself. Christopher's safety depended on how well she could hide her distress and not give away the game. Making an effort to calm her flighty thoughts, she drew a deep breath and conjured an image of a regal lady, holding it firmly in her mind until she grew comfortable with it. Her chin raised a notch. She was Lady Saxton, she told herself, the mistress of her husband's manor, and she would not be intimidated in her own house.

Once again she opened the door and retraced her steps to the master's chambers, only to find it deserted except for Aggie, who was hastily arranging the bedcovers and tidying the room. It came to her as she paused in the portal that the housekeeper probably knew more about the manor and its occupants than anyone else outside the family. She decided to settle one of many questions right here and now.

"Aggie?"

The woman turned quickly. "Aye, mum?"

Erienne swept a hand to indicate the tome that lay on her husband's desk. "You once told me that book held an accounting of every birth and death that happened here in this house and on these lands. If I were to look into it, would I find Christopher's name entered as the younger brother of the Saxton family?"

Aggie twisted her hands in sudden consternation and glanced away nervously.

Erienne read the answer in the woman's manner and sought to relieve her obvious anguish. "It's all right, Aggie. I understand your loyalty to the family and do not ask you to reveal anything that I haven't already guessed."

"Please, mum," the housekeeper pleaded, "hear the master out 'fore ye think ill o' him."

"Oh, I intend to hear him out," Erienne assured her, but as far as the other she feared she had already begun to have some very doubtful thoughts about the master of the manse.

Erienne left the woman and made her way to the stairs, intending to await the visitors in the common room. Paine was on station at the front door, and she gave him a gracious nod as she passed. She swept through the archway leading into the great hall and then froze. Her dignity dissolved, and consternation raged in its wake, for seated calmly in his usual chair beside the hearth was Lord Saxton, the right leg gathered behind the good one, the gaze behind the blank helm fastened on the doorway, and his gloved hands folded atop his walking stick. Though crippled and scarred, he was in truth a most formidable figure of a man.

Erienne stammered a jumbled apology. "My lord, I did not . . . I was not informed you had returned."

"Our guests are nigh." The hoarse whisper was not unkind, only flat and emotionless. "Come here and take a seat beside me." His left hand briefly indicated a chair before it returned to rest on the cane.

She crossed to the proffered chair and sat erect on its edge, but the position left her knees to tremble all the more. Her nerves were as taut as the strings of a harpsichord, and she rose to stand close beside him, half behind his chair, her hand resting on the top of the ornately carved back. They waited thus in silence, a regal lord and his pale, stiff lady, while the tall timepiece in the great hall ticked the moments away with maddening slowness.

Erienne started slightly when a rattle of many hooves sounded outside, coming up along the front lane to cease beside the tower door. Paine turned the knob, but before he could open the portal, it burst wide at the inward rush of Sheriff Parker followed closely— indeed, too closely—by Haggard Bentworth, that worthy ever-ready-for-battle crony. A whole flock of fellows came at their heels and crowded into the entry. Seeing the open door of the common room, the sheriff brushed arrogantly past Paine, then stepped spritely aside as the naked blade that Haggard bore prodded him in the backside. He yelped and whirled, swatting the harrying sword down with his hand and causing it to rake the sheepskin vest and closely threaten his manhood. It was only when the danger had passed that Allan dared release his breath, then a menacing glare came into his eyes and bored into Haggard, who fumbled sheepishly with the weapon.

"Put that thing away, you fool!" Parker snarled through gnashing teeth. "And this time not in me!"

Good Haggard eagerly nodded and thrust the weapon into its sheath with a vengeance, then flinched and sucked his left thumb where a small droplet of blood welled up.

Paine raised his chin and sniffed loudly, managing to speak without a hint of a smile. "Lord Saxton awaits in the common room."

Allan Parker snorted once at Haggard and, mumbling beneath his breath, strode angrily through the tall, welcoming archway. He advanced a pair of paces into the room and, with an officious frown, surveyed the scene that met his eye, giving the master and mistress of the house a curt nod before he turned and beckoned a man to him.

"Sergeant, set the men to searching the house and put a guard on this door. Then see that those outside are . . ."

His words were halted by a loud double click, and both he and the sergeant turned warily to face their host. They found themselves returning the unwinking gaze of a pair of oversized pistols and could not find the courage to doubt their priming and loading. Lord Saxton's skill with weapons was a well-known fact throughout the countryside, and neither of them wished to test it at a close range.

"No man searches this house but on my word or the King's." Lord Saxton's rasping voice resounded through the hall. "I have issued no such directive, but if you have a warrant from the other, then I would see it."

Both men kept their hands carefully away from their sidearms while Parker, with a decided change in manner, made haste to apologize and explain.

"Your pardon, my lord." He doffed his hat as he acknowledged the presence of the lady and nudged the sergeant with his elbow until that one followed suit. "I have no warrant from the Crown, but 'tis my good intent to seek your permission for a search. We are looking for the night rider. A dastardly crime was committed several days ago, and we have proof that one Christopher Seton is that rogue, the very same who laid Squire Becker in his grave, brutally slew his coachmen, and kidnapped the young daughter."

Erienne stepped forward, her hand raised in hot denial, but her way was suddenly blocked by a gloved hand bearing a pistol. She looked down at her husband in angry urgency. "But 'tis not . . ."

"Shush." His subdued whisper came for her ears alone. "Control yourself, my love. Trust me."

She returned to her position, but when her hand came back to the chair, she gripped it until her knuckles were white.

The sheriff continued as he regained Lord Saxton's attention. "The man is also wanted for the murders of Timmy Sears and Ben Mose, not to mention a host of lesser crimes." He rubbed the back of his bandaged left hand. " 'Twas said in town that he was some kin of yours."

"Are you sure of your facts, Sheriff?" The hollow voice chuckled lightly. "Christopher Seton and pistols, that I can believe, but he seemed too clumsy an oaf to be well skilled with a blade."

Parker slipped his left hand into his coat and shrugged. "Skilled enough at least to best a drunken sot and a brawling lad untutored in the matter of blades."

A bitter laugh came from the blank mask. "Or an aging squire who would defend his daughter?" The low, coarse voice took on a note of concern. "Your hand, sir? Have you hurt yourself?"

The sheriff reddened a bit and stumbled over an excuse. "I . . . I cut it. 'Tis little more than a nick."

Lord Saxton lowered the hammers and tucked the pistols away. "I will allow your men to search. Only tell them to be quick about it. My housekeeper will not take kindly to all these muddy boots tramping through the place."

"Certainly, my lord." Parker jerked his head at the sergeant. "Attend to it."

The sergeant stepped before his men and flung out his arm in several directions as he gave them orders. When they had been dispersed, he took to the stairs, leaving the sheriff to poke about the corners of the common room.

Lord Saxton shifted his weight carefully in the chair and lent his attention to Erienne. "My dear, if you would be so kind. A brandy for the sheriff."

Without a word Erienne crossed to the sideboard, struggling with the nervous tension that had sapped the strength from her limbs. After pouring a draught from the decanter, she turned with the glass in her hand, but her husband gestured again.

"A little more, my love. 'Tis a foul day out, and the sheriff will no doubt need the fortification for the ride back."

Parker perused the comely feminine form as he took the glass, wondering how the girl could content herself with such a husband. He remembered Avery's difficulty in finding a suitor to please her and had to believe the girl was handling her guise of devotion very well.

Upstairs in Erienne's chamber, Aggie watched the men rudely search the armoire and tramp behind the draperies that secluded the bathing room. She cringed as Haggard's sheathed sword fanned out behind him, bumping against the furniture and threatening costly vases and lamps. His face lit up as he passed Erienne's dressing table, and he paused to sample the intoxicating scent of a dusting powder. Curiously he raised a crystal vial and, with his thick fingers, ever so gently lifted the stopper. He poked his large nose near the top and sniffed. An expression of dreamy ecstasy transformed his face, and for a moment he forgot the world existed.

"Aren't you . . . ?"

Haggard jumped, and the perfume vial flew from his hands, doing a spiraling cartwheel through the air, in the process dousing him with a liberal portion of the contents. He juggled his hands about, trying to catch the crystal container, and breathed a sigh of relief when he clutched it safely to his bosom. Finally he met the woman's pained stare with a hesitant smile.

"Aren't you supposed to be looking for a man?" Aggie reminded him.

A light seemed to dawn in his brain, brightening his face, and Haggard hurriedly set aside the crystal vial. He glanced about, then dusted his hands, content that no one was hiding in the room. Beckoning to his confederates, he passed on into the hall. In his absence, Aggie waved the air in front of her nose and looked heavenward, as if she offered prayer for such a clumsy buffoon.

A second libation had been offered to and taken by the sheriff when his men returned to the hall. Haggard was grinning in joyful innocence for a task well performed and missed the widely skeptical stares of his companions. He crossed the hall to stand beside the sheriff, who choked on the remainder of his brandy as the overpowering fumes hit him. Coughing to catch his breath, Parker looked about with a mild tearing of the eyes. In the background Aggie smiled smugly, content that she had been present to see the expression on the sheriff's face.

"No sign of a wounded man in the house, sir," the sergeant announced.

"Satisfied, Sheriff?" Lord Saxton inquired.

The man nodded reluctantly. "I am sorry to have inconvenienced you, my lord. We will look elsewhere for the knave, but should he come here, I beg you detain him and send a rider to inform us."

No answer came from the mask, and the sheriff pushed Haggard out ahead of him. Erienne held her place, listening to their departure until an overwhelming silence filled the manse. Lord Saxton gestured to Aggie, bringing the woman close, and spoke in a low voice to her. The woman straightened, cast a quick glance at her mistress, and hastily left the room.

Once they were alone, Lord Saxton raised himself slowly from his chair and half turned to his wife. "I would like a private word with you, madam. Would you be so kind as to join me in my chambers?"

Now that the moment of truth was at hand, Erienne was not nearly so certain that she wanted to proceed. Considering that Christopher had only recently vacated the chambers, she wondered if she should direct her husband elsewhere, but the suspicion that Aggie had already told him about the Yankee made Erienne hold her silence. Meekly she crossed the room and then paused at the entry leading into the tower to wait for Stuart, who came at a more awkward pace than usual. As he climbed the stairs, he seemed overly tired. Erienne ran ahead to open the door for him and was amazed to find that the bedcovers had been turned down and the pillows fluffed and piled in one heap. It was apparent that Aggie had already been there to prepare the room, and Erienne could not resist a question as Lord Saxton passed her with his slow, halting gait.

"Are you ill, my lord?"

"Lock the door, Erienne," he rasped and, without appeasing her curiosity, made his way carefully to the chair by the hearth.

Erienne turned the key and stared dismally about, wondering what the next moments would bring. Her husband's stoical manner boded ill, and she held no hope that she could approach him on the matter of their marriage without feeling greatly hampered by her trepidations. Hesitantly she moved to his desk and idly turned several pages of the tome as she tried to think of an opening.

Lord Saxton hitched the chair around to face his wife. "Will you pour me a brandy, my dear?"

The request startled her, and casting a curious glance at him, she reached to take the stopper from the crystal decanter that resided with several glasses on a silver tray. She poured a draught and felt his gaze as she brought him the libation. The fact was firm in her mind that he had never taken any substance in her presence, for doing so would have necessitated the removal of the mask. Unable to cease her trembling, she hurried back to the desk and lifted the crystal stopper to replace it.

"So, my dear . . ."

She faced him with thudding heart, the crystal piece clutched desperately in her hand, but she was hardly aware that she even held it.

". . . You say I have let another man into my bed."

Erienne opened her mouth to speak. Her first impulse was to chatter some inanity that could magically take the edge from his callous half statement, half question. No great enlightenment dawned, however, and her dry, parched throat issued no sound of its own. She inspected the stopper closely, turning it slowly in her hand rather than meet the accusing stare.

From behind the mask, Lord Saxton observed his wife closely, well aware that the next moments would form the basis for the rest of his life or leave it an empty husk. After this, there could be no turning back.

"I think, my dear," his words made her start, "that whatever the cost, 'tis time you met the beast of Saxton Hall."

Erienne swallowed hard and clasped the stopper with whitened knuckles, as if to draw some bit of courage from the crystal piece. As she watched, Lord Saxton doffed his coat, waistcoat, and stock, and she wondered if it was a trick of her imagination that he seemed somewhat lighter of frame. After their removal, he caught the heel of his right boot over the toe of the left and slowly drew the heavy, misshapen encumbrance from his foot. She frowned in open bemusement, unable to detect a flaw. He flexed the leg a moment before slipping off the other boot.

His movements seemed pained as he shed the gloves, and Erienne's eyes fastened on the long, tan, unscarred hands that rose to the mask and, with deliberate movements, flipped the lacings loose. She half turned, dropping the stopper and colliding with the desk as he reached to the other side of the leather helm and lifted it away with a single motion. She braved a quick glance and gasped in astonishment when she found translucent eyes calmly smiling at her.

"Christopher! What . . . ?" She could not form a question, though her mind raced in a frantic search for logic.

He rose from the chair with an effort. "Christopher Stuart Saxton, lord of Saxton Hall." His voice no longer bore a hint of a rasp. "Your servant, my lady."

"But . . . but where is . . . ?" The truth was only just beginning to dawn on her, and the name she spoke sounded small and thin. ". . . Stuart?"

"One and the same, madam." He stepped near, and those translucent eyes commanded her attention. "Look at me, Erienne. Look very closely." He towered over her, and his lean, hard face bore no hint of humor. "And tell me again if you think I would ever allow another man in your bed while I yet breathe."

This revelation was so different from what she had assumed, Erienne had trouble grasping the facts as they were presented to her. She knew the two were one, but reason failed to knot the elusive ends and brought the plaintive questions to her lips. "How? Why?"

"The one you thought was Lord Saxton is dead. He was my older brother, Edmund. He bore the title before me, but when the east wing burned, he was trapped in the fire. His servant found him . . . or rather what was left of him . . . in the ruins, and laid him in an unmarked grave atop the cliff overlooking the firth." The muscles flexed in his cheek, giving evidence of his constrained anger. "I was at sea at the time, and the letters bearing news of his death never reached me. When I came to England, I was presented with the fact that someone had murdered him."

"Dead? Three years ago?" Erienne repeated numbly. "Then when I married, it was really you . . . ?"

"Aye, madam. I could not court you otherwise, nor could I think of a better ploy to confuse the ones who torched the manse than to resurrect the older brother whom they thought was dead. 'Twas you who gave me the guise and challenge when you said you would rather wed a scarred and twisted cripple."

Erienne glanced about, unable to settle her misting gaze on a single object while her mind flew in frenzy. He reached to take her against him, but she eluded his hand.

"Please . . . don't touch me," she said sobbing, and ran to the windows, there refusing to yield even the smallest glance in his direction. A heavy guilt came upon him as he moved to stand behind her. He saw her slender shoulders jerk with her silent weeping and heard her racking breath, and the muted sound drove a piercing pain through his heart.

"Come, my love . . ."

"My love!" Erienne whirled, and her tear-filled eyes blazed at him as she choked on her sobs. "Am I in truth your love, a respected wife to bear offspring with a proud and noble name? Or am I just some tender tidbit you've taken for sport? A simpleminded wench to fill your needs for a night or two, perhaps? What amusement you must have had playing your game on me!"

"Erienne . . . listen . . ."

"Nay! Never again will I listen to your lies!" She swept the back of her hand across her cheeks to fling away the streaming wetness and snatched free as he tried once more to take her arm. "What was it that you wanted? A paramour to while away the hours with? Aye! A tender virgin to entertain you while you're here in these northern climes. That was your first proposal, wasn't it?"

She strolled toward him, hips swaying suggestively while her eyes flashed through their moisture. She caught her finger in his shirt and flippantly jerked the tail out of his breeches. "What does a good trollop earn in the time I've been with you? Fifty pounds? That *was* what you paid for me, wasn't it? 'Tis so hard to recall. You gave with one hand and took with the other."

Christopher cocked a dubious brow, somewhat amazed at the spirit of this woman he had wed. "No such miserly sum, madam."

Erienne deliberately misinterpreted his answer. "Oh? Then you must consider that you bought me for a real bargain if most doxies earn more than that." Her lips turned upward in a coy smile as her eyes grew dark and sultry. "Am I not worth more than that now that I've learned some of the duties? Perhaps my speech is too refined." She leaned her bosom against him and tauntingly rubbed her thigh against his as she slid a hand beneath his shirt to slowly caress his lean, naked waist. "Ain't I worth more'n a couple quid a night ter ye, gov'na?"

He raked her with a brazen stare, able to give as good as he got, yet after a brief consideration he decided it would not be prudent to tempt Fate too far. She had a right to be angry, and it would behoove him to weather the storm with patience.

"What's the matter, gov'na?" she asked in a feigned tone of hurt when she failed to win a response from him. "Ain't I good enough for ye?" She twined her arm about his neck and, catching his hand, brought it to her breast and slowly rubbed the palm against the rising peak. "Don't ye like me?"

"I do indeed, madam," he drawled leisurely. He reached behind him, flipped open an armoire door and, taking out a sheaf of papers, held them before her eyes. "These are the rest of the receipts for your father's bills I paid in London." He tossed the stack in the direction of the bed, careless of how they scattered to the floor. "They account to more than ten thousand pounds."

"Ten thousand?" she repeated in questioning astonishment.

"Aye, and I would have paid twice that had there been a need. I couldn't bear the thought of letting you wed another man. So when your father banned me from the roup, I took my rightful title as Lord Saxton and had my man bid for me."

She stepped away, not willing to relent. "You tricked me. You tricked my father . . . and Farrell . . . the whole village. You tricked us all," she sobbed, tears brimming in her eyes again. "When I think of all those nights you took me . . . held me in your arms . . . and all the while you were laughing at me. How you must have laughed at us all."

"Madam, I never laughed at you. I wanted you, and I knew of no other way I could have you."

"You could have told me . . ." she cried.

"You hated me, remember, and scoffed at my proposals." He tugged off his shirt and threw it aside. Rubbing his knuckles in the palm of his hand, he began to pace slowly about as he sought some discourse that would soothe her ire. "I came to these climes to seek some clue to the identity of my brother's murderers, and in the course of that venture, I viewed a maid whose fairness seized my heart. She entrapped me as surely as any southern water siren or sea maiden, and I desired her as I have never desired any woman.

"Fate decreed that we should be at odds from the start, and I was commanded to ignore the very one I wanted. The warnings only sharpened my desires to have her. I plied her at every opportunity, and though her words chilled my hopes, I glimpsed some wee chance that she might in time yield to me." He lifted his right arm and rubbed the bandage with his other hand as if to ease a pain. "However, the moment wherein she would be wed to another quickly approached. 'Twas a choice I had to make . . . to let her go and forever regret that I had not been allowed time to woo her, or to present myself as the beast and take advantage of a ploy that could also aid me elsewhere. The longer I debated the matter, the more possibilities it presented. It seemed plausible, and it would allow me to court the lady at my leisure."

Erienne's voice was ragged with emotion. "So you duped me into believing I was marrying an unsightly beast. If you had really cared for me, Christopher, you would have told me. You would have come to me and eased my fears. But you let me suffer through the first weeks of our marriage, when I was so frightened I wanted to die!"

"Would you have been relieved to find yourself married to me?" he inquired. "Or would you have gone back to your father and set the word out against me? I had this matter of my brother's death to settle, and I had no way of knowing I could trust you. Many had sought to kill us. My mother booked passage to the colonies after the attempt on her sons' lives. She was frightened, for the hand of our foe seemed widespread. She hired a man with a daughter to sail with her and traveled under his name. When she arrived in the colonies, she adopted her maiden name and made a new life for us all. She feared us coming back, but 'twas meant to be. The rebellion in the colonies interfered, but nonetheless, after friendly relations were resumed, my brother came to claim his rightful place as lord. Nothing had changed. He was here only a short time, and they came with their torches and gave him no quarter. I was determined to be more wary, even with the one I had become enamored with. Her father was untrustworthy, and she had often confessed her hatred of me."

Tears blurred her vision, and she wiped angrily at the twin trails of wetness that continued to course down her cheeks. "I tried so desperately to be an honorable wife, but all the while I was just a pawn in your ploy for revenge."

"Justice, madam, and I will yet have it, though I see the sheriff is working diligently to destroy me."

"Allan Parker?" She forgot her anger for the moment as she stared at him in amazement. "Does he not work for justice, too?"

"Hardly, madam. He is the one whom the highwaymen call their captain. He led the attack on the Becker carriage, and that is how he came to know I am the night rider."

Erienne could not doubt his accusation, though the shock of it lingered on, but she had some claims of her own to make. "You have been involved with so many games. The night rider is not the least of them." Her unrelenting distress was evident in her tone. "You played the rutting stud with me and worked diligently to tear through my honor and destroy my self-respect. You seduced me in the carriage. You played your game with me there, and you would have taken me, too, and let me think that I was cuckolding my husband. Then later, when I came to this bed, you made love to me, deceiving me as you did, letting me believe you were another man while you made love to me."

Christopher's brows creased. "My desire for you was hard-driven, Erienne. I saw you as a man craves to see his wife . . . in the bath . . . in the bed . . . always so close under my hand, and so damned beautiful, it became torture for me just to look at you. I was soundly caught in a trap. I never dreamt you would yield to me as Lord Saxton, and when you came, I could not for the life of me deny myself or your plea in that moment, though in the taking of you I made the truth more difficult to tell. After easing my desires, I only wanted you more, and I was afraid I would lose you entirely."

"Have you no ken how I suffered because of your charade?" she asked, choking. "Every time you came to me as Lord Saxton, I was tormented with images of Christopher Seton. It became impossible to separate the two of you in my mind. And now you say 'twas but a game? Do you realize you nearly drove me mad?"

"My apologies, madam." His eyes were soft and yearning as they rested on her. "I was never sure you cared for me until you whispered my name in the dark."

Erienne was beset with confusion. She knew him to be a man who went after what he wanted, yet his method to win her seemed somehow less than honorable. Still, had he not done so, she would have found herself wed to Harford Newton or any one of a number of suitors she had despised. She had resented Christopher after the roup because she had thought he had done nothing to save her from a distasteful marriage. Could she be too distraught because he had done exactly that?

"You told so many lies to me," she said, sniffing, "I wonder if I can believe you at all."

Christopher stepped toward her. "I love you, Erienne. Whatever you may think, I never lied about that."

She stumbled back, knowing that if he touched her she would crumble, and there was much yet to be settled. "You lied about everything else! You said you were scarred . . ."

"And so I am. I bear the scar of your brother's shot . . . and a half-dozen other . . ."

"Burned!"

"That, too. There was a fire aboard one of my ships and in quenching it, a clot of flaming tar struck my leg and stuck there, burning. It left a scar, not great"—he stared at her, half smiling—"but enough to quench a maiden's curiosity."

Erienne stared at him in bemusement until she recalled the night her hand had moved along his thigh while he slept, and she suddenly realized that he had not been asleep at all. She turned away abruptly. "You said you were Lord Saxton's cousin."

"If you'll remember, my love, Anne said the Setons and Saxtons were cousins, which is true. You assumed the rest. I only played out the game."

"Oh, and how well you did, sir," she jeered. "In bed! Out of bed! You had me either way, whether it was as Lord Saxton or Christopher Seton."

He grinned. "Madam, I was not willing to gamble with so precious a prize."

Erienne backed around the bedside table as he advanced on her. The wall halted her retreat, and she found no other course of escape from the beast that stalked her. Christopher's eyes burned into her, and she could feel the resistance melting within her. The thought began to run through her mind that he was, after all, her husband, and it was quite proper to yield to his caresses, to his kisses, and to anything else he had in mind. Still, her pride had been stung, and she sought to rally a flagging will to her obedience, for in her mind he sorely begged a sound chastising.

An iron-thewed arm slipped about her waist and brought her against that broad, hard chest. She thought to remain passive in his embrace and did not struggle as his mouth lowered upon hers. As soon as their lips touched, however, she realized the idea was ludicrous and a gross miscalculation of her power to deny him, for the kiss went through her with the impact of a full broadside. His mouth slanted across hers with a ravening urgency that would not be denied, and the searing lips sent little tremors of delight boring down through her body, flicking every nerve until they were aflame with desire. Her world began to tilt, and she was lost in a dreamy limbo where the only thing that mattered was the closeness of his muscular body and the circling protection of his arms. She became aware that her arms were looped tightly about his neck, and she was returning his kiss with a fervor that betrayed her own longing. Her fingers brushed the familiar scar, and she thrust aside any lingering thoughts of resistance. There was, after all, no need to play the injured maid when she was very, very content with the turn of the day.

Christopher raised his head to caress her lips tightly with his own and then stepped backward toward the bed, drawing her with him.

" 'Tis daylight," she murmured, glancing toward the windows.

"I know." His gaze probed with flaming warmth into hers, compelling her to follow. There was no need for words. They were no longer bound to darkness, and he desired her now. When the back of his legs touched the bed, he halted and lowered his face to hers once again. His mouth leisurely possessed hers while his hands plucked at the fastenings of his breeches.

"Will you unfasten me, please?" she breathed against his mouth. He raised his head, and his reply burned in his eyes. She turned, lifting her hair aside, and waited while he complied. He pushed the gown over her shoulders, and a shiver of pleasure ran through her as his hand caressed her naked skin. His lips replaced his fingers, and she bent her head forward, closing her eyes in ecstasy as his warm kisses traced a path along her nape. She leaned forward, dropping the bodice away from her, and tugged her arms free of the sleeves. The bed creaked as he sat on its edge, and she cast a glance over her shoulder to find him ridding himself of the breeches. He tossed them aside, and Erienne did not miss the slight wince of pain that flickered over his countenance as he leaned back into the pillows. It was quickly gone, and he seemed unconcerned with his manly display as he awaited her.

"You're lagging, madam," he chided with a grin, eliciting a small start from her as he gave her rump a light, playful slap with the back of his hand.

Erienne struggled with the pangs of uncertainty. Making love in the dark had kept much from view, and though her hands had become familiar with his body, to see him naked in the full light of day was rather startling. Despite the scars, he was a most impressive specimen, and since she was his wife, she would just have to get used to seeing him without the adornment of clothes.

She smiled as she faced him, deciding such a task would not be so difficult. "You ought to be coddling your wounds instead of embarking on such activity, my lord."

"Never fear, madam." His smile was almost a leer. "I have a thing or two more to teach you in the way of pleasing a man."

"You would have me please you, my lord?" she asked warmly.

The heat of his gaze set her blood on fire and struck sparks along her flesh. "My fondest dream, madam."

Her mouth curved in a sublime smile while her eyes grew dark and sultry, burning into his and promising him more than he had ever expected. She moved with sensuous grace before him, and his eyes followed where she led them. Deliberately she pulled the straps of her chemise off her shoulders, allowing the garment to dip low over her breasts while she worked behind her waist at the ties of her petticoat. When she bent to push the gown and petticoats free of her hips, the stiff-boned corset pressed her bosom upward, threatening the sagging chemise with an overflow. The garments fell to her feet, and the straps slid another degree, exposing part of a soft peak above the lace trim as she worked to free her stays. The corset was thrown atop his breeches, and she shrugged, letting the chemise slip over her hips and then to the floor.

Christopher's eyes smoldered with desire as they moved with leisured thoroughness over the soft, delicately hued breasts, on downward to the slender curve of her waist and the long, sleek limbs. He held out a hand in invitation, and her eyes in turn slowly raked the long length of him, nearly taking his breath away when they paused in bold admiration. She knelt on the bed beside him and leaned down to press her lips to his. Her small, darting tongue played chase with his, tasting the stronger brew of brandy, while her roaming hand made him catch his breath at the pleasure it evoked. Her mouth dipped to where his heart pounded in his chest, and a kiss touched that broad expanse above the bandages, then her lips came back to press against his throat while her tongue lightly traced his skin. Her fingers glided over him, and the building force of passion threatened the crumbling wall of his restraint, and each kiss that touched his skin pushed him farther to the brink. He was a fuse ready to be ignited, and her touch was the flaming torch that sparked and teased.

His hands lifted her, and he led her with purposeful intent, bold in his knowledge and gentle in his regard of her. He felt the warmth go through his body as she covered him, and he saw her eyes go soft and limpid, her lips part as a small shiver went through her. She moved against him with silken grace, turning their passions end over end in an ever-rushing race. It was a moment meant to be, a time when they came together in full awareness of each other, eternally bound by their love and union, like the stars in the heavens, the fish in the sea, unable to exist long without the other. She was his; he was hers. The world could fall apart, and they'd still be one. Conflicts and angers were banished, and whispered words of love mingled with sighs of ecstasy as they were caught together in a rapturous expression of their love.

Twenty-one

A fortnight passed in heavenly peace, yet with a speed that equaled the degree of its pleasure. The spring weather was nervous and seemed determined not to settle on any path. On an evening it spat great clinging flakes of snow, and with the dawn, drizzling rains misted the gently swelling bosom of the moors and ran in crystalling rivulets down the stoic, rocky faces of the seaward cliffs. Seabirds mounted swirling currents in spiraling pairs, while hawks hurled piercing cries of challenge to all who ventured on their lands. In the greening bushes tits and peewees chortled the reveling songs of spring. Another evening fell, and the gloaming brought the throaty croaks of frogs and the distant trill of a bashful nightingale.

For Erienne, it seemed that she could hardly start upon a day before it was gone. In the evenings she nestled in her husband's arms, and when not stirred to impassioned heights, she simply rested upon that oak-ribbed chest, feeling the brush of his lips on her brow or a nuzzling kiss against her ear. She came to know his face, the way his lips twitched or the corners dipped when he was about some inanity. Though his eyes wrinkled slightly when a mediocrity smote his fancy, he could just as easily give uproarious vent in rich appreciation when she failed to see the cause for mirth. She came to learn there was a baseness to him too, when he would lift her in his arms and brook no denial, when his kisses could be fierce and demanding, his passion all-consuming. His amorous zeal left her panting and breathless but thoroughly content in the warm security of his embrace. In those moments after their passion was spent when she could still feel the heat of him burning through her, she would look up into his face with eyes warmed with love. He was the husband that women dreamt of having for their own, and Erienne was still somewhat stunned by the realization that he was hers.

In those days she also found in him a sensitivity that made him capable of perceiving her need for tenderness. With quiet serenity he could admire the darting flight of a swift or sit for long moments with his arms folded about her while they silently enjoyed the dying glories of a day.

His moods were like the changing character of the seasons and weather, sometimes infinitely gentle, at other times curt and angry because of some injustice or offense. She learned to read the tensing muscles in his cheeks and the lowering of the brows as forewarnings of a storm and was thankful that his anger was never carelessly applied or anything but just. He could be a source of delight as he displayed a depth of brawny tenderness that lent him an almost boyish exuberance, and yet he was totally a man, sure of himself and at ease with the world.

At first, Christopher rested to let the healing progress. Before the first week was past, he began to rise at the first gray light. Easing from her side, he would draw a pair of breeches over his naked loins and stoke the fire to chase the chill from the room, then in the growing light near the windows, he would lift the sword to test the arm and try a thrust, only to wince and rub the side when it would not bear the stress. He moved slowly, trying not to aggravate the wound, stretching forward and back, lifting and lowering the piece, attempting a thrust again, and then starting over.

As the second week began, he could swing the sword with enough force to snip a candle or a finger-sized twig. The blade twinkled as he executed a series of attacks and ripostes too fast for the eye to follow. Erienne watched silently from the bed with a mixture of pride and worry, marveling at the flexing muscles across his shoulders and back, yet dreading that time when he would be well enough to venture forth as the night rider.

"You make me afraid," she murmured one morning when he came back to sit beside her on the bed. "The thought plagues me that I will see you slain and, like your mother, will have to flee to find a haven for our babe."

"By the grace of God, madam, I will prove wiser than my enemy." He lay back across the bed, resting his head in her lap while he reached up a hand to caress softly her smooth, flat belly through the light fabric of her nightgown. "I have a fancy to see our offspring and plant other seeds where this one grows, so you needn't fret that I'll be foolhardy, my love."

Erienne ran her fingers through his hair. "I hope the hour quickly approaches when you may give up the mask and guise. I want to tell the world and all the women in it that you're mine." She shrugged lightly. "'Twould not overburden me to tell my father of our marriage, either."

Christopher chuckled. "He'll croak."

Erienne giggled and leaned over him. "Aye, that he will. Louder than any wily toad that e'er's been born. He'll stamp and snort and claim injustice, but with your babe growing in me, I doubt that anyone will lend an ear to the question of annulment." Her eyes gleamed with twinkling humor. "Besides, what suitor would look twice at me when I've grown fat with child?"

Christopher raised up an elbow and leered at her. "Madam, if you think your father or any suitor could get past me to try to separate us, then let me assure you that the highwaymen have not yet seen such a wrath that I would display should that happen." His brow raised in question. "Do you doubt what I say?"

Erienne gave a flirtatious shrug, then rolled to the edge of the bed and bounced to her feet with light, lilting laughter floating behind her. Before she could catch up her robe, however, Christopher swung around the end of the bed and caught her close against him, slipping his arms around her waist and holding her tightly to him. Their lips met in a long, slow kiss of love, and after he drew away it was a full moment or more before Erienne opened her eyes to find the grayish-green ones smiling into hers, and her arms tightly clasped about his neck.

"I believe you," she breathed unsteadily.

His mouth returned to savor hers for another blissful eternity, and when he raised his head again, she released a long sigh.

"I can understand why you never kissed me as Lord Saxton. I'd have known you instantly."

" 'Twas what I feared, madam, but you don't know how hard it was to resist the urge." His kisses played upon her lips, touching as light as a butterfly's wings, then he set her away from him and released a long breath. "As much as I would rather spend the day with you, madam, I suppose I must don my disguise and venture from these chambers."

"There's always tonight," she whispered.

He grinned down at her. "I won't be bound to darkness again."

"We could always light a candle," she suggested sweetly.

"Better yet," his grin widened, "just come when I beckon."

Except for Bundy and Aggie, none of the other servants knew the truth. When the master's chamber was not in use, Aggie kept it locked, and no one entered Erienne's rooms without approval. The others wondered at the seclusion of the master and his lady, and despite their many guesses, none came even close to the truth. When Lord Saxton finally descended to the realms of earth with his lady at his side, their worries faded. Even then, some detected a subtle change in the mistress. They laid the reason for the buoyant spirits to her husband's convalescence and continued to admire her devotion to such a fearsome man. This attitude was seen in her unhesitating acceptance of the hand or arm he offered, the quick, sweet smile when she looked up into the face of the mask, and her readiness to be near or to touch him.

The Lady Erienne was most beautiful, and her airy laughter and light, ever-ready humor infected them all. With her presence, it seemed the sun shone brighter and the day grew warmer. Their hearts were lightened, and they attacked the chores of spring with a zealous determination to please her. The great stone hall came alive and began to function and once more took on an air of being something more than a dark, gray mansion.

Spring spread across the countryside like ripples over a pond. The tenants dragged out plows, curried horses and trimmed and re-shod their feet, and otherwise prepared for the vernal breaking of the land. The enchanted couple strolled about the grounds of the manse, and the pace of the crippled one gave the spry one ample time to investigate each wonder. In the folds there were newborn lambs, and near the stable a new filly tippled along on shaky limbs behind her mother. An arrogant pair of geese led their furry goslings to a pond, then they hissed and stretched their necks as the couple passed. Erienne's delighted laughter gave them pause, and they tipped their heads in wonder at this unknown sound, then returned to count their brood with diligence as the master and his lady moved on.

The path wound outward, down behind the house, out across the open space, and among the trees. Once in the shadows and out of sight from those above, Lord Saxton straightened and moved with more agility as they hurried hand in hand through the dappled gloom. They reached the cottage, and the black-garbed man scooped the lithe form into his arms before plunging through the doorway. Had a spy been set to observe, they would have seen nearly an hour's space of time elapse before the two emerged again. That very same spy could only speculate as to the activities within, for when they did come forth, it was as Christopher Seton and Erienne Saxton.

Around the glade this pair of woodland nymphs danced. He swept her in a waltz to a duet that was sometimes off tune, sometimes rent with giggling and laughter as they made their own music. A breathless Erienne fell to a sun-dappled hummock of deep, soft moss, and laughing for the pure thrill of the day, she spread her arms, creating a comely yellow-hued flower on the dark green sward while seeming every bit as fragile as a blossom to the man who watched her. With bliss-bedazzled eyes, she gazed through the treetops overhead where swaying branches, bedecked in the first bright green of spring, caressed the underbellies of the freshlet zephyrs, and the fleecy white clouds raced like frolicking sheep across an azure lea. Small birds played courting games, and the earlier ones tended nests with single-minded perseverance. A sprightly squirrel leapt across the spaces, and a larger one followed, bemused at the sudden coyness of his mate.

Christopher came to Erienne and sank to his knees on the thick, soft carpet, then bracing his hands on either side of her, slowly lowered himself until his chest touched her bosom. For a long moment he kissed those blushing lips that opened to him and welcomed him with an eagerness that belied the once-cool maid. Then he lifted her arm and lay beside her, keeping her hand in his as he shared her viewpoint of the day. They whispered sweet inanities, talked of dreams, hopes, and other things, as lovers are wont to do. Erienne turned on her side and taking care to keep her hand in the warm nest, ran her other fingers through his tousled hair.

"You need a shearing, milord," she teased.

He rolled his head until he could look up into those amethyst eyes. "And does my lady see me as an innocent lamb ready to be clipped?" At her doubtful gaze, he questioned further. "Or rather a lusting, long-maned beast? A zealous suitor come to seduce you?"

Erienne's eyes brightened, and she nodded quickly to his inquiry.

"A love-smitten swain? A silver-armored knight upon a white horse charging down to rescue you?"

"Aye, all of that," she agreed through a giggle. She came to her knees and grasped his shirt front with both hands. "All of that and more." She bent to place a honeyed kiss upon his lips, then sitting back, spoke huskily. "I see you as my husband, as the father of my child, as my succor against the storm, protector of my home, and lord of yonder manse. But most of all, I see you as the love of my life."

Christopher raised a hand to sweep aside her tumbled hair, then resting it at her nape, pulled her to him. The kiss was long and mutual while she lay upon his chest and his hand caressed the silken softness of her shoulder.

"Aye," he breathed, "and one day soon I shall throw away the mask, and we shall stride the world as nothing more than what we are." He looked at her and with a finger traced the delicate outline of her ear. "There is much evil yet to set at rest, and to that end I still am sworn, but 'twill be soon, my sweet. I promise you. 'Twill be soon."

They finally rose and wandered farther, at one point pulling off their shoes and stockings to stroll barefoot along the soft turf that edged the brook wandering through the glade. Though they would have held it back, the sun crossed the sky, and as it lowered in the west, Lord Saxton led his lady up the hill. The pair was silent, somewhat subdued, for the disguise weighed heavily upon the youthful cheer of the afternoon. They supped leisurely in her chamber and sat with hands entwined across the narrow table. With heads close together, they spoke in low voices of things best known to lovers and the like.

The fortnight waned and then was gone, and like a signal from the depths of Hades, the seclusion of the hall was broken. The rattletrap livery from Mawbry clattered down the road behind an ancient nag and careened on wobbly wheels up the drive to halt before the tower. Avery descended first, letting Farrell attend the baggage. The mayor waited patiently until the load was down, then strutted toward the driver, fumbling in his waistcoat and drawing forth several coins. He selected a smallish one and laid it boldly in the man's hand.

"Here! Keep it all," he magnanimously insisted. " 'Twas a goodly distance out so there's a little extra for yer trouble."

Avery turned away and completely missed the driver's dubious frown as that one stared at the meager wealth in his palm. The man bit the coin to test it, then giving a disgruntled snort, thrust the coin in his pocket and snatched up the reins angrily to set the horses into motion.

"Ye see?" Avery jerked his head in the direction of the departing conveyance and hefted a pair of small bags while Farrell struggled with a heavier one, a pair of muskets, and several pistols. "Ye gots ter figure it all. Now, at least, we'll get us a free ride back in that fine, fancy coach of his lordship."

"You should have let me warn Erienne we were both comin'," Farrell mumbled.

"Nonsense, lad. Ye're out here all the time, a body would think ye live here. I can't see as how they'll be offended if I come along with ye."

"Lord Saxton did not take kindly to you threatening Erienne the last time you were here."

"The little twit," Avery fussed. "She needs more'n me hand laid to her for her high-minded arrogance." He gestured angrily to the tower looming overhead. "She's got all this, and still she ain't offered ter share a bit o' it with her poor father. Such a grand, huge place, 'tis a pity they have so much and we so little. If it weren't for me, the two of 'em would not be together now."

Farrell gave his sire a doubtful stare, but the mayor seemed oblivious to the fact that any could find fault with him. Avery dropped his bags carelessly beside the front door, then tugged his waistcoat down over his sagging paunch before he reached forward and swung the heavy knocker against the door.

Answering the summons, Paine admitted the visitors into the foyer, solicitously assisting Farrell with his cumbersome burdens and earning a dark frown from the father. "The master hasn't been feeling well these past weeks," the servant announced. "He's in his chamber now taking the noon meal with the mistress. Would you care to wait in the hall for them."

Avery turned a jaundiced eye upon the man and tried not to sound too hopeful. "Ye say his lordship's sick? Anything serious?"

"I suppose 'twas bad enough for a while, sir. The mistress hardly left his side, but the master is coming along very nicely now." Paine reached to take the weapons from Farrell. "I'll take these upstairs with your bags, sir." He looked to Avery. "Will you also be staying?"

Avery nudged his bags to one side as he cleared his throat. "Aye, I thought whilst Farrell was here, I'd spend some time visitin' with me daughter."

"Very good, sir. I shall return for your baggage when a room is readied for you."

Paine climbed the stairs with his burden, and when he had disappeared out of sight, Avery gave a contemptuous snort. "Stupid girl! His lordship bein' without next o' kin, she'd be a wealthy widow if he were to keel over dead."

Farrell remained mute, but the gleam in his eyes became brittle, and the lines of his mouth tightened in aggravation. He was beginning to understand Erienne's disenchantment with their sire and wondered if he would be able to enjoy any part of this visit. He spent less and less time at home, preferring to travel to York to visit Miss Becker and her mother rather than listen to the mewling complaints that persisted from morning till night.

Erienne descended the stairs in a rush, smoothing her hair and arranging her collar in place. She paused at the archway leading into the great chamber, discovering she had left her bodice partly undone in her haste, and gave herself a moment to catch her breath and repair her appearance. Her cheeks were flushed, and she felt slightly misaligned for the moment, for Aggie's knock had sounded on the master's chamber door at a most inopportune time. The noon meal had been left to cool on the small table while Christopher's amorous bent had warmed them both. The untimely interruption and the announcement that the mayor had come for a visit had descended upon them with the effect of a chilling bath, and they had broken apart in ruffled haste.

Erienne crossed the hall, managing a guise of serenity as she greeted her kin. Going to her brother, she raised on tiptoe and left a kiss on his cheek before she turned and bestowed a smile upon her sire.

"Father, it has been some time since you were out," she stated pleasantly. "Will you have time to stay with us for a while?"

"I thought I would, though I might o' felt a wee more welcome if I'da been asked ter come." He thrust his thumbs into the armholes of his waistcoat and peered at his daughter, whose smile had not wavered, noting that she did not rush to apologize or make excuses.

"Come sit before the hearth and have a glass of wine," she bade, unaffected by his reproach. "You both must be famished after your long ride. I'll have the cook prepare something for you while we chat."

At her summons Aggie came in and bustled about the table, setting out plates and silverware while Erienne poured a light wine and handed the goblets to the men. Avery sipped and frowned heavily, then cleared his throat loudly to gain his daughter's attention.

"Ah, girl. Do ye s'pose ye have somethin' more fittin' ter clear the road dust from a man's throat?"

Erienne laughed disarmingly. "Drink your wine, Father. 'Tis better for you. In another moment there'll be food and a good brandy afterward."

The man sulked, but not being one to set aside an undrained glass of any brew, he reluctantly proceeded to the task.

As she handed Farrell his libation, Erienne gently touched his motionless right limb. "How is your arm, Farrell?" she ventured. "Is it better?"

Farrell brightened a bit. "I was to York several weeks ago. If you'll remember, I borrowed Lord Saxton's carriage for the journey. I met a surgeon there, well acquainted with gunshot wounds. He believes the ball is still there, lodged against the joint, and that it might be what is blocking the movement. He thinks he can cut it out, but there's some risk with the arm." He lifted the mentioned member and shrugged. "I don't know which is worse, a shortened stump or a useless branch."

Erienne patted his shoulder soothingly. "We'll ask Lord Saxton. He has had much acquaintance with surgeons." She took a chair and gestured him into the one near her own. "But tell me, how did you manage with Miss—" The limp arm swung clumsily against her, and with the blow she caught his warning frown. "Mister . . . ah . . . the one who was going to hire you at the shipping office in Wirkinton?" It was the only thing she could think of on the spur of the moment. "What was his name?"

"Mr. Simpson." Farrell nodded slowly and smiled as he tasted his wine. "I'm thinking of looking for work in York now so I've dismissed that idea." He gestured with his glass toward Avery. "Of course, Father is fairly certain I am deserting him."

His sister laughed and tugged at his sleeve, leaning toward him and speaking as if in confidence. "He dotes upon you, Farrell. Humor the man in his old age."

"Harumph!" The throaty grunt indicated that Avery was following their conversation, at least close enough to catch the comment. He mumbled sourly. "Needles and darts and yer tongue-borne barbs are enough to prick me skin, girl."

"Salt seasons skins very well, Father, or haven't you heard?" Erienne replied pertly. Avery stared at her blankly until she waved a hand and laughed. "Never mind, Father. Finish your wine, and if you would like, I'll have Paine fetch a jug of ale from the larder. Perhaps that will be more to your liking."

"Harumph!" he grunted again and took a healthy draught, then wiped the back of his hand across his mouth. "Ye cannot buy a father's love with sweet temptations, girl."

She raised a brow and inquired sweetly, "You do not want the ale?"

Avery came from his chair in a huff. "Ye twist me words just like yer mother did! I said nothing o' the kind!" He paused and calmed a bit, seeking to temper his gruff tone, for he realized he could lose the very thing he desired. "I'll take the ale."

Amusement twinkled in Erienne's eyes, brightening them to a dazzling radiance. The suspicion that she was laughing at him was too much for Avery to bear. He thought to squelch her gaiety with a little prodding.

"There's some talk in town, 'bout yer Mr. Seton bein' the night rider." To his disappointment the smile stayed. He tried again. "In fact, Allan thinks he might be badly wounded or even dead, since he's not been about doin' mayhem."

Erienne shrugged casually. "With everyone chasing about the countryside after him, 'twould seem they would have found him by now. The sheriff came here to search for him . . ."

"Eh?" Avery came upright. "Why would Allan come here for the likes o' that blackguard?"

"Didn't you know?" Erienne asked in the perfect guise of innocence. "The Saxtons and Setons are cousins. Christopher has visited here several times since my marriage. He even escorted me to Lord Talbot's ball."

"He *what?!*" Avery barked, and then in sorely vexed aggravation, demanded, "Ye mean to tell me yer husband trusted that bastard with ye?!"

The dishes clanged on the table, and Erienne glanced quickly over her shoulder to see Aggie fumbling and snatching with the silverware. The woman's lips were tightly compressed, and when she looked up, it was to cast a glare at the mayor.

"Father, do be careful of your language here," Erienne advised, barely managing to maintain her own poise. The slur he cast was against the one she held most dear. "Someone might take offense."

He snorted. "Bah! I haven't a care what the servants might think."

"I wasn't speaking of the servants, Father." She met his bemused stare with a cool smile, almost daring him to question her.

It was Farrell who made the inquiry. "Erienne, you haven't come to tolerate the man, have you?"

Her manner softened as she faced him. "Farrell, I have heard many accusations against the man, but I have come to learn that most of them are false."

Farrell frowned. "But he accused Father of cheating."

Erienne gazed directly at her father, who lowered his head sheepishly between his shoulders. "I know that, Farrell, and I would suggest that you get to know the man yourself before you form a definite opinion. He might prove to be a valued friend."

"Have ye gone daft, girl?!" Avery asked sharply. "Look at what the man did ter poor Farrell's arm! He made the lad a useless cripple . . ."

"Father!" Erienne's eyes blazed with outrage, and in the face of her confrontation Avery's anger subsided. "Farrell is not a useless cripple, and I resent you calling him one!"

Aggie had drawn near and stood in polite silence until her mistress looked around. "Will the gentlemen"—she plied the word with a sidewise glare toward the mayor—"like to eat now, mum?"

Avery came out of his chair, indicating his eagerness, and Erienne nodded. The woman hurried back to the table and poured more wine, and the men followed. Erienne waited until Farrell and her father had settled themselves at the table, then made her excuses.

"I really must see what's keeping Lord Saxton. While I'm gone Aggie will serve you. Please enjoy yourselves."

Avery was not at a loss as to the procedure of helping himself to the bread and wine that had been placed on the table and, with both hands occupied, pointed his chin after his departing daughter.

"Gone ter swab his majesty's arse, no doubt." He swung a glare on Aggie, who gasped in surprise, then continued defiantly. "Why, the twit probably has ter bathe him like a babe."

Aggie met his gaze for a moment and glanced at the blushing face of Farrell, then hastily left them to serve themselves as she went to the kitchen. In an effort to control her rage, she braced her arms against the cutting table and, with narrowed eyes, perused the long length of a sharp knife, considering what such a weapon might do for the relief of Avery's belly. She dismissed several bloodthirsty alternatives before her gaze fell on the rack where a drying clump of cooking and medicinal herbs hung, and her eyes took on a definite gleam. She was well acquainted with the benefits of senna and flea-wort, and when liberally applied, either or both might create the reaction she desired.

"Just about the time he'll be eatin' again," she murmured to herself.

She set to work with a vengeance, adding the stuff to the bowl she had set aside to serve the mayor. The rarebit would hopefully hide the flavor, and since the man dined with such enthusiasm, he'd probably not even notice.

When she entered the great chamber again, she carried the steaming bowls on a silver tray. A smile aglow from ear to ear, she hastened to seat a serving before Farrell and then another in front of the mayor.

"A sample of rarebit, sir?" she sweetly cajoled as the aroma wafted through Avery's testing nostrils.

He lifted a spoonful and delicately tasted from the edge. He found it delicious and wasted no time devouring the dish until he was fully sated. Finally he pushed back from the table with an eruptive belch to demonstrate his admiration of the cook.

The rest of the afternoon was passed in a relaxed manner. The guests were taken on a tour of the stables, where some fine, hot-blooded mares were lovingly displayed. The only puzzlement was that no stallion seemed in attendance. Avery yawned his way through a tour of the grounds, which pointedly did not include the ruins of the east wing, and yearned for the comfort of the bed in his chamber upstairs.

The discussion turned to firearms, where Farrell was wont to lead it, and Lord Saxton expounded on the accuracy of a new Yankee gun of unusually light caliber and a newfangled barrel. Here Avery found some meat to chew and bluntly discoursed at length on the robust reliability of the English "Brown Bess" musket. Avery declared its accuracy to be phenomenal at thirty paces and scoffed at the idea that any gun could consistently kill a squirrel at better than a hundred. The unflinching mask gave no indication as to the effectiveness of his arguments, but a small demonstration was provided by the master of the house, and much to the mayor's chagrin, the matter was settled in favor of the colonial gun. Red-faced, Avery took note that both his daughter and son seemed pleased by the outcome of the exhibition, as if they favored the scarred one as their champion. He could excuse the girl, for she appeared unreasonably attached to the man, but his own son . . .

Avery's mouth drooped. Of late, Farrell had grown overly fond of guns and spent his hard-earned money to that end, leaving only a shallow pittance now and then for his doting father. It was also marked in Avery's mind that his son had lost his love for a night at the tavern amid good friends and many mugs of ale. More often than not, he traveled to York, and Avery was beginning to wonder if the journey was all for want of new employment.

I'm losin' the lad, he thought morosely, and to the likes of that black-garbed deformity, a man who's probably never sat a horse or shot a weapon in a good, hearty battle.

Avery hurried forward to join the other three, noticing that they had drawn ahead and again conversed in muted tones. Farrell seemed more inclined to converse privately with the two of them than with him, and on several occasions had grown silent when he came near, as if the lad were afraid to let him hear.

Avery trailed the group to the study, where that same foppish cripple withdrew to the protective shadows surrounding the harpsichord, removed his gloves, and ran through a long series of tunes. Avery hung close to Erienne, hoping that he would find a moment to broach the subject of his visit, that of his need for a liberal portion of her wealth. He had carefully planned his plea, and just this afternoon had enhanced it. Surely she would see that Farrell needed money and attention for his arm.

Much to his disgust, his daughter moved to the harpsichord and stood beside her husband. He dared not join them, for the moment seemed almost private between them as her soft, lilting voice combined with the notes of the instrument. It was a silly song of love, and he thought the girl daft to fill the man's head with such ideas of devotion. During the day Avery had taken special notice of statements indicating the lord and his lady had separate chambers, and he concluded that the show of affection did not extend to her bed.

It was to Avery's great relief that Paine entered to announce that dinner would be served. The four of them gathered at the candlelit table, Lord Saxton in the massive chair at the head, Erienne close upon his right, and the two men together on the opposite side. Both Farrell and Avery were quick to note that services were set only for the two of them and that Erienne merely accepted a glass of wine to sip. It puzzled the mayor, but he shrugged it off as some foible of the rich. As for himself, he accepted this opportunity to dine wealthily on the delicately prepared foods.

It was Farrell who made the inquiry after he had raised a glass to the health and fortunes of their host. He gestured to his sister's empty place and asked in puzzlement, "You do not eat with us tonight?"

Erienne smiled and began with an apology. "There is no affront intended, Farrell." She reached out and laid her hand upon the black-gloved one that rested near her own, squeezing it fondly. "My husband, as you know, prefers to dine in privacy, and I have chosen to join him this evening."

Avery was astounded that the girl would openly prefer the company of that twisted face while she dined rather than take her food with normal people. Pondering this development, he pursed his lips and leaned back in his chair. Women had always confused him, but this twit was waxing insane in her selectivity. First she dismissed all the suitors as being an ugly, ancient lot, and now she slavishly doted on her husband's every need, seeming ignorant of the fact that most folk thought him a monster of sorts. Why, she even clung brazenly to his arm and gazed upon him with idolizing tenderness, as if he were some noble knight.

A bowl containing a rich broth liberally laden with bits of vegetable and meat was placed before Avery, interrupting his musings. Paine refilled their goblets and set warm loaves of bread within their reach before withdrawing to a safe distance. Disdaining the knife, Avery broke off chunks of bread and began to dunk them in the soup. With the bread in one hand and the spoon in the other, he set about his meal. Every three or four spoonfuls, he sopped the bread and filled his mouth from the dripping piece. As he progressed, a path began to form between his shirtfront and the edge of the bowl.

Of a sudden, Avery paused. His eyes widened and his cheeks bulged with a half-squelched belch. A wet, gurgling rumble echoed through the room as his stomach rebelled, and Avery's neck grew red as he struggled with an unquenchable urge. Slowly it passed, and he relaxed. After a quick, sheepish glance about the table, the mayor bent himself to his task again. The bread dipped. Avery slobbered. The spoon made several round trips twixt dish and lip before a pained look came across his face again. The spoon clanked onto the plate, and his hands went beneath the table to clench each other. He squirmed and shuffled his feet while a red-and-white mottled appearance overtook his face. His jaw grew rigid, while his feet moved faster.

At last the pain receded. He glared down Farrell's questioning frown and stared at Erienne until she sipped her wine, though she continued to watch him over the rim of the glass. He might have imagined it, but even the blank helm of his host seemed to lift a puzzled brow. Avery pushed back the half-finished bowl, tossed down some wine, and morosely chewed a piece of dry bread. The combination seemed to settle his stomach, and the chatter between Farrell and Erienne gradually resumed.

By the time the second course arrived, Avery was well disposed to deal with it. In fact, when he caught a whiff of the fare, he was eager to accept it. Aggie even ladled an extra portion onto his plate, casting a smile in his direction. By the time Paine placed the dish before him, his mouth was watering, and before the man withdrew his arm, Avery held the knife and fork at the ready. He delved to the depths of his dish and, stuffing a large piece of meat into his mouth, chewed it in pure delight with eyes half closed. Swallowing heavily, he muttered as he dipped again.

" 'Tis good. 'Tis very good." He waved his knife about. "The best I've had in some time."

He plunged the laden fork into his gaping maw and was searching for another piece when suddenly the butts of both the fork and knife struck the table, still in his fists. He leaned forward, half rising. A slow groan of agony squeezed out between his clenched teeth, and his entire body went as rigid as some bronze statue, while his face turned much the same hue. He dropped the knife and fork, and his hands clenched the edge of the table until his knuckles grew white.

His teeth ground together, and he sucked in a quick, whistling breath. He held the pose for a moment, then in rapid syllables and an overloud voice he barked out, " 'Tis-such-a-comely-night-outside, urp! I-think-I'll-take-meself-out-for-a-little-walk."

He nodded an abrupt pardon, then fairly flew from the room, his coattails sailing out behind with the speed of his passage. The tower door thundered wide, then slammed back to latch solidly.

Farrell glanced at Erienne and shrugged. She looked at Paine, who in absolute stoic pose held his usual calm expression. Aggie's manner was much the same, though a darker shade of red was slowly creeping up her neck, and she seemed to have gained an odd twitch about her shoulders and a slight tic at the corner of her mouth. As Erienne continued to stare, the woman gave a strange choking cough and hurried from the room. When the door closed behind her, a muffled noise, much like the sound of suppressed laughter, drifted back to them.

By the following evening Avery's stomach had finally calmed enough to allow him to leave his room in quest of Erienne's quarters. The house was late, and everyone had retired for the night. He had determined it would be the last chance he would have to meet with her in private, for he and Farrell were planning to return to Mawbry the next morning. The previous night had been spent in a frenzied effort to find relief for his roiling bowels. He had no idea what malady had struck him; he would have blamed it on spoiled vittles except for the fact that none of the others seemed affected. Thus he felt considerably frayed by the worry that it might be of a serious nature, which only made him all the more anxious to secure a wealthy sum from his daughter.

Only a few candles remained lit along the wall of the upper hall. At his seemingly innocent inquiry, Farrell had given him instructions to the bedchambers of the lord and his lady. Avery followed the way carefully, stealthily creeping close to Lord Saxton's door to listen. No light came from beneath the portal, and no sound issued from the room, which encouraged him to believe the man was slumbering in peaceful repose.

More confident now, yet still wary of making a noise until he was assured that his daughter was alone, Avery went down the corridor to Erienne's room. This time he found a thin shaft of light shining from beneath the base of the door. Stepping near, he leaned an ear to the wooden planks. Much to his disappointment, he heard Erienne speaking in a muted tone, but hoping that it was only a servant she was with, he stayed. A burst of masculine laughter came from the room, and Avery almost stumbled back in shock before he collected himself and pressed his ear tighter against the door.

Erienne's bubbling reply erased any doubt as to her companion's identity. "Christopher, be serious. How can I even concentrate on finding a name for our babe if you tease me like that?"

Avery's eyes shot open wide, and his face took on a crimson hue comparable to the prior evening's. He wanted to bolt through the door, tear the filthy scoundrel from the girl, and pound him to a bloody pulp, but the fear that the man might do worse to him halted such a foolish idea. His caution did not slacken the rage that built within him. He despised Christopher Seton, and he fumed at the thought that the man had gotten to the twit and filled her belly with his seed. Kin or not, Lord Saxton was a fool to have trusted him with her. No wonder she could look so happy with Lord Saxton when this Seton rascal was crawling between her thighs at night.

Avery left the hall and made his way back to his room. The good he could see from this cuckolding was that his daughter might be willing to pay to hide the fact of her unfaithfulness, and that could prove beneficial to him.

Erienne left her husband's arms and ventured downstairs at an early hour the next morning. She was amazed to find her father waiting for her. The expression on his face, however, made her wary. His lips were pursed thoughtfully and his head was nestled in the collar of his frock coat, giving him the look of a smug turtle. His stare followed her unflinchingly as she crossed the room, and when she stepped close to set a cup of tea next to him, Erienne thought she detected a sneer.

"Is something wrong, Father?"

"Possibly."

She took the chair across from him and leisurely sipped her tea. "Is it something you wish to talk about?"

"Might be."

Not willing to prod him into a discussion that would no doubt be bent toward self-pity, she sipped her tea and waited.

Avery leaned his head against the tall back of the chair and let his gaze sweep the artifacts of chivalry, tapestries, and portraits that lined the walls. "Ye know, daughter, I was a generous man ter yer mother and me family. While I could afford it, ye wanted for nothin'."

Although she could have argued against his claim, Erienne held her silence. Avery Fleming had long been known as a man of self-indulgence, and it was only through the efforts of their mother that she and Farrell had had a home and as much tutoring as they did. She was not moved by his high opinion of himself.

"I've been hard pressed since yer mother died," he lamented. "While grievin' for her, I forgot meself sometimes, and I buried me sorrow at the gamin' tables. The day was filled with woe when I met that Yankee scoundrel and he accused me o' cheatin'."

"But you were," Erienne stated bluntly. When he gaped at her in surprise, she lifted a questioning brow. "You did admit it to me once, remember?"

Avery cleared his throat sharply and glanced away, shrugging. " 'Twas done in desperation." He flung up a hand as he defended his actions. "Besides, the man was well able ter afford the loss. 'Twas him or me, girl, and he wouldna've gone awantin', whereas I . . . well, ye see what he left me with."

"Father," Erienne's voice was flat, "cheating for a purse is no better than stealing, and you were cheating."

"And what do ye call it when yer mighty Christopher Seton flies about the countryside doin' murder?" he demanded.

Fire blazed in the dark blue eyes. "He has killed outlaws who, for the wanton murder of innocent folk, deserved to be slain." She waved a hand. "As for that, I have also killed. And Farrell. We came upon a band of thieves attacking a coach, and we fired upon them, killing several to save a girl."

"A girl?"

"Miss Becker." Erienne supplied the name with a cool smile. "If need be, she will support my statement and verify the fact that the night rider attacked the highwaymen and helped her and Farrell to escape."

Avery's curiosity was pricked. "Farrell didn't tell me 'bout her."

Erienne remembered her brother's reluctance to confide in their father and was not willing to say more. "Farrell probably prefers to tell you himself. I shall say no more."

A brief silence ensued before the mayor spoke again. "You seem ter be content with yerself, girl. Living here with his lordship 'pears ter agree with ye."

"I am most content, Father. Perhaps more than you are able to understand."

"Oh, I understand, all right." His chin lowered into his collar, and his smile was blatantly smug.

Erienne contemplated her father, wondering what little tidbit he was savoring. "Do you have something else you wish to discuss?"

He studied his short, stubby fingers for a brief span of time. " 'Tis come ter me that ye've not been at all generous with yer kin since ye've gotten yerself a title and all."

"I haven't heard Farrell complaining," she replied.

"The poor lad's been blinded by yer meager show o' kindness, but what really have ye done for him? Have ye been in the least bit charitable or sympathetic to his lameness? Is he any richer for comin' out here? Nay, he's had ter work hard for the bit o' coin he has."

"In my opinion Farrell's character has advanced considerably since he stopped rolling in self-pity and did something for himself," Erienne stated with conviction and a bit of anger. "Charity or sympathy, if carried to extreme, can be the ruination of a good man. A person builds self-esteem after seeing the labors of his own hands reap a plentiful harvest. Aye, we should be charitable and kind to the less fortunate, but helping them do for themselves is infinitely more chari-table than allowing them to mope about in self-pity. Good, honest work is valuable to one's well-being. Besides," she couldn't resist add-ing, "it gives them less time to dawdle around a gaming table."

Avery shot a glare at her. "Ye've never forgiven me for sellin' ye off at the roup, have ye?"

"I detested the way you sold me," she admitted. A slight smile curved her lips as she smoothed her skirts. "But I can see naught but good from it. I love the man I married, and I bear his child . . ."

"Is it his?" he asked sharply. "Or that bastard's ye had in yer room las' night?"

Erienne's gaze flew up in surprise, and her heart gave a fearful lurch. "What do you mean?"

"I come 'round ter have a talk with ye, and ye had that devil Seton in yer room with ye, right 'neath yer husband's nose. An' I heard ye laughin' 'bout the babe ye had made together. Ye're carryin' Seton's bastard in yer belly, not yer husband's."

Erienne's cheeks warmed considerably. She wanted desperately to retort with the truth, but she knew the folly of that. It was far better

if her father thought her unfaithful than to jeopardize the life of the man she loved.

"Ye can't deny it, can ye?" Avery's half-sneering, half-gloating grin tore at the mettle of her pride. "Ye've played Seton's doxie, and ye've gotten yerself with babe. O' course, ye ain't plannin' on tellin' Lord Saxton the seed what's sprouted ain't his."

Erienne suffered through his sneers with a tight-lipped silence, but inwardly she seethed.

"I suppose I'll be havin' ter hold me tongue too." He eyed her narrowly. " 'Twould make it easier for me if I knew ye cared 'bout me more'n ye do, if ye sent a joint o' lamb or a fat goose for me table now and then. Why, I even have ter cook me own vittles, without nary a one ter do for me, either ter wash me clothes or keep me house tidy. Considerin' all the servants ye have here, I don't see where 'twould hurt ye none ter send someone ter care for me. But then again, any you'd send would be wantin' wages, and I've little enough coin ter spare. As ter that, I could use a new coat, a pair o' shoes, and a few shillin's or so ter jingle in me purse. I'm not askin' much, ye understand, just a bit ter see me comfortable."

Erienne came up slowly from her chair, incensed at his gall. The idea that he could try to gain a reward for keeping quiet was despicable. As usual, he was only concerned about what he could reap from this affair. "How dare you try to wheedle coin from me. All my life I have heard you complain about your poor lot, but I will hear no more. I have seen how you use people to gain some wee bit of wealth for yourself. You used my mother, my brother, and myself. You tried to use Christopher, but he would have none of it, so you set Farrell to fight for your pitiful honor, such as it was. Now you seek to use me again, but I will have none of it."

"Ye've a hard heart, girl!" he accused angrily. He flung himself from his chair and paced irately in front of her. "Ye act so high and proud, even when ye're takin' a criminal in yer bed, and ye cannot even yield yer own father a few coins ter make his lot in life easier ter bear. I've gots ter walk 'bout the village and face me friends, tryin' ter hold me head up high." He stopped and banged his fist on the table beside her, demanding, "Dammit, girl! What would ye do if I informed Lord Saxton 'bout yer cuckoldin' him with that Seton bastard?"

He glared at her and would have spoken further, but a scrape of a hard sole against the floor made him turn and stare with sagging jaw. Lord Saxton was coming across the room toward them from the tower, dragging his cumbered foot across the stone. Taking up a stance beside his wife, he faced the mayor.

"Did I hear my name mentioned?" His low, grating voice filled the sudden silence of the room. "Was there something you wished to speak with me about, Mayor?"

Nervously Avery glanced at Erienne and was amazed by her serenity. It seemed she almost dared him to speak. Avery could not make the words come forth, though Lord Saxton waited patiently for an answer. His lordship was the one person he was afraid to rile. He knew too well that the man doted on the girl and would not take kindly to being informed of her indiscretion, and when roused, his rage might spill over on the one who bore the news. "Me girl and me were havin' a discussion, milord." Avery cleared his throat awkwardly. "It has naught ter do with ye."

"Anything to do with my wife concerns me, Mayor," Lord Saxton assured him almost pleasantly. "I fear my fondness for her tends to make me somewhat overly protective. You do understand, don't you?"

Avery nodded, not daring to say ought against her, for surely this man would not heed his counsel in any kind of a gracious manner.

Twenty-two

Regret can be a worrisome thing sometimes, especially when the matter done or not done can lead to rather serious consequences for those involved. Erienne did not trust her father, and if he spilled his precious news to the sheriff or anyone else, it might prove disastrous for the one she loved. She had begun to fear that she had been too hasty in denying his request. A tasty morsel had been known to keep a whining dog quiet.

Coming to a conclusion, Erienne dressed in a gown of iridescent blue silk, the bodice of which closed with a multitude of tiny buttons running from the high collar to the pointed waist. She called for the carriage to be brought around, then went to her husband's chamber to inform him of her intention to visit her kin. Christopher was involved with the account books for the hall, but he readily pushed them aside to bestow on her a lengthy kiss, ardently given to remind her throughout the day that he would be eagerly anticipating her return. She giggled as he whispered a wanton promise in her ear, then with a sigh drew away, blowing back a kiss as she stepped to the door. He enjoyed the swig of her bustle until she was out of sight, and it was almost a pain to return to the dry, dull figures written on parchment.

Spring had touched the North country with fresh color. The hills were greener, the sky bluer, the streams and rippling rivulets shone clearer as they tumbled over their rocky beds. White, puffy clouds glided overhead, pushed before a light, airy breeze, while the short, new grass was ruffled beneath its touch. It was a fine day to be out and about, and as Erienne journeyed southward she hoped that it would not be torn asunder by her visit to the cottage.

The anxiety that had plagued her since her father's departure from Saxton Hall the week before diminished somewhat as she came in sight of Mawbry. The wheels of the conveyance rattled over the bridge, and Tanner pulled to a halt before the familiar cottage. The footman jumped down and hurried to open the door and place a step for his mistress.

During her absence from the dwelling, Erienne had always held the same vision in her mind of the way it had looked when she had left it. Though only a brief few months had passed, the façade seemed strange to her. The small garden in front of the cottage had known no spring tilling, and dried stalks bearing yesteryear's blossoms were sad reminders of their earlier beauty.

Bidding Tanner to wait, Erienne approached the door, pushing back the hood of her cloak. She paused on the step with her hand poised to knock, recalling that ecstatic moment when Christopher had first come to call and her heart had raced with the hope that he would be the one she would wed. She smiled at the memory. Compared to the men her father had paraded before her eye, he had seemed like a flawless knight.

Her knuckles rapped lightly, and in a moment she heard footsteps plodding to the door. The portal swung open, and Avery's rumpled form appeared. The long tail of a nightshirt was stuffed haphazardly into a pair of loose breeches that hung from tattered braces, and from it all issued forth a sour odor of sweat and ale. When he saw her, surprise momentarily touched his unshaven face, then an almost leering smile spread across his lips.

"Lady Saxton!" He stepped back and swept his arm inward in a mockingly gallant gesture. "Won't ye step into me humble dwellin'?"

Erienne's eyes passed lightly over the cluttered interior as she moved in. It was immediately evident that her father lacked the ambition to set his house in order in more ways than one.

"Have ye come ter see me, or is it Farrell ye be wantin'? The lad went to York, and heaven only knows when he'll be back."

"I came to see you, Father."

"Oh?" Avery closed the door and came around to stare at her as if he found her reply hard to believe.

"I thought over what we talked about." She could not manage a smile as she drew a small purse from beneath her cloak. "And though I detest the idea of being threatened, I have determined a small allowance could be offered for your comfort."

"That's grand o' ye!" He chortled sneeringly and moved on into the parlor. As he poured himself a libation, he spoke over his shoulder. "'Tis strange ye comin' here today."

Erienne followed him into the room and removed a rumpled shirt from a chair before perching on its edge. "Why is it strange?"

"The sheriff came ter see me."

"Oh?" It was her turn to use the single word in a questioning tone, and she waited to hear what that brigand was up to.

"Aye." Avery moved to stand beside the window and peered through it, speaking in a museful vein. "I had a long discussion with him. It seems Lord Talbot has grown displeased with me over some frivolous matter and has threatened to dismiss me." When no answer came from his daughter, he continued. "I sought some way to placate him, and thought perhaps if me and the sheriff were ter bring in yer lover and string him up before the townfolk, Lord Talbot might prove ter be in a more forgivin' mood."

Suspicious fear reared up like a sharp-fanged beast in Erienne's breast, and her sudden wariness was evident in her tone. "What have you done, Father?"

He casually strolled about the room until he stood between her and the hall. Seeming to settle himself in place, he lifted his thick shoulders in a careless shrug. "I told Allan Parker what I knew . . . about ye and yer lover, I mean."

"How could you?!" She came to her feet in outrage. "How could you so blithely betray your own kin?"

Avery snorted. "Ye're no kin o' mine, girl."

Her hand flew to her throat as a shocked gasp emitted from it. "What are you saying?"

He braced his short legs slightly apart and folded his arms across his chest. "Ye ain't no daughter o' mine. Ye're that Irishman's brat."

Erienne shook her head in disbelief. "Mother would never have played you false with another man."

The mayor jeered. "The seed was already growin' before I met yer ma. She had taken up with the bloke, married him against her family's wishes, and then hardly a fortnight later he was hanged. Yer ma would not wed me unless she told me the truth 'bout ye bein' there already growin' in her belly, but all these years I've wished I'd never known. "Twas a sour thing ter swallow. All I could think o' was her in his arms." His upper lip curled back. "She never stopped lovin' him. I saw the way she'd look at ye, and ye bein' the very image o' him."

"If you met my mother after my father was hanged," Erienne inquired slowly, as if she found it hard to grasp what he said, "how could you have known—"

"What he looked like?" Avery finished for her. He laughed caustically. "Yer ma never knew it, but I was the one what gave the final orders ter hang the man." He shrugged beneath Erienne's stunned stare. "I didn't know yer ma at the time, but that wouldna've stopped me. The man was arrogant, claimed ter be some lord instead o' the bastard he was. I can still see him stridin' in front of the guards as if the thought o' dyin' was something ter be laughed at. Oh, he was a handsome one with his black hair and deep blue eyes. He was tall and lean-waisted, like yer lover. A man like me could never have taken a maid from his arms. All those years yer ma lived, she mourned after him. When ye were born, I saw the joy leap in her eye. Ye were his, all right, and none o' mine. Riorda O'Keefe, a man who has haunted me all these many years."

A frown furrowed Erienne's brow, then slowly faded as a rueful smile replaced it. "And you, Father? Nay, never that title again. Henceforth, I shall address you as anything but that." She reformed her statement. "And you, sir, have haunted me all these many years."

"Me?" Avery shook his head in confusion. "What do ye mean, girl?"

"You will probably never fully understand, but you have lifted a great burden from me. All these years I thought your blood was mine, and I am most relieved to find that false." She tucked the small purse back in her cloak and approached him, looking him squarely in the eye. "I give you a warning, Mayor. I shall not be as forgiving as my mother. If you pursue the hanging of Christopher Seton beyond this moment, I shall live to see you hanged and many with you."

Avery wondered at the spine of steel the twit had found. His own was pricked by little barbs of apprehension, for he was convinced that she meant every word she said.

"I will give you a bit of further advice in return for your tender care, sir," she stressed the last words sneeringly. "If you would avoid a hanging yourself, I bid you hold yourself a goodly distance from Sheriff Parker and his friends."

"And why, pray tell? Tell me," he bade derisively, taking high offense at her words. "Perhaps yer lordly Saxton has a comfortable position for an old man. After the whole tale is told, will he ever listen to his wife? Why should I cast off me friends on the say o' an adulteress?"

Erienne's eyes glittered with a coldness that should have chilled him to the bone. "I have given you a warning. Do with it as you will. Allan Parker has no friends, and he may learn something new of ropes before all this has come to an end."

"And what will that be, Lady Saxton?" a new voice from behind her questioned. "Who will teach me more about ropes?"

She whirled on her heel, and her breath froze as Allan Parker moved with leisured stride into the room. A pair of his henchmen followed close on his heels. The kitchen door swung shut behind them, and the sound made her start. The cruel horror of the robbery she had witnessed came back to her, and the almost gentle smile on his face became a savage leer of evil. She spun about to flee, but Avery's arm shot out, and she was caught and held fast in his grasp. Her intended scream was cut short by the sheriff's hand clamped ruthlessly over her mouth.

One of the men snatched a cord from the drapery, and as Parker pulled a gag across her mouth against a possible outcry, the man bound her wrists firmly together in front of her. The sheriff shoved her down in a chair and jerked his thumb toward the door.

"Fleming, get rid of that coach and driver," he commanded tersely. "Send them home. Say that she's spending the day."

Avery's concern was rampant. The purse she had tucked away was uppermost in his mind, and he was loath to lose the possibility of others that could follow. "Ye wouldn't be hurtin' me lil' girl, now, would ye?"

"Of course not, Avery." Parker threw his arm across the other's shoulder and guided him toward the door as he explained, "But with bait like this, we could just catch us a Mr. Seton. That should put us on Talbot's good side, eh?"

Avery nodded eagerly in newfound wisdom and opened the door

as the sheriff stepped out of sight. The mayor cleared his throat and called, "Ho there, Mr. Tanner."

The coachman looked around. "Aye, sir?"

"Ah . . . me daughter wants ter spend the day with me. She said ter take yerself on home."

Tanner and the footman exchanged uneasy glances, and frowning, the driver slowly approached the cottage. "Lord Saxton bade me to watch over his lady. I must await her return."

Avery waved him off with a loud guffaw. "Have no fear, laddie. She'll be safe enough with her own father." Avery gestured toward the inn. "Have yerself an ale or rum ter warm yer innards. Tell them ter put it on the mayor's account, and I'll send her ladyship home in the livery before dark. Now be off with ye."

Tanner was reluctant to leave, but there was not much point in further argument. Climbing to the driver's seat, he clucked the horses into motion, swinging them past the inn without a pause and urging them into a fast gallop when they cleared the indistinct outskirts of Mawbry.

Avery returned to the parlor and avoided Erienne's accusing glare as much as he could. Her face was flushed above the linen gag, and her eyes snapped with a promised vengeance.

Parker rubbed his chin thoughtfully as he stared down at his prisoner. "The Lady Saxton is, after all, the mistress of a known criminal and an adulteress. That should be enough reason to hold her captive, and in the meantime we'll spread the word for Seton's ears that she's taken. That will bring him in."

He motioned to one of the men. "You. Go to the livery and hire the carriage. Assure the driver that we will not need his services and will bring it back before nightfall." He counted out a few coins into the other's palm. "That should be enough to satisfy him." As the man departed, he admonished, "And try to get a decent horse for it."

Parker glanced at Erienne again. "Have no worry, my lady. You are as safe with me as in your own home." He chuckled briefly at the doubt visible in her eyes, and added, "At least until Lord Talbot returns from his business. Then I fear I'll have to leave you to your own resources."

A bristling glower was bestowed upon him before Erienne deemed to turn her face away, dismissing him as effectively as with her voice. She might be trapped and bound, but she was not dead yet, and she promised herself to give them whatever trouble she could.

A rattle of loose-jointed wheels announced the arrival of the rickety livery as the sheriff's man drew it to a halt in front of the cottage. After a glance out the window, Parker caught Erienne by the arm and lifted her from the chair. "Come, milady. I'll escort you to your carriage."

Avery interposed his bulk again. "Uhh, Parker, ahh. She had a purse." In a lame gesture he held out a hand and waited for it to be filled.

The sheriff stared at him as a laconic smile crept across his face. "You'd thieve from your very own daughter? Tsk-tsk. Avery, how could you? Here, take mine if you have a need." He fetched out his own much lighter one and dropped it in a greedy palm.

Avery frowned sharply as he hefted the purse. "I've got more comin' than a few shillin's. Why, his lordship owes me for the past two months and this one. And then there's me services of late." His eyes narrowed above a greedy snarl. "Aye, he owes me a lot more'n this."

"The purse should buy you rum for a few days." Parker shrugged. "You can discuss it with Lord Talbot when he returns. I'll see that a meeting is arranged." His smiled broadened. "I suppose you know who will come when the Lady Saxton doesn't return this evening. Were I wearing your shoes, Avery, I would visit Wirkinton, or Carlisle, or some other place a good distance off."

The sheriff touched the brim of his hat in farewell, and adjusting Erienne's hood well forward to hide her face, he led her from the cottage. He was just stepping past the garden when she abandoned her meek guise and brought her heel down sharply on his booted toe. Before he could react with anything more than a grunt of pain, Erienne came around with her bound hands clenched together and struck hard at his throat, right where his Adam's apple protruded. Her assault jolted the breath from him, and he stumbled back with a hand clutching his throat as he choked and gasped for air.

Erienne's attempt to flee was abruptly curtailed by the man who had followed them from the cottage. Flinging long, thick-hewed arms about her and lifting her off her feet, he shoved her into the carriage. She fell upon the seat but was immediately clawing at the opposite door to get it open until the man reached in and dragged her back to the side nearer him. Erienne was not finished yet. She turned on the seat and thrashed out with her sharp heels, kicking him wherever she could until a broad fist thrust forward, catching her alongside the jaw and abruptly blotting out her world.

Still holding his throat, Parker glanced about and was relieved to find an absence of witnesses. He climbed into the interior of the carriage and taking a seat beside the crumpled form, began to lower the shades. As they departed, the second henchman mounted his own horse and, leading two other steeds behind, trailed the time-worn conveyance.

Avery slammed the door and made his way toward the kitchen, still hefting the purse. He had found a good rasher of salted pork in a crock, and the very thought of it made him drool in anticipation. There would be time enough to relieve his hunger before he had to set to flight.

His eyes widened and he came to a sudden halt as he realized the sheriff had taken the only available livery in town. "But how will I leave Mawbry when I have no mount?"

"Try walking."

The sneer came from the kitchen door, and Avery froze in fear as his gaze raised along the booted, tan-garbed figure who stood there. His knees began to tremble before he recognized his son.

"Farrell! 'Od's blood, lad! Ye nearly frightened me ter me grave." He tossed the purse and caught it. "Ye see this, lad? I've found a way ter turn our fortunes, and there's plenty more where this came from."

"I heard, Father." The sneer had not left Farrell's voice. "I saw the sheriff and his men skulking by this door, and I heard . . . enough."

"Now, Farrell, me lad," Avery coaxed. "Our woes are over, but I have a need for your horse . . ."

"You sold her again." The younger man's tone was flat as he ignored his father's request. "And this time for a pittance."

"There'll be more, laddie. Much more!"

Farrell stared at him as a new light of knowledge began to dawn. "You really did cheat Seton at cards, didn't you?"

"Well, the man didn't need it." Avery's voice took on a whining note. "He had so much, and we had so little . . ."

"So you left me to a duel with no honor in it, and you didn't care about the outcome." He looked down at his stiff right arm. "A settlement with the Yankee was beyond your pride."

"I had no money ter pay the man off!"

"So you sold Erienne on the block!" Farrell's lips twisted in vivid repugnance. "It wrenches my belly to think that I took part in it."

"Ye feel no worse than I do, lad, but 'twas the only way!"

"You sold her then! You sold her now! Your own daughter!"

"Not mine!" Avery shouted, half crouching as he tried to make the stubborn lad understand.

"What?!" Farrell stepped close until only a handsbreadth distance separated their noses. His eyes, so much like the elder's, blazed with fury.

"She was never mine! Only some Irish rebel's brat!"

"She is my sister!" Farrell shouted.

"Only half . . . only half sister!" Avery insisted. "Don't ye ken, lad? Yer mother bedded down with an Irish bastard and got herself with a wee one! Erienne is his! Not mine!"

Farrell's rage took on new heights. *"My mother was not that kind!"*

"Oh, she married the bastard, all right," Avery cajoled. "But still, don't ye see, lad, you and me . . . we're blood kin. Ye're mine!"

The younger's lips turned in contempt. "You sold us all—my mother, my sister . . . me—all of us into poverty with your love for drinking and gaming."

"I raised ye on me knee," Avery protested. "And I've shown ye a wealthy share o' the good life. I've carried ye home in the wee hours when ye were too sotted ter stand."

"In the past months Erienne has done more for me than you ever thought of doing!" Farrell charged. "She gave me understanding . . . and love . . . and the will to stand on my own two feet . . . and the strength to stop feeling sorry for myself and blaming others for my state!"

"Ye take her side against yer own true father?" Avery barked.

"I will no longer claim you as kin!" Farrell's voice softened and grew deadly calm as he continued. "I will move out of this house and take up residence in York, where I will be married shortly. You, sir, will not be welcomed to either the wedding or my home. Now I will leave you to whatever ends you might find."

"But, lad, ye see I need a horse. Lord Saxton will be comin' . . ."

Farrell nodded. "Aye! Lord Saxton will be coming. Were I you, sir, I'd find a deep, deep hole to hide in." He wheeled about on a heel and as he strode through the kitchen, he hurled back over his shoulder, "Good day, sir!"

Avery filled his belly, donned his boots, and drew a coat over his rumpled garments. He tugged the collar high to hide his face and stomped out of the cottage, the thin purse tucked safely in his pocket. He carried with him a jug of ale and the balance of the pork wrapped in a cloth tucked beneath his arm, not knowing when he would be able to return to his home. The day had grown blustery, crisp, and dark, as if some menacing omen had sapped the warmth of the spring sun, though the hour was only slightly past noon.

He wandered aimlessly for a while, then went to stand on the bridge. When he was certain no one watched, he crossed over and quickly ducked off the roadway. He doubled back under the span and entered the heavy brush that bordered the water, pausing only briefly at the spot where they had found Timmy Sears. The hackles rose on the back of his neck, for the word was out that Christopher Seton had done the killing. If that were so and the wrench carried his child, the Yankee might come looking for the one who had sold her. It gave Avery more reason to worry.

It was said that old Ben Mose had built himself a crude shelter somewhere in the marshy tangle of undergrowth above the town. If he could find it, he could wait out the wrath of both Seton and Saxton and still be handy for a summons from Talbot or the sheriff.

Farrell Fleming hurled his steed around the last sharp bend before Saxton Hall and prodded him on with thumping heels. The coach stood in the lane before the manor, and the horses were well lathered from the breakneck pace that Tanner must have demanded of them. The landau was being brought around by a footman, while Keats ran to the larger conveyance and climbed into the seat. Taking up the reins, he urged the four-in-hand toward the stables, making room for the landau in front of the door.

Farrell hauled back on his own reins as he drew alongside, and his feet struck the ground almost before the steed had stopped. He threw his body toward the portal and flung it open, nearly plowing Paine over as the servant reached to open the door for his master.

"Lord Saxton . . ." Farrell gasped, seeing the one he sought hop-skipping across the hall toward the tower. Bundy and Tanner were puffing along in his wake, trying to keep up with the agitated man.

"I don't have time now, Farrell," Lord Saxton said bluntly, slowing his stride only slightly. "Erienne did not return with the coach when she went to see your father, and I am concerned for her safety. I must go."

Bundy and Tanner managed to maneuver past and hurried to

mount to the driver's seat of the landau. Lord Saxton stepped to follow, but the younger man caught his arm.

"She's not there, my lord."

"What?" The master of the manor halted and the blank mask pivoted with eerie effect to stare at the younger man. "What did you say?" His voice had lost its customary hoarseness but still echoed hollowly from the openings.

Farrell released his hold on the lord, and rubbed his brow. "As much as I would have it otherwise, my lord, I fear the mayor has handed Erienne over to the sheriff."

Lord Saxton snarled beneath his breath, "I should have killed that . . . !" With amazing agility, he spun on his heel, sweeping the heavy cane about him like a saber. "And Talbot? Where is he?"

"I believe the sheriff said he was away."

"Where did they take her?"

"I don't know," Farrell answered lamely.

"Which way did they go?"

"I'm sorry." The young man gave his admission shamefacedly. "I was in the kitchen, and I did not see."

For a moment Lord Saxton cast his leather-covered head from side to side like an enraged bull seeking an elusive foe. He straightened and barked out the doorway, "Bundy!"

The man vaulted from the carriage seat and came running. "Aye, milord?"

"Send men on fast horses to Carlisle, Wirkinton, out the York road, every direction! Have them search out word of . . ." He turned to Farrell with the unspoken question, and that worthy filled in the information required.

"The town livery. They took it without the driver."

"Tanner!"

"Aye, milord?" He was already at the door.

"I won't be leaving just yet. Prepare the coach, and be ready to move at any time."

"Aye, milord!"

"Bundy," Lord Saxton faced his man again, "I have letters to write. See that men are set to guard the Saxton roads, and be ready yourself to ride." He turned and made his way back into the great hall, with Farrell close at his side.

"What can I do to help, my lord? She's my sister. I've got to do something."

"You will, Farrell," the older man assured him. "I have a need for someone to ride to Wirkinton to seek out Captain Daniels on the *Cristina* and give him a letter."

"But that's Seton's ship. How . . ." Farrell seemed confused. "Why would you want the Yankee's help when Erienne . . . I mean . . ." He did not find the words to finish. If Lord Saxton was ignorant of his wife's infidelity, Farrell vowed that he would not be the one to tell him. "Of course I'll go. Anything to help."

Passing on to the chamber beyond the great hall, Saxton pulled a chair out from a desk and took up quill and parchment, then sat for a moment with the former poised above the latter. Of a sudden he sat back in the chair with a growl.

"That damned fool Avery! His luck will be exceptional if I don't see every bit of his hide flayed from him!" Remembering the other's presence, he glanced toward him. "My apologies, Farrell. I did not mean to insult you."

"Rest easy, milord." The younger spoke wryly. "I have preceded you. I no longer recognize the mayor as any kin of mine."

In the next hours there arose a current across the Saxton holdings that only much later came to the lord's attention. Bundy rode to several farms seeking out his choice of men to guard the lands and to be ready if the need arose. Though none declined this service to their lord, he bound them to silence, lest some careless word further betray the Lady Erienne in her duress. Still, by the gloaming's end, hardly an ear remained that had not heard of the lady's fate. While the men cleaned muskets and sharped their scythes, the wives made plans to take their carts to every village, town, or market they could reach within a day's ride and back. They vowed they would not see this lord driven from his rightful place.

Erienne came awake in slow stages. She was first aware of being uncomfortable and cold, then of a stricture about her wrists and mouth. She raised her head to find that she was lying on a pallet of straw stuffed into an ancient bed frame and covered with a blanket loosely tucked in at the edges. She suffered from a clear sense of disorientation, unable to recognize anything of her surroundings. Thick patches of plaster had crumbled away from the stone walls, and what was left of the windowpanes was not enough to keep the crisp winds out. A rickety table and chairs were tumbled together, as if they had been hauled in and dumped. A heavy, planked door with a small barred window seemed to be the only access to the room, but it bore no handle or knob that might have encouraged her to try it. Near it, a small cubicle gave evidence of being a privy closet. Its door gaped open, sagging from a broken hinge.

She pushed herself up on an elbow, and the room swayed with the onset of a pounding ache in her head. She recalled the same feeling that had come upon her after her fall into the stream. With that memory came another one, firm now in its clarity, of Christopher leaping from his horse with hooded cape spreading wide, and charging across the rivulet, heedless of its cold, to lift her in his iron-thewed arms and bear her up from the chill morass. She remembered the warmth of his body and the tantalizing man-smell that had haunted her through the months with Lord Saxton.

Her mind cleared, and she realized the full import of her fate. She was a prisoner, and to what end she could all too readily imagine. They would demand that Christopher Seton surrender himself in return for her release. If that event should occur, she could hardly believe that either of them would long survive.

She twisted around until she sat on the edge of the bed, then raising her hands to the gag, began to work at the knot that still chafed her cheeks. She winced as the cloth shifted and brushed a tender spot alongside her jaw. She tossed the muffle away and, with her teeth, plucked at the cords tied about her wrists. When freed, she rubbed the red marks that had left visible evidence of the tightness of her bonds. A bucket of clear water near the window gave her the best view of the dark bruise on her cheek, and she gently waggled her jaw to see if there might be a deeper hurt. It seemed serviceable enough as she tested it, but she had doubts that she could withstand another such blow without the bones giving way.

Footsteps grated against the narrow stone stairs outside the door, announcing the arrival of visitors, and Erienne straightened to await her gaoler. A key rattled in the lock, then after a loud "clank," the thick portal swung inward as Allan Parker made his entry. He was followed closely by another man bearing a tray with a covered bowl and a half loaf of dark bread.

"Good day, my lady." Parker gave the greeting in good humor. "I trust you slept well." Ignoring her glower, Allan came to her and leaned near, inspecting the purplish swelling just above the line of her jaw. "I must warn Fenton about his heavy hand. He is rather brutish with things of delicacy."

Thinking of nothing pertinent to say, Erienne simply turned away from the man, denying him the benefit of a reply. The other man had straightened the table and chairs and placed the tray on the former. He caught the meaningful jerk of his leader's head and, without a word, beat a hasty retreat, pulling the door closed behind him.

"Come, Erienne," Allan coaxed. "Do not ignore me. You know I have always been more than a little fond of you, and it pains me to see you abused because of this situation. You will surely stay here for a while until we bring this Seton fellow to heel."

Erienne faced him at last. *This* was something pertinent. "Do you think Christopher will ever yield to a pack of thieving murderers?"

"What are you saying, madam?" Allan feigned amazement. "We are well within the law. Christopher Seton is the murderer, and you are his mistress."

"You are part of the murdering band that has laid waste to this country for years!" she accused irately.

His brows lifted in a tiny shrug. "A man must survive, madam."

"Survive! Do you call this surviving?" She looked about in derision. "Hiding out like frightened rabbits?"

"Only until the hawk is caught, my lady," he answered easily. "We have felt his claws much too often not to be wary of him, and we have the bait we need to bring him to ground."

"Christopher will never be snared by your trap! He knows it would mean his death and no doubt my own. You could not long tolerate either of us in your midst."

"Seton, certainly not! But you, fair Erienne, are quite a different matter." He brushed a hand over her tumbled hair but dropped it again when she jerked her head away from his fondling. "I bid you consider your predicament. Lord Talbot will return in a few days, and I think his persistence will prove most trying to your reserve. Even I cannot deny him. His power extends to areas beyond these climes. And there are others."

Erienne raised a brow in mute question.

"The men below," he explained. "They believe a woman has but one task, and they pursue that talent diligently. They have a tendency to be rough, and though stalwart fighters, they make less than worthy lovers."

"So I am caught between a lascivious, mincing lord on one hand, and a pack of lusting wolves on the other." She scoffed. "I cannot perceive which would be the lesser of evils."

"There is another port of escape, my lady," he assured her, and met her searching gaze with a smile. "Given the incentive, I can provide Talbot with a lusty wench who can exhaust his appetites to such a point that he will be hard pressed to stay out of her reach. As for my men, they will not dare step beyond the bounds I set. You need only yield to me what you gave Seton. I might point out that if I so desire, I can take what I want from you."

Erienne tossed her head in a sardonic gesture. "Aye, I saw the way you prepared the Becker girl."

Surprise briefly touched his face, but he waved away her comment with a flip of his hand. "My men become overzealous in their lust. Of course, she would not have lasted out the night. Nor would you if I were to give you to them." His smile came back. "You ought to be thankful that I want you for myself."

Erienne gave him a scalding glare that could have sundered the largest ice floe in the north Sea. "And you think you are man enough to take Christopher's place?"

"I have proven myself with many other ladies," he answered casually. "I have no doubt as to my abilities. I can be most caring of one with your charm and grace."

"Your care!" She laughed in disdain and swept her hand toward her cheek. "If this be a sampling of it, Milord Sheriff, I would not want to taste of your anger."

"My apologies for that, dearest Erienne. Fenton was warned that your escape was not a tolerable condition. In his zeal, he chose the rudest but simplest path to assure his duty met. If you would only speak of your wishes, I would heartily strive to see them served . . . in recompense, of course."

"Oh, kind sir," Erienne mocked, "your concern touches me. My needs, of course, are legion. A bushel of rags to stuff the windows, a cloth or two to wash with, and a basin. A broom, brushes, and a shovel to move aside the debris." She cast a hand about to indicate the leaves and dirt which rounded every corner of the floor and lay in duneline ridges across the stone. A staff of servants could clean the place in a fortnight or two, but despairing that, I would apply myself to the task. A clean blanket and some linens would not be beyond consideration either."

"I shall do what I can, dear lady," he said, laughing. "In between time, is there a possibility that you will consider what I have suggested?"

"Aye, a possibility." Nodding slowly and turning, she stared out the window, then sneered over her shoulder. "As much possibility as there is of a man soaring to the moon and bringing me back a piece of it."

Allan Parker regarded the Lady Saxton's rigid spine for a moment, not without a certain appreciation for the shapeliness of it, and was of the firm opinion that she would change her mind in due time. After all, he was the best of the choices presented her. "I can wait for your answer. I'm sure after Lord Talbot arrives, you will come to a different frame of mind."

Erienne tossed a glare toward the door as it slammed shut behind him and heard the solid lowering of an iron bar across its planks. She paced the room for a while but could find no relief from the anxiety that filled her. She prayed that Christopher would ignore their challenge and remain safely hidden in the guise of Lord Saxton. She would not want to live without him, and while she knew he was free, she'd carry the hope that somehow she would escape and join him.

In want of something better to do to settle her mind, she tasted the stew, but the venison was too fresh and lent it a gamey taste that did not appease her pallet. She ate only out of necessity to keep up her strength and for the wee babe resting within her. For several months to come, she would carry her precious burden and take comfort in the fact that she had a part of Christopher with her. She grew wistful as she thought of a tiny girl or boy with her husband's reddish-brown locks and eyes that caught the light of every flickering taper or burning lamp. She would nurture the babe against her breast and be filled with memories of how his father, so boldly a man, had dared to snatch her from beneath the noses of all those who had hated him.

Would he do it again? Her head came up as a thought struck, and her serenity of the moment was shattered. She could expect him to come. It was just his way.

"Oh, please nooo," she moaned. "Please don't let him come. Please! I could not bear it if I lost him!"

She stumbled back to the bed and curled into a knot against its straw tick, not wanting to face the thought of losing him. She sought sleep to block out the worry in her mind, but an hour or so passed to no avail. The key turned in the lock, and she came up from the bed with a gasp, expecting to see the sheriff enter with more of his demands. She was as much surprised to see Haggard.

"Yer pardon, milady." He bobbed his tousled head. "The sheriff sent me ter fetch ye some stuff."

In wonder she watched him stuff rags in the window and move aside some of the debris. He was well meaning when he took up a well-worn broom and applied it to the floor, but the dust he stirred soon had her coughing and begging for mercy. Chagrined, he wiped his hands nervously on his breeches and departed.

Another bowl of the same venison stew and the other half of the loaf were brought for the evening meal. She had been effective in making her cell more presentable, though it was far beyond the help of any immediate repair. She received from Haggard a half-dozen short, thick candles and a tinder box by which to light them. Darkness was settling across the land by the time she finished her repast, and she managed to light two of the candles, placing one on the table and the other atop one of the headposts of the bed. They gave the ancient chamber an eerie, shifting light as the night gained hold and a last magenta glow waned in the west. A subtle chill invaded the quarters, and Erienne took to the bed, wrapping herself in her cloak and the single blanket.

The sharp assaults of loneliness and despair thwarted sleep. She struggled to lift her mood with childhood games of the mind, but they were only half remembered and ineffectual. There was little to hold her attention away from her fears, and slowly, inexorably, her thoughts turned inward. She closed her eyes and imagined her husband's arms around her, his kisses touching her and bringing to life her passions. She shivered and pulled the blanket tighter about her as she relived the fortnight of undisturbed bliss they had shared. She yearned for the gentle caress of his hands and the heat of his body next to hers, warming her, rousing her.

Like a dark demon in the night, doubt and dread rose up to haunt her, sapping the strength of her will. Tears came in a copious flow, and a slow sobbing racked her as her spirit searched frantically for any shred of hope, however remote. Then she felt a calming touch in the back of her consciousness, and like the ebbing of the tide, her burden lifted. While there was life, there was hope.

Exhaustion and the stress of the day overcame her, and slowly, step by step, a kinder invasion took place, and her defenses crumbled as slumber mercifully put her to rest for the night.

*   *   *

Lord Saxton sat at his desk and with mechanical precision dispensed his duties as master of Saxton Hall. He felt a helpless impatience as he waited for some word of his wife's whereabouts to come. None did, and the lord of the manse sat silent at a lonely evening meal as Aggie wrung her hands and fretted because he made no effort to eat or to converse except to answer curtly and briefly when questioned directly.

Bundy returned, and for a while Christopher's mood lifted, only to plunge again when it became clear that the man bore no news. The servant reported that all had been completed as the master had ordered. In despairing loneliness Christopher bade the man to take a seat and partake of the meal, but what followed was a stilted, silent charade. Although they had shared food before under many varied circumstances, Bundy was agitated with his own inability to relieve his lord's ill-concealed distress.

The time proved painful for them both, and as soon as he had taken enough to satisfy politeness, Bundy excused himself and departed to make a late check of the watchers and seekers for word of the Lady Erienne. He returned to the manse near midnight and, seeing the dim light in the lady's chamber, knew the master agonized in his own frustration. The very stones of the manor house seemed to groan in sympathy.

There was nothing Bundy could do. He could not bear to face his master again and tell him there was no hope, no word, that all their searching had yielded nothing as yet. He put away his horse and, seeking out his pallet, laid his weary body to rest.

Christopher Saxton stood alone in the middle of his wife's chamber, finding no relief for the heaviness in his chest. He saw her combs and brushes neatly laid to one side of her dressing table and knew the wealth of soft, gleaming tresses that fell in long, luxuriously thick cascades and fairly begged for a touching.

"How deeply has this wench entrapped me?" he mused. "She has snared my spirit and my soul. Like a hawk, she has snatched them in full flight." He shook his head. "But unlike the wild bird, she harmed them not. Nay, rather took them to her breast and breathed new life into them, and they have been so blissfully refreshed, my heart is nigh to bursting. Before I came to these shores, I would have sworn my ships would ever be my love, for no maid had so captivated me as the thrill of skimming the seas beneath billowing sails.

"Then on the path of revenge which I sought for my brother, I stumbled on that fair one who denied me every way and gave me no quarter, yet her beauty bound me ever closer to her side until she became the essence of my joy. Without her near, the day is empty, and all things pointless ploys."

He leaned a shoulder against a post of the bed and drew to mind the moments of bliss they had enjoyed therein. In a sudden flare of anger he jerked the draperies shut, closing off the view of that feathery, silken nest of pleasure. His eyes roamed wildly and came to rest on the tub beyond the arras. He envisioned again the curve of her bosom and the beckoning warmth of her smile as she welcomed his caress and kiss. He ran a shaking hand through his hair as he fought the urge to kneel in despair and sob out his agony. The ache in his chest became a physical thing, and he strode about the room to ease its tightening grip.

"She haunts me!" he flung at the dark shadows in the corners. "Damn! She haunts me every moment! How can I touch the thought of life without her? The mere idea of it chills my heart and sets my fears to flight within my head, like great, black bats harrying my peace!"

He could stand the place no more and fled to pace the hall. There was no one to share his roweling disquiet. Farrell was gone to Wirkinton. Bundy would share, but punished himself for his inability to solve the thing. Aggie would fret and grow distraught. He roamed the house goaded by his dilemma until the clock chimed the hour of two. He sought out his chamber, but even there her presence mocked his helplessness.

He flung himself back upon the bed and stared at the canopy overhead, not daring to close the velvet hangings lest his imagination refresh his torture. Slowly, imperceptibly, Morpheus soothed his plight with dreams of dark, silken tresses against his cheek, of pale arms entwined about him, of a kiss as light as thistledown, and finally the mercy of an ebon rest.

The slanting rays of an early sun lit the chamber, and Christopher roused and then came to his feet, glaring about him for some foe to attack. Reason flooded back, and his sense of rage was subdued beneath a firm grip of will. He stripped off the wrinkled clothes he had slept in and, after a quick ablution, garbed himself in fresh raiment. Aggie brought the morning meal to his room and, after a brief worrying glance, refused to meet his gaze. She puttered about in nervous embarrassment, as if something burned in her mind, then bobbed a quick curtsy and left.

Christopher donned the garb he had grown to detest, and Lord Saxton made his way slowly down the stairway to enter the routine of Saxton Hall. He signed a handful of papers and waited for word of his wife.

He inspected the grounds with Bundy and the gardener, approving several proposed changes, and waited for word of his wife.

He heard the arguments of a dozen or so conflicts among his tenants and passed judgments he hoped would benefit all sides . . . and waited for word of his wife.

He ate a lonely lunch, and a messenger brought a letter from Farrell. The young man stated that he would accompany the *Cristina* north when she sailed. The ship would have to beat a laborious, tacking path northwestward against the winds and should arrive offshore some time in the late afternoon of the morrow.

Christopher sought activity to fill the hours of the afternoon and wished they would have moved as slowly when he had held Erienne in his arms. His mood grew snappish and sharp as evening approached, but an understanding staff had compassion and gave him room to exercise his dismay at the continued absence of any news, good or bad.

For Erienne, the day passed on much the same. The notable differences were tied to the continued state of her incarceration. She stacked the dishes neatly on a tray after a breakfast of the same stew, this time served with a poor, half-burned excuse for bread, and swept the room. She bathed as well as she could from a bucket of cold water, using a shallow pan and no soap. She worked her fingers through her hair to relieve the tangles and restore some semblance of order to it, then swept the room again. She fretted when the evening meal was brought and again it was the same venison stew, only this time much thicker, as if it had spent the day simmering above the fire.

She watched the day die through one of the few intact panes that still filled a leading molding. Tears swam in her eyes as she wondered whether Christopher also viewed the same magnificent hues. It settled in her mind with a firmness that could not be set aside that he was thinking of her, just as she was of him.

"Oh, my love," she said, sighing and wiping at the tears, "I would be brave for your account, but your babe rests in my womb. 'Tis said the unborn are marked by trials such as this, and I would have this one free of any hatreds I bear."

She recalled a day long passed when she had wielded a phantom blade and made bold threats, albeit in privacy. She faced the room at large, standing straight and bold, and steadied the airy sword at her side. Casting up her hand in the best rhetorical stance, she spoke to her audience of none.

"Were I an argent knight sworn to mete out justice in the name of right, I would set upon this nest of knaves who seek to revile your name. I would test them all with the might of arms till the end and bid them bend a knee and beg forgiveness ere I smite their heads loose from their shoulders and claim the victor's truth."

She paused in her diatribe, and slowly her arm sagged. The flair was gone. The tears fell unheeded now. She knelt beside the straw-filled bed and wept upon it.

"Oh, Christopher, my dearest love," she whispered, "were I that knight, I would never have known your touch, your tenderness, your arms enfolding me, your kiss upon my lips, your warm, sweet flesh on mine, your babe." After a while she sat around and watched the last light fade in the crystal pane. "I must be brave." She sniffed and dried her cheeks on her skirt. "Be the babe a lad, I must be strong for him, or a girl child, I would have her know the strength of true love.

"My darling Christopher," she brought her hands together in a prayerful pose, "I would not have you risk yourself, but find a way to free me and slay my beast forever. I have found my rose in winter. You are my own precious love, promised to me evermore. Come, my love, the beast can only flee the two of us together."

Christopher viewed the irresistible approach of the day's end with total abhorrence. He knew the specters the dark would bring, having met a host of them the night before. He stood at the end of the western hall and ran his finger over the leading of a window his grandfather had put in place, and Christopher watched the fading light of the sunset dwindle in a few long-hanging clouds. Its reddish-purple shade brought not fear but dread at what his own mind could set against him.

Suddenly it became clear to him. If he did not leave the manse, his energy would be spent in waiting and tearing himself to shreds. He would seek out the highwaymen wherever they lurked and ravage them until one would tell him what he had to know. Then he would hunt the sheriff, drag him down like a hunting wolf hamstrings a stag. And if one hair of her head was harmed, he vowed, that man would beg for death a century or longer.

The night was solidly fixed upon the hills when the lower door of the bolt hole opened and a tall, darkly cloaked man came out with strides as bold as a venging lord, carrying at his side a long-bladed claymore, one that had known the death grip of his father's hand. The stallion sensed his master's mood and pranced and stamped in its eagerness to fly. The man took to the saddle, and vengeance rode the moors as the wan, pale moon hid its face before the promised bloodbath. This man's beloved had been taken by his foes, and no savage had ever set foot to earth with a blacker rage filling his heart.

The black steed's breath snorted forth like a dragon's breath in the crisp night air. His hooves struck sparks from stone as they thundered forth into the night. They rode here and there, back and forth, pausing at a lonely barn, there finding neither man nor horse, only a recent sign of an encampment. A hidden cave shed no greater revelation of the thieves' whereabouts.

"They are gone," he growled. "They have gathered in to set their trap with a bait they know I cannot resist. But where? Damn them! Where?"

The hour was late; the low moon still flitted bashfully behind the clouds, as if it feared the boldness and anger of the man. The high rage all but consumed him as he urged the stallion into a reckless run. They were a fleeting shadow across the vales and moors, soaring low with the widespread wings of a hunting hawk seeking prey.

Twenty-three

Some people thought it was old Ben returned from the grave. The ragged man huddled in the shadows near the rear door of the Boar's Inn and slowly sipped his ale. He hadn't appeared in the day, only after dark, slipping into the corner chair without a word and banging a coin on the table until Molly brought him a mug of stout. He reminded her of the mayor, but he reeked of smoke and sweat, and his grease-matted whiskers defined recognition in the shadows, so she discounted the likeness and went her way. His coin was miserably husbanded, and he never left extra. Thus she was not wont to dally overlong in serving him.

Avery Fleming's eyes never rested as he sat in his nook. He was ever primed to fly whenever any cloaked figure reminded him of Seton or a chair scraped the floor, bringing to mind a clumsy, deformed foot. The slim purse Parker had tendered him was almost empty, and his hope was fading that the sheriff would remember him with Lord Talbot. With both Seton and Saxton after him, he was unsure of his life from one moment to the next. He had no way of knowing when they would find the hovel in the marsh, but he was sure they were beating the brush for him. The previous night a hunting dog had nearly frightened the wits from him, rousing him from a dead sleep with its baying, and he had fled the shack in sudden panic, sure that Saxton was upon him. He had plunged waist deep into the brackish waters, and it was only the cold that had driven him back to the cottage for dry clothing. Even there, a soft bed was denied him. He had tried to spend the night, not daring to light a fire or even a candle, but in the darkness each sound had sent a shiver of terror through him, and several times he had sworn he saw that horrible leather helm floating toward him or heard the swish of a black cape or the click of a boot heel in the parlor. At least in the shanty he could sleep!

A man entered the inn, no one he recognized and, after obtaining a tankard of ale, roamed about the room, peering into faces until he came to the shadowed one in the corner. He sipped from his mug and spoke softly for that one's ears alone.

"Fleming?"

Avery jumped, then calmed when he realized no threat was forthcoming. "Aye?"

"Parker sent me. 'Ere's a horse out back. He'll meet ye at the first crossroads north o' town." The man moved on unconcernedly and soon was chatting with Molly at the bar.

Avery slipped out the back and found the mount as promised. A few moments later he was racing north, his spirit much lifted with the prospect of money in his hand. He would leave them all and seek out a place where a warm south wind blew off the sea.

Parker was awaiting him as advertised, with a fair half-dozen men for company. With Christopher Seton unaccounted for, the sheriff was taking no chances. Avery lit from his horse, and Parker drew him some distance away from the others, who held carefully to the darkness provided by a small group of oaks. Recalling too well the slash of the venging blade and flashing hooves in their midst, they were nervous to such a point that they had nearly bolted when Avery came pounding down the road.

Avery, himself, was not in a trusting mood and carefully kept his hand on the pistol he had tucked in his waistband. His mind was filled with the frozen scream of Timmy Sears' face, and he was not totally convinced that Seton was the only suspect. His fears subsided somewhat when he saw that both of Allan's hands were filled, one with a letter, the other with a purse of considerable weight.

"I'm afraid I have some bad news for you, Avery. Lord Talbot has sent a messenger from York relieving you of your duties effective a month ago. But take heart. He instructed me to give you a purse of two hundred pounds, double the compensation owed you for the past two months. If you treat it carefully, it should see you well away from here. As to giving you payment for the girl, he is aghast that you should sell your own daughter . . . again."

"But without her, ye can't catch Seton!" Avery protested.

Parker held out the money bag and the letter purportedly written by Talbot and smiled at the shrewdness of his own game. Talbot had made up his mind to dismiss the man, all right, but word had not yet reached his lordship of the most recent happenings, and Allan had taken it upon himself to deal with Avery. It would amuse him to see the erstwhile mayor hounded from village to town with the jaws of fear forever snapping at his heels. Avery had no vital information to harm anyone, as Timmy had held, and could therefore be dealt with in a frivolous manner. "Take them, Avery. 'Tis unlikely you'll get anything more."

Grumbling in disappointment, Avery accepted the offering. He had hoped for much more, but he was intimidated by the way the sheriff's hand came to rest on the handle of his pistol. Avery jammed the letter into a coat pocket and tucked the purse carefully into his waistcoat.

"Now, Avery, in view of our friendship"—Parker placed an arm across the man's shoulders—"I will gift you with the horse you rode here and a piece of advice. One of my men reported seeing a tall, caped man poking about your cottage just after dark." He smiled as Avery drew in a sharp breath. "The fellow had a big black horse and went down by the marsh. Apparently he was looking for you. If I were you, Avery, I would put a great distance between me and Mawbry, just as soon as possible."

Avery nodded in total agreement. "I'll not take meself back there again. Now that I gots me a horse and some coin, I'll head south and keep on goin'."

"Good fellow, Avery." Allan Parker patted him on the back. "I wish you luck wherever you go." He stood back and watched the ex-mayor scramble to the horse and haul himself into the saddle, then waved him off. "Farewell!"

"Eh, Cap'n?" One of the men called to Parker and drew alongside him. "Why'd ye give the mayor ol' Charlie Moore's horse? Ye know

Charlie'll be ready ter kill someone when he comes back and finds his best saddle and horse gone."

Parker chuckled as he swung astride his own steed. "Poor Avery. So many wolves will be chasing down that one miserable hare, Avery will be afraid to poke his head out of the ground for fear he'll be snared. I wonder which one will get him first." A hearty chorus of laughter rose up, but he waved an arm for silence. "Be quiet, you fools! Seton may be around here somewhere, and I, for one, don't wish to feel his fangs in me. Let's get back and see how Haggard has fared with that Saxton wench."

Avery felt content, not overly so, but at least well enough to set Mawbry behind him without regret. He had put a fair distance between himself and the sheriff, and he was just beginning to breathe easier when the thunder of hooves on the road behind him made him glance back over his shoulder in sudden apprehension. Fear pierced his quaking body and a low, rising moan escaped him as he saw the apparition materialize from the shadows of the trees. His mind froze with the one thought: Death had found him!

He whimpered and flogged his mount with boot heel, wishing for spurs and a whip. Over his shoulder, he saw the rider's cloak flying wide until the man seemed to float above the horse like a giant bat which was certain to suck the life from him if it caught him. Eerie laughter filled the night, sending cold shivers along his spine. He began to beat the racing steed with fist and rein, but the horse had already sensed its rider's fear and, having partaken of it liberally, was now laboring at the limit of its gait. They entered a twisting place where the road passed along the edge of a deep gully, at the bottom of which meandered a tumbling stream. The night rider was lost from sight for a moment, but that fact did not ease Avery's plight. Indeed, his worry grew more intense, for the way was well shadowed and marked by ruts. The horse stumbled, and his rider lost the stirrups. The beast seemed fraught with clumsiness, for no sooner had he recovered his footing than he found another hole. This time Avery lost the reins in his struggle to stay seated. Alas! It was his undoing! The path ahead was covered with tumbled rock and gravel. The flying animal skidded, lurched, and careened along the very brink of the gully. Without guidance he wheeled abruptly from the precipice, and Avery found himself truly aflight, without a horse.

He sailed over the tops of some bramble bushes and a tall, jagged stump of a dead tree. There was a sharp tug at his braces, then he crashed, rolled, slid, tumbled through brush, careened around tree trunks, bumped over rocks, and tested the density of long-thorned bushes. A solid blow expelled the wind from his lungs, and another blow brought it back again along with a flash of stars before the night closed in tightly around him.

A mile or less down the road the night rider caught the horse and stared dubiously at the saddle, unable to mark in his mind the spot where the man had left it. The frightened, unburdened beast had led him a merry chase, and the fleeting shadows had hidden the empty seat too long. With a wry glance back, Christopher led the steed with him as he turned once more toward Saxton Hall. Perhaps it had been his imagination that had brought Avery to mind when he had glimpsed the man, but whoever he was, he would continue on his way without the aid of a horse.

The manse was dark and silent when its master returned, as if it had lost a vital portion of its life. Christopher roamed the halls for a while in abject loneliness. For the first time in his life he had tasted the richness of a close companionship of a loving and loved wife. Now it was gone, and he had only the aftertaste to quench his burning thirst.

The common room was dark but for a single taper near the window. The hearth was cold, and the shadows brought him painful memories of laughter, a giggle, and warm, rich mirth. He grasped convulsively the hilt of the sword he carried, and his mind dwelt on the shedding of blood. The old lord's study was stagnant with age, and he absently touched a finger to the keyboard of the harpsichord. The single note rang hollow and flat without her voice to give it word and warmth.

Christopher stood with hanging head as the tall clock in the hall struck the second hour. He went to his chamber as the echoes of the chimes died away and, removing only his boots, stretched out on the bed. With an effort of sheer will, he blanked his mind and filled it with the creaking masts of a ship on the high seas. Rest was a necessity, even if it was for only a few hours. Soon it came, and mercy made it undisturbed.

The sun shining against Avery's eyelids cast a red glow in his mind. He ached in every limb and joint, and he could barely move his left arm, though a quick touch assured him the pulse was still in place. His head throbbed, and the exposure to the night's chill had seeded a tremor in his bruised body that could not be uprooted even by the warming sun. He lay as he had fallen, feeling sharp pebbles protruding into his back and the stinging sores where thorns had rent his flesh. he had not the courage to move, for to do so would have caused undue pain in his overly strained muscles.

A bird flitted overhead and then dipped to earth, settling on a nearby branch to survey this mangled sight of humanity. Avery rolled one eye around and squinted at the feathered thing that trilled so gallantly in the new day. He was certain the bird was mocking him.

A breeze wafted over him, and Avery blinked as he realized it touched the bare skin of his legs. With a grimace, he raised his head and saw that his breeches had been completely stripped from his lower half, leaving the ends of empty braces dangling from beneath his waistcoat. He leaned his head back against the rising bank and looked upward. There, high above, flapping from the ragged stump of a dead tree, was what remained of his breeches.

It was a long while before Avery assured himself that no bones were broken. He turned slowly, painfully, pushing himself to his hands and knees, and crawled ever so carefully around shrubs and trees toward his breeches. It was hardly worth the effort he expended, for the garment no longer resembled its former shape. The best he could manage was an apron of sorts that would questionably guard his modesty.

There was, of course, no sign of the horse the sheriff had given him, and he moaned over the loss of the fine saddle. Both would have brought him another fifty pounds or so, enough at least to sit down at a game of cards and begin rebuilding his fortune. Ah, well! The two hundred pounds in the purse would serve him toward that end.

He could not resist an accounting of his treasure and drew out the purse, emptying it on a flat stone between his straddled legs. Then he stared agape. The greater portion of the purse was thick, dark-colored disks. He lifted one and bit into it, and its softness readily took the marks of his teeth. It was lead! Lead balls had been split into a semblance of coins to weight the purse. After he counted out the worth, he found only a few pence over twenty pounds.

Avery cursed and threw a handful of the lead into the brush. A fool's game, it was! Tears filling his eyes. All his planning, all his scheming and maneuvering were all for naught except for a slim twenty quid!

Angrily wiping away a tear, he vowed to seek out Lord Talbot and face him with this affront. He jammed his hat down over his ears, then rolled and crawled upward toward the road. He would have gotten to his feet, but he caught the distant sound of thundering hooves coming toward him, and he scrambled to hide himself. After a moment, a large black coach and a team of four came into view. He watched until it drew near, then gasped and ducked down, recognizing the crest of the Saxton family emblazoned on the door.

Claudia slapped the missive against the palm of her hand, sorely chafed with curiosity as to what message it bore. She had assured the man who had delivered it that she would give it to her father as soon as he returned, but even then she was not sure that she would learn of its contents. At times her sire waxed secretive and refused to inform her of his affairs. Of late she had overheard bits and parts of his conversations with Allan Parker, and the frequent mention of Christopher's name had not escaped her notice. She was aware that they suspected the Yankee of being the dreaded night rider, and the very idea filled her with excitement. She was wont to imagine him as a gallant figure riding about in the dark of night, not to murder, as the reports claimed, but to expend his lust upon beauteous maidens and hold them captive for a few delicious hours. Of course, she would not have really cared if the night shade had murdered Timmy Sears and Ben Mose, for they had seemed somewhat useless anyway.

Thoughtfully she tested the seal that secured the parchment and drew close to the fireplace, where she held the letter close to the warmth. The wax softened, and taking the letter quickly to her father's desk, she pried the wax carefully away from the lower half of the paper. She was sure that her father would never notice anything once she rewarmed the wax and pressed it carefully into place again. But she must hurry. He had told Parker before he left that he would return before noon of this same day.

Eagerly she unfolded the parchment, and as her eyes skimmed over the words, her tightening lips began to form them, and they were gritted out between gnashing teeth.

". . . informed me that his daughter, the Lady Saxton, is with child by Seton. I have taken her in my custody as bait to bring in the Yankee dog. I will hold her upon your arrival at the castle ruins on the western tip of the firth. Allan Parker."

Claudia's face twisted in a savage snarl as she flung the parchment away from her and stormed from her father's study, not caring how that one might react to her tampering. She had a need to vent her fury on that Saxton bitch, and she would not be stopped in that cause.

"*Charles!*" She fairly screamed the name as she strode across the foyer toward the stairs.

Sounds of running feet came from the back of the mansion, and the butler burst through the door, completely ruffled by her summons. Catching sight of her on the stairs, he skidded and stumbled to a halt beside the balustrade.

"Yes, mistress?" he managed breathlessly.

"Have Rufus bring the carriage around," she snapped. "I will be taking an outing shortly."

"Yes, mistress." He gave a brief bow and hurried toward the back again to see to her bidding.

Shouting in strident tones for her maid, Claudia continued her ascent, and the trembling girl rushed out of her mistress' chambers to meet her in the hall.

"I will be going out for a while," Claudia stated sharply. "Lay out my clothes."

"Whi—"

"The red traveling dress and the plumed hat," her mistress barked. "And this time, don't dawdle! I am in a hurry!"

The young maid whirled and was about to dash back into the chamber, but she remembered herself and stepped quickly aside to let her mistress enter first. Claudia glared at her as she passed, and the girl shivered in trepidation. The bruises had barely healed from her last reprimand, and seeing the temper her mistress was in, she fully expected more to follow.

A half hour later, Claudia came from her chamber and descended once again to the elaborate foyer, snatching on a pair of gloves as she came down. She watched curiously as the butler hurried to the door well ahead of her, but what she had thought was an eagerness to please was no more than a part of his regular duties. Though she had not heard the knock on the front portal herself, she was sure it had come, for when Charles opened the door, there stood a man whom she stood in great fear of: Lord Saxton.

"I have come to see Lord Tal—"

Lord Saxton halted his announcement as he caught sight of the crimson-garbed figure on the stairs, and in sudden panic, Claudia glanced about for some place to flee, but she was held fast to the step as the cripple, brushing past the gaping butler, moved with his halting gait to the bottom of the stairs, where he stood looking up at her.

"Miss Talbot"—the rasping voice seemed to hold a sneer—"I was hoping your father had returned, but you might provide the information I seek."

"I don't know where they've taken her!" she lied, her tone reaching a high squeak.

"Ahh." Lord Saxton leaned on his cane and tilted his masked head thoughtfully as he peered up at her. "So you know why I came."

Claudia bit a trembling lip, daring no reply, and nervously pulled off her gloves.

"I'm sorry to intrude," her unwanted guest apologized in the same snide tone. "I see that you are going out."

"I"—she searched for an excuse—"need some fresh air."

His gloved hand swept in a downward motion, indicating the stairs. "Please, you needn't fear me." His chiding laughter mocked her obvious anxiety. "I rarely harm anyone . . . unless provoked."

Claudia gulped and glanced up, wondering if she could reach the safety of her chamber before he caught her. She saw her maid standing near the balustrade on the landing above, nursing a bruised and bloody lip, and distantly mused on what tricks her imagination was playing on her. She could have sworn she had seen a smug sneer on that one's face.

"Miss Talbot, join me," Lord Saxton bade in a flat, harsh tone.

In compliance she carefully descended the stairs but could not bring herself to move from the last step. There was no need. He came to her instead, making her cringe away to escape his imposing nearness.

"Do you know where the sheriff has taken my wife?"

His words, though deadly calm, jolted her. She read in the rasping tone many implications that caused her concern for her well-being.

"Charles . . ." she whined fearfully.

Lord Saxton turned as the servant took several hesitant steps forward. "Stay where you are if you have a care for yourself. I will tolerate no interference."

Charles retreated an equal number of strides and nervously closed the door in want of something to do. Claudia blanched as the masked head came around, and she caught the hard glint of his eyes behind the holes.

"Well?" he barked. "Do you know?"

"Allan sent a note to my father," she rushed to explain. "I had no idea what he had done until I read it. He's keeping her in an old deserted cottage somewhere south of York, I believe. I was just going to see to Erienne's welfare now. Is there some message . . ." She stumbled to a halt as the eyes hardened behind the leather and sensed that he had seen through her lie.

"If you have no objections, Miss Talbot, I will go with you. My coach can follow us."

"But . . ." She sought some excuse to deny him, but as he stared at her with that fixed, leather smile, she felt the trap close about her. In an effort to escape it, she questioned, "Do you know that your wife is with child . . . by that renegade, Christopher Seton?"

The brittle light never wavered.

"Did you hear me?"

"Aye, I heard." The hooded head slowly nodded. "I have much to talk with her about."

Claudia's brows raised as a new thought struck. Perhaps there was much to be salvaged of her revenge by leading this beast of a man to the other woman. He might become violent with Erienne, and she could witness the beating the wench rightfully deserved. A smile touched her lips as she thought of such a comeuppance. After Lord Saxton finished with his wife, Christopher Seton would not want to look upon her again, and of course she, Claudia, would be quick to offer him condolences at his loss of a mistress.

She waved a hand almost cheerily as she beckoned the cripple to follow her. "Come along then. We'll be on the road for some time, and we'll need to get started now if we intend to reach the castle by noon."

Lord Saxton followed in her wake, dragging his cumbered foot past the butler, who stared after them in amazement. He knew his mistress was flighty of moods but wondered at her wisdom in going off alone with the beast who had all but threatened her on the stairs. He closed the door behind the pair and shook his head as he crossed the foyer. A movement on the landing made him pause, and he glanced up to where the maid leaned against the balustrade. The hatred on the girl's face had grown quite obvious now that her mistress had gone.

"I hope he drops her down a well-used privy somewhere."

Avery had managed to obtain himself a ride on the back of a cart to the edge of the Talbots' property, though the sheepman who had provided it had cast a deeply skeptical glance toward the pasty white legs jutting out from beneath the strange skirt that covered his loins. But as Avery scrambled to his fastest and most painful gait up the lane leading to the Talbots' manor house, he gave no thought to what the man might have thought of him. The Talbot coach had passed them a short distance down the road, and he had espied Lord Talbot himself sitting within it. Avery was too anxious to catch the man before he left again on some other business to worry about his own attire.

He jerked down the skirt of his britches as an errant breeze wafted up to caress his backside, but he did not slow his puffing pace as he saw the manor house just ahead of him and Talbots' coach standing in the drive before the portal. He smoothed his bedraggled garments as best he could and climbed the full dozen steps to the front portal. His insistent banging on the door plate brought him face to face with the dignified butler, who suffered a momentary spasm of repugnance from the sight that greeted him. His gaze disdainfully measured the tattered man before he regained his arrogant stance and sniffed. "Yes?"

"Ah, I see his lordship's at home." Avery cleared his throat. "I would like ter talk with him for a few moments."

Charles's eyebrows jutted up with a quick twitch, then he raised his head and loftily explained, "Lord Talbot has no time for visitors now. He is about to leave on important business."

" 'Tis urgent that I speak with him!" Avery insisted.

The hooded eyes of the butler flicked down him again, and almost reluctantly he replied, "I shall ask his lordship if he wishes to speak with you, sir. Your name?"

"Avery Fleming!" the former mayor announced in aggravated tones. "Don't ye know me? I've been here before!"

Charles's surprise was evident. "You do bear a resemblance to the mayor." He looked Avery over more closely and shook his head doubtingly. "Excuse me, sir, but it looks as if you've fallen to a bit of misfortune."

"I have!" Avery heartily agreed. "And that's why 'tis necessary for me ter speak with his lordship!"

"I shall return shortly, sir."

Avery waited, barely able to control his fretting impatience as the servant's footsteps retreated into the house and dwindled into silence. In a moment the sound came back, and Avery brightened as he caught sight of the butler again.

"What did he say? Can I come in?" he asked the servant eagerly.

"Lord Talbot is pressed for time, sir. He will be unable to see you."

" 'Tis important!"

"I'm sorry, sir." Charles haughtily apologized and would say no more.

Avery's shoulders slumped in defeat, and he stumbled away from the door, hearing it close behind him, and made his way down the steps. His legs felt weak of a sudden, and he leaned against a carriage wheel, entirely drained by the events of the past days. If he could just present his case to Lord Talbot, he was certain that the man would understand and feel compassion, at least enough for a few more quid and maybe even a horse.

Avery raised his head and gingerly touched a tender spot on his brow. He had not the energy to get to Mawbry, or anyplace else, for that matter. It seemed he was doomed without a mount or even food to sustain him. What could he do? He was bereft of all of his belongings, cast out by family and friends, and now with no chance to talk with his lordship, there seemed no hope for him.

Suddenly his attention perked as his eyes settled on the canvas-covered boot of the coach. It was big enough for a man, and not only would it provide him with transportation, but by hiding in it, he also might even be allowed the opportunity to present his claim to Lord Talbot after the man's business was done.

Avery glanced around furtively. The driver was paying no heed to him as he sat in his seat, dozing. The two footmen were talking together near the lead horses, and after dismissing him from mind with a derisive sneer, they paid him no further mind. No one else seemed to be about to stop him. It was his chance, perhaps the only one, and he would be a fool if he did not at least try.

Twenty-four

The ground grew barren and rocky as the coach bearing Claudia and Lord Saxton approached the western shore overlooking the heel of Solway Firth. The winds whipped wet and cold off the western sea. A granite bluff reached high, then plunged in shattered parapets to the sea crashing white with foam and froth far below. Retired from the brink and half behind the shelter of the bluff, the ruins of an ancient castle squatted like some wounded hare upon the barren slope of stone.

It was to this tumbled structure they journeyed, the Saxton coach halting a hundred yards or more short, well beyond a normal musket's range. Tanner made a half circle, turning so they faced away, ready for flight should the need arise, while the Talbot coach passed boldly on, laboring up the steep incline, across a once-dry moat now bridged with salvaged masonry and planks. A shout heralding their approach rang out, and the coach entered the broad courtyard, unimpressive in its size and half filled with the scattered blocks of once-proud walls. On the right, a timbered portico sheltered the entry to the barracks. To the left, only the first and second level of the watchtower remained intact, while the higher floors had crumbled away.

Ahead of them, the central keep lay in tumbled disarray. There, a place had been cleared to stable horses, and short of that, a turn-around for carriages.

Allan Parker stepped casually from the doorway of the barracks and watched the familiar coach sweep in and come to a stop. Lord Talbot had made good time finishing with his business in York and arriving before noon, Allan mused as he went to greet his employer.

The footman hastened to fold down the step, then reached up, pulling the door wide. The opening was immediately filled with crimson skirts and a wide-brimmed, plumed hat of the same hue. Allan gave a mental groan and ground his teeth as he recognized the one he least wanted to see. Recovering his aplomb, he proceeded as propriety dictated and, putting on a welcoming smile, reached out a hand to assist in Claudia's descent. His fortunes quaked in the still-young day, for if the wench's presence was not enough to darken it, the door was quickly filled by another. Parker stared in open bemusement as Lord Saxton swung his twisted, booted foot to the ground.

"You amaze me, Lord Saxton," he stated his thoughts bluntly. "You are the last person I expected to venture here."

A rasping chuckle came from the mask. "Miss Talbot informed me of her intent to visit my wife, and I thought it only prudent that since our ends were alike, she and I might travel across this hostile countryside together. I brought my own carriage, as you can see if you choose to look, and men for protection. Oh"—he held up a hand to make a point—"my men are quite well armed, Sheriff, and perhaps more than a little nervous. You know the stories going about." He flicked his gloved fingers casually. "If any of your men should . . . ah . . . wander too close, I cannot answer for the consequences."

It was Parker's turn to chuckle. In a way he admired the boldness of this cripple. "From most men, sir, I would consider that a warning, even a threat."

"Forbid it, sir," Lord Saxton assured. "Strike it from your mind. I meant nothing of the kind. I only know my servants are ill at ease of late. You know, the highwaymen, this night rider, and these murders and all. Most dreadful and frightening times."

Lord Saxton noted the half-dozen indiscriminately attired and rather brutish-looking men who had wandered out to lounge behind the sheriff near the barracks door. They stared in unbridled curiosity at him, and several gestured at Claudia, leaning heads together as they exchanged whispered comments with leering grins. The girl was accustomed to a loftier style of gentry and grew uneasy beneath the lecherous stares.

"I came to see the mayor's daughter, and I would be about it," she declared, and then questioned testily, "Where is she?"

The sheriff ignored her a moment. "And you, Lord Saxton? Have you also come well armed? It seems the last time we met . . ." He let the comment hang unfinished.

Lord Saxton clumsily braced himself with his twisted foot. "But for this." He handed his heavy walking stick to the man, then spread his cloak and coat wide. "You may search me if you wish. I have no other weapon, unless you see something I have missed."

Allan hefted the cane in his hand. "A most formidable one, at that." He twisted the silver head to no avail. "But I will give it to you. Perhaps the temptation"—he spoke this last loudly and over his shoulder—"would urge you to use it unwisely."

He tossed the cane back and laughed, while his men picked up the play with loud guffaws as they fondled the butts of their own pistols in hopeful glee.

"Well, then," Lord Saxton sighed impatiently, "as Miss Talbot suggested, let us be on our way to see the Lady Saxton."

"As you will." Parker gave his arm to Claudia and tossed back over his shoulder, "If you will follow me, sir." He led off without pause, and it was only Claudia's careful, mincing gait that allowed Lord Saxton to hobble along apace with them. Still, he almost stumbled several times as his cane skidded on loose rocks, and each misstep was marked by mocking laughter from the porch of the barracks.

"Eh, he must be blood kin ter Haggie," one chortled.

A path had been cleared on the debris-strewn steps that led to the erstwhile tower, and the sheriff stepped ahead to open the door to the room within. There, five men cast lots on a blanket-covered table in a corner. As the sheriff entered with his guests, one of the men jumped to his feet and was recognized as that ever-eager worthy, Haggard Bentworth. He stepped forward to greet them, not noticing that the hilt of his sword had snagged a corner of the blanket, and with his movement pulled the teetering table over, spilling coins, cubes, and cups of ale to the dust-laden floor. He ducked beneath the swing of a ham-sized fist and ignored a bevy of curses and threats as he disencumbered himself, slapping down the wayward blanket. With a cheery smile, he started forward but stumbled over a broken chair and plowed headlong into the sheriff.

Parker cursed and threw the man off, wondering why he had ever allowed Haggard to come along, except that the oaf was too innocent—or too stupid—to force himself upon their prisoner and was therefore worthy to be trusted as her keeper.

Haggard's ear twitched as he cast an uncertain glance toward the masked one, then he peered at the sheriff wonderingly. "Be there ought I can do for ye, sir?"

"Aye! Give me the key to the lady's cell." Parker's lips almost twitched into a snide sneer as he regarded the fellow, but he won the battle and managed a noncommittal frown as he received it. "See that some tea and vittles are prepared for our guests."

With a quick nod, Haggard left, and the sheriff set his feet on the first of the steps that spiraled upward along the wall.

"This way if you please, but be wary," he warned. "As you can see, there is no balustrade." He led them upward until they came to a heavy door that blocked the way. The steps continued on past the door, curving along the tower, but ended with blue sky showing beyond the crumbling stone. Parker thrust the key into a lock that held the end of a thick bar across the door. The fixture, like the barred window set high in the panel, had the appearance of being a most recent addition to the door. Leaning near the opening, the sheriff called through to the prisoner.

"My lady, I have returned."

An angry voice came from within as he pushed the door open. "I gave you my answer before! If you doubted me then, perhaps this will convince you!"

Parker ducked as a missile sailed toward him, and the shattering crash of a cup against the door resounded in the barren chamber. On its heels came a plate, which took a more positive course toward his head. He batted it away and, in three long strides, was across the room, throwing his arms about the she-cat as she searched about for something else to throw that would help vent her fury with the man. He lifted her feet clear of the floor and turned with her toward the door as Claudia stepped through.

"I've brought you company, my lady," he chortled.

Erienne ground her teeth as she kicked and struggled in his arms. "I have no more need of Miss Talbot's company than of . . . !" She caught her breath sharply as Lord Saxton came through the open portal, ducking his head as he passed beneath the low frame. "Nooo! Oooh, nooo!" she moaned. "Why did you come?"

"Tsk-tsk! Is that any way to greet your husband?" Parker chided. He looked toward the other man and feigned a look of sympathy. "She doesn't seem to be overjoyed at seeing you, my lord. Perhaps she would have preferred the Yankee to come in your stead."

"Put her down," Lord Saxton commanded in a harsh tone.

"Certainly, my lord." Parker obeyed most amiably and held his smile as he observed the pair.

Erienne would have flown to her husband, but his cane came up abruptly and halted her.

"Stay where you are, madam. I will not be moved by the whimperings of an adulteress." His curt tone brooked no disobedience, and Claudia smiled smugly as he continued. "I have come to hear it from your own lips. Did you indeed bed the Yankee and take his seed within your belly?"

Erienne nodded hesitantly, realizing she was expected to play out the game for the benefit of the other two. Wringing her hands, she glanced toward Claudia, who mistook the cause of her distress. The woman gave her a superior smile as she doffed her gloves, and Erienne turned back to her husband, answering him in a timid voice.

"He was most persuasive, my lord. I could not help myself. He persisted until he had his way with me."

"And do you love him?" the rasping voice demanded.

The blue-violet eyes grew soft as she met the dark gleam behind the shaded eyeholes. "Would you have me lie, milord, and say nay? I would gladly spend the rest of my life here in this prison if I knew he was safe. If he were standing here with me now, I would entreat him to flee before they took him."

"How generous you are," Claudia sneered. Tossing her gloves aside on the table, she strode forward arrogantly until she stood beside the couple. Settling well manicured hands on her tightly cinched waist, she smirked. "Would you be so generous if you knew your precious lover had had his way with other women hereabouts?"

Lord Saxton hobbled around until he faced the woman. Claudia felt a shiver go through her but thrust aside her aversion to the man as she confronted the prisoner again.

"Molly herself said she caught a woman in Christopher Seton's bed at the inn, and from his own words he seemed to be well taken with the wench."

"The rumors had it that you also enjoyed his company, Miss

Talbot," Lord Saxton stated dryly. "Did you, too, fall to the man's ploy and entertain him while your father was away?"

"Certainly not!" Claudia gasped. "Allan can vouch for the nights my father was away! He . . ." She halted as the sheriff cleared his throat sharply, and she became aware of what she had spilled. "I mean . . . he came to see to my welfare . . ."

Allan's lips twitched with amusement as he made his excuses. "I have duties elsewhere. I shall leave you to visit for a while." He strode to the door where he half turned, glancing toward Claudia. "There are guards downstairs, as you saw. Should you need anything or choose to leave, they'll be most eager to come to your aid."

He opened the door, then leapt aside as Haggard, bearing a tray with teapot and cups, tripped on a loose portion of granite and came rushing through. Haggard's large, booted feet worked in one continuous motion as he tried to steady himself and balance the tray at the same time. He bumped into the table and, with a loud clatter of dishes, deposited his burden abruptly on its planks. After a brief examination of the cups, he heaved a sigh of relief, then turned a happy grin to his awed audience.

"I brought you tea!" he announced. "The vittle'll be a while."

Allan Parker strived for control and, placing himself well out of the path of harm, angrily gestured the man out.

"Would ye be wantin' me ter stand guard at the door, sir?" the man offered with alacrity. "Just in case the lady be needin' anythin'?"

The sheriff glanced toward the hooded one. He did not think the cripple was foolish enough to try anything, even if he was of a mind to forgive his wife, but he guessed it would do no harm leaving a guard at the door.

"Should Miss Talbot need your assistance," he counseled, doubting the possibility, "try not to harm her in your eagerness."

Haggard nodded enthusiastically, then paused as if suddenly perplexed by the sheriff's statement. Parker cast a dubious glance toward him, wondering if he had ever met anyone as slow of wit, then with a nod to the ladies, he took his leave. He heard Haggard's footfalls coming close behind him and hurriedly descended several steps lest mayhem befall him.

The door closed, and the solid bar fell into place. Claudia strode about the room, glancing about in disdain. She paused beside the narrow window in the far corner and smirked as she contemplated the rags stuffed into the opening. "You really have come down in the world since I last saw you, Erienne. You gave the gossips enough to banter about that night at my ball when you all but threw yourself at Christopher." She swept around to challenge the other woman, arching a dark brow as she jeered questioningly, "Where is your lover now? I don't see him rushing to your aid."

Lord Saxton seemed to ignore the woman as he gently lifted his wife's chin with a gloved finger and examined the dark bruise on her jawline. Erienne leaned toward him, wanting to touch him but afraid to show her emotions. Her eyes, probing the shadowed eyeholes, spoke of her love.

Claudia grew annoyed at the couple's lack of attention and smirked. " 'Twould seem they've handled your wife roughly, but 'tis no more than she deserves for what she's done to you. Getting herself with child by that renegade, Seton. Tsk-tsk. Why, there's no telling how many other men she's been with, or even if she really knows if it's the Yankee's child or not. Maybe it isn't his at all, but some hired man's whelp. I suppose that really doesn't matter, though. She admits that the Yankee has bedded her"—her words dwindled as the master of Saxton Hall came to peer out of the same window where she stood, and she finished in a weakening tone, realizing she was well out of sight of the door where Haggard stood—"and cuckolded you."

Lord Saxton braced his cane against his leg and tilted his hooded head to the side as he thoughtfully regarded her. "Cuckolded? Pray tell me, Miss Talbot, how can a man cuckold himself?"

Claudia's eyes widened as a gloved hand reached up to the side of his throat and freed the laces. She gasped as the other hand joined the first and began to drag the leather mask from his head. She would have bolted past him, but he stepped before her, blocking her flight, and she stared in petrified horror as he swept the leather helm from his head. Then her mind reeled in sudden confusion as the handsome, unscarred face of Christopher Seton was revealed.

"Miss Talbot?" he greeted in a chiding tone.

Claudia's bemused stare moved from him to Erienne, whose worry had not dissipated. "But where is"—her reaction was no different than Erienne's had been at the discovery of his identity—"Lord Saxton?"

Christopher swept his hand before him and gave her a shallow bow. "At your service."

"Lord Saxton?" She repeated the name in widening bewilderment. "You . . . . ? But he"—her eyes flew downward to the heavy boot—"is crippled."

"Merely a ruse, Claudia. As you may have noticed, I suffer no such impairment."

The woman's eyes narrowed as the situation became clear. "If you think you will escape from here with your mistress, you are sorely mistaken!"

"Not mistress," Christopher corrected and smiled blandly into the woman's inquiring stare. "Erienne is my wife and rightful lady of Saxton Hall. She carries my child, and she has been with no other. Of that, I have no doubt."

"Wife of a renegade who is shortly to be slain!" Claudia snapped back and opened her mouth, but before she could draw breath enough to scream, Christopher caught up the walking stick and, with a flick of a small catch, slid a slim rapier from the wooden sheath. Claudia suddenly found herself facing the sharp end of the sword, and when she glanced up, slowly closing her mouth, the grayish-green eyes bore into her.

"I've never killed a woman," he stated softly. "But then, I have never been so tempted before. I suggest that you be as quiet as possible."

Claudia's voice trembled as she asked, "What are you going to do?"

A leisurely smile lifted a corner of his mouth. "I've come to fetch my wife, and you, Miss Talbot, are going to help me."

"Me?" Her eyes had widened. "What can I do?"

"'Tis said that wisdom comes to those who seek it." Christopher's eyes wrinkled at the corners as his smile deepened. "Miss Talbot, would you be so kind as to remove your hat?"

Much bemused, Claudia obeyed.

"And now, Miss Talbot, if you don't mind, the gown also." He ignored her gasp of indignation and turned to his wife. "Erienne, we must take advantage of the resemblance you bear to our guest. I know they are gaudy, but would you be averse to wearing another's clothes?" He was answered with a sudden smile and a quick shake of the head, then he glanced back at the other woman, letting a shade of anger show in his frown. "My dear Claudia, you need have no fear that I will be tempted by anything you display. But I do insist. The gown, if you please."

She stared at him in rage, her lips parted as if she might scream. The end of the sword described a small figure eight in front of her eyes, capturing her total attention with its clean, sharp tip. Her hands began to move, undoing the catches and laces as a note of fear replaced the anger in her frown. Being held captive in this manner was not exactly the way she had imagined it.

Christopher held out his hand to Erienne, and without a word she laid in it the same cord that had bound her own wrists a pair of days ago. As soon as the gown fell to the floor, he folded Claudia's arms across each other and bound them close to her chest, looping the cord behind her elbows so she could not tug free and making the final knot beneath her arms, where it could not be unfastened with her teeth.

"The minute you leave this room," she hissed furiously, "they'll find you out and kill the both of you!"

"I'm willing to chance the escape rather than wait here for them to kill us," Christopher responded lightly and reached out his hand again to Erienne. This time she gave him the same cloth that had silenced her, and in a moment that serviceable rag applied the same duty to Claudia.

Christopher glanced toward the door and was satisfied to see the broad back of Haggard filling the opening. Christopher laid his cloak about Claudia's shoulders and jerked the leather helm down over her head. Her protestations were adequately muffled beneath gag and mask, and he led her struggling to the table and chairs. Turning the back of the chair to face the door, Christopher pushed his prisoner into it, and Erienne hurriedly tore strips from her petticoat for use as bonds. These he used to wrap Claudia's hips and legs to the chair, and then he draped the cloak to hide the wrappings. When he stood back, he weaved the sword in front of the mask where he was sure his prisoner could see it.

"Silence now," he whispered. "One sound or warning and your father will outlive you by at least some hours."

The eyes behind the leather helm followed him as he backed away to the edge of the bed. There he opened his arms to receive his wife, who came eagerly against him. Their lips met in a kiss that, to Claudia's way of thinking, displayed more passion than the situation allowed.

"Oh, my love," Erienne breathed as he pressed his lips to her brow, "I was afraid you would come, and yet I hoped you would."

Light kisses rained upon her cheek and brow as he held her close, savoring the nearness of her while he could. "I would have come sooner had I known where they had taken you. I had not expected this of your father, but he will answer. I promise you that."

Erienne shook her head and replied in the same muted tone. "He is not my real father."

Christopher held her away, looking down at her wonderingly. "What is this?"

"My mother married an Irish rebel and got with child before he was hanged. Avery married her, knowing the facts, but he never told her that it was he who had given the final orders to hang my father!"

Christopher gently brushed a tumbled curl from off her cheek. "I knew you were too beautiful to be kin to him."

She nuzzled against his chest as she slipped her arms about his waist. "Oh, Christopher, you have become all things to me. I love you, my darling."

He raised her chin, and his eyes drank of the brimming devotion he saw in the amethyst depths. "And I you, milady. Perhaps more than even I was aware of until they took you from me." He lightly kissed the bruise on her jaw. "I will see that they pay for this."

"It doesn't matter, Christopher. As long as I have you and your babe within me, nothing else matters."

"Our escape must be our concern now. We must make ready." He stepped away, doffing his coat and waistcoat, then pried at the block of shaped wood that wedged his right boot to an unnatural angle.

Erienne had succeeded in freeing only a few of the intricate buttons that secured her bodice when a falsely bass voice from Haggard announced in booming tones, "The lord high sheriff approaches!"

Erienne snatched her husband's garments and the crimson gown and thrust them in the privy closet, then hurriedly sought to repair her bodice while Christopher bobbed the tip of the sword before Claudia's eyes to remind her of its presence.

"Remember, 'twill be but a few inches from your throat."

He belied his threat as he moved across the room and flattened himself against the wall beside the door. Erienne gave up trying to refasten her gown and took a seat across from Claudia at the table, quickly pouring tea and setting a cup in front of Claudia. She caught the hateful glare behind the eyeholes and, despite the seriousness of the situation, gestured to the cup. "Don't drink it down too hastily, my dear. You might choke."

The sheriff jogged up the last few steps and tossed a question to Haggard. "All is well?"

"*Aye, sir!*" he barked, much too loudly.

Allan Parker flinched and stepped around the man as if he were some strange white and purple cat. He looked through the window, but made no effort to open the door. "Where is Claudia?"

Erienne rose and came toward the door, noting how his eyes dipped to her parted bodice. She felt Christopher's gaze on her as well but refrained from glancing in his direction for fear she would give him away. She gestured toward the privy as if embarrassed. "Claudia is indisposed. The long ride . . . in the carriage, I think." She indicated the helmeted figure at the table as that one leaned forward and a muffled groan sounded. "Lord Saxton is also a trifle ill."

"I can understand why," he replied meaningfully. His eyes passed over her in bold appreciation. "Have you given some more thought to what I requested? Lord Talbot will be here in an hour or so, and you'll have to make up your mind before then."

"Shhh!" Erienne glanced toward the hooded figure. "He will hear you."

"It doesn't matter," he assured her.

She turned an inquiring gaze to him. "What do you mean?"

Parker shrugged. "Your husband has made me curious to see what the mask hides. Believe me, before he leaves these chambers, I will see what lies underneath that helm."

Erienne twisted her hands in a fretting, anxious manner. "I am most certain that you will not be pleased with what you find."

"Be that as it may, I will appease my curiosity," he promised. He glanced at Haggard and directed harshly, "Summon me when Miss Talbot is ready to leave."

With that, he turned and hastened down the stairs. Haggard stepped in front of the door, and his broad back once again filled the small opening. Erienne released a long, ragged sigh and faced her husband, accepting the crimson gown from him.

"Quickly now!" he whispered urgently. "Get dressed!"

Claudia writhed against her bonds, and Christopher ventured back to stand before his prisoner, meeting her vicious glare with a smile.

"My apologies, Miss Talbot, but I fear you must suffer with the mask a bit longer."

"Mmmm!" She shook her head wildly.

Christopher restored his sword to the cane and lounged lazily in the chair across from Claudia as he awaited his wife, enjoying the view Erienne presented as she dressed in the corner beside the door. Though the gown hung lose about her waist, it stretched tightly across her bosom. There was, of course, little time for a proper fitting. Hurriedly she coiled her hair on top of her head, securing it with pins, then donned the hat.

"How do I look?" she asked worriedly as she came to stand before her husband. She could not help but wonder at what depth the deception would be tested and if she could carry it off.

"The color becomes you, my dear." He caught the empty fold at her waist in his hand and peered up at her with a grin. "Perhaps you'll even grow into it in a few more months."

A derisive snort echoed from the mask, and the cloaked figure twisted as Claudia fought against her bonds. Christopher was undismayed as he took Erienne on his knee. Slipping an arm behind her waist, he laid the other across her lap, and once again they enjoyed a long, blissful kiss, though the ire of the one across from them grew by leaps and bounds.

Haggard's stentorian announcement intruded into the moment. "The food is coming!"

Footsteps came up the stairs, and Erienne moved to stand beside the window in the corner, turning her face aside, while Christopher hefted his cane and slipped into the privy. The key rattled in the lock, and the door was pushed open to admit two swarthy, unshaven men, one bearing a tray with several bowls of the usual, while the other stood guard inside the door with Haggard.

"Put the food on the table," Haggard directed the man unnecessarily, then nudged his companion sharply in the ribs with an elbow. "Ye'd best keep an eye on his lordship there," he warned from the corner of his mouth. "A man what wears a mask is always tryin' ter hide some'in'."

The logic of his statement was lost on the man as that one admired the feminine form dressed out in crimson. Hitching up his britches, he swaggered toward Erienne. Talbot's daughter was even prettier up close than what he had first thought, and he cleared his throat to express the idea. "Me name's Irving . . . yer ladyship, and I want ye ter know, I think ye're a right fine-lookin' woman."

Erienne glanced around nervously, seeing the man and Haggard coming toward her. The other who bore the tray set his burden down on the table and was about to place the bowls on the planks when he noticed the seated one wiggling his knees. The cloak slipped aside, revealing a goodly wealth of petticoats. The hooded head bobbed vigorously, and curiously he reached forward to pull away the mask. He never heard the one who came upon him from behind. A solid thud of Christopher's cane at the back of his head abruptly darkened his world, and before he completely crumpled, he was hauled backward toward the privy.

Erienne glanced from the leering guard to Haggard, trying to find some semblance of an encouraging smile to keep their interest, but Irving glanced back over his shoulder at the almost imperceptible sound of something being dragged and saw the boots of his companion disappearing into the alcove.

"Eh! What're ye doin'?" he demanded, snatching for the pistol in his belt as he came around. Haggard followed the man's lead while Erienne caught up a broken arm of a chair that was near at hand. She was dismayed at which man to strike first, but since Haggard was nearer, chose him as her victim. She raised the club to apply it with force against Haggard's thick skull, but to her amazement he lifted his own weapon and brought the butt of it down hard on Irving's head. That one slithered to the floor, as if the air had been expelled from his huge body. Throwing back a grin at Erienne, who had not fully recovered from her slack-jawed astonishment, Haggard quickly removed the pistol from the man's hand and tossed it to Christopher as he stepped from the alcove.

"How many?" Christopher asked as he checked the loading.

"Three downstairs. Parker's probably in the barracks with the rest."

Erienne closed her mouth as her husband came to stand beside her and eased her bemusement with an introduction. "If you have not met him before, my dear, this is Haggard Bentworth. Though no one knew him as such, he was my brother's servant. A most loyal one, to be sure."

"A pleasure," Erienne responded, fighting a sudden mistiness in her eyes, and extended a hand toward the man, who took it and bobbed his head.

"The pleasure is mine, mum, and I'm sorry I couldn't tell ye sooner." He faced Christopher with a small, disjointed shrug. "I couldn't get away ter tell ye where they had taken her either, milord," he explained. "They didn't trust me."

"Perhaps your heart isn't black enough for their liking." Christopher smiled and then gestured toward the door. "We'd better get another one up here to even the odds."

Haggard stripped the waistcoat from the unconscious man, giving it to Christopher, who quickly donned it. Together they carried Irving into the privy and dumped him beside his companion. After renewing his warning to Claudia, Christopher took up his position beside the door, while Erienne returned to the window and Haggard moved to the head of the stairs, where he called down. "Eh, ye blokes, Miss Talbot wants some wine ter go wit' her vittles. Fetch her up 'at bottle what we set aside for his lordship."

Haggard went to stand beside the table, and after a moment plodding footsteps came up the stairs. A burly rogue paused at the doorway and thrust out the bottle, making no attempt to enter the room. Haggard nodded toward the crimson-gowned figure.

"Yer ladyship be wantin' ter speak wi' ye."

The man pushed his hat back from his brow and peered into the room suspiciously. "Where's Irving and Bates?"

Haggard waved his hand casually to where Christopher stood flattened against the wall beside the door. "There's yer man."

Unable to see anyone, the burly fellow stepped into the room. His head jolted back as a solid fist met his face, and for good measure Christopher lowered the butt of his pistol on the man's head in a powerful downward stroke. Christopher caught the sagging form and carried him into the privy to add to their collection. He confiscated the man's hat and pulled it low over his brow.

"Two left, you say?" Christopher questioned Haggard, tucking the pistol in his belt. He received a nod. "Then let's be about it."

Leaving the room together, Christopher trailed behind as Haggard stumbled his way down the stairs. Erienne waited tensely, hearing their laughter mingle as they neared the lower level.

Only one of the men glanced up from the blanket as Haggard came into sight. "C'mon, Haggie," he urged with a chortle. "We needs yer money if hit's ter be a game at all."

The second man turned his head and managed only a brief squeal of warning before Christopher's fist snapped his head about. The man spilled to the floor as Haggard stepped forward to deliver the butt of a pistol with abrupt results to the first one's skull. The first man lit rolling, scrambling for his weapon, but Christopher pinned his grasping arm beneath a boot and chopped down with his fist again. Slumping into a quiet, uncaring slumber, the man gave up his struggle.

Christopher accumulated the weapons, shoving them into his own belt, then returned with Haggard upstairs. Erienne's relief was visible in her face, and catching her hand and taking her with him, Christopher went to lean against the table where Claudia could see him. "The time has come for us to depart your company, Miss Talbot. You may keep the mask and cloak, of course, more or less as trade for the gown or, if you prefer, a memento of our undying gratitude. Show them to your father when he arrives and tell him Lord Christopher Stuart Saxton has come to these climes to avenge the death of his brother and father. His greed for power and wealth has been his undoing."

Her snarl was muffled by the gag, and her foot twitched as if she yearned to kick him. She glared at him through the eyeholes, and if looks could kill, he should have fallen in a million delicate slices.

Christopher touched his fingertips to his brow in a casual farewell salute. "Good day, Miss Talbot."

One of the highwaymen in the barracks leaned against the frame of the open door and watched as two men and a woman left the tower. "Look at that, will ye?" he laughed. "That Haggard can't even walk without stumblin'. Why, he nearly knocked the Talbot bitch on her arse."

"No more than what she deserves," Parker muttered as he tipped his hat back away from his eyes. He had been dozing in front of the blazing hearth with his feet propped on a low stool while he awaited the summons from Haggard.

A long moment of silence passed, then the man guffawed again. "There he goes again. I swear, he'll kill himself afore they gets through the gate."

"The gate?" Allan's feet came to the floor as he suddenly sat up. "The Talbots' coach is by the stable, not the gate." He moved to the door to see for himself, then his eyes flared wide. "You fool!" he bellowed. "That's Lady Saxton, not Claudia! And Seton! How the hell did he . . . ? To arms, you blithering dolts! To arms, I say! They're escaping!"

Men scrambled everywhere in wild confusion, slamming into each other as they searched out weapons. The loud commands and the commotion sounded the warning for the three. They were almost at the gate and made a dash for it. Erienne lifted her skirts to her knees as Christopher pulled her along with him. The red, plumed hat sailed off unnoticed to mark the point of their passing.

As soon as he cleared the gate, Christopher gave a piercing whistle that seemed to shatter the quietness of the countryside. "Run!" he yelled to his companions. "The coach will be coming around! I'll see if I can discourage them."

"Oh, please, Christopher!" Erienne cried fearfully. "Come with us!"

"Haggard, see to her!" he commanded.

The man caught her arm and dragged her from her husband's side, urging her into a run down the sloping side. Christopher halted a short distance beyond the gate and took aim with one of the pistols. The ball plowed through the open doorway, narrowly missing Parker, who was leading the charge out. Another shot smashed through a boarded window and whined viciously through the room, making men dive for cover. It was just enough to keep them worried for a while and fearful of raising their heads.

"Up, you laggards!" Allan shouted when no further shots were fired. "To horse! Run them down!" His eyes filled with rage as the men delayed, and without warning, he raised his pistol and fired a shot into the timbered ceiling, winning their undivided attention. "After them, damn you, or the next shot will be in one of you!"

There was a mad scramble for the door, and the men crowded through it in a mass of jumbled bodies, all willing to obey at once. Once past the barracks' portal, they stumbled over each other as they ran toward their horses.

Erienne's slippers were hardly meant for running on the uneven stones, but even so, she surprised Haggard with her speed once Christopher turned to follow them. He gained on them rapidly as the coach emerged from the trees. Tanner had stoked the team up with several cracks of the whip, and they were coming on fast. Erienne's heart fell as Christopher halted again some two score yards beyond the moat. A musket ball plowed into the turf beside him, and another whipped overhead as three men on horseback charged through the gate. He seemed in no hurry to take aim, but when he did, his movement was sudden and sure. The piece bucked and roared, giving forth with a puff of smoke, and the lead rider was plucked from his steed. The rider's companions were greatly discouraged when Christopher turned the sights of another pistol toward them. They dove headlong from their horses into a gully, heedless of its rocky bed and the pain it caused them.

The coach came forward, and the thunder of charging hooves filled the air as Tanner cracked the whip high over the horses' heads. Almost immediately he was pulling on the reins and standing on the brakes to halt the team beside the two who were running toward them.

"Where's Lord Saxton?" Tanner yelled down to them.

"That's Lord Saxton!" Bundy pointed toward Christopher, who was quickly gaining on the pair with his long-legged reach. "That's him without his mask!"

"But that's Mr. Se—!"

"Saxton!" Bundy barked and took up a pair of long, wicked-looking Yankee rifles he had tucked beside him and tossed them down to Christopher as that one halted beside them.

While some men were still chasing down loose horses in the courtyard of the castle, others had mounted and were charging across the planks that bridged the gully. Christopher knelt in the dust beside the coach while Haggard lifted Erienne inside. Christopher wet the bead at the muzzle of a rifle, then brought it up quickly to his shoulder. The light gun barked and jumped, and though the cloud of smoke was small, one of the men cried out and tumbled from the saddle. He hefted the other gun, and another man fell to the dust.

Haggard had climbed inside the coach, and a musket roared as he followed Christopher's lead.

"Got 'em!" he cried in enthusiasm as Christopher swung inside. His feet had no more than left the ground than Tanner slapped the reins and set the team in motion.

Sheriff Parker jerked his arm toward the departing conveyance. "After them! Don't let them out of your sight! I know where they're going, but I want you to nip at their tails all the way home!" As some more men swung up on their steeds to give chase, he yelled to one, "Ride and get more men! Join us at Saxton Hall! I'll be along after I see to that Talbot brat!"

Parker ground his teeth as he strode across the courtyard toward the tower. He had come into Lord Talbot's services more than five years ago, though a bit more than three of those had been as the sheriff. It had been a guise both of them had laughed about, but it had helped to lead suspicion away from him. It had been his own idea to burn the east wing of the manor after Edmund Saxton had ridden into their camp by accident and recognized him among the raiders. Talbot had heartily agreed with the deed, of course, for he had hated the Saxtons from the first and coveted their wealth and lands. Some score years ago his lordship had led his own raid on Saxton Hall and had slain the old lord when his accusations of treachery against Broderick Saxton had been dismissed as having no merit. Though Talbot had friends at Court still pleading for his cause to cast the Saxtons from their lands, it seemed that that family also had acquaintances just as powerful working to reestablish the Saxton house and honor.

Despite all of Talbot's efforts, however, things were going swiftly awry. Christopher Seton was to blame for much of it. It seemed he had no more than touched feet on the soil of these northern climes but that he began to thwart and torment them. He had frightened Timmy Sears near to death, and Timmy, the big man that he was, had come blubbering of all he had confessed to the night rider. He had held back the names of the leaders and therefore had to be slain before he also spilled that information. Ben Mose had also known more than he should have, and it was for that reason he was killed. Now, with Seton free to wreak vengeance for the taking of his woman, their woes were sure to increase. Claudia would be the first one of those to surmount.

Parker stepped over the inert bodies of his men in the tower and took the stairs three at a time. He stepped into the cell cautiously and frowned at the scene that greeted him, most of all at the black-garbed figure beside the table. With saber drawn, he approached carefully from behind and quickly snatched the leather helm free. The curled coiffure of Claudia Talbot greeted him before her head turned and her glare came upon him. Her eyes fairly crackled with rage. He loosed the gag but realized his mistake as she launched into a venomous tirade.

"You fools! Could you not see that Christopher was playing a game with you?! He is Lord Saxton!"

The sheriff's surprise dwindled readily as the full realization dawned. Of course! Why did he not think of it himself? Timmy Sears had whined that the night rider was the lord of Saxton Hall who had returned from the dead to haunt him.

Fool! he thought. You let that many-faced man deceive you with his tricks!

Claudia was not timid about placing the blame on someone else, quickly forgetting that she had also been duped. As he labored at the knots that held her imprisoned, Allan heard his reputation be-smirched—nay, flogged and slain—his parentage reviewed with rampant speculations as to its legitimacy and content of humankind, and even a few choice epithets leveled at her sire. By the time he freed her, he was of the firm opinion that his own well-seasoned soldier's adjectives had just been put to shame.

Claudia threw off the long black cloak and grabbed up the iridescent blue gown Erienne had left. As she pulled it over her head, she spoke through the cloth, "I want to see that bastard drawn and quartered before this day is through!"

The skirts settled over her petticoats, and Claudia reached up to pull the bodice together. Her eyes widened and her face flamed as the two edges refused to meet around her waist, leaving a gap as wide as the breadth of a large man's hand.

Allan choked as he tried to subdue his laughter and won a heated glare for his effort.

"Help me to fasten it!" she barked.

"I fear there's no time," he replied and refrained from indicating that it would be a hopeless task. He had often observed the trim, well-curved form of the Saxton wench, and though the two women favored somewhat in looks (though there, too, Claudia was wanting), that had not been true of their shapes.

A moment later they were striding across the courtyard toward the Talbot carriage, and as Claudia struggled to keep from stumbling over the long ends of Lord Saxton's black cloak, Allan strenuously stressed the need for her to return home.

" 'Twill be no place for a woman," he argued.

"I insist! I want to see Erienne's face when you cut down her husband."

Allan sighed wearily. He already knew that neither of the Talbots were the forgiving sort and were rather bloodthirsty when they set to the path of revenge. "You have your coach. I cannot stop you, but your father will deal with me harshly if some harm comes to you."

Claudia's head raised slightly as she looked past his arm, then she smiled smugly. "The blame for this at least needn't be placed on your head. My father is coming now. He will take me with him."

Allan mentally sighed his relief and went to meet the coach as it swept through the gates. Before it even halted, Lord Talbot was at the window.

"Was that Saxton's coach I passed down the road a piece?" he demanded.

"Aye!" Allan replied. "And we must be after him. Lord Saxton is none other than Christopher Seton."

The gasp that accompanied Talbot's explosive expletive made the three glance at each other in bemusement.

"What was that?" Talbot barked, looking around. He was sure the sound had come from behind him.

"It doesn't matter! We must be off if we hope to get to Saxton Hall with the men."

"I'm coming with you, Papa!" Claudia declared, reaching up to open the door.

"The hell you are!"

"I am!" Claudia flung the door wide. It hit the side of the coach with a resounding crash that made Avery's ears ring as he huddled in the boot.

"Dammit, girl! Have you no mind?" Talbot roared. "This is war!"

"I now hate the Saxtons as much as you do, Papa, and you're not going to cheat me out of seeing Christopher Saxton laid low! Now, move over! You know I hate riding backward."

Talbot had given many orders to many men, but once again he failed to win his point with his much-coddled daughter. The muscles in his face tightened with suppressed ire, but nonetheless he slid over, making room for his offspring. His brows came together in a sharp frown as the black cloak parted, revealing the open bodice of the blue gown.

"What happened to your clothes?" he questioned sharply and suspiciously glanced toward the sheriff. He might have dallied with scores of harlots and easy wenches himself, but he had always demanded more of a moral code for his only daughter.

" 'Twas Christopher!" Claudia explained bluntly as the carriage began to swing around in the courtyard. "He made me undress, and he gave my gown to Erienne. He said it was gaudy and held a sword at my throat, threatening to kill me. I think he would have, too." She began to mewl and then to sob, sniffing dramatically. "Oh, Papa, it was terrible! He's such a madman. No telling how many men he's killed getting her free. Why, look at them." She gestured out the window. "Does the sight of those dead men convince you of the danger I was in?"

The coach crossed the planks of the bridge and gained speed rapidly, hitting ground with a jarring jolt that brought Avery's teeth together with a solid "clunk" and restored the pain to his bruised body. He would have moaned his misery but was afraid the Talbots would hear him. Thus he suffered in silence . . . for once.

The racing team plunged ever onward, sweeping the Saxton coach through the vales and over the hills, ever shadowed by the shifting flock of riders that flowed out behind. Christopher had bade Tanner to ease the pace of the racing steeds to save them for the long ride to Saxton Hall. Almost immediately there was a surge forward of the horde who trailed them, but they were quickly dissuaded by the long-reaching Yankee rifles, which seemed to pluck them from their saddles at the will of Lord Saxton and that one they had most recently considered naught but a bumbling oaf. Haggard proved his own skill with the weapons and, more than once, scattered the chasing flock by sending one of the brigands tumbling in their midst.

With the easier gait, it was not long before the sheriff, riding just ahead of the Talbot coach and joined by other men, overtook the ones who followed the Saxtons. A cackle of glee came from Claudia as she saw ahead of them the prey they sought.

"We've got them now!" she exclaimed and jiggled her father's arm excitedly. "They won't be able to escape."

Nigel Talbot, himself, was elated, but wondered why the band had not already swarmed around the conveyance and dragged them to a halt. Leaning out the window, he saw that the sheriff had pulled back his mount to match the pace of his men rather than lead a charge forward. It incensed Talbot that Parker could waste the advantage of having Saxton outnumbered and so close within their grasp.

Talbot barked an order up to his driver, who in compliance pressed the team on ahead until the men on horseback were forced to move aside or test the wicked shot of another rifle by riding ahead. They were eager for a respite and did not argue because some had to draw back behind the Talbot carriage.

"Why haven't your men stopped them?" his lordship barked at Parker, who came to ride beside the door. "You've got weapons! Use them to kill the driver. That should bring them to a halt."

"Pistols and muskets are useless," Parker yelled back over the din of the thudding hooves. "Whenever a man tries to get close enough to use them, Saxton lets loose with one of those damn rifles Avery told us about."

"Damn!" The expletive exploded from Talbot's tightening lips, and his rage mounted as he questioned, "Is there not one among you who is willing to take the chance?"

Parker had felt the chiding taunts of his men much too often when he had ordered them to risk their lives not to give vent to his own frustrations now. "You are welcome to try it yourself, my lord, if you are prepared to face the results."

Talbot's visage grew red with rage, and his eyes blazed. He picked up the challenge, but not in such as way as to threaten his own life. "Set a marksman on top of my coach and double-load an O'l Bess. That should reach them well enough as we pull forward."

Parker doubted the results but did as he was commanded. Soon a man with a large-bore musket was swinging from his racing steed onto the coach and climbing to take a place beside the driver. The coachman urged the team forward, and the marksman, bracing himself against the swaying ride, took careful aim. He squeezed the trigger, and instead of a sharp report, a hollow, double-throated roar came forth. There was a sudden yelp from the driver as the gun backfired, flipping the one who had held it onto his back. The man's eyes stared wide from a face that was a bloody, mangled mess, and with a last twitch of his legs, he lay still.

"What happened?" Claudia inquired eagerly. "Did he kill the driver? Did he stop them?"

Parker gestured to the coachman, who nudged the dead man over the side. The body tumbled to the road, giving the occupants a start as it fell past the window. Allan Parker did not hide the smirk that turned his lips as he reined his mount close to the carriage door.

"Have you cannon for the task, my lord?" he asked snidely. "I fear less is hardly equal to the task."

At his lordship's orders, the Talbot coach pulled back, letting the gang of highwaymen pass them. Though the effort was continually made to harass the Saxton conveyance, none was successful in daunting the determination of the group it carried. When the attempt was made to ride out wide and then move around the coach to halt it from the fore, the obstacles proved too much to overcome. If the rugged terrain allowed it, then the riders presented themselves as easy prey to the long rifles, or Tanner would once again stoke up the team to a breakneck pace that could not be overtaken.

Thus the entourage, such as it was, gained the Saxton lands. Tenants paused where they stood to gawk at the passersby. It was the crack of the Yankee rifle from the familiar Saxton coach and the resulting fall of another brigand from the saddle that bespoke of the seriousness of this procession. Anger flared in their hearts as they realized that another Saxton lord was being threatened. Spurred to action, they grabbed pitchforks, axes, scythes, clubs, old muskets, and an odd assortment of anything worthy of being a weapon. Like angry hornets they swarmed in the direction of the manor house, scrambling as fast as their legs could carry them.

The Saxton carriage swept up to the tower portal and pulled to a halt with wheels locked as Tanner stood on the brakes and sawed on the reins. While Haggard and Bundy discouraged the onrushing flock, Christopher threw open the door and leapt out. He turned to lift Erienne down, then scooped up the rifles and followed his wife through the central portal. Bundy and Haggard pushed through behind them as Tanner took the coach out of the way of the crossfire.

The returning party was met just inside the great chamber by Paine, who seemed somewhat confused by the presence of Christopher Seton instead of the master of the house. Behind him, Aggie wept in her apron, which was gathered in both hands and pressed to her mouth. Tessie stood in the background, elated to see her mistress but bewildered by the housekeeper's manner. Only a few moments prior, before they had heard the rattle of wheels, the elder woman had been comforting her and assuring her that all would end well. Perhaps with the absence of Lord Saxton, Tessie mused, the housekeeper perceived some ill had befallen him and was already mourning his loss.

"There, there, Aggie," she soothed, patting the woman's shoulder, "the master'll be along soon no doubt. Don't grieve yerself."

Aggie raised her teary gaze and looked at the girl as if she had grown two heads of a sudden. "What are ye talkin' 'bout? This here's the master. Lord Christopher Saxton, he be."

"Oh." Tessie's large eyes came around to the one who was ordering Bundy and Haggard to take positions near the windows. A shattering of glass evidenced their readiness to defend the manor as they broke out the crystal panes and thrust out the bores of the long Yankee rifles.

Christopher surveyed the faces that surrounded him as he took his wife into the shelter of his arm. The cook was even there, grinning from ear to ear. "Those of you who would are free to leave. Erienne can show you the way out."

"No!" The word came from several lips at once, then he realized that Erienne had spoken also. He looked down at her, and she clung to him with a tenacity that revealed her intent as strongly as her word.

"I shall not leave your side. I will not rear my babe without a father."

Aggie enlarged upon the theme. "When the old lord was slain, the servants were sent to safety. He faced his murderers alone. We'll stay, milord. Maybe I can't shoot one o' them fancy muskets o' yers, but I can swing a wicked broom."

"You should be aware that I am the night rider," Christopher explained for the benefit of those who were still torn with confusion. "I am the one whom the sheriff has been seeking, but my cause has been just, and that was to root out the thieves that Allan Parker and Lord Talbot led. They killed my father, and they torched the wing to murder my brother. Many have fallen prey to the highwaymen, and I only sought to end their reign of terror."

"Are you really Lord Saxton?" Tessie asked timidly.

Erienne laughed and wrapped her arms about her husband's lean waist, hugging him close. "I know 'tis hard to believe, but this is the same one who nearly frightened us out of our wits."

A shot from outside brought their attention around to more serious matters. Each hurriedly took up weapons of their choice, some as unusual as those the peasants had assembled, and as Erienne loaded a pistol with powder and shot, she caught Christopher's eyes upon her.

"My darling wife," he murmured softly, " 'tis probable that I shall be most heavily set upon within the next few moments. The front door, as solid as it is, cannot be properly defended, and they will come before long to ram it down. 'Twould please me much if you . . ."

Erienne's head was already shaking before he finished. Strangely she experienced no fright, no fear. She was in her home, and a grim determination lay beneath her composed exterior. "I will stay with you." She tapped the pistol with the tip of her finger and informed him bluntly, "The man who harms you will not live out the day. I will see to that."

There was a level sternness in her gaze that made Christopher glad she was his wife and not a foe.

A shield of sorts was quickly formed to protect the ramming brigade, and the door suffered from a relentless pounding of an oaken log. Even so, any man who did not make full use of the cover fell by the wayside, his life snatched from him by a shot from the manor. Talbot stood in the shelter of some trees near the manse, safely out of the line of fire but not so far away that he could not claim the victory that was close at hand. He watched the proceedings with a smug smile, while Claudia surveyed the happenings from the comfort of the carriage. Neither of them were aware of the one who peered out of the boot, for Avery was content to remain hidden lest some action be demanded of him in the taking of the manor.

The door cracked and splintered beneath the strain of the invading timber, and the dozen who clustered behind the wooden shield guffawed, for the next few blows promised to see them through. Parker was behind them, urging them on and lending his weight to the task. Then out of the corner of his eye he caught an unexpected flash of color coming across the field. He paused to look and found a pack of enraged peasants running toward them, brandishing their weapons and setting up a hue and cry as they neared.

"Get this damn door open quick!" he yelled.

The log hit the planks once again, and the door crashed inward. Talbot had also seen the peasants, and when the sheriff and men surged forward, he was immediately behind them. Some of the other highwaymen started to run across the clearing to join them but fell back as the tenants charged them. The highwaymen were hard pressed to defend themselves against the angry attack and gave no further consideration to joining the few who had entered the manse.

The rushing tide of eager foes was met by an assault of pistols fired from very close range. The first few fell, but the others charged forward over the bodies of their dead companions as Christopher, Haggard, and Bundy fell back into the great hall. There the brigands were immediately confronted by another form of attack. Ears rang with the almost musical notes of heavy iron pans laid to thick skulls. Aggie and Paine were there in the midst of the fray, while the cook in nervous agitation awaited a worthy target for his long, vicious-looking knife. The men in the fore had to meet the slashing blade of his lordship, Saxton, and the clumsier hacking of Bundy and Haggard's swords. Parker pressed through this mélange of experienced and novice fighters and leapt clear. His goal was the Lady Erienne, whose capture would assure surrender, but a single pace in her direction brought him face to face with the lord of the manor and the long, blood-darkened blade of a claymore.

"Your time has come, Lord Saxton," the sheriff threatened as he drew his dagger and lifted the saber for the attack.

"Aye!" Christopher returned with a slowly spreading smile. "You have for too long ravaged this land and escaped your fate. You took my wife and held her captive with no other cause but to draw me out. You have succeeded to that end. Aye! Your time has come!"

Erienne pressed a hand tightly across her mouth as her heart throbbed in sudden dread. Fear rose within her, and she could not beat it back as she watched her husband taunt his enemy with the bloodied claymore. The sword described a slow arc back and forth before the other's eyes.

"Death, Milord Sheriff," Christopher promised. "Death!"

The sheriff launched the attack with all his considerable skill, the saber slashing, thrusting, cutting, while the dagger was held ready to test the flesh of the other. The long, straight claymore, as heavy as the saber but with a double edge that was whisker sharp, denied his thrust and lunge and met each with a threat of its own.

The great hall rang with the sound of the clashing swords, which was echoed by the conflict near the entry. Talbot, not knowing where to turn, met the menacing glare of the cook. The knife threatened him, and being quite squeamish about bloodletting when it concerned his own, he raised his cane and lowered it over the man's head, crumpling him to his knees. Talbot would have reversed his direction then and there, seeing that his best choice for survival was outside, where the tenants were being beaten back, but when he turned to leave, his jaw sagged, for another horde was swarming up the hill to give aid to the peasants, this one led by Farrell and a man in a blue coat. The new wave of recruits had the look of seamen, and it became quickly apparent that they were experienced fighters. Talbot turned back into the hall and snatched up the cook's knife. Haggard, Bundy, and the rest of the servants were too busy subduing the brigands to notice as he slipped past them into the hall. His eyes settled almost gleefully on the back of Christopher Saxton as that worthy fought for his life. Talbot hefted the knife and charged to the attack, preferring to sneak up on a man from behind.

Suddenly the hall filled with a thunderous sound as Erienne made good her threat. Talbot was thrown backward by the force of the shot she fired from the pistol, and Christopher glanced around in surprise to see the man fall with limbs sprawled in a grotesque fashion and with a hand still clasping the knife. The sheriff saw his advantage and plunged forward to deal the death blow, but the saber was struck down by the claymore as Christopher's attention returned to him.

Lord Saxton's eyes seemed to flash with a renewed strength, and the claymore dipped to the attack. It flashed beneath Parker's guard, then whipped up. A sharp pain pierced the sheriff's left arm, and the dagger fell useless to the floor. He beat down the plunging thrust of the other, retreating a step. Another attack was launched, and Allan swept it aside, but there was no pause, no time to counterthrust. Another came, and then another until Allan Parker's lips twisted in a snarl at the helplessness of his defense. He never felt the thrust that pierced his ribs and heart, only a slight tug at his vest as the blade withdrew. The strength faded from his arms as he stared at Christopher in stunned surprise. A sudden darkness came upon the hall as his saber clattered to the floor, and Allan Parker never knew when he fell beside it.

There was silence in Saxton Hall as Christopher glanced about. Those few thieves who had entered and survived were being nudged outside by the prodding sword of Haggard Bentworth, and they knew by the gleam in his eye he was serious. Christopher tossed down the claymore and gathered Erienne in his arms as she came to him and softly sobbed out her relief against his chest.

"I must thank you for defending my back, madam," he whispered against the fragrant hair. "Our babe might yet grow up with a father."

Her weeping grew more intense as the stress of the day was released and her fears were put to rest. She clung to him, wetting his shirt with her tears, and she felt the gentle stroking of his hand and the touch of his lips against her hair as he held her close against him.

Finally she quieted, and holding her against his side, Christopher moved outside to stand in front of the manor and allow the spring sun to warm them. They saw the multitude of people who had come to their defense, and even Christopher suffered from a mistiness in his eyes as he realized the tenants had risked their lives for him. They came to assure themselves that all was well with the Saxton family and met a lord they could look upon with ease. In a few moments they set to work clearing away the dead. It seemed for them at least that of their own forces no more than a handful had suffered serious wounds.

Bundy and Tanner carried out Lord Talbot, and there was a duo of gasps in the Talbot carriage as both Claudia and Avery recognized the limp and bloody form. The tars from the *Cristina* had passed Claudia by after glancing in the carriage to make sure it held no threat to them and thus made no attempt to stop the coach as she yelled up to the driver to be on his way.

Defeat came as a crushing blow to the man and woman. Avery could see no hope for his life; he was bound to roam in endless fear, always afraid of that moment when he would meet Christopher Seton again. Or was it Saxton? He shrugged mentally. One was as bad as the other.

Claudia's outlook was hardly any better. She had gleaned enough knowledge in the past few days to settle the suspicion in her mind that her father had been a thief and perhaps even a murderer. His holdings would no doubt be stripped away by the Crown, and she could not bear the humiliation that would be forthcoming. With no one to take care of her now and to coddle her with the riches of life, she did not know how she would survive. Perhaps she should gather what wealth she could find in the Talbot mansion and travel elsewhere.

Christopher observed the passage of the coach from his sight and then turned his gaze to the pair of men who approached them. It was Farrell and Captain Daniels, and while the latter was smiling broadly, the former frowned in sharp disapproval at the couple. Christopher thrust out a hand in greeting to his captain, then looked at his wife's brother.

"Farrell, I don't think we've been properly introduced," Christopher smiled as he extended his hand. "I am Lord Saxton."

The young man's eyes widened, and he searched the softly smiling visage of his sister as he mechanically accepted the hand. "Lord Saxton? *The* Lord Saxton?"

"Aye, I am the one who wore the mask and walked with a limp," Christopher confessed. " 'Twas done partly to fool the thieves into believing the man they had murdered was still alive, and then too, I desired to wed your sister and found no other way. I hope you will value the friendship we began when you knew me as a cripple."

Farrell tried to grasp all the facts and put them together in their proper places. "You are really married to my sister, and you are the father of her . . ."

Erienne blushed as she glanced hesitatingly toward the sea captain, who seemed to be enjoying the whole exchange. His smile broadened as her husband gave a reply.

"You needn't sharpen your skill with firearms to avenge your sister's honor," Christopher replied. The teasing gleam in his eyes shone brighter. " 'Twas quite properly made, I assure you."

They paused as a coach came into view, followed by a score of riders. Erienne immediately recognized the entourage as the same they had passed on their return from London some weeks before and was puzzled by its presence here. The conveyance swept up the drive and pulled to a halt. A footman rushed to open the door, and the Marquess Leicester descended the steps that were set before the door.

"Have we come too late?" he inquired with an amused smile twitching at his lips. He glanced about, surveying the scene of the tars carrying away the dead and piling them in carts. "I say, you didn't need my help at all. It looks as if you've put these thieves to rout once and for all." He turned back to question the occupants of the carriage. "Ladies, 'tis a dreadful sight you'll see here. Are you sure you're up to it?"

"I want to see my son," came a smooth feminine voice.

Christopher took Erienne's arm and led her forward as the marquess reached in a hand, lending assistance to his wife, who sat nearest the door. As soon as she stood to the ground, Anne held out her arms to Erienne.

"My dear, what a dreadful experience it must have been. We were gone when Christopher's letter arrived, and when we found it awaiting us, we rushed here from York, where we've been since leaving London. Thankfully my sister had just come from Carlisle to be with us."

"Your sister?" Erienne peered within the interior, and her face showed surprise as the marquess moved aside and the Countess Ashford appeared in the doorway. The woman descended and lifted a cheek expectantly to receive a kiss from Christopher, then he led her to Erienne, who stared in bemusement at the woman. His eyes twinkled as his voice filled her mind.

"Erienne, my sweet, I would like you to meet my mother."

"But you are the Countess Ashford." Erienne's mind stumbled in growing confusion. "I remember you from the assembly. You played cards with me."

The countess smiled gently. "I wanted to meet you, and since my son was determined to keep his identity a secret from you, I could not tell you I was his mother, though I dearly longed to. Will you forgive me for the deception?"

Tears started in Erienne's eyes, but they were joyful tears, and of a sudden the two women were crying together and embracing each other. The countess drew back and, with a lace handkerchief, dabbed at the girl's tears, ignoring the ones that brimmed in her own eyes.

"I came to stay in Carlisle so I could be near my son," she explained amid sniffles. "I am a widow again, and it was lonely in

London without him there. Besides my sister, Anne, Christopher is the only family I have left, and I was so afraid something would happen to him. I bade Haggard to watch over him as much as he could."

"You came back to England to live after your marriage?" Erienne inquired.

"By then my sons were grown, and the earl was an old friend of ours. It seemed fitting that I should marry him, though Broderick was the only real love in my life."

Christopher placed an arm about his wife's shoulders and smiled at his mother. "I have not had the chance to tell you, Mother, but you are to become a grandmother this year."

Mary caught her breath, and her face lit up with sudden happiness. "I think a boy would be nice. But then again, I never had a girl, and I've been so anxious for Christopher to wed and settle down. Aggie and I have worried that it would never be. Oh, Erienne, Erienne." Tears reappeared in her eyes. "You will be so good for my son. I just know you will."

The silence of the lord's bedchamber that evening was thwarted by the whispering voices that came from the bed as Erienne Saxton lay tucked securely in the curve of her husband's body. Together they observed the glowing coals of the dying fire, and now and then his lips dipped to touch the spot below her ear where the pulse gently throbbed.

"I think I should like to see America someday," she murmured in the dark. "Your mother talked about it so much at dinner, it must be quite a country. Do you think it would be possible for me to see it?"

"Whatever my lady desires," he breathed, nuzzling the fragrant tresses beside her ear. "My world is where you are, and I follow where you lead."

Erienne giggled as his teeth nibbled at her earlobe. "Nay, sir. I will never lead you, for my hand will be tucked firmly in yours. We are one, in truth, and by your side I will gladly walk or stand if you will have me there."

"*If?*" There was amazement evident in his tone as he repeated the word. "Have I fought for you all these many months just to place you behind me, where I cannot view your beauty? Nay, my lady, beside me is where I would have you, always close to my heart."